"RICHLY ATMOSPHERIC."
Publishers Weekly

"Clarke assembles two sets of characters to play out a pair of parallel stories which manage to intersect in mysterious ways."
Los Angeles Times Book Review

"Compellingly tense . . . Contains just enough of the supernatural to be called fantasy . . . The story's juxtaposition of poesy and practicality are immediately involving, and holds one's involvement."
The Philadelphia Inquirer

"Fascinating . . . A new genre has arisen that might be called scholar-thrillers—ideas that offer entertainment and insight as you follow them down their labyrinthine paths. . . . Entertaining."
The Hartford Courant

"THE CHYMICAL WEDDING finally reveals a sinuous, aching beauty in its languid and graceful pages."
Booklist

"Powerful and earthy . . . Intriguing and rewarding."
School Library Journal

Also by Lindsay Clarke:

SUNDAY WHITEMAN

THE
CHYMICAL
WEDDING

Lindsay Clarke

IVY BOOKS • NEW YORK

Ivy Books
Published by Ballantine Books
Copyright © 1989 by Lindsay Clarke

Library of Congress Catalog Card Number: 89-45304

ISBN 0-8041-0702-5

This edition published by arrangement with Alfred A. Knopf, Inc.

Manufactured in the United States of America

First Ballantine Books Edition: April 1991

Cover art by Marty Blake

For Maddy

Is not this, perhaps, the secret of every true and great mystery, that it is *simple*? Does it not love secrecy for that very reason? Proclaimed, it were but a word; kept silent it is *being*. And a miracle too, in the sense that *being* with all its paradoxes is miraculous.

C. KERENYI, *Introduction to a Science of Mythology*

Reality favours symmetries and slight anachronisms.

JORGE LUIS BORGES, *The South*

Contents

1 ▨ The Green Man

In that part of the world the sky is everywhere, and the entire landscape seems to lie in abasement under its exacting light. It gets into church towers and between the narrow reeds along the river's edge. It glances across undulant acres of barley and beet, and takes what little the flints have to give. Everything there feels exposed, so keeping secrets is hard. It's not the easiest place in which to hide.

Also, if you don't have a car, it's quite difficult to get about. In fact the journey to Munding was simpler a century ago. These days the train takes you only as far as Norwich, then it's a leisurely bus-ride through some of the roomier parts of the county to the market-place at Saxburgh, and there's still a four-mile walk along the lanes to Munding. Just outside the village you cross the old branch-line: its rails have been scrapped, its sleepers disturbed, and the small halt closed. So much for Victorian progress!

I was in no hurry. Looking down from the bridge at the silent gravel-bed I reflected that the journey across England had been quite long enough to make specific a sense of banishment. By the time I reached the village my defection was complete.

It was a late Spring afternoon in the early '80s. I was 27 then.

The name of the cottage was painted in white on a spruce-green ground: *The Pightle*. There was something diminutive, almost elfin, to the ring of it. The name matched the dumpy lime-washed walls and poky interior. It matched my mood.

The Pightle was built of wattle and daub, timbered throughout

1

in oak, with a reed thatch cocking a snook at the world from either gable end. It was set in a stand of beech and chestnut a quarter of a mile from its nearest neighbour. The small garden at the front was already overgrown enough for a hen-pheasant to risk nesting under a clump of fern. At the rear the cottage overlooked the water-meadows on the wilder fringes of the hamlet and you could see the round flint tower of Munding St Mary's glinting in the sunlight across the stream. The windows were leaded and small; even at midday the rooms were shady, almost dark. The Pightle felt perfect for my needs at a time when I was no longer sure what my needs were.

Shortly after my arrival I was puzzled by a noise that grated the air outside like the tearing of tin. Then I recognized it: someone somewhere was feeding a lot of pigs.

There was a gale on that first night. It rolled out of a starry sky, a crass wind racketing among the trees and, though there was no rain, lightning floodlit the window-glass behind the blind in quick bright pangs. I counted the seconds till the thunderstroke. Eight, nine miles away.

I lay awake for a long time thinking how strange it was that the quiet lane should be so turbulent by night, and queerer still that I should be lying on this brass bed, listening to the flux and the way the timbers of the house creaked like a ship.

When I slept I slept badly, dreaming myself ringed by a band of crazy women, their eyes bright with malignant purpose. They wanted to change me, refashion me to their taste through some ordeal of humiliation. And when I woke again I was troubled by the dream, and the gale still shuddered about the house, and I lay there thinking how complicated it is to be a man.

'Go to Norfolk,' Clive Quantrill had said. 'The cottage is there, I shan't need it this summer, and it could do with an airing. So could you. You're all fouled up with other people. Be on your own for a time. Get clean.'

Clive was my publisher as well as my friend, and perhaps in that order. His press had barely covered its costs on my first collection, but he'd gambled on a second which did better. I'd done my best to make both slim, softback volumes intact and chinkless—too guardedly so, according to at least one reviewer. And, yes, there were moments when one would rather be a kitten and cry mew, but the responsibility remained to be as good as a poet as one could. Especially now that everything else was in pieces. Clive's offer was a moment's grace. I took it.

After all, there were few constraints on my time. I had been released from my job at the Polytechnic. My salary would be paid through till the end of the summer, so money was not yet a problem. Also I knew I could have the job back if I wanted it.

But once you've stepped out on to the wire it seems paltry to think of the net below.

Clive had warned Bob Crossley that I'd be coming. He was a retired psychiatric nurse, a widower, living on his own down the lane. Like Clive he was a foreigner in the village, and kept an eye on The Pightle for him. He had a blotchy nose, a balding head, and the newcomer's enthusiasm for local history.

Pightle was a local word, he said, of unknown origin. 'It means a small enclosure. A sort of croft, or smallholding, I suppose.' He told me how he'd looked up the tithe-maps in the county archive and found that The Pightle, like most of the land round there except the Easterness Estate, had once belonged to King's College, Cambridge. 'Maynard Keynes sold it all off when he was bursar there, invested the proceeds in stock. Made a fortune for the college out of properties that brought in a pittance. Clever man . . . if you approve of capitalism?'

I said, 'I gather you don't.'

'Tory heartland, this,' he regretted. 'They haven't heard that feudalism is over. I'm a lone voice on the Parish Council.'

'Can't let them have it all their own way.'

He smiled, encouraged, 'If only . . .' then shrugged. 'The motto of this county is *Do Different*, but not many of us do. Will you be about here long?'

'A couple of weeks. Maybe longer, I'm not sure yet.'

'Not much social life in Munding. You might find it a bit dull . . . without a car, I mean. Only one bus a week.'

'I'll be fine.'

'Mind you, the Feathers keeps country hours . . . no bobby here, you see. And it's a decent pint.' He sized me up again. 'You can always drop in on me if you're at a loose end. I can do with some intelligent company . . .' Bob was that brand of exiled Yorkshireman who, on meeting another, assumes instant affinity, but my smile disappointed him: *take no interest in me*, it said; *pin no hopes*.

There was, however, a tactful soul under his cardigan and

plaid shirt. 'Well, if there's anything you need,' he said as he left, 'you know where I am.'

From my bedroom window I could count the towers of four churches. Only they and the scattered spinneys were vertical. All else lay supine—acre after acre of barley and wheat, patched here and there with the yellow dazzle of the mustard fields. Outside The Pightle one was as exposed as the rat flattened to the narrow road by a passing car.

Munding was what the locals call a 'pig-village.' When the wind veered it smelled of cabbages and the sties. There was a little shop which doubled as the Post Office crammed into a converted front room of the house of its owner, Mrs Jex, a comfortably proportioned woman who knew everyone's business but mine. There was a row of council houses tacked on to the end of the street, their brick injuriously red against the cooler colours of the landscape. Most had corrugated iron shacks at the back in which chickens and rabbits were kept, and one had several cars in bits and pieces parked across the front garden. Almost all the older houses had been refurbished as commuter-homes and retirement cottages: pink-washed plaster, timbers exposed, roofs rethatched. Unless you counted the church there was no other community centre but the pub. The primary school had been axed and sold off for conversion, so there were no sounds of children around. It was a quiet place except when the din of aircraft out of the nearby base at Thrandeston shattered its sky.

Those first few days I slept late and walked a lot, and wherever I walked I seemed to stand at the centre of a vast circumference of space, as though the pace of my tread was matched by the turning of the earth under my feet. The margins of the lanes were laced with cow-parsley and you could smell wild garlic in the hollows. There were larks and plovers over the fields, and the tall blue days seemed amazed by their own candour. My introspection insulted them. I knew it, just as I knew that Bob Crossley was injured by my dance-step distance from his advances; but there was a thing on my mind that resisted such exposure. It needed solitude. Cover.

I took to the little copses and the gloomy carrs, the places where starlings thronged, where willow and alder brooded over a flooded marl-pit or hankered for the river's edge. I had the engrossed, purposive air of a man looking for something—

which, in a way, I was; for among the many pieces into which my life had fallen there was one that seemed to offer some rudimentary promise of renewal. It was that I was after.

I called it the Green Man.

Day after day the figure prowled my imagination. I could sense him there, almost smell him, in his rough green fell; yet whenever I came close he stole from shade to denser shade where the trees packed deep. All I knew about him for sure was that he was a woodland-dweller, so it was inevitable that the search should take me at last through the forbidding perimeter of barbed wire into the Great Wood to the north of the Easterness Estate.

There noble beeches, three or four hundred years old, were ranged almost equidistant at its heart. They were still spectral in a smoky woodland mist, and not yet canopied in full summer green. Boughs dripped in the silence. The beech-mast crunched beneath my feet. Pheasants whirred away at my approach, and if the hares were crazy in the Spring then I was crazier—Alex Darken, escape-artist of the moral universe, dropped like a leveret on the run in the middle of Norfolk deeps.

And it was not that I expected to encounter him *out there*— in the flesh, so to speak, this clumsy, feral creature sired sometime in the dark between the Fifth Day and the Sixth, and neither man nor beast. But this, if ever, was the season of the Green Man, and this almost medieval wood was Green Man country. If I looked long and quietly enough he might one day shiver into focus, print himself across the page, and I would know then what kin he was to me, and whether he was likeliest to injure me or aid.

Such, anyway, was the dream in which I lived those days.

Then, one hot afternoon, I was no longer alone in the wood. From somewhere down the galleries of beech the sound of laughter echoed across the glade and stopped me short. The laughter was brief, as though a joke had been cracked—almost it felt at my expense, though I could see no one—then the air was stealthy and green and very still once more, until a blackbird chattered its indignant cry, and the laughter came again, female, a little hectic, over where the ground fell away to bracken.

It puzzled and excited me; worried me too with its reminder that I trespassed there. Covertly I stepped between the trees.

Pale and naked in an auburn glow of sunlight, a man and a

woman were clasped in each other's limbs, tussling and rolling in a hollow where the glade banked into mixed woodland. Beyond them a dense drift of bluebells threw their flesh into white relief.

They were laughing as they fought, the woman over the man now, holding him spreadeagled by the wrists so that he was hidden beneath the arch of her back. Her legs were astride him as she tossed her head from side to side, teasing him with the dangle of breasts above his face.

'All right. All right. I take it back,' the man laughed.

'Every word?'

'Every word.'

'Say "uncle!" '

'To a mere chit of a girl? Never.'

'Say "I'm an old fool and I don't know which side my bread is buttered, and I should count my stars that I'm lucky enough to have such a hotshot intellectual as a partner." '

'Consider it said.'

'Say it.'

'I can't talk with my tongue in my cheek.'

'Say it.'

Then the man lurched up suddenly. The woman squealed, stretched back upright on her heels, and said, 'Dammit, Edward, that hurt.'

She pulled herself to her feet and turned away, one hand to a breast, rubbing the nipple. She was tall, sturdily built, the patch of hair at her groin thick and barbarous among the smooth planes of her body. Her tan was un-English and complete, except for the white flaw of an appendectomy scar. She tossed her hair back across her shoulders, and stood biting on a knuckle as though to distract some other pain.

Hands cupped beneath his head, the man wriggled a little in the sunlight, chuckling still. His body was scrawny, hollow-chested, the belly rounded like a wineskin over the grizzled cloud of his pubic hair. He must have been over sixty—some forty years older than the girl who walked away from him to where her clothes were piled.

'You can be really hurtful, you know that?' The soft, transatlantic accent to her tones was distinct now. As she slipped an arm into the sleeve of a faded purple shirt, I saw the reddened flesh where the old man must have closed his teeth. 'Sometimes I wonder about you. I really do.'

'If you will sin in the sunshine with a man quite old enough to be your grandfather you should expect something other than the simperings of pimpled youth.' The voice was measured and resonant, picking its way deliberately among the consonants, and he was smiling still; until he realized that the girl was distanced from him, unamused. 'Are you all right, my dear?'

'I'll live.'

'If you hadn't jumped . . . It was only in sport, you see . . .' He essayed a smile. 'Not the true serpent's tooth at all.' The face was handsome still in a punished, ruinous way, the hair shiny, iron-grey curling to white, its wildness made wilder by the two bluebells threaded through his locks. He too was tanned, but there were manifold wrinkles round his eyes and mouth, and a salt-and-pepper moustache emphasized his moue as he muttered, 'And we are feeling contrite. Do look.' He pointed down to the limp member slumped at his thigh. 'Did you ever see such a sorry-looking fellow?'

Despite herself the girl smiled. 'You're impossible.'

'But amorous with it.' The old man stroked the ground beside him. 'Why don't you come back? Let me tender you some comfort.'

'No way.' Head averted, the girl resumed the buttoning of her shirt.

He shook his head regretfully. 'You're absolutely right: I'm a perverse old fool. I don't know which side my bread is buttered and . . . what was the rest?'

'Too late,' she declared, lightly aloof, 'far too late.'

'But such a day . . . such a day,' he sighed. 'Time has no business here at all.'

It was true. The girl paused in her dressing. Eyes closed, she seemed to draw in some of the sunlight with her breath. The man lay still. The two figures might have been drowsily patient under the eye of a French painter—soft impasto light, green wood-shadow, and the dreaming mist of bluebells beyond. There was nothing Anglo-Saxon here, not even a breeze to ripple gooseflesh on their skin. Nor, while they were silent, was the long moment of this century even. It felt closer, much closer, to Theocritus—and I, squinting like the Cyclops from the shade.

Again the blackbird chattered its dismay. The girl opened her eyes. 'Are you asleep?'

'Adream.'

She bent to pick up the discarded denim shorts, then stopped, straightened herself, and stood listening, as though sensing they were watched. Her eyes—they were narrow, dark-lashed—surveyed the trees.

I shrank into the shade of a beech, one hand against its smooth bark for support. I could have sworn for a moment that our eyes met, but the girl showed no sign of alarm. She pursed her lips slightly, stretched her neck to tilt the chin, and then brushed back a stray tress from her face. The toes of her right foot drew a segment of a circle through beech-mast and leaf-mould.

'Do you feel anything?' she said quietly.

'Lust?' the old man suggested lazily. 'A certain consuming nostalgia for your body. Remorse for a squandered opportunity . . .' He might have gone on but she frowned impatiently, shushed him, listening to the air. After a moment she said, 'I think *she* used to come here.'

The old man sat upright, suddenly intent. 'You can feel her?'

Again the girl's eyes scouted the glade. 'I'm not sure. There's something.'

'Close your eyes. Keep absolutely still. Let your other senses work.'

The girl raised a hand to still his urgency. The air of the glade was glassy and brittle. She stood at the centre of a silence, radiating pure attention. The old man watched, mouth ajar, as if an untimely word or gesture might break a spell.

'Yes, it's there,' she said softly, '—an intense yearning . . . hunger . . . it's everywhere here.'

'The emotional hunger,' the man said, ' . . . the ache you described before?'

'No, it's different.'

'How?' The demand was a quick, clipped breath.

Suddenly, startlingly, the girl's voice and posture changed. 'It's me,' she said, 'I'm starving. Let's go home.' She looked back at the old man and burst into bright laughter at his outraged scowl. 'Got you.'

'God damn,' he growled, beating the ground with the flat of his hand. 'I told you never to fool about with that. Never, do you hear?'

'Serves you right.'

'I'll serve you right.' As he pushed himself to his feet she giggled again, snatched up her shorts, slipped her feet into sandals, then ran, fleetly, through the bluebell drift and up the bank. From the cover of the beech I watched the old man lumber after her, shouting, and saw the girl turn between two sycamores to call, 'Better not leave your clothes. I might double back and pinch them and leave you to make your way back without.'

'Then I'd garland my nakedness like Lear,' the old man bellowed, 'and walk home via Saxburgh bidding copulation thrive. But I'll have you first.'

Long after they'd gone from sight I could hear their squeals and shouts, the crashing of their tracks through bracken. Part of me wanted to laugh out loud, break cover, join the mad chase. Instead, astonished by the brief spectacle, feeling cheated, envious of the old goat, I turned away.

And there was movement behind me.

A quivering in green foliage. A disturbance of sunlight off the leaves.

Swiftly, I turned my head, certain for one hot moment that I too was observed. The scent of bluebells was in my nostrils, heady and raw. My own skin might have been glowing green as nettles now. I shook my head, blinked—there was nothing but the stir of light and leaf, and the flimsy swaying of a branch; but I was trembling a little.

After a long moment, though in a different direction from that in which I could still hear the laughter of the girl, I too began to run.

You get by, an hour at a time, mulling things over, nosing for a future, not content, but managing; then the wires cross with someone else's world and suddenly you're a shambles again. Actuality is elsewhere. You're dispossessed.

The encounter in the wood had been like a hot dream. For a few minutes it took me outside myself, then it left me chafed and restless, critical of my vacant days. And it turned chilly that evening. Or was it merely in contrast to the heat of a day in which a bare-arsed wood-nymph could frolic unflinching over a paunchy Silenus with bluebells in his hair? Either way I was cold, so I carted a basketful of logs from the shed and looked for old newspaper to start a fire.

It seemed odd that Clive hadn't mentioned such neighbours. He'd suggested I look up Ralph Agnew at the Hall ('He has a soft spot for verse'), and warmly recommended Bob Crossley. 'And while you're there,' he'd added, 'give my love to Gypsy May,'—about whom no more, except that I was bound to come across her.

From his smile I'd pictured a batty old Romany woman thrusting clothes-pegs at me and muttering darkly about the future. It seemed an improbable name for the American Amaryllis of the glade, though there had been a gypsy air about her—sallow-skinned, nomadic at a guess, and—if her joke on the old man had travestied some serious business—psychic withal!

With an arsonist's interest I put a match to the paper and watched the kindling catch. Smoke wavered towards the cowl.

So what were they up to here?

And why, once more, was I relegated to the status of voyeur?

Like most of my generation I'd grown up with a dangerous illusion: that once you were adult you were also, by a kind of evolutionary osmosis, a reasonably coherent individual. A person, no less. Only recently had events disclosed the shabby menagerie beneath the skin; and some of its creatures were bedded down in very dirty straw. In particular I distrusted the scrawny beast which eked out the narrow consolations of the voyeur's role. It was contemptible. I could do without that shade of green.

I jumped from the trance with smarting eyes.

The parlour was a cloud. The smoke had bent back on its tracks to explore the room. There'd be soot-dust everywhere. I prised open a window—too small to make much difference—made for the door, pulled it open, and saw Bob Crossley standing at the step with a fist poised to knock. We stared at one another in amazement as smoke swooped round us.

'Good God, are you on fire?'

'It's the chimney, I think. I just lit a fire and this happened.'

'Let's have a look.' Bob pushed past me into grey billows. 'Chimney's blocked. You've probably got a starling's nest up there. Or it could be damp. There hasn't been a fire in here for ages . . . *Christmas*!' He came back to the doorway, fanning the air. 'Come on. Outside. It's caught too far to pull it off yet.'

We stood in the garden and he grinned at me. 'Damp,' he decided. 'I remember Clive had the pots netted. You shouldn't have any trouble once the flue dries out.'

'The thatch?'

'Hmmm.' He stepped back, craned up at the pot where a thin feather of smoke wistfully aspired. 'No, that's all right. It'll clear soon.' He looked back my way. 'The thing is, Clive just rang. He's ringing back in ten minutes . . . wants to talk to you.'

My confusion was compounded. One of the attractions of The

Pightle had been its phonelessness. It was Clive's bolt-hole, and I'd thought myself uncontactable there, but here was the world at my shoulder again. It was like a bill dropping through the door.

'Did he say what he wanted?'

Bob shook his head, and looked at his watch. 'Better nip on down to my place. I'll keep an eye on this.'

'If you don't mind . . .'

'What neighbours are for. Handy timing really. On your way.'

Bob's house was larger, more permanently homely than The Pightle, the garden trim and well-worked, and everywhere, in the chintzed pelmets and loose-covers, the traces of a woman's hand. I found the phone in his study and, beside it, a photograph of his wife. There was a sturdy, Quakerly plainness about her, composed and unsurprisable. Her smile was patient of the camera, and vicariously, it seemed, of me. She was still the tutelary deity of the place. Other framed snapshots on the windowsill showed the couple on holiday together in Venice, and on a CND rally somewhere, in matching parkas. I sensed that, for Bob, every glance upwards from the desk must be an act of memory. There were Open University textbooks there, a scribble pad, and a paperback titled *Karl Marx: Social and Political Thought* splayed on its spine. The room smelled of Bob's pipe.

I picked up the phone at first ring and said, 'Clive?'

There was a moment's silence at the other end, then an unfamiliar voice demanded, 'That you, Bob?'

'Er . . . no . . . He's out at the moment.'

'Well who's that?'

'My name's Darken. I'm living in the cottage up the lane—The Pightle?'

The stiff voice softened. 'Oh I see. Clive's friend?'

'That's right. Look, I'm expecting a call. Bob should be back in a few minutes if you'd like to call again.'

'No, no need. Quite glad to speak to you, in fact. Listen, this is Ralph Agnew. From the Hall. Just ringing to tell Bob I'm having a few people for drinks on Friday. About eight. Like him to come.'

'I'll tell him.'

'Oddly enough, was going to suggest he bring you along. Want to meet you.'

'Thanks. I'll see . . .'

'Do come. Poet, right? One of Clive's stable? Yes, you really must. Someone you should meet. Nothing formal, you understand? Shall you be there?'

Damn Clive!

'I'm not sure what I'm . . .'

'I really think you should. Eightish then. Friday. Okay?'

Before I could answer he put down the phone. I did the same, but it rang again almost immediately.

'Bob?'

I recognized Clive's voice. 'No, it's me.'

'Oh it's you, is it? Nose still above water then? Bob tells me you haven't been showing your face.'

'I'm settling in.'

'Everything okay? Managing all right?'

'Fine—except that I've just set the place on fire.'

'What?'

'Don't panic. The chimney was smoking, that's all. Bob says it's damp. He's up there now. The cottage, I mean, not the chimney.'

'Well thank God it's in capable hands. Listen, mooncalf . . . why didn't you tell me that Jess didn't know where you were?'

'Has she been ringing you?'

'Course she has. Half off her head. You really are too much.'

'Not really her concern these days.'

Clive savoured the edge in my voice. 'She does still care about you. We all do, though God knows why we should.'

I said nothing.

'And there are the kids. I mean, a vanishing act's a bit hard on them, don't you think?'

'I was going to send a card.'

'Well get on with it, lad. I've got better things to do than shuttlecock about between you and Jess.'

'Did you give her this number?'

'And drag old Bob into your catastrophes? No way. But she did wring the address out of me. Expect a letter. She chewed my head off for not letting her know where you were before.'

'Look, I'm sorry about that.'

'So you should be. Anyway, I think I cooled her down. You writing yet?'

'Not yet.'

'Dug the garden?'

'Look, Clive . . .'

'Well do something useful for God's sake. You must be sick of the sight of your navel.'

'I've just been invited out.'

'Good. Who by?'

'Ralph Agnew.'

'Better still.'

'Was it your idea?'

'Mine?'

'He knew I was here . . . who I was.'

'Village life has no secrets. You're going, I trust?'

'Maybe. Haven't made up my mind. Who's Edward?'

'Edward who?'

'Here. In the village. Oldish man. Sixty or so. American girl-friend.'

'No idea.'

'I saw them romping in the wood today. In their birthday suits.'

'Good Lord! Sixty, you say?'

'At least.'

'Not hallucinating, are you?'

'For God's sake.'

'It's just that I don't remember the woods being quite that lively. Mind you don't get shot at, by the way. There are some mean keepers round there. Oh yes . . . one other thing. I've got that cheque. Royalties on *Shadowgraphs*. Not exactly a princely sum. Shall I send it on?'

'No, hang on to it. I'm not sure how long I'll be here.'

'I thought you were settling in?' Clive said and, after a silence, 'Well, it's up to you. Listen, post that card will you?—if it's the best you can do. And go and see Ralph, okay?'

'Okay.' I put down the phone, then said aloud, twice, 'Damn!'

Bob Crossley was standing at The Pightle door. 'I've managed to rake some if it out,' he said, 'but it's still a bit thick in there.' He took in my preoccupied frown. 'Don't worry. It's only smoke.'

'It's not that. Look, I'm really grateful . . .'

He shrugged off my thanks. 'Problems?' The vague shake of my head did not deter him. 'Things do catch up,' he fished.

To no avail.

'I was just going down to the Feathers for a jar. Why don't

you come? Leave the windows open here. It'll have cleared by the time you get back.'

There were things on my mind, but, 'You can't sit in there,' he pressed. 'Anyway, it's your civic duty. If you don't use the pub the brewery will shut it down. Things are measured by the till these days. The school's gone already. The bloody accountants are tearing the heart out of the villages. Dormitories, that's what they'll be. Geriatric wards. Even the church can only run to the occasional service. Not that that's any great loss. But the pub . . . I mean, a pint's worth fighting for, isn't it?'

His grin was seductive.

Within the hour I was tipsy. An hour later I was drunk.

'Ah Gypsy May!' Bob had said. 'Now thereby hangs a tale.'

'A tail and a half,' Bill Rush had added. He was the pigman at Home Farm, a man with a long thirst and a Sagittarian eye for the doubles on the darts board. The whole Snug sniggered— the verb might have been the active principle of the noun. Even George Bales, the dour gamekeeper, joined in the laughter from his solitary corner. Clearly the joke was an old friend, but I was having trouble enough with the singsong local accent, and the pun escaped my innocent ear.

'So are you going to tell me?'

'I'll do better than that,' Bob had winked. 'You come along to church with me tomorrow morning and I'll introduce you.' The laughter enlarged itself, masculine—no women about; the old, smokily reassuring alliance.

It was the next morning now as Bob and I strolled down the green lane to the church. To my eye the tower should have been taller in proportion to the nave, but funds must have run out back in the Middle Ages for the church looked hunchbacked now where it stood on a hummock across from the Feathers, outlined against a marbled sky. The Rectory, a yew-shaded Georgian manse of rosy brick, stood empty over the way from the lych-gate. It was up for sale.

'Riddled with dry-rot,' Bob told me. 'The last Rector to live there died of gangrene. It's true, I promise you. The present man lives over at Thrandeston. He has four parishes to look after and not enough Christians to go round.'

We entered the churchyard through a narrow wicket-gate off the lane where a path had been trodden through thick grass freckled with dandelions and buttercups among the gravestones.

'He wanted to keep goats on the grass here,' Bob explained, 'but the old biddies wouldn't have it—said they were creatures of the Devil. If he'd kept goats he'd have lost his congregation. Creatures of the Devil, I ask you! So we have dandelions instead, till someone puts a scythe to it.' He plucked a blade of grass and stood, sucking on it, looking up at the flints of the church.

I walked on round the tower taking in the view across the village street. No one was about, and the morning was silent save for birdsong and the distant rumble of an aircraft out of the base at Thrandeston. The breeze was rich from the sties. Two stone angels shook censers over the entrance to the porch, and there was a dead fledgling inside. I pushed the door open on to a hollow silence. Light shafted down across the narrow pews from clear-glass lancet windows. Except for the usual church furnishings and more angels at the high beam-ends, it was plain and white as a dairy in there, smelling of stalled air and damp hassocks.

These days, at the end of the Christian era, the solemnity of a country church has less the air of a temple about it than that of a museum. Yes, it makes you feel you have to speak in whispers, but even the noise of your feet on the flags sounds like an intrusion, and entering such ancient space is like stepping out of time. Yet there is an awesome sense of continuity too. Here in Munding St Mary's, for instance, a board near the west door recorded the incumbents from William de Witneshame in 1190 down to Neville Sallis who had recently taken the living. There were fewer names than I would have guessed: apart from Nicholas Launce in the plague years and one Edwin Lucas Frere who'd lasted only from 1848 to 1850, most of them seemed to have had good innings. Only boredom could have tested their nerves in this quiet retreat.

Somewhere in this building lurked Gypsy May, about whom Bob had remained teasingly reticent. Yet apart from the old propane heater with its twin gas-bottles nothing anomalous caught my eye. The two brasses let into the flags were undistinguished, and only one of the swagged memorials on the chancel wall was imposing. Commemorating Sir Humphrey Agnew, Bart, 1622–1695, it was flanked by a fanfare of Resurrection angels and bore a familiar quotation from Virgil:

Facilis descensus Averno;
Noctes atque dies patet atri ianua Ditis;
Sed revocare gradum superasque evadere ad auras,
Hoc opus, hic labor est.

The Agnew family were well represented here, and no doubt
Ralph would eventually join these dead ancestors whom time had
turned to tablets of stone. Like Louisa Anne, for example, whose
name and dates, 1821–1913, were carved on the open pages of a
marble book with the brief inscription *Mutus Liber*. It felt a sad
little epitaph—to have lived so long and be remembered only as a
silent book. I was pondering it when Bob came up the nave behind
me and said, 'Were you married in church, Alex?'

I hadn't told him I was married at all; but, 'The works,' I
admitted, '—monkey suit and all. What about you?'

He shook his head. 'Registry Office. Never had much time
for these places. Too tied up with this for my liking.' He indicated another tablet commemorating Capt. Henry Wharton Agnew, 1894–1916, and Lt Hilary Louis Agnew, 1896–1916;
brothers presumably, and probably killed in the same battle. The
words *Haec Manus Pro Patria* were inscribed beneath the names.
My Latin was fresh enough to recognize a clever if sombre pun,
for I remembered that *Manus* meant both 'a hand' (in reference
to Mucius Scaevola's sacrifice of his right hand for Rome) and
also 'a little band of soldiers.'

'*Pro patria,*' Bob said aloud and sniffed. 'No marble slabs
for the other ranks, you see—just a list on the cenotaph outside.
Would you believe that even this small village lost nine men in
Flanders? There was nothing for the poor sods here, and not
much in Flanders either. But I'll bet the Yaxleys grieved over
their two lost sons just as bitterly as the Agnews did.'

There was something faintly depressing in the air of the silent
church. 'So where is she?' I asked.

Bob looked back from his pondering and grinned. 'You
walked right past her.' I glanced round the white walls again.
'Outside,' he said, and led me back down the nave. The heavy
door banged shut behind us. The light seemed harsher out there,
and the morning was loud with the sound of a chainsaw somewhere. 'This way.' Bob pushed through the long grass away
from the church, then turned and pointed upwards.

I shielded my eyes from the sun as they followed his finger.
It took a moment or two to distinguish the slab of stone from

the surrounding flints, but there was shadow enough to define the rough contours of the figure carved there. I was uncertain whether simply to gasp or to laugh out loud at the improbable sight of it.

'That's Gypsy May,' Bob said.

2 ▣ The Figure in the Stone

In 1848, a few years before the railway cut past the hollow on its way to Saxburgh, the view from the mound of the church across the village of Munding had not been so very different. The street was untarred, of course, and there were no wires for electricity or telephone, but the same copse masked the hamlet from the west, and the same water-meadows on the south and east were flooded most winters by the stream that crossed the lane to Saxburgh in a shallow ford. A wrong turning among the warren of hedgerows approaching the village (though, sadly, too few of these would survive the aggressive farming of a later age), and a traveller might pass within a slingshot of its reed-thatched cottages without knowing they were there.

There has always been something reclusive in the way Munding St Mary's clasps the Norfolk light, and in that it perfectly matched the temperament of Sir Henry Agnew, and the undemanding taste of his daughter, Louisa Anne.

For a long time that young woman had been at her window watching the clouds ferry the October light across the sky as though they were the carriers of urgent news. Except for the rise and fall of her breath she was still, one hand lightly pressed against the pane, the other at her side holding a Michaelmasdaisy, head downward, by the stem. Her dress was of grey silk, its sheen answering to the tilt of the evening light across the lake, so that she was now little more than a marbled shadow among shadows.

For three days, since the month had changed, an easterly had fretted among the trees and would not back, but now she sensed

18

a veering in the air, a softness where things had been gritty and bitter before. Or perhaps it was no more than her own uncertain mood which had veered all day between expectancy and swift, inexplicable fits of sadness. Her customary poise had absconded. Disagreeably. Even arranging the flowers in the vase she had found herself reflecting how there had been a war in Heaven once, and these Michaelmas-daisies—neither angel-white nor wholly serpent-darkened—were its wounds. Which was a solemn and untypical thought. And with guests about to arrive at any moment such moroseness would not do. It would not do at all.

Perhaps too warily, and for too long, she had held the world at bay, and now she was just a little afraid. Not that she was discontented with her life and with her work—few people had ever been entrusted with a task of such pressing gravity—but an offended suitor had once consoled himself for her failure to swoon at his feet by comparing her to Mariana of the Moated Grange, and the remark, however unjust, had stayed with her. On such vulnerable days as this she could wish herself ordinary enough to fit such simple expectations as his; but she shuddered at the diminishment this would mean. On the lozenge of the glass closest to her lips her sigh made a small mist which blurred the park and the distant trees a moment, and then, as she turned away, dispersed.

There was nothing more to do, but she must do something. And what she did was decidedly unwise—she knew it even as she laid the flower on the sill and crossed to her writing desk. From the compartment at the back she took out a small wooden casket, turned the key, and opened the lid on the piece of velvet in which the cards were wrapped. It was of a blue so dense it glimmered on the brink of blackness.

There was no time, and she was not composed enough, to attempt a thorough reading. She knew too that it was wrong to approach the cards in so restless a way; but it might still be illuminating to see which particular image would present itself out of a long shuffle and a single, decisive cut.

Neatly she folded the velvet aside to reveal the golden floral pattern on the reverse of the top card, then seated herself more comfortably and picked up the deck. The cards were too large for nimble shuffling—one must rearrange them a few at a time, passing them from one palm to the other, making sure that none should fall. The surfaces were cool and shiny to the touch. As she changed the order of the procession in her hands she called upon an old meditational device to still herself. She made her mind a mountain-spring, which became a stream that coursed through crevices of rock until it reached a point where it must plunge in a long fall to the lake beneath. As her imagination plummeted, cold and clear, down into the black abyss of the waiting lake, the cards travelled, tapping and sliding, one against the other, from hand to hand.

Now she was ready. Eyes still closed, she patted the cards back into a solid deck and laid it flat on the palm of her left hand. The fingers of her right tested the thickness of the deck, then cut.

She opened her eyes and, in the same instant, there was an inward pang like that of breaking ice. A man was smiling up at her from the face of the top card where he dangled upside down on a gallows, his arms fastened behind his back, the loose leg crossed behind the one from which he hung, and money was falling from his pockets to the ground.

It was the twelfth and, to her, the most mysterious of the Trumps: The Hanged Man.

And then she heard the sound of horses in the drive.

'Damnation!' said Henry Agnew, who had heard the same stamping hooves, the same jingle of harness, through the window of his library. With a sigh of exasperation he put down his magnifying glass and closed the volume of Ashmole's *Theatrum Chemicum Brittanicum*. At 69, though still reasonably sound in health, he resented every hour that kept him from completion of his life's work, and in recent weeks he had been pestered by more distractions than he could patiently abide.

The Rector of the parish had died in scandalous circumstances. The locum had seized the opportunity to admonish the congregation on its more pagan than Christian standards of morality, and his overlong sermons had proved tiresome even to the virtuous. Agnew, as local squire, had been under some pressure to hasten the appointment of a more congenial incumbent, but the living was not in his gift. It lay with the Provost and Fellows of King's College, Cambridge, to whom the spiritual welfare of a remote Norfolk hamlet was not of pressing moment.

There had been much correspondence between Agnew and King's, between the Dean and the Bishop, until at last a possible replacement had been found. The eligible man was circumspect, the Dean's last letter had advised, and would, of course, wish to visit the parish before committing himself. The Rectory had been closed since the last parson's death, and it had fallen to Agnew to entertain the Reverend Edwin Lucas Frere and his wife while they considered how they should answer God's call to link their destinies with that of a parish so far from the main highways of preferment.

Not for the first time Agnew mourned the early loss of a wife who had been so much better equipped for this kind of ordeal than he was himself. Thank God at least for a daughter as capable as Louisa Anne. In her he was truly blessed. If his son was too immersed in the passing excitements of the great world to recognize the importance of Agnew's work, that certainly was not the case with the girl. Each day as he returned to his desk he could expect to find there, penned in her elegant hand, a lucid redaction of the texts with which he was currently engaged. With the same delicacy of touch she would do her best to shield him from this intrusion now.

It was Louisa who opened the library door on her way to receive the guests, and said, 'The visitors are arrived, papa.' She seemed elated at the prospect, a little breathless.

'I know. I know.' Agnew's eyes sloped to the corners under their lids, and a large, gnarled nose jutted between. Displeasure was writ large.

'Then will you be so civil as to come? They will not go away again for wishing it.'

'Two,' Agnew growled beneath his breath. 'Two miserable couplets today. That's all.' He got up from his chair and allowed Louisa to straighten his collar, which she did a little sternly. 'You are to swear on your honour that you will not play the Trappist,' she responded. It was marvellous convenient the way a vocation of silence descended upon her father the moment visitors arrived—unless it chanced to be Tom Horrocks, or Mr Speedwell with a fresh consignment of books for his approval. She planted a kiss on his grimace and said, 'Who knows but that the parson may prove an agreeable fellow? A university man should have some wit to commend him.'

'But the woman . . . I never yet met a parson's wife who wasn't a confounded stickler.'

'Then you must charm her. Now come, sir. Best foot forward, if you please.' She had placed in parenthesis for a moment the

thought of that disturbing Tarot card. Besides, the drag of a dull
pain in her loins had now explained much.

Having prepared herself for barbarous discourse on the merits
of gun dogs and the adventures of the local hunt, Emilia Frere
was relieved that intelligent conversation should be so readily
available. The baronet himself did not greatly entertain, but the
girl . . . a vivacious mind, suitably responsive to maturer guidance, a most winsome smile (those angled eyes were quite beguiling), and with a lightfoot wit. A surprising find in these rural
deeps, with as yet no major fault to be seen. It could only be a
kindness to restrain her immoderate enthusiasm for the novel
under discussion.

'One must indeed be compassionate with anyone in Mrs Huntingdon's plight,' Emilia was saying of the novel's heroine, 'but
as a clergyman's wife I can hardly condone a woman who de-
serts her husband, no matter how grievous the provocation. No,
my dear, a vow is a vow, and those of marriage the most sacred
of all. I confess myself amazed that any gentleman could recommend their abrogation as Mr Bell's narrative appears to do.'
Once more she found herself wondering at the mild precision
of the young gaze across from her. Hard to conceive how the
girl had escaped marriage for so long herself—though 27 was
no great age. Later she would console her with the thought.

Louisa Agnew, calmer now that the guests were met and measured, avoided controversy. 'But can one be quite certain that
the novel is a man's work?' she enquired. Since she had taken
The Tenant of Wildfell Hall on loan from Saxburgh subscription
library (looking to find there no more than a refreshing contemporary companionship after a hard day's work over Latin texts),
Louisa had felt too close a kinship with the author not to put
that provocative question. The light in her eyes contrived to be
sprightly and earnest at the same time, and their blue sorted well
with the black tresses of her hair. 'Do you not feel a woman's
sensibility in its insights?'

'Thus the gossip runs,' said Emilia, who had learned much
in the fencing-school of Cambridge conversation, 'but I prefer
to believe otherwise. Were it conceivable that one of our own
sex should publish such a questionable narrative, well . . . I
could only think my reservations more strongly founded.'

'Or the passion with which it is written more intensely felt?'
Louisa suggested, and smiled.

Henry Agnew cleared his throat, glowering at his daughter the while. He had long since decided the parson's wife a cold fish. Dinner was over, and as neither he nor Frere had read the novel in question he felt it high time the sexes took their separate ways.

'That sound,' Louisa interpreted, 'is the cry of the male Agnew impatient for its brandy. Shall we withdraw, Mrs Frere, and leave the gentlemen to mend the troubles of the world in peace?'

Edwin Frere added water to his brandy and prepared himself for inquisition. Above the crackle of the fire and a hoarse draught in the chimney, moorhens could be heard across the lake outside, like the squeezing of tiny horns in fog. Otherwise, with the ladies departed, there was silence in the room. Agnew had settled back in his chair, lit up a pipe, and was now staring into the fire as though into the deeps of meditation.

Uncertain whether his host was marshalling a line of enquiry, or simply absorbed in the business of digestion, Frere sat out the silence for a while. Like many large-boned men he was rather shy, and rarely gave a new acquaintance the full advantage of his ardent brown eyes which, in consequence, appeared more shifty than soulful beneath the dark curls of his hair. A keen observer, however, would mark the long eyelashes (*like a giraffe's*, Louisa had thought) and their silent agitation when, as now, he was a little at a loss. He admired the panelling once more, and worried over the lubricious glint in the stare of the portrait above the fireplace. Eventually it became clear that if there was to be conversation then he must open it.

'You have a fine house, Sir Henry. I greatly look forward to seeing the park by daylight.'

Agnew grunted on his pipe. 'I'm content enough at Easterness. Give me my library and the Norfolk light and let the busy world go hang, I say.'

'It is a peaceful spot.'

'It's that all right. I should warn you, Mr Frere, I've had guests from town who complained they could not sleep for the silence.'

'I believe I could sleep on a clothes-line tonight.'

Agnew eyed his guest dubiously. His thoughts had been elsewhere and the preposterous image of a parson on a clothes-line was momentarily perplexing. Then he returned to his preoccupation. 'I'm trying to find a word other than *mixed* to rhyme with *fixed*,'' he said, as though no further explanation of his abstraction was required. 'Damned if I can.'

Frere took the problem upon himself. 'Betwixt?' he suggested after a moment.

'Hmmm. Hadn't thought of that. Might do. Might do very well.'

Frere was encouraged. 'I see you share my enthusiasm for versifying, Sir Henry.' He had once dreamed that he might one day be numbered among the Anglican poets—the work of George Herbert lay close to his heart—but it had been a long time since the verses flowed, and if he had hoped to stir his host's interest he was disappointed. Agnew was nodding his head in time to the tap of his finger on the chair arm—counting out the numbers of a line perhaps. After a time he scowled, rubbed his chin, then glanced awkwardly at his guest. The suggestion of the rhyme had at least secured the parson a larger place in his attention.

'But you, sir,' he said, 'you're a youngish man still. Will you not find country life tedious after Cambridge? Munding Street is a far cry from King's Parade, you know.'

The clergyman smiled. 'My fears are not on that score. Believe me, on a January night with an east wind cutting across the fens Cambridge can be the most desolate place on earth.'

'And then,' said Agnew, as though in mitigation, 'you have a wife for company.'

'Indeed.'

'Unlike Matt Stukely. His undoing that, I say.'

'I don't believe I follow you, Sir Henry.'

'The flesh, you know. Our late lamented Rector burned with it. Did you not hear tell the manner of his passing?'

'An apoplexy, I understand.'

Agnew snorted. 'He ate well, drank well, and took precious little exercise save of the kind that brought him to his maker. A big man—built like my bull Jonas. That night he was riding his housemaid full gallop when his heart burst on him like a fig.' Agnew snapped thumb and finger. 'Poor Amy Larner lay across the mattress with this great corpse dropped on her and couldn't move an inch. Screamed till half the parish was awake. It took two men to lift him off her, and she with her shift up round her neck.' He took another philosophical puff on his pipe. 'On reflection I doubt that Matt could have wished for a choicer way to go.'

A shy man, anxious to be exemplary, and aware that his resilience was under trial, Edwin Frere smiled, then instantly blushed. 'I had no idea,' he said.

'Don't mistake me. Stukely was a good enough sort in his way. Didn't terrorize his parishioners like some Rectors in these parts. But he had a weakness, you see . . . I'd surmise that his favourite text for his housemaids was "Sleep not, for you know not when the master cometh." There's more than one brat about Munding that's half-parson already. Will you take more brandy?'

The clergyman raised a hurried finger and lowered it across the snifter like a lid.

Agnew contemplated without enthusiasm the confusion he had caused in his guest. *Put two shy dogs together,* he was thinking, *and you'll soon have a confounded mess on the floor.* He looked for another stone to turn. 'I hear you are a travelled man, Mr Frere? India, the letter said.'

He had tried to put the man at his ease and could not understand why the parson should now shift even deeper into recoil. Frere was overly diffident perhaps, with a curious way of pinching his earlobe as he listened; but rather that than holy condescension or the locum's sanctimonious rantings.

'I was there for a time . . . when I was still a single man. The Evangelical Mission to the Heathen . . .'

'You found it not to your taste?'

'Not exactly that . . .'

Things were going badly for Edwin Frere. He was attracted to the figure of the old eccentric across from him, and would dearly have liked to discover some ground where they might both relax, yet from the first the conversation had slipped out of his control. Now he must find a way of steering round this innocent enquiry.

'India is a great mystery, Sir Henry,' he suggested. 'Alexander could not encompass it, and neither could I.' He had attempted a witticism but he had little gift for such matters and it had come out sounding as though some serious comparison were intended. He fumbled for a handkerchief and, behind its cover, sought to slow his breathing and, with it, the heart. 'I discovered,' he said at last, 'that mine is not a missionary spirit.' Then he saw how the question might be turned. 'Have you been a traveller yourself, Sir Henry?'

Agnew shook his head. 'No time for it. It's my contention that there are mysteries enough in here to keep a man occupied without meddling in foreign parts.' He had tapped his breast with the pipe-stem to indicate the direction of his own explorations. 'I could wish the boy had seen as much.' Agnew's only son was active in Lord Palmerston's Foreign Office, and Frere had been surprised earlier to discern in the father a certain scepticism towards the son's ambitions.

'Indeed,' he agreed, a little hastily. 'I see you are a philosopher, Sir Henry, as well as a versifier.'

Agnew's eyes were half-closed in scrutiny of his guest. 'And perhaps something more than either,' he offered, '—as they are commonly understood.'

The baronet, Frere sensed, was as little at ease as he was himself with the trivia of social conversation. Perhaps here was an opening on to more substantial ground. 'I have often thought,' he returned tentatively, 'that mystery is what I know, not what I don't know.'

'Indeed?' said Agnew, interested, though he was already regretting his admission of a moment before. 'But then,' he added cautiously, 'as a wise man once said, "Mysteries profaned and made public fade and lose their grace. Therefore, cast not pearls before swine, nor spread roses for the ass." '

For an instant Frere wondered whether he was being rebuked as such himself, but there was a glint of enthusiasm in the old man's eyes, and something akin to hunger. And that quotation—referring to Matthew's Gospel, but not of it—was puzzling. 'If you would take me with you, Sir Henry,' he said, 'you must say more.'

For a long time Agnew considered the younger man over his pipe. Out of such approaches either a true friendship or a confounded nuisance might be born. Yet for the first time in many years he sensed himself in male company that would not find his own heart-deep convictions entirely ridiculous. Stukely's had been an indolent mind. The rest of the local gentry were a philistine rabble. His only close friend, Tom Horrocks, was a doctor of the new school, a rationalist and a man of science, excellent for an honest dispute or a game of chess, but good-naturedly sceptical of Agnew's 'mumbo-jumbo.' It had been a long time since he had met a kindred spirit. So long that he had thought the need outgrown. But, yes, this one ran deep. Somewhere along the line the fire had touched him. And yet . . .

Frere sensed the man's hesitation. Yes, Agnew too was shy. A small risk perhaps? Something light?

'I can assure you a more discriminating eye for pearls than

you might fear,' he said, venturing a smile, 'and, if Apuleius is to be believed, even asses have been initiated into mystery.'

The smile was answered. 'I take you for no ass, Mr Frere. On the contrary . . . But one wonders . . .'

'Sir Henry?'

'The Rectors hereabouts. One has not found them overly tolerant of question.'

'At King's, Sir Henry, one encounters little else.' Frere's confidence had grown with Agnew's manifest uncertainty. The baronet was no free-thinker—that much was clear; so what was the secret he was clutching to his bosom with such reticent fervour? 'I have always found an open mind the surest ground of faith,' he added, smiling again.

'Then consider this,' Agnew responded with the gusto of a man launched upon his favourite theme. 'Christ came into the world eighteen and a half centuries ago. He taught love of one's neighbour and forgiveness of sins. He healed the sick, raised the dead, resisted the Devil, took our sins upon himself, suffered for it, died, and rose again. All that could be done for the world he did. Yet it remains a sorry place, sir, and man a sorry creature within it.'

Frere was a little startled by the sudden vehemence. 'But our Redeemer liveth, Sir Henry,' he protested mildly, 'and God's grace abides.'

'Precisely so. But is that the end of the matter, sir? All the evidence proclaims that the work of redemption remains incomplete. It is up to us now. We were created in the Divine Image, Mr Frere, and a residual germ of that divinity remains occulted within us even in the fallen state. We are more, far more, than the beasts that perish. But if we are to raise ourselves from the blind world of sense into which, like poor Stukely, we have fallen, there is much to be done.'

'For which reason we have a church surely?' Frere answered; then added, ' . . . with all its frailties.'

'And I remain a faithful member, sir. If you take the living you will find me praying and singing with the best of them. But is it enough, I wonder, to put on our Sunday faces and recite the Apostles' Creed?'

'Indeed not,' Frere began.

'Is it enough even to practise good works, to keep an open, charitable heart? How am I to love my neighbour as myself, sir, if I remain in ignorance of who I myself deeply am? And how is a man to know himself, to discover the elemental constituents of his own being, unless he takes a conscious part in the great experiment of Nature? As you yourself opined, man, there are great mysteries.' By now there was a hot light in Agnew's eyes.

And a flutter of anxiety in Frere's. 'There are also great dangers, Sir Henry.'

'Of which, Mr Frere, your Hermetical philosopher is more aware than most.' There, it was out. Let the parson make what he might of it.

'You consider yourself to be . . . an Hermetic?' It was difficult for Frere to keep the surprise, the incredulity from his voice.

'That question was once put to a philosopher by a king,' Agnew returned. 'I might answer with him that I am a Christian, and it is no disgrace to be that and an Hermetic at the same time.'

'You see no conflict?'

'On the contrary, sir: I see a complement.'

There was a silence between the two men, pensive, a little uneasy, into which there came the sound of a piano from another room. A moment later they heard Louisa's voice lifting with graceful, lucid confidence between the lower and upper reaches of an air. For a moment Frere found himself regretting that they were not with the ladies. His own voice, a polished baritone, was never so poised as when raised in song.

Perhaps Agnew was grateful for the reprieve as well. Frere sensed the old man's loneliness like an ache on the air where he sat in silence staring into the fire. The clergyman felt warmly towards his host, and displeased with himself. Had he not invited the challenge, encouraged intimacy, only to slip away the moment it was offered? Must his entire life always stretch itself on this rack of contrary impulse? Perhaps he was wrong to imagine himself cut out for the pastoral role? The edifice of his reconstituted life was frail. Perhaps frailer than he had thought.

The two men listened in silence until the song in the next room came to an end and they heard the sound of Emilia's applause.

'Your daughter certainly has the voice of an angel,' said Frere, uncertain as yet how to respond to the old man's asseveration.

'And an angel's intellect and disposition too.' Agnew was disappointed by the withdrawal, remorseful at having said too much. Had he not yet learned that such impulses of candour were invariably occasions for regret? 'In this life,' he said, 'she is my one true friend. And often enough my inspiration. Without her . . .' He faltered there, grimaced, tapped the dottle from his pipe against the fire-dogs, then composed himself with a sigh. 'I have been too long among my books, Mr Frere. I am a poor host, I fear. You must forgive an old man his enthusiasms.'

'On the contrary, Sir Henry . . .'

Agnew waved a dismissive hand. 'You've had a long journey and you must be weary. And tomorrow you must face the church-wardens and their lady wives. I hazard you'll find that there are already two or three Rectors and at least six Rectors' wives in the parish . . . if you take my meaning.'

Edwin Frere smiled. Perhaps he had not lost the man after all. 'It is my earnest hope, Sir Henry, that if I should prove acceptable to the parish we may enjoy more hours of stimulating conversation together.'

The face was frank and guileless. Though Henry Agnew pre-ferred his solitude he had a magnanimous heart. It was his cus-tom to keep under restraint that prodigality of spirit which, in his father, had warped to extravagance and vice. He was like a shy animal, hungry somewhere for the hand it shunned. 'Dam-mit, man,' he said, 'it's not us but the Provost of King's you must please, and you would appear to have done that already. If you want the living it's yours.'

The wind gusted to rain beyond the casement. It was as though the night were throwing small stones at the glass.

This evening (Louisa Agnew wrote in her journal) *the great world came to Easterness to see whether it might squeeze into our parish without too tight a pinching of its heels. As a growing testiness all day foretold, father left the burden of entertainment largely to me, though it was far from unwelcome as an easterly has made a dreary time of it of late, and I have been a vexation to myself. What, however, to make of this admirable pair?*

Was Mrs Frere merely out to impress a country maid, I won-der, or is Cambridge so emulous an environment that even such a simple soul as she must continuously aspire to brilliance? Yet I must not be too censorious, for she listened sweetly while I sang and responded most sincerely in her approbation.

As to the aspirant himself, he seems a tender spirit, with more of the dove's harmlessness about him than the serpent's wisdom. I have seldom seen so roseate a blush in a man his age (unless it be from an excess of port); though I would judge him of a more melancholic than sanguine disposition. He wants a touch of Jupiter to lighten his humour a little, or perhaps a dash of Mercurius' mischief. When he is in a consternation he will so tug upon his ear that my chief anxiety is lest a few tea-time conferences with Mrs Bostock and Eliza Waters will leave his left lobe so distended he might be able to pass a saucer through it as they say the savages do in the darker parts of Africa!

I am unkind, and one day I shall answer for it.

No, my truer intuition is of a profound, unanswered darkness in our Mr Frere. Behind the reticence of his manner I scent a seeker. One wonders what promptings of the spirit should lead him to this rural fastness? I have a fancy he will take the living, though whether his lady wife will rest content with that I hesitate to judge. She will certainly follow, however, if her husband has the will to lead.

The closing chords of the hymn ascended through the light and settled in dust upon the hammer-beams. In the gallery the bassoonist and key-buglers lowered the instruments from their lips. There was a general shuffle and coughing along the nave.

Frere had mounted his pulpit and stood now, hands gripping the woodwork to steady him. How white, like so many china beakers, was the blur of faces below. The air was redolent of dust and jaded lilies. From where it hung in chains a clock ticked out his hour.

Frere announced and repeated his text: 'Have ye not read that he who made them in the beginning made them male and female?'

He began to preach extempore; but there was some commotion among the pews. He spoke on, though that shifting of feet and exchange of glances was breaking his transport. Only moments into the sermon and he had lost them. His eyes travelled down to the rear of the church where Agnew and his daughter were seated. And this was strange: why were they not in their family pew at the head of the nave? Stranger still, Agnew observed him with a rudely sardonic eye. He seemed the one attentive person in the congregation, but detached, ironical, finally dismissive. *How long*, the bored smile seemed to say, *will you detain us with this pap?*

Then, astoundingly, Agnew stood, raised a single finger to beckon Frere, and walked out of the church.

Frere dried. It was hot beneath the vestments. His knuckles

were white against the oak. To go or stay? The summary crook
of Agnew's finger had indicated some urgency. Everywhere now,
a whispering. In a hot trance the Reverend Edwin Frere stepped
down from the pulpit and walked along the flags of the nave.

Outside the light was a falling blade. Agnew was crouched
on the grass like the yogins Frere had seen in India, and the
grass was luminously green. Agnew reached a hand inside his
coat and took something from his breast. Something small, slender, mobile, that quickly wrinkled around his arm. It glinted,
crackle-glazed and green as emerald. Still smiling, Agnew held
Frere's eyes. His fingers caressed the head of the snake, and it
luxuriated beneath his touch. Under the blunt stub of its nose a
thin tongue flickered languidly.

Nothing was said. No words were needed. The urgent matter
was now. Both understood its nature. The question was simply
whether or not the priest would allow Agnew's snake to bite
him.

Already he sensed what it would be like: the hot dart of the
fangs, the swirl in the bloodstream, a singing in the ears, the
interminable spinning seconds before . . .

There was a rime of sweat behind the priest's ears. Agnew's
smile was an invitation, a summoning, a dare . . .

Edwin Frere lurched awake in a strange room.

In the thin light he made out Emilia stretched beside him.
Below the little bonnet in which her hair was piled the eyelids
were closed and the lips a little open. Frere was trembling.
Immediately he thought to look to his wife for consolation, for
if there was an absence of passion in their life together there was
much affection. Yet it seemed indulgent to waken one who slept
so peacefully. He wondered at the simple human trust in sleep:
how easily it was betrayed. One was consigned there to a world
which derided far more than the laws of time and space. Again
and again one encountered morally dubious figures—tricksters
and faithless lovers who rejoiced in the old anarchy of things.
So often one fell asleep in Hell and, waking, dared not sleep
again.

Quietly he slipped from the covers, crossed to the window
and opened the curtain a little. Dawn was unfolding among the
birches in the park at Easterness. The rain had stopped in the
night, and under high banks of cumulus smaller pinnaces of
cloud were scudding eastwards. Between them flooded a soft,

drenched light in which the spinneys were dusky islands still, and the lake a dim hammered pewter.

He wanted to be out there. He wanted to look at the church alone.

By seven, when Louisa came down to the servants' hall to discuss the day's arrangements with Mrs Tillotson, the housekeeper, Frere's dawn pilgrimage to the church was a matter of common gossip. He had been spotted from an attic window by one of the kitchenmaids whose early duty it was to light the fire in the range and raise the dough for the day's bread.

'And what time do you say this was, Tilly?' Louisa asked.

'Nelly says a little after five, Miss Louisa. The gentleman do seem a deal less partial to his bed than Parson Stukely were.'

'Perhaps he slept badly. You say he has not yet returned?'

'Not so far as I know.'

'And Mrs Frere?'

'Not yet come down, miss. Shall I tell Sarah to give her a knock?'

'No, let her sleep a while. The poor thing was quite exhausted. It's a fine morning, Tilly. I shall take Pedro for a run in the park.'

It was Pedro who discovered Edwin Frere. Like all setters he was gifted more with heart than sense, and having been kept kennelled the previous evening to shield the guests from his promiscuous adoration, he was delighted now to find the clergyman sitting on the stump of a felled oak and gazing out across the lake.

'Pedro, here. To heel,' Louisa called, observing the guest's embarrassment at such passionate attention. 'Pedro, get down. Get down, sir.' Only when she came up to them was she able to disengage the parson from the dancing dog. Frere waved away her apologies, but she sensed something deeply discomfited in the man.

'See, the brute has muddied your coat, Mr Frere. Oh Pedro, you are an ill-mannered cur. You disgrace me. Be off about your business.' The hound skulked, shame-faced, for a yard or two, then decided that was contrition enough. The outraged ducks were settling beyond his reach, but his nose would start some other quarry. Confused, Frere watched him bound away.

'I fear you did not sleep well, Mr Frere.'

'Well enough. Well enough, thank you.' He flushed at the polite lie and conceded that he had been a little restless.

'This is a difficult decision for you?'

He was taken aback for a moment by this direct enquiry. 'No one should lightly undertake a cure of souls, Miss Agnew,' he answered, but how pompous the words appeared against the fresh, early morning complexion of the young woman's face. One could only leave the soft breeze to scatter them.

Louisa wondered how far this man was victim to his own career. What would he have been like, for instance, if he had been put to sea rather than to the cloth? Switch his canonical black for a captain's blue and he might swagger to devastating effect. Either way, he was clearly not yet himself.

'And did your prayers in church this morning clarify the matter?'

Frere looked down upon this young woman in surprise. 'You know about that?'

'The good Lord is not alone in seeing every sparrow that falls in Munding. Your dawn devotions have been the gossip of the kitchen for the past hour.'

'I wanted to view the church alone . . .' He might have been confessing to some escapade.

'And did you approve of what you saw?'

Frere looked above the crowns of the beech trees for guidance. 'Indeed, I had begun to feel I might be of some service here . . .'

Louisa waited for him to continue as she walked beside him. She saw the hand slip to his ear. She said, 'Do I see a *but* upon your lips?' He stole a quick glance at her. 'Some reservation?' she encouraged.

'It is a . . . It is not a . . .'

She smiled at his hesitation. 'I see you have a fondness for riddles. But it is early still and not all my wits are about me. You must give me more of a clue or I shall never guess the answer.'

She felt his spirit hurrying away. Had it not been altogether impolite his body would eagerly have joined it. 'I fear it is something of which I am not quite ready to speak, Miss Agnew,' he muttered. 'You must excuse me.'

Louisa stopped, puzzled, and looked around for Pedro who was scurrying, nose to the ground, towards the Great Wood. Already too far to call and anyway he would not obey. 'Oh dear!

I seem to have lost my dog and you your enthusiasm, Mr Frere. Do you think we are in for a trying day?'

He glanced across at her face. Her skin was shiny in the light, and the blue eyes were tilted slightly, teasing his perplexity. From somewhere beyond his general grave humour a smile surfaced suddenly. It was like a fish nibbling at the air—a momentary spasm of the waters, then gone. Perhaps, after all, his gloom had been disproportionate.

'Is it perhaps that we are too rude a community for your taste?' The candour of the question was nicely calculated—no reproval in her voice, no sarcasm. She might have been asking about his choice of tobacco. It was his weakness, however, to imagine some offence taken.

'Good gracious no, Miss Agnew. Not that. Not that at all.' Having said so much he saw that a larger explanation of his demeanour was now required; he was a poor deceiver. 'It may seem a slight thing to others,' he ventured, 'but I was examining the fabric of the church . . .'

'And wondering how much effort you must expend exhorting the parishioners to its upkeep?'

'Miss Agnew, you misunderstand me. I was pleased to find the church in excellent repair.'

'There is a small leak in the vestry,' she conceded. 'Mr Starling has tried to repair it many times but it has proved recalcitrant.'

Frere waved a hand as though erasing her remark from an invisible slate. 'No, please, do not concern yourself on that score. The church is clearly well cared for . . .' This was a most disconcerting young woman.

'Yet something has discountenanced you,' she pressed. 'Come, Mr Frere, I think we should be friends. You may unburden yourself to me, and then it will be easier when you confront the church-wardens.' Again an encouraging smile. How fluently she reversed the conventional roles; but he could hardly share his discomfort with one of her sex. He was uncertain even how to speak of it to Emilia. He turned and walked on.

'You disappoint me, Mr Frere.'

He stopped.

'I have a name in the parish for a sympathetic ear. I promise you may repose your confidence in me.'

He turned again.

And blushed.

She stood, perplexed—amazed and amused by this sudden rubicund haplessness. Her mind was fleetly at work—what could it be that had so silenced him? Something to do with the fabric of the church?

Of course!

'Ah!' she exclaimed, 'I think I have it.'

He looked down upon her, wide-eyed under raised brows.

'You have met Gypsy May.'

He frowned, puzzled. 'I met no one, Miss Agnew.'

'On the south wall,' she said, smiling, 'above the windows?'

He felt the blood in his face.

'Gypsy May,' she said, triumphant.

He was astounded to find her less embarrassed than amused. 'It is,' he muttered, 'a most extraordinary feature,' and could see no delicate way to pursue the matter.

'In this part of the kingdom, yes. I understand such curios are found more commonly in Ireland where, father tells me, they are called *Sheelagh-na-gigs*. There is, however, one other example in the eastern counties—on the church at Whittlesford in Cambridgeshire.'

'Really? I do not know the building.'

'The carvings are of Celtic provenance, I believe,' the young woman persisted as though they were discussing an entirely innocuous matter. 'Or perhaps older still than that. There is something positively aboriginal about her, don't you think?'

'Indeed.' Frere was incapable of thought.

'Poor May has become nothing of more account than a bogey to frighten naughty children. You must not let her mortify you, Mr Frere.' She gave him a quick, elfin smile, then added—and the clergyman could not entirely conceal his shock—'I am rather fond of her myself.'

He struggled for composure, jerked the chin a little higher on his neck. 'I would hardly have thought it a figure to inspire affection.' He was determined to keep to the impersonal pronoun—they were talking about a stone slab after all.

Louisa studied him, head tilted again in a wide-eyed glance, demure, yet with a faintly derisory curve to her lips. 'I have grown up with her,' she answered simply. 'Perhaps to a newcomer she must be somewhat startling.'

'Indeed,' he said again.

They walked on in silence for a while. The flight of a mallard returned Frere's eyes to the outer world, and he observed with relief that it would not be long before they entered the parterre garden to the rear of the hall.

'This prospect of the park is very gratifying,' he said. She acknowledged the diversion with a nod. 'You are most fortunate in your home, Miss Agnew.' It was necessary somehow to fill the silence between them.

'Yes, Mr Frere, I have many blessings and I am far from unconscious of them.'

As they came to the small iron gate he opened it and stepped aside to let her enter first. She halted in the gateway between two vigilant stone lions, and turned to face him, holding the brim of her bonnet away from her face. 'Compose yourself, Mr Frere. I fear you will find other ladies in the parish quite as dragonish as Gypsy May, if certainly more proper.' She paused, smiled, and added, 'It would be a great pity if you were to allow any of them to drive you away.'

He stood, dumbfounded by her frank smile—utterly other than the grotesque staring head of Gypsy May where the image squatted, high on the church wall, naked with drooping dugs, and both hands holding open the organ of her sex, as though she were about to drop a child in labour, or as though she might engorge a man.

Then, suddenly, as if she had realized the inner reaches of his discomposure for the first time, or some tardy awareness of how far she had overstepped the bounds of strict propriety was rising within her, a reticent shadow fell across Louisa's face. It was like a modest fan raised briskly to her lip. She twisted the little button at her throat, then turned on her heel and drifted along the paved path with so smooth a motion that she might have been walking on water rather than on stone.

3 ❧ The House of God

Mellowed with lichens, the stone lions kept their vigil still across the prospect to the lake, and the parkland could not have greatly changed, but Louisa Anne Agnew was no more than a small marble tablet to me, and Edwin Frere only one among a list of incumbents' names in the church at Munding, when I went, reluctantly, with Bob Crossley to the gathering at Easterness.

As soon as I saw Bob in his suit and tie I knew I'd taken too literally Ralph Agnew's promise that this was to be an informal affair. Yet when I suggested I go back to The Pightle to change out of my jeans Bob wouldn't hear of it. Nor would he lend me a tie. 'No need to make concessions,' he said. 'You'll be a breath of fresh air, and Ralph won't mind. As the local gentry go, he's all right, and if any of the Range Rover Brigade are there it'll do them good to bump up against a free spirit.'

'I note you're wearing a tie.'

'And this,' he countered, flourishing the CND badge at his lapel. 'Make the buggers think, says I.'

For an informal gathering it was also large, but the evening was warm and we were able, thank God, to spill out through the French windows on to the terrace from where you could see the lake glimmering in the dusk and envy all things wild.

'So glad you could come,' said Ralph Agnew with more than mere politeness—he seemed almost relieved. He was a burly man, older than I'd expected—around seventy I guessed—with a well-groomed gloss of silver hair, and would have been handsome still but for the asymmetrical twist to his face. A mild

37

stroke must have permanently disturbed its stresses, and now the narrow lips lifted towards the downward slope of his half-closed left eye, and his speech was slightly slurred. But the overall effect was roguish rather than paralytic. 'Someone I want you to meet,' he said. 'In fact, to be perfectly honest, that's what this whole shindig's about. I'm counting on you to keep an old friend at ease.'

'Who would that be?'

'He's not here yet . . . probably still stiffening himself on Scotch. Bit of a shy bird, you see. Poet. His name's Edward Nesbit.'

'Edward Nesbit?'

'You know him then?'

'I know of him, of course, but . . .'

'Old friend. He's staying with me here. On the Estate. At the Decoy Lodge.'

'That's extraordinary.'

'Why so?'

I was about to say that I thought he was dead, but pulled up in time. 'I mean, nothing's been heard of him for years.'

'Been lying low. Abroad mostly. Anyway, when he turns up I'll introduce you. Look . . . if it's not too much to ask, keep an eye on him, will you? Should have plenty to talk about. Got my own hands full, otherwise wouldn't ask. Not at his best at this sort of thing, you see. In the meantime Bob here will help you to meet some people. Right? By the way, your last book . . . enjoyed it. Touch of the true flame there, I thought. Clive has an eye.'

I stood mumchance, in slight shock, as I watched him make off to greet newcomers. 'So what was all that about?' asked Bob.

Edward Nesbit, I explained, had been among the half-legendary poets of the '40s and '50s, one of the more flamboyant denizens of Fitzrovia, a colourful and dissolute wordsmith whose early promise of grandeur had burned itself out into silence. Nothing had been published under his name for years and, in the gossip-riddled world of the poets, so little had been heard of him that I had assumed him dead.

What I did not say was that it had been Nesbit's work that first turned me on to verse. I was fifteen at the time, restless in the drab, secular desert around me, and his poems had seared across my sky like a prophetic shower of meteors. It had been a cold day when I woke to the realization that, in my own first efforts at verse, I was aping the idiom of Nesbit and his contemporaries with no access to their experience. Later, at university, where I lost my god and found a social conscience (however well-guarded behind some glassy ironies), I had come to prefer a cooler line of descent; but I had never been able to hear myself dismiss Nesbit's work as 'cryptic bombast' without feeling that I was fouling my own first springs of speech.

To learn that he was here now, and that I was expected to shepherd him through a gathering that had already left me half-cataleptic with unease, was to receive a summons from my own dead youth.

It was a moment before I realized that someone else was at my shoulder inviting attention. I looked up to see an eager, youngish man in glasses, sporting a thin white tie over a black shirt, and was surprised therefore to hear Bob introduce the Reverend Neville Sallis, current Rector of Munding and three other parishes. His beam embraced me with interest. I presumed that the absence of a dog-collar announced a liberal theology behind the smile.

'I was telling Alex about the goats,' said Bob.

'Oh dear, that story,' Sallis shrugged, not greatly discomposed. 'Can't seem to get away from it. It should be explained that I was a mere novice at the time. I had no idea that people would take the business of separating the sheep from the goats quite so literally.' The joke had a well-used air. 'Fortunately things are a little more forward-looking at Thrandeston.'

'If you regard nuclear bombers as forward-looking.'

'Now you won't draw me on that one, Bob.' Sallis smiled amiably and turned to me. 'Shall you be at Munding long? It's St Mary's turn for Evensong on Sunday, if you're so inclined.'

'No joy there, Neville,' Bob answered for me. 'Alex's only interest in the church is Gypsy May.'

'Ah yes. She's rather jolly, don't you think?'

'Extraordinary,' I said. 'What on earth is she doing up there?'

'I suppose it was a way of christening her,' Sallis suggested. 'Missionary politics, you know. This too has been among the dark places? The best way to convert the heathen was to consecrate their holy sites. You must have noticed the mound? A lot of churches round here are built on them. Under the patronage of St Michael now—victory over the pagan serpent and all that.'

'But not Munding.'

'No, not Munding.'

'I was wondering about the name—Gypsy May?'

'Ah, I have a theory about that. I think May is a corruption of Mary, and of course there was more than one St Mary. Do you know about Maria Aegyptica?'

'The prostitute?'

'That's the one.' Bob had pricked up his ears and was looking puzzled. 'A rather unusual saint,' Sallis explained. 'She was a temple whore in Egypt who worked her passage to the Holy Land, was converted to Christianity and ended her days as a mystic in the Thebaid. They say when she died a lion came out of the desert to bury her. She was commonly called Mary the Gypsy.'

'So you think the church was consecrated to her?'

'I wouldn't say that. But the legend was popular in the Middle Ages, and with Gypsy May's . . . er . . . posture . . . well, the confusion would have been understandable. The carving's clearly of the old Mother goddess. She couldn't be entirely suppressed so some progressive priest blessed her instead, and there she sits. Good thinking really.'

'Like Easter.'

'Exactly. In fact, I've often wondered about the name of this place. Eostre, the old Spring goddess, might be in there somewhere, don't you think?'

'And none of this bothers you?' Bob asked.

'Why on earth should it? I wish there were more time to research it thoroughly.'

'But the Bishop wouldn't approve?'

'Oh I don't think he'd mind; but the Mothers' Union . . . well . . .' Sallis raised a dubious brow. 'So tell me about yourself, Alex.'

Bob was drawn away into Parish Council business by a fat-cat farmer in a hacking-jacket. I chatted with Sallis for a while and disappointed him by saying I was sure I wouldn't be in the area long enough to read my verse at a concert-party he was organizing, and then endured an hour or so of trivial gossip with some of the other people there. My surly eye discouraged the approach of the more formidable ladies of the county, but I was growing desperate by the time Ralph Agnew came, puffing and blowing, to button-hole me. 'There you are. Edward's arrived.

He's in the library . . . rather the worse for wear. Do come along.' I might have been an indolent employee.

Clad in elephant-cord trousers and a woolly cardigan, with a touch of dash in the scarlet and green scarf knotted loosely round his neck, Edward Nesbit presented a burlier figure than I remembered from his naked appearance in the wood; but the iron-grey hair, the moustache, and the disreputable, Cretan-black glitter to his eyes were unmistakable. And that roué's face, so lined it might have crackled when he laughed. He stood by a window, glass in hand, a cigarette smouldering between his fingers, shoulders hunched slightly, as though a lifetime of listening through bar-room din had left him permanently stooped. The girl was not with him.

'Here he is,' said Ralph—to both of us it seemed. He made some introductory noises, murmured uncertainly that it was best if he left us to it, and slipped out. We stared at one another, dubious beneficiaries of someone else's good nature, until Nesbit grunted and looked away. 'Shouldn't have come,' he said.

Did he mean me or himself?

'I've been told to keep you company.'

'Ralph's idea,' he added in mumbled explanation. 'Didn't want to offend him.'

'I see. Me too.'

'Good man—Ralph.'

'I hardly know him.'

He cast an eye over me, wondering blearily which stone I'd come from under, then looked around for a chair, and slumped into it. 'Drink?'

'I forgot my glass.'

'Use the bottle for God's sake.'

I did, and sat across from him, under a suspicious eye.

'Can't stand this sort of thing.' With the fingers of one hand he mimicked the empty yapping of mouths. 'Tried to tell him. Probably disgrace myself.'

I'd met old poets before. They could be sweet as pie or venomous as nettles. This one looked uncomfortable, a little helpless now. I said, 'I sometimes think there'd be less boredom in the world if people weren't at such pains to organize it.' He nodded his agreement, smiling faintly, but said nothing. That was the other thing about them: they commanded the high ground; they could afford to wait.

'Ralph tells me you're living on the Estate.'

'Over the lake.' His hand gestured vaguely at the window. I volunteered that I was in Clive Quantrill's cottage but the name stirred no response, and the information no interest. I cast about for something that wouldn't be swallowed up by the sign of the yapping hand.

He sniffed, looked away, and said, 'I'm told you're something of a versifier.'

'For my sins.'

'What'd you say?'

Under repetition the remark receded further into absurdity; as he'd known it would.

'Good God,' he said, 'you'll not convince me you've many of those to your credit. Not with a face like that. Look at mine, dear man. All seven deadlies writ large.' I could see the possibility of six in his stare, but Envy was absent. 'If it's sin you want to talk about . . .' A wave of his hand dismissed the subject.

'I'm always interested in listening to an expert.'

A hint of a smile, but he was not to be so lightly seduced. I began to understand why Ralph Agnew had needed a keeper for his friend, and resented the appointment. Unhelpfully, Edward Nesbit stared into his glass as though innocence were drowning there.

I recalled my adolescent fantasies of the glamorous young man who'd stormed London in the late '30s, hat stuffed with images, scattering his wit like loose change and declaiming his verse to anyone who'd listen. Significantly, the aged Yeats had listened, and Eliot had respected a talent so different from his own. Had Nesbit been killed in the war, or drunk himself to death, the critics might have lamented the loss of his great promise. Less satisfactorily the man had simply abjured the place on the public stage that his early profusion of verse had briefly won for him, and disappeared into obscurity. His *Blitz Litany* remained a standard anthology piece, but surveys of modern verse accorded him only passing mention now: a significant if minor figure whose spendthrift way with words had led to bankruptcy. It seemed they were right.

'I've read your stuff,' he said abruptly, eyes aimed my way a moment, then darting away.

I waited.

'Beautiful.'

Magnanimity was not what I'd expected. I concealed my pleasure behind a deprecatory smile.

'So beautiful'—he looked up, gimlet-eyed—'I wanted to smash it.'

Even in the shadows of the dimly lit library the impact of the remark must have been obvious. Yet he smiled in reparation, leaned towards me, almost consolingly. 'What you don't yet understand,' he said, 'is that poetry is not enough.'

'I see.'

'No, you don't see,' he snarled.

'Then you'd better explain.'

He turned away again impatiently and dragged on his cigarette. His eyes closed in a frown—hunting a difficult thought perhaps—then he stared at me again and made a wide gesture to the walls that slopped the whisky in his glass. 'Use your eyes,' he said. 'Look at 'em all.' Evidently he meant the books in their glazed cases. 'Thousands of them. Thousands. And the one that counts . . . Not here, you see. Burned. Up in smoke. Abolished.'

I had no idea what he was talking about. He looked around the room almost anxiously. 'Where's Laura?' he demanded.

'I don't know.'

'I want Laura.'

'Do you want me to look for her?'

He eyed me suspiciously.

'She did come with you?' I checked.

'Of course she came with me.'

'Look, I'll go and find her if you like.'

'Sit down.'

I did.

'Wanted to tell you something.' His mind seemed to be wandering. Just drunk? Or some more permanent insult to his cells? Surely not yet entirely senile?

'That poetry isn't enough?' I reminded.

'Something like that.'

'It's enough for me.'

'Then you're asleep. Your *taròcchi* need shuffling.'

'My what?'

'Thousands of you out there, scribbling away. Metre-ballad mongers. Petal-counters. Pen-suckers. All secretly convinced they're God's gift to English poesy. And it's over. Finished.' It was an outrageous generalization from a personal loss. Had it been less absolute it would have been pathetic. Or was it merely perverse? For he was peering at me now, one eye closed, the other inviting and defying demurral.

'Is that why you gave up?' I said.

He drew in, and released noisily, a deep breath. 'None of your damned business.'

'If you say so.'

'But I'll tell you.' Again he made me wait, *'Je ne sais plus parler,'* he whispered. *'Ma santé fut menacée. La terreur venait.'*

'That was Rimbaud's answer,' I began. 'What's . . .'

'Better poet,' he interrupted. 'More reason.' And then, louder, 'And it's too good for the likes of you.' He emptied his glass, reached for the bottle again, unsteadily. I poured a measure for him.

'You're a gentleman,' he said. 'In my cups, you see. Pay no heed.' Then he beckoned me closer to his face as though about to share some drunken confidence. I leaned cautiously towards him, saw his face approach mine, eyes glittering up from under his brows, then he planted a damp but surprisingly tender kiss on my lips, and slumped back in his chair. 'English poets have kissed one another from Gower onwards,' he mumbled.

'And will,' I declared.

'If there's time, dear heart, if there's time.'

For a moment there was a frail bond of sympathy between us—two poets in a darkened library while the party went on around us. There we sat over a bottle, surrounded by people who, for the most part, couldn't care whether we penned another line or not; for whom Edward Nesbit was a curiosity, like an eighteenth-century anchorite paid to look picturesque in a parkland grotto, and I, a nobody in jeans. Once more I was overwhelmed by the futility of the poet's craft. Perhaps after all he was right.

'Let me tell you a story,' he said. 'It's about a country. A country where, after centuries of shame over their base animal nature, the people thought they'd finally broken free. Suddenly it was all body beautiful, *capito*? Sex was everywhere. Everyone wanted their share. Appetite and sensation were the order of the night. Are you with me?'

I nodded, amazed by the sudden lucidity of his voice.

'And then something entirely unanticipated transpired. At the centre of their foreheads the men began to sprout horns—single, cartilaginous little horns. Like unicorns, you might think, but without the grace, without the mythic majesty. No, these horns were stubby little spigots right at the centre of their brows. In some, inevitably, they took the shape of pens.' He smiled at me, sulphurously, again. 'Being an educated young man, you will, no doubt, have recognized them already as secondary pricks. And what fun they were! Giving head took on a delicious new twist. Also, unlike the true generative organ skulking between the thighs, they carried with them no risk of pregnancy. Everyone could be as horny as they liked and all that was e-jac-u-lated from these splendid little temple stopcocks was a thin thrill of ideas, a harmless spurt of ink.' He sniffed, downed the measure. 'The only pity of it was—and some said it was a small enough price to pay for so neatly ducking the inflexible laws of genera-tion—the only pity of it was that when they tried to make love the damned things got in the way.'

I laughed, as much at the doleful expression on his face as at the story. 'It's a true story, damn you,' he growled. 'A true story. And I need to pee.' He got up and staggered out of the library. I waited a longish time, and when he didn't come back, went out to look for him.

In the panelled hall the party was dispersing, hurriedly. I saw Neville Sallis, pale but beaming as he dismissed Ralph Agnew's apologies. 'Water off a duck's back,' he was saying without conviction. 'Really. Don't give it another thought.'

'He can be . . . difficult, I'm afraid,' Ralph persisted.

'Poetic licence no doubt. Not every day one meets a sacred monster.'

Ralph saw me over Sallis's shoulder and excused himself. 'Look,' he whispered urgently, 'could you find Laura for me? She's out in the parterre I think.'

'What's happened?'

He shook his head. 'Edward's through there with Bob but he wants Laura. Do you mind? My fault really. Should have lis-tened to him. Be a good chap?' He turned back to the rest of the departing guests as I slipped out wondering why, behind its apologetic mien, a certain kind of breeding should command instant obedience.

There was no one in the garden. I followed the path to the lion-gate and looked across the park. I could hear the plash of duck among reeds but the lake was no more than a thin glimmer on the darkness. Swift pangs of sound quivered across its surface—the small cries of moorhens and the muted Klaxons of Canada geese. A few stars ticked mistily among cloud. She— Laura—the girl, presumably, whom I'd seen with Nesbit in the wood—could be anywhere, and I wasn't about to shout.

The air was sweet. I took in a few cleansing breaths and would have turned back but I heard a small rasping noise somewhere in the gloom. It was repeated four or five times, quickly, un-identifiable, until a feather of flame appeared twenty yards away in the shadows at the water's edge. In its brief glow I made out the profile of a woman's face lighting a cigarette. Unaware of my presence she was sitting cross-legged at the shore end of a small jetty that ran out into the lake. As I walked towards her the moon stepped out of the cloud.

'Laura?'

She turned her head, frowning.

'It's Edward. There's been some sort of upset. He wants you.'

'Upset?'

'I wasn't there.'

'You mean he's insulted someone?'

'I suppose so. The vicar I think.'

'That figures.' She turned her head away but made no other move.

'Ralph asked me to find you.'

She gathered a shawl closer about her shoulders and stared intently out across the lake as though her attention was drawn there by something more interesting.

'Are you coming?'

She drew on her cigarette. 'When I'm ready.'

'I think Ralph would appreciate it.'

'He can handle it.'

The indifference of the soft American voice irritated me. I said, 'Edward's pissed out of his mind. You should take him home.'

She looked back at me, mildly surprised by my tone. 'Sounds like he got to you too.'

I shook my head. 'But I don't much like being used as watch-dog and errand boy.'

'Then why are you here?'

Nettled, I answered, 'You don't make any concessions, do you? Either of you, I mean.' She shrugged and looked away.

Detesting the stupid, liminal figure I'd become I went back to the house in a foul mood, and heard Edward's voice perorating through the open French door. With the taste of blood he seemed to have gained his second wind, or perhaps the dispersal of the party had freed his spirit. Either way, he was now in full rhetorical flood.

'Consider the history of History itself,' he was saying, '—a gradual degeneration from the sublime dream-time of myth into heroic legend; an even more rapid and much more dismal decline into patriotic fiction; and then finally—God save the mark—into Eco-nomics. And there's a bastard foundling of the academic mentality if ever I smelled one. One, if I may say so, my dear . . . dear?'

Bob supplied his name.

'Yes, dear Bob, one that an intelligent soul such as yourself should hesitate to inflict on a free spirit as the iron hand of necessity. It won't wash, dear man. If what you call history has any value at all it's merely as an object lesson in human stupidity, against which even the gods themselves are helpless. Which brings us back to the ground we should never have left in the first place—sacred ground. My old heart faints at the thought of the utopian palace of conformities you'd have us build upon it. At best I see it as a hideous, coeducational public convenience. At worst—a secret policeman's dream.'

'That's the old Tory line,' Bob returned. 'For my money we either remember the past or repeat it. History shows . . .'

'If history shows anything it's that a great deal more than memory is required to avoid the recurrence of calamity. It requires—I think you will agree—some spark of insight into the darker operations of the human soul. And for that we shall need a more luminous exercise of the imagination than your naïve materialism has on offer. Speak to me from your best self, dear heart. Recall your glassy essence.'

Bob had the air of an earthquake survivor—patient and dazed beneath the fallen masonry, but managing a gallant, good-natured smile. 'I don't think it's my materialism that's naïve.'

'And I don't care what you think. It may be our common misfortune to live in a vast supermarket of opinion, but your particular brand loyalties are no concern of mine. What interests me is what you know. You call yourself a materialist, but do you know, for instance, what matter is? Have you given the matter any thought? Have you tried taking the word back to its roots? It goes right back to Sanskrit and doubtless beyond. Push through the fissive nature of matter, penetrate to its roots, and where do you find yourself? Not, I assure you, in the kingdom of the Leptons and the Quarks, but in the black hole of the Magna Mater. Yes, the Great Mother herself, and it is a terrible thing to fall into the lap of the living Goddess. Now there's a thing we might do well to remember. Isn't that so, Ralph?' Nesbit nodded briefly at his host who had entered from the hall and was pouring himself a much-needed drink as he listened in resignation to the soliloquy.

The old poet seemed oblivious of, or indifferent to, the embarrassment he had caused, and paused for no answer. 'If we accorded her the reverence she demands we might begin to recover something of the sacramental quick of life. We might come alive again to the tremendous symbolic dignity of things.' I watched him silence Bob with an imperious hand. 'But perhaps you prefer to suck your thumb in the literally dia-bolic junkyard that such bright opinions as yours erect around themselves with—yes, I grant you—historically determined inevitability. If so, Heaven help you, for you leave me at a loss.'

Nesbit had spoken throughout in measured tones, polishing his syllables like a lapidary. When he had ended he looked away, as though in despair, and his eyes fell on me. 'Darken,' he growled, 'you call yourself a poet. Come. Instruct our friend in celestial dialectics. I doubt the fellow really knows what dia-bolic means. He's cut off his roots, you see, and he won't listen to a superannuated old fool like me.'

I'd had more than enough of his pontificating, and liked even less his attitude towards Bob. I said quietly, 'If I thought there was a shred of evidence for divine order in this dog's dinner of a world I wouldn't hesitate to do so. As it is, I'd say that Bob's red flag has more life in it than your sacred cow.'

Loosening his tie, Ralph Agnew relaxed into an elegant velvet chair and murmured, '*Touché.*' There was a hint of requited glee across his stricken features. It brought to mind some plump senator settling himself in a good seat at the Colosseum.

Nesbit sighed extravagantly and said, 'Oo-la-lah!'

Our eyes were fixed on one another. I could sense the other two men pegged on the sudden tension between us. Then Nesbit smiled and shook his head. 'Forgive me,' he said, and I thought he was about to relapse into bleary lassitude; 'but that remark,' he added, 'betrays a lack of attention excusable only in the autistic or the drunk.'

There was a retort at my lips, which I arrested when I saw

the sadness etched into the latticework of lines around the old
poet's eyes. It offered a bleak complicity. It was as intimate in
its way as that between headsman and victim at the moment
when silver changed hands. Then we were all startled by a new
voice in the room—duskily sonorous with an American lilt to it.
'You being a pig again, Edward?'

I turned and saw the girl standing by the French door, dark-
haired, sallow-skinned, arms crossed at her chest as though she
were hugging herself against the cold. Her fingers held the shawl
in place, and her clothes concealed the lines of her body, making
a bid for invisibility; but she drifted into the room like a cloud
of loose electricity charging the air.

'Laura, my dear,' said Ralph rising.

There was little pleasure in Nesbit's smile. 'How gratifying
that you've deigned to join the party after all, and in such striking
style. No doubt everyone is savouring the brilliance of your observation; but it seems a pity to shift the focus at such a tanta-
lizing moment. I was just about to discover why this young man
is so intent on laying waste the palace of his mind.'

The girl eased herself on to a leather pouf by the fireplace and
said with no great urgency, 'Why don't you give it a rest, Edward? Leave him alone.'

'He's perfectly at liberty to tell me to go to hell if he likes.'

Bob stepped back in unhappily. 'I think Alex was only saying
what I was trying to say—there's no rational evidence for what
you're on about, whereas . . .'

'No,' said Nesbit patiently, 'I think he was saying rather more
than that. Still, if it's evidence the lad's looking for, then evidence he shall have. Ralph?'

'Edward?'

'Louisa's cards. Where are they?'

Ralph grimaced. 'Don't you think it's a little . . ?'

'Do bring them. It might be . . . entertaining.'

The two men studied each other in silence for a time. They
were of the same generation—children of the Great War, or of
the late Edwardian summer that vanished forever with it—but
how different was the feel of their presences: Agnew refined,
polite, the diffident English gentleman; Nesbit volatile and
louche. Of the two I would have guessed Agnew the elder but,
despite the spasm of the stroke across his face, there were moments when he appeared junior to the rumpled, experience-

ravaged figure of the old poet—who fixed him now with a pe-
remptory smile.

Their silence was contentious. Was Ralph finally tiring of his
difficult guest, I wondered; or merely recommending a more
gracious taste in entertainment? Eventually he opened his hands,
Pilate-like, got up and excused himself a moment.

Bob Crossley, the third man of that generation, but of another
class, another less extravagant world, cast a quick uncomfortable glance my way. He wanted to leave, but said nothing. Having precipitated this clash with Nesbit, I could hardly make the
suggestion myself. In this handsome room, with generations of
portraits gazing down on us, Bob and I were stuck. The evening
had turned perilous.

Laura pushed back the hair from her face. 'Edward, we should
go.'

'Nonsense, my dear. The fun hasn't yet begun.' His eyes
returned to me. 'This will not, of course, be irrefutable evidence
of the presence of the gods, nor yet of the existence of the prophetic soul. But I think I can promise you a small demonstration
that there are things in heaven and earth that your entirely reasonable assumptions will not explain away.'

The four of us sat in uneasy silence until Ralph returned bearing an elaborately carved wooden box. 'Edward,' he said, 'is
this altogether wise?'

'Of course not.' Nesbit took the box, placed it on a low table
before the fireplace, patted the lid, then looked up at me. 'Sit
down, for God's sake.' He indicated the chair of his choice, next
to the table, across from him. As I sat, he opened the box, took
out an oblong package wrapped in a velvet cloth of midnight
blue which he unfolded to reveal an unusually long and thick
deck of cards. 'You are familiar with the Grand Tarot?' He
spread a few cards in a fan across the table. Unfamiliar symbols
that might have been illuminations from a medieval Book of
Hours were hand-painted on them with exquisite care. Each
motif shone against a golden ground which was itself textured
with swags and furbelows, and the margins of the cards were
inscribed with glosses in a tiny, cursive script. I saw arrangements of chalices and swords, and other cards bearing curious
heraldic figures which had names capitalized at the foot. I saw
LA COURONNE DES MAGES, LA PAPESSE, LE PENDU.

'Only from Eliot,' I said, '—*The Waste Land*?'

'My major complaint against Mr Eliot—sweet, strict man that

he was—is that he made use of the cards without taking the trouble to know them. In any case, I am not Madame Sosostris, nor is this an ordinary deck.'

Curious, Bob made to pick up one of the cards, but Nesbit forestalled him. 'I'd much rather you didn't.'

'Well, I'm going to have some brandy,' Ralph said. 'Anyone join me?'

'Excellent idea.' Nesbit collected our nods and passed them on to the host, then looked back at the cards. 'These wondrous things have been in Ralph's family for a long time,' he said, 'but I associate them particularly with that splendid lady whose portrait you see by the window.' He indicated a heavily-framed oil of a mild, very old woman who gazed into the room, untroubled, interested, with serene repose. 'Louisa Anne Agnew,' he announced proprietorially. 'As a boy, Ralph was fortunate enough to know her. He tells me the likeness is just. Note how she seems to gaze into

> That time when no more change shall be
> But steadfast rest of all things firmly stay'd
> Upon the pillows of Eternity.'

His rich voice savoured the cadences.

'Spenser,' Ralph supplied from where he decanted the brandy into snifters. 'One of her favourite poets.'

'But not among yours, I can see,' said Nesbit, looking at me.

'Not particularly. So what do you propose? To tell my fortune?'

Nesbit's face crumpled with distaste. 'Nothing so juvenile. I merely thought you might not be averse to a small experiment.' As he spoke he sifted through the cards, selecting some, rejecting others.

'What kind of experiment?'

'Patience, dear man.'

On the whole I preferred his earlier, less sinister taste for insult, but I watched, smiling, as he continued his search. Laura received her brandy, sipped at it, then looked at me. 'You don't have to take any of this, you know.' In its way her cool regard was more of a challenge than the words had been.

Nesbit looked up from the cards. 'Of course, if you'd rather not . . .'

I was strung between two contradictory taunts: either way loser. I said, 'Go on.'

'Good. I promise it won't take us long, and then . . . we shall see.' For a moment longer he searched the deck. 'Ah, here she is. Now, I think we are ready.' He counted the cards he had chosen and stacked the others neatly beside the box, then looked back to me. 'There are things known to you alone—things in the privacy of your past from which the rest of us in this room are entirely excluded. Agreed?'

'Of course.'

'Nothing, however, is secret from the cards. Predictably you asked if I was going to tell your fortune. I could have done so, but it would not have served our purpose. As the future is not yet with us there is no way you could have known whether what the cards had to say was true. Not tonight at least. So I am going to perform the exact reverse: I am going to foretell your past.'

'There's no great mystery about that.'

'Then you must be a singularly dull young man—which, despite all the evidence to the contrary, I do not believe. Now be silent. All you have to do is take these cards and shuffle them patiently. Take as long as you like, and while you are doing it concentrate upon your recent past. I do not mean yesterday or the day before, but that recent moment which seems to you to be charged with the most significance for your personal destiny.'

'Why only these cards? Why not all of them?'

'These are the Major Arcana, the Trumps or Triumphs. There are 22 of them, though only 21 are numbered. The other is the zero card. *Le Mat*. The Fool. The Joker of the deck. Now shuffle please. And concentrate.'

I found the cards too large to shuffle like a normal deck, so fumbled for a moment then began to rearrange them one or two at a time. My mind, however, was not where he'd directed it. I was wondering about lines of communication. How much had Clive told Ralph about me? How much had Ralph passed on to Nesbit? Also, by their own admission, both had read my verse: to another poet there were clues enough within and behind its ironies and allusions. But the very recent past? No, that was not there, not even a hint of it, for I'd been too blind myself to see it coming. But Clive certainly knew enough—a discreet hint to an old friend in Norfolk, the suggestion that he might, in the circumstances, keep an eye on me? And what about Bob? How much did he know? How much of a gossip was he?

I saw that my life might be more public than I cared to think
. . . that this business with the cards might be no more than an
elaborate charade.

'That'll do,' I said abruptly.

Nesbit nodded. 'Good. Now I want you to select a card and
lay it face down on the table without showing it to anyone,
including yourself. Good. Now give the rest to me.' He took
the remainder and added them to the discard pile.

'Pick a card, any card . . .' I said.

'Precisely.'

'And you're going to tell me what it is?'

'Either that or make an utter ass of myself. An interesting
moment, don't you think? Two brittle vanities at stake over a
single card. Much riskier than gambling for money, for more
than the ego is riding here. The question was: is there or not an
order in the universe, an order beyond mere causality? I say yes,
you say no. At the moment the odds are all on your side. You
shuffled. You picked. I haven't touched the card since. I did not
look at the discards, and there's nothing to distinguish the back
of this one from all the others. Agreed?'

I looked down at the simple floral design printed there, and
nodded. 'So what is it?' I demanded. 'The Fool, I suppose.'

There was silence in the room. Ralph and Bob were staring
at us in fascination. Even Laura was attentive now.

'No,' said Nesbit, a finger crooked at his lip, his head shaking
slowly from side to side, though there was nothing remotely
drunk about him now. It was as though he'd entirely sloughed
off his earlier feckless state. His eyes were shining like surgical
instruments. 'No,' he said again, 'I think what we have here is
The House of God.'

The card lay between us, the eyes of the entire group on it as
though it were a trapdoor through which, in a puff of smoke, a
summoned genie might appear. Tense still, aware that the moment was—must be—absurd, I flipped the card.

Before I took in the picture I saw three words neatly capitalized:

LA MAISON DIEU

I heard Bob say, 'Good God!' and laugh.

The oldest trick of all, pranked out in fancy dress, and I had
fallen for it. There had been no gamble. I didn't know how he'd

done it, but of course this was the card Nesbit had predicted. Yet, in its way, my own guess had been quite as accurate: it should have been The Fool, for there I sat, sweating in the ass's head; yet damned if I would bray.

I stared, not at the card, but at Edward Nesbit. I was filled with the cold thought that the old fraud should have his moment of glory if, to console himself for the loss of his true gift as a poet, he so badly needed it. He should have it, and taste to the full my contempt for its emptiness.

Nesbit's eyes were closed. Where I had expected to meet a smirk of triumph I found instead the distracted gravity of an invalid. For a moment I wondered whether he'd even seen the card, whether he was eking out the spurious drama. But no, he had seen it. He knew.

'Clever stuff,' Bob said, 'but I don't see that a card trick proves anything very much.'

Nesbit opened his eyes. 'There has been no trickery,' he said. Then looked up at me.

I saw, with sudden dreadful certainty, that he was telling the truth. This was all happening, and it was real. No trick. I felt a kind of fatality loom between myself and the old veteran of pain across the table. It was an almost tangible presence, like a veiled figure in the room.

'Don't look at me,' he counselled gently. 'Study the card.'

I held his gaze a troubled moment longer then looked down again, more closely, at the card. It portrayed a tower struck by lightning. The bolt, elaborately stylized in curlicues of vermilion and gold against a livid sky, had hit the parapet which was dislodged, about to topple. The tower was in flames, and two figures were falling through the air. Had it not been for the inscription there was nothing to indicate that Nesbit had named the right card.

Then, as I stared at the image, for a terrifying hot instant I became it. The body of the tower was my body. I could feel the riot of flame within. The toppling crown of the parapet was my head lurching away into space under the impact of that excruciating stroke from the sky. Beneath me everything familiar had begun to keel and slide, and I was falling—not a free fall, but that sickening, bottomless plummet with which one sometimes jerks from sleep. And Jess stood across from me again, her white face that of a frightened stranger now as, with cold unreachable lucidity, she broke her dreadful news.

I was no longer at Easterness, but there in what had once been my home, the kids asleep upstairs, my heart a faltering donkey-engine as, finally, irretrievably, in words as plain as they were devastating, something was stolen from me without which life would no longer be supportable. And how rapidly things had teetered into travesty. Wronged kings might have acted thus, or madmen driven to a frenzy of despair—but *me*? All measure, irony, restraint—the qualities to which I'd pinned my stance—were gone. My language became coarse and platitudinous. Only in insult had it range and flexibility. Even physically I'd felt myself altering as my nervous system trembled out of control. Wife, children, home were vanishing; and when I'd looked in the mirror I'd seen Agamemnon's mask.

I could feel the sweat on my palms, struggled to collect myself, looked up and away. And caught Laura's eyes. She was playing with a twist of her hair, waiting, lips slightly pursed in—what? Mockery? Disdain? No, there was another subtler message in those unremitting eyes. 'I tried to warn you,' she might have been saying, 'and now it's too late. Well, somewhere inside yourself you were asking for this. Use it.'

'Are you all right, Alex?' It was Bob's voice.

I nodded, swallowed, and looked up at Edward Nesbit.

He averted his eyes, frowning in what seemed an agony of self-recrimination. He might, suddenly, have been very ill.

'Laura,' he said, 'take me home.'

4 ◆ A Disagreement at the Rectory

Of the small circle gathered about the breakfast table that first morning at Easterness only Edwin Frere knew how violent had been the shock when he gazed up at the crude dawn-lit figure of Gypsy May. Indeed, Sir Henry and Emilia were quite unaware of the incident, and though Louisa Agnew was sensitive to Frere's discomfiture, she had ascribed it to a too prudish sensibility and therefore made light of it. This was perhaps as well, for even under the patronage of a general ignorance, Frere was finding it hard to attend either to the ladies' chatter or to the bones of his smoked herring. He was trying, silently, to come to terms with his confusions—among them the dread that Miss Agnew might thoughtlessly let slip some further reference to their meeting, though such an embarrassment now seemed unlikely. But the day was scarce begun and already it had proved unreliable. Shock had followed quickly upon shock, and Frere could not confidently contend with more.

None of this could have been anticipated. Disturbing dreams were common enough in his experience and, once out of his bed, things had appeared to take an encouraging turn. The Hall had been still as he made his way along the gallery and down the stairs. In the courtyard the first light came damp and sweet on the wind. Passing through the stable-arch, down the yew-hedged drive, he could see the church in the distance, hunched like an immense snail peering at the day. There was no one about.

The ancient door had opened on to a sparse, cool space. His footfall startled the air. It was not (praise be!) the church of his

dream, and the dream itself receded swiftly to oblivion as he
took in the sturdy columns, the narrow pews, the carved canopy
of the font. He walked towards the chancel and knelt at the
simple rood-screen, but he was too excited to sustain more than
a brief prayer. He turned again to survey the nave. How compact
this space was, how unassuming! So intimate after the soaring
vault of King's; and where he had delighted there to a rainbowed
stippling of air among high pillars, here were narrow shafts of
clear-glass light—plainsong, faintly elegiac. God's scouring-
stone.

It was to his taste, his scale. It had the repose of simplicity,
as of a gull alighting and folding its wings in one smooth motion. In all modesty he might fill this space with praise as it was
already filled with the domestic peace of God.

He looked up at the pulpit but, no, he would not mount, not
yet—though in his mind's eye he saw a congregation assembled
there below him, the well-born and the lowly joined in common
prayer. He thought of the long generations committed to the
earth outside; of parson succeeding parson down the centuries.
He was part of a long procession through time, and already, by
a quiet friendly stealth, this bare, barn-like church was becoming an enlargement of his life. In the still air faintly chrismed
with damp he experienced anew the consoling mystery of his
faith—one that needed no ornament save the soft devotions of
this English light. His heart lifted to embrace the little parish.

It was in this state of mild exaltation that he had eventually
stepped outside to inspect the outer fabric, and there the shadows of the early light picked out the living's permanent incumbent, agape and waiting for him.

For a dreadful moment he had felt his heart stop. Then, with
a violent lurch, as though he had been thumped across the chest
by a giant fist, it restarted. The October dawn shimmered gid-
dily about him.

When thought eventually returned it was to question, though
no more coherently than in a gasp of inward pain, what monstrous perversity in the scheme of things could have lured him
to the one parish in all the vast reaches of the county where, it
seemed, his madness might recur. Then he had staggered away,
turning his back on the church for which his shaken heart had
brimmed with affection only moments before.

He had wandered the lanes for a time, turning through a gateway to avoid the approach of a farm-labourer clad in sacks and

leggings. The diversion brought him back into the Easterness
parkland from the south where the lake glimmered before him.
On the rot-riven stump of a felled oak he sat gazing out across
the fretted surface of the water, trying to collect himself, but his
mind was impervious to the gathering brightness of the day. He
felt the old dark crowding there—the hot darkness of the Gan-
getic plain, the place where his reason had been unseated once
before. He strove to remind himself that, in contrast to those
Hindoo effigies with their flagrant appeal to the sensual beast in
man, this image was primitive and crude. It was coarse as a
lewd and vulgar joke. But the point was it had no business there
at all; yet there it was, as though appointed for his particular
confusion. Small wonder his mind had reeled.

He should have been warned of this. Someone should have
advised him that this church was distinguished from all others
by a grotesquely unchristian feature . . . But why should they
have troubled to do so? He alone knew the true nature of the
mental turmoil he had suffered in India. He alone could have
anticipated that what might seem to others no more than an
antique curiosity would be to him a memorandum of despair.

He could not live with it. He could not take this living. Apologies must be made. He and Emilia must take coach for Cambridge now, that day. Somewhere another living would be found.

It was on this gloomy figure that Pedro had come bounding.
There had followed the difficult, stammered conversation with
Miss Agnew, which effected a shock of another order. The young
woman had been alarmingly direct, and when the facts of the
case emerged, or as much of it as he dared admit, there had
been no hint of falsity in her response. Neither a coy reserve on
the one hand, nor shamelessness on the other. There was rather
a glow of sanity about her which sorted well with the morning's
breezy light. It made his sombre self-absorption seem disproportionate. It was like being smacked lightly across the face
with a flower.

Edwin Frere had returned to his room, and his wife, in much
hastily concealed disarray.

Later, while Emilia completed her toilette, he turned for guidance to the only book he had brought with him on the journey.
It was a small calfskin copy of *A Priest to the Temple or the
Countery Parson, his Character and Rule of Holy Life*, published in 1652 under the authorship of Mr G.H.

The Countery Parson, he read there, *is exceeding exact in his*

*life, being holy, just, prudent, temperate, bold, grave in all his
wayes. And because the two highest points of his life, wherein a
Christian is most seen, are Patience and Mortification; Patience
in regard of all afflictions, Mortification in regard of lusts and
affections, and the stupefying and deading of all the clamorous
powers of the Soul, therefore hath he thoroughly studied these,
that he may be Absolute Master and commander of himself, for
all the purposes which God hath ordained him.*

. . . *the stupefying and deading of all the clamorous powers
of the Soul!* How precisely the limber Jacobean prose prescribed
his need! And how high the standard set to which the country
parson must aspire! Yet the author of this little book (who was
much better known as the composer of some of the most exquisite verse in the English language) had proved in his own life
that such standards might be met—for who had laboured more
sweetly than George Herbert to make Humility lovely in the eyes
of men? His was a spirit that Frere had long revered. Under the
gentle influence of Herbert's exhortations the unhappy man had
begun to think more calmly.

Now, over breakfast, entertained by Miss Agnew's banter, he
was beginning to wonder whether he had been, perhaps, too
hasty . . . fallen too quickly prey to his own infirmity. It would
be quite wrong to run so soon, improvising whatever excuses
he could find. Far from being temperate and bold, that was the
coward's way. And, in any case, Emilia would demand explanation; and what could he say, after his earlier enthusiasms, that
would not be immediately transparent? No, he must still himself. He must wait for some guiding word.

That something untoward had ruffled Frere's composure did
not escape his wife, but she had found scant opportunity to
question him before breakfast and certainly none there. Nor was
it possible that Emilia should fail to observe a certain diffident
complicity between her husband and the young mistress of the
Agnew household that had not been evident the previous evening. True, it was a slight thing—so slight that had their roles
been reversed, Edwin would have noticed no alteration in her
own demeanour—but then women are more sensitive registers
of such nuance than men; and, by that same token, Emilia was
also sure that Louisa saw that she saw. Moreover, the change—
slight as it was—would not appear explicable by a simple sharing

of the morning air. Curious that Edwin had omitted to mention this.

Not that Emilia was jealous; she was too little a sentimentalist to fall prey to such self-inflicted distemperature of the feelings. In any case, she had confidence enough in her hard-won ascendancy over her husband's spirit not to doubt his loyalty. Emilia Davenport had been the companion of Frere's youth. She had wept on his departure for India, and was there at the quayside to receive his returning shade. It was she more even than his own mother and sisters who watched over him when the brain-fever returned. It was she who supplied him with the necessary resolve to live which had seemed at times the only bar to his extinction. The illness had been prolonged and mysterious, but at last his health returned as a portion of her own. Their spirits had become inextricably mingled. Thus, when he asked her to become the wife and helpmeet of a life to be remade, the proposal justly ratified a secret conviction of her own: that the God he had perversely sought to serve among the heathen had found means to work what she had known all along to be Edwin's true spiritual destiny. If he was here in Norfolk now it was because, and only because, they were together.

Still, it was mildly irritating to witness her husband's coy attention to Louisa's chatter. After a restless night had left her longer abed than was her wont it made for a disagreeable start to the day.

It was not to be denied that Louisa had an engaging tongue—so much so that Emilia's smile was not entirely contrived. Yet listening to the young woman's picturesque thumbnail portraits of some of the parish worthies they must meet that day, it was hard not to regard the condescension of her views as disproportionate to her youth. The young châtelaine of Easterness appeared to consider herself apart from the generality of the human lot. She might have been some buskined Olympian tripping impishly among the affairs of men, and, though her vivacity drew one willy-nilly into a warm sense of alliance, Emilia remained detached enough to recognize that it would require no other condition than one's absence for that agile wit to conjure one's own foibles into graphic focus.

There was, in brief, something about Louisa Agnew that Emilia did not entirely trust. The discovery added to her uncertainties about this eastward enterprise.

By now Sir Henry had heard enough. Not for the first time

he tapped his watch as though dubious of its progress. 'Mr Frere is a man partial to mystery, my dear,' he muttered. 'Say more and you will quite dispel whatever mysteries our small parish might hold for him.'

The remark stopped Frere short in his thoughts. He could hardly protest that the young woman's sparkling flow had made the world feel real around him again, and a little ridiculous even, for she had made him laugh—no mean feat, this morning, that. And now the baronet's interruption reminded him of the glib manner in which he'd professed his knowledge of mystery the previous evening. How could he have dared such arrogance? Had he really believed himself intimate with the dark, often painful, always perplexing working of its ways? If so, he had been sternly schooled.

Emilia hastened to cover her husband's inappropriate silence. 'Have no fear, Sir Henry. My husband has mysteries enough of his own. Certainly he is often a mystery to me.'

'Then you are fortunate indeed,' Louisa replied. 'I could imagine no sadder plight than marriage to the predictable.'

Emilia had intended her remark as a prompt to her husband, not as an invitation to comment upon her marriage. In her early thirties now, late married and still childless, there was a strictness to her finely boned nose and narrow lips that seemed sharpened at moments of careful thought by the way the lids of her hazel eyes reclined among shadow. Some of the more cavalier intelligences of Cambridge society had wilted a little under that chill appraisal. Miss Agnew, however, did not. And still Edwin did not speak.

'Oh yes,' Emilia said, 'Mr Frere is a man of surprises.'

'Better still,' Louisa enthused, observing the parson's fingers reach for the lobe of his ear. 'In my limited experience I have yet to meet with a surprise that did not turn out to be an unexpected blessing.'

'However thickly disguised?' Emilia enquired without great interest, for she was irritated that the burden of this conversation should be left so completely on her own shoulders.

'I have often thought,' Louisa answered, 'that the thicker the disguise the greater the blessing.'

'Perhaps that is your good fortune.' Emilia turned upon her husband. 'Your silence is certainly surprising, Edwin. I trust it holds a blessing for us all.'

Frere smiled in some confusion. Wrongly, he had believed

Miss Agnew's remarks directly addressed to his own preoccupations. They had fallen on his ears as the guiding words he sought. Mystery thickly disguised as surprise, as shock . . . Perhaps that was it? For a dreadful space that dawn he had seen himself as victim of some malignant cosmic conspiracy. Now, under that engaging smile, he wondered whether the pressure he had felt on his heart might not be an insistent pushing by the hand of an all-seeing but compassionate God. He lifted the napkin to his lips.

'Good Lord,' said the baronet, 'is that the time already?'

'I was thinking . . .' Frere began. 'I was thinking . . .'

'That much was evident, Edwin. It is the nature of your thoughts that interests us.'

'My thought was that if all Munding proves as hospitable as the Hall we are indeed fortunate.' Which was, of course, only partially true. He was thinking that George Herbert was right: a man was not priest to the temple because he had no loud clamourings of the soul, but because he had studied and mastered them. He was thinking that to spend a life in flight from demons was to remain their obeisant slave. He was thinking that if he was ever to become what he believed himself to be—a devout and worthy servant of his Lord—then he must eventually turn and face those demons. And now, having uttered only a small portion of his thought, he was thinking: *Very well, let a start be made.*

'The mountain has laboured,' said Emilia, offering her hosts the benefit of her patient smile.

'But the mouse,' Louisa responded, 'is very genteel.'

It was with renewed commitment and a less entirely rigid smile than he would earlier have believed possible that Edwin Lucas Frere proceeded to meet the more distinguished residents of the parish later that day. In some matters still an innocent, he was not sufficiently so to entertain high expectations of their Christian charity. Nor had he needed Sir Henry's warning that no parish is without its self-appointed monitors of virtue. No doubt in Munding, as elsewhere, the Pharisees had long since requisitioned the choicer pews.

There was Mrs Bostock, for instance, whose iron will must have supplied some of the sharper nails in Matthew Stukely's cross. Her friend, Miss Waters, had less vinegar blended with her balm but might prove equally problematic in her precise knowledge of what form of service was acceptable in the sight of Munding's God. As to the gentlemen, Mr Bostock was a lantern-jawed drone content to let his lady-wife rule in matters spiritual; but Mr Wharton, the wealthiest of the local farmers, was more exacting. Fierce memories of the agricultural disturbances of the previous decade burned in his mind undimmed; he was unimpressed therefore by Frere's conviction that care for the parish poor should rank high among a parson's priorities. 'If it's care you're concerned with,' Mr Wharton recommended, 'then have a care that the rascals do not abuse your good nature, sir. I warrant you'll find hard work and a healthy terror of Hellfire a surer road to their salvation.'

In short, Frere found himself facing a not untypical selection of the rural gentry, as characteristic in their established prejudices as in their shrewd evaluation of the parson and his more assertive wife. Mingling among them, Frere felt his confidence grow. Yes, there were a number of hard hearts to be opened here, but that prospect did not daunt him. In contrast to the steelier intellects of Cambridge society they were manageable enough. A little light, air, warmth, and their shrivelled thoughts might soon green again.

In a moment alone, a glass of sherry in his hand, he watched Emilia chatter happily with Mrs Bostock, and found himself smiling. And over there—how patient Miss Agnew was with Eliza Waters's tattle! Even Sir Henry had troubled to engage with his neighbours on matters closer to the land than the sky. The whole room was lively with a sense of community. There was work to be done here. He was up to it. He might make his stand.

His sole regret was that circumstances should allow so little opportunity to meet the poorer families of the parish; but there would be time enough for that in weeks to come, and he was resolved not to be hamstrung in a client-chaplaincy to the local gentry.

He turned, beaming, as Mr Bostock approached. Yes, he responded, he would be most interested to hear the man's view on the vexatious case currently before the ecclesiastical courts. Also—though this he did not express—he took quiet satisfaction in the discovery that Miss Agnew's amusing observations on her neighbours had not greatly misled him.

Louisa, however, was less confident of her judgment.
Though I have schooled myself in discretion, she would write

in her journal later that day, *and though time upon time my dear father has counselled me in Patience and Prudence as the faithful handmaidens of the work, I remain—and it shames me to confess it—an impetuous spirit. There is that in me which seems wilfully seditious of all probity—will speak when it should keep silent, will act when it should hold still; and which, like Pedro (who is my joy and my despair) loosed momentarily from the leash, bounds recklessly to start what birds it may for the sheer joy of seeing them in flight.*

I have striven to master it, but this mischievous spirit has been particularly virulent in recent weeks, and I must bring it to a reckoning. The better to know it and the better, mayhap, to conjure the imp more readily to my control, I shall give it a name. I dub it MERCURIUS, *for it is a masculine sprite inhabiting my female form and, as surely is the case of our true philosophical Mercury, it is of a duplicitous and antinomian nature.*

On the one hand I know it to be a vital and procreative energy—the little silver tongue of flame that flickers at the heart of such vivacity I have. On the other the sprite remains a prankster and deceiver; one who, if I do not have a care, will prompt me to extremities from which a nimble tongue, a ready wit, and the most earnest protestations of my good intentions will not easily reprieve me.

So, Sir Mercurius, you are named now, and I must needs consider more carefully how you have recently beguiled me.

Item: it was you who provoked me to meddle so lightly with the Tarot cards, and sprang upon my casual attention the mystery of The Hanged Man's smile—a perplexity I may well have merited, but which abides to trouble my more sober contemplations.

Item: it was your insouciance that prompted my teasing of Mrs Frere, laying snares to catch the frightened rabbit which twitches behind her formidable smile without her suspecting what you are about. However, after this morning's satirical conspectus of local society the good lady is doubtless the less deceived as to our naïvety, and I shall now have the greater work to prove myself worthy of her benevolence. It is a fault that must be made good if I am not to stand, as I do already with Mrs Bostock et al., in her patronizing disapprobation.

Item (and this most vexatiously of all): you have lured me into a most questionable encounter with that gentle and diffident man, her husband, who must now entertain the gravest doubts of my propriety. How—I am left wondering—how am I to engage with him in the niceties of trivial conversation, which is the proper mode of intercourse between the parson and a young spinster of the parish, when there is the knowledge between us that we have both looked upon the private parts of Gypsy May and I have impudently advised him to take her to his bosom?

Come, my Mercurius, I must learn to keep a tighter rein upon your mischief or one day, surely, it will quite undo me.

Now that the spider was caught and Edwin had safely deposited it out of the bedroom window, Emilia expressed a guarded satisfaction with the spacious Rectory. 'It is an airy and elegant place,' she agreed, 'though certainly too large for our immediate needs.'

'Ah, but when—as surely He shortly must—the good Lord sees fit to grace us with a family . . . will this not prove an excellent situation to raise them happily? The garden alone, my dear . . . It can soon be restored. It must have been a glory once. And all these rooms . . . Why, it makes our house in Portugal Place seem positively pinched.'

Emilia's eyelids flickered at this infelicitous alliteration, though the complaint was one she had often expressed herself. 'It will be difficult to heat in winter,' she suggested.

'I see no shortage of fuel in these parts. And the temporalities . . . They are substantial. Almost disproportionately so. I think that we might live very comfortably here.'

Emilia stood by a window, gazing westwards. 'You do not find Munding largely bare of diversion? I cannot but think that I shall miss Hattie and Charlotte and all our . . .'

'But there are new friends to be made. Did I not see you getting on famously with Mrs Bostock?'

'She is an admirable woman . . . if a little restricted in her interests.'

'And then there is Saxburgh at no great distance. I am told there is an Assembly Room at the Black Boys Hotel, and a subscription library . . .'

'And the promise, one hopes, of a wider circle of acquaintance.'

'Well then . . . And Norwich itself is none too far away. Wharton tells me the railway will reach here soon, and that will bring all the world much closer.'

Emilia sighed. 'I confess that it still weighs heavily with me that we shall be a long and dreary distance from my father.'

Frere's own heart fell a little under that weight. He had counted it among the advantages of the location that it was not too far to Cambridge in case of actual emergency, yet far enough to counter trivial demands. That he should harbour such thoughts would not impress his wife, however, and the railway card was already played.

'It will not be possible to pay the same close attention to his welfare that residence in Cambridge allowed. As you know, Edwin, he was quite desolate at the thought of our leaving, though he sought to conceal it, and he is not well.'

Once more Frere could not bring himself to admit that he did not entirely trust the nature of Mr Davenport's needs. 'But Hattie is there, and the journey not insufferable.'

For a long moment Emilia held her husband in a steady gaze. Why, oh why could he not have been happier in Cambridge? She had tried so hard to make him so. And it was hard that she should now be required to choose between the two people who mattered most in her life. Of course, should she put her foot down, she might remain in the place where no choice was needful; but then she must live with Edwin's disappointment, for it appeared that his heart was now set on this move. And certainly something in their life must change.

If only she had fallen pregnant in Cambridge. He would be such a good father, his happiness would have been assured, and she need never have faced this difficult decision. Again she looked out of the window, beyond the far wall of the neglected garden, where a plough-team drudged across the long flank of a stubble-field. The turned sods glinted in the chill light. And it was all very well for Edwin to wax lyrical about this lucid air and spout lines from the *Georgics* at her, but was not this the bare reality of country life—this dogged tussling with mud? She was a child of the city. Its gossip, its passing show, the toings and froings of witty company were her daily cordial. So must she accept this dull yoke? Almost she might have wept. But it had been many years since Emilia had shown her weakness to the world, and—much though her heart might flinch from the consequence—she was a dutiful wife.

This was all too difficult for her.

'The decision must rest with you, my dear,' she said eventually. 'If you hear the vocation then we must trust to it.'

His heart went out to her. He could feel the sacrifice, was sensible of the responsibility it placed in his hands and, nervous of this, he too was uncertain again. 'Munding is a little remote,' he conceded. 'There will be hardships and deprivations. Also it may well be that the larger opportunities of life may pass us by.'

She smiled at him then, a wan reflex of sympathetic affection, for she was long reconciled to the knowledge that his ambitions reached no higher than an eventual canon's seat in some cathedral chapter. Edwin was not the stuff of princes, but she cared for him no less for that. 'I have only modest demands to make on life,' she said, 'and foremost among them is your contentment.' But this was not the whole of her truth, and she must speak the rest. 'What I must have is your assurance that you will be content in this parish, for it is not rich in such resources as we have learned to take for granted in Cambridge.'

She sensed immediately that it had been an error to mention Cambridge again.

'I believe'—Frere was frowning as he spoke—'even that may have its advantages. In such a small parish as this . . . the closeness of such a community . . . a man might make a deeper mark upon the hearts of others. And that, surely, is where true contentment lies?'

It was hard for him that he felt unable to share with his wife the fruits of his earlier reflections. Their occasion scarcely permitted it. And yet, with the source of his new resolve concealed, there was an incompleteness to his answer. He was left with hints, implications, and the hope that his wife might gather from his earnest gaze that much of importance to his moral fibre was here at stake. 'If that were so,' he added, 'then one might begin to feel . . . worthy again.'

'The parish would be more than fortunate to have you.' It was her pride that spoke, yet Frere felt her subtly withheld from him, as though her will was momentarily in abeyance rather than harnessed eagerly to his cause. A mantle of service and consideration seemed to muffle the pulse of life between them. He must venture more. But he paused for a long time in solitary contemplation before speaking again.

'Yes I do feel . . . have felt . . . a kind of summoning. It is very curious . . . almost as though I knew the place already . . . have been in the hamlet before. As though to take the living would be a kind of return.' He looked up in search of understanding, but Emilia was staring out of the window now.

He was decided then. She must be practical about it, and she was not patient with metaphysical speculations when practical issues crowded upon her mind. There were moments when it was wiser to yield than to resist, and this was one of them. She must give him his head and make her own dispositions accordingly. It had already occurred to her that the temporalities of the living were substantial enough whereby, when this backwater proved tedious, a curate might be appointed and they could still enjoy a prosperous life in Cambridge. For the moment, however, this planning against contingency must be kept to herself. She was too well-apprised of her husband's present disapproval of absentee parsons.

So even as their sentences tacked towards agreement, somewhere, deeply, they were at odds. They spoke together as they might have written letters apart—affectionately, yet from regions of experience at a far and dark remove.

Throughout the day dark rain-clouds had lowered across Easterness so that dusk when it came—earlier than usual that drear October evening—seemed a sealing of an already insuperable gloom. Henry Agnew sat alone in his library meditating no longer on the volume at his desk. The small flame of the candle beside the book was, in any case, insufficient for reading without further injury to his sight, and he was feeling out of sorts. He was a little breathless from the dense weight of depression gathered at his stomach, and in the past few moments an unfamiliar tingling sensation, fiery and heavy, had begun to shoot from his chest along his arms. In other circumstances he might have dismissed it as writer's cramp, but today . . . He had written so little. In fact, the first clear day since the departure of the Freres had produced no more than a scrumple of paper. And now, suddenly, this pain that brought with it a queer, sickly giddiness. It frightened him a little.

Nervously, as though to test his own vitality, he reached for the candlestick, gripped and lifted it. There was the remote numbness of a hand gone to sleep. It was unsteady, and he would have replaced the brass sconce instantly but the glow of the small flame reached out across the gloom to animate the face of his distant ancestor, Sir Humphrey Agnew, where it smiled down, full-wigged, in the gilt frame against the panelling. It was a smile from outside time, unlined except where the skin tones had been crazed and mellowed by a varnished craquelure. Humphrey had been a young man when he sat for that portrait—for by Henry's standards one's forties were still a youthful season—yet the triumph of achieved intellectual consciousness was fully evident in the angled three-quarter face. During more than forty years of assiduous study, most of which had been passed here under the patronage of that smile, Henry Agnew had found a source of constant inspiration there. Now, in that uncertain light, its serene composure had taken on the aspect of a taunt.

For so long had Agnew been the autocrat of his own solitude that nothing had been permitted to stand in the way of an ambition cherished since his youth. It had begun before he was twenty as a golden enterprise; yet now, when the harvest of those long years should at last come home, he questioned whether his metrical epic of the Hermetic Mystery would ever reach completion. Daily the crisis of the age cried out for it and he made no progress. Had he left it too late? Had he made the old adage that haste is the Devil's part a mere excuse for procrastination? The fear that this was the case lay close to the root of his present gloom, for the consequences . . . The consequences were unthinkable.

Trembling, he replaced the candlestick on his desk. The pains in his arms—he was convinced of it—were the first alarums of a heart threatening to fail. With a touch of malign irony he imagined its final spasm—an inward explosion of light, the sudden dark, and then a servant coming to the library, finding his body slumped across a book. A condign end to the intellectual arrogance of one who had persuaded himself—poor fool—that he too was of the *Catena aurea*, that golden chain linking across the generations all those who had striven to keep the fire-soul live and burning in the world of men. Yet to have escaped from the mad shadow of his father for that, no more . . .

These dismal reflections were interrupted by a rap that came lightly at the library door. It was followed, when he did not speak, by Louisa's voice. 'You are sleeping, father?' Wearily he lifted his brow from his hands and answered, 'No.'

The door was opened. Louisa stood for a moment in the aura of the lamp she held, then shook her head. 'How often must I beg you not to read by candle-light?'

'I was not reading.'

She heard the glum defiance in his voice, sighed—though not impatiently—she came across to share her light. 'It has not gone well?' And, when he did not reply, 'Perhaps if you chivvied the

Muse less furiously she might prove readier to take you un-
awares.'

She found no answering lightness in his face—only the black
crow that haunted him so much of late. 'Tell me,' she said,
'what impedes your progress?'

'It is a madness,' he said with sudden bitter vehemence. 'A
forty-year madness in which I have bruised my brains to no
advantage and laid waste the best years of your young life.'
Appalled by his own acrimony, he stared at her wide-eyed a
moment, then looked away, shielding his face from her gaze
with a quivering hand.

She too was taken aback. Wondering, she looked down at his
freckled crown, the ruffled silver hairs glistening in the lamplight. She saw the ink-stains at his thumb. After a moment she
said, 'You know it is not so.'

'I know nothing. Nothing.'

She placed the lamp on the desk, and her lowered glance took
in the spoil of paper at his feet. Perceiving that in this black
mood only some indirection might reach him, she put a hand to
his shoulder waiting for inspiration.

'I have misled you,' he said. 'All those years when you might
have been out in the bright world among your peers, tasting the
very quick of life, I have kept you here . . . letting you fust away
with an obsessed old man and his delusions . . .'

She essayed one further lightness. 'I am no fusty old maid,
sir, and I would not have you think me so. Nor will I hear your
priceless knowledge slandered—not even at your own lips.'

He would not look at her, sat shaking his head. 'There is no
justification for what I have done, and no meaning in it. It is
waste. All waste and dereliction.'

An exclamation of protest was at Louisa's lips. Then, for a
moment, she was on the point of sharing with him an enterprise
which had been quietly incubating in the privacy of her mind
for some weeks now—one which would demonstrate how utterly
wrong he was to judge her years of study waste. She saw instantly that this was not the time. In his present mood her father
would negative all hope. He simply would not hear, and what
she had in mind required his full assent. No, she must hold her
peace a while, and find some other means to strengthen him.

'Then you have forgotten all you taught me,' she said quietly.
'I see you do not remember what I recall most vividly—those
prescient words that John Pordage wrote for Jane. Must I remind

you now?' He did not stir. She waited a moment then, softly, as though the music of her voice was an echo of a muffled whisper deep in his own mind, she quoted the old adept: *'Now it seems to the artist that all his work is lost. What has become of the Tincture? Here is nothing that is apparent, that can be perceived, recognized, or tasted, but darkness, most painful death, a hellish fearful fire, nothing but the wrath and curse of God.'* She paused, stroking his shoulder with her hand. *'Yet he does not see that the Tincture of Life is in this putrefaction, that there is light in this darkness, life in this death, love in this fury and wrath, and in this poison the highest and most precious medicament against all poison and sickness.'*

As she spoke his left hand moved from his temple to lie gently upon hers at his shoulder. His head was still bowed, but his breathing had slowed a little. It had ever been so, that she could quiet him like this, but today he could hardly bring himself to look at the child who had been the one great consolation of his life.

A blinder man might have seen only that the birth of this daughter had cost him the loss of his wife; and indeed so deeply had Agnew grieved that it had been a long agony of time before he dared to look upon the babe for fear that he should hate her. Yet what awaited him, when finally he found the heart to see, was a priceless gift.

If evidence were needed that we enter this life not from darkness but out of a radiance remembered by the infant soul then it lived and breathed in that small child. Here was no common rag-doll of a babe but a shining presence, and as the years passed that pristine clarity remained undimmed. Even after the accession of knowledge when so many children changed into wilful tyrants and conspirators, the subtle enquiring grace of her imagination astounded and delighted him. Swiftly she had learned Latin, Greek and Hebrew at his knee. Her intellect had been trained for his great purpose. Without her able secretarial assistance the long years of research might never have been completed. And she was more, far more, than a gifted amanuensis: she was his muse. Again and again her words had come like the rap of a wand on rock, freeing his thought. Such was the communion of their minds there had been times when he entered an almost trance-like condition. A mesmeric stillness would descend between them, then he was rapturously possessed once more with the gift of tongues. It might last for hours this state, and was as exhilarating as it subsequently proved exhausting; and he had come to trust that such insights as might otherwise have perished with the passing of the trance were later to be found, impressed as in wax, on the clear tablet of Louisa's memory. She had been indispensable to the work. She was—and still he quailed at the thought—his mystic sister.

As Jane Leade had been mystic sister to John Pordage, as Peronelle to her husband Flamel, as Theosebeia in ancient times to Zosimus, and as—much closer to home—Janet Dyball had served his own glorious ancestor, Sir Humphrey, so Louisa had become mystic sister now to him. But that a man should use his daughter so . . . This was not the first time the thought had troubled him; but there it was—she had served him so with pride; she had done all that was possible to bring him to the moment where he must work alone. Only success could justify the demands he had made upon her; and should, as now seemed probable, he fail . . .

'See,' she urged, 'I at least have learned my lessons well. And what says Trismegistus in his *Golden Treatise*?—"Know, my son, that that which is born of the Crow is the beginning of the Art." '

Eyes closed, he fetched a great sigh from a heart foundering on its own despair. 'Dear God, Louisa, I am seventy years old . . .'

'And all the wiser for those years.'

'But there is so little time.'

'Yet we know the Lord will hasten all up at last, and quickly enough. Where is the trust you taught me?' In some concealed distress herself she saw the shaking of his head. 'I think perhaps you stand in your own light. If you would look you might see, at least, that I am by to help.'

But guilt still kept bitter company with such consolation. 'And if I am not poet enough?' he demanded.

She reached out a hand, turned his face towards her. 'Do you dare tell me you are not, sir?'

What Agnew dared not do was let his eyes meet hers. Never before had she encountered such resistance in him. It was as though something perverse in his will was bent against her; something that must be exorcized before its grip should tighten. Louisa considered a moment then decided that where gentleness had failed sternness might serve. 'Well,' she insisted, 'if that is so, then say it. Say it aloud to me. Say "I am not poet enough for this essential task." '

For a moment longer Agnew tried to hang his head. Her pride, her certainty, shamed the act. He must look up and when he did so the fire-soul shining in those eyes was irresistible.

'You see,' she exclaimed, 'the thing will not be said.' She took in the sadness unassuaged by his reluctant smile, '. . . though I know how bitterly the thought must come to trouble you. And will,' she added, lightening her voice again, 'as long as you persist in brooding longer at your desk than common sense would commend. Now come, sir. Close your book. If you remain here a moment longer I vow I shall fetch a crop to you.' She held out a summoning hand.

Certain only that he could not bear to disappoint the confident trust those eyes reposed in him, Agnew took the hand in his own. Perhaps she was right; perhaps he had simply sat here too long, stupefied by his own company. This was not, after all, the first time he had been overwhelmed by gloom. But his heart was heavy still as he lifted himself from his chair.

Short of actual catastrophe there can be few more nerve-racking experiences than moving house; and when one has spent many years assembling a precious collection of chattels that must now be carted on rough roads across three counties from an old home to a new it is not to be expected that the upheaval will be completed without loss. Nor could a woman who placed such high value on order as Emilia Frere be expected to cope with the consequent period of muddle without, at some point, showing signs of strain.

Frere himself was not a handyman, and his determination to be of assistance in places where fingers might be trapped or questions of weight, volume and angle of approach must be nicely calculated, proved less of a help than a hindrance to the stout fellows in his employ. Too often his eager person was situated in precisely the wrong place, and his apologies were rarely reserved for the moment when a heavy armoire had been put down, or other more pressing matters had been given the full attention they required.

The move was, in fact, achieved. By the end of it the Rectory at Munding was in handsome order. However the translation from Cambridge to Norfolk was made only at some cost to the wife's esteem for her more spiritual than practical husband. Perhaps it was for this reason that only the day after their arrival they found themselves in dispute.

Already Emilia was impatient with the way Edwin bumbled about the rooms, questioning her disposition of the ornaments, fretting over misplaced books, and generally impeding her. 'Have you no business of your own,' she demanded eventually, 'that you must hinder me at mine?'

Surprised by the asperity, Frere stood blinking. Emilia sighed over a list from which fewer items than she would have liked had been deleted. 'Surely there are things in this parish that require your attention?'

Frere saw that he was indeed procrastinating, and on a matter which must be addressed before he could take confident charge of his Munding flock. For a moment it felt almost as though Emilia had intuited the need, though that was impossible, for the absurd name that whispered in his thoughts had never been mentioned between them. It remained a private care, one that— now they were here, the carters gone, the commitment irrevocably made—had returned to trouble him. It left him nervy and restless. Irrationally so, he recognized, but it was a trial to him as he had now become a trial to his busy wife, and something must be done. Immediately.

Without explaining himself he left the room, reached for his topcoat, hat and cane, and strode out of the house. Even then, though it stood only a little way down the lane, he did not go directly to the church. There were people about and, for what he had in mind, he must be unobserved. How was it that his moments of resolve were rarely timely?

After the morning's rain there was a scent of decay on the air. It rose from the mulch of fallen leaves. If drifted on the breeze. There was already a taint of winter on its breath. His nostrils flared, and he decided that a long walk out across the water-meadows might serve his present need. It would pass the time till dusk and would, moreover, act upon his mind in the manner of a pilgrimage, bringing him back at last to a pacifying encounter with the source of his unease.

Quietly he went back indoors to change his shoes.

Almost two hours later, under a sky that was all pearl and madder where it was not yet touched with dusk, Frere approached the church across the water-meadows. His mind had been fortified by prolonged meditation on the psalms. The 115th—*Wherefore should the heathen say, Where is now their*

God?—had restored perspective. The idol on his church was not of silver or gold, but it remained the mere work of man's hands. Like the images David had derided, it had a mouth but spoke not, and eyes which did not see. Furthermore, David's prayer for the remission of sins resounded in the dark places of Frere's own soul: *Behold, I was shapen in wickedness, and in sin hath my mother conceived me. But, lo, thou requirest truth in the inward parts, and shalt make me to understand wisdom secretly.*

Frere was resolved: here, in Munding, his ghosts should at last be laid. Alone, by dusk, he would stand beneath Gypsy May and christen her, as once, centuries before, the first founder of the little parish had elected to do. He would make a reconciliation there.

His purpose was forestalled, however, by the discovery that he was not alone in the churchyard. As he rounded the chancel Frere saw the figure of a small boy in a patched shirt standing near a gravestone, whistling. The shirt was too large for the pinched chest and bulged about his trouser-tops. He had not observed the parson's approach.

Frere halted, at a loss. Then he moved into the shadow of a buttress wondering what was to be done about this unanticipated audience to his rite. Some minutes passed, and the boy showed no sign of leaving his post. He might have been appointed sentinel for the very purpose of obstructing Frere's intent. The dusk was gathering quickly. Rooks complained. A breeze had got up and it fetched to Frere's impatient ears the tuneless sound of the boy's whistling. Frere took out his watch—it was late, would soon be later than he had intended. He was fretful, angry even. He had taken such pains to prepare himself for this moment, and was he to be driven off by the half-starveling figure of a ten-year-old idling the dusk away in grubby trousers? The child had no business here, whereas he . . .

After a further indecisive moment Frere stepped out of the shadow. 'What are you doing here, boy?'

The urchin jumped, turning a pallid face in the direction of the voice. Beneath a cowlick of ash-blond hair the eyes were bright with terror. Instantly Frere felt a pang of remorse to have startled him so. He saw that the child was about to turn and run and, before he could do so, said, 'Stay where you are.' The moment for which he had prepared himself was vanished now, and he would not have the child rush round the village with tales of hobgoblins among the graves.

The command tethered the boy to the spot. He was shivering a little in the thin shirt. Frere's hand impeded further thought of flight. 'Well, boy, I asked you a question. I am the Reverend Frere, your new parson, and I believe I deserve an answer.'

The boy said nothing, looked around, askance, as though for aid. Frere asked his name, more mildly now. The child looked down at his clogged feet and mumbled.

'Louder, boy, and look at me when you speak.'

Gulping, the boy glanced up. 'Sam Yaxley, sir.' His first terror was passing now, though only to be replaced by a second anxiety which pinched his narrow features: that his trousers offered thin protection from the parson's cane. Frere saw it, and the residual irritation in his manner fell away. 'Well, Sam Yaxley, I ask you again: what are you doing alone here at this hour?'

'Nothin', sir.' The face was feral almost, rueful that its name had been so unwisely surrendered.

'Is that the truth, Sam?' Kindly but with the bulk of his clerical dignity looming large, Frere looked down into those shifty eyes. 'I don't believe it was. Tell me, now—what were you up to?'

Again no more than a mumble.

'I don't understand you, boy. Speak up.'

Sam Yaxley sniffed and cast his eyes around the gravestones for inspiration. Regrettably he found nothing but the truth and some possible mitigation in sharing of the blame. 'Nelly Jex,' he said.

'Nelly Jex? What about her?'

'She hev bet me I daresn't stand here . . . not in the dark.'

Frere remembered it was All Souls' Night. 'Among the graves, you mean?'

'Under 'er, sir.'

Frere frowned, incredulous. 'Under whom, Sam?'

The boy nodded upwards. ' 'Er, sir. Gypsy May.'

Involuntarily Frere looked up. He took a moment to recover himself, and when he did he smiled. 'But you weren't afraid, eh?'

Reassured by the smile, Sam answered derisively, 'Tha's only a lump of owd stone.'

Frere's smile broadened, then he remembered himself. 'I see. And do you believe in the Lord Jesus, Sam?'

Sam perceived that much might depend on his answer. Solemnly he said, 'That I do, sir.'

Again Frere smiled at the instant innocence and the guile of it. That scruff of blond hair reached right back to the Angles. He remembered Gregory in the slave-market at Rome. *'Non Angli sed Angeli,'* he muttered aloud, and then, seeing the boy's bewilderment, cautioned, 'The churchyard is no place for games, you know.'

'No, sir.'

'But you're a brave boy, Sam.' Frere reached into his pocket. 'Here's a penny for you and be off with you now. And tell Nelly Jex I shall want a word with her after church on Sunday.'

Amazed at his good fortune, omitting any sign of gratitude in his relief, Sam turned on his heel and ran. Smiling, Frere watched him go. A few moments later he heard a muttering and giggles in the gloom beyond the wicket-gate, and the sound of children running.

Well, the time had not been entirely lost—a start had been made with the youngsters at least. He must remember to seek out the boy's home for there was poverty there, a need for kindliness. Sighing, Frere looked up again among the flints where the image of Gypsy May was shrouded in shadow. *Nothing of more account than a bogey to frighten naughty children,* Miss Agnew had said. Frere saw how disproportionate his own lonely thoughts had been.

'What a booby you are, Edwin Frere,' he whispered quietly. And then, a moment later, 'I think you are going to be happy here.' A little laugh escaped with his breath. This was not at all the encounter for which he had summoned strength, but how much more satisfactory, how much more sane. Whistling, he walked towards the lych-gate through the failing light. He looked back at his church and felt a sudden elation.

It was in this happier condition, eagerly anticipating his return to the new home, that he came upon Amy Larner, crouched beneath the blood-red hips of the dog-rose hedge in the lane outside the Rectory. When she looked up he saw that she was in tears.

Again he was discountenanced. He stood for a moment over the weeping housemaid, then bent slightly and put his fingertips on her shoulder. 'Come now, Amy, what is all this?'

The young woman looked up at him through ruined eyes, then released a further, louder sob of inconsolable misery before covering her face with her apron.

'Come, come,' he said. 'Hold up your weeping a while and let's see if I don't have a moment's comfort for you.'

Amy sniffed and shuddered, looked up into his gentled eyes for an instant and then, as if the very thought of comfort only exacerbated her wretchedness, she burst into a further torrent of tears. The apron was lifted to her face again. It was clutched in both hands, so Frere could see only her whitened knuckles. He tried another tender question or two, apprehensive that some calamity must have befallen either the girl or her family to provoke such speechless grief. 'What is it? What is it now? You must tell me and share the burden of it, or how am I to help you?' But Amy could only shake her head while biting her lip so fiercely that Frere was certain it must bleed. 'Come inside, my dear,' he said, ' . . . we may speak more easily there.' The invitation elicited only a broken howl. Then Amy pushed herself to her feet and ran off sobbing down the lane.

For a moment Frere wondered whether to pursue her but decided that further enlightenment was needed before he could be of any real help. He turned into the house and found Emilia rearranging the pictures in the sitting-room, white-faced and overly precise in her gestures.

'The strangest thing, my dear,' he said. 'I just came upon Amy in the lane, sobbing out her heart beneath the hedge, and when I tried to comfort her she ran off without a word of explanation.'

Studying her adjustment to a picture, Emilia drew a taut breath and said, 'If she had nothing to say I am quite sure it was shame that silenced her. She is dismissed from our service, Edwin.'

'Dismissed?'

Emilia nodded, and returned her attention to the unsatisfactory tilt of the frame.

'But why? What has she done? Has she been impertinent?'

'She is not a suitable person for this house.'

'But I had thought her such a good-natured soul.'

'I had thought so myself. We were deceived. I can only be thankful that Mrs Bostock informed me of her true character in good time.'

'Mrs Bostock? She was here?'

'She arrived shortly after you had left and was disappointed not to find you at home. However she took advantage of our solitude to caution me about that young woman. I was left with no choice but to dismiss her instantly.'

By now a clearer picture had begun to form in Frere's mind. Frowning, thinking quickly, he said, 'I see.'

'I very much doubt you do. But I have no desire to discuss the matter further except to assure you that I have acted in our best interests.'

Frere studied his wife in silence a moment as she sighed, shook her head and took the picture down again. Then he said, 'I should have preferred to be consulted on this.'

Holding the picture at her breast, his wife looked across at him, surprised by the sharpness of his voice. 'I assure you there was no need. Had you too been apprised of . . . the facts . . . you would have felt compelled to do the same.'

Frere sat down, fingers drumming on the arm of his chair. 'I presume,' he said quietly, 'that it is the matter of Amy's relationship with my predecessor to which you refer.'

Emilia had been about to hang the picture once more but she froze at his words and then, in stark amazement, turned to face him. 'You knew of this?'

Frere swallowed. 'Sir Henry Agnew informed me of . . . the matter, at our first meeting.'

'And you did not think to share it with me?'

He looked away.

'You could allow me to take that . . . that woman into my employ when you knew what scandal she must bring upon the house?' Emilia's face was glacial. There was a spark of cold fury in her eyes that only an act of will restrained to pained bewilderment in her voice.

'I gave much thought to the matter.'

'But little wisdom, it seems. I cannot say whether it is your secrecy or your poor judgment which has injured me more.' She turned away again with only the gilt frame in her hands to control her trembling. Frere was alarmed by this coldness. Such temper was alien to their exchanges. They were both unnerved by it.

'There was no injury intended,' he said. 'I meant only to spare you . . .'

'To spare me! To spare me what? I assure you a greater candour on your part might have spared me much humiliation. I cannot think what possessed you.'

Distressed that his renovation of spirit at the church should have no warmer reception than this, Frere said quietly, 'I was weighing the benefits of charity against those of retribution. I was remembering that forgiveness of sins is at the heart of the ministry. I was considering how it might be thought doubly unjust if one parson were to cast a harsh stone at a woman whose fall was directly attributable to the frailty of another. It did not seem to me a simple matter, or one that I could share without embarrassment to us both. And so I took it upon myself to keep silent in the certain knowledge that there was more hope for the young woman under our influence than in Saxburgh workhouse, or on its streets . . .'

'And you gave no thought to the scandal that must attach itself to your own name in the circumstances? Or to the consequences it must have for me—without my knowing it—each time I showed my face in society? I must be thankful that Mrs Bostock has a firmer grasp upon reality, and proved friend enough to risk some embarrassment to herself in sparing me the shame of it.'

'I had trusted that a charitable act would be perceived for what it was, and not be perverted by gossip in such an ignoble manner. It seems that I was wrong.'

'Indeed you were. You were very wrong. I can hardly believe your judgment to have been so at fault.'

'My judgment of what?' Frere demanded more severely now. 'Of the meaning of the Christian message, or the capacity of local society to understand it? On the latter I am prepared to stand corrected. On the former I believe myself a sounder judge than Mrs Bostock.' He took in the startled dismay on his wife's face, but he was angry now—an anger born of the sudden shock of this collision. 'I regret that you feel yourself to have been injured by my keeping my own counsel, but I do not accept your impeachment of it. We shall not make ourselves loved in this parish by a deficiency of care in our own hearts.'

'Nor shall we win respect by appearing to condone behaviour that it pains me to speak of even. Would you have the Rectory mocked as a house for fallen women? Shall we hand placards at the gate—*Come forth, ye sinners all; there is a warm welcome to be found at Munding parsonage. It is Liberty Hall!* Oh Edwin, I do not see how you could be such a . . .'

The sentence ended in a horrid frozen silence between them. They were both trembling now, Frere's mind reeling at the contrast between his access of cheerful clarity at the church and the awful confusion of this disagreement.

'Well, it is done now,' he said at last.

'Yes, it is done.'

'And you have given thought to what is to become of her?'

'She is paid until the end of the month.' Emilia shook her head, eyes closed, for such considerations were now far from her thoughts. 'I believed I acted for the best,' she said.

Frere nodded. Astounded by the heat of his own passion, he struggled to remember that forgiveness, as much as charity, begins at home. 'I understand,' he said. 'It was indeed a tortuous matter. But I must see what can be done for the young woman now.'

'I had not thought to displease you.'

'Nor I to cause you distress.'

Then they stood, with the yards of carpet stretching between them, and the clock ticking, and nothing to be said.

5 ▨ In Dreams

As though she'd turned over a body in a street-accident and recognized the face she saw, the girl frowned down at me, then was gone. The old man had already vanished with his wicked pack of cards, and I was wondering what was happening when the letter-box flapped downstairs, and I came fully awake. My watch showed the morning half over. I heard the postman's van change gear as it pulled away up the lane.

I'd forgotten that the only mail I could expect was a retributory letter from Jess. This was it, and I was in no shape for retribution. I leaned the envelope, unopened, against one of two idiotic Staffordshire figurines on the mantelpiece, then sat scowling at it. The cottage was very still. It was like sitting inside a stopped clock. It should have been peaceful, but the letter was as disruptive as that Tarot card had been at Easterness. Both spoke of dilapidated dreams.

I shaved, made coffee, charred some toast, then saw I had a choice: I could evaporate on that tall blue vacancy outdoors or stifle in The Pightle's gloom. I was washing out my coffee-cup when the knock came at the front door.

It had to be Bob wanting to mull over the business of the night before, to reassure me again that Nesbit was a fraudulent old ham, as had been proved by the way he'd backed off. I was in no mood for rational consolation. Or for politeness. One simply asked to be left alone, for God's sake. Another two minutes and I would have been gone, out, unreachable among the trees. I snatched open the door.

The girl—Laura—was standing there, her car—a battered old

Countryman—parked in the lane. She wasn't looking at me but gazing into the ferns beyond the little box-hedge that led from the gate to the front door. She raised a hand to hush me and, after a moment, whispered, 'There was something moving—over there, in that clump of fern.'

Unbalanced that she should have stepped from dream to door-step like this, and without prior arrangement on either occasion, I said, 'It's a pheasant. She's nesting there.'

'So close to the house?'

'She was here first. The place was empty when she was building.'

'And you haven't disturbed her?'

'We try not to give one another any trouble.' It was said without humour. I was still switching channels in my mind.

She smiled, draped a strand of hair behind her ear, and said, 'Hello.' The amiable greeting was out of key with my mood. It elicited a churl's response. Undeterred she asked if she could come in, and brushed past me, tall and casual in belted jeans with a long, thickly-knitted cardigan over a petrol-blue T-shirt. She took in the shady parlour—the worn velvet Chesterfield before the hearth, Clive's watercolours on the white, rough-plastered walls, the scatter of half-read books. 'What a cute place.' (I winced at the Americanism.) 'And all to yourself?'

I nodded, instantly aware of the mess around me—unemptied ashtrays, the corduroy jacket with its leather elbow-patches slumped like a drunk across a chair, one green wellie leaning against another for support.

'Don't you go crazy here?'

'I haven't been here long enough to find out.'

Her nod seemed to accept this as a reasonable assessment.

I said, 'I was just on my way out . . .'

She was still taking in the feel of the place as though there were more of interest there than its occupant. Her frown disapproved of the state of the Weeping Fig on the window-sill. 'You really should water this.'

She was right, though my first thought was, *I'll let the damn thing die if I want to*. Then she turned, suddenly business-like. I saw that she wore nothing beneath the T-shirt—a further disconcerting candour that brought memories of her nakedness in the wood. 'It's about last night,' she said.

My shrug and its silence were non-committal.

'When Edward came round this morning I told him what a

pig he'd been. He felt badly about it.' She looked for a response and found none. 'I don't think you realize how unusual that is. Anyway, he wants you to come to lunch. I'm here to fetch you.' She read the imminent refusal in my face, and forestalled it. '. . . if you'd like, that is. It's a fine day. We thought a picnic . . . cheese and wine, by the lake? He wants to make amends.'

There was a cheerful appeal in the face, an assumption that such largesse was unrefusable, that I couldn't possibly have anything better to do with my time. 'In that case,' I said, 'why didn't he come himself?'

'Ha . . . well, the thing is . . .'

'Yes?'

She turned away slightly, fingered one of the figurines on the mantelpiece, noticed the envelope. 'You haven't opened your mail. How can you bear it?' The expatriate innocence to the question did not, I thought, preclude a calculated evasion. My face left it plain that the answer was none of her business. 'Hmmm,' she said. 'He really got to you.'

'He didn't bowl me over with his charm.'

'Edward's not easy,' she conceded. 'He's an old man. He doesn't have time to mess around. Also he has his pride . . . He was afraid if he came himself you might say no.'

'And he doesn't like to take the sort of treatment he hands out so freely?'

She accepted the remark unflinching. 'He was very nervous last night.'

'He could have fooled me.'

'He fools most people.'

'But not you?'

She held me in silent appraisal for a long moment. It was like being stared at by a gypsy, that naked regard devoid of all social grace, skin-stripping. I refracted it back, reminding myself that I was the injured party, until she released her breath, shrugged, and said, 'My mistake. Okay, if you like we can forget about it. I'll leave you in peace with your pheasant.' She reached into her jeans-pocket for the car-keys, swung the ring on her index finger. 'Don't forget the plant.' She made for the door, and turned there so briskly that we were both speaking at once. I gave way.

'For what it's worth,' she said, 'we're sorry about last night. I wasn't exactly sweetness and light myself.' The soft American voice contrived to suggest that a bigger man would have found a handsomer way to acknowledge an olive-branch when he saw one. It was at once just and unjust, contrite and judgmental; and besides I didn't want her walking out morally victorious, leaving me in still deeper spleen.

I said, 'It was pretty weird.'

She heard the concession, nodded. 'Bizarre things tend to happen around Edward.'

'That business with the card . . . ?' I looked up, saw the interrogative tilt of her head.

'It was for real,' she answered, and then after a moment, 'Look, he knows he left you on a hook last night. He was pretty shaken himself . . . wouldn't talk about it when we got back. He was smashed, of course, but it was more than that. I haven't seen him that way before.'

'You've been with him a while then?'

'Two, nearly three years, on and off.' Her glance quietly defied me to broach the deeper layers of the question.

'Here, in Norfolk?'

'God, no.'

We were standing uncomfortably across from one another, strangers, hazard-met. Either this awkward conversation must expire or move, and my voice had relented already. I was showing interest. I said, 'I'm sorry. I woke up in a foul mood. Would you like some coffee?'

She shook her head. 'I've already had. Too many cups make me jumpy. But . . . a cigarette?'

I offered my packet, and took one myself. 'Why don't we sit down?' She opted for the window-seat, one arm draped along the sill, her fingertips consoling the parched fig.

'All right,' I said, 'I'll feed it.'

I brought a milk-jug of water from the kitchen-sink and began to pour. She said, 'You should get a spray for the leaves. There, that's better, isn't it?' That question was for the plant, the next for me. 'Do you talk to it? You should. It's good for your own soul too.'

'My father told me never to speak to strange plants.'

'Then he should have known better. I bet your mother did. Look, I think you should come . . . to lunch, I mean. Make Edward cringe a little. I doubt he'll actually apologize, but he should be half-way decent. He's interested in you.'

I left the jug half-full on the sill, sat down and looked across at her. 'I should be grateful for that?'

The bitterness was gone from my tone. It was wryer, and

there was a smile between us as she said, 'You never know.' It was hard not to admire the way the window light descried the tawny variations of her hair.

'The strange thing is,' I offered, 'he was a sort of hero to me once. A long time ago . . . when I was a kid and first started writing.'

Her nod suggested that she had heard this kind of thing before. 'I'd never heard of him before we met,' she confessed. 'Part of what he calls my "vincible ignorance," I suppose.'

'How did you meet?'

'I was a student at a crazy college in Connecticut. Edward was visiting professor.'

'Creative writing?' I tried to keep the distaste from my voice. In the light of his remarks the previous night, it seemed an unlikely profession for the old poet. 'Is that what you were studying?'

'Parapsychology,' she corrected, and smiled at my frown. 'I told you it was a crazy college.'

I flashed back to the scene in the wood—that trance-like state that had relapsed so rapidly into joke. 'So what are you doing here—ghost-hunting?'

She caught the note of condescension, smiled, lightly sibylline, and looked out of the window. 'In a manner of speaking.'

'Not seriously?'

'Seriously.'

'Any luck?' One had to say something.

'Some.'

'With or without heads?'

Again that gypsy stare, not offended, but with a wry brow admonishing my flippancy.

'And Edward's into this?' I asked.

She nodded and drew on her cigarette in silence.

'So you're his research-assistant?'

'We're lovers,' she said, and looked out of the window again.

I was on the point of admitting that I knew as much, but hesitated. 'He certainly seems to need you.'

'Yes.' The answer came matter-of-fact, unemphatic but absolute. I had the feeling that she was using this queer mix of frankness and mystification to her own advantage. A kind of pre-emptive politicking to mask whatever reservations she might have about her own choice. It was a game that two could play.

'So it wasn't just a joke?'

'A joke?'

'The other afternoon . . . in the wood.' I held a finger in the air, tilted my head as though alert to invisible presences and, in a portentous voice, quoted her own words: 'I think *she* used to come here.'

Her lips were open, her eyes narrowed. I expected but did not receive a blush. 'I knew there was something there,' she said.

'It was me.'

'So it seems.'

There was an awkward gap before I said, 'I heard you laughing . . .'

'Do you often play Peeping Tom?'

It was I, after all, who coloured.

'I hadn't meant to pry, but . . .'

But what? I was lonely; nosy; horny as only a blocked and solitary writer can be?

Then suddenly, surprisingly, she laughed. 'For God's sake, don't tell Edward.'

'He wouldn't find it amusing?'

'He'd never forgive either of us. I told you, he's very proud.' She did not say, but I guessed, also very jealous.

Her laughter had let me off the hook. 'Then I'll hold it in reserve—in case he takes another shot at me.'

'Does that mean you'll come?' she asked and then, in swift afterthought. 'Or have you seen all of us you want to see?'

Was there an air of flirtation to that *double entendre*, I wondered? Or was I merely flattering myself that any attractive young woman who had impulsively mortgaged her days to an old man's lust must, somewhere, be gratified that a younger man had seen, and admired, her nakedness? Certainly the thought in no way mortified her.

'Who is *she* anyway?' I changed tack. 'The ghost?'

'You don't believe in ghosts,' she smiled.

'But you do.'

'Do I?'

'I thought . . . Parapsychology?'

'Has many branches.'

I shook my head, smiling at the puzzle of her. 'What are you up to?'

'I think you should ask Edward.' She looked at her watch. 'Now are you coming or not?'

During the course of those few brief minutes she had completely altered my mood. I was intrigued, looking out again. In her eyes challenge and invitation were renewed. To a man at a loss what to do with the day, with the whole weekend, or, for that matter, with the rest of his life; for whom the alternative was another solitary walk, a drink at the Feathers with Bob Crossley perhaps, and an eventual return to the unopened, unwelcome envelope still waiting on the mantelpiece, to such an unsatisfactory man as I then was, for whom recklessness seemed a possible, if unpredictable, remedy, both challenge and invitation were irresistible. I said, 'I suppose Edward and I do have some unfinished business.'

'Good,' she answered. 'I'm glad.'

Sequestered a good half-mile down a gated but unsigned, and unmade-up, woody lane, the Decoy Lodge would have been a hard place to find without a guide. It stood far down the lake from the Hall, out of its sight, across the water; even the tall barley-sugar chimneys were concealed by the bend of the opposite shore round a thinly-wooded, man-made mount where a flock of Jacob sheep were grazing. The little hill was crowned with what looked like a neo-Gothic folly, a pinnacled fairy-tale fastness in rosy brick, which turned out, under question, to be nothing more romantic than a water-tower.

The Decoy Lodge might have been a water-bailiff's cottage once, but at some point in its history it had been extended and refurbished as a summer-retreat—a place where duck-shooters or boating-parties might make landfall; or, such was its secretive nature, a place for other, more intimate assignations. Apart from an upward extension at the eastern gable, it was two-storeyed and low-visaged under a reed thatch, with lancet windows looking out across a lawn that dipped to the lake-shore. There were croquet hoops and a peg set out across the grass. A narrow wooden jetty ran a few yards into the water, and an old boathouse with cracked and missing pantiles and much-lichened weather-boards fronted the lake to the west where dense rhododendrons bordered the garden before yielding to the woods. Beeches and a full-candled chestnut sheltered the house and its outbuildings from cold easterlies. On a day like this, high and bright, the effect was of a sunny arbour hidden among the trees, invisible from everywhere save the private, mounted pasture on the opposing shore.

Edward had fallen asleep in a deckchair beneath an expansive white parasol. A large pair of binoculars hung round his neck and, beneath them, the shirt was open revealing a fuzz of grey hair at his chest. The neb of a dark blue hat was pulled down over his nose. A pair of bright red braces drooped at his sides. Beside him on the grass an antique, brass-bound volume lay open, its heavy paper densely printed in Gothic black letter with a framed woodcut illustration at the head of the text: I caught a brief glimpse of a female figure, winged and crowned, sprawling across a naked winged man, and the single-word caption—FERMENTATIO—before Laura flipped the book shut and said, 'Wake up, Edward. We're back.'

The old man grunted beneath the hat. There was a twitching of the moustache. He sniffed and stirred, then pushed back the hat, turned his head and squinted up at us. 'I wasn't asleep,' he growled.

'Liar.'

He grinned, amiably enough. 'She got you, I see.'

'And it wasn't easy,' Laura forestalled me. 'He expects an apology.'

Edward grimaced up at me. 'Does he indeed?' For an instant I foresaw a resumption of hostilities, then he wrinkled his nose. 'Then he must have one. Laura informs me that I was what she inelegantly termed an "ass-hole" last night. If an ass-hole's apology is acceptable to you would you be so gentle as to consider it offered?'

Little though I trusted his smile I could hardly refuse it. 'As I gather it's a rare event,' I said, 'wouldn't it be irresponsible of me not to?' His smile further puckered the manifold lines of his face.

'I told him that apologies are an endangered species in these parts,' Laura explained. 'This is only the second I've seen. Perhaps they'll breed.'

Edward stretched in a yawn. 'Then we should all be in a sorry state. Sit down, Darken, for God's sake—you make me feel like a small cripple. It lacks only the rug about my knees. Did you have a bad night? I trust you did.' And, before I could respond, 'Laura, my dear, do you think—the wine?'

In parody of a slave-girl's obeisance to her sultan—fingertips reaching from a bent brow out to part the air before him—Laura stepped backwards a few paces, then straightened. 'Try to be human, Edward,' she said, 'or we'll never see him again.' Without waiting for an answer she turned towards the house. Edward chuckled after her then tipped me a confidential glance. 'I'd be lost without her, you know? Keeps me sane. Up to the mark. Never have got you here on my own.'

'She's very persuasive,' I agreed. 'She suggested I might make you cringe a little.'

He affected a wince. 'Wasn't good, that business. Should have kept my mouth shut or seen it through. Never learn . . . The booze, you see? Not good.'

It seemed that the effort of contrition was genuine enough, however back-handed his enquiry about my night. In the drooping braces, with the absurd binoculars around his neck, he looked a harmless old man, wilted a little in bright sunlight. I said, 'I think I might have been asking for it.'

'No doubt about that. You certainly were. And I should have followed through, but . . .'

He shook his head, scowled down at the binoculars and removed them. We sat in silence for a while. He seemed a little at a loss, as if, once belligerence was dropped, no alternative mode availed itself. I guessed at a lifetime of masks, of protective coloration to keep the world at bay. I remembered that moment of pained intimacy immediately after the card was turned—the suggestion that the turmoil it exposed was not mine alone. I began to relax.

'Found her in America,' he said abruptly. He might have been drawing my attention to a piece of Shaker furniture, proudly, with a connoisseur's eye. 'Something about American women, don't you think? The real ones, I mean—not the corporation whores.'

Wondering privately how an intelligent American woman could tolerate such unabashed sexual bigotry, I told him I didn't have much experience of either. He tutted, avuncular. 'Recommend it. No moral sense, you see; only a sort of evolutionary appetite. It's a libel, you know, that woman was made from Adam's rib. Quite the reverse: man was entirely the product of woman's sense of adventure. You should wound yourself on an American someday.' He winked and then, as a humorous afterthought, cautioned, 'Not mine, of course, not mine.'

'Don't worry,' I said, 'I'm not in the market for wounds.'

He quizzed me a moment through narrowed eyes. 'I hope, dear boy, you're not *in the market* for anything.' He made the catch-phrase sound contemptible. 'Unless, of course, you're speaking of that "desolate market where none come to buy." '

I recognized a quotation but had lost its provenance.

'Blake,' he supplied. '*The Four Zoas*. Read it. You might find it answers. Anyway, that's the only sort of stall we run here. White elephants and wisdom. Stuff nobody wants. Never once made a decent killing all my days.'

I looked around at the spacious, sunlit garden, the vista of the lake, the elegant lodge at our rear. 'You don't seem to have done too badly.'

'None of it mine, dear man. All skimpoled from my good friend Ralph. As far as possessions go I'm angel-naked . . . a breathing testament that economic survival without compromise or capitulation is entirely possible.'

I wondered whether Ralph Agnew was content to view things so, but had no desire to cloud Edward's humour. I said, 'You'll have to teach me how it's done.'

'Bravado,' he answered. 'Bravado in the face of all except Providence—in which, as I recall, you do not believe.'

'No more than in ghosts, I'm afraid.' The word elicited no more than a mildly puzzled response. I tried again. 'Laura tells me you were a Professor of Parapsychology in the States.'

'Good God, no. Must have got the wrong end of the stick. That's her field, not mine.'

'I thought she was your student.'

He scried me with a canny glance. 'She sat in on a course I gave there, yes.'

'On?'

His eyes twinkled. 'Pushy young sprat, aren't you?'

'Interested.'

'In an old man's sacred cows?'

I winced at the reminder. Already it was obvious that Nesbit remembered more of the previous night than a true drunkard would have done. In the Lodge Laura pushed open a window and shouted, 'If one of you two would move his male butt we'd get to eat faster.' Edward sighed and fished for his braces. I said, 'I'll get it,' and walked across to the window where I was handed a tray with three cheeses, a butter dish and a loaf of home-baked bread, its crust neatly braided. 'Human?' Laura asked.

'Human,' I smiled.

'Good. Can you handle this as well?' She proffered a carafe of wine and said, 'I'll bring the rest. Keep him sweet.'

The sun was high over the lake now, the day blue and drowsy, very still, no sound save the plash of ducks bobbing to take the bread we tossed them as we ate. Our conversation was light, a little desultory, but the silences were not uncomfortable—a quiet relishing of the day rather, and the way the light hung across the lake like a veil.

There were moments when Edward and I might have argued. He wrinkled his nose, for instance, to hear that I was a teacher as well as a poet. 'Contradiction in terms, dear man,' he disapproved. 'It's not the least crime of our benighted education system that it seeks to deafen its pupils to the inward voices of the deepest self. The poor little buggers are persuaded it's in their interests to neglect, to deride, even to deny them . . . doubtless because the teachers are dimly aware that nothing they themselves have to say is a tenth as relevant to the welfare of the child. And, of course, if the children were seriously encouraged to attend to these inmost promptings of the soul, they would immediately pull the schools down round their ears. And who could blame them?'

Not I, not that afternoon, dubious already of my own career, nor was I looking for an argument. Careful as I was with my words, it felt good simply to be in company again, with none of the formality that had blighted the previous night's gathering, and none of the animus. Good too to acknowledge that—whatever reservations I still held about Edward—we appeared (as Laura observed) to have kissed and made up. I found myself remembering how his verse had once seduced my youthful imagination—all the more intriguing to the adolescent mind for its obscurities. It had long since lost its power to beguile, but one could only regret its decline from music into rodomontade. And then, the silence. It was a sad bankruptcy and, watching him bend from his chair to feed the ducks, I saw only a mild eccentric, taking pleasure in small things. After all, I had no real quarrel with him.

Laura had changed into denim shorts, their edges frayed at her thighs. Barefoot and long-legged she lay sprawled in sunlight. Edward smiled at her approvingly. His glance invited my appreciation. Then he reached out a hand to stroke her inner thigh. It was an affectionate rather than a lustful gesture and was accepted as such. Perhaps for that reason it left me conscious again of my own loveless condition. It seemed a long time since I had touched, or been touched, with such gentle candour.

I shifted my gaze and saw two swans beating down across the

lake, a crisp light flaking from their wings. 'Oh look,' I cried, but the others had already heard the thud of swept air.

'It's Humphrey and Janet,' Laura said. The names seemed oddly drab for such majestic creatures, but they sprang from her tongue in delight, and her eyes were bright witnesses of that swift act of grace. Stately, frigate-like, the two swans sailed to where the ducks still squabbled among the reeds.

'We know them well,' said Edward. 'They're our familiars.' He reached for the remains of the loaf and got up to throw more bread. His baggy corduroy trousers were held a little high at the ankle by the scarlet braces. The shirt was rumpled at the waist. After a while he turned to grin at me. 'There you have it all, Darken. Keep a swan's neck and a duck's back, and cast your bread upon the waters. You won't go far wrong.'

The remark was offered lightly, and the moment itself would have been light enough except that I had taken advantage of Edward's turned back to look at Laura, and as he turned he must have realized how intent my gaze. She was sitting up on the grass, one leg resting across the other, her weight carried on the slender arms flexed behind her, utterly immersed in the presence of the great cob-swan preening itself by the edge of the lake. It was the first time I had really looked at her since that afternoon in the wood. She was closer to me now, known. Reclining there, she seemed unconscious of both Edward and me as she gazed at the swan, lips slightly parted, in profile to my angle of vision. I could feel her *seeing* the swan, and I too was deeply drawn into the act of seeing her. Her poise and rapt attention compelled it. Then Edward spoke and, when I turned to acknowledge his remark with a smile, I saw that he had not missed the effect of her realized presence upon me. One of his eyelids was flickering a little, and there was a sudden uneasiness to his smile that left me conscious of how exclusive of him was this new, sharply focused picture of Laura that had impressed itself on my senses. Then we were nodding and smiling at one another like puppet-heads as Laura sighed and relaxed back on the lawn to deliver herself up to sunlight again.

Later Edward suggested that he and I take a turn around the lake. I looked to Laura who shook her head. Edward and I were to be alone. 'Need to keep in shape,' he said as we moved off. 'Too much time on my arse.'

'Writing?'

He merely shook his head, murmured, 'Reading mostly,' and walked on through the small wicket-gate out of the garden. The path between the rhododendrons and the lake's edge was narrow. He strode ahead of me, swishing at the bushes with his ferruled ashplant now and then.

'And you?' he said over his shoulder. 'You working?'

'On and off.' The casual lie was no sooner out than I regretted it. It sullied the frank air. 'Actually,' I said to his back, 'I've dried.'

He received the amendment without surprise. His stick swept a fallen branch from the path. 'It happens,' he said, and I was thinking myself a fool to expect further sympathy when he added, brisk as a doctor, 'How long?'

'Weeks. Months now.'

'Scary feeling.'

'The worst.'

'There are worse,' he said. For two or three hundred yards he led the way in silence until, at a place where a riven oak leaned towards the water, he stopped and turned. 'That card . . . last night. You should think on it.'

'I have.' I held his stare a moment. 'I'd like to know how you knew which one it was.'

'I didn't. Not for certain.' He turned away again, walked on. 'Keep your eyes skinned—we might still see wood-anemones. Wind-flowers. Laura loves them.'

'Then . . . chance?'

'Never that. Not with the cards. But I shouldn't have gambled. That was . . . braggadocio. Ego. The booze.' He sniffed. 'Paid for it, of course.' He cast an almost shy, certainly rueful glance up to where I walked beside him.

'Which was why you left?'

'Felt bad. Memories. Knowing what it was like. That I should have kept my mouth shut . . . That there are times when it's wrong to be right.'

'But you were.'

The path narrowed again. He pushed on ahead as if embarrassed by his admissions, relieved to sever the link, to show me only his back as he said, 'Wasn't too hard, of course. Written all over you.'

'What was?'

Without turning he placed his thumbs to his temples and waggled the antlered splay of his fingers. 'The cuckold's mark. The horns and the need to use them.'

'It was that obvious?'

'My dear man, even sainted martyrs make a public display of their pain. How much more then injured husbands feeling sorry for themselves?' Then he added less brusquely. 'Besides, when you've worn them yourself . . .' He looked back at me, saw that I was still stinging a little. 'It's a kind of rite, you know,' he offered. 'That's why they do it to us . . . want us to change, grow up. It lops off the head, and once the head's off there's a chance we might learn to think with the heart. You have children?'

'Two.'

'Then you must truly bleed.'

He strode out along the narrow margin of the lake. I followed, staring down at the path, uncertain whether that last quick comment stemmed from genuine sympathy or out of a jaded weariness with the banality of it all.

I knew the latter was possible. Marriages vanish like disposable waste these days, and because they are not entirely biodegradable their relics litter the land. It had struck me when I'd tried to share the news with Clive. It upset him, yes, but what can you say? We'd quipped laconically around the facts, sealed them in irony, because no one, least of all a poet, likes to be caught mouthing the platitudes that spring so promptly to the lips for such occasions. Yet the fact remains: however well-trodden the path to ruin, our own calamities are never banal. To me this was not banal. The pain, grief, rage were virginal. To think of it still made me reel—the first brutal shock of Jess's confession; then the hours spent in ever more futile wrangle with her, the kids in tears upstairs; and, later, the ghastly, fumbled three-way negotiations in which she and Martin tried to explain themselves, while I, rank with the injustice of it, turned the pair of them on a sharp spit. He was my friend, for God's sake—a guest in my home, invited there in his own hour of need; and to do this, to me, at that moment, when he must have seen I was struggling myself . . .

And I'd been dunce enough to listen—what choice was left?— to take in dazed seriousness their protestations of care for me. For love, they'd said, like liberty, was indivisible, and somehow, together (ha!), we'd find a way through, we'd make things work.

Then the long nights listening. The lonely dark.

Edward noticed I'd stopped in my tracks. He turned, took a few paces back to where I stared into the shallows of the lake. 'I know,' he said quietly, 'I know.' The face which had mapped the seven sins the previous night was now a catalogue of remembered woe. But one could be ruined by sympathy; and, anyway, after the event the solace of the uninvolved always seemed overblown. If my stomach still turned turtle to think on these things then no more than a rueful smile must show.

Edward studied my smile for a moment then answered it, though not necessarily in collusion, and the brisk twitch of his moustache made him fat Puck of pensionable age, still entertained by mortal folly, except that he too was not exempt.

'So that was the cuckold's card?' I said.

Edward smiled. 'Not only that. Look, the sluice-gate's just a few yards round the bank. Shall we sit down there?'

The air was nimble over the rush of water where the lake drained to a small swift stream. Edward leaned his ashplant against the brickwork of the sluice and heaved himself up to sit dangling his legs above the water pouring from the arch below. He fished a blackened briar from his pocket, then a tobacco-pouch and matches.

I climbed up beside him and lit a cigarette, watching the stream wrinkle through green wilderness towards the Munding water-meadows. Somewhere among the trees a woodpecker yaffled derisively. Edward listened, smiling, then gave a little snort, and glanced sidelong. 'You want me to follow through?'

The question, like the choice, was open. It was clear he had no investment in my answer. Any thought that he had designs on my mind was mere solipsism. But the offer made me conscious of my loneliness; and that, alone, I was getting nowhere. I said, 'Why did you call it The House of God?' It was assent enough.

'That doesn't matter. Not yet. What matters is what you make of it.'

'The symbol?'

'And the experience it mirrors. I don't just mean the hurt. I mean the shock, and why you chose to incur it.'

I said, 'I think you've got the wrong idea. It wasn't my choosing.'

'I see. You were the innocent bystander? The passive victim? The poor me who can think of nothing better to do than bawl out the unanswerable *Why*?' Whatever warmth I had fancied between us seemed to fade as he added, 'I don't believe it.'

'Then why call it shock?'

He savoured the edge in my voice a moment. 'The shock of recognition?' He shrugged, looked away. 'Towers invite the lightning.'

'I thought an Englishman's castle was supposed to be his home.'

He snorted, impatiently this time. 'Listen, then be truthful with me. Even though you'd never seen it before, when the card was turned you recognized it. Right?'

Almost against my will I nodded.

'How could that be?'

'You tell me.'

'Because it was yours. You'd chosen it.'

'I didn't know which card I was choosing.'

'Just as you didn't know you were asking your wife to shatter the dreary tower you'd built around yourself, I suppose?' Edward shook his head. 'I doubt that you're as ignorant of your own dark side as you pretend. I asked you to be truthful with me. Think again. You knew what you were doing—you got what you wanted, didn't you? The tower was down. You were out. Free.'

'I didn't want to be free,' I snapped; then took in the wry lift of his brows. 'Not that way,' I added lamely.

'Was there another? Why didn't you take it? Sooner. In time.'

'You're making some very large assumptions.'

'They're not assumptions. It's what you told me yourself—through the card. You were speaking to yourself there, of course; but it seems that I was the more attentive listener. It's high time you listened too. To yourself. To your best self.'

I sat in silence, glowering at the stream.

'All right,' he pressed after a moment. 'Let's put it another way. Your wife—am I to assume that you married a mere wanton?' And, when I didn't answer, more softly: 'I think you were asleep, my friend. Holed up. In retreat from the claims of life. Ouspensky said of the card that if men could see that almost all they know consists of the ruins of destroyed towers they might cease to build them.' He sighed, drew on his pipe. 'You were asleep. You should be thankful that your wife had the courage to waken you.'

'She wasn't doing it for my benefit.'

'Perhaps. But in my experience women rarely act from a single motive. Their intelligence is more sensitively diffused than ours.' He gestured across at me with his briar. 'Somewhere, I suspect, you knew you could count on that.'

'If you're right why aren't I more cheerful about it all?'

'Because you like the taste of your wounds?' he suggested. 'Because you're infatuated with the role of Aquitanian prince? Because your abolished tower once felt safe? Because freedom scares you? Because you have not yet recognized that you're a lucky man?'

I gasped at that last sally. 'I've lost my wife, my kids, my home. I can't write. I can't think straight. And you call that lucky! Who the hell do you think you are?'

He shrugged, knocked the dottle from his pipe and answered mildly. 'An old fool who believes that we lose nothing that is truly ours.'

His words echoed on something that Jess had said to me. How free all these mystics were with 'truth' and 'truly'! How pious their cracker-barrel maxims! How would he feel, I wondered, if some sly wolf were to snatch Laura from his lap?

'But your question might be more profitably addressed to yourself,' he went on. 'Who do you really think *you* are? And you should address it to your best self—not the injured ego for all its hogging of centre-stage!'

He must have seen that if he taunted me further he would lose me, for he sighed and said, 'Of course, you're feeling dazed. Why should you not? You've been struck by lightning after all. It takes time to recognize that it's a privilege to be singled out by the gods that way.' He raised a finger to forestall a sarcastic retort. 'Think about lightning,' he said quietly. 'It doesn't only destroy—it fructifies. It energizes the ground for new growth. And those little figures on the card—were they falling or flying? Perhaps when the shock has passed, they will begin to savour life outside the tower. They might have felt safe in there, but it was a prison as much as a stronghold. Now that it's down . . . well, they might recognize that they have become conductors of new energy back into the world of men. Tell me, have you been dreaming lately?'

Further dazed under this provocative assault of images, I said, 'It feels as if I do nothing else.'

A nod of acceptance. 'But do you remember your dreams?'

I recalled the bad dream of that first night at The Pightle—the

band of crazy women, the humiliating ordeal to which they would
subject me . . . Nesbit now sat in judgment on my deepest hurt.
I decided not to give him the satisfaction of knowing he had
inward allies. I shook my head.

'You should try. "In dreams begins responsibility"—wisest
words Willie Yeats ever uttered. How else can your best self
speak?'

It was the third time he had used the phrase, and I disliked it.
There was a Sunday-school ring to it, the odour of sanctity. It
had no bearing on the old dark anarchy rife inside me—the rage,
the hurt; my black menagerie. Plainly the old man had no idea
what it was like in here.

'However varied our dreams,' he said, 'they all have the same
punchline. It is: *Wake up!* You should listen. And what of your
waking dreams? Your daylight fantasies? Behind the adolescent
lust for comfort and revenge, is there nothing else? No shoot of
something new?'

The green image budded in my mind, became the Green
Man—that mute, shambling creature, feral and furtive, arrested
somewhere along the evolutionary line to man. Green as envy.
As youth and its callow folly. He was there, watching from my
own dark glades. I glimpsed him for a moment clearer than ever
before; but then he was gone, slipped away, too canny to declare
himself in public. No one's Caliban but mine.

I looked up and saw that Nesbit sensed we had not been alone
in those instants. 'I don't ask you to tell me about them,' he
said. 'Simply to pay attention to whatever they have to say.'

We sat for a long time in silence.

Aware that, for all his sententious manner, the old man had
been trying to help, I was gripped in a sort of shame. It was, I
suppose, the obverse of my stubborn pride, and I was gripped
rather between the two, in a vice of my own making. For half
of me ached to pour out its heart, while the rest, charier, conscious that the cost might beggar all dignity, held that softer self
in check.

I thought about the image on the card—the lightning, the toppled tower, the falling men. I tried to imagine them as fledglings
and dizzied at the thought. I thought of what Edward had said
of the experience it mirrored; of what Jess and Martin had tried
in their time to say. Only through thought could the dam hold
fast. And yes, I wanted to believe them; but I could feel the old
atheism creep like couch-grass through my mind. I wanted to

be on my own and could find no gracious way to cut and run; and only the empty Pightle waited, with that envelope still on the mantelpiece. I wanted to be back in what had once been my home, with the children, in the time when our two names—Jess and Alex—had flowed from the lips of our friends in a single cursive polysyllable, and we were surrounded by what felt now like an antediluvian sense of peace . . . In which too, God help me, I could not really believe.

Edward grunted beside me and shifted his weight. 'Talk too much,' he muttered. 'Always did. Damn fool.'

'I asked for it.'

'Should know better. Everybody has to find their own way out of hell. Just don't fall asleep there, that's all.' At that moment the sky above our heads was seared by a jet aircraft flying at low level, murderously swift, and with so violent an impact on the air that even the grass around us quailed. Instinctively we both recoiled, then glowered up where its trail might have scarred an otherwise immaculate blue. Edward growled deep in his throat. 'When eventually I form a government,' he said, 'my first appointments will be Minister of Mirth and Secretary of State for Extramarital Affairs. There will be no Department of Defence but the Chancellor of Common Sense will see to it that every peasant is supplied with a bazooka for use on occasions such as this.' Awkwardly he swung his legs back over the brickwork and down on to the path. 'Shall we go on round the lake or would you rather go back?'

I slipped down from the sluice-gate and looked back at the lake. It would be a far walk round—too long now to continue alone in Edward's company. Yet I felt unready to face Laura again so quickly with so much disturbed and unresolved inside me. Edward observed me uncertainly. 'Listen,' I began. 'I want you to know that I appreciate . . .' But he shook his head, shushed me silently. I saw that the gesture was not meant merely to spare my pains, and that he had more faith in my resistance than in this formal half-measure of assent. Still, both ways some sort of acknowledgment was made.

I cast about a moment longer, and remembered. 'The windflowers. We didn't pick any.'

'You don't pick them,' he growled. 'Pick them and they're dead in half an hour. But we should look for some, yes. Might learn something there.' I watched as he walked away, hunch-shouldered, parting the undergrowth with his stick—old man again, and oddly lonely.

When I got back to The Pightle I took the envelope down from the mantelpiece and opened it:

Dear Alex,

I know you think that words have come to an end between us so I'll keep this brief.

I could wish for the kids' sake that you'd left in a different spirit, but even before you disappeared Martin and I had already begun to see how wrong we'd been to try to keep you here. Though we'd never intended things so, it was—as you said the last time we talked—a bastard sort of half-life for you, and as long as you felt that way none of us could be happy. Not that we're entirely happy now. Marcus and Lily still don't accept that you're gone and very much need to hear from you. Martin has been marvellous with them, but he's feeling miserable with guilt, and I . . .

Well, I'm prepared to pay the price that honesty exacts—my honesty and yours. If your truth is that you need to be away from here, out of touch, then I can't blame you for that. Not any more. There is no blame. I simply want you to know that there will be no more demands, of any sort, from me. The children are another matter but, as far as I'm concerned, you have your freedom now. I suspect it's what you always wanted.

One last word: I realized something right at the start of all of this—that once you admit the truth there is no ending. Alex, there have been other truths between us than the ones we face, and they too do not end. So, whether you want it or not, you have

my love,
Jess

P.S. Meanwhile life goes on:

The police came round on Wednesday. They were a bit annoyed that you'd disappeared, but you'll be relieved to know that they're not pressing charges. I rather think that in the circumstances their sympathies were with you. Also Derek rang from the Poly. He needs to know whether or not you want the job back next year. Can you get in touch with him by mid-June at the latest?

Unaccompanied the letter would have brought all kinds of remission, but there were two enclosures: a drawing from Lily—a signed self-portrait with our dog, Bracken, executed in a rainbow of bright felt-tips—and another, typically laconic, letter:

Dear Daddy,
    I hope you are all right. I am all right.

> Love,
> Marcus

The tears came entirely unexpectedly. I thought they had all dried.

Later I tried to write an answer. Not to Jess—I had been transparent to her for so long that she would expect no answer now. But the children . . .
Draft after draft lay screwed on the floor. The only simple things I found to say were lies, and lies they should not have. Finally I drew a picture of The Pightle with myself standing in the doorway waving. On the back I told them about the pheasant in the garden and the smoke I'd brought into the house. I told them that I needed to be on my own for a time, that I would be back to see them soon, and they weren't to worry because I was safe and loved them very much. It was less than they needed and as much as I had to give. It left me feeling male and inadequate. But it was done.

I shook myself free of it, sat back, and tried to take stock of what was happening. What, for instance, would Clive make of this dishevelled figure inhabiting his house? What, for God's sake, had happened to my style? Where were the ironies now when I needed them, the studied cool with which my whole generation had sidled between cynicism and sentiment? If nothing in that wry detachment could pass for wisdom, there had been at least a fine, cavalier defiance. Its bravura was never entirely at a loss. It had salt.

I resented Jess's pious certainty that she understood me. My freedom wasn't hers to give: I'd taken it. It was mine. And anyway, nobody really wants to be understood, not deeply. Complete understanding would rob us of our private mystery, of the secret we keep even from ourselves. It would put out the light. Which was why I had a problem with Edward Nesbit now. He was coming very close.

I'd begun to warm to the man. I liked his oddball angle on the world. I admired his derision and his vanity. I was intrigued by Laura's spirited mix of American candour and something more elusive, vagrant. In that hour together by the lake I'd begun to open myself again. We'd shared more than bread and wine in our silences. It may have been the place as much as the people—that flawless sky, the beaten-metal shimmer of the lake—yet even in that difficult exchange with Edward I'd felt myself nudged by the tide of things. But where? And now I was lonelier than if I'd never met them. Still more provisional. Restless.

I'd brought a small tinfoil screw of grass to The Pightle with me and had been saving it for the right time. I made up the joint with tobacco and a cardboard roach, lit it, and sat in the sweet stink, feeling time cloud slowly round me.

Whether it was because I was smoking on an empty stomach, or long unused to the effect of the drug, or whether my body had risen in fierce insurrection at this attempt to sidestep its grief, I do not know. What I know is that I was drifting swiftly from a bitter-sweet reverie of that afternoon when I'd first taken Jess by punt up the Granta (kingcups, candock, green river-shadow); away from that, through the shock of her pregnancy, into the wedding; the labour pangs soon after (Marcus entering the world like a salmon at a leap); the post-natal tensions of that tiny house in The Kite, the move (financed by Jess's parents at the news that Lily was on the way); and then the ups and downs of our years together, the adoration and the bitchy withdrawals, the rows and contrition, all slipping by, until Martin turned up after his disaster in Africa; and, eventually, the first quick green glow of suspicion, and the sudden gaping hole in my life . . .

I felt my life slide past me like a raft, the children receding, smaller and smaller, down the wrong end of a spyglass . . . space lurching away . . . And I was up and out the front door, heaving my guts in the darkened garden.

I came back, white as lime, and dragged myself to bed where I lay for a long, bleak time. There was no moon. It was dark, thick dark in the bedroom. And, inside me, blacker, I think, than it had ever been. I was shivering at the cold and dizzy blackness of it. Not even in the worst moments with Jess and Martin had I known it so. Not in the black rage of the brawl at the college-dance, nor in the chill aftermath. It felt as though I'd vomited up the last thin shreds of light. What was left was nullity.

Then, as if in confirmation of this final clarity of dark, I heard the drone of aircraft overhead, flying out of Thrandeston on a midnight sortie. Merely keeping their evil hand in, or for real this time? There was no way of knowing but to wait. Either way, regardless of my existence, or of my children far away across the country, the obedient young men up there would execute their duty. The sound throbbed around me like an emanation of the dark. Its voice.

Things could not continue so. In the emptiness of The Pightle I was unravelling again. I might dwindle to a jelly there.

Monday was market-day in Saxburgh and I was short of supplies, so I walked into town and found my way to the auction-ground. It seemed that half the county had come: a throng of farmers and dealers and housewives, shrewdly eyeing the live-stock, picking over the deadstock—bales of wire-netting, sheets of chipboard and asbestos, the furniture and pathetic bits and pieces drawn from houses of the dead. The air was fat with the warm smell from a fish-and-chip van, loud with the shout of money. Florid auctioneers quipped slick jokes as they knocked down the lots. Deal after deal was struck, stuff changing hands, bids made and regretted, roof-racks loaded, trailers crammed, as though time itself was up for grabs and Want waiting at every door.

After the stillness of The Pightle, the hush of the woods, I felt an almost agoraphobic panic among the throng. What was the need of all this clutter—the dubious TV sets, the ugly For-mica tables, the painted pine cupboards that would be stripped and sold on, the job-lots of lockless keys and tin-boxes filled with junk? Yet this was it—the human community in focus, jostling for gain amid a muddle of stuff. And with a sense of occasion, as though everyone was tipsy on the fraught air. Odd to think of these dead objects moving around the country from one niche to the next as if in quest of some specific destiny. And people could spend their lives this way, producing nothing, merely moving it on, or accumulating, to what satisfactory end? And who was I to judge, mesmerized in the middle of it, owning almost nothing now but the clothes I stood in, and lonely as a stone?

In the shed where fresh vegetables were sold I saw Laura, tall among the circle of buyers, bidding for a bunch of irises. Parcels of leeks, parsnips and carrots were held in the crook of her arm. Presumably Edward was somewhere about, but it was she who held my gaze again, joking with the auctioneer, taking an expatriate's delight in local colour, adding to it with the bright garments she wore, un-English, slightly brash. It would have been simple enough to sidle alongside her, to offer a hand with her load, to pass the time of day. It wasn't shyness that stopped me but some more obscure resistance. And she was too involved with her purchasing to notice me.

I slipped away.

That nervousness in Saxburgh bothered me. Even crossing its streets had begun to feel risky after Munding's quiet lanes. I needed to connect with the world again, so when Bob Crossley told me he was driving into Norwich that Wednesday and offered me a lift, I decided to go.

Bob was interested to hear that I'd seen Edward Nesbit again, and mildly amazed that some effort had been made to apologize for his outrageous behaviour.

'I think we caught him at a bad time,' I said. 'He was very drunk.'

'Some such thought had occurred to me.'

'I don't think it was typical.'

Bob eyed me dubiously. 'Sounds as though you're developing a soft spot?'

'He's an abominable old bugger, but . . .'

'You like him.'

'He intrigues me.'

Bob sniffed. 'He's different, I'll say that much. But . . . I don't know. I'd be careful if I were you.'

'Why so?'

Bob pondered a moment, watching the rear-view mirror, said, 'I'd say he's obsessed,' then scowled as a car overtook us too close to a bend. He changed down, giving way. 'Damn fool!' The remark, I saw, applied to the driver not Edward.

'Obsessed?'

'I'd say so.'

'What with?'

Bob shrugged. 'Ask me another. But it shows. He doesn't listen. If you watch his eyes, he's always thinking ahead—not really in touch with the feel of what's happening, too busy making his own case. You must have noticed.'

'But obsession?'

'There's something there, something biting him. Doesn't leave much room for ordinary folk like you and me—unless he has a use for us.'

I smiled at his concern. 'I doubt he'd have much use for me.'

'You're a poet, aren't you?'

'And, therefore, by definition, useless. Edward would be the first to say it.'

'The girl—you don't think he's using her?'

'She seems very attached to him.'

'Of course.' Bob sighed. 'I've seen something like it before—old men, scared by their own mortality, possessed by some visionary idea or other, and needing disciples . . . and sex. Young sex. To blow on the embers. It's a way of colonizing—deceptive and self-deceptive. Sad really.'

'If I didn't know you better . . .' I smiled.

He grinned back across at me. 'Think I'm jealous, do you?'

'Well she is . . .'

'Yes, she is. And I'm not yet past it. But I'm old enough to know it can be disastrous all round. And the magic bit . . . that business with the cards. Didn't take it too seriously, did you?' A quick glance took in my shrug. 'They're murky waters, Alex. I came across a man once who'd set himself up as a "perfect master"—claimed he had all the answers and persuaded a lot of people to believe in him. "Perfect bastard" would have been more to the point. He came unstuck when it turned out he'd been having it away with all the women—secretly, conning each of them into thinking she was the chosen handmaid. You can laugh, but one of the girls ended up on a section-order after she'd tried to cut her wrists.'

'Edward's not like that,' I said with more conviction than I felt, then tried to lighten the mood. 'Anyway, I can't imagine he fancies me, and I think Laura can look after herself.'

'I'd say she was running scared. Father trouble probably. You may be right, but I'll lay you ten to one it can't last—Nesbit and the girl, I mean. Someone's going to get hurt.'

'Isn't that par for the course?'

Bob didn't look at me, simply pursed his lips, then said, 'It doesn't have to happen, you know.'

'I think you were lucky, Bob.'

'I know I was. But people don't have to go looking for disaster.' After a moment he added, 'Will you be seeing them again?'

'I don't know. I have an open invite to go back . . . But I'm not sure how much longer I'll be about.'

I had the feeling he was about to say more—something avuncular if discreet. I looked away. In the window the pale ghost of my reflection stared back. We were silent for the rest of the drive.

Bob had business at the Labour Party offices so I had a couple of hours alone in the city. He'd recommended a good secondhand bookshop which I found and liked. It was a warren of staircases and dusty rooms where the books huddled like refugees—displaced aristocrats fallen on hard times sharing the shelves with a motley crowd of paupers, special-pleaders, eccentrics and bores. I was at home amongst them. This was where most of my life had been lived. By the time I was twenty I'd married my mother with Oedipus, rioted with Mercutio, murdered an old pawnbroker in St Petersburg, seen eternity in a grain of sand before drowning at Lerici only to rise again on the third day and proclaim the death of God. And here I was now—cover battered, several pages soiled, others missing or foxed, author's copy, signed, and with a host of errata or what used to be called 'faults escaped.'

I found a nice nineteenth-century edition of Catullus and passed a wry quarter of an hour savouring the acid that the young Roman had thrown at Lesbia in his hurt. I recognized that voice. Failing verses of my own, I thought it might oil the works if I tried my hand at translation. I bought the book and was about to leave when I was stopped by the complete Blake I'd spotted on the shelves. I remembered Edward's tip and decided to take a look at *The Four Zoas*. What I found there was this:

What is the price of Experience? Do men buy it for a song,
Or Wisdom for a dance in the street? No! It is bought with
 the price
Of all that man hath—his house, his wife, his children.

The words printed themselves on my mind with corrosives quite as fierce as any Blake had used in engraving his Prophetic Books.

Sod you, Edward, I thought, and baffled the amiable bookseller with a grim smile as I paid for the Blake too.

The air of Norwich was crisp and blue and bright, as though the city stood at altitude. I'd arranged to meet Bob by the cathedral and spent some time wandering around the cloisters where, visually at least, there was nothing between me and the Middle Ages. Those vaults had been raised in a time when poets were honoured and feared, when they were prized as the living memory-bank of experience. There had been a time too when I was confident of a place among them. I remembered how the verses had flowed from my first ardour for Jess—how she'd divined the poet in me and made him thrive. Such adoration there had been, such expectation of the life between us. Even the rows, the bitchiness and spleen had given tongue. And where had it all gone? Given away, made public, finally spurned.

So what was Blake daring to say? Out of such loss what wisdom but bitterness? To hell with experience bought at such a price. Damn Edward and his electric towers . . . unless . . .

Unless somehow one could find a way to bring back home what had been so unwisely surrendered.

There it was: as though the thought had been striding the flagstones too, coming the other way to meet me. And, like all such realizations, once it was made it was blindingly obvious. So obvious I wondered how it could have taken me so long to get there.

In placing my centre of gravity between myself and Jess I had invoked collapse. She had only to move and I was down. It was as simple as that. I had given myself away. In all senses I had given myself away, and I had to get myself back.

Suppose Edward was right—that it wasn't possible to lose what was really yours? Suppose there was a difference between surrendering yourself in meeting and . . . whatever it was that I had done? Suppose that the real self was inalienable? And what if that was what Jess had been after—a restoration of myself to myself—however uncertain and ruthless her intuitive act? What then?

Standing in the cool shade of the cloisters I raised my head, looked up and, from the centre of a boss where the ribs of the vaulting surged to meet, I saw the face of the Green Man grinning down.

The Pightle was no longer empty. It was crowded with my thoughts.

What I had surrendered to Jess was female: so much was

clear. I had insisted that she be it, do it, for me, on my behalf.
I needed it, and she *was* it, so I'd needed *her*. I'd called it my
love and without it I was a shell. Yet, once deprived, I understood only the kind of passionate rancour to which Catullus had
given immortal voice. I could relish every poem of his that
screamed out 'Bitch!' between the cadences. I wasn't proud of
my translations, but they were my business, peculiarly mine.
Working at them was an oblique twist of the quest to bring *her*
back. Not Jess, but whatever dream of woman I had squandered
on her . . . though not fruitlessly, for Marcus and Lily were
there, the product of our meeting. Uniquely, irreplaceably themselves. Were they the sole reason for our marriage then, its only
final justification—whatever pain inhered in that strict thought?
Or was it all far more subtle than that, more elusive, like the
dream of woman dancing a dance of veils between my senses
and the real?

Certainly, until I let go of Jess—let go of the loss—there could
be no clear space for something new to enter. But how to do
that? You can't simply make up your mind. I tried and found
that the mind was a blunt instrument. It couldn't cut water, and
water felt closer to what woman was. Water and also, when
occasion demanded it, cold stone. I thought of Gypsy May on
the church at Munding—each comer's whore and mother. No,
not funny. Not funny at all. Voracious. Immolating. To be
feared.

Catullus had known and feared her, or whatever equivalent
was worshipped in the temple of Cybele on the Palatine Hill at
Rome—so close to the house of Clodia Metelli, the Lesbia on
whom he'd wrecked his heart:

> Great Cybele, Mother Goddess, Dindymian Queen,
> Let not your fury fall on Catullus' house;
> Drive others mad, trap others in your frenzied toils.

The passage was already scored in my copy of the book. Some
other man, some other fool, had trembled there before.

I found myself thinking mythologically. It was the old, old
story: the king slept or went to war; when he woke or returned
it was to find his wife in love with another man. He saw he'd
foolishly divulged his secret weakness, but the realization came
too late for there was murder in her heart, and he saw it only as

his head was off. But then—as Edward had suggested—once the head was off perhaps you might start to think with the heart.

With such strange and untypical thoughts I kept myself awake far into the night.

And then:

Stepping through the darkness I approached Munding church. Something queer had happened to its proportions. There was something very odd about the porch. When I looked up I saw that Gypsy May was no longer a small stone figure half-lost among the flints. She had grown enormously. She straddled the church, and the porch was no longer a porch but the wide-held maw of her cunt, through which—a mote at a minster door—I was inexorably drawn.

When, slowly, as at the turn of a dimmer-switch, the darkness yielded to a faint red light, I saw that I had entered an underground laboratory or operating theatre. It was raked like an auditorium. I stood at the top of a steep descent of pew-like benches and looked down. Far below, two shadowy figures were at work behind a table crowded with apparatus—test tubes, bell-jars, crucibles. At the centre of the table two glass retorts, curiously shaped like hour-glasses, though more bulbous in the lower than the upper chambers, were clamped together in such a way that the slender spout from each upper chamber was inserted into a flanged aperture on the lower chamber of the other, and sealed. The single, circulatory vessel thus formed was glowing with an intense ruby heat. This was the only source of light in the room.

Even as I watched it seemed to gather in intensity, and the colour of the light was changing as it flowed around the system, becoming iridescent, glowing rainbow-like but brighter in the surrounding gloom. The two figures were bathed now in the full spectrum of its radiance so that I could make out how strangely they were dressed—the man in a full frock-coat of the seventeenth century, peruked under a wide-brimmed hat, with a lace jabot at his neck; and at his side the woman was smocked and long-kirtled, her hair bunched in a white mob-cap. As though expecting me, the man looked up from the retorts and, with a brisk crook of his finger, summoned me down the central aisle of the auditorium. For the first time I noticed the acrid odour on the air. Apprehensively, half-afraid that I was to be the subject of some dubious experiment, I descended the stair and stopped a few paces away from the glowing retorts.

The old man smiled at me. For a shocked instant I thought I recognized Edward Nesbit's wrinkled features beneath the wig, and looked to the girl, expecting to find Laura's features over the seventeenth-century dress. But it was a momentary illusion only. These were strangers out of antiquity; not of my time, yet oddly familiar. Both turned their heads, directing my attention away from the now dazzling retorts to the hidden source of their energy: naked in the shadows, two other figures, a man and a woman, were making love. Gently. In passionate innocence, as though entirely alone in a dream of their own, and unobserved. Even before I saw their faces I knew who these lovers were.

Wistfully, with a strange absence of surprise or bitterness, I watched until the two figures began to fade. All that tender energy was gathered now into the still. The old man nodded, took the hand of his companion and then, with a final imperious gesture, indicated the shimmering radiance of the glass.

'This is the one true philosophical Pelican,' he announced— promised? warned?—'and none other is to be found in all the world.'

6 ❧ Approaches

As the arrival of correspondence was not a frequent event in Louisa Agnew's life she was surprised to receive two letters in the space of a few days, both of them from her brother. The first had been little more than an affectionate postscript to a lengthy newsletter written for joint perusal with her father. The second was unusual, and had been penned only because young Henry was deeply disturbed by his father's cursory reply to the first.

I have long been reconciled (he wrote) *to father's indifference to my career, and I shall not pretend it has not been hurtful. Nevertheless I confess my breath quite taken away by the enclosed response to my latest (perhaps ill-conceived) effort to persuade him that my role in these turbulent times is not entirely without significance. My first thought was that he had outdone himself in his resolve to make plain his derision. My second was more alarming, and it is that which prompts this hasty confidence.*

Read his letter, dear Lou, and ask yourself whether I am not justified in my suspicion that father has begun to drift quite beyond the pale of sensible discourse. I begin to fear it may be so, and if the thought greatly concerns me it is not least for your own welfare.

I know of old your capacity for patience and forbearance; know too that it may have done you greater harm than you yourself readily apprehend. Therefore I insist: if all is not well at the Hall I must be informed at once. In particular I seek your immediate assurance of father's continued competence to manage our family's affairs. Though my duties here remain onerous, I shall, if occasion requires it, come down to Easterness with all possible despatch.

You will remember my good friend Charles Mortimer. He sends you his kind wishes and often asks after you. I believe he regrets (as I sometimes must myself) that your life should be so entirely circumscribed by the whims of a tiresome old man.

In much dismay Louisa unfolded the enclosed sheet of paper. It read:

My Dear Son,
*   have received and digested yrs of the 20th ult. It confirms my expectation that in the boardroom of Hell there will be increased satisfaction at the annual report.*
                         Yr affectionate father,
                                         H. Agnew

Louisa's first response was a relieved smile, for she immediately recognized a brisk exercise in bubble-pricking. Small wonder brother Henry was nettled . . . to have written at such eloquent length and receive such meagre return! If only he would not wallow in his glory so, for whether the issue was insurrection and the fall of kings in Paris, the unsatisfactory government of Spain, the frequent resignation of Prussian cabinets or violent discord in the Austro-Hungarian Empire, he was ever at pains to impress upon his family that Lord Palmerston did not have to look far for sound advice. Sadly, the effect was to make her brother appear only slightly a less self-regarding ass than Mr Mortimer (whose kind wishes Louisa could happily forego). Then too there had been his vehement account of the Chartist agitation in London. Aware as she was of the human anguish behind that chapter of afflictions, Louisa had hardly been able to restrain a smile at the thought of Henry and Charles needlessly barricading the windows of the Foreign Office with bound copies of *The Times*.

And yet . . . there *was* something troubling in her father's reply. Louisa herself had occasion enough to complain of his taciturnity: when the mood took him he could be a man from whom even monosyllables must, like oakum, painfully be picked. But this letter to an only son—one of whom he was

prouder than he might readily admit . . . It was disconcertingly
brief and dour. Grim even.

Unlike her father, Louisa had an instant understanding of its
burden. In her estimation, as in her father's, the grave questions
of the age reached fathoms deeper than mere policy. The real
battleground for the future was not Paris, Baden, Vienna, Venice, or even London itself: it was that of the beleaguered human
soul. As, of course, it had always been, though the present crisis
was grave indeed. Yet when she looked at the grim little letter
again, when she remembered her father's recent fits of spleen,
his morose presence at dinner, his complaints of sleepless nights,
she realized suddenly—and it came like a chill at her heart—
that this was a battle her father might himself be losing.

She brought his tray of tea to him that day. She had included
an ample slice of his favourite blackberry and apple pie—the
last of the year, for the Devil had spat upon the blackberries the
previous night—and as he ate she chattered inconsequentially.
Then, against some resistance, she persuaded him to take a turn
in the park.

Once outside she encouraged him to speak his anxieties, refusing to accept his first gruff demurral. 'There is something
troubling you,' she insisted, 'and you shall have no peace till it
is out between us.'

Henry Agnew sniffed the autumnal air like a badger dragged
into the light of day. He saw a resolute glint in his daughter's
eye, one which would allow no easy retreat. Something must be
said to satisfy her.

Yet much was omitted from his grudging confession. He made
no mention, for instance, of his recent fears for his health. There
had been no significant return of the pain that had frightened
him, and he saw no point in alarming her unduly. Nor did he
admit to the grave doubts that nagged at him through the empty
hours alone: the growing suspicion that the prime obstacle to
his progress was something unregenerate in the dark places of
his own soul. He had battered his brains and could find nothing
to obstruct the free flow of his knowledge if it was not some
obdurate flaw in his own character; but the nature of that flaw
he was reluctant to examine too closely . . . certainly not here,
aloud, in his daughter's company. Still, he must say something,
and to complain of the difficulty of his self-appointed task would

appear mere belly-aching. Only after several moments of anxious thought did he hit on a theme that might answer.

'Is it not obvious, my dear? The pace of my work . . . it is, of necessity, slow, while with every day that passes I have a more agonized awareness of the urgent need for its completion.' And he was launched now on a passionate jeremiad against the iniquities of the age.

Surely he need not remind her of the convulsive events recounted in young Henry's letter? And beyond the immediate turmoil, he insisted, the world continued to mistake for progress its accelerating descent into the prison of matter. He reflected gloomily on the drift from the land into the noisome inferno of the cities, on the terrible speed with which machines disordered the ancient balance between man and nature. 'And how rapidly,' he growled, 'those brute, obedient servants must soon turn master. They will diminish men to desperate creatures, void of all dignity, and ever more violent as their efforts to lay hands on life prove ever more vain. Believe me, Lou, in my blacker moments I foresee a time when all reverence for the divine spark occluded in man will be mocked out of court. And what shall our pains have been worth if unregenerate matter finally triumph over spirit?'

That can never happen, Louisa was thinking, but he pressed on in his ferocious misery. 'The vision of a golden world will be cashed in for muck and brass. Already men's minds are so infatuated with the brisk profits of material gain they take no heed for the consequences. And the church—ha, the church! Those reverend gentlemen are consumed with their own quarrels . . . heat generated without illumination, authority without knowledge, a monstrous preoccupation with the trivial while the dark powers range.' Agnew glowered as though the entire Anglican synod quailed before him, then murmured, 'There is so little time, Lou, so little time . . .'

Louisa listened, her head tilted slightly so that the dark ringlets crumpled at her shawl. The fingers of one hand fondled the locket at her throat—it contained a tress of her mother's hair. Around them, under a racing sky, the parkland gleamed. The windy light disavowed each sombre prophecy, yet so tight was the grip of her father's beetled brows he was able to see none of it.

Nothing of what he said was new to her. Was not this precisely why they had worked together all those years? And if the crisis of the age was grave, graver perhaps than it had ever been, an age-old tradition of wisdom was still alive in them, still available to answer it, still filled with golden promise as the elms and beeches here were crowned with golden leaf.

No, none of this was new—nothing except the note of despair threatening to undo their long years of perseverance. She had heard the uncertainty in his voice and it confirmed what she suspected: her father was indeed in great distress, though not at all as her brother believed. Even now he spoke truer than he knew, for in his weariness and frustration he had become so obsessed with time he was no longer free to use it. His imagination was imprisoned by his doubts. No wonder his verses would not flow, for they were dammed by a rock that could and must be lifted. She glanced quickly his way and saw that she could tell him this and it would make no difference. He would nod, contrite, ashamed—or maybe he would bluster; and either way it would do no good. Something new must enter the situation.

'Tell me,' she responded, drawing lightly on the air, 'do you trust my understanding of the work?'

Agnew sighed and looked away. 'There are times when I trust it more than my own judgment.'

'Very well. Then I have a proposal to make.'

He looked across at her, a little puzzled, though he had sensed her eyes bright with purpose when she insisted they take this walk together.

'However,' she added, her voice assuming that pretence of sternness which was a mark of her endearment, 'there is first a statement I must make, and you must promise to be patient with me.' She took in the mild distraction of his nod, then stopped in her tracks to look out across the lake. When she spoke again her tone was graver. 'I understand that the full resonance of the work can only be communicated in verse. I know it is of the nature of truth to deplete in the telling, and that only poetry can offer sufficient resistance to such depletion. It is clear to me that no substitute, however well-endowed with reason and lucidity, could stimulate the minds of men with equivalent power. Nevertheless . . .'

He thought he caught her drift and hastened to forestall it. 'Do not suggest that I abandon verse for prose. There is . . .'

A raised finger reminded him of promised silence. 'Can you

think I have given my assistance all these years only to deter you from your true vocation?'

His cane chastised the grass. 'Then what . . . ?'

'That I *know* what you too gloomily forget—that your work in verse must *and will* be brought to fruition.' She paused to adjust her shawl, then added before he could interrupt again, 'But it occurs to me that your epic might meet with a yet more receptive audience if the way for it had first been prepared.' How yellowish, she saw, had the corners of his eyes become: she had been remiss not to notice it before. 'Is it not also possible,' she persisted, 'that a prose treatise on the work might go some small way towards meeting the immediate crisis of the age . . . arouse the proper attention, at least, until the moment when the true voice shall be heard?'

He shook his head in exasperation, and resumed his walk. 'Have I not already said there is little enough time for verse without the additional burden of a work in prose?'

She had not followed his steps. Her voice was carried by the breeze over his shoulder. 'You have not yet understood me. I do not suggest that *you* should be the author of this preliminary treatise.'

Five or six paces away by now, he stopped, and turned, and saw the sole alternative candidate for this difficult task. Louisa held his troubled gaze a moment, then turned the delicately-boned oval of her face—the chin tilted a little, the tip of her tongue at her upper lip—to look across the lake once more.

Somewhere, he realized, he still thought of her as a child—as his creature, whose life he had shaped and possibly disfigured by the intellectual discipline he had imposed. In this, as in so much else, he was wrong. Here was a free spirit, adult, autonomous, freely choosing to remain at his side, and not for his sake alone. Quietly he said, 'I see,' and looked away.

Already she was regretting that she had not found a way to make the idea spring from his own lips. That would have been shrewder, more efficient, for she could sense the lines of his jaw begin to set in resistance; but it would also have been manipulative, and therefore wrong. She said, 'Do I trespass too far?'

He heard disappointment, a genuine anxiety in her voice. 'My dear,' he procrastinated, 'it would be an awesome task.'

'But one for which I have been well prepared.'

'Indeed.'

'All those years of note-taking and redaction,' she encour-

aged, observing the quick activity of his eyes, '—more than half
the labour is already done. Surely what remains would be the
joyful part?' She hesitated, remembering that in his own work
he had not found it so of late. Better to press on, however, while
she held the initiative still. 'I have an outline in my mind . . . a
plan of the chapters that would take me from our speculations
on the early mysteries, the Chaldaic Oracles and Pythagoras,
through to the Alexandrian Platonists; then on by way of Geber
into the medieval sages—Albertus Magnus, Aquinas, Bacon,
Lully. Thence to Ficino, Pico, Agrippa, and all the grand adepts
of the Paracelsian school . . .'

There was more, but she faltered there at the uncertain expression on his face. What thoughts was he mustering behind
that darkly furrowed brow?

Agnew listened as the great names rippled from her tongue
like a register of class-mates, or friends she would eagerly invite
to some grand occasion. Then—almost as though she had divined this latter thought—she added, more shyly now, 'I have
even conceived a title for the treatise.' She waited a moment for
a response that did not come. 'It is: *An Open Invitation to the
Chymical Wedding, being a Modest Prolegomenon to a Fuller
Revelation of the Hermetic Mystery.*'

Out of nowhere, it seemed, jealousy flickered across Henry
Agnew's mind. It seared with the full biblical force of the word.
This was *his* knowledge, *his* learning. He had given it to her.
Then how was it that she should be so blithely confident of its
public dissemination while he laboured like a mole in grudging
darkness? He turned his back, began to walk again. 'It would
appear,' he muttered, 'that you have long contemplated this.'

She had seen the dark cast to his face, heard the resentment
in his voice. She followed him, saying, 'I had thought only that
my project might relieve you a little from the burdensome pressure of time . . . that it would free your spirit for the greater
work.'

Agnew stared up at the hurrying sky. He was shamed by the
injury imminent in her voice. Dear God, had he not burdened
her often enough with his complaints? Had he not avowed at
times that she was more naturally equipped for the work than
he? If this tremendous vocation had fallen to her now, he was
himself in large measure responsible.

To his credit Agnew did not doubt his daughter's capacity for
the task. He may, as any doting father might, for too long have

regarded her as a child; but that she was a woman—that in itself
was no objection. Women such as Paphnutia and Maria Pro-
phetissa had been amongst the greatest exponents of the Art.
Indeed, certain aspects of its mysteries were accessible only
through female wisdom, and for that very reason his need of her
had been so great. If she was ready, eager even, to undertake
this solemn charge should he not rejoice in that—rejoice that the
living flame had been passed on, and take strength in the knowledge that this lesser work would be in safe hands while he resumed the higher task?

Yet there was still an obscure heaviness at his heart.

By now she had caught up with him. They advanced a few
paces side by side. 'It goes without saying,' she offered, 'that I
could proceed only with your full approval.'

He sensed the quick appeal of her glance but did not raise his
eyes. 'Certainly,' he conceded, 'your proposal merits further
thought.'

And let that be the end of it.

Yet what a dismal response was that to this further gift she
brought him. And the unfamiliar formality of their tones—it was
an estrangement. Must he lose touch even here, in the one place
where solace might still be found? *I am the walking grave of my
own dreams,* he thought, *a vision's carcass.* Afraid of this sudden coldness, he said aloud, 'Child, I wonder how well you
appreciate the rigours of even this preliminary task?'

Suddenly Louisa was strong again, stronger than this uncertain, too morose old man she so dearly loved. Her glance was
proud, at once respectful and reproving, as she answered. 'I
have had a great teacher; one who has exampled me in perseverance. In this endeavour—as when I was a child indeed—I
would be carried on your shoulders.' Again she halted on the
path, and this time he was arrested with her. The touch of her
fingers at his wrist assured it. 'But it is true,' she added, 'that
one thing further would be needful.'

'Which is?'

'The knowledge that such an enlargement of our work together would bring you greater happiness.'

Agnew was assailed by an enormous grief. As though a rough
gust of wind had shouldered past him he lurched away, and the
distant elms blurred against the sky, which was itself a drenched
and melting opalescence now. For a space he knew that only
tears might answer her. What else? To confess again that he had

been wrong to lead her into this labyrinth where he had lost himself? To prevent her from entering deeper now while it was not too late? Such was her faith she would never hear him. How could she when her life and her faith in him were one?

On all sides he was oppressed and vulnerable. He was old and tired and lost. He was in contention now with death itself, and could not tell her. She asked for happiness and all he had to show was grief; which was, if truth were told, no more than the last thin shift of his despair. Some paces ahead he saw the stump of a felled oak. He made for it, his breath labouring, and sat, head down, crabbed hands crossed at the pommel of his cane.

Briefly Louisa recalled another troubled figure seated there with Pedro dancing round him; and then she was suddenly concerned at something feeble, unshored, in her father's posture. 'You are quite well?' she asked, the breath cold at her throat.

He nodded, murmured, 'Well enough . . . A little weary perhaps . . .' but would not look at her.

Louisa approached, aware how short his breathing. For so long had his hale condition been a fact of her life that she was shocked to see how suddenly old he was become. Her concern was sharpening to alarm as she crouched at his knees, forcing him to meet her anxious gaze. 'You are sure?'

Wanly his face contrived a reassuring smile.

Which she wished to believe. Yes, he was tired. He had taken too little exercise of late. She must, at some more auspicious moment, remind him of this. 'I have presumed too much,' she said.

He saw that her dress was crumpled among damp leaves, took her hands, and made her rise to her feet again. 'Child, all the happiness I have known since your dear mother died I owe to you alone.' He eased his breathing in a sigh, and looked at the surface of the lake where a sere autumnal glow of sunlight had scattered, quivering, like a trash of leaves. 'I have no right to ask for more.'

'You have every right,' she exclaimed. 'There is not a man in all the land I would sooner serve.'

Agnew reached out to hold his daughter close against him. He pressed his head to her bosom, felt her hands at his shoulders, and heard the steady beat of her heart almost as clearly as when he had listened once, experimentally, through Tom Horrocks's stethoscope. 'Is this what you truly wish?' he said.

'It is,' she whispered. 'It is why I am here.'

His own tired heart was ravished by her certainty. 'Then perhaps it must be so.'

'I have your confidence?' she urged.

'My every confidence.'

She pulled away a little, smiled down, eliciting a response from the mesh of lines about his lips and nose. 'Then I promise that if my efforts can win it for you you shall have your happiness again.' She saw that more than the wind glistened at his eyes and, fearing that they might both be overwhelmed, gripped the old hand at her side. 'Now come,' she encouraged. 'I think in your despondence there is something you have overlooked. Tom Horrocks will come by tonight. Good food, good wine, the port, a game of chess and Tom's bluff company should soon restore your spirits. Then tomorrow,'—she straightened his collar, planted a quick kiss on his brow—'tomorrow we begin anew.'

The plight of Amy Larner weighed heavily on the Reverend Edwin Frere, and all the more so because he was now ignorant of her whereabouts. Enquiries of Amos Starling, the sexton, had produced only the information that she had last been seen walking to Saxburgh, that she was a bad lot, and a good riddance—sentiments expressed with such animus that, had Frere been of a less charitable disposition, he might have perceived himself speaking to a rejected amorist. Other tentative researches took him no further. The villagers had not yet taken the full measure of the new parson and seemed, at best, sceptical of his motives. Conversation was impeded by the still unfamiliar cadences of the local accent (designed, Frere was coming to believe, more for concealment than communication) and, as he walked away in confusion from a brawny gossip of the parish and her squinting friend, he blushed to imagine their subsequent opinion of his interest in the fallen young woman. It had, after all, not been quite possible to be specific, and his predecessor had set no good example.

Doubtless Mrs Bostock and her friend, Eliza Waters, would have proved a mine of information, but that was a mine he had no present wish to enter. In any case, his wife was in their company at the moment and would not relish further embroilment in this unhappy affair.

Throughout that gloomy day Frere brooded on the problem

and on his own inadequacy before it. Had not Goethe proposed the life of a protestant clergyman as the finest subject for a modern idyll—the priest-king of his small community, furthering the spiritual education of his flock, blessing them at each milestone of their way, consoling them in adversity, and strengthening their hope of bliss to come? What a poor start to such an idyll was this! That he should be so swiftly compromised before his wife and his parish by a matter so delicate. Unless steps were taken a shadow would fall across his ministry that would not easily lift.

Frere was a man of imagination: there were strengths in that, and there were weaknesses. As rapidly as his finer thoughts could scale spiritual heights so could their darker equivalents plunge into purgatorial gloom. Before many hours had passed he had watched Amy Larner's progress from the hedge of Munding Rectory to the streets of Saxburgh and down into unspeakable shame. If she ended, as he feared she might, selling herself outside the ale-houses and dingy gin-palaces of Norwich, then he was answerable. At his door the first stone would have been cast. It was not enough to console himself with pious hopes for her welfare.

As he could not release himself from this preoccupation, and his wife did not share it, dinner at the Rectory that night was an unhappy affair. Emilia, it seemed, had banished the unpleasant events of the previous day from her mind, and Frere was reluctant to conjure the spectre of Amy Larner back into the house. He had no wish to aggravate the dour humour that seemed to have settled over his wife with the recent cold weather. In springtime Munding might have its charms, but Emilia's first not entirely satisfactory adventure into local society had left her apprehensive of the long dull winter to come.

Consolingly Frere suggested that she must still be exhausted from the exertions of the move. It would take a little time to recover and respond to the pleasures of this new environment. Emilia could not detect their promise. A wearisome afternoon feigning interest in rural tittle-tattle at Mrs Bostock's well-appointed but not altogether fashionable home had left the refinements of Cambridge society livelier to her mind. She was, she must admit, more than a little homesick for their house in Portugal Place. Nor would she have believed how draughty this great barracks of a Rectory must prove. How were they ever to make it homely? The mere thought of the difficulties worsened the headache that already troubled her composure. Would Edwin mind if she retired early that evening? Her day had not been the success she had hoped. She would like to bring it to an early close.

Frere sat unhappily over his notes for Sunday's sermon. His attention, fitful at best, was distracted from his appointed text by memories of the second lesson read earlier that week on All Saints' Day. It had been from the Book of Revelation: *After these things I heard a voice of a great multitude in heaven saying, 'Hallelujah, Salvation and Glory, and power belong to God: for true and righteous are his judgments; for he hath judged the great harlot which did corrupt the earth with her fornication, and he hath avenged the blood of his servants at her hand.'*

As witness to the Christian triumph over pagan idolatry this was consoling, and he had taken it so at first reading; but it was hard now to picture the great harlot with Amy Larner's crabapple cheeks and injured eyes. Try as he might he simply could not make the description fit. Not unless she became so raddled by her experience as an outcast that she were remade—or unmade rather—in this hideous image. How he envied Emilia's untroubled conviction in the rightness of her judgment. Why could he too not put the matter out of his mind, and attend to the problem of preserving other young women of the parish from a similar fate?

He could not. Therefore something must be done.

And soon.

He checked the clock. Still before nine. It was perhaps not too late, if a little unconventional, to put in action a plan he had conceived during the course of the meal. If he did nothing he would sleep badly again, and one troubled night was enough. There was, after all, a place in the hamlet where he might receive sympathetic and, perhaps, productive attention.

A maid answered his knock, still drying her hands on a white apron, and so perturbed by this late demand at the door that only after a moment's suspicious scrutiny did she bob to receive him. Sir Henry had company, she informed him, but if the parson would care to wait a moment she would apprise the master of his arrival. She disappeared, and Frere shifted from foot to foot, holding his wet hat in the entrance hall. The chime of a tall-case clock startled him from his consternation. He should have anticipated that there might be company. He had been in error to arrive without prior notice, particularly on business that required some discretion. But he could not now vanish.

'Mr Frere, how kind of you to call.'

He looked up and saw Louisa Agnew at the head of the stair. She wore a full-skirted gown of silvery-blue sheen, and her ringlets were clasped back in braids which emphasized the slender line of her neck. Her smile as she descended was one of gratified surprise, though it masked, he feared, some mild confusion.

'Good evening, Miss Agnew. I must apologize for presenting myself at this late hour.'

'It is an unexpected pleasure,' she answered, smiling warmly, 'I have been meaning to call upon you at the Rectory . . .'

But he was already speaking over the second of her sentences, and she laughed lightly at the collision of their words, gesturing for him to speak again.

'I had hoped for a brief word with your father, but he has company, I understand. The moment was ill-chosen.'

'I am sure he will be as pleased to see you as I. It is already a gentleman's evening. Father is at chess with Dr Horrocks of Saxburgh, who is a frequent guest, so please do not discompose yourself.' She knew already that the parson was a diffident man, but had she detected a greater discomfort on his face than simple shyness would warrant? 'Is there perhaps some difficulty?'

'A small . . . er . . . matter has arisen. I thought perhaps the baronet might be able to advise me. However, I would not wish to disturb his leisure with a friend. Perhaps tomorrow? The matter is of no immediate urgency.'

'Urgent enough to bring you out on an inclement night. We shall not let you leave disappointed. Alice,' she said to the returning maid, 'take the Reverend Frere's coat and hat. I will show him through myself.'

Even as he unbuttoned his topcoat Frere continued to demur, but Louisa would not hear of it. 'Father and the Doctor spend too much time in silence over the board. A distraction should restore their powers of speech.' She led him through to a room at the rear of the Hall and opened the door saying, 'Here is Mr Frere, father, in need of your counsel.'

The baronet and the doctor rose from the studded leather chairs before the fire. There was a low chess table between them on which few pieces remained standing. A pale mantle of tobacco smoke was draped about their heads.

'Come in, Frere, come in.' Agnew brusquely overrode the

parson's apologies. He was in much finer fettle than earlier in the day. The conversation with Louisa had strengthened his resolve and, as she had foretold, the evening with Tom Horrocks had greatly brightened his humour. His friendship with the doctor was a meeting of opposites in mutual relaxation, and their debates a kind of intellectual wrestling-match conducted without hostility and always with a warmth of affection that consoled Agnew for the long hours of solitary study. He had been further heartened by Tom's apparent failure to discern any signs of strain to his health. Furthermore it was already clear that the evening's game was his. 'Come and meet Tom Horrocks,' he invited, '—one of the few civilized heads in Saxburgh Hundred . . . if a confounded materialist can qualify for the epithet. Fortunately he's a better physician than he is a philosopher.'

The doctor grinned amiably at this pejorative introduction and offered a large hand. He was a handsome, long-boned man in his forties, with a Romanesque head and gaunt cheeks fringed by grizzled Dundrearies. 'You have arrived just in time to save me from humiliation, Mr Frere,' he said. An engaging smile puckered the wrinkles about his eyes. The grip was firm.

Frere glanced quickly at the board. 'I think you are polite, Dr Horrocks. This still looks to me a hot engagement.'

'I would have had him in four moves,' Agnew said a little ruefully.

'I think my knight has more fight in him than that,' Horrocks protested, 'but . . .'—he toppled his king —'I confess myself resigned this past ten minutes. And now the parson is here to bury the dead.'

'You will take some brandy, Mr Frere?'

'I had not meant . . .'

'Come. A little will counter the effects of that damp easterly outdoors. Sit yourself down before the fire.'

While Agnew attended to the decanter Frere flipped the skirts of his coat and settled in the proffered chair. Louisa had made no motion to leave, and already he was worrying how best to raise the matter on his mind in this mixed company.

'So—you are a chess-player yourself, Mr Frere,' the doctor observed. The parson made a deprecatory gesture with his hands but his smile hinted at a larger answer.

'Excellent,' said Agnew, handing the unexpected guest a fuller snifter than Frere would have preferred. 'Matt Stukely had no head for the game. As often as not I'd look up from some move I'd long pondered and find him in the land of Nod.'

'Am I to be excluded from this masculine conclave,' Louisa asked, 'or may I share your fire for a while?'

'Sit down, child,' said Agnew. Frere's consternation grew.

'I was wearying of your father's smirk,' said Horrocks. 'Now with the parson's company and the addition of your beauty, the evening takes an altogether fairer turn.'

Evidently Louisa was accustomed to such blandishments from this family friend. 'And Mrs Frere?' she said, turning to the other guest. 'She is quite well?'

'Very well. Yes.'

'And happily settled in her new home?'

Even polite lies came hard to the lips of Edwin Frere. He nodded, contriving a smile, though his eyes shifted away. A silence fell over the little group. Frere's hand strayed to the lobe of his ear.

After a moment Louisa said, 'I believe Mr Frere has a small problem to share with you, father. I have emboldened him to make free with it.'

Thus, too rapidly for calculation, Frere found himself confronted by expectancy. 'I fear this is not quite the occasion . . .'

There was something in this characteristic diffidence that made Henry Agnew fidget. Not that he disliked the man, but a greater firmness of purpose on the parson's part would economize with everyone's time and embarrassment. 'Come, be forward with us, man,' he urged, as he thought, warm-heartedly. 'We're all friends here. Speak up. What help we can give we shall.'

Frere's hand stiffened about the snifter. 'It is a matter of some delicacy.'

A log tumbled in the grate sending a constellation of sparks up the chimney. The baronet and the doctor glanced at one another, then Horrocks reached for the poker and began to chivvy the embers. After such a generous exhortation it was not possible for Agnew similarly to shift his attention. Observing the manner in which Frere avoided Louisa's thoughtful face, he was wondering whether he should ask his daughter to leave after all.

'It has some bearing on my legacy from Mr Stukely,' Frere murmured into the silence.

'You refer to the matter of Amy Larner, I think?'

Frere looked up at Louisa in surprise. 'You have heard?'

The young woman smiled, pleased with herself. 'Did I not once tell you that Munding has few secrets? You may relax a little, Mr Frere. I am already apprised of the situation.'

'What situation?' Agnew demanded in some perplexity.

'Amy's departure from the Rectory, papa. I told you of it yesterday evening.'

Agnew grunted and frowned. 'Ah yes. Poor old Amy . . . Good enough soul, that one, I should have thought.'

Dr Horrocks looked up from the fire. 'Is this the young woman I am thinking of . . . the one . . . ?'

'The very one,' Louisa smiled. Aware of the parson's discomfort, the doctor averted his own broader smile.

'I had hoped,' Frere said, 'that there would be no great difficulty . . . about retaining her in employment, I mean. I exercised my conscience on the point considerably. However . . .'

'Her sins have found her out?' the doctor suggested drily.

Louisa hastened to Frere's aid. 'I understand that Mrs Bostock acted as celestial detective on this occasion.' Frere nodded unhappily. Agnew growled in his throat. 'I am quite sure,' Louisa continued, 'that she left Mrs Frere with no choice but to act as she did.'

'I fear so.' Frere was about to add that his wife was not naturally of a hard-hearted disposition but he was prevented by his host's sudden expostulation. 'The woman should be muzzled. That damned Pharisee of a husband too. Sanctimonious boors, the pair of them.'

'They are not among my favourite patients,' Horrocks agreed.

'One day, Tom,' said Agnew, 'you may get to dissect their miserable flesh. If you find a heart in either I'll burn my books.'

'As to that,' said Frere hastily, 'I cannot say. But as you yourself opined, Sir Henry, Amy is a good soul, whatever her . . . weaknesses. I feel in a manner responsible for her present plight.'

'Matt Stukely would have seen her right had he not been taken off at such short notice. He may have been a gull to the senses but he had a conscience.'

'After the event at least,' Louisa said quietly.

Agnew smiled. 'Amy wouldn't have been the first he set up with a small pension.'

Dr Horrocks saw that the new Rector was not entirely happy with the turn the conversation had taken. 'I am glad to see you take such a charitable interest, Mr Frere,' he said. 'Were more of the cloth to follow your example I might incline more seriously towards the faith myself.'

'Tom is an inveterate rationalist,' Louisa interposed. 'Perhaps you may persuade him of the soul's existence, Mr Frere, where the rest of us have failed.'

'Had you cut up as many cadavers as I did in Paris, young woman,' the doctor beamed back at her, 'you too might be puzzled as to its whereabouts. You will forgive my scepticism, Mr Frere, but I have my hands full keeping flesh this side of the grave without bothering my head with speculations about the other. I mean no offence, you understand?'

Frere had taken none, for his own head was far too busy contriving ways through this embarrassing situation. 'I was wondering . . .' he began, looking again to Agnew, who grunted his encouragement. 'The thought occurred that you might perhaps be able to assist me to secure another place for the young woman? As I am yet new to the district I find myself a little . . .' He looked up and met only a puzzled frown. 'I thought some charitable family in need of another pair of hands perhaps . . . ?'

'I am afraid,' said Louisa lightly, 'that where such matters are concerned my father is not entirely of this world. However, I have already given thought to it myself. I even wondered whether we might take her into service here.' She saw the light of gratitude dawn in the parson's eyes and knew she must disappoint it. 'Sadly, there is no love lost between Amy and Mrs Tillotson, I'm afraid.'

'Tilly is a prude,' said Agnew. 'Even I know that. It wouldn't work. We can't have Tilly bristling about the house.'

'So I concluded.'

'I certainly had no intention of putting you to personal inconvenience.' Frere masked his disappointment, observing as he did so that Agnew would not, in any case, have allowed that to happen. 'But is there not some other household in the district?'

Louisa studied the man more seriously now, a little ashamed that she had been privily amused by his earnest and awkward presentation. Here was a Rector who intended to honour the pastoral role however much it might personally disoblige and embarrass him. Here, in fact, was a charitable heart such as he sought among his parishoners, and to find its equal outside the Hall would be no easy matter. 'The Bostocks you will have excluded already,' she sighed. 'The Whartons offer no better prospect.' She took in Frere's dismay then turned to the other guest. 'What of Saxburgh, Doctor? Your acquaintance is wider and more current than ours.'

Tom Horrocks fingered the mutton-chop whiskers at his cheek. 'Well, I suppose we must keep her out of the Union workhouse if we can. There are already too many poor devils on the parish.' The hand rasped down across his jaw. 'She's a good-hearted soul, you say?'

'I can vouch for that,' said Louisa. 'All the children in the village love her. Indeed she is almost a child herself.'

Much as he agreed with it, Frere thought this opinion came strangely from one who was little older than the person in question. 'And industrious,' he added. 'In the short time she was in our service she gave no cause for complaint. I had thought her a blithe presence about the house.'

'No doubt she considered herself lucky to be kept on,' Horrocks remarked. 'Where is she now, by the way?'

Frere's opened hands conveyed his regrettable ignorance. 'However, she is not without means. My wife has paid her to the end of the month.'

'She has relatives in Saxburgh,' Louisa supplied. 'They are poor people but they will surely have given her a roof for a time.'

'No doubt,' said the doctor, 'if she has cash in hand.' He took out a pencil and pocket-book. 'Their name?'

'Larner,' Louisa answered. 'I'm afraid I do not know their address in Saxburgh.'

'Well, I shall make enquiries.' Horrocks pencilled the name. 'A question or two at the Angel or the parish-pump should sort the matter straight enough.'

'You see some possibility?' Frere asked.

'There is a situation I have in mind. The wife is ailing and there are a number of children to care for. If Amy is good with youngsters, and learns to mend her ways, she may do well with them.'

Frere's delight was as open as his earlier discomfort had been. 'I am deeply obliged to you, Dr Horrocks.'

'I make no promises, mind.' The doctor's sternness relaxed into a smile. 'But they are good people and there is a need.'

'I think,' Frere hazarded, beaming with relief and gratitude, 'that you may be a better Christian than you know.'

'Religion has no monopoly in human decency, sir. Nor in my experience do the two always run together. But be persuaded,

Mr Frere—it was your own manifest concern that elicited my
finer instincts.' He took a watch from his fob and frowned.
'Well, it seems I am roundly trounced at the board, I am charged
with Christian charity, and I have a damp ride back to Saxburgh
for my pains. It was a privilege to meet you, Mr Frere. If—
which is unlikely—I have need of a parson ever, I shall know
where to come.'

'And you shall find me conscious of my debt, I promise you.'

Despite the bitter wind Frere was glowing as he walked up
the lane to the Rectory. He had been right to go to the Hall. He
had been right to come to Munding. Emilia should be persuaded
of it. And, if he needed further reassurance, he might think of
the warmly approving and—surely he was not wrong to imagine
it?—already fond smile with which Louisa Agnew had favoured
him before turning back into the Hall.

A few minutes later he climbed into bed beside his sleeping
wife. His grateful prayers were said and he knew he would sleep
soundly. Yet before he did so Frere found time to reflect on the
way he and his three new-made friends had been able to deter-
mine the fate of another human being, secure in the knowledge
that only some monstrous convulsion in the fabric of society, or
some inconceivable act of folly, could put their own rich lives
so completely at the mercy of a charitable providence.

Eager as she was to begin work on her treatise, Louisa knew
that other matters would require attention first. Soon she would
have little time to supervise the running of the household and,
though the domestic round was well-established, she must provide against all contingencies if interruption of her task was to
be kept to a minimum. The staff must understand that absolute
authority lay with Tilly now, and that only the direst need could
be allowed to intrude on her own privacy. Then a letter must be
sent to Henry, putting his mind at rest, soothing his injured pride
and, above all, ensuring that he did not come bustling down to
Easterness at this critical juncture.

Also her father's needs must be met. Not until she was quite
certain that he was provided with sufficient material to keep him
occupied throughout her own seclusion could she happily enter
it. This was more complex, demanding much forethought and—
more even than advance secretarial assistance—a sensitive care
for his still volatile condition. Already he had begun to wonder
how he was to manage alone without the daily, sometimes

hourly, encouragement she had given to his spirit. He understood well enough what concentration her task must exact, and knew that once it was begun he would have almost as little right as Tilly or Alice or any of the other servants to trouble her with demands. The prospect daunted him.

His consternation increased when he learned that she had no intention of working in the library with him, and that not even the muniments room next door would satisfy her needs. Louisa had known all along that such proximity would not serve. Her father's fits and starts, the outbursts of spleen, the exclamations of delight and groans of frustration to be heard through the library door were an indispensable portion of his working rhythm, and firm though her powers of concentration were, they could not easily exclude such rumblings. Nor would he be able to resist the temptation of turning to her with some brief triumph of prosody or some problem that he must finally solve alone. It was best, for both their sakes, that such temptation be removed in advance.

'But how will you do?' he protested. 'I mean, the books, the texts, they are all here, in the library, where they belong. Surely it is better to have you here at a desk of your own rather than stealing in and out like a burglar?' Before she could speak he anticipated her reply. 'And if you take a volume elsewhere suppose it be the very one I need myself? What then? No, we can't have that. You must think again.'

She smiled at his flustered grimace. 'All the texts I need I have by heart. You shall not find I have burgled your shelves I promise you. Nor will you have any interruption other than Alice with your tray of tea when you ring for it. As for my own needs, they are simple—pens, pencils, an ample supply of ink, a ream or two of good rag-paper and a bobbin of green ferret to bind my chapters. Nothing more.'

His lips wrinkled beneath the promontory of his nose. 'I don't care for it,' he said. 'I don't greatly care for it.'

What he did not care for was this transfer of his solitude on to terms that would no longer be entirely of his own making. Louisa saw it without resentment—there was not a man in the land who had taken upon himself a higher and more difficult task, or a lonelier one. If he chafed a little at this severance from his sole intellectual companion that was to be expected; but there was more at stake here, for both of them, than mere convenience.

'How shall I do without you?' he said mournfully. 'You are as needful to my work as light itself.'

'Perhaps I have been so,' she answered quietly. 'But do we not both know that what I have been able to do for you is accomplished now—apart from this last service which requires seclusion if it is to be done well?'

Agnew sighed and leaned his cheek against the hand she had laid softly at his shoulder. It was true. One could travel so far with a companion but a moment eventually came—perhaps the most sacred moment of all—when one must stand alone before the elemental powers and make one's report as best one might. It was as true of work of this order as it was of death itself. If an old heart quailed at either prospect that was only to remind oneself of what must never be forgotten—one's own human frailty. Yet the thought came hard.

'Also,' Louisa added, 'I have recently begun to wonder whether my attentions may not have impeded as much as they have assisted the free flow of your own particular thought . . . That in ways neither of us could have anticipated, I may have come to stand between you and your inward light.'

'Never think so, child.'

'But I do. And you should consider it too.'

'I cannot count the hours I should have lost without you.'

'Nor those you might have gained had I not been there to break the tension of your mind. It may be that both statements are true. It may be that when you return to your own true solitude all that has been arrested flowers there again. I truly think it may be so.'

He looked up into her anxious face and smiled, shaking his old head in resignation. 'It seems we must find out.'

'We shall. It may even prove that—apart and invisible—we shall be all the more deeply present to one another as we work.'

'You make it sound as though you would take to some desert island,' he said in an attempt at levity.

'Almost I think I shall.'

'Your rooms are no desert, my dear.'

Aware that a critical moment had been reached she kept her own voice light. 'Nor can I work there—hearing the servants bustle about, knowing what is being done and what remains to do, wondering who is at the door, or how some squabble between kitchen-maids might soonest be sorted.'

Agnew frowned. 'Then what did you have in mind?'

Louisa gathered her breath. 'I thought—the Decoy Lodge.'

And her father's frown darkened. 'That place. I cannot hear of it. The Lodge has been empty for years. The thatch . . . You will freeze to death. Whatever has possessed you to imagine that . . .'

'I think you are forgetting that Henry had the roof re-coated, father. You know how fond he is of the Lodge. You humoured his desire to make use of it at times.'

'But it is no place for you.' There was a note now in Agnew's voice which would brook no further argument.

Louisa heard, and ignored it. 'On the contrary, I think it perfect for my needs. I shall work there like an anchoress in her cell, untroubled by the daily round, with a fine prospect of the lake to inspire me, and all the peace the contemplative life could ask.'

'It is an unwholesome place, I tell you. The atmosphere is not . . . not conductive to . . .'

Louisa waited a moment for the end of his sentence and, when it did not come, smiled in gentle exasperation. 'But you have not been there for years. You would not even cross the lake to admire the improvements which Henry made. In any case, I shall bring my own atmosphere with me.'

Agnew's frown became a scowl which he sought to avert from his daughter's gaze. Privately he was appalled to discover that, even after all these years, the very mention of the Decoy Lodge should send this thrill of horror coursing through him. The child could have no notion of the turmoil provoked by her senseless fancy. The Lodge was an evil place. If it had not been so before the time of his own father—'Madcap' Agnew—then that depraved man had certainly defiled it. Whatever changes young Henry had made, they could never exorcize that shadow. Nothing could.

There was much in his son of which Agnew disapproved, and not least the boy's brief and perverse attachment to the Decoy Lodge—an attachment which had been formed (Agnew sometimes believed) only because he himself was so evidently discountenanced by it. Yet there it was, and to preserve his own quiet life Agnew had given young Henry a free hand in the matter of the restoration. The work had been finished some years before, and he had wished no knowledge of it. Nor had he been displeased when his son's interest in the place had faded almost as quickly as it had arisen; but that Louisa should now plan to make use of the accursed spot—this more than any other aspect of her enterprise was incomprehensible to him. Alarmed that she would not accept his first refusal, and unable to confess the true reasons for his resistance, he cast about for further argument.

'It can hardly prove convenient,' he blustered. 'By the time you have walked around the lake the morning will be half lost.'

'I shall go by skiff. It will be a large part of the pleasure of the thing—to strike out each day across the lake and make land-fall on another shore. By the time I arrive my head will be as clear as crystal, ready for the pen.'

'And if it rains?'

'I shall get wet.'

'And catch your death.'

She laughed at his disgruntled moue. 'I have asked Jem Bales to lay in a store of fuel. I shall be cosy as Christmas there.'

'You have begun to make your dispositions already then?'

'I had not thought you would object.'

'I do. It is a solitary place. Who knows what . . .'

'Pedro will be with me there.'

'To roll his belly for an intruder to tickle?'

'He has more fight in him than that. But who should intrude?'

'One never knows.'

'Would you have me take your old fowling-piece with me?'

'I would not have you go at all.'

She was breathing quickly now. Not until this conflict had she realized how largely the occupation of the Lodge had figured in her vision; and more painful than the prospect of its loss was the knowledge that this was the first time her father had sought to refuse her anything. At a moment when she had believed herself launched at last on the independent creativity of an adult life, it seemed he was determined to keep her confined.

'Of course,' she said quietly, 'if you forbid it . . .'

Agnew looked up into eyes where defiance and disappoint-ment contended. He too was conscious that such conflict be-tween them was unprecedented; conscious also of how uncharitable must appear this bitter repayment of his debt to her. 'Need it come to that?' he asked.

'Only if you insist.'

He saw that her heart was set upon the thing and could not credit it. 'It seems I have no right to forbid you anything.'

'You have a father's right.'

Restrained as it was, never had there been such heat between them. He shook his head and sighed. 'But you have been more than an obedient daughter to me.'

'Then be more than an overzealous father,' she demanded. 'Let me have my way in this one thing.'

She had no idea what she was asking of him, and therefore how arbitrary his resistance must seem; yet the truth could not be told. With a failing spirit he said, 'This matters greatly to you?'

'It does.'

There was a winning brightness to her eyes, a wistfulness that melted his resistance. Perhaps the fears were only his own, and the real wrong would be to inflict them now on her? It must be so, for to cast his own shadow across her eager enthusiasm would be to do to her, though far less vilely, what his own father had once done to him. Somewhere that curse must cease. 'I cannot for the life of me see why,' he said at last, 'but on my soul, dear Lou, if that is what you want and need, then you must have it, I suppose.'

So warm was her embrace, so filled with delight the kisses planted on his crown, he could almost forget the uneasiness incited in him.

Three days later Louisa rowed across the lake to light the first of her fires in the Decoy Lodge. It was a chill November morning, the wildfowl bending their flight against a stiff breeze, Pedro panting in the stern of the skiff. The Hall receded before her sight with Tilly waving from the boathouse as though her mistress were embarked on an Atlantic voyage to the New World—which, in a way, Louisa told herself, she was. She was coming at last into her own kingdom, for though the work awaiting her remained ancillary to her father's greater task, it was for the first time truly her own.

She rounded the bend of the lake and the Hall vanished behind the Mount. The moon still shone, a shadow of itself by day, but clear and cold as a lucid mind. She heard the water gurgle beneath the skiff. The morning was damp at her lips. Already as she rowed an opening paragraph was taking shape in her thoughts, yet every sense was alert to the raw, quick mystery of things being *there*, around her, in a mist-lit array of detail that no human mind could ever have conceived. This was truly to live, and with such a glittering sense of purpose that her heart was in her mouth to think of it.

Then the skiff was bumping against the jetty at the Decoy Lodge, and Pedro bounded barking ashore. She made her vessel fast and looked up at her waiting hermitage. She saw the neat stack of seasoned ash that Jem had laid for her, the pump new-primed and straw set ready there against the frost. Though the Lodge had been aired these past two days she had insisted that this morning no fire be lit, for this was to be her own small ritual. There in the hearth of the room overlooking the lake she would kindle her own flame. This was her furnace, her athanor. By its heat the clear alembick of her mind would make the fixed volatile, the volatile fixed, so that eventually, at Nature's pace, the stone of her work might shine.

The kindling caught and flame enthused among dry logs. She warmed her hands then stepped solemnly towards the desk at the lakeward window. All her needs were waiting there. Pedro stretched before the fire. The room was very still. She leaned across the desk and cleared the condensation from the glass to look out over the lawn, the lake, the park and distant woodland. 'Nature takes delight in Nature,' she quoted to herself, softly aloud. 'Nature contains Nature; and Nature can overcome Nature.'

Then she seated herself, took a crisp sheet of paper, dipped her pen in the inkwell and, in her fine copperplate hand, inscribed:

An Open Invitation
to
The Chymical Wedding
being
An Enquiry into the Great Experiment
of Nature
and
A Modest Prolegomenon
to
A Fuller Revelation of the Hermetic Mystery

Beneath which in a smaller hand she added this epigraph from the *Rosarium Philosophorum*:

Nota bene: in arte nostri magisterii nihil est celatum a Phi-

*losophis excepto secreto artis, quod non licet cuiquam reve-
lare: quodsi fieret, ille malediceretur et indigniatonem Domini
incurreret et apoplexia moreretur.**

Carefully she blotted the page and laid it to one side, then
took another sheet and sat, smiling, as she sucked the end of
her pen.

*Mark well: nothing is concealed by the Philosophers in the art of our
magistery except the secret of the art which may not be revealed to all; for
he who should do so would be accursed and incur the wrath of God, and
die of the apoplexy.

7 ▨ The Lady's Name

The door of the Decoy Lodge opened at my second knock.
The instant of irritation on Laura's face became embarrassment;
then—perhaps—relief, though not quickly enough to forestall
my mumbled apologies for having turned up unexpectedly. She
recovered quickly and ushered me through to the kitchen where
Edward sat at a scrubbed pine table, the sleeves of his sweater
rolled back, one hand holding a tumbler of whisky so tightly I
could see the veins at his wrist, gnarled and blue. The twitch of
his moustache was his only concession to my smile, while the
dubious eyes plainly regretted that earlier invitation to return.

When he turned away from Laura's welcoming chatter it was
obvious that I'd walked in on a row. She offered me a drink,
poured it before I could demur, then indicated the empty chair
between Edward's and her own. Less than a minute had passed
and already I was appointed buffer-zone.

Laura helped to make the running in a conversation that was
falsified at every turn by Edward's silence. The sensible course
would have been to admit the moment badly chosen, but the
more I saw of Laura's nervous relief and Edward's rudeness, the
less sensible I felt. I had come with a purpose: better to broach
it and see what happened. It would be interesting to watch the
old man answer to his own rhetoric.

'I've been thinking over what you said about dreams, Edward.'

The turned face admitted having said nothing.

'. . . That one should take them seriously, I mean.'

'Of course.'

138

'However preposterous?'

There were moments when Edward squinted at you as at small print. 'Do you know what happens if you stop a man dreaming?' he demanded after a moment. 'Persistently, I mean. He goes mad. One should take that seriously, don't you think?'

'From lack of sleep?' I suggested.

Edward scowled. 'We don't sleep to sleep, dammit, any more than we eat to eat. We sleep to dream. We're amphibians. We live in two elements and we need both. Only the ego in its ignorance could be so preposterous as to pretend otherwise.'

'But why should the ego do that?' I pressed, '. . . if dreams are so important, I mean.'

For a moment Edward wondered whether this conversation was worth the breath, but the opportunity to air his thoughts got the better of him. 'Because dreams have a knack of undermining the ego's self-esteem, that's why. They out-trump its impoverished efforts at control at every preposterous trick. They offer nightly demonstrations of what malleable stuff reality is made. Their invention is endless, insatiable, because they insist on the truth. On the whole truth.'

'And nothing but? Didn't Freud suggest that they might conceal sometimes . . . disguise things . . . lie even?'

'Freud was . . .'

Whatever Freud was I was left to guess, though the ticking of Edward's brain implied that it was, at best, unsatisfactory. He emptied his glass and sniffed. 'No doubt he had his reasons for saying so.'

'But you don't agree?'

'I do not. Lies are a mere social convenience. In the dreamworld we pass beyond the reach of social control. Which is why the dream is the last citadel of the free spirit. It's the Archimedean Point—the place outside the world from which the world itself can be moved . . . if we dare to take it seriously enough.'

Large claims; outrageous even; but I was used by now to his oracular manner, and was on the point of a deflationary reply when Laura said, quietly, 'At the very least a life can turn on a dream,' and gave me pause.

'You think so?'

'Of course,' she answered. 'It happens all the time.'

'To you?' I demanded. 'Has it happened to you?'

She held my gaze a moment—her eyes in that light a dark lobelia-blue—then nodded, and looked away.

'Why is it,' Edward glowered at me, 'that even when you're asking questions I find it difficult to believe a word you say?'

'Because that's the effect you have on people.' It was Laura who answered, and my own confusion evaporated in the hot glare of hostility across the table. 'You make them so damn picky about their words they hardly believe themselves.'

'My dear,' said Edward, innocent, 'I did not instigate this unsatisfactory conversation.'

'Look,' I put in, standing, 'perhaps I should . . .'

'Sit down,' Edward growled. I didn't, not immediately, and his head swivelled up to fix me in its stare. 'Don't flirt with me,' he said. 'I don't like it. It makes me feel old. If you have something to say, say it, for God's sake.'

I looked to Laura who was fingering the small silver star at her throat, tight-lipped. After a moment's hesitation I reached into the inside-pocket of my jacket, took out the sheet of paper on which I'd written the dream, and put it down on the table beside the whisky bottle, under Edward's nose.

I might have been serving him with a court-order, but he picked up the paper, unfolded it, frowned, then—in some irritation—looked around the room. Laura sighed, got up, crossed to the dresser where a red glasses-case lay on an open book among the crockery, and returned with it. The case clicked open in Edward's hands. He eased the wire frames gingerly over his ears—the lenses gave him an owlish squint—then looked at the paper again. I sat down, waiting. After a time, he pushed the glasses up on to his brow and rubbed the bridge of his nose between a nicotined thumb and forefinger. 'You wrote this down at the time?' he demanded.

'No. This afternoon.'

'I thought as much from the literary flourishes. You've edited it.'

'It's as accurate as I could remember.'

He grunted, dissatisfied. 'Should have done it at the time.'

'At four in the morning?'

''Immediately. Whenever. Dreams of this order are too important to tamper with.' He must have noticed the glint in my eyes, for he added. 'All dreams are.'

Relieved that I'd said nothing about the vain and frustrating hours in which I'd tried to turn the dream into verse before settling for this prose version, I watched him turn the paper over on the table and take a pencil from the pocket of his shirt. With a few swift strokes he made this drawing:

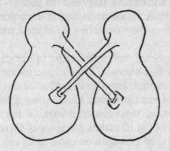

'The retorts,' he demanded, '—they looked like this?'

'More or less.'

'Well did they or not?'

'They were more elegant, subtler.'

'Gemini,' he said. 'A double Pelican.'

'What's that?'

His scowl was challenging, resentful, as though he could barely bring himself to believe that a dream of this quality had been wasted on an idiot. His incredulity appeared to have deafened him.

'You told me to look out for my dreams,' I said. 'I thought you might be able to help me understand it. Particularly as . . .'

'Yes?'

'Well, as you've read, there was a moment when I thought the old man in the dreams was you.'

'Do you think I have nothing better to do with my nights than make guest appearances in other people's dreams? It most certainly was not me.'

'I know. I saw it at the time. It was someone else. A stranger. But . . .'

'It was you.'

'No,' I began to explain testily, 'I was watching the whole thing from . . .'

'It was you. Everything in the dream is an aspect of your psyche—not only the watcher. The church, Gypsy May, the theatre, the figures, all of them, male and female. Even the Pelican. Dear God, yes, even that.'

I was about to insist that the two lovers at least were identifi-
able—even while dreaming I'd recognized Martin and Jess with
a wistful pang, and that memory had not faded—but Laura said,
'Edward,' and there was a reprimand in her voice, an injunction
on her face. Then she turned to me. 'May I read what you've
written?'

I shrugged, pushed the paper across to her coolly, yet in the
knowledge that this was why I had come to the Lodge. It was
her response I wanted. Even now, ruffled as she was, there was
a candour about her that might tease when it chose but finally
felt honest. Behind the enigmatic haze of her interest in the
paranormal, I thought I'd caught glimpses of a trustworthy spirit.
It was as unfazed by Edward's excesses as by my own first surly
reticence, and there was nothing of stupidity there, or acquiescence; rather an impenetrable thoughtfulness hanging on the air
like scent. It exuded a quiet sensuality. I contemplated it in
silence as Edward and I watched her read. Then she looked up
at me, as if the days since we'd met had been a long, slow
process of recapitulation and I was finally recognized.

'But this is a marvellous dream,' she said, and, and, for an instant,
my heart was in my mouth with delight and gratitude. Then we
were both aware of Edward's stare. She turned towards him,
smiling still. 'Edward, you do realize . . . ?' She caught her
breath, shook her head. 'I think,' she said quietly, 'that we should
take this more slowly.'

The agitated twist of Edward's moustache, the biting of his
lip, relaxed in a long exhalation of breath. 'You're quite right,'
he said. 'Darken, I'm sorry. It's just that . . . Damnation, at this
moment I'd give my eye-teeth for a dream like that.'

'But we have it,' Laura exclaimed. 'It's here. Alex has brought
it to us.'

On Edward's face bewilderment contended with mounting
interest and a still reluctant scepticism. 'You think . . ?' he said
to Laura, who nodded, smiling. 'It has to be,' she answered;
and I was left feeling oddly included and excluded at the same
time by this elliptical exchange.

Edward's frown deepened, then he seemed to take some sort
of decision. 'Darken, I'm sorry about this but Laura and I need
to talk.' He signalled that they should go through into another
room. Now Laura frowned, unwilling to move. Edward got up,
and I was caught between them. I said, 'Look, I'll step outside

a minute,' and when I saw that Laura was about to demur, added, 'Really, I'd rather,' and got up and let myself out into the garden.

There was a cool breeze out there, a fresh eastern night, very black, against which the constellations were fretted, sharp and brilliant—Orion striding out, Venus twinkling under the thin sliver of a moon. I heard the sounds of disagreement indoors, then Edward looked out after me. 'We won't keep you a minute. I promise.'

I didn't care. They could take all the time they liked. I had stepped out into the night as into my own principality. I knew now that, however obscure the dream, it had taken me through into another place. Watching the shades of Jess and Martin make love there had somehow consigned them to themselves. At a deeper level than conscious intention I felt I had finally accepted the fact of their togetherness, and I'd shed the poison of it. I was single again. Lone wolf. What was done was done. Over. What remained was a hunger for new beginnings.

For less time than it took to smoke a cigarette I stood out there under the starbright night, relishing its taste, listening to the moorhens and the coots, oddly detached from whatever consternation my arrival had caused indoors. Edward's rudeness didn't bother me. I was amused rather that my dreaming mind seemed to have turned the tables on him. Nor, in that moment, did I feel in need of interpreters. I had invented the dream; now it was reinventing me. I knew from the quality of Laura's first response that this was real. For the first time in weeks I felt good about myself.

When Laura called me in I turned from the lake to the Lodge with an amused, ironical curiosity about what awaited me there.

Edward's manner had changed. There was still a hint of suspicion in his face but I had the impression of a man under orders to behave himself.

'The thing is,' he said, '—your dream—you must have guessed—it appears to have a bearing on what we're doing here . . . Laura and myself, I mean.'

I decided to make things no easier for him and kept silent.

'I saw it immediately, of course, but . . .'

'Admit it,' Laura interrupted, '—it took you by surprise.'

'I'm not denying that . . . Accounts in part for my clumsy response. The thing is . . .'—except when he was drunk I had never seen him so incoherent—'I don't care to talk too openly about our work, for all kinds of reasons. I wouldn't be doing it now if . . . Well, Laura thinks I should and, God knows, I've reason enough to trust her intuition. She seems to think that you're . . . involved.'

'Why else is he here?' Laura asked. 'Why else the dream?'

'Involved?' I repeated, the word no less dubious on my lips than on Edward's.

'Yes.'

'In what?'

'Our work,' said Laura.

'Which is?'

'. . . not easily explained,' Edward answered. 'Like your dreams.'

'But you'll try?'

'Yes.' Edward sighed. 'I'll try.' He closed his eyes in thought a moment, and when they opened again they were bright with defiance. 'Listen. You brought your dream to me tonight because it puzzled you, right? It was a riddle to which you had no answer. A mystery.'

I nodded uncertainly.

'All right. Let me answer your riddle with another.'

Both Laura and I watched in surprise as he got up, went through into the next room, and came back after a moment flourishing a sheet of paper. 'Here, see if you can sort this out.' He thrust the paper in front of me. I picked it up, quizzing the now mischievous glint in his eye, then looked at Laura. She too was smiling in sudden comprehension of what Edward was about. They were together again, and I the outsider. 'It's the name of the game,' he said. 'It's what we're doing.'

I looked down at the paper and read:

My name contains 6 and 50, yet has only 8 letters. The third is a third part of the fifth, which added to the sixth, will produce a number whose sum will exceed the third itself by just the first, and which is half of the fourth. The fifth and the seventh are equal, so are the last and the first. The first and second together equal the sixth which contains four more than the third tripled. Now, my lord, how am I called?

I read it through again in complete bafflement, then looked up. 'You made this up?'

'No, it's from an old text called *The Chymical Wedding of*

Christian Rosenkreutz. Laura, fetch him some paper. He'll need it.' Smiling, without protest, Laura did as she was bidden.

'I have to work this out?'

Edward nodded.

I looked back at the cryptic sentences. 'Look,' I said, 'is this really necessary?'

'Essential.'

'Maths was never my strong point.'

'Simple arithmetic, dear heart.' Edward handed me the pencil. Laura put a clean sheet of typing paper in front of me. I was expected to play.

'The answer's a name?'

Again Edward answered with no more than a nod.

'And it has eight letters. But all the clues are numerical. A code presumably?'

'Like your dream,' said Laura. 'All the best things come in code. You have to work for meaning.' There was challenge in her eyes. And mine is a competitive spirit. I applied myself.

Having re-read the conundrum I made a line of eight dashes and numbered them below. Then, after a moment's thought I bracketed the fifth dash to the seventh, and the first to the last.

'More whisky, I think,' said Edward, and refilled our glasses. He was almost jolly now. Now that things were back on his terms, I thought. He sat across from me, grinning.

'Roman numerals?' I suggested, for I had seen that the six would give me the letters V and I, and the fifty L, but Edward's smirk offered neither encouragement nor dissent. I was on my own.

I played about with the idea for a while and got nowhere with it, so I abandoned it for the little I remembered of algebraic equations and made no significant progress. No matter how I tried to get a purchase on the clues, the only conclusion I'd reached after several minutes' thought was that, if we were not dealing in Roman numerals, then the sum of all the numbers would be 56 . . . which might be useful if I had seven of the answers and needed only the eighth but was otherwise unhelpful. Also there was an ambiguity in that second sentence which bothered me.

I took off my jacket. Then sucked on the pencil trying one fruitless hypothesis after another. The fifth number, for instance, was divisible by three, and if I could identify it I would have the third and the seventh too. But was it 6? 9? 12? 15? Any, and more, were possible. There was no way of cross-checking and no clear route open to further deduction. Either I was missing something obvious or this was a maze with no entrance.

I put down the pencil.

'Is there some problem?' Edward asked mildly.

I smiled. 'I have the feeling this can't be done.'

'Your noble predecessor, Christian Rosenkreutz, managed to do it when the riddle was first presented to him by the lady whose name it conceals.'

'Then he was brighter than me.'

'Certainly. But the problem was not solved by the rational intelligence alone.'

'Then how?'

Edward eyed me sardonically. 'He knew very well that certain problems are only solved through special acts of grace. As he was not too proud to beseech one he had the good sense to ask the lady for more help.'

Unruffled enough to recognize another clue when I heard it, I turned to Laura. 'Well?'

'Not exactly gracious,' she smiled, 'but I'll give you one of the numbers.'

'Which one?'

'That's up to you. You only get one, so choose carefully.'

I examined the riddle again, conscious of the vehement heat inside me, that my pride was now at stake. A moment's consideration revealed the most profitable option. I asked for it.

'Nine,' said Laura.

Thereafter, with a little ferreting among the words, the rest was indeed simple arithmetic. I looked at the line of numerals. None over twenty-six, therefore probably a crude alphabetical cipher. I transposed the letters for numbers and found myself looking at an unfamiliar version of a familiar word.

'The lady's name,' said Edward.

And, quite obviously, not only that. If this was a lady's name then she was a figure from some queer medieval allegory. It represented something else—the thing that Laura and Edward were doing. But—for God's sake . . .

Like the account of my dream, the word lay there—an intriguing object of dubious use, a relic. But I remembered the antique figures from my dream, the ancient, acrid laboratory . . .

Stalling for time, I said, 'Why the riddle? Wouldn't it have been simpler to tell me?'

The question must have smacked of youth's specious patience with the oddities of age, and it was immediately clear that Edward had no taste for such simple expectations. I saw sarcasm shaping at his lips, but Laura said, 'It's a bit like dreams, Alex—if the meaning was immediately obvious without having to work for it then we wouldn't value it—in the same way that none of us really has much use for good advice from other people. We have to make it our own through experience. There was a point to the riddle. Edward was . . .'

Edward was not about to let someone else speak for him. 'Look, you have just demonstrated to your own satisfaction that in some matters unassisted rational effort is not enough. Am I right?'

'But it was set up that way.'

'Exactly. Once Laura gave you the key there was no problem. But the key could not be teased out of the clues because it had been deliberately omitted. The rest was self-sealing—like the retorts in your dream. To unravel it you needed something else—something that was not written down and could not be manufactured by the agile mind on which you appear to pride yourself. You had to find a new, humbler relationship to the problem, right? You were, in fact, dependent on direct oral transmission from an adept—someone already in on the secret.' There was no satisfaction in this explanation, only a further weary sigh, as though whatever pleasure he'd taken in the game had long since faded.

I looked back at the answer to the riddle, then up again at Edward. I said what I saw: 'You *are* serious about this.'

'I'm a serious man, dammit. There's no time to be not serious. I'm impatient with everything except the truth. I've got no time for cleverness . . . no use for it. I'd rather keep silent than waste my breath . . .'

The sentence might have ended 'on fools,' but Laura curtailed it. 'It's not a game, Alex.'

'Not *only* a game,' Edward corrected.

'Then what?'

Laura looked resolutely across at Edward, an appeal for patience. 'Tell him,' she said. 'Tell him you know exactly how he feels.'

Edward shunned her eyes. The index finger of the hand on the table began to tap. The other hand masked his scowl. I heard it rasp across the blue-grey stubble of his chin. 'It's true,' he muttered. 'I too am looking for a key to unlock a mystery. So far there has been no special act of grace.'

Laura shifted in her chair. I caught a further exchange of glances before Edward arched his brows again. 'Laura seems to be of the opinion that your arrival, and that extraordinary dream, may provide it.'

There was a silence. I looked across at Laura. For a moment, aware of my gaze, she avoided it; then she looked up, decisive. 'Listen—we're doing some research together here . . . into something that happened to the Agnew family last century. We're trying to find out as much as we can about it because we think it matters. We think it has a bearing on things that have gone badly wrong in the world . . . that it might offer some hope of a way through.'

'And it has to do with my dream?' I had seen the tension between resolve and vulnerability in her eyes, heard it in her voice; but it was hard to keep the incredulous edge from my question.

'Yes.'

'I don't see the connection. You'll have to say more.'

She drew in her breath, glanced across at the old man who frowned down at the table, dubious of Laura's intervention, dubious of me. 'Edward,' she said, 'I think you'd better explain.'

The thing about riddles is that the answer is always more mysterious than the puzzle. Sure, once you have it, the pieces click into place. It fits. But what are you holding? Like that ancient riddle to which the answer is 'the wind'; or, better still, like the Sphinx's riddle to which the answer is 'man.' Fine; you get the point; all very clever. But what *is* the wind? What *is* man?

This was much the same. I had the answer and it answered nothing; and Edward clearly was none too happy about explaining. I thought I saw why. I mean—alchemy! ALCHIMIA! It had to be an elaborate piece of chicanery. I arranged my face accordingly; but when I looked across at him I had the impression of an old dragon coiled about its hoard, and fuming jealously.

Under question it quickly emerged that I knew precious little about alchemy—no more than the fragments I'd picked up from literature: Chaucer's mockery of it, Jonson's satirical play, the conceits of the Metaphysical poets. I saw it as an eccentric quirk of history, a dodo-hunt in which credulous men had tried to transmute base metal to gold. It was the quest for the Philosopher's Stone, wasn't it? Or the Elixir of Life? I'd never been quite sure which, and did it matter? I knew—but did not say—that the whole thing smelled of fraud.

Edward girded up the weary swags beneath his eyes and—I hadn't been prepared for this—agreed. 'Yes, the men whom Chaucer and Jonson despised were quacks, con-artists, knaves. Lacking the patience to woo the lady Alchimia they tried to rape her. They failed, of course, and their failure made the enterprise appear contemptible. But that is not the whole story. Regrettably the darker powers at work inside us know exactly how to muddy the waters so that a spiritual child goes down the drain with them unseen. Then meaning goes with it, and with meaning value . . . and we are left darkling.'

He observed my frown at the reference to dark powers, and said, 'They are there, I assure you. You are not exempt.' He brooded over the words, and the words brooded over me. I was beginning to feel uncomfortable.

'True alchemy,' he declared, 'is one among the sacred arts . . . For we Europeans perhaps the most vital.'

Now in my world only one art was sacred and it wasn't alchemy. I retreated into flippancy, said that this all sounded a bit mystical to me.

'But do you know the meaning of that word?' Edward returned. 'At root it has to do with closing, with sealing . . . the closing of the eyelids, the sealing of the lips, the closing of a wound. It has to do with making whole or holy . . . with healing. Alchemy is the effort to heal the split in consciousness. And, yes, in that strict sense of the word, I agree, it is mystical. But it is an art which is also a science . . . one which acts on the understanding that all true science is also a matter of poetics.'

I saw his eyes shift at Laura's impatient signals, but his frown silenced her. 'We'll get nowhere,' he said, looking back at me, 'unless you start to think as you dream—symbolically. Alchemy sees the world as a great dance of symbols. A delicate web of correspondences in which nothing is finally separable from everything else. It starts from the premise—from the experience—that the germ of life plays everywhere. It has long known what the physicists ''discovered'' yesterday—that the observer and the observed are members of a single interactive field. But it knows also what we have yet to learn—that the field is far from neutral. What we do to it is done also to ourselves. We are implicate. We create only in our own image, like God, and therefore self-knowledge is of critical importance. Without it the consequences are diabolic.' He paused to let the full force of the word strike home, then added, 'Hence the disaster of materialism. It's like the polystyrene muck it makes—rot that won't rot. There's nothing regenerative in its relationship to the world. How could there be?—for rebirth is a science of the spirit.'

'A science?' His first use of the word had bothered me; this second was unacceptable.

'A science. A way of knowledge.'

'But hardly scientific?'

'Rigorously so—though not the scientific method of the materialists—a method which is, I may point out, increasingly aware of its limitations.'

'But at least materialism . . .'

I was about to suggest that it offered a solid purchase on the world, insisted at least on verifiable fact, but Edward winced, extravagantly. 'Spare me,' he groaned. 'Isn't it enough that it proliferates around us daily, atomizing as it goes, making a junkyard of our world? Don't bring it in here. Not in my house.'

'Edward.' Laura's reproof was again forestalled.

'All right. I'm sorry. But look where it's got us. At obscene expense and considerable inconvenience to those with humbler need of the money, the physicists smash their way into the mirror of matter, and what do they find? That it breaks. That matter is fissive, right? Remarkable! Except that alchemy has always known this. It also understands that the more we are entranced by the dance of matter the more we fall victim to its fissive nature. It's not only the atom that splits. *We* are in the mirror. Consciousness splits too. It shatters like china. And then— howlback. Heat death. The big chill. Cut.'

He left a silence in which I might reflect on this brisk potted history of nuclear physics. I said, 'So you'd rather we went back to counting angels on pinheads?'

Edward sighed. 'It might be saner than counting quarks— charmed or otherwise. Or counting universes for that matter. I suppose you know what the physicists are up to now? I presume you're familiar with the Many Universes Theory?' Gratified by a further confession of ignorance, he explained. 'It's a fancy little number cooked up by the fissive mind in its efforts to account for the schizophrenic behaviour of smashed particles. We are now asked to bend our imaginations round the thought that at every instant of choice the universe forks. In this world only one thing may appear to happen, but in countless unreachable others all the alternative possibilities spin off happily doing their thing. Matter splits, you see, and thus, with fine paradoxical flair, nothing really *matters* any more. If a few million Jews are murdered in this world, never mind—there are others in which they find Jerusalem. If Africa starves here and now, elsewhere it waxes fat. If the missiles eventually incinerate this madhouse reality, worry not—in a more sensible dimension we beat them into ploughshares. Nothing matters. We have an elegant, theoretically sound explanation of a fissive world. Which I, for one, don't buy. Do you?'

He gave me no time to collect my thoughts. 'Don't you get it yet? Materialism leaves us trapped in a world that won't hold together. It's centrifugal. It splits at every turn into the Ten Thousand Things each neatly labelled with a Ph.D. thesis. In the meantime we become more and more obsessed with what we mistake for our real needs, hopes, fears . . . and more and more estranged from our birthright membership of a coherent universe. Hence this century's endless harping on the theme of exile—typically misconceived in merely political terms, or as the dreary job-description of being human. If we were less arrogant we might see ourselves for what we are—children sent on an errand, who first forget our instructions and then realize we have forgotten the way home. How to find our way back? How to realize a whole vision of life? Not some self-sealing intellectual construct; no shabby, patchwork compromise, but a regenerative, transcendent change. One that reconciles matter with spirit, heart with mind, the female in us and the male, the darkness and the light. That was the problem which engaged the spiritual intellect of the true alchemist. That was the Elixir, the Stone, the Gold . . . *aurum non vulgi*—no common gold. They are all symbols for what cannot be said—only experienced. As is,' he added pointedly, 'the chymical wedding—the promise of which you saw celebrated in your dreams.'

He took in the impact of this last remark, and left a further silence which, this time, I did not break. The strange phrase chimed through my mind. For an instant I was possessed by an image of the mind as a glass bell—an intangible but lucid elision of bell-jars and wedding-bells, the sound and the shape—temple-bells even, ringing like glass across the valleys of the brain. Momentarily I was hooked. And he saw it.

'You were given a glimpse of the thalamus,' Edward said quietly, '—that chamber of the mid-brain which is also the bridal-chamber. It is where the mysteries are consummated while the world makes its rough music outside, wanting it to happen, yet excluded from the secret. The Agnews were the guardians of that secret. If you have understood anything you will see it is a secret we desperately need to know.'

Slowly the dragon uncoiled from his hoard, and he did it by telling a story. It began back in the seventeenth century in the time of the first baronet of Easterness, Sir Humphrey Agnew, an ardent royalist who had founded the family's fortunes at the Restoration. A gallant, somewhat mysterious figure, he had also been a profoundly learned man—a friend and correspondent of Robert Boyle and Isaac Newton and, more particularly, of Thomas Vaughan, author of the *Magia Adamica* and the *Lumen de Lumine*, and twin-brother of the poet Henry Vaughan. All four of them, it seemed, had been explorers of the Hermetic arts, though Boyle and Newton's enquiries in this area had largely been forgotten.

Humphrey Agnew was himself an adept who had conducted his own important researches in collaboration with a remarkable woman called Janet Dyball. Edward explained that many alchemists had worked with a female assistant—a *soror mystica*—for the Art required that both aspects of human nature, the male and the female, the solar and the lunar, be reconciled in harmonious unison if the chymical wedding was to be celebrated.

It was a moment before I made the connection with the names of the swans—Humphrey and Janet—and began to perceive what Edward might have meant when he called them their *familiars*. At the same moment his need of Laura was thrown into a context quite different from any I had guessed. I wanted to press him further on the relationship between alchemist and mystic sister, but already Edward had moved on.

Regrettably he couldn't prove it but he had a strong suspicion that Sir Humphrey was the adept who had written under the pseudonym *Irenaeus Philalethes*, the greatest master of the golden age of English alchemy, whose identity had never been established. Agnew had been born in 1622 and would therefore have been 23 in 1645, the age and the year in which Irenaeus attained to the Stone of the Philosophers. Whether or not this theory was right, Agnew had certainly been an important link in the *Aurea Catena*—the golden chain by which knowledge of the alchemical mysteries was transmitted orally from adept to adept. The library in the Hall was still packed with the Hermetic texts he had collected. It was one of the finest private collections in the world. Furthermore, some of Sir Humphrey's alchemical instruments were now in the Kensington Science Museum. 'There is a particularly fine example of a Pelican such as you saw in your dream,' Edward said. 'It's a retort designed to facilitate the circulation of the vapours during the sublimation of volatile substances.'

I hadn't the faintest idea what this meant, but without pausing to explain he went on to insist that, though there was never again to be a Hermeticist of such distinction in the family, he believed that the tradition had been kept alive from generation to generation—oral transmission of the inner secret while the rest of the world plunged headlong into blind materialism.

'And you think that Ralph still has it?' I remained unclear what the secret might be, but when I recalled that portly gentleman with his bland high Tory manner, he seemed an unlikely carrier. My voice conveyed as much.

'If only it were that simple.'

'Then what happened?'

'That's exactly what we're trying to find out,' Laura said. 'That's why we're here.'

'The chain was broken,' Edward added. 'I am trying—God help me—to mend it again.'

The break had happened in the time of the eighth baronet—Ralph's great-grandfather, Sir Henry Agnew. In revulsion from his father's rakehell excesses Henry Agnew had chosen the contemplative life. Having distinguished himself as a philologist at Oxford he retired to Easterness where his studious disposition could devote itself entirely to metaphysical enquiry. His wife had died at a relatively early age and, after her death, he became ever more reclusive. He had one son who made a successful career at the Foreign Office, but his real pride was his daughter, Louisa Anne, who lived with him at the Hall.

'She was an extraordinary woman,' Edward said, '—intellectually brilliant, entirely devoted to her father. You have to understand that she was much more than a daughter to him. She was his intellectual comrade. His collaborator.'

'His mystic sister?' I put in, thinking that this was a very strange way for a man to regard his daughter.

'Precisely. After Henry died in 1850 Louisa was the last link in the chain. You saw her portrait at the Hall the other night, remember?' To refresh my memory Edward showed me a photograph of an old lady—in her seventies, I judged—sitting in a basketwork garden-chair, wearing a long gown of black, buttoned taffeta with lace at her neck and a shawl round her shoulders. The slender, almost flimsy hands rested on an ebony cane. At first glance she appeared a typical, late-Victorian matriarch— one could imagine her smelling of camphor and the family Bible. On closer inspection the aged, delicately chiselled features seemed to peer out at the camera with alert, benevolent interest. The eyes were steeply angled and must have been quite devastating in her younger days. Even here in the old sepia photograph they were bright with intellectual mettle, and her lips seemed mildly amused that she had survived long enough to witness this moment so distant from her youth. I sensed a quality of innocence reconciled to experience such as only the very old, or the very holy, seem to have.

'This was taken on her ninetieth birthday,' Edward said. 'A formidable figure, don't you think?'

'And well-preserved. She must have been a beauty once.'

'Laura can tell you,' Edward answered. 'She has seen her.'

I stared up from the photograph. Laura looked down at her hands. 'It was in the Hall,' she murmured. 'A few weeks ago. She was wearing a long dress of grey silk and holding a Michaelmas-daisy in her hand. She was gazing out of a window as though waiting for someone. And, yes, she was very beautiful.' Laura lifted her eyes and held me a moment in a quietly defiant gaze.

But my critical faculties were bristling again. Edward saw it and smiled. 'Laura has unusual gifts which is only one of the reasons why I have such great need of her. Have you ever heard of psychometry? It's the ability to divine from an object the qualities of the person who has been most strongly in contact with it. A rare ability, but real. At the time Laura was holding something that had been very precious to Louisa—her deck of Tarot cards. The very deck you held yourself the other night.'

Once again, as when I'd puzzled over the riddle, I felt that for obscure purposes of their own the pair of them were out to make a fool of me. I half-expected it of Edward, but that Laura should be in collusion with him bothered and heated me. I didn't really want to look at her. Nor did I want her to think they could get away with this. So I ignored Edward, mentally cancelled him out, and studied her obvious embarrassment before saying, 'And that was enough to cause an apparition of her?'

'It wasn't really an apparition,' she answered quietly.

'Laura doesn't care to talk about this,' Edward put in. 'But as she has already decided that we be open with you . . .'

Laura drew in her breath. 'It's a way of tuning in to time,' she said. 'I can't explain it . . . No one saw her but me.' It was clear from her voice and face that she was sincere. Clear too that she would welcome no further question.

As though both in confirmation and reparation Edward added, 'Laura estimated that she was about 24 at the time—a year or two before the crisis.'

He hesitated. I was aware of the uneasiness between them, and momentarily my sympathies were with Edward. After all Laura had insisted on these disclosures. She could hardly draw the line at her own peculiar involvement. There were moments when she resembled Jess a little too closely in her desire to have things on her own irrational terms.

'How do you do it?' I demanded.

'I don't. It happens. It's a matter of relationship, of receptivity. Like dowsing. Anyway, it's not the main point. You don't have to believe.'

'On the contrary,' Edward insisted, 'it's very much to the point, but as our friend is obviously unhappy with it let's try and keep things simple. I have explained that Henry and Louisa had been working together for some years. By the late '40s they had conceived the idea of publishing their findings. Already they foresaw the consequences of the accelerating drift into materialism. They felt that something must be done to stem the tide— something more radical than the Evangelical revival which had already hardened into pharisaical conformity and mawkish sentiment. Something more truly Catholic than the odour of papist sanctity in which the Oxford Movement had foundered. They knew that in their knowledge of the Hermetic tradition they held a key to spiritual regeneration which would challenge materialism at its very root . . . which would redeem the century's debased and debasing perception of the nature of matter. More than a century ago they saw the crying need to resacralize experience through the reconciliation of opposing forces. This was around 1848, remember. The old order was breaking up. Industrialism had seized the minds of men. Europe was in the throes of revolutionary unrest. As Blake and Wordsworth had foreseen, the split in human consciousness was growing ever wider. Think about it—that very year, not much more than a hundred miles away, Marx was in the British Museum writing the Communist Manifesto—developing in the name of the brotherhood of man his tragically misguided dialectical materialism. Lyell's principles of geological dating had knocked the bottom out of a literal interpretation of Genesis. Even Paley's elegant argument from design would soon be called into question by Darwin. In a few years Sigmund Freud would be born to darken counsel by dragging the sexual skeleton from the closet as though it explained everything. These were no mere pigeons coming home to roost but vengeful eagles. The church had no answer to challenges of that order.'

I was left breathless by this brisk dismissal of the century's intellectual giants. 'And the Agnews had?' I interjected.

Edward narrowed his eyes. 'Yes,' he said quietly, 'I believe they did.'

'And you don't find it strange that nobody's heard of them?'

'All right,' Edward said after a moment, 'in historical terms their endeavours to blow on the divine spark in man may have been hopeless. Just as we too—Laura and I—may be whistling in the wind. But at least they were determined to try. For God's sake, man, they knew that the battle for the human soul was joined, that the world was teetering towards desecration and despair. Look around you—consider this appalling century— were they right or not? We have seen where materialism has led. Oh yes, it freed us to do many ingenious things, but now the bill is presented. Apart from the manifold horrors we perpetrate upon ourselves, forests die, even the seas are fouled, we can no longer trust the air. As bills go it is, I think you will agree, quite staggering.' Edward stared into my silent face, shaking his head. 'Infatuated by our own clever minds, we turned our backs on the old redeeming symbols. We forgot that the *symbolic* is that which holds together—it is the very meaning of the word. In our blindness we have preferred its exact etymological opposite— the *diabolic*—that which tears apart. For again, in that strict sense, materialism is a diabolic attitude. By its careful inventory of the multiplicity of things it has succeeded only in creating a schizophrenic world, powerful but fissive. It should be no sur-

prise, therefore, that—unless we wake up—its most characteristic achievement may soon tear the planet apart in a final clash
of unreconciled opposites. Think about it, man. Do you really
believe that such atrocity is inevitable as anything other than a
direct consequence of human blindness . . . of the collective
madness spawned by countless failures of individual responsibility? In any case,'—he lifted his eyes to hold me in an unremitting stare—'is not this what has been happening to you?'

I was shocked by this abrupt return from the general to the
particular. It stunned the reservations at my lips, for suddenly I
glimpsed that there might indeed be a connection. Almost
against my will I had heard his argument drawing together the
fears I had felt alone in The Pightle listening to the drone of
aircraft out of Thrandeston—the dread of, the perverse appetite
for annihilation—and the obscure, fragile hope embodied in my
dream. His case had been more assertion than argument; I was
dubious of its logic; but now, at the feeling level, I was placed
by his last question at the very cockpit of processes I did not
understand.

'You have engaged with life blindly,' he insisted. 'You have
suffered a little cataclysm. Your tower has been shattered and
you have perhaps begun to see that what you took for your integrity was a sham. If you are honest you will acknowledge that
you are a man in pieces, with few of the pieces in their proper
place. You have just begun to sort the fragments out . . . at a
much deeper level than you know. And now, it seems, the tutelary spirits of the Hermetic Art have appeared in your dream,
announcing their willingness to help. If you are wise you will
listen. For if the best of us refuse to understand ourselves what
hope is there? I say that our very survival depends on such
knowledge. I mean, our survival as coherent human individuals
grounded in the real. I mean our collective survival as a species.
That, my friend, is the wider import of your dream. That is the
real name of the game.'

I looked across at Laura who had sat for some time in silence.
She held my gaze a moment and then, almost as if in embarrassment, looked away. Most of this she had heard before—had
it become no more than noise to her? Was it any more than that
to me?

At least two voices argued inside my head, scepticism warring
with a half-mesmerized desire to believe. It was precisely this
sort of secret promise that had excited me in Edward's work

when I was young. It was precisely his weakness for inflated rhetoric I had come, later, to reject. And this emphasis on secrets—I shared Bob Crossley's distrust of 'perfect masters' with their claims to knowledge from which we ordinary mortals were, for our own good, shut out. Whatever else, I wasn't buying that.

I might have rejected the whole thing out of hand, but behind it all I recalled the emblems of my dream—the old man and the young woman over the shimmering retorts; Jess and Martin, the female and the male, celebrating their own chymical wedding while I—voyeur, outsider—watched and knew—God help me, how I knew—what I was missing.

But that was dream. In the real world the bombs were still targeted, the doomwatch prophecies pressing close, my life a wreck. Over against all that where did this high talk get us? Where did any of it lead?

I looked back at Edward, remembering Bob's intuition that he was a man obsessed. He studied my dark frown. 'No,' he answered the unspoken demand, 'it is not futile. The vision is still accessible. Your dream insists on it. It is immanent within our very being. We are the case for hope as well as the authors of our own despair. This is what the Agnews understood. They had the guts to work at the problem. They devoted their lives to it—Henry in his library; Louisa here, in this very room.'

I looked around me, grateful for the moment's remission. I tried to imagine the place as it had been more than a century before. The room couldn't have changed that much. It was a weird sensation—the continuing presence of the past; of a figure who, like those of my dream, stepped out of time in fancy dress to insist that she was my contemporary. I saw myself half-hypnotized by Edward's voice, by Laura's diffident claim that the past was contactable, and shook my head to clear it. Then an obvious objection presented itself. If Henry and Louisa Agnew had possessed the answers why didn't they share them? Why were they not public knowledge?'

'So what went wrong?'

Edward closed his eyes, leaned his head so far back I saw the tendons stretching in his neck. The question might have punched him there. 'Disaster,' he said. 'Totally unanticipated disaster.'

I sensed shaky ground. 'Well?'

For the first time he avoided my eyes as he answered. 'They were working on two separate books, you see. Henry was composing a verse epic of the Hermetic Mystery—honouring the ancient tradition of alchemist as poet, like Norton in his *Ordinall*, like Ripley of Bridlington. Louisa was working on a prose treatise—it was to be an introduction, clearing ground for her father's greater work.'

'He was a poet then?'

'He was a hermetic philosopher working in verse.'

I sensed Edward's unease at the distinction. I guessed at a bad poet. A poetaster. Doggerel.

'The point is,' Edward continued, 'that Henry had barely finished the first canto of his epic when Louisa brought her treatise to completion. She called it *An Open Invitation to the Chymical Wedding*. It was supposed to be no more than a modest prologue to her father's work, but . . .'

Whether he was growing tired, or seized by recurring doubts about sharing such matters with a still sceptical intruder, I don't know, but at this point in his narrative Edward sighed and seemed to lose heart. He reached for my packet of cigarettes, took one, and drew on it with closed eyes. Then he looked across at Laura. 'You started this,' he said. 'Tell him. Tell him what happened.' Then he slumped in his chair, apparently indifferent now whether I was interested or not.

Laura looked from him to me. Her voice was quieter, less passionate than Edward's, though the gaze was searching. 'You have to understand that Henry had complete confidence in Louisa's abilities. He'd taught her himself. I guess he thought of her as his creature almost. Anyway he was probably too caught up in his own work to take more than a passing interest in hers. The fact is he didn't even read it when it was written.' Laura shook her head. 'Can you believe that? All those years she'd worked for him—secretary, handmaid, muse, housekeeper even—keeping his mind clear of all domestic responsibilities. And then when she brought her own work to show him he simply told her to send it off to the printers. Sure, he'd pick up the tab and take a look at the book when he had time . . . but, I mean, can you imagine how she must have felt?'

'He trusted her,' Edward interjected. 'You said it yourself.'

Laura drew in her breath. 'Am I telling this or you?'

Edward made no answer, simply shook his head and withdrew. Laura looked back at me. 'You'll gather we don't always see eye to eye on this. Whatever the reason, it wasn't till the first copy came back from the publisher that Henry bothered to read what Louisa had written. That was when the storm broke. Edward claims he was seized by a sort of moral panic. I'm not so sure—there could be other explanations. But Henry decided that Louisa's book was too explicit, that she'd said too much. According to him, secrets that had been preserved for generations were written there in black and white for all the world to read.'

'She neglected the first premise of the alchemical writer,' Edward interrupted fiercely again. Laura sighed impatiently, turned away.

I said quickly, 'But I thought that's what they were trying to do—share the secret?'

"God damn,' Edward snapped, 'have you understood nothing? The secrets are dangerous. The alchemists were investigating the structure of matter—not for crude purposes of exploitation, not from mere intellectual curiosity, but as the very stuff of life itself. They knew that terrible energies lay sleeping in matter as in our minds—gunpowder was a direct result of their experiments with sulphur and saltpetre. They knew the dangers of waking those energies because they experienced and *contained* them. Within their own being they strove to make of themselves a vessel strong enough to hold together all the warring forces that might otherwise be released—inwardly, in the form of monstrous psychic inflation, or outwardly, with massively destructive power. They knew that in the wrong hands their knowledge could have appalling consequences—which is why, unlike the brilliant fools who tinkered with matter this century, they would have no truck with princes. Secrecy was of the essence. It has always been so:

> So this science must ever secret be,
> The cause whereof is this, as ye may see,
> If one evil man had hereof all his will
> All Christian peace he might easily spill.

I said, 'Is that an example of Agnew's verse?' My tone implied that, if so, I was not impressed.

'No, it's damn well not. That's fifteenth-century verse from Norton's *Ordinall of Alchemy*, and you can keep your Cambridge lit-crit standards to yourself. They're irrelevant. The point is, the girl wasn't careful enough. She said too much.'

'Or so her father said,' Laura retorted.

'She said it herself. She agreed.'

'She loved him.'

'That's beside the point.'

'It's the whole point. Why won't you see it?'

This hot exchange ended in silence. After a moment I said, 'So what happened?'

Laura looked fiercely across at me. I too was male, and she was on her own between Edward and me, representative suddenly of all women in their struggle to make their voice heard in the oppressive din of male debate. 'I'll tell you what happened,' she said coldly. 'He burned her book—that's what happened. He went to the printers and called in the whole edition. The publishers made a stink about it. Agnew had to pay over the odds to make up for their lost profits, but he got the whole lot back and made a bonfire of them—right here in the Decoy Lodge. On top of that he burned his own work too. Never wrote another word. He died of a stroke a few months later.'

Edward had relapsed back into his chair, shaking his head— either at the tone of Laura's account or at an unrightable wrong. It was unclear which, but Laura seemed to assume the former and withdrew into cold silence. I was left at an impasse, more aware of the immediate conflict than concerned about the fate of the Agnews.

It was a curious story certainly, but I couldn't share their agitation over it. The nineteenth century had produced other fish quite as queer as Agnew and his daughter, and—for all Edward's assertions—I failed to see the critical relevance of these odd events to our contemporary predicament. He could hardly be suggesting that some naïve Victorian bluestocking might have let slip the secret of nuclear fission, or that her indiscretions had altered the course of European history. By his own admission the Agnews' enterprise was hopeless. Marx, Darwin and Freud were not to be out-trumped by a quixotic country squire and his daughter. When I thought about Henry Agnew I could see little more than a private psychological crisis in the mind of a man obsessed.

And, when I looked back where Edward frowned down into space, it occurred to me that I might be witnessing a re-enactment of that crisis in contemporary terms—that Edward was more haunted by the past of this place than he knew . . . That both of them were.

I said carefully, 'It's an extraordinary story, but I still don't see what you hope to do with it?'

Edward looked up fiercely from his abstraction. 'But it's all

here, somewhere. It has to be. Don't you see? Agnew and his
daughter were the last links in a living chain. They had generations of the oral tradition behind them. They knew what we
desperately need to know. It's vitally important that I recon-
struct their knowledge.'

I recalled what he had said about the risk of psychic inflation—perhaps he was hankering after 'perfect master' status
after all. But the pathos of his words disturbed me more than
their vehemence. I looked to Laura and met no response. She
was dealing with frustrations of her own. For the moment I
would have to handle this directly, alone.

'You're absolutely sure that the whole edition was destroyed?'

'Of course I am,' Edward snapped. 'Do you think I would
waste my days . . .' But neither was he prepared to waste his
breath.

Throughout the evening power had been shifting around the
room in unpredictable ways, and for much of it I'd been the butt
of Edward's condescension. But it was clear now: I held the
sane, objective ground. The last time we met Edward had been
direct enough with me about my own troubles and, however
obliquely, I had learned from him. It would have felt a dereliction of both reason and responsibility if I ducked this moment
now.

'Isn't it possible that Agnew destroyed his daughter's work
from some other motive—one that even he may not have recognized?'

'You mean envy?'

'You said the girl was brilliant. She had finished her work . . .
Perhaps it was done too well for him to accept—that it made his
own work seem redundant? It could have been a hard thing for
him to face. And the fact that he burned his own manuscript—
doesn't that raise questions?' I looked to Laura for support. She
was icily remote, aware perhaps that I was hedging a deeper
question—one that she did not share.

'I've looked at that,' Edward answered. 'I'm no fool, Darken.
Whatever other faults he may have had, Agnew was not a mean-
spirited man. There was more to it than that.'

'There is another possibility,' I risked, '—that once he'd read
Louisa's book he realized that they were both labouring under
a delusion. That it was nonsense.'

'No.' Edward's reply was instant and absolute.

'Then you think he did the right thing?'

He was caught on the question. I saw the skin at his temples tauten. 'By his lights,' he said at last. 'I don't know. What I do know is that the subsequent demoralization was a tragedy. Something vital and specific to the health of western man got lost with it. Something that should have been preserved—in secret if need be, but none the less preserved. I know that the mainstream view of reality is corrupt and corrupting. It drives us out of our minds and arrests the feelings. It leaves us helpless. We can't live that way, not for much longer. And the world can't live with us—not like this. We have to change. We have to find a vision that will help us to change—that will restore dignity and meaning by altering our relationship to the delicate web that supports our life. Everyone knows it deep down; but we're lost, confused, complicit in our own bad dreams. The Agnews were part of another tradition—one that has always seen life whole, however painful the process of holding its contradictions together. They knew that matter and spirit are indivisible—that everything is translucent, permeable, infinite in its marvellous covenant of meaning. The Hermetic tradition has always offered a vision whereby men and women might recover their experience in its wholeness. It offers a technique for achieving that vision—and we need to know how to know it now, for that is how things deeply are, and not only human life depends on it . . .'

I pondered the old man across from me for a long time. He looked intolerably forlorn, as a man must who has a truth to speak and no language but an archaic dialect ridiculed by his times in which to speak it. Haggard as he was, I saw suddenly why Laura must first have found him attractive. He had fire, vision, a compelling certainty that the surface of life had been barely scratched, that there remained enormous opportunity for visionary invention, and urgent need for it. No, it wasn't power for himself he wanted—he had that already. His ambitions were at once larger and more modest.

My doubts about his sanity felt suddenly shabby—symptoms of an intellectual vanity so unsure of itself that it could thrive only by diminishing other less palpable but richer ways of seeing and feeling the world. In his preoccupation with alchemy Edward might be misguided—there was every possibility of that— but there was no way he was crazy, unless craziness in an uncaring world is another word for care. I found that I very much wanted to believe him.

'What about Louisa herself?' I suggested. 'She lived on into this century—sixty or more years after the crisis. Her book might have been burned, but her knowledge . . . You can't burn ideas, experience. Did she never speak about it to anyone?'

Edward must have sensed the altered tone of my approach, though his face was still creased with something approaching despair. 'As far as I know she kept it to herself. She lived in more or less permanent seclusion . . . never married. Ralph says there was a deep emotional shadow over her life which surfaced every now and then behind the calm exterior, but the aftermath of 1849 and her father's death would account for that. She must have felt the responsibility of it even though Henry was already an old man.'

For a moment I thought Laura was about to speak—the breath was drawn before she decided otherwise. Unaware of it, Edward sighed and continued. 'Ralph knows no more of the details than I do . . . only that she was an old lady of extraordinary strength and resolution and calmness of mind . . . much loved by everyone and, at the same time, impenetrable.'

'Then what about Ralph's father—didn't he know more?'

Edward snorted. 'Ralph asked him once. Apparently on one occasion his father tried to talk to Louisa about her work. He pressed her quite hard, I gather, and when she refused to answer he demanded to know why. She simply directed him to one of the most beautiful texts in the library, the *Splendor Solis* . . .' Edward laughed, drily sardonic. 'What he must have read there was this: *Alphidius, one of the old Philosophers said, "Everyone who does not care for the trouble of obtaining the Philosopher's stone will do better in making no enquiries at all than only useless ones."* If he bothered to read any further he would soon have got bogged down. He was driven by curiosity, you see . . . no genuine desire to understand. He told Ralph not to waste his time over it.'

'So the secret—whatever it was—died with her?'

Edward nodded. 'I've been through her correspondence— apparently there was a moment in the 1880s when her interest in the formation of the Theosophical Society reawakened hope for the possibility of sharing her knowledge. But she seems to have measured the movement and found it wanting. She would have seen through Madame Blavatsky like a shot. In any case, none of her associates at the time could press her very far and she soon withdrew into seclusion. She spent most of her time with her brother's grandchildren. One of them, Hilary, appears to have had the makings of a poet and it's just possible that she confided in him. But it was a kindness she died when she did, for Hilary and his elder brother were both killed in Flanders. It would have broken her heart to see what the world did to them . . . to see the inevitable catastrophe of it all. Ralph himself was too young to know her as anything other than a delightful old lady. Most of what he knows of her early life comes at second-hand and much edited. Had Hilary survived perhaps . . .' Edward opened his hands in a gesture of futility. He sighed, then looked uncertainly across at Laura. 'Are you all right, my dear?'

Laura fixed him with a sharp resentful glance, then averted her eyes.

'I'm sorry,' he said, 'I didn't mean to cross you.' But she was not to be won back so easily. She sat, locked in her own thoughts, apparently impervious to either of us. While Edward and I had talked she had withdrawn into the cold angry space that is left for women while men jostle their ideas, their minds. I myself had pushed Jess into such a corner many times. I too had struggled, as Edward did now, to draw her out when I was ready . . . when I saw, too late, what was happening.

'What is it?' he demanded.

'Isn't it obvious?'

'Look, Laura, there are some things on which we disagree . . . that's all.'

'Dammit, Edward, it's not that.'

'Then what?'

She drew in her breath fiercely. 'Look, I'm tired and I feel used. I've done all I can and where's it got us . . . Scenes like tonight—earlier, I mean—before Alex came . . .' She shook her head as though to dispel the memory. 'We can't carry on like this—you getting more and more bad-tempered, me at a loss—expected to be there when you need me, blown away when you don't. It's doing neither of us any good. We're going nowhere fast but down.'

Shocked by her vehemence, hating that it happened in my presence, Edward murmured, 'It's only frustration . . . Forgive me. I'd be lost without you, you know that.'

'The truth is you're lost *with* me as well. Look, I don't really care about what happened just now. I'm used to it. But face it, Edward, we need help. I thought when I read Alex's dream . . .'

But she faltered there, seeing the mask of despair on Edward's face, softening despite herself.

'What did you think?' I asked.

She looked across at me, a glance somewhere between doubt and defiance. 'I don't know now if you'll understand, but I've learned to trust coincidence—that if you're in touch with something real there's a kind of symmetry to things. Like my meeting Edward in the first place. I was drawn to his class—it was an option, not even in the mainline of my own work, but the moment I heard him speak I knew that it mattered to me, that I was part of it. I knew that he needed me, and that . . .' She hesitated, looked across at Edward who sat, eyes closed, with his head resting on one hand. 'And now,'—she had changed course—'when we're really stuck, you turn up with a dream that might have come straight from the pages of Louisa's book . . . I don't know . . .'

'It's true,' Edward murmured quietly. 'Laura's done all she can. She's helped me to build a clearer picture of what Louisa was like. But much of what we've learned is as confusing as it is clarifying. We don't know what to make of it, and at times, as you've seen, it leaves us at odds. And for the rest . . .' He sighed heavily. 'I've been working through all the remaining documents. Ralph has given me access to the family papers—notebooks, journals, letters. And there's the library—hundreds of volumes are annotated. There's a vast file of index cards. I'm trying to take bearings from them, using deductive logic, intuition, guesswork—anything that might shake the pieces into some sort of pattern, but the material is vast. They were working on it together for the best part of a decade, and Agnew had been preparing his notes for almost thirty years before that. Many of the references are in Latin—mine's rusty, Laura doesn't have it, and on my own I . . .' He looked up, haggard-eyed.

The room was very still.

Then Laura spoke again. 'Tell me something,' she said quietly, looking at me, 'hasn't any of this reached you?'

I sensed immediately that much might hang on my answer, that this was a yes or no moment. And, if she wanted me to believe, it didn't feel like a desperate search for a fellow-conspirator. Nor did she have the evangelical ardour of a true-believer. It was, uncomfortably, a little like looking into Jess's eyes after the event—that vulnerable reservoir of care which had been at the time entirely unacceptable to me. Except here there was no shadow of guilt, no need to prove anything. This woman and I were virtual strangers, distinct, with no claims on one another. No need even to prolong the acquaintance beyond the end of the evening. Yet what I thought I saw in her gaze was a mild hope—no more than that—that I wouldn't wilfully blind myself to some richer possibility.

'I mean,' she pressed, 'given the fact of your dream—and it was that which started all this, remember—didn't it ring any bells at all?'

For a moment I felt cornered by the direct appeal. Yes, of course bells had rung—lots of them, and some of them were alarm-bells, such as the one that was ringing inside me now as I held her gaze.

I was conscious too of Edward's silent attention. Behind that wrinkled frown lay a hero of my youth—a man who might, with luck, have evolved into a master of English verse, yet had abandoned that promise for this chimerical quest he clearly believed essential. One thing was clear: however he might mask it, the man really cared. He cared about what was happening in the world. He was striving, by his lights and against the odds, to come to terms with it. What's more, and amazingly enough considering the spoken and unspoken contention between us, he seemed to care about what was happening to me.

In some way I could not grasp we were all implicated in one another.

Then I remembered how the figures of my dream had been illuminated by the light radiating from the Pelican—that soft warm blur of belonging that suffused the other-world of dream, and in which all things appeared subtly interfused. For an instant I glimpsed it again. Less vividly, but with power enough to excite, I saw how it was possible that everything—each one of us—is the condition by which all else exists. I saw that reality might not be a fixture—crudely, inescapably *there*—but a continuing, spontaneous enterprise of the imagination. It might be shaped, remade, revalued, again and again, through each act of perception, each inventive gesture of relationship.

I could diminish Edward to a deluded eccentric or make him my friend, and my own being would be enlarged or diminished by the decision. I could make a fantasy out of Laura—a figment concocted from my lovelessness and the memory of her naked in the glade—or I could cleanse my senses and discover who she might really be. More immediately, I must answer yes or no to her question. One reply would put a stop to this, leaving my rationality intact if not my honesty. The other might open on all manner of new beginnings.

Wordlessly, I reflected how much of my life had been spent waiting for the present to happen: here, suddenly, was a moment in which a delicious sense of risk was all the more present because the future hovered about it ready to alight.

'Yes,' I said, 'of course it did. And I don't know if this is at all wise, but—if it helps—I do have Latin.'

The words came like a change of atmospheric pressure in the room. For an instant it felt as though their lives too had hung in the balance. Then I smiled at their astonished, upturned faces.

8 ❧ A Season of Ice

After the first success in the matter of Amy Larner, who was now comfortably situated with Dr Horrocks's friends in Saxburgh, Edwin Frere found himself a little at a loss, for his parish proved less permeable than he had hoped to the motions of the spirit.

He had inherited a sleepy congregation from Matthew Stukely. Only the church band—two clarionets, a serpent, a bassoon and an ill-tempered violoncello—brought much vigour to the services; after the harmonies of King's their enthusiasm fell stridently on the Rector's ear. His wish that the entire community might join in the responses had met with no immediate assent and so, apart from the hymns, his own voice and the clerk's must remain the sole conductors of divine energy. There were, however, some lusty singers among his parishioners, and he looked forward to the time when it might prove possible to fill the chancel with an unsurpliced choir. Otherwise they were a dour lot these rural East Anglians. Though the village seemed blessedly free from active dissent, even those most in need seemed more suspicious of than grateful for Frere's efforts of charitable service. His visits were regarded as occasions for embarrassment rather than pleasure or consolation, and he was left wondering why, when his motives were generous, these people should find it so difficult to respond with a matching warmth. Sadly, if patiently, he came to recognize that, though he might be their Rector, he remained—and would, he feared, for some time remain—a foreigner first.

Neither had Frere derived much encouragement from his fellow clergymen in the area. The best of them, Canon Ivory in Saxburgh, brought more diligence to the care of his hives and garden than to the needs of his parish. The worst were spreaders of terror, like Cuthbert in Thrandeston, or crassly negligent, like Jackman of Shippenhall who spent his days ruing the loss of his investment in a bogus railway company, and took pleasure only in riding to hounds. The sole promise of rewarding friendship had come from Sir Henry Agnew and his daughter; yet both now, it seemed, were deeply engaged on speculative work of their own, and had taken to a life of almost complete seclusion.

Despite the difficulties Frere was committed to his new life and regretted only that enthusiasm came less easily to his wife. An educated woman, attuned to the refinements of Cambridge society, Emilia found it hard to relate otherwise than *de haut en bas* even to the local gentry. Though she tried as faithfully as she might to devote herself to the needs of this rude community, she knew that she was not greatly liked and the knowledge injured her. It was not that she felt a need for approval, but it was disheartening that these people should show so little comprehension of the sacrifice she had made in wedding her life to theirs. Nor would Edwin concede more than a spineless encouragement that she be hopeful and humble in their work together. He seemed incapable of accepting that she was very lonely.

Frere dared not silence, but neither could he see the value of, Emilia's recurrent nostalgic reveries over their former life; but he was deeply troubled when she drew his attention to the fact that the services of a curate could be acquired for as little as thirty pounds a year. He knew what was suggested by her apparently abstract interest and would not hear of it, yet the price of his deafness was high. Emilia's subsequent ill-temper spent itself on the domestic staff, and she interpreted his own efforts to placate the ruffled servants as treachery.

'You will always seek the easy way, Edwin,' she complained, 'and it will not serve. The softness of your manner may appear to win their loyalty but only feeds their impertinence. And it is I, not you, who must bear the brunt of it. Were you to bring a tenth of the consideration that you show them and your parishioners to needs that lie closer to home you would find a more contented wife at your side. I would not *be* like this. It is not native to my disposition. Were my friends in Cambridge to see the change in me I vow they would not believe it. I can hardly believe it myself.'

As the days grew shorter, the Rectory colder, the pleasure they took in reading together or playing backgammon before the fire began to pall. Their prayers beside the bed were more articulate in their silences than anything that was uttered aloud. And then, miraculously it seemed, the most fervent of Frere's prayers was answered.

Shortly after a delay in her monthly courses Emilia fainted and both knew that, at last, she was pregnant.

To all who heard it—even if they did not understand the full depths of the resonance he intended—Edwin Frere's first Christmas sermon to the congregation of Munding St Mary's was clearly an inspired delivery. There, at the heart of the cold season, at the very dead of winter, he spoke in bright impassioned terms of the birth of the Christ-child as the abiding promise of new life. His previous sermons had been pitched a little too high for their comprehension. The words had sailed over their heads to be lost among the hammer-beams. One could not doze easily as one had done in Matt Stukely's day for there was something too insistently personal in this new parson's efforts to reach them; yet they had remained stolidly unreached till now when the fervour of his exhortation spoke to them as with an angel's tongue. It was cold inside the little candle-lit church but each heart was briefly warmed by the Rector's words and yearned again for its lost innocence. At the first chords of the carol—'O Come, All Ye Faithful'—they raised their voices as though they sought to equal in adoration the praises of the angels in Bethlehem long ago.

To complete the picture it is necessary to add that, at each reference to babies and new life, Mrs Bostock and Eliza Waters had exchanged meaningful smiles. They knew the secret of the Parson's enthusiasm. They knew too that the parson's wife was distressed by a persistent sickness that left her retching and queasy; and though there was some satisfaction in seeing her humbled, the two friends were quick to remark on how little such eagerly expectant fathers as the parson truly understood of the tribulations of the woman's role in these mysteries.

Nevertheless it was out of his own immediate sense of the renewal of life, his very own good news that seemed to match the eternal Good News out of Bethlehem, that Frere spoke to his congregation that Christmas. He knew that, for the first time, his words had found them. He was glowing like an altar-candle as he spoke, and the words presented themselves like gifts. They were hardly his own yet sprang from his heart as though, in those exalted moments, it were itself a living vessel of the Christmas mystery. New life, green as the holly leaf, was at work inside him as surely as it stirred inside his wife.

Around him the voices of his congregation swelled in jubilant carol. His own rich baritone rang out with joy, and at the words *Lo he abhors not the Virgin's womb*, Frere thought briefly, almost affectionately, of Gypsy May in the cold and dark outside those walls. What was she, after all, but a crude precursor of the Divine Mother whose labours they celebrated here in a church consecrated to her name? At all times all wise men had revered the mysterious organ of generation through which alone might life be entered. It was no devourer but the very portal of life.

So, *Sing, choirs of angels, Sing in exultation, Sing, all ye citizens of Heaven above. Glory to God in the highest.*

Glory.

In excelcis Gloria.

Early that January a bitter wind blowing off the far Urals seized East Anglia in a grip of ice. After a night-long blizzard the villagers of Munding woke to find the water-meadows glittering and still, the ford across the lane crusted over. The repose of snow was everywhere. The wind had dropped but the still air winced with frost. All the pumps were frozen and had to be freed with burning straw. Mattocks were taken to the ice-bound troughs. Icicles dangled from roof-thatch and porch. Each window pane hung dizzily fronded.

Cattle moaned in the stalls. When they staled in the yards it quickly froze. The geese seemed driven off their heads with ice as the nights became a vast gallery of frozen stars, the air so stiff it scarcely yielded breath. The moon itself was not colder or more silent than this strangely arctic Munding landscape. Already it felt as though the earth would never warm again.

Like it or not, Louisa Agnew was driven back upon the Hall. Observing her return from the Decoy Lodge one afternoon, blue and chapped about the lips, her father forbad further voyages across the lake until that frozen wind relented. So well had her work progressed at the Lodge, and so greatly—for all the discomfort—had she enjoyed her solitude, that Louisa momentarily tried defiance; but she was shivering uncontrollably even as she did so. She knew it was with good reason that she had brought her papers back across the lake that day. There was no virtue in having her fire-soul expire in ice while she laboured to make it burn more brightly for the world. If Nature herself sought to impede her progress, then resistance was mere pride and folly. There would be time enough in more clement days to come.

By the next dawn—a Saturday—even the lake at Easterness was frozen over. For the first time in years it was thick enough to bear. Furthermore the wind had dropped, the sun shone brilliantly over the ice, and already, early in the morning, small boys were sliding through the radiant air, whooping and hallooing, and sending broken boughs skidding across the frozen surface with a hollow, reverberating whoosh. Few people in the village had skates but those who did were not the only ones to gather at the lake that morning without invitation or fear of rebuke. Such a rare marvel had instantly become public property.

Even Sir Henry came out of his chill library to stand for a time, wrapped in greatcoat and mufflers, surveying the Breughel-like gathering at the lake. 'Tundra,' he said with distaste, the word accompanied by a white plume of breath. 'Don't much care for it myself but it seems the people do. Louisa, we should have Ducker get out the stove . . . roast some chestnuts . . . mull some wine. If any of these poor beggars die of cold old Starling will have a hard time digging a hole for them.'

'You arrived at the thought a moment before I did,' his daughter answered. 'It's good to see you outdoors again, father. To see some colour in your cheeks.'

Henry Agnew sniffed. 'Well, I've tasted the air and found it frigid. Enough is enough.'

'You will not stay to watch me skate?' She pouted at the shake of his fur hat. 'And surely once word reaches Saxburgh that the lake is bearing Tom Horrocks will ride out to take a turn on the ice?'

'Then he may join me indoors when he's had enough, as I already have.' With that the old man turned away to give orders that the assembled villagers be shown the hospitality of the Hall. Privily he would have liked to enjoy the fun but his heart was already labouring against the cold. It frightened him a little.

Louisa had been skidding unsteadily about the ice for the best part of an hour when a carriage came round the rear drive of the

Hall and, after a moment's debate, Edwin Frere sprang down to give a helping hand to his well-muffled wife. Louisa was surprised by the arrival and glad of it, for young Frank Wharton had been ragging mercilessly her occasional graceless descents to the ice, petticoats and undergarments protruding from her skirt, skates flailing above them. Frank's incorrigible efforts at flirtation had become tiresome to her and, the truth of the matter was, he was no great dandy on the ice himself for all his mockery. It was a relief therefore to make for the frozen shore where the parson was protesting that his wife would be safer and more comfortable if she remained in the carriage. She might observe the proceedings equally well from there.

'I am no invalid,' Emilia replied. 'If you will not permit me to skate you must at least allow me to stand near the ice. This is as close as I have felt to Cambridgeshire for some considerable time.' She turned to greet Louisa with a ruddy-cheeked smile. 'Good morning, Miss Agnew. Do I discern that skating has not been a frequent pleasure in these parts?'

'Sadly so, Mrs Frere, as my inelegance attests. The lake rarely freezes so we have little opportunity to discover our ice-legs. But you are looking well this morning. It is a great delight to see the glow of health about you. We have wine on the mull. May I offer you a warming glass?'

Emilia sighed and waved a weak, refusing hand. 'I fear it will not agree with me. It is a pleasure, like that of the ice, I must forego . . . in the interests of the third of our small party, you understand?'

'Of course. But, Mr Frere, surely I can persuade you?'

'In a moment, Miss Agnew, I would be delighted—but first I must try our Norfolk ice.'

'It seems from the eager glint in your eye that you are a practised hand . . . or do I mean foot?'

'In my day, Miss Agnew, in my day.'

'Then you must impress us, Mr Frere. If you skate with the same passion as you preach I dare say you will have the whole parish at your feet.'

It was perhaps more than the chill air that flushed the parson's cheeks as he bent to fasten his skates. 'After the narrow dikes of Cambridgeshire,' he said standing again, 'the span of this lake offers an exhilarating prospect. Will you accompany me, Miss Agnew?'

'I should rather keep company with Mrs Frere. We shall stand breathless in admiration together.'

'Then here I go.' Frere stepped on to the ice, sniffed at the cold air, and then, hands clasped at his back, the tail of his frock-coat lifting a little in the breeze, he sailed off. One confident stride after another pushed him out across the ice until he wheeled sharply, shedding a spume of flakes at his feet. He smiled back at them, shifting his weight smoothly from foot to foot as he reversed, turned again and was off at an ever accelerating pace round the bend of the lake and swiftly out of sight. Louisa gasped with delight to see the man and his reflection travel together so fluently. The party of astonished villagers raised a spontaneous cheer at this virtuoso performance. Openmouthed, a little aghast perhaps, Frank Wharton pushed himself stealthily further out across the ice where he could view the parson's progress, the better to see how the thing should be done.

'Upon my soul,' Louisa exclaimed to Emilia Frere, 'your husband is a man of surprises. Why, he is as proud as a regimental stallion. I confess his grace amazes me.'

Emilia smiled with satisfaction but said nothing. Inwardly she chafed a little that she too could not take to the ice and show this country maid a quicksilver pair of heels. How exhausting it was the way circumstances conspired against her simple pleasures.

Momentarily Louisa was troubled by her companion's silence. Had a too open show of admiration given offence?—for she had felt a flame leap to her throat to watch the man's confident pride in his body, the actuality of his skill, the sheer command. Who would have thought the ear-tugging parson to have such grace? Who would have thought it?

Then her eyes were caught by Frere's swift return around the bend of the lake. Imprinted against the sculpted white drifts of the opposite shore he sprang from the ice in a swift, frisky curvet, landed with perfect balance, and sped towards them with a lithe, energetic swing from foot to foot, faultlessly timed. The shores rang to the sound of his skates against the ice, a resonant hollow warble drawn at each stride from the depths of the lake. He pulled himself erect and floated effortlessly across the shining surface to brake in a shower of ice-shards at their feet. He was panting and smiling, an ice-glow radiant at his face. 'This is heaven,' he said.

'Certainly you skate like an angel, Mr Frere.' The male voice came from behind Louisa and Emilia. They turned and saw Tom Horrocks smiling there, a pair of skates slung over his shoulder. 'If the road to Heaven ever freezes over you'll be there before the rest of us. But then I suppose you would be anyway. At least I shall be warmer in the opposite direction.'

'I very much doubt you will have the chance to discover,' Frere laughed. 'Take a turn with me, Doctor, and I'll lay my faith to your scepticism that I make the weir and back before you.'

Tom Horrocks snorted. 'I'm too old a hand to make wagers with sharpers, Mr Frere—even those sporting bands. But if a stately progress to the other shore and back will serve your turn then I'm your man. Provided, of course, I'm furnished with a glass of good red mull before we set out. It's been a cold ride from Saxburgh. And are those hot chestnuts that I see?'

'They are indeed,' Louisa answered. 'Come, help yourself.'

Horrocks chatted affably a moment with Tilly who presided over the hot griddle amidst a ring of ragged children. He took a chestnut from the pan and bounced it from hand to hand as he turned cheerily to enquire after Mrs Frere's welfare. 'It's good to see you out and about. Fresh air is what you need—that and time will see you through these early discomforts. And you must eat. Here, have a chestnut.' Laughing he tossed the hot nut, and Emilia, squealing, caught it in gloved hands. 'You'll take a glass with me, Mr Frere?'

'Indeed I will.'

The mull was hot, well-spiced and laced with brandy. Horrocks smacked his lips. 'Ichor!' he exclaimed, '—the gods' own blood. I shall need it if I am to race with Mercury here.'

Louisa started a little at the name so casually used. Mercury, or Mercurius as he was known to the alchemists, had been much on her mind of late. He was the tutelary deity of the Hermetic Art—a slippery, ambiguous figure who was, according to that great master Gerhard Dorn, 'the true hermaphroditic Adam.' Only the previous day Louisa had been pondering a passage from the *Aurelia occulta* in which Mercurius promised to bestow on the adept the powers of male and female, of heaven and earth. *By the philosophers I am named Mercurius,* he said there, *my spouse is the gold; I am the old dragon found everywhere on the globe of the earth, father and mother, young and old, very strong and very weak . . . often the order of nature is reversed in me.*

I am dark and light. I am known yet do not exist at all. I am the carbuncle of the sun, the most noble purified earth, through which you may change copper, iron, tin and lead into gold.

As the familiar words passed through her memory again Louisa was gazing at Edwin Frere where he stood on the ice, warming his hands on the glass of mulled wine, smiling in chatter with Tom Horrocks. In this moment all contraries seemed reconciled in him—shyness and strength, awkwardness and grace, the spirit bright within the balanced body, his parson's black against the white of the distant drifts. Beyond him a gleaming snow-light travelled across the lake, and, for a moment, it appeared to flake from his hair. It shimmered even more vividly around the sunlit icy reflection at his feet with the bright iron of the skate-blades between. Frere stood tall on the ice, his head thrown back in laughter. The breath was cold at Louisa's lips. There was a faltering, unanticipated agitation within her. This day was turning strange. She felt as though something quite terrible was about to happen.

Then she knew herself addressed by Emilia Frere.

'I'm so sorry,' she answered.

'An angel passing, my dear?'

Louisa smiled uncertainly. 'It is so strange, don't you find? This sudden ice . . . our little world so utterly transformed. It feels almost as though it might stay this way for ever.'

Discreetly Emilia dropped the unwanted chestnut in the snow and gathered the collars of her coat about her. 'It is my earnest hope that it will not.'

Frere turned towards her in concern. 'You are cold, my dear? You wish to leave?'

'Perhaps a few minutes more,' she answered. 'You must not disappoint the Doctor of his chase . . .'

Horrocks looked up from the strapping of his skates. 'You are well-wrapped, Mrs Frere. The air will do you no harm. And this light. Just look at it. What do you think, Mr Frere? Do you not agree that if God ever did say *Let there be light* he must have been over Norfolk at the time?'

'He is still there, Dr Horrocks. Look, his angels are shining from those great hammer-beams of cloud.'

'To a believer's eye mayhap. For me the light alone is enough.' Horrocks saw the shadow of disapproval cross Emilia's face and smiled. 'Come then, Frere,' he said, 'humiliate me. You will join us, Louisa?' He stepped down among the frozen reeds.

'I fear the two of you will leave me far behind.'

'Not at all,' Frere answered. 'Come, we shall skate three-handed, like the horses of a Russian sleigh.'

'Excellent,' said Horrocks, 'that way I am sure to stand.'

'Or I shall drag you both down with me.' Louisa stepped on to the ice, crossed her hands and held them out to her escorts. She was breathing quickly. 'This is very gallant.'

'By the left then,' Horrocks urged, 'and off we go.'

Slowly at first, then ever more rapidly, she was drawn out across the lake. Ahead of her glittered the tracks of Frere's previous solitary excursion. The wind came cold and fast to her face. Supported by her two companions she found that she need not even move her feet. Once they had turned the Mount, with the full span of the ice shining before them, the two men gathered pace, at once in harmony and contention, drawing vigour from the presence of the young woman between them, who cried out, not in fear but encouraging them on to greater exertions. Her lips were open so that the cold air came gasping there like water flowing much too fast to drink. Helpless other than in the firm clasp of their hands, she was all exhilaration; sweeping, it seemed, down a steep cylinder of ice and air. Both the sun and the pale moon were in the sky above her, and she was, in the words of an old adept, 'running without running, moving without motion.' Ice shot from their feet like sparks, scattering behind them. And on they sped so swiftly that she might almost have cried out with Ostanes, less in trepidation than delight, 'Save me, O God, for I stand between two exalted brilliances . . . Each of them has reached me and I know not how to save myself.'

Then Tom Horrocks was panting beside her. 'Enough,' he called, 'enough. This old horse is jaded.' Firmly clutching her hand he slowed, and Frere arced around them on still skates so that he made a sweeping circle on the ice before they came, breathless, to a halt.

Tom Horrocks dropped his head, hands at his knees, groaning and smiling up at them. 'Another ten seconds,' he gasped, 'and I should have been down, or Louisa torn limb from limb between us. You are a fit man, Mr Frere . . . You must carry me back.' He stood erect again, reached a hip-flask from his pocket and proffered it.

Smiling, Frere declined. Seized by an impulse of delight, and with an untypical desire to impress, he pushed away again and

was suddenly spinning like a top on his skates, arms outstretched. Pigeon-toed beneath her crinoline, Louisa clapped
his performance, and the sound of her clapping sped across the
ice to echo back from the trees. Ducks, disgruntled among
barbed reeds, took flight. Further down the lake, back in the
direction whence they had come, children were playing coach
and horses with a sled. The sound of their cries tinkled on frigid
air. Tossing his head, Frere braked to a sudden stop. Horrocks,
who had watched with the flask arrested half-way to his mouth,
said, 'Here's to you, Mr Frere—a true prince of the ice,' and
swigged at his brandy.

Frere stood feeling the park sway around him as he panted,
and when the dizzy motion stopped he was looking through the
brilliant air at a thatched dwelling, snow-laden, secreted among
the trees, its dark jetty seized in ice. 'What a splendid situation,'
he said. 'I had not noticed it before.'

'The old Decoy Lodge,' said Horrocks.

'But who loves solitude enough to live there, I wonder?'

'That is my phrontistery, Mr Frere,' Louisa smiled, '—my
retreat in more clement weather. That is where I go to be myself.'

'In my experience,' Frere answered, 'you are that everywhere, Miss Agnew.'

'But I have secrets, Mr Frere, and one needs a place to keep
them.'

He gazed at her, puzzled, for a moment, then assumed that
he was teased. 'You could not have found one more sequestered,' he said, '—or more lovely.'

'I thought the Lodge had been shut up,' the doctor put in.

'I have opened it again.' Louisa rubbed her hands for warmth.
Even inside the gloves her fingers were stinging a little.

'And Henry does not object?'

Louisa arched her brows. 'He does not greatly care for it, but
I need its solitude if I am to accomplish what I am about.'

'May one be so inquisitive as to enquire what that is?'

'Nothing of which you would approve, Doctor Horrocks,' she
teased, and saw immediately that the Rector might misunderstand. She turned towards him, 'Nor of which you would dis-
approve, I hope.'

'More mumbo-jumbo?' Horrocks laughed.

'I am sure you would think so.'

'Henry should know better than to keep you cooped up with

his books. If I were ten years younger, my girl, I should come and carry you away myself.'

'And ruin your bachelor peace with my tattle? I think you deceive us both.'

'This is where you belong,' the doctor protested, 'out here, in the light of day. There is more to life than the mind, young woman.'

'Indeed there is. More too than the flesh—for all your assertions to the contrary.'

Tom Horrocks shook his head and slipped the flask back into his pocket. 'Either way,' he said, 'the flesh has its needs, and they must out or fust. Am I not right, Mr Frere?'

Frere stood flustered at the turn their banter had taken. Such intimate familiarity was no part of his normal intercourse with the parish. He was surprised that the doctor should seek to draw him into such boldness with one who was of the other sex, and the daughter of a friend. He tried for abstraction. 'There is a case to be made for asceticism . . .'

'A damned special case,' Horrocks grunted. 'Louisa is no nun. Look at those eyes. If there is not more mischief there than . . .'

But his comparison was interrupted by a shouting down the lake. All three of them turned their heads. Young Frank Wharton stood unsteadily on his skates, waving one hand and calling, 'Mr Frere. Mr Frere. You must come at once.'

The chill air was suddenly colder about them.

'Something is amiss,' Frere said. 'You will excuse me . . .' At a speed that neither could match Louisa and Horrocks saw him hasten back down the lake. They were still some distance away when he slewed to a halt beside Frank Wharton and, after the briefest confabulation, sped on. Frank shouted, 'Doctor, you must come too. It's Mrs Frere.'

Louisa and Horrocks exchanged anxious glances. 'You can make your way back without me?' he asked.

'Of course. Hurry.'

On his way to the lake-head Horrocks learned from Frank that the parson's wife had swooned all of a heap by her carriage. 'As soon as we get back,' Horrocks ordered, 'fetch my bag for me. It hangs by the saddle of my bay. Be sharp about it.'

The doctor was sweating from his exertions as he pushed his way through the silent ring around Mrs Frere. 'Stand back there,' he snapped. 'Give the woman air.'

Panting and frightened, Frere cradled his wife's head in the crook of his arm. A cape had been laid beneath her and she was wrapped in Frere's own coat. Emilia's face was white almost as the snow, but she was conscious and moaning now.

Mrs. Tillotson stood wringing her hands. 'That happen all of a flash,' she was saying. 'One minute she were up by the carriage, the next she were down on her back like a tumbled ewe.'

Horrocks knelt, put his hand to the woman's brow then to the pulse at her wrist. 'All right, my dear,' he murmured, 'we'll have you right as rain in a moment. Are you in pain at all?'

Emilia closed her eyes and nodded. 'I think . . .' she faltered, opened her eyes again. Horrocks saw the fear there. He cast a quick glance into Frere's anxious face.

'It is the morning-sickness?' Frere asked.

'Stand over her a moment,' Horrocks said. 'You too, Tilly. You must forgive me, Frere.' He moved the coat aside, quickly lifted Emilia's skirt and the petticoats beneath, then drew them down again. The glance had confirmed his suspicions. He looked up at Mrs Tillotson. 'Can we fashion some sort of stretcher? We must bring her into the Hall.'

Emilia heard the urgency in his voice. For a moment she stared, wide-eyed, then her head drooped to her shoulder. 'Where the devil's Frank with my bag?' the doctor snapped, for —as much in shock as in pain—Emilia had fainted away again.

'I should have taken her home sooner,' Frere was saying. 'We should not have come at all.'

'Don't berate yourself, man,' the doctor answered gruffly. 'If this was going to happen it would have happened anyway.' He saw the terrible realization dawn on Frere's face. His voice softened a little. 'It may not seem so now, but I promise you a miscarriage is one of nature's mercies.'

Louisa arrived in time to hear this and to see, a moment later, the tears start to Frere's eyes, then she was down beside the unconscious woman, holding her head. When she looked up again she saw the tears roll in silence to Frere's chin. 'I'm so sorry,' she heard herself saying. 'I am so terribly sorry.'

Frere was stunned with grief. It was Louisa as much as the doctor who supervised the carrying of Emilia into the Hall, holding her cold hand, murmuring small phrases of consolation and encouragement as the improvised litter was lifted carefully up the stairs and the invalid laid in the same bed where she had

passed her first night at Easterness. There was an expression of
frozen terror on Emilia's face. It stood between her and tears,
as though they too were frozen even before they might reach the
air. The careful procession into the Hall had felt like a kind of
funeral.

At the doctor's bidding Frere waited outside the bedroom,
awkwardly attended by Henry Agnew. 'It may be for the best,
man,' Agnew was saying, 'though God knows I know how you
must feel. My own wife, you know . . .' But he halted there,
seeing more cause for anxiety than consolation in his path. 'Perhaps some brandy . . . for shock?'

Staring at space, Frere shook his head. There was a great
gash torn in his world. Nothing would focus. Everything was
frozen yet strangely unstill. Outside he could hear children
shouting on the lake. The world went on, ignorant how everything was changed. The Hall had become an island in space, its
time altered, its atmosphere scarcely breathable. Everything
there was very fragile.

There had been some error. This was not how it was to be.

Edwin Frere looked into Agnew's old face and saw only hopeless consternation there, as though he too were overwhelmed
with feelings so vast and flood-like that no word might answer
them.

Somewhere a clock was chiming.

Louisa Agnew was feeling not faint but dazed. The contrast
with her exhilaration on the frozen lake had come so swiftly. In
the bedroom she had done everything that Tom Horrocks had
bidden her, reflexively, without panic; yet she had known herself
for the first time up against the frailty of the human organism—
the mess of it, the degradation. There had been a great deal of
blood. Emilia was tallow-pale, a frail parcel of flesh, shedding
a life that was her own and not her own. There were things to
be done, and they had been done, and everything was inexplicable. Tilly and Alice, she knew, would be able to speak of it;
already, below stairs, the events were becoming narrative, being
talked into a kind of submission. She herself was silenced now.
There was no adequacy of words—only this tranced awareness
of mortality, and of the pain that the Rector and his wife must
share to the exclusion of all others, alone in the bedroom, while
Louisa stood between her father and the doctor in the hall, her
limbs aching, her mind strangely uncertain of itself.

'It would be unwise to try to move her back to the Rectory,' Tom Horrocks was saying. 'Not for two or three days, I think. There is some risk of infection, of fever.'

Henry Agnew cleared his throat and nodded.

Louisa saw that some further response was required. 'Of course, she must stay here,' she answered. 'I will care for her myself.'

'I'm as much concerned for her emotional as her bodily welfare,' the doctor warned. 'I understand that the Freres had long wanted this child. She may seek to blame herself. She may feel that she has failed her husband. Such feelings are understandable but she must not be allowed to brood on them. They are without foundation and can only injure her.' Tom Horrocks reflected for a moment on the little he knew of Emilia Frere. 'It may not be easy, I fear.'

'She's not an easy woman,' said Agnew. 'Mrs Frere is less strong than she would have us all believe.' Secretly, and with some self-reproach, he found himself resenting the circumstances of this imposition.

'The husband too will require attention. The shock of it will come hard.' Remembering the parson's delight on the ice, Tom Horrocks shook his head. 'I tell you, there are times when I could agree with the good doctor of Norwich, old Tom Browne, that it were better if we humans propagated in the manner of trees. There would be a sight less suffering in the world.'

'And less joy,' Henry Agnew muttered quietly, remembering his wife and finding his better feelings in the memory, 'less joy.'

With a sudden access of cold doubt Louisa Agnew recognized that, beyond the narrow world of her books, of neither suffering nor joy had she any great understanding.

Emilia Frere passed three nights in the bedroom at the Hall before Tom Horrocks professed himself satisfied that all danger was passed and she might return to the Rectory.

At first—perhaps under the soothing influence of laudanum— she had seemed grateful for, even to enjoy, the attention she received. Soon, however, she confessed to finding Mrs Tillotson a fusspot and Alice a tiresome chatterbox. She would receive visits only from her husband and Louisa.

Louisa was patient with this choice. Though she was not entirely at ease with Mrs Frere her heart flooded with sympathy for her loss. As best she might she encouraged her to speak her grief, but soon saw that her efforts, however tender, were experienced as intrusion, as invasion almost. Emilia showed little wish to speak, Louisa had to content herself with reading aloud beside the bed, though the books she suggested were soon rejected in favour of such verses as those of Felicia Hemans and Anna Letitia Barbauld—works that were not at all to her own taste. Yet the reading appeared to bring Emilia a kind of doleful peace.

After both his first two visits Frere came unhappily from the bedroom, managing a brave but unconvincing smile and admitting only his boundless gratitude to Louisa for her pains. He had the look of a punished dog, but he too was unwilling to speak whatever troubled feelings lay behind his mien.

Louisa felt a little helpless before his diffident manner, and she was surprised when Emilia insisted that she remain in the room throughout Frere's third visit; surprised and discomfited, for it was not a happy interview. The parson was as effusive in his attentions as circumstance would allow, but Emilia petulantly resisted them. Louisa was left feeling that she had been appointed audience to a play of the wife's devising, one in which the heroine's suffering was the principal theme and which might, indeed, have been moving had not the sense of theatre been so pronounced, and had the script been less expressive of a plaintive heart than of its tribulations.

In the hope that it might cheer his wife Frere had brought a letter from her dearest friend in Cambridge, who was, of course, as yet unaware of Emilia's condition. The letter was opened and read in silence. 'How Charlotte misses me,' she said at last, 'and how well she understands! She quotes Hazlitt, Edwin: "There is nothing good to be had in the country, or if there is, they will not let you have it." ' Emilia smiled across at Louisa. 'Of course, my dear, it is not entirely true. When I am quite well again I must inform her so. Edwin, I would be utterly desolate were it not for my faithful companion here. We owe a great debt of gratitude.'

'Indeed we do, my dear.' Observing Louisa's embarrassment, Frere tried a change of course. 'I have written to your family,' he said. 'I am in hopes that your sister Hattie will come to ease your convalescence at the Rectory.'

'Is it yet posted?'

'Not yet. I was intending to . . .'

'I should not wish her to come yet. Nor that my father be

made unduly anxious on my account.' She looked to Louisa again. 'My father is not at all a well man. Indeed, I had the greatest reservations about leaving him.' Her gaze returned to her husband. 'I think you have been too forward, Edwin. We should wait until we are quite certain that all is well. Then I myself shall write in reassurance.'

'If you think it best.'

'I do. Do you not agree, Louisa?'

'As I do not have the good fortune to know your family, Emilia, I am hardly in a position to say, though I feel sure they would wish to know of your distress.'

'They shall. In good time they shall. But one must not burden others unnecessarily. I am already distraught that you yourself have been put to such pains.'

Even as she reassured Emilia once more that her concern was groundless Louisa found herself reflecting on the power of the weak, its hold upon the minds of others. How sad was the Rector's face, she thought; sad as the sound of a cello on a rainy afternoon. Deeply as she sympathized with the woman's condition she saw no reason why the husband should be made its victim. She was troubled by the contrast between Edwin Frere, ice-dancer, and this submissive comforter. Yet even as she felt humiliated on his behalf she recognized that she too had been drawn into complicity with Emilia's will. Where had the woman learned such stratagems?

Like father, like daughter, she guessed—but then had she not herself devoted her days to a father's needs? And with what consequences, she wondered, for her own development? How complex was the human world! How much more so than the enigmas of her books! All that had once seemed clear was clouding now, and she chafed under the demand for moral adjustment to this difficult guest with her very real needs. Did she have so little charity after all? Almost she disliked herself.

On what was to be the patient's last night at the Hall Louisa looked up from her reading and saw that Emilia was in tears. Something akin to gratitude overwhelmed her. Many times Louisa had wished that the woman might weep as her husband had done, might permit something deeper than care for her creature comforts to reach her. Delicately Louisa had tried again and again to create the opportunity, but she had been allowed no room. Whatever pangs of grief and guilt and shame Emilia

might suffer had remained locked inside her, an unapproachable
wound. Astringently if politely, Louisa had been held at bay;
till now, when at the lines:

> Here must I stop;
> Or is there aught beyond? What hand unseen
> Impels me onward through the glowing orbs
> Of habitable nature, far remote,
> To the dread confines of eternal night,
> To solitudes of waste, unpeopled space,
> The deserts of creation, wide and wild,
> Where embryo systems and unkindled suns
> Sleep in the womb of Chaos?

she heard Emilia sniff and saw the tears in her eyes.

'My dear.' Louisa put down the book, crossed to the bed and
wrapped an arm about Emilia's shoulders. There was no deep
release of grief, but a tense shuddering of the muscles, a stifled
whimpering behind the handkerchief held tightly at Emilia's
face.

'You must let the tears come now,' Louisa murmured. 'You
must own your grief. You have tried to be too strong.'

'It is true,' Emilia cried, and her breast shuddered again, and
the handkerchief was pressed more tightly against her face. For
a long time they clung together so until, with a haggard shaking
of her head, Emilia freed herself from the embrace, struggled
for, and found, a measure of composure. Louisa sat back a little
on the bed to allow her greater room to breathe, to speak.

'We are friends, are we not?' Emilia asked weakly.

'Of course we are.' With her own handkerchief Louisa dabbed
the tears from Emilia's cheek. It was not precisely true, but since
Emilia's first frail arrival in the room there had been no such
promise of intimacy between the two women.

'My dear, since we first came to this terrible place you are
the only person to show me true consideration.'

Astonished as she was by this bitter description of the home
she loved, Louisa kept her voice gentle. 'I am sure that cannot
be so. Everyone here cares for you.'

Emilia was shaking her head. 'Be true with me,' she said.
'We must be true with one another or I fear I shall go quite . . .'
The handkerchief stifled at birth the terrible thought.

Alarmed now, Louisa stroked the woman's shoulder. Too well

she knew how difficult the others in the Hall had found her, how most of the parish regarded the Rector's wife as an aloof, critical figure who acted solely from duty, with little warmth. And this was not the moment to suggest that Emilia, with her refusal to let go of Cambridge, to be truly present in the parish, might herself be at fault. 'I think at least,' she suggested carefully, 'that you are forgetting your husband. He is . . .'

'My husband is a man,' Emilia interrupted from the impatience of her pain, 'with a man's insensitivities.'

'He is grieving very deeply.'

'For his child, don't you see? He is grieving for his child.'

'But not that alone. My dear, he is distraught with anxiety for you.'

Breathing heavily Emilia stared at the younger woman as though bereft of all hope that she might be understood.

'You should hear the poor man . . .' Louisa began again, but faltered when she saw Emilia close her eyes and shake her head in the little bonnet she wore. Then the head was turned aside on the pillow, staring across the room.

'It is natural that you should suffer from such doubts,' Louisa attempted. 'Dr Horrocks told me that you would feel the pain of this experience as . . .'

'You do not understand.'

Distressed by the dull anger in her voice, Louisa waited.

'I am so alone.' If there was an element of self-pity there it was also a statement of fact. Louisa received it so, and her heart went out to the suffering woman.

'Oh my dear.'

Emilia withdrew at her approach.

'I think I am not long for this place,' she muttered quietly.

'Oh come now,' Louisa answered. 'The Doctor is more than happy with your progress. Why, I would guess that after tomorrow's visit he will send you packing back off to your home. You are on the mend, I promise you. This very distress is a sure sign of it.'

'That is not my home,' Emilia said.

Louisa saw immediately that she had misunderstood. Emilia turned her head to look at her again. 'You are such a child,' she said. 'You cannot know.' The expression on her face was strange—part sympathy, part derision—and the weakness had gone from her voice.

'Then you must try to tell me.'

Emilia lay in silence for a long time, biting her lip. Louisa saw that she had misjudged this woman. So little had been released from that tight grip, and there was so little natural affinity between them that, for all the hours they had spent in this room together, they remained strangers to one another. Louisa had lied when she said they were friends. If she had spoken in charity to an unhappy invalid it had also been negligent of a larger truth: that they were representative of two very different principles—principles that might meet only in an hour of need, or in honest confrontation with one another. They might almost have been of different species. That Emilia thought her a mere child revealed how little she understood; but then Louisa herself had only limited comprehension of what remained dark and unspoken in this woman who studied her, almost coldly, summoning resolve.

'You will listen to me now?' Emilia said.

Swallowing, Louisa nodded. She held Emilia's eyes in her own grave gaze.

'And you will hold everything I say in confidence? In sacred confidence?'

To demur would be to banish the woman still deeper into the wastes of her own loneliness. Away from the fireplace now Louisa was beginning to feel cold. She pulled her shawl closer about her shoulders and said uncertainly, 'Of course.'

Emilia sighed. One hand seemed to test the quality of the coverlet between her fingers. 'You have not known a man,' she said. 'Really known, I mean . . . not as a daughter knows her father, however deep the affection she holds for him. You have not yet suffered at their nakedness, and therefore you have never known how blind they are, how weak. Nor do you know how cruel that blindness and weakness can be—and all the more so when they are sugared over with sentiment and concern, with the pretence of tenderness. I promise you, it is quite terrible. Until you have known it you will have no conception of what it is to be truly lonely. To feel yourself a shell-less creature, bereft and vulnerable. Emilia stared up, sharp-eyed, at her listener, who was amazed, almost horrified to see the narrow smile at her lips. 'I think, my dear, you have not yet learned what a curse it is to be born woman. You think it is all a matter of love and loving, of care and caring . . . Very well, I too have had such thoughts. Before I came here I too believed that love and duty were the compatible ingredients of a woman's life . . . that loy-

alty and patience and service were all. I had not seen that hatred
might prove an indispensible friend.' Again she studied Louisa,
smiling at the impact of the word. 'Now you will misunderstand
me again. You will think that I hate my husband. I assure you
I do not. He is too weak to bear the force of that . . . even if I
felt it, and I am not a cruel woman. But I hate this life here. I
hate this place. And I have grave doubts that I will be able to
endure it for long after this . . . *débâcle* . . . this hideousness.'

Appalled by the woman's candour, aware that no word of
demurral would answer, Louisa looked down on her unspeaking. Emilia wished only to be heard. She sought neither argument nor consolation. She was a woman alone, making as best
she might a terrible virtue of her solitude. A time might come
when she would regret these words, when she would hate Louisa
for having heard them. But they must be heard. And in silence
that passed no judgment, that neither condoned nor denied.

Louisa's hands were very cold.

'You are wondering why I tell you this. It is because if I tell
no one it will drive me mad, and I have no wish to be mad. That
is why I must leave this place. There is nothing for me here,
don't you see? It is a wilderness. There are no people.' Emilia
was breathing quickly now, almost panting. 'I cannot even grieve
over this child, for it would have kept me here. I didn't want it
. . . not here. It would have been my gaoler.' She looked up at
Louisa in appeal. 'I have to get away from here, you see. It must
be done. Not yet. Not quite yet. But soon.'

'Your husband,' Louisa said, '—does he know of these feelings?'

Emilia narrowed her eyes. 'He knows but he will not hear.
He will not speak of it. He dare not. But it will happen . . . not
quite yet but at the point where he will no longer hinder me with
the pretence that he would have me stay. He must want me to
go.'

Louisa was held by those urgent eyes, drawn more deeply
than she would have wished into the darkness behind. 'Can you
be so sure that that will happen?'

'I shall make it happen.'

'And your husband. What shall become . . . ?'

Emilia silenced her with a raised finger. 'That also is why I
am telling you this. Edwin is a weak man. You will discover that
for yourself, if you have not already done so. He will suffer, of
course . . . as I have suffered . . . but he will not leave. Not at

first. He will not feel able to leave, and so for a time he will strive to manage alone. He may even make a good appearance of doing so. And he will have the sympathy of the entire parish, of course. But eventually he will need help. He will need care. He will need to be told what he must do.' Emilia stared at Louisa. 'You will think me a terrible woman. Perhaps I am. But I am not without feeling. And I meant what I said about you at the start of this. You may still be a child but you are the only person in this dreadful place who understands the meaning of care. You must promise that you will show it to him as you have done to me.'

Louisa was transfixed by the woman's gaze. She felt as though a web had been thrown over her, the same web in which—however little he knew it—Edwin Frere was deeply entangled. As though to tighten it a hand came to rest on hers. Cold as it was, Louisa could feel its power. She felt that all compassion must have passed from Emilia with the emptying of her womb except for this last residue that smouldered in the promise she exacted now. For a moment they were both looking at the gold band on Emilia's wedding-finger. Louisa was breathing very quickly. Something must be done to free her from this grip.

'Mrs Frere,' she began, ' . . . Emilia, I think it of the utmost importance that . . .'

'Promise me.'

'I cannot believe that . . .'

'It is true. Promise me. I implore you.' The grip tightened. 'Promise me, or I shall have no peace.'

As she looked down into that face on which all tears had long since dried, Louisa had the deranging sensation that she was in the presence of a dying woman.

'Should it come to pass . . .'

'It will. There is no other way. It will come to pass.' And Louisa saw the finality of the woman's will. It was quite absolute.

'Then I must promise.'

But the hand was still held.

'Edwin must know nothing of this. This confidence is sacred. You have accepted it.'

Confused, almost in tears, Louisa nodded.

Emilia sighed and released her grip. Her head relaxed back on the pillow. 'Leave me now,' she said. 'I must say my prayers.'

In a trance of dismay Louisa saw that the woman was very far from death; she was no longer ill; not even, as she had earlier been, unhappy. She was gathering her strength for the season of ice that must settle over Munding Rectory.

9 ▓ The Firing

Back at The Pightle, outside the magic circle of the Decoy Lodge, I woke to the Monday sound of rain. A fine drizzle dripped from the thatch-eaves and brought the scent of the box-hedge through the open window. When I switched on the radio a sober voice intoned the day's bad news. I lay there trying to square what I heard with the new enthusiasm derived from Edward and Laura, for I'd left the Lodge around two in the morning, ready to set off with them the next day in search of the horizon.

The whisky had helped, of course, and something anarchic in me responded to Laura's brightened mood. Edward had become sparkier and we laughed a lot. I remembered peeing with him under the stars, asking questions about the danger of translating a private spiritual vision into social action. After all, fanatic ayatollahs and born-again Christians eager for the Rapture set no encouraging example. He talked about those who had been fired by the spirit but had lost touch with the soul; about unassimilated shadows which foisted evil on to enemies rather than bringing responsibility back home; he talked of tight-ropes and sword-bridges and the narrow course between the clashing rocks. Then, fastening his zip, he said, 'One must trust to that star in man which is the visionary imagination. It wants to live, to thrive. And the star'—he tipped his head in the general direction of the galaxies—'is the perfect symbol for the hope it brings because, like a star, it is glimpsed most clearly from the corner of the eye.'

Heady stuff, and to reject it outright with a condescending

intellectual leer would have felt like a return trip down the chute into futility; but now, with the radio offering a bleaker view of things, I was less certain why I'd agreed so eagerly to meet him in the library of the Hall this morning.

Bob came by, his umbrella dripping at the door. Apparently he'd called the previous evening and been surprised I wasn't there. He was just checking that I hadn't left for good, was glad that I hadn't, and was that real coffee he could smell?

I liked Bob. He was predictable but that contrasted happily with Edward's slippery shifts of mood, and there was nothing abstract about either his neighbourliness or his politics. Both were a generous extension of human decency. For him, humanism and socialism were the logical development of that common sense which was his strength and, perhaps, his limitation. Now he was a retired countryman with time on his hands, looking for company. It felt churlish to tell him that I was in a hurry, that the coffee would have to be quick. In Munding nobody was in a hurry.

'I see,' he said when he learned that I was meeting Edward. 'That where you were last night?'

I nodded, placing a steaming mug before him. He sipped it hot, hummed his appreciation. 'So have you found out what it is yet?'

I looked across at him, unconnected.

'His obsession.'

'I'm not sure I'd call it that.'

'What would you call it?'

'He is working on something. In fact, that's why I'm meeting him. He thinks I might be able to lend a hand.'

'I see. The man he wouldn't have a use for is now lending a hand.'

I'd forgotten that I'd said that, and was, in any case, already regretting the admission. I was also beginning to see why Edward had been loth to speak openly about his work. Incredulity in one's listener is a great silencer, particularly when it verges on ridicule, and Bob was likely to prove a milder critic than I had been.

'May one ask what with?'

I had been thinking quickly. 'Some historical research he's doing.'

'I thought he didn't believe in history.'

'It's about the Agnew family. Some of Ralph's ancestors.'

'Did they do something interesting then? Struck me as a dull lot by and large. On the wrong side in the Civil War, profiteering from the Napoleonic Wars, dutifully sending two sons to get butchered in Flanders. Mindless gentry—with a single decent exception. One of them made a stand for repeal of the Corn Laws, which must have taken some guts in this neck of the woods.' Then Bob smiled as if in dawning realization. ' 'Course, I suppose our friend might be interested in old Madcap Agnew. Kindred spirit there perhaps. Notorious boozer and woman-izer.'

'I don't think so.'

But Bob had warmed to the idea. 'Your typical Regency rake-hell, that one. Declared incompetent in the end and locked away. G.P.I.' Bob tapped his nose and added, 'Syphilis to you. But hardly worth a book, I'd have thought.'

'That's not what he's doing.'

'Then what?'

How to answer? How to account for the improbable mating of a dream and—yes, Bob was probably right—an obsession. If I were to try to explain the little I understood about alchemy it would run through my fingers like water. I would do no better with my dream. Though he had been a psychiatric nurse Bob attached more value to medication and group therapy than to dream interpretation. He would have steered well clear of the wilder shores of analytic enquiry. He had been a sort of excellent Ambulance Brigade man in a world of psychological casualties, and was in no doubt that the cause of mental stress was largely social: people went mad in a mad world. So far, and no further, would he and Edward have agreed.

I said, 'I'll tell you when I understand it better myself.'

'Curiouser and curiouser, said Alice. Which ancestor is it then?'

'Henry Agnew—mid-nineteenth century—and . . .'

'The Corn Laws man.'

'I didn't know that.'

'What else is interesting about him?'

'He was . . . a poet.'

'Ah, I see. I didn't know *that*. Was he any good?'

'I'm not sure.'

Again the dubious regard—it seemed I wasn't sure of very much. 'Nesbit needs help making up his mind?'

'There's a lot of stuff to read. It's still in manuscript.'

Lamer and lamer, but Bob was discreet enough not to press. Or perhaps he'd simply lost interest in the diversions of aesthetes. 'I should have thought your time would be better spent studying the common people. The leisured classes have had more attention than they deserve. What about the poor beggars who were worked to death to feed them? Have you any idea what it was like round here in those days?—women and kids out in the fields till all hours, gleaning, stone-picking, hauling the wagons when they got bogged down. Life in this place'—a tilt of the head took in The Pightle—'must have been squalid. Short commons, endless insecurity, real fear of losing the roof over their heads, and all the best men cropped—packed off to Botany Bay for poaching. This was a real village once—none of your weekend cottages and retirement homes like mine. And England wasn't very merry, I can tell you—not in the hungry Forties.' He sighed, shook his head gloomily. 'The way things are going we'll be back there soon. Victorian values! Power and money with a bit of sanctimonious charity thrown in to square the consciences—that's what your Victorian gentry cared about. Like this bloody government.'

Listening, I felt still more unsure of the meaning and relevance of Edward's enterprise. Bob knocked back his coffee, and I was about to stand when he said, 'Listen, Alex, I don't know if I should say this to a poet, but there are some things a damn sight more urgent than the doggerel of a dead country squire. Have you heard the news lately?'

He took in my grimace and sniffed. 'Makes you sick. I mean, how the devil did we let things get this way?' He looked up, not expecting an answer, but to fix me with his stare. 'It's our fault—my generation. Two bloody wars and we're still content to snooze and let that lot get on with it. Gave our power away, you see, and there are always people ready to grab it. Time we woke up again. Are you in CND, Alex?'

'I'm not a joiner, Bob.'

'You should think about it. Bet you didn't know, for instance, that there's a nuclear siren right here in the village? In Munding, for God's sake! Horrible little black box it is, bang over Mrs Jex's head at the Post Office. A sort of gauge with a dial that shifts from red alert to black alert . . . to warn of fall-out. Mrs Jex says it gives her nightmares. I mean, what's she supposed to do if it goes off—waddle round the village telling us all to duck? It's bloody madness. That'll soon put a stop to Nesbit's historical research . . . put a stop to history altogether.'

'He's not blind to the facts, Bob.'

'But what's he doing about them—card tricks?'

Casting about, I found only platitude. 'It takes all sorts . . .'

Bob harumphed but saw the quick glance at my watch. Sighing, he got up. He had tried. At the door he turned. 'How's the girl?'

'Laura? She's fine.'

A searching moment indicated that it was my motives rather than her welfare that were under question.

The conversation had been unsettling in other ways. As I walked through the drizzle I imagined showing up at Bob's CND group and saying, 'Don't worry. It's okay. If Edward and I can sort out the secret of the Hermetic Mystery your problems are over. It's all a matter of Pelicans, you see . . .'

Only Bob, with his experience as a psychiatric nurse, would take me seriously.

No, what drew me to the Hall was personal. Profoundly personal. The aftermath, perhaps, of the panic-stricken self-absorption that had seized my life after Jess's defection. The sense that something new was needed if I was to learn to breathe on empty air. Booze had not worked. Sex had not worked. Both had ended in the humiliation of that brawl at a dance and me taking a swing at a hapless policeman. It was that sense which had brought me to Munding, which had set me hunting the Green Man in the woods. It had been intensified by the mysterious directive of my dream, and by the provocative conversations with Edward. What I was doing now was no crazier—and no less crazy—than they; but I was not about to pretend that the future of the planet depended on my explorations. Only me—my future: Alex Darken taking another step in the daft jig of his life, pushed from the rear by his own dark dreams. No rationalist after all: a terminal romantic.

Ralph Agnew was standing in the porch of his Estate Office, talking to his gamekeeper, George Bales, a tall, booted man wearing a green nylon anorak ripped at the sleeve. I'd seen him in the Feathers, surly in his own corner of the Snug, not liked by, not liking, the other villagers. Had I known I was trespassing on his domain I would never have entered the woods so lightly.

He nodded as Ralph greeted me, touched the neb of his flat cap, and walked away.

'You're looking for Edward, right?' Ralph said. 'Expected you sooner. He's up in the library already.'

'Bob Crossley called in—held me up.'

'No hurry, old chap. Those papers have been there for more than a century. Drop more dust won't hurt. Glad you and Edward have hit it off. Had a feeling you might. Bit of a shaky start though?'

'He's an unusual man.'

'A rum'n—that's what they call him round here. Solid gold, though. Solid gold.'

'Aurum non vulgi.' I smiled.

Ralph narrowed his eyes at me, further dislocating the lop-sided twist to his face. 'Latin scholar, I hear.'

'Hardly that.'

'Not what Edward tells me. Anyway, you should be some help to him and he needs it. Frankly, what he's up to . . . Well, it's all Greek to me, but so long as it keeps him happy.' He glanced away, almost as though in embarrassment. I had the feeling of a patron drawn deeper than he would have liked into the unpredictable consequences of his generosity—a lonely figure, heir to the Agnew fortune and tradition, yet unmarried, childless, last of his line. Edward could not be typical of his friends, but I remembered that Clive had called him a friend to verse, and that he had read my work. There must be more to this country squire than was disclosed by his clipped mannerisms and his habit of smiling each time he spoke, as though to ease his way through a dubious world. He looked at his watch. 'Well, I have an appointment in Saxburgh, and Edward will be wondering where you are.' He leaned towards me, confidential. 'Take care of him, won't you? He's not nearly as tough as he makes out. Been through some bad times, you see.' The smile had gone. The corner of his lips twitched a little with a solemnity which suggested only a matter of some gravity would persuade him to venture this close to the personal. Then, before I could respond, he resumed the seigneurial stance. 'You know your way up?'

I did, and to my disappointment, I found Edward alone in the library.

'Thought you'd backed out,' he muttered as I took off my damp coat.

'Sorry. I got held up. Laura not here?'

Edward sniffed and looked away. 'Laura has work of her own.'
I waited for further explanation and none came. Edward's fingers drummed on the edge of the desk. I was the new boy at the office, he the old hand wondering what to make of me; but if he was having second thoughts he dismissed them in a sudden grin. 'Right, there are some books I want you to look at—general background to give you the feel of the thing. But I thought we might take a quick look at the muniments room first. Come on through.'

A door from the library led through into an oak-panelled room with tall mullioned windows. 'I've sorted out all the stuff from our period.' he said. 'It's over there.' He pointed across to where a corner of the room was stacked with coffers, cabin-trunks, packing cases, pile upon pile of what looked like shoe-boxes and other cardboard containers. 'They're all full of papers,' he said. 'You see my problem?'

I saw. But already I was half in love with the old library. I hadn't been there by daylight before and my bibliophile heart had lifted at the sight of those tall glass cabinets, shelf over shelf of finely bound volumes, each of them a door on the possible. The air was still as a church in there, the rainy light playing through the leaded windows with their view across the parkland and the lake. It was a dream-chamber, redolent of leather and polish and the scented dust of books. And, yes, smelling of centuries of privilege too, of aloof refined seclusion. In the normal run of things I would have had no business there, no access. This, however, was not the normal run of things.

Nor were the books that Edward showed me the kind of thing I would normally have read—not, at least, as anything more than a casual browse among the dustier nooks of human eccentricity. It was like stepping from the main street into a cobbled alley's curiosity shop—that shock of surprise to discover again what an intricate and peculiar organ the imagination is, what extravagant uses it has found for time.

Even under Edward's guidance it proved difficult to feel my way into the texts he gave me to read. They were tantalizingly obscure—no sooner did you think you'd begun to grasp the gist when it slipped through your fingers. Again and again apparently rational lines of argument suddenly congealed into a porridge of images, while some texts dispensed with argument completely and the mind was left to wrestle with Olympian assertions that left Edward's own rhetoric sounding like cool logic. Witness the Smaragdine Tablet of Hermes Trismegistus, which was, he assured me, the seminal document of all alchemical thought:

> True, without error, certain and most true; that which is above is as that which is below, and that which is below is as that which is above, for performing the miracles of the One Thing; and as all things were from One, by the mediation of One, so all things arose from this One Thing by adaptation; the father of it is the Sun, the mother of it is the Moon; the wind carries it in its belly; the nurse thereof is the Earth. This is the father of all perfection, or consummation of the whole world. The power of it is integral, if it be turned into earth. Thou shalt separate the earth from the fire, the subtle from the gross, gently with great sagacity; it ascends from earth to heaven, and again descends to earth; and receives the strength of the superiors and the inferiors—so thou hast the glory of the superiors and the inferiors—so thou hast the glory of the whole world; therefore let all obscurity flee before thee. This is the strong fortitude of all fortitudes, overcoming every subtle and penetrating every solid thing. So the world was created. Hence were all wonderful adaptations of which this is the manner. Therefore am I called Thrice Great Hermes, having the Three Parts of the philosophy of the whole world. That which I have written is consummated concerning the operation of the sun.

Faced with such rhapsodic prose I felt it would take more subtlety and sagacity than I could command to make obscurity flee before me.

'But don't you see?' Edward encouraged. 'The whole point is to excite curiosity, to stimulate the sleeping powers of the mind. If I talk about "psychic integration" or reunion with the Divine Archetype, these are abstractions on which the mind has little purchase. But if I speak of a stone that turneth all to gold, or a treasure hidden in the menstruum of whores, then the imagination is set to work. The rational intellect is side-stepped and one must look within. I mean even the highest spirit of Reason which, according to Nicholas of Cusa, guards the gate in the wall around Paradise—a wall which is built of contradictions. If we are ever to pass through what a shrewd American has named the "moronic inferno" into what I call "the oxymoronic paradiso," then responses from a deeper level are required. That's what these texts demand.'

'You don't think it's more likely to put people off altogether?'

'That too is the point. The one-sided man who clings to rationality will dismiss it all as gibberish—a word, incidentally, derived from Jabir, one of the greatest of Arab adepts. If he goes hunting through the texts for a quick recipe for gold or earthly power he'll soon get lost, give up. But the man who desires to know himself more completely—however strange and confusing his discoveries may be—he is drawn further within until he finds in the texts a mirror of his own complexity. And—if he is lucky— of the simple secret at its heart.'

'So the language acts as a kind of filter?'

'On one level, yes. But as a poet you will appreciate that some experiences are communicable only through symbols—symbols which lose all virtue in any attempt at paraphrase or analysis. Symbols are the deep grammar of experience, and the alchemist inhabits a symbolic universe. He means precisely what he says—but one must enter the language on its own terms or the meaning vanishes. However, without access to the transforming experience from which those symbols spring they remain impenetrable.'

Like much of your own verse?' I hazarded.

Caught on the hop, Edward frowned. For a moment I expected a knuckle-rapping response, but after a brief hesitation, he said, 'My verse was obscure because I was obscure to myself. I was a young man then . . . a young fool. I heard the music but I had no inkling how serious these matters were. Or how dangerous.' He returned from a pained abstraction, and smiled at me a little ruefully. 'I was much like you—infatuated with my own talent, worshipping only my own intellect . . . A crime for which, as Ficino points out, a capital punishment is appointed. And in the symbolic domain the punishment is entirely appropriate—dismemberment, beheading.' His thoughts shifted quickly away. 'Ficino. *The Asclepian Dialogue of Hermes* . . . Now there's a text that speaks plainly enough.' He wandered to the shelves and came back thumbing through an old volume. 'Listen to this: *No one shall look up to Heaven. The religious man shall be counted insane; the irreligious shall be thought wise; the furious, brave; and the worst of men shall be considered good. For the soul, and all things about it, shall not only*

be the subjects of laughter, but shall be considered as vanity.
Every divine voice shall, by a necessary silence, be dumb; the
fruits of the earth shall be corrupted; and the air itself shall
languish with a sorrowful stupor. The language may sound archaic,' he commented, 'but he got his facts right. Henry Agnew
saw that time coming. Look here.' He showed me the page of
the book—the passage had been furiously scored with a pen nib.
'Well, it's here now—and it's time that silence was broken.'
Edward looked up again and stared into my frown. 'Stay with
it. Eventually things will come clearer. Or better still—ignore
the words for the moment. Concentrate on the pictures. I think
you'll find they speak the language of your dreams.'

From the densely stacked bookcases he took down some lav-
ishly illustrated volumes and left me alone to wonder at them.
Those illustrations were like admission to someone else's
dreams—at times glowing with visionary fire, at others the
pitchblende hallucinations of a tormented mind. Set in rich Ve-
netian palaces or wild surrealist landscapes, they might depict
the slow death of a bearded king, or miners at work beneath an
enchanted hill. There were chariots driven by demons, pulled
by strange winged beasts. Sun-kings and Moon-queens stood in
stately adoration of each other or, in other guises, warred.
Childish lovers sported in a glass retort. A black three-headed
hell-hound rent and devoured the pathetic human figures in its
power. I was an innocent let loose in an exotic, heraldic kingdom of mythical beasts and grotesque hermaphroditic figures
that rose from the copulations of the kings and their sister-
queens. Yet in that fantastic cavalcade of monsters, freaks and
angels, there were two moments in which I recognized something of myself.

The first was when I came across a picture of a heavily ar-
moured man jousting with a naked woman, like knights at a
tournament. He had the sun for his head, she the moon. He was
riding a lion, she side-saddle on a black gryphon, and they were
fighting. But they both had shields against which the lances
struck, and the beauty of it was that on her shield was the insig-
nia of the sun, on his that of the moon; so they were each pro-
tected by the principle they opposed. The background against
which they fought was arid red desert; they might have been
fighting to make it green again; yet one had the feeling that if
either defeated the other it would be disaster. More eloquently
than a thousand words the picture showed the need for, and the

difficulty of, reconciliation between the sexes. I began to loosen my armour.

Later I turned a page and uttered a gasp of stunned surprise that made Edward look up from the manuscript he scrutinized. He came across to look at the image open on my lectern: a wild man covered in shaggy green fur was fighting a little lion with a club. The drawing had a sprightly vigorous line, and there was a pleasing rhythmic balance between the sway of the wild man's body and the crouch of the snarling beast. The Green Man wore a coronet of leaves and a girdle of stems at his waist. The unknown artist had painted the fur with such a delicate brush you felt you might stroke it. The bearded face smiled in its mantle of green hair.

'You recognize him?' Edward asked.

I nodded, silent.

'Another dream?'

'I keep bumping into him. I've been trying to write about him for weeks.'

Edward looked up from the picture and studied me for a long moment. 'Perhaps you will,' he said eventually. 'Perhaps you will.'

I wasn't left to ramble through this new realm for long. Edward brought me a box of Louisa's file cards and a scholarly Latin dictionary. 'Time you got stuck in,' he said. 'You've seen how much there is to do.'

The plain fact was I had not grasped the magnitude of Edward's task when he first unfolded it to me. There was a mountain of paper in the muniments room, the neglected monument to decades of industry, neatly hand-written in paling ink. It was worse than a mountain—it was a maze; and how intricate its twists I soon discovered.

I tried to picture what she must have been like, the young woman who had diligently allowed her life to fade away working at this solitary chore. The years of her youth had been sacrificed to her father's obsession. Why hadn't she rebelled—gone crazy even? Perhaps she had; but there was nothing mad about the composed face I'd been shown in the portrait and the photograph, only an infinity of patience. That patience must have been well-schooled here, and I would need lots of it myself if I was to follow her tracks from card to cryptic card through all the boxes. Still, I wasn't being paid—I'd resisted Edward's offer of money; I was pretty sure he didn't have much and, for the moment, I didn't need it. Unpaid, I could drop this when I chose.

Yet once I started work I became increasingly absorbed. The oddly medieval flavour of the Latin notes intrigued me, and there were occasional memoranda in the formal English of Louisa's day. *Here is evidence*, I read on one card, *that the Pagan Mysteries were instituted pure*. And on another: *Here it is manifest how the Way of Life is found only through a Death, and that, without the deprival of all other knowledge, Self-Knowledge itself is not to be achieved. An admirable paradox!* It was like listening to a voice whispering across time, an eerie sensation that became a frisson when I read: *Time was, Time is, and Time shall be, but here the Adept stands outside of time within the penetralium of mystery.*

Though much of what I translated defied comprehension, it was provocatively enigmatic. I began to see what Edward had meant about secrecy being a great enticer, about how the sleeping powers of the mind might wake. And there was something else. Daunting and preposterous as the task appeared, I was glad to be busy again, of use. When Edward saw that I was willing to work, and that the ground covered in a day could be almost doubled with my help, he relaxed and became more open with me.

As the days passed in the library I increasingly understood why Laura had been attracted to Edward—the wry, sidespin dart of his humour, the sudden shy warmth of expressed affection, the uncompromising certainty that in all things meaning inhered, and the strict honesty which refused glib answers. Had I not worked closely with him I would have seen little of this. He wouldn't have bothered to show it; I would have been too arrogant to look. But work is a firm bonder, and never more so than when a task is both fascinating and absurdly difficult.

What we were faced with was an enormous puzzle—a cryptic crossword with the clues in Latin, unnumbered, and not much of a grid for guide. I translated the clues and passed them across to Edward who frowned over them, making entries in his own files, collating cards with texts, referring often to Louisa's journals and Henry's copious notes, trying to piece a pattern together. Confronted with such vast heaps of material one had to think of it as a game. That was how I saw it: Henry and Louisa Agnew, long dead but mysteriously alive under this mountain of paper, were one team; Edward and I the other. It began to feel—

though I suppose this is true to the essential beauty of all sport—
that we were working together, the four of us, for the love of the
game.

Gradually the outlines of the Hermetic myth came clear to
me. Like more orthodox Christians, the alchemists maintained
that mankind had suffered a fall; but this lapse from grace was
not seen merely as a matter of original sin. It was a critical
moment in the great experiment of Nature. It was the very access of consciousness—life's arrival at the moment where it
might contemplate and shape its own existence. But consciousness comes at a price, and the price is banishment from the
Garden. When we wake it is to find ourselves alone and separate, trapped in the toils of matter.

There were close links between the alchemists and the gnostics, and for the gnostics the picture was bleaker still. Life in
the material world was tragic, they claimed—so evil that it could
not be the work of a benevolent God. The universe itself was
cracked. It was the creation of the Demiurge, the Archon, the
mad lord of this world. It was wrong to value it, wrong to bear
children even, for that was only to add to the sum of suffering.
It was the task of the spirit to resist complicity, even to the point
of burning for this belief—this *knowledge*—for it was, of course,
entirely unacceptable to orthodox Christianity.

For the Christians the only answer to the human plight was
trust in the redemptive love of Christ. For the alchemists such
passive dependence was not enough. In every human body, they
insisted, there remains a spark of the Divine Principle which
once irradiated its entire being. Cased in the base metal of our
fallen state, this 'star-fire' yearns to return whence it came. It
longs to be golden again. The alchemists maintained that through
the correct disciplines such a return might be made. If one knew
how to go about it the Fall was reversible.

The transmutation of base metal to gold was the paradigm of
this sacred task. Unlike the Indian mystics they did not regard
the material world as mere illusion, though they were not blind
to its illusory aspects. A seed of star-fire lay imprisoned in all
things. It might be freed. Matter itself might be redeemed and
made translucent. In working to change the substances, the alchemists also changed themselves. In changing themselves they
added their own weight to the effort by which the world itself

might be changed. It was clear that their economy was based on no common gold.

But what to make of this? Much as I might personally long for a world where sun and moon danced together and all the trees clapped their hands, it remained intangible. It remained a myth. And, yes, Edward could point out that we live in a time when the very meaning of the word *myth* has been debased, that it has come to signify only what is untrue, false, misleading; and, yes, I could largely agree that it is nevertheless by myths we live, and what matters is how large the contrary truths a myth reconciles in its embrace. But here I still sat, unenlightened, puzzling.

I saw only that, in this magical new view of the world to which I had been introduced, scepticism and gullibility must be harnessed in tandem if nothing was to be missed. Such an attitude required fresh springs of energy, and the effect—I was delighted to sense it as I woke each day—was to make me more bouncy and mettlesome than I had been for weeks.

For three days I went into the library at the Hall hoping to find Laura there and each day I was disappointed. Each evening when we tidied away our papers I expected Edward to invite me over to the Lodge for a drink or a meal, and the invitation was not extended. Much as the work fascinated me, and fonder each day as I became of Edward, there was nevertheless a growing sense of frustration. It was Laura who had first recruited me to this task, she who had seen that I might be involved. It was the thought of her that had drawn me back to the Lodge with my dream, and if this odd enterprise had any meaning at all it must lie, I believed, somewhere between the three of us. Yet studiously, subtly, with no obvious exertion on Edward's part, Laura and I were being kept at a distance. Was that perhaps what she wanted? Or need I look no further than the old man's unspoken mistrust of my intentions? I suspected the latter.

It both peeved and amused me. From my angle Edward and I were now firm friends. His charm had seduced me. He had my affection and my loyalty, and I thought I deserved his trust. Yet he had a way of manipulating our conversations on to ground of his choosing where he spoke so admirably that only afterwards did one realize how other issues, other questions, had been delicately side-stepped. So Laura remained, like Louisa herself, a silent, invisible presence between us.

The next day Edward came late to the library in an untypically gloomy mood. As I worked at my translations I heard him mutter and grunt at his desk. He seemed fixed in a dour, obsessive concentration that defied approach. It was a hot day. Through the tall leaded windows the bright span of water flittered and shone. It felt absurd that we should be indoors poring over papers when we might have been out there, basking in dappled sunlight, bathing in the lake. I was restless, sticky under the armpits, for the first time a little bored. Laura was more on my mind than Louisa. What was she doing? Had she begun to resent my usurpation of her role as Edward's collaborator? Our silence about her was ridiculous. I made up my mind to broach the issue over lunch.

I suggested that it was a waste of a glorious day to eat indoors. Why didn't we make a picnic by the lake? 'Might as well,' he agreed. 'I'm getting nowhere here.' When we had eaten in silence I asked him what the trouble was.

'I sometimes think Sisyphus had an easier task,' he said without humour. 'Just when you think you're on to something it all unravels.'

'Do I detect the voice of the demon Doubt?'

'I don't know. Take no notice of me. I had a bad night.'

I smelled some recurrence of the tension between him and Laura and looked for a way to open the subject. 'It's a pity that Laura didn't just ask Louisa what her secret was—when she saw her, I mean.' It had been intended lightly but Edward was not amused.

'I'd rather you didn't joke about that.'

'You really believe that she saw her?'

'I know she did.'

I sat in silence, waiting.

'And Ralph knows it too. There were details to her description she could have known no other way.'

'I'm impressed.' I caught the dubious lift of Edward's brow. 'It was only the one time?'

'There have been other experiences.'

'Such as?'

'As you clearly don't trust them there seems little point in going into them.' His tone was final. A cold silence came between us. After a time I said, 'I'm sorry. My flippancy . . . habit of a lifetime.'

'Not a lifetime. Merely a trick you learned in college. As a child you would have known better.'

'Before my star-fire dimmed?'

Edward saw that he was teased, and smiled. 'Only your brain is dim. But I imagine even that is bright enough to recognize an extraordinary woman when it sees one.'

'No argument. Tell me about her.'

'Laura can speak for herself.'

'Except that I don't get to see much of her.'

The web of lines around Edward's eyes wrinkled in a frown. 'Your tone would seem to imply that I am some sort of Blue-beard who keeps her incarcerated. The fact is she is busy.'

'At what?'

'Her own work.'

'Which is?'

Wisdom teeth have been more easily drawn. A long moment passed before he sniffed and said, 'She is a potter.'

'Really? I'd no idea. She has a wheel at the Lodge?'

'She doesn't work with the wheel. Her pots are hand-built. She makes her own glazes from vegetable ash and fires them in a small wood-burning kiln we built together.'

'A sort of practical alchemy?'

'Precisely.'

I began to realize how inadequate my picture of Laura was; that I had made no room in my thoughts for an independent life of her own, let alone one as earthed and pragmatic as the potter's craft. No wonder I'd seen so little of her. She was busy, making, while Edward and I ballooned through the intellectual strato-sphere with nothing to show for our efforts but an increase of paper. I was intrigued by what we were doing, but no one would ever eat or drink from it. It lacked substance—almost as much as had my fantasies that Edward was deliberately keeping us apart. I said, 'I'd very much like to see some of her work.'

'I doubt she will let you.'

'Why not?'

'It is a private matter. No one goes into her studio. I have seen little of her work myself, and she won't thank me for men-tioning it. Most of it she destroys.'

'But why?'

'Because she has no wish to add to the sum of things in the world unless they answer. To her dream of the real, I mean. It

is very exacting. Also I am quite certain she would wish me to
say no more about it.'

'So Louisa isn't the only one with secrets?'

Again Edward did not smile. 'There is much in Laura's world
that is private. It is a matter of protection. She is best understood
as a refugee. Her confidence is . . . fragile.'

I tried to marry this judgment with the memory of the sturdy
young woman I'd seen joking in the glade; who had come breez-
ily into The Pightle telling me to water the plants and daring me
to a duel of wits with Edward; who had seemed so certain of
me over against his cautious vacillation. *Fragile* was not the first
word that would have occurred to me, unless I had overlooked
something vital—something which, I remembered, Bob had
noted.

As for Edward—it was clear that I'd stumbled on to sensitive
ground. He was staring at the lake, regretful perhaps that he'd
said too much not to say more. 'There have been . . . difficulties
in her life.'

No further question was invited, so I said, 'It must get pretty
lonely out at the Lodge.'

'She likes it that way.'

But I remembered her asking whether I didn't go crazy on my
own at The Pightle. 'Not all the time, surely? I mean, the other
night—she seemed to cheer up then. You're sure she doesn't
need company?'

'I've tried to tell her that. But she's working very hard right
now. Perhaps too hard. Now that you've freed her a little from
my demands, you see . . .'

I saw that I might, in more than one way, have been used.

'Don't misunderstand me. She's very much with us in spirit.
What you saw the other night . . . it happens, yes. We get tired
and sometimes we take it out on one another. But . . .' He
turned to look across at me. 'We mean a great deal to each
other.' There was an appeal in his eyes, almost a throwing of
himself upon my mercy. 'I helped her through a bad time, you
see. One that involved disturbing experiences of her gifts . . .
They weren't understood. Which is why she still prefers not to
speak of them. No one understood their importance until . . .'

'She met you.'

'Yes.'

His eyes shifted away again. I wondered whether he was not,
after all, over-protective. It wouldn't be the first time that a man

had lovingly supported a woman through crisis only to discover that when she was strong again his own need was to confine her in a dependent role. There were gentle ways of playing Bluebeard too.

'I wouldn't want you to think it's all one way,' he resumed uncertainly. 'For me . . . Well, when we came together . . . It renewed my own sense of meaning. I had been preoccupied with the alchemical vision for some time, but it had become words, ideas, a mere prejudice in favour of the angels, if you like. But Laura *was* what I could only think. What I have to struggle for again and again is instinct with her. She makes it real for me. Sometimes I think to her cost . . .'

Something wondering and recapitulatory in his tone brought to mind the way I had often spoken of Jess in her absence: odd, I thought, the way men tended to prize their partners more highly when they were elsewhere; almost as though the idea of relationship was more satisfactory than its practice. Neither of us had been prepared for this sudden release of feeling; Edward seemed embarrassed by the confession, I embarrassed by his embarrassment, and regretting my earlier ungenerous thoughts . . . Embarrassing too, the recognition that my interest in Laura remained less innocent than I'd persuaded myself. Edward clearly adored her; I had no wish to hurt him, so perhaps things were best as they were—he and I working alone. But my heart dipped at the thought.

In the meantime Edward had been thinking too. This was the first time he had shared anything personal with me, and that he could let the mask slip a little was a measure of his growing trust. A shy smile hinted that he did not entirely regret it. Then he slapped his thigh, stood up, leaping from embarrassment to action. 'But you're right, dammit. She needs to get out of herself. We all do. We should do something together. We should go to the sea.'

I looked up in amazement at the abrupt shift.

'That's it.' He clapped his hands together. 'Come on.'

'But if she doesn't want to leave her work . . .'

'I'll seduce her. I'll charm her from the tree. Great God, I've become a bore. I've forgotten how to laugh. I need to dance again.' He did a sprightly two-step, twirled, and was off across the lawn, shouting. 'Come on, Darken. On your feet. *Thalassa!* The sea, the sea!'

* * *

Friends then, the three of us—me sitting in the back of the old Countryman as it rattled along, Edward at the wheel singing Verdi as though he'd just found the key to the Hermetic Mystery if not that of the aria he'd chosen, while Laura, who had taken some persuading, groaned and laughed beside him. We headed for the north Norfolk coast, careering through the bright afternoon until Edward parked by a staithe where a creek coiled across a salt marsh, and we all piled out. The mastheads of beached yachts tinkled in a stiff breeze. It was a place of sea-pinks and oyster-catchers, where small birds dusted their wings in fennel and made the air smell of aniseed. Mudbound tideposts staggered out into the creek, and out across the flats a marram-fastened line of sand-dunes concealed the distant sea. Edward was the only one of us who had been here before. Clearly he loved the place.

He struck out on the diked path that sheltered a corn-field from the sea wind. It was the still afternoon of a weekday in term-time, and we had the world to ourselves.

After a long walk we came out between the dunes and were staring at the sea. The tide was far out over a wide plain of sand but you could see its many colours silvering towards those reaches where sky and horizon misted together. The expanse of beach was so denuded of any trace of the present century we might have stepped out on to a distant planet. Again I wondered at Edward's way of making me feel like the useless son out of a folk-tale who had stumbled by chance into the hollow hills. I stood with the breeze flapping at my collar, watching the spin-drift sand, promising that one day I would write about this place. When I turned I saw Edward dancing on the shore.

'He really needed this.' Laura was standing a little behind me, smiling as the wind tousled her hair.

'He said much the same about you.'

'Then he was right. He usually is . . . in the end.'

'About everything?'

'About what matters.' She glanced across at me, flicking the hair from her face. 'What about you?'

'Oh I'm usually wrong.'

She caught my smile. 'Dumb-bell! I mean how are you?'

How was I? Glad to be here. Feeling good about the air and sea. A little sad suddenly. I said, 'Fine. In better shape than I was.'

'That's good.'

'Also slightly cross-eyed over those texts.'

For a second she was puzzled by the change of tack, then smiled, wrinkling her nose. 'They're really weird, don't you think?'

'I'm surprised you think so.'

She shrugged, looked out to sea again. 'They're Edward's thing, not mine. I can't read them—not for long. They pile up on me. I mean, they're so dense—the language, the symbols. Like an Austrian church—too full of stuff. I like things simple.'

'I'm glad to hear it. I was beginning to think it was me who was dense.'

But she ignored the joke, looked out across the duneland expanse, the wide acreage of sand and sea. 'They go on and on about Nature, but just look at it. No clutter. Nothing superfluous. Just light and air, changing all the time, moving through places that words won't reach.'

'But unaware of itself? It needs us to give it voice.'

'Maybe that's just our need. It has voices of its own—the necessary sounds. Not like all those books. It's my guess that Louisa came to feel this way—that that's why she burned her book. I think she might have done it without regret.'

'Does Edward know you feel this way?'

'I've never said it before. I'm not even sure what I mean. Perhaps that's why we sometimes find it hard to talk about her. I have a feeling for her, that's all, and it frustrates him.' She gave a little snort and smiled across at me almost mischievously. 'He claims I have unfair advantages.'

'Your gifts?'

'Just being a woman, I think. He says he has to go bat-fowling for what I take for granted—whatever bat-fowling may be.'

'If it means stumbling about in the dark I sympathize.'

'But then,' she added, 'he has a way of finding the right words—when he's sure of his ground, I mean. And it's like magic—everything suddenly takes shape, makes sense. I can't do that.'

'He's a poet,' I said, '—whether he's writing or not. Do you know why he gave up?'

She shook her head. 'He won't say, and I've learned not to ask. I know there's a lot of darkness there and he won't share it. I think he thinks he's protecting me, but . . .' She faltered there, shrugged.

'And you find that frustrating.'

'Not really. But it makes me sad. I'd rather have him like this.' She smiled across to where Edward still frolicked on the sand. 'I'm glad you've helped him back.'

'I wasn't even sure he liked me at first.'

'That was never true. But he didn't trust you. I remember after that first night at the Hall he said there was something unnerving about you.'

'Unnerving?'

'If I remember right he said, "There's something unnerving about such energy so unaware of itself." Something like that. It might have been "power." ' She thought about it, trying to recollect, then shrugged again. 'I told him you were someone who was too used to getting his own way, and probably still dumbstruck that you hadn't got it. Was I right?'

Her breezy smile left little room for more than a grin of agreement. 'Something like that . . . though I wouldn't have thanked you for saying so.'

'But I didn't know you were a big dreamer then. So we were both right.' She looked away, not coyly but with an elusive smile. 'The fact is, he likes you very much, and I'm really glad you found each other. It makes my life a whole lot simpler.'

Which was not, in that moment, quite what I wanted to hear; but it was so transparently sincere I had to accept it. After emerging from one three-way wreck so recently, I reminded myself, it would be crazy to look for anything other than simplicity. After a moment I said, 'How's your own work coming?'

'Edward told you about that?'

'A little, but he was very discreet.'

She wrinkled her nose, sighed. 'I'm building towards another firing, but it's slow . . . getting things right . . . not getting in my own way. I've been too close up against it. I needed a break as much as Edward. Look at him.'

I looked up and saw Edward jumping up and down, performing an elaborate semaphore with his hat.

'He wants us to play. Come on.' She ran down the dune, calling, 'Okay, I'm coming.'

I watched smiling as they owled and pussy-catted along the beach. Then she snatched his hat and teased him with it, threatening to throw it in a runnel of sea-water among the banks. Edward chased her, shouting, 'Rescue, Darken—this trollop has hijacked my hat.' I joined in on Laura's side with Edward as pig-in-the-middle, windmilling for the hat that sailed like a Frisbee between us, until we collapsed, panting with laughter, then stared in silence at the sea.

Laura collected sea-shells, looking for forms and colours she might work into her pots. She found a shapely length of salt-stained driftwood with a whorled grain. It was water-logged, half-buried in the sand, and surprisingly heavy but she insisted that we bring it back to the car with us. She needed it. It had value.

We had tea in a still half-deserted seaside town and when we came out of the cafe Edward produced from his pocket a tomato-shaped ketchup-holder which had taken Laura's fancy and amused Edward with its outrageous farting noise. Neither of us had noticed him pocket it. 'Steal for you?' he answered Laura's astonished protest, 'I'd do time. I'd swing for you, my dear. I'd willingly die.'

On the way back we stopped at a pub where Edward regaled us, and disturbed the landlord, with hilarious anecdotes of raff-ish nights around Fitzrovia as a young man. They were elicited by my questions about his earlier career, and most of them seemed new to Laura for she laughed with unfeignable gaiety, her head at moments in helpless tears against his chest. 'What are you grinning at, Cambridge?' he demanded—he'd given me the nickname after some reference I made to my own past; it was an affectionate pan of coals for my head—'It's perfectly true. And I should know. I made it up myself.'

'I was grinning,' I said, 'because I was thinking how lucky I am to know you two.'

'Lucky he calls it! Such a privilege comes only as a gift of Providence. And if you don't believe me, ask a Bushman. "There's a dream and it is dreaming us," they say. Know a thing or two, those clever little buggers. Damn sight more than that boor behind the bar. I've had enough of this particular sip-well. Let's go.'

They dropped me at The Pightle door. I heard them laughing still as the car pulled off down the lane. A little to my own amazement I found myself happy for them.

Two or three weeks passed surprisingly quickly. Apart from the accumulation of translated index cards, Edward and I made little progress, but our humour was good. When he did show signs of depression I could usually shake him out of it, and we took a schoolboyish delight in finding ways to disconcert Ralph's snooty man, Talbot, who brought morning coffee and afternoon tea up to the library, and evidently disapproved of both us and our enterprise. Ralph looked in on us every now and then with awkward, undemanding enquiries about our progress, and received Edward's sardonic remarks with a reticent grace. I was glad to be Edward's colleague and friend rather than suffering the indignities he subtly laid on his patron. It must have been odd for Ralph, I thought, to feel like an intruder in his own library.

In breaks in our work Edward entertained me with curious stories of the old alchemists. Raymond Lully featured among them, though in apocryphal form, as the subject of a singular conversion experience: inflamed by illicit passion for a married woman, he would brook no denial until she took him to her house and there, in the presence of her husband, bared to Raymond's astonished eyes a breast almost entirely devoured by cancer. Thereafter he became a missionary of heathen Africa, wrote a seminal alchemical text called the *Clavicula*, and was reputed to turn himself into a red cock when occasion demanded. He seems to have lost the knack when he most needed it, for he was stoned to death by unimpressed heathens.

Then there was Denis Zachaire, a young gentleman of Guienne, who invested all the money meant for his education in the furnishing of an alchemical laboratory—regrettably to no better effect than the loss of his tutor who died from the quantity of soot he inhaled. But Zachaire was bitten by the gold bug and wandered around Europe, one jump ahead of the plague, seeking to learn from the motley swarm of alchemists to be found in the abbeys and cities. By his own account, after much expenditure of charcoal and years of failure, he discovered a powder through which he made a successful projection of sufficient gold to pay off his creditors. According to one story (though this was told of others too), he was later murdered in his sleep by a servant who ran off with both the powder and Zachaire's wife. Alchemy, it seemed, was not an entirely happy affair. The man known as Helvetius might have produced gold which withstood the tests of assayers, but Bernard Trevisan was duped out of a fortune before finally performing the *magnum opus*, and Thomas Norton prepared the Elixir twice and was twice robbed of it before dying in poverty. Michael Sendivogius was imprisoned by the Emperor Rudolph on pain of yielding his secrets, and it was he who wrote what struck me as fair comment on the Hermetic enterprise in an imaginary complaint of the alchemist to Nature:

> Now I see that I know nothing, only I must not say so for I should lose the good opinion of my neighbours and they would no longer trust me with money for my experiments. There are many countries and many greedy persons who will suffer themselves to be gulled by my promise of mountains of gold. Thus day will follow day, and in the meantime the King or my donkey will die, or I myself.

Edward advised me not to be fooled by this open confession of fraud: it was an early exercise in disinformation. Each of the alchemists, he claimed, was in his way an incarnation of Mercurius—the ever-ambiguous tutelary spirit of the Art who promised much and was not to be had for the asking. The true face of the Hermetic philosopher was to be seen in the final picture of the *Mutus Liber* where the adept and his mystic sister raised their fingers to their lips in the gesture of the secret. This was why Louisa Agnew had chosen the title of that text for her epitaph; and if he and I were ever to unravel that secret, he said, we should get back to work.

Inevitably I saw more of Edward than of Laura. She was hard at work in her jealously private workshop, though she called in briefly at the library from time to time, and I was invited back to the Lodge for meals some evenings. I delighted them once with a return invitation to dine at The Pightle. The soufflé made up in ambition for what it lacked in accomplishment, but the wine was good. We talked a lot, laughed a lot, drank a lot— another round in the warming game of friendship that left me happy at the time, and aching afterwards as I contemplated the lonely bed.

Under question, Edward told me a little more about Laura's past than she herself was willing to volunteer. Her father was president of his own securities corporation, an East Coast patrician—'a Mammonite,' Edward called him—'a man whose feelings have been arrested by money, power, the dead hand of his ancestors. He's a kind of Giant Holdfast who both loves and terrorizes his children. His wife is a doer-of-good-works. She keeps their home as clean as a refrigerator and about as warm.

Sadly, they lack both the elegant wit of the eastern intelligentsia and the street-irony of those who do not share their advantages. You can smell dead redskins in the woods about the house.'

Pressed more closely he told me that for a number of years Laura had lived an almost schizophrenic life, symbolized by two quite different wardrobes—one for her parents 'the Goody-Twoshoes suits,' the other for what she believed to be her real self. He claimed that her private world had been little more than an experiment in frenzy, and that a breakdown had been inevitable. It came when her parents pried into her secrets and were horrified by what they found. In particular they were appalled by the discovery that their daughter was deeply in love with a young Jew. Neither Laura nor the young man had been strong enough to withstand their frigidly withering assault.

'After that,' Edward said, 'she wouldn't speak, scarcely ate. She was afraid that her very capacity for love had been defiled. Her feelings were frozen. She had no great wish to live, and slipped into an anorexic depression which kept her to her room, resisting all approaches. She tells me it felt as though she was living in a violent void, that she was losing touch with everything until . . .' He hesitated, decided, continued. 'What happened was the first recurrence of an experience she had not had since she was a child. I really don't feel free to tell you about this, but it seems to have been both deeply deranging and profoundly helpful. It was also kept intensely private. It happened many times over a period of weeks and, between the . . . visitations . . . there were moments when she doubted her own sanity. It can still frighten her, though she has learned how to handle its tensions, how to guide such experiences and use them. But if you wish to know more you will have to ask Laura. I doubt she will want to tell you.'

I gathered that her parents had seen only that Laura was losing touch with reality. They insisted that she consult a psychiatrist and, fortunately, Laura had the strength to insist that it be a woman. One was found—'a pragmatic, civilized feminist who did not pretend to understand all that had happened to Laura but had the good sense to see that she was a great deal saner than her parents. It was she who eventually recommended that Laura go to a college she knew of—one where she would find an environment supportive of her experience. The college is in Connecticut. It is called the Heartsease Institute. I have a long-standing association with its work. That is where we met, and the rest you know.'

He would say little more for my questions infringed on what he considered Laura's private domain. When I asked him about the college he volunteered only that it was an experimental community of researchers and students—'the kind of imaginative endeavour you will find only in the States.' It offered, I was told, 'a variety of approaches to the more inclusive aspects of speculative enquiry into the natural order.'

It seemed an unlikely sort of place, and even more unlikely that Laura's conservative parents should entrust their daughter to it. 'But they were desperate,' Edward answered, 'and desperation is often strangely fruitful. Somewhere they knew they had crippled her life, and their own responses were inadequate. They're sad people really.'

'You've met them?'

Edward sighed. 'Yes . . . I tried to talk to her father . . . by the poolhouse. Over root-beer, would you believe? For a moment I thought he was about to dare to let himself like me, but the wife was watching, alas. Mind you, he was also daunted by the fact that I was some years his senior. The poor devil wasn't sure whether to call me "sir" or "scoundrel." Had the idea I was after his money, I suppose. And the thought that I was bedding his daughter . . .' Edward winked mischievously up at me. 'You should go to America. The action's there. It's the alembick of the age—one that might blow up in all our faces, and yet . . . I don't know. I only know that Laura is well out of it.'

'She doesn't want to go back ever?'

'Why should she? She is much loved here. Her life has meaning now.' Edward looked at his watch. 'Cambridge, you're a great waster of time. I have things to do.'

Reflecting how Laura herself invariably shied away from mention of her gifts, I was left with my thoughts. Either Edward's account was true, or there was some bizarre pattern of collusion between them—he providing cover for her insecurity, or—equally possible—she reinforcing his. For the life of me, I couldn't say which was the case.

Later that afternoon he came to me with some of my translations from the index cards. 'I'm puzzled by something you've turned up,' he said. 'These parenthetical references to a mystic brother.'

'*Frater mysticus meus,*' I said. '*My mystic brother*, right?'

'Yes, but the term means nothing to me. There's no precedent for it. The female assistant was known as the mystic sister, but the man was always the Adept, the Master, Magister. Louisa wouldn't have thought of her father as a mystic brother.'

'Could she have been thinking of her real brother?'

Edward wrinkled his nose dubiously. 'He took no interest in the work. He rarely even came down from town.'

I smiled at him. 'Perhaps they were in telepathic communication?'

Edward was not amused.

'There was something I noticed about those references,' I added in recompense. 'They all looked as though they'd been written at a different time from the rest of the notes on the cards. The ink's different. Even the handwriting. See what you think.'

Edward studied the original cards—most of them contained quotations from the *Rosarium Philosophorum*, a text I hadn't read. They were principally concerned with the *Coniunctio Solis et Lunae*, the marriage of the solar and lunar principles. One was from the *Arisleus Vision*: 'With so much love did Beya embrace Gabricus that she entirely absorbed him in her own nature and dissolved him in inseparable atoms.' I'd thought about that one for a long time, wondering who Beya and Gabricus were, and had paid little attention to the note in brackets which had been added afterwards: (*Frater mysticus meus.*)

'I think you may be right,' Edward said after a moment. 'This is closer to the handwriting of her later letters. She must have gone back over the cards much later, when she was old. But what did she mean by it?'

'No clues in the journals?'

'Not as far as I remember. She stopped making entries when she began work on the Treatise. The last entry is in January 1849. She must have been too busy after that. If only she'd kept it up.'

'Was there anything significant about that last entry?'

'Not really. Just her regrets about the Rector's wife who'd had a miscarriage . . . *Frater mysticus meus.*' He whispered the words aloud as though to conjure the hidden meaning from the card.

'You think it might be important?'

'It's certainly puzzling . . . But then what isn't, dammit?'

'Might Laura have some idea?'

'She might,' Edward said dubiously. 'I'll ask her this eve-ning.' Puzzling still, he returned to his desk. I riffled through the shoebox of index cards and found several more with the same cryptic postscript. Marking the places from which they'd come with scraps of paper, I decided to translate them first.

I had another dream that night, less orderly and dramatic than my dream of alchemy, but it felt significant. I was checking the rooms of The Pightle for leaks and other necessary repairs when I discovered an entirely new wing. There were several rooms, all in good condition, which seemed to have been rented out though I was aware that they remained my responsibility. One room had the smell of a hospital ward, and there were patients asleep there with a nurse in attendance who was not surprised by my intrusion. I passed down the ward and opened a door at the end of a passage. A whole order of nuns was waiting to welcome me. I remembered that they had been there all along, and wondered how I could ever have forgotten them.

The scene shifted and I found myself at the head of a stairwell, aware that yet another place might be reached but only by som-ersaulting over the banister and walking my feet down the op-posite wall as one might descend a defile in a crag. Others had done it, I knew, but I felt nervous about accomplishing the tricky manoeuvre. Then Laura appeared, and there was something odd in the manner of her appearance. She felt more substantial than the other figures in the dream, almost as though she had troubled to step out of her own dreams to assist me with mine. I was relieved to see her and encouraged by the confidence she gave me. I gripped the banister and swung myself head over heels, then came out on the roof of a tower. When I made my way down its spiral staircase I found myself in the main thoroughfare of the town where I was born. The dream ended with the thought that if I had known this was the main road I need not have resorted to the acrobatics that had brought me there.

I woke feeling good, eager to get back to the Hall, and I wrote down the dream first, thinking I would tell it to Edward. Then, over breakfast, I decided I'd keep it to myself.

Edward was in a foul mood, applying himself obsessively to his studies, encouraging no conversation. When we broke for coffee I asked him whether he'd consulted Laura about the references I'd turned up.

'Yes.'

'Well?'

'Nothing helpful.'

'You're sure?'

'Of course I'm sure.'

'What did she say?'

Edward scowled at me. 'Her mind wasn't really on it. She's at a crucial point with her own work. We were at cross-purposes.'

'You mean you had a row?'

'Yes, we had a row. Not that it's any of your damned business.'

Except that I had to live with the aftermath.

It was the first time the old coldness had returned. For a moment I thought he was about to apologize, but he didn't. He resumed his work. I looked across to where he sat hunched like a crow over carrion, and thought what a cantankerous old sod he could be when he chose.

Around three Talbot came up to the library with a telephone-set in his hand. 'There's a call for you, sir. If you'd care to use the extension plug by your desk no doubt the Estate Office will connect you.'

For once Edward was in no mood to bait the man. He glowered at the instrument, plugged it in, then picked up the receiver. I returned my attention to the papers on my desk as Talbot left the room. Though I had the distinct impression that Edward would have preferred me to leave too, he said nothing, merely drummed his fingers on the desk top, then snapped, 'Well?' into the receiver.

I heard the faint warble of Laura's voice but could discern no words.

'Oh for God's sake, why couldn't you wait till the weekend? I thought we agreed. You know I'd have helped you then.'

There was a mixture of irritation and concern in his voice. He was shaking his head as he listened.

'I *know* you'd prefer to do it on your own, but it's obvious you can't. You were bound to run into trouble. Do you need me to come right now?'

' . . .'

'What on earth for?'

' . . .'

'But that was an accident. My concentration slipped. I'm not about to do it again.'

There was a further prolonged warble, to which Edward replied, 'I think we can manage perfectly well on our own.' He swivelled his chair away from me and stared out of the window. 'But if you weren't even sure you wanted me around . . .'

'. . .'

'All right. On your own head be it.'

Laura said something else, Edward grunted and put down the phone. His chair swivelled back my way. Again the fingers drummed. 'Listen, Laura's having rouble with a firing. She's running out of chopped wood and needs help. Last time I practically took my thumb off and apparently she doesn't trust me to do it again. She wondered whether . . .'

'I'd love to,' I said.

It was another stunningly hot, windless day, the sky an unclouded eggshell-blue, the temperature in the high seventies, so it was good to hang my head from the open window of Edward's car and let the air come pelting at my face. I had never seen a kiln fired before and the unpredictable behaviour of live flame could only add to the already restless sensuality of the afternoon. The prospect exhilarated.

Yet somehow Edward must be appeased, so I sought to make a virtue of my ignorance, asking questions that would allow him to air his greater experience. He knew what I was doing, and answered only in clipped, unhelpful sentences. 'All you have to do is chop. And keep out of her way. She does the whole thing by feel . . . listening to the kiln.'

'But something's gone wrong this time?'

'It's a delicate business. Not like a machine. It's alive. You have to nurse it along. She must have got the balance wrong and it's stuck. She should never have tried to do it alone.'

He braked in the yard at the rear of the Lodge, and through the windscreen I saw a plume of smoke rising almost vertically beyond a pantiled outbuilding which I assumed must be Laura's studio. Edward saw it too and his mood changed. His eyes glinted at me. I saw the excitement there. 'Come on then,' he said, 'let's make the elements dance.'

He led the way round the studio. I saw an open shed stacked with timber, graded according to its thickness, and then, as we turned the flint gable, there was Laura crouched before the kiln in a muddle of faggots and fire-irons, her rump in the air, legs bare beneath the sawn-off fringes of her denim shorts, wearing a blue-grey sleeveless T-shirt that had ridden up around her waist. One of its shoulder straps had drooped to her upper arm. Her hair was piled at her head, tied in a scarlet bandanna, and when she turned her face to look wanly up at us there were soot-marks on her brow and cheeks where she had wiped away the sweat with the back of her hand. 'I can't get the draught right,' she said. 'I need more wind.'

'Where've you got to?' Edward demanded.

'About 900 I think. But I've been stuck here for ages. It was going fine till I tried for a reduction. Then the temperature dropped and I can't get it moving again.' She stood up, adjusted the strap of her shoulder, and smiled at me. 'Hello. Am I glad to see you.'

Edward crouched to his knees before the firebox and peered into the sickly blaze. 'What's the atmosphere like?'

'Pretty soupy. See what you think.' Laura moved round to the side of the kiln—it was a roughly built cube of fire-bricks the colour of pale sand, with a bricked-up Norman door-arch on one side and a narrow throat at the rear which led to a tall, cast-iron stovepipe wired for support to the studio wall and a bough of a late-flowering cherry tree across the yard. The whole thing had the odd appearance of a brick-built Mississippi steamboat beached and panting to get back to the lake. Laura removed a wedge-shaped bung from the wall and peered in. Sighing, Edward moved round to join her, muttering again that she shouldn't have started the firing on her own.

'Don't give me a hard time,' she begged. 'I've got troubles enough.'

A hand at his brow, Edward squinted into the chamber. 'Murky. Too much uncombusted carbon in there. Thought so from the firebox. You've choked it.'

'I know I have, dammit. I needed more of the thinner timber, but I can't fetch, chop and feed it at the same time.'

'What did I tell you? Where's the bloody hatchet?'

'Edward, I'm not having you chop. Not after last time.'

'Let me,' I put in.

Edward glowered.

'It's his hands, you see. They're not steady enough.' Laura shot a quick glance Edward's way. 'It's stupid, Edward. You know it is. Look, what I really need is to have more of those old floorboards brought round. They're tinder-dry. They should get it moving again. Would you mind?'

For a moment Edward stood there, assessing her with a cold eye, then he slipped off his linen jacket, and looked at me. 'Come on then. Give me a hand.'

Together we brought round a pile of boards and I started chopping while Laura fed the slender faggots to the flame, and Edward tinkered with the loose bricks that controlled the air supply. It was hot beside the mouth of the kiln and I was soon sweating; but the air was bright around me, the narrow prospect of the lake still and cool in the distance. I pulled off my shirt and threw it beyond the woodpile. It felt good to be active again after the days cooped in the library's shade.

'It's all a question of balance,' Edward muttered. 'All the elements are here. They want to work together.' He stared suddenly at Laura. 'You did remember to bless the kiln?'

' 'Course I did. We just need a bit more breeze, that's all.'

'We could whistle for one, like sailors,' I said.

'Or work for it,' Edward snapped. 'We need to waft the air.' He looked about for a thing to waft with, saw nothing satisfactory, scowled and said, 'I suppose I'll have to find a fan of some sort.'

Laura made a mischievous moue as he walked away.

'He's been in a bad mood all day,' I said.

'I'm not surprised. We had one hell of a row last night. Look, it's great of you to come. Edward and I would only have gotten in each other's hair.'

'My pleasure. At least I know how to chop—if I'm ignorant about everything else you're doing.'

'It's very basic really. When the draught's okay the flame gets drawn over the bag-wall at the back of the firebox, then it sweeps round the arch of the kiln-chamber, down through the pots into the throat and out up the chimney. That's the theory anyway. I didn't reach temperature last time. We had a real struggle, then Edward practically took his hands off. Disaster. But he might be right about this. Kilns are temperamental—if you get the balance wrong you can feed it till you go blue in the face and get nowhere.'

'What temperature do you have to reach?'

'The glazes flux at 1280 centigrade.'

'That's hot.'

'Very hot. You'll see the whole kiln shake before we get there.'

'How will you know when you're there?'

'Give it another couple of minutes and I'll show you. This is coming better. The wood's just right.' When she was satisfied with the state of the blaze Laura led me round to the side of the kiln, removed the bung and gestured for me to look in. I felt the heat hit my face as I stared through the opening with narrowed eyes. I saw two small spires through the spy-hole, and beyond them the intense red haze of the kiln chamber. The atmosphere was less turbid than I'd expected from Edward's description—a glowing, orange-red furnace of heat in which I could make out the shadowy profiles of two pots.

'You see the cones? One of them will melt when we reach a thousand. The other goes at glaze temperature. But you can tell from the colour as well.'

'I think the top of one's bending a bit.'

She pushed me aside, peered into the chamber. 'You're right. And the atmosphere's cleared. We're on our way again. Great! You've brought me luck. Come on, more wood, more wood. Let's keep it moving.'

I started to chop furiously again, the dry wood riving and splintering under the hand-axe. Laura crouched beside me feeding the fire with a smooth, regular rhythm, sweat shining at her shoulder-blades, the T-shirt damp at her back. When Edward reappeared carrying a wicker carpet-beater she called, 'it's all right. We've done it. We're on the move.'

He stood disgruntled, staring down at us. Again I felt his displeasure. I tried grinning up at him. 'I think you've done it between you,' I said. 'Made an alchemist of me, I mean. I've got the bug.'

He nodded, smiling thinly, and fanned himself with the now redundant carpet-beater.

'We'll give it another quarter of an hour or so,' Laura said, 'and I'll try for another reduction. What do you think, Edward?'

'They're your pots,' he answered unhelpfully. Again Laura shot him an uncertain glance, then returned her attention to the fire. 'Would anyone else care for a drink?' Edward asked.

'I put some cans in the fridge,' Laura said. 'Alex must be gasping. Me too. It's a great idea.' Edward turned back to the Lodge.

'Reduction?' I asked, pushing across another stack of faggots.

'You cut off the air and starve the atmosphere of oxygen. The atmosphere has to find it somewhere so it goes after the molecules locked in the glazes and that's when the real magic happens.' There was a sheen of elation in her eyes which had widened, sparkling, at the word *magic*. It was as though she herself were under a spell, transmuted suddenly to a higher pitch, animated and volatile—as the alchemists were altered by their work. Even with the soot-stains on her skin—perhaps because of them—I had never seen her look so radiant. Her mouth was open slightly, the tongue damp at her lower lip, her whole face eager, capable of every challenge. I looked and saw nothing remotely fragile there. Then she was aware of my gaze, glanced away, blew a puff of air upwards at her face, pinched the T-shirt between her fingers and flapped it for draught. I returned my eyes to the axe.

By the time Edward returned with a tray of beer-cans the fire was blazing with famished enthusiasm. I pulled the ring-top from the can and drank greedily, for the heat of the day and the kiln's hot breath had parched my throat. More decorously, Edward lifted his can before drinking. 'Here's to a successful firing, my dear.'

'I'm sure it will be. I can feel it.' She looked up suddenly where a shower of blossom swirled from the cherry-boughs. 'Even the breeze is getting up. It's going to be all right.'

'An extraordinary exercise of trust, don't you think, Cambridge. To craft the pots so patiently from earth and water and then deliver them over to the mercies of fire and air.'

'That's what I love about it,' Laura said, '—the risk, the trust.'

'The unpredictability,' Edward added. 'The surprise.' He turned to me again. 'One never knows what the fire will do, and it has so many aspects. Look at the way this merry rage had risen from the sullen beast we found earlier. Consider the immense energies slowly eating out their heart up there,'—he nodded upwards at the sun, dazzling westwards across the lake— 'and the Pentecostal flame which brings the gift of tongues. Then there is the darker, unintelligible fire of the inferno, which burns and gives no light.' He grinned across at me darkly. 'Nor should one forget the *ignis fatuus*, familiar as it is to us all.' He took a swig from his can, smacked his lips. 'There is a story of a Japanese potter who was commanded by his Emperor to reproduce a marvellous glaze he had chanced upon as a mere hazard of the fire. He tried for years without success until finally, in utter despair, he threw himself into the kiln. When the pots

were taken out . . . Of course, you bright boy, you have anticipated me . . . Yes, the Emperor's command had been fulfilled.
Which is why, of course, all artists burn.'

Laura had no time for such abstractions. 'Come on, Edward,' she interrupted. 'Alex needs more planks. Would you
mind . . . ?'

'As my words appear to have lost their power to charm I
suppose I may as well diminish myself to beast of burden.'

'Don't try to carry too many at once.'

'I am not yet a total incompetent,' he muttered walking away.

I chopped. Edward came back struggling with a load of
planks, and I got up to help him. 'I can manage,' he said
brusquely, threw them down, and went back for more. The pine
boards snapped beneath the stamp of my foot. I swung the axe
in swift rhythm, glad of the release it gave to the tension I felt
building inside and around me. Then, when she judged the moment right, Laura shut down the damper in the smokestack,
sealed the air-vents, and the whole kiln began to throb and pant
black smoke. 'Look out,' she cried as tongues of flame blow-
torched from the crevices around the bung and came licking
back at us from the firebox. A dragon might have been suffocating there. It was hard to believe that this clumsy box of bricks
was strong enough to withstand the pressure of its wings. The
whole enterprise felt suddenly dark and dangerous. For the first
time I began to recognize the power of the forces that Laura was
summoning to her need.

Fascinated, I watched the flames gasp for air, the carbon-
black exhaust of smoke billowing from the chimney-mouth, the
throb of imprisoned energies. Laura stood, tall and lithe, glowing with sweat, listening to the growl of the kiln, hands clenched
tightly at her sides. Edward came back, dropped the planks, and
stared at the kiln as into a mirror of his own increasing frustration. For longer, much longer than I would have dared, Laura
held us all there, sustaining the kiln's turbulent rage, then said
quietly, 'Alex, take this glove. Go to the damper and open it
when I give the word.'

The damper was no more than a thin sheet of steel inserted
into the stovepipe. I waited, feeling the heat thrown from the
chimney, then Laura cried, 'Now!' and pushed open the air-
vents with a fire-iron. I pulled the damper out: it was glowing
red-hot along its length, 'Great God, look,' Edward shouted, 'a
pillar of fire,' and pointed upwards where a rush of living flame

burgeoned from the chimney like a fiery tulip against the vivid blue of the sky.

'That should have done it,' Laura whispered. Then more briskly, 'Quick, we'll have lost temperature. Keep the wood coming, Alex. We might just catch it right.'

I had been working for more than an hour and my wrists ached from the continuous chopping, but I was filled with an immense exhilaration. The release of flame had swirled right through me. I was as much arsonist as alchemist now, swinging the axe glee-fully, impervious to everything but the fire's appetite. Never in my life had I done anything like this before. I remember thinking that this was to be alive. Even the air I breathed—charred with smoke, sweetened by the scent of surrounding trees—had a dif-ferent taste. It was the taste of Spring at climax, of an afternoon in which, at the touch of the rising breeze, cherry-blossom floated from the boughs in a frail pink torrent of petals that drifted through the shimmering heat-haze to cling at the sweat on one's skin.

Rapt in her attention to the kiln, Laura demanded finer and finer splinters of wood. She slipped them rapidly into the hot mouth where they were instantly consumed in a shower of sparks. Sweat was running from my temples, stinging at the corners of my eyes, and when I paused to wipe them Edward shouted, 'Come on, come on, give me the bloody axe.' I glanced quickly at Laura. 'You need a break,' she said. 'For God's sake be careful, Edward.' Reluctantly I handed over the axe and made way for him, then stood, stretching my back.

When I looked at my watch I was amazed to see that it was well after six. I realized I was hungry and it didn't matter. There was no way I could care about anything now till this kiln was fired. It would be done this time. If I had to sweat blood it would be done. But it made sense at least to stretch my cramped legs, so I strolled down to the edge of the lake and lit a cigarette. Sunlight glittered across the water as though that too tingled with golden fire. I remembered what Edward had said about the presence of all the elements, wanting to work together, to meet and merge. And Laura—if she had been earth and water as she shaped her pots, she was now, like Cleopatra, all fire and air.

Alive inside my skin, indifferent to the blister smarting in the soft cruck of my thumb, I sensed the world changing round me—a sensation of risk, of things poised on a hot brink where anything might happen and never be the same again. I think I already knew then that I would not return to my job at the Polytechnic, for the security of that monthly cheque had lost all meaning. The job was a cage where the wild man in me fretted and chafed. I could step out between the bars, and a day like this declared every reason for the risk. Why settle for the predictable, it demanded, when nothing truly attuned to the precarious magic of being alive can ever be predicted? I thought about Marcus and Lily, how they would have loved it here—the lake, the kiln, the excitement of the firing. I released a long, tense breath, flicked the stub of my cigarette into the lake, and turned to look back where Edward and Laura squatted before the smoking kiln, for all the world the alchemist and his mystic sister, except that the roles were powerfully reversed, and—I realized suddenly—they were arguing under their breath.

'They're still too thick,' Laura complained.

'Goddammit, I'm doing the best I can.'

'Every time you fumble I lose ten degrees. Look, give the axe to Alex. He knows what he's doing with it. I don't want you to hurt yourself.' Before Edward could answer she sprang to her feet. 'Alex, I'm losing it. Can you come?'

'It's all right,' Edward growled. 'Just have some patience, will you?'

'It's not me, dammit. It's the fire. You know this last haul's the hardest. I'm not going to lose it this time.'

Edward looked on scowling as I came over. There was a long, hot moment in which all three of us were penned in a triangle of critical regard—Laura fiercely indifferent to everything except the health of her blaze; me awkwardly between, holding out my hand for the axe; Edward, old man suddenly, hating his years and his uncertain hands, humiliated, furious with Laura, resentful of my youth, and profoundly unwilling to surrender the axe. He held it there like a weapon. For an instant I seemed to be staring into smoke. What I saw was scary enough to make me lower my hand.

'Edward,' Laura said quietly, 'be reasonable. Look, why don't you go and get some food together? I can't leave this and we'll all be starving by the time we reach temperature.'

He stared at her incredulously. Her gaze shifted away to where the fire craved fuel, then turned back to him again. 'Please, Edward. I can't cope with everything.'

Ignoring me, cancelling me from the face of the earth, he glowered at her a moment longer through narrowed eyes, then let the axe drop, turned on his heel, and walked away. Laura called after him, half-reproachfully, half in appeal. There was no answer.

Laura and I looked at one another uncertainly. She pushed back her hair where it had slipped from the bandanna, then tried to shrug off the tension with a sigh. 'Oh come on, let's feed the fire.'

I picked up the axe and began to chop. She crouched at the firebox, shooting the wood into its mouth as quickly as it came, then cowered back from the sudden heat as the blaze was roused again. 'I'm not going to let him spoil it,' she muttered. 'Not this time. This really matters to me.'

'I think I know how he must feel.'

'His feelings aren't the only important thing in the world.'

'He knows that. Let him cool off. He'll be all right. I've seen him like this in the library—grim as hell one minute, chortling the next.'

'You don't know him like I do. He's just impossible sometimes.' She sighed, shook her head and picked up more faggots. 'Come on, fire, be sweet to me. We're nearly there.'

For the best part of an hour I chopped and Laura fed the flame. We said very little—simply worked together, sweating, sniffing, aware of each other bent in crazy service to this marvellous beast she'd roused. Eventually she got up, removed the bung once more with a gloved hand, and stepped back as a tongue of yellow flame licked out at her. Then shielding her eyes with her arm she craned to peer inside. 'Oh yes,' she cried. 'Alex, come and see. It's incredible.'

I dropped the axe, wiped my temples and joined her where she held the incandescent bung away from her skin. For a moment I thought the heat from the bung-hole might incinerate my brows, but when I squinted beneath an outstretched palm the sight stole my breath. What had been only a dense red glow when I first looked into the chamber was now a torrent of liquid flame. It swirled among pots and tingled and glimmered in a dance of fly-ash. The first cone was melted to a puddle, the second was bending in obeisance to the blaze—as I felt myself to be, stooped there before the kiln, wanting to gaze and gaze, but the vision was barely supportable. In the instant before Laura replaced the bung I understood how that ancient Japanese potter might have flung himself into those dazzling fountains. I turned to share the wonder of it, but she was gazing up at the bloom of flame surging from the chimney's mouth, and beyond where the evening-star glittered against the deepening blue sky. We stood together in silence for a long moment. Her lips opened in a half-dazed smile of speechless delight. She bit her bottom lip, brought her arms together at her chest so that her hands met at her mouth. 'We've done it,' she whispered into the little cave made by her fingers. 'We've really done it.' Then she was jumping up and down, turned suddenly, threw her arms around me, eyes tightly closed, squeezing me against her. I tightened my own grip, felt the soft blur of her hair at my cheek. Then her hands were at her back, unclasping mine. 'Quick,' she said. 'I've got to soak the kiln. We need to hold it here for another half hour. Come on, before it drops.'

I stood, thrown, watching her leap back to the firebox. 'Come on,' she cried eagerly, 'I need more wood.'

So we were back before the firebox, exhausted and happy, and Laura had just shut down the kiln, when Edward came round into the yard again.

'We've done it,' Laura called. 'Edward, we've done it. I've put it to bed. Be happy for me. Be happy, please.'

I gazed across at him, willing him not to wreck this moment. I could see the contention in his wrinkled face. Then an arm lifted, as though of its own accord, and came to rest on the crown of his head. He had missed her moment—he knew he had missed it—yet his eyes softened suddenly, and you could almost see the shadow fall from his shoulders as he twinkled down at Laura where she knelt before her dying fire. As if it was the most natural thing in the world he said, 'God bless you, my dear, I knew all along it would be all right. Come and give me a hug.'

Laughing she sprang to her feet. He moved towards her, opening his arms, and I saw there were tears at the corners of his eyes. 'Well done,' he whispered, eyes closed, holding his cheek against her. 'Well done.' They hugged each other in silence for a long time. I stared at the mess of faggots round the hearth of the closed kiln, supernumerary now. Then I heard Edward's voice. 'You too, Cambridge. Come join this orgy of delight. You've earned a kiss.'

'That's right,' Laura exclaimed, 'I couldn't have done it without you. Without both of you.' They each held out a free arm. Smiling, I rose to join them, and when they both pressed their lips to my cheeks I caught the smell of whisky on Edward's breath. 'What Nature leaves imperfect,' he quoted, 'we perfect with our Art.' Then we were all clasped in a threefold embrace, Laura calling out her thanks to the sky. I felt Edward's pressure at my hip wheeling the hug until the three of us circled in a scrum of affection. 'Nature takes delight in Nature,' Edward whispered as we turned; then, a little louder, 'Nature contains Nature'; and shouting then as though the triumph of the hour was entirely his: 'And Nature can overcome Nature.' Laughing, we broke apart.

'I know what my nature needs right now,' Laura said.

'A feast awaits you indoors,' Edward answered. 'The burgundy breathes. The chef has done his worst.'

'Wonderful. But there's a thing I have to do.' She grinned, said, 'I'm going to jump in the lake,' and she was off, sprinting and skipping, pulling her T-shirt over her head, round to the front of the Lodge. Edward and I stared at one another. A moment later we heard a splash and a squeal, more splashing, a flutter of duck, whoops of delight. A little blearily Edward laughed.

I said, 'That sounds like a good idea.'

'Be my guest.'

'You don't mind?'

'Should I?'

We were each held for an instant in the other's dubious quiz. 'You're smelling a little high,' he said, 'and we have no shower.'

'What about you?'

'I have already bathed my wounds.'

'Then . . .'

'After all, there's nothing you haven't seen before.'

'She told you?'

'Laura tells me everything . . . eventually.' He sniffed. 'Go on, for God's sake. Let's see what you're made of.' He followed me round to the jetty where Laura's clothes were scattered across the lawn.

'Come on in,' she shouted. 'It's bliss.' Her hair was loose, shining where it floated on the surface around her head. Smoothly she lifted her arms in a back-stroke, then twisted the blur of her body and struck out into the lake with a fluent, practised crawl. Edward watched as I kicked off my shoes and socks, unbuckled my jeans and let them fall. I handed him my watch, stared at his grin for a moment, then slipped out of my shorts and ran out on to the jetty to plunge into the sudden cold

shock of the lake. When I surfaced, gasping, the sky was intensely blue and I saw the moon, cratered and radiant, high over
the tower on the distant Mount.

We were some distance out in the lake when Edward eventually called from the shore that supper was spoiling. Until that
moment no single glance had suggested more than shared pleasure in the lake by night, two friends at swim. Laura's challenge
to race back was uttered in that spirit, but she was the better
swimmer and reached the jetty strokes ahead of me. She must
have known I was watching as she lifted herself from the lake,
water running down her long back, the skin glistening in the
light cast from the house across the lawn. I couldn't take my
eyes off her as she swivelled to rinse the mud from her legs, then
flexed her arms, swept back her hair to shake it, and the motion
rippled through her body. She opened her eyes, smiled down
where I stood waist-deep in water still—the smile itself a quick
gasp on evening air—then she was upright, running along the
jetty to where Edward waited with the towels. He wasn't looking
at her—he was looking at me, and there was a snakeskin feel to
his face.

It was the glance of an instant only. I tried to shake it from
my mind as I shook the water from my hair, but I knew what
that face felt like from the inside. It was imagining its own
absence from the scene, and disbelieving innocence. As far at
least as I was concerned, it did so with due cause.

And Laura?

I didn't know. If she'd relaxed in her skin after the hot work
over the kiln, she hadn't flaunted it; not till that moment, and
even then, had she been clothed, the smile might have signified
no more than amused affection. But she was frank and inaccessible as a Modigliani nude; and I was back in the green glow of
the glade—except that this time I too was observed.

By the time we came to eat it was evident that Edward was
already drunk. He ate little of the meal he'd prepared, but added
more than half the wine to the mix of beer and whisky inside
him. I tried to engage him in conversation about the analogy
between pottery and alchemy, and Laura prompted him to share
ideas that had long been familiar to them both, but he showed
little interest. Self-consciously, I shifted the ground to literature,
regretting that the emblems of alchemy were now too arcane to
be of service to modern writers.

'If you'd had your eyes open,' he growled, 'you'd have seen that such is certainly not the case,' and muttered, 'Numbskull,' under his breath. The charm—that demon glitter of narrowed eyes which had given the lie to all previous insults—was conspicuously absent. He turned to Laura. 'The man's half-educated. Barely that.' He downed more wine. Suddenly I was back in the presence of the unpredictable figure I'd met in the library at Easterness that first night, and as uncertain now as then.

'Who did you have in mind?' I asked.

'I didn't have anyone *in mind*. I have them by heart, where they belong.'

'All right. But who?'

'James Joyce modern enough for you? Or is he old hat already? "The first till last alshemist"—that's what he called himself.' For a moment I thought his tongue had slurred the word, then I remembered Joyce's fluent way with puns. 'But I don't suppose you've taken the trouble to read *Finnegans Wake*?'

'I had a hard time getting through *Ulysses*,' I responded as lightly as I could.

'See what I mean?' he demanded of Laura, who gave me a quick, apologetic glance, then looked down at the table.

'It's been a marvellous day, Edward. Don't spoil it.'

'Man asked me a question, didn't he? Or made some asinine observation or other. Don't remember now. *I* didn't start it. Know that.'

'He was just making conversation.'

'And I was just responding. Or am I not permitted to speak in my own house?'

'Tell me about Joyce,' I said quickly, and found myself fixed by a menacing leer. Slowly his head turned from me to Laura. 'With Laura's gracious permission,' he said, sarcasm spacing the words. She sighed and looked away. Then he studied me again, breathing heavily, the corner of his mouth twitching a little. 'Joyce knew it . . . chymical wedding, I mean. More than you'll ever know. Listen to this: "equals of opposites, evolved by a one-same power of nature or spirit, as the sole condition and means of . . . means of . . ." ' He screwed his eyes, pressed the thumb-knuckle of the hand holding a cigarette into his forehead, struggling to remember, then jerked his head up, scowling. The ash fell from his cigarette on to the table-cloth. 'Laura, how's it go?'

'I don't remember.'

'Yes you do, dammit. You're just being pissy with me. How's it bloody go. Man wants to learn.'

Staring at him coldly, Laura completed the quotation: 'as the sole condition and means of its himundher manifestation and polarized for reunion by the symphysis of their antipathies.'

'That's it. *Symphysis of their antipathies.* Pure alchemy. Twentieth-century state of the art. Satisfied? Any wiser, you little Cambridge shit? And what about Yeats, for God's sake? The *Rosa Alchimia.* Haven't read that either, I suppose? What do they teach in crammers these days? Manage your own hand-jobs, can you? And then there's Lowry—sweet, sozzled Malcolm Lowry. He tried. He tried. We're talking men now. Real men. We're talking burning-ground. None of your navel-lint, tit-licking pen-fuckers so infatuated with the twitchings of the ego they remain sublimely indifferent to the obscene fact that their words are worth less than the flies tormenting the eyelids of an African child. And who gives a toss about litter-a-chewer anyway? Is that what you're in this for? Scratching round our backyard for pickings to pad your lines out with? That it, eh?'

Laura stepped in to cover my obvious discomfort. 'Please don't do this, Edward.'

'It's all right,' I murmured.

'It is not all right,' Edward snarled, and pointed an unsteady finger at me. 'You stay out of this.' He turned on Laura, with a caustic grin. 'Fancy him, do we? That the game? That what it's about?'

'Oh for God's sake.'

'Think I'm blind, do you? Old and blind. That what you think?'

'I think you've had too much to drink, that's all.'

'Liar. Lying bitch.'

I could see the breath shaking in Laura's voice as she said, quietly, 'Edward, if you're not careful you might regret this very much.'

He stared at her, swaying in his chair, then all the malevolent rage seemed to collapse inside him. 'Done it before,' he muttered. 'Done it before.' He looked across at me with watery, beseeching eyes as if he had just told me the entire, intolerable story of his life. His hand was trembling, half-open, on the table-cloth. He looked at the cigarette, almost burnt-out between nicotine-stained fingers, and stubbed it on his plate again and again until it was quite crumpled. He sniffed, and looked up at Laura. 'You're quite right, my dear. Darken,'—his great, wrinkled head revolved slowly towards me—'forgive. Old fool, you see. The booze. No good for me. Pay no heed.'

'It's forgotten,' I said, but my own hand was trembling a little as it reached to take the unsteady, hairy hand he offered across the table.

'Hope so. Didn't know what I was saying.'

There was a long silence in which he sat, nodding, before he released his grip. His free hand reached for the bottle again, then pulled back. He beat the edge of the table with the flat of it—an old gorilla, caged—shook his head as though to clear it, then jerked uncertainly to his feet. The chair would have fallen to the floor had Laura not reached out to catch it. 'Had enough,' he said. 'Going to bed.' He lurched towards Laura, kissed the crown of her head, and mumbled, 'Forgive, forgive,' into her hair.

'It's all right,' she said.

'Yes, it's all right. It's good. It's as it should be. All is for the best in the most impossible of worlds.' Then he smiled across at me, a doleful witness for his own prosecution, and shambled from the room.

Laura and I sat in tense silence, listening to the creak of the stairs. She opened her lips to speak. I said, 'Don't say it. It wasn't your fault.'

'I really wanted us to be happy.'

'I know.'

'He's impossible.'

'But he loves you very much.'

'He needs me.'

'That too.'

'And I owe him . . .' She closed her eyes, sighed, frowned down at the table where the ash lay like his spoor.

'Does this happen often?'

'It's been getting worse.'

'Is that my fault?'

She looked up, puzzled by the question. 'Why should it be? No, it's not that. It's . . . I don't know. It's happened before. I tried to leave him once when he got like this. In the States.'

'And he went to pieces?'

She shook her head. '*I* did.' When she looked up at me there was a kind of glazed defiance in her eyes. 'I left him because I couldn't handle the shadow his expectations threw over me . . . the way he cast me as a member of his dream. I started to think he finally made it impossible for me to be myself.' Again the eyes were lowered. 'I came back because I discovered that without him my head splits into a thousand pieces. I couldn't work, couldn't feel my way. Nothing made any sense.'

I tried to say that I understood, that I'd felt much the same way when I lost Jess. 'But you came through,' she said. 'On your own, I mean. Without Edward I . . . There are things I can't explain.'

'Try.'

'Look, if it wasn't for him . . .' She had been prepared for none of this, stalled now, changed her mind. 'It wouldn't make any sense to you. He's the only one who really understands.'

'He told me a little about what happened to you in the States,' I encouraged.

'About Hester?'

Immediately I saw that if Edward had mentioned that name it would have been deemed a great betrayal. 'No. Only that you had some very confusing experiences . . .' I waited. Agitated, she made no move to change the course of the conversation or to end it. I took a further risk. 'Who's Hester?'

She glanced up warily, found nothing but sympathy in my gaze. 'That's just it. She's not. Not any more. She was an ancestor of mine. She's been dead longer than Louisa, but . . .'

I could feel the hairs rise at the back of my neck as I said, 'You've seen her?'

She nodded, reached for a cigarette and lit it. 'I used to. I used to a lot. Whenever things were really bad we'd talk . . .'

Had Edward told me this I would not have believed. Even now, despite the patent honesty of her eyes, there was resistance.

'You see what I mean?' she said. 'It sounds crazy, right? Well, I was crazy . . . sure I was for a time. But not about that.' It was as though she was accruing power over against Edward's earlier impossible behaviour, against my possible disbelief. 'And not about Louisa either . . . Edward knows it, but he won't hear. He thinks I've got it wrong and . . .' Her breath came in a shaky release of tension. 'That's one of the things that's come between us. But—what I was talking about—he knows it's not crazy. He knows it's real.'

Whatever the crux of their disagreement she was not about to disclose it. She had no such trust in me.

I said, 'Why shouldn't it be real? I only have to switch on the news to hear things a whole lot crazier than that.' I'd tried to keep my voice light, coaxing, but she studied me coolly as though she'd picked up my unspoken reservations and would not forget them. The expression on her face read my last remark as no more than a condescending gesture of patient sympathy such as she must have met many times before. Or perhaps she wasn't considering my words at all, for she said suddenly, 'I should stick to clay. That's real.' And then, a moment later, 'Oh God, I was a bitch to him today.'

'Come on, that's not fair. There's no point punishing . . .'

'Look,' she interrupted, 'I can't leave him too long. I know him—he'll just be lying there miserable . . .' The appeal in her eyes was asking me to leave.

'You'll be all right?'

She nodded, summoning strength. I saw the candle-lit flash of the little star at her throat; saw too that to contrive a longer stay would only put her under further pressure. Already there were shadows of exhaustion round her eyes. I pushed back my chair and got up. 'Well, at least the kiln's in good shape.'

She smiled, though wanly. 'Bless you for that.'

'I wouldn't have missed it for anything.'

'I'd offer to run you back but . . .'

'It's okay. I like to walk.' I saw the mess on the table and said, 'Oh God, the dishes . . .'

'Don't worry. You've done enough. Really.'

At the door I turned to look at her.

'You don't have to be haunted by the past—or by that abominable old sod upstairs. You're alive here, now, entirely in your own right. No mother, no father, no ghosts. You're a kiln-firer. A free spirit. I think it might be an excellent idea if you forgot about everything else for a minute and let me hold you.'

I might have said all of this, and I said none of it. I felt many things for which, in these confused circumstances, there were no permissible words. And it was impossible to tell whether her own gaze held anything more than the bewildered gratitude and regret that were clearly there. So I silently willed her to know that if life with Edward became insupportable there was a place for her to come. Yet she would have been upstairs with the old man before I was out of the moonlit yard.

10 ❧ Symbolic and Diabolic

It was the morning of Emilia Frere's departure from the Hall and for a few minutes Louisa found herself alone with the Rector, who fingered the brim of his hat and beamed like the milky sun outside.

Though she had foreseen the need for such a private moment Louisa would certainly not have chosen it to occur so quickly. Her thoughts were muddled still, and her feelings scattered in small exclusive groups like members of a difficult meeting yet to be called to order. They kept slipping away, as her father had already slipped away, with no more than a mumbled excuse, to jot down a line of verse that had presented itself while he stood in some abstraction. Tom Horrocks, who might otherwise have furnished a convenient buffer, had been drawn to the kitchen by the smell of newly baked bread, and was doubtless flirting disgracefully with Tilly and the kitchen-maids. In the meantime Emilia was in her room still, fussing for an unconscionably long time over her appearance. So Louisa must decide how best to employ the unsought opportunity of her confinement with the Rector, and she was entirely unready.

'Fortunately,' she said in belated response to Frere's remark of a moment before, 'the drive to the Rectory is not far.'

'And the day,' he observed, 'moderately clement.'

'Emilia will be well wrapped.'

'Indeed.'

And there yet another exchange of platitudes gravelled on silence.

She had been trying to marshal a persuasive line of argument in her mind. *If the truth is at last unavoidable,* it ran, *and if it must bring consolation in its train, then surely there should be no need to dread its disclosure?* But there was something unsatisfactory about its far from syllogistical terms, and she was left unconvinced. As her eyes strayed, yet again, to the clock on the mantelpiece, she wondered whether it was, after all, a matter of timing—that what in auspicious circumstances might be helpful could, in others, be quite devastating. How difficult this was!

Evidently the Rector felt himself obliged to remedy the silence. 'Tom Horrocks has put my mind quite at rest,' he said.

'He is a considerate man.'

'And an excellent physician.'

'Yes. His reputation reaches behind the county, I believe.'

'We are fortunate to enjoy his services,' said Frere, though he immediately regretted the choice of verb: heartening though Horrocks's manner was, there was small occasion for pleasure in a doctor's professional attendance.

'I know him better as a friend,' Louisa confessed, 'having always enjoyed good health.'

'It is a great blessing.' The hat took a further turn in Frere's hands. 'We must count our blessings, Miss Agnew. They are manifold.'

For a moment Louisa wondered whether this platitudinous sentiment might be turned to advantage, but it could not be done without contrivance; and when she looked up she saw how the Rector's face aspired to bravery. During the past few days anxiety had shadowed his eyes like bruises; they were brighter now and eager in their attention to the door through which his wife must soon enter. Plainly he was recovering himself. Were Louisa to speak what pressed upon her mind it would, she saw, quite undo him.

'I was wondering . . .' Frere began again, hesitantly.

But Louisa was elsewhere still. She was reflecting once more how her continued silence might preserve the unsought trust confided in her, but it remained a betrayal of her friendship for this man. Never had she been so confused.

'I thought, once Emilia is with us . . .'

'Yes, Mr Frere?'

'I thought . . . a prayer of thanksgiving?'

'It would be entirely appropriate.'

'You would join us?'

'It would be a great joy.'

'Your father?'

'Has promised to return in a moment.'

'I felt sure you would consent.' Yet behind the grateful smile one cloud remained. 'But the Doctor . . . Tom? I would dearly wish him to be there and yet I would not impose on his convictions.'

'Nor, I feel sure, would he wish to give offence by abstention.'

'Then you think . . . ?'

'I do.'

This was, apparently, a burden lifted from his mind. It was more than that, for now all anxieties were dispelled. The smile was clear. Handsomely, warmly so.

Louisa was filled with a terrible wonder at Frere's ignorance. Again she found herself astounded that Emilia should have so little feeling for him. His diffidence was the shy guise of uncommon sensitivity. Other parsons of her acquaintance would have nothing but commination for Tom Horrocks's head; they would have demanded brusquely that all kneel and at least pay lip-service to their own self-righteousness; but this man . . .

She wanted to cross the room. She wanted to press her hand on his, say, 'My dear, Mr Frere, I beg you to forgive what must appear an intolerable intrusion, but I have reason to believe your present happiness must be short-lived unless . . .'

Unless what?

In her imagination Louisa saw the man confronted by the chill implacable will which had seized her own hand the previous night and imprisoned her in confidence . . . that *sacred* confidence. How fiercely Emilia had insisted on it. It lay now like a stone across Louisa's tongue. And there was nothing sacred there. It felt like a curse rather. It profaned the very bonds of speech. If she herself was at a loss to cope with the perplexities it wrought, what chance would this tender spirit stand before it? Such happiness as had returned with his wife's recovery would wither as she spoke. Her candour, however delicately phrased, would blight it. What was meant for a joyous occasion would shrivel to a general wretchedness.

Yet if she did not speak . . .

There might *be* no other moment.

Louisa felt the palpitation of her heart. There was a flutter in her throat as she drew the breath to speak. 'Mr Frere, there is a matter that I must . . .' She faltered at his eager eye. He waited, unwitting, ready to be of service. He was all unprepared. Again his encouraging smile discomposed her.

The door opened and Emilia was there, caped and bonneted, a pale disgruntlement in her face. 'Ah, here you are. I had begun to believe the Hall quite deserted.'

Frere sprang to his feet. 'Emilia, dearest, do you imagine I could abandon you now at the very moment I have longed for? Miss Agnew and I have been patiently awaiting your appearance.'

Emilia deflected the warmth of his approach. She turned an exact gaze upon Louisa, then a studied flickering of eyelashes affirmed complicity. 'My dear,' she said, 'you look a little wan this morning. Have I quite worn you out with my demands? Edwin,' she added, without moving her gaze, 'Louisa has been so great a comfort to me I can hardly bear this parting.'

For a moment Louisa could not bring herself to answer the frail smile. How she loathed this web that had been spun so swiftly round her. She felt soiled by it.

'I believe it is possible,' Frere was saying, 'that there may be some small service we can do in return. Miss Agnew, you were about to say?'

And she was caught between them. *Fool*, she was thinking angrily, and she could not restrain the quick glance that sought Emilia's eyes. In a shocked instant she saw it: had she seized the moment that was lost for ever now, had she spoken to Frere, unfolded the unhappy fate in store for him, it would have spelled disaster. The scenes were acted swiftly in her mind: when Frere turned in bewilderment to Emilia the woman would deny that any such confidence had been exchanged; accused of mischief, Louisa would be forgiven by neither; the 'intolerable slander' (for such it would be called) would furnish a pretext for Emilia's immediate departure from Munding; and Frere, if he remained, would be friendless.

Was it possible then that, in its impotence before a lie, the truth could do great harm?

She stood, numb with shame, fingers tugging at the bracelet round her wrist until it caused her pain.

'My dear?' Emilia encouraged.

Louisa looked away, out of the window—how she wished she was out there in the frosty air, in the simplicity of the Lodge, alone, in the one place where her tarnished star-fire might begin to gleam again.

But she must speak.

'It was nothing,' she said, ' . . . a passing thought.' Then she willed herself to look back at them. 'Nothing that may not be answered by the prayer that Mr Frere would have me join.' She took in his mild perplexity. 'Excuse me a moment,' she added hastily, 'I must find father and Dr Horrocks. And I am sure that Tilly and the staff would wish to join us in expressing their heartfelt relief.' Before either the Rector or his wife could speak again Louisa hurried from the room. Behind her she heard Emilia say, 'I think the child will be quite desolate to see me go. Her life is very empty here.'

When the thaw came to Munding it came as rain, a wind-driven chilling rain that flooded the water-meadows and made the ford impassable. Pipes, sprained by the ice, burst now, reed-thatches leaked; at least one low-lying cottage in the hollow was awash. Water, it seemed, was everywhere; the lanes were mired with it, dikes deep, clogged here and there by flotsam into dams that would sunder and flood under the pressure of constant rain. A sodden pedlar out of Saxburgh brought the news that the millrace there had broken its banks and the pond lay right across the Norwich road. The bridge at Pottisham was down. Further along the river, it was rumoured, a wherryman had drowned. Certainly people in Shippenhall were out on their roofs for boats to rescue them, and still there was no let up in the rain.

Only in Munding Rectory had there been no thaw.

Clearly Emilia Frere's decline was more emotional than physical, for it would respond to no remedy. Visitors were not welcomed upstairs, and if Mrs Bostock haughtily insisted on the sovereign nature of her companionship she met with little encouragement in that belief.

Mrs Frere's refusal to respond (Mrs Bostock later informed Eliza Waters) was as dreary as the rain, and as impervious to her visitor's desire that it should cease. My dear, one had positively risked an influenza to bring her some good cheer, and to what end? There had been nothing achieved by the expedition save the coachman's cold which now threatened to lay low the rest of her staff. However, one knew one's duty even if the parson's wife seemed negligent of hers.

Eliza Waters, who was herself venturing upon a cold, would have found it difficult to agree more. Yet, to be quite fair, Mrs

Bostock conceded, one must consider the possibility that the fault might lie with the husband.

Miss Waters was certain that this was so, but she would be most interested to hear how her friend had arrived at that conclusion.

Was it not obvious (she was answered) that the man felt sorrier for himself than for his wife? He was all milk and water. He lacked the fire to take a firm hand with the woman. Why, if Bostock treated her that way she would be inclined to fetch a stick to him, for the vapours (as Mrs Frere so dismally attested) would be the sole alternative. One must pity the woman, however tiresome she made the task. The fact was, the Rector had no sense of priorities—he would be happier washing the feet of the poor than ordering a dignified social life such as a woman in Mrs Frere's position had the right to expect.

'If only she would not go on about Cambridge so,' Miss Waters regretted.

'My dear, the woman no longer does even that. Indeed, some tattle of Cambridge life would have been a pleasurable relief. The poor thing can hardly bring herself to speak at all. One might as well not be there.'

'And the Rector showed no gratitude for the interest taken?'

'But you know the man as well as I,' Mrs Bostock protested. 'He bumbled and tugged at his ear and said he hoped I might call again at a more opportune moment, though I did not believe a word of it. He wanted me out, my dear. That much was evident. I greatly fear that there is something not right about the man.'

'Not right?'

'Not right.'

'I do agree,' said Miss Waters, then regretted that she had agreed too quickly, for Mrs Bostock would venture no further except to opine that the Reverend Frere was, at the very least, too little of this world to serve as a useful guide to the next. 'Charity begins at home,' she concluded, 'and that is not a home I shall seek to enter again in a hurry.'

And what more could Miss Waters do but affirm that if one could not perform one's Christian duty without being treated as a busybody then the parish had come to a sorry pass?

Having fought to overcome his grief at the loss of the child, the object of this critical review had, in fact, sought every means he dared to stop the great gap it opened in the domestic life of the Rectory. Frere's thanksgiving for his wife's recovery was heartfelt, for *that* loss would have been irreparable; and his rejoicing at her return was genuine enough; but how short-lived. Muted as it was in consideration of Emilia's still frail condition, the joy, which was inevitably tinged with sadness, had been allowed small room to breathe. Indeed, it had expired almost on the short journey home.

For Emilia, as for himself, Dr Horrocks's reassurance that miscarriage was a kind of mercy had brought no deep comfort, and Frere would not remind her of it, for he had quickly seen that, in some way he was far from comprehending, the loss was more secondary to her than it was to himself. Was she then secretly distressed by the thought that she had failed him? If so, he would not have her blame herself. The failure was less hers than his own for not having taken better care. He would never forgive his absence at her moment of need—the fault was freely confessed in an agony of self-reproach; but such, it seemed, was not Emilia's unspoken thought. *Failure* was not a word that answered.

Nor did his attempt to view their shared suffering as part of the Lord's mysterious providence—a present ill from which a future good might spring—in any way ameliorate her condition. She listened to his earnest philosophizing and did no more than that.

Where she must take comfort, he insisted, was in the doctor's assurance that there was no reason why she should not conceive again. Had Tom Horrocks not promised her so himself? Out of their love for each other, in God's good time, another child would grow. An hour was sure to come when this very room would ring loud with infant cries. Why, on cold winter nights like this, they might even briefly rue the desire that had brought a howling babe between themselves and sleep.

Emilia was neither comforted nor amused. She sighed, her pale brow resting on the fingertips of the ringed hand. If Edwin did not mind, she wished only to be left alone. Conversation exhausted her. After a long moment's unhappy shifting from foot to foot, Frere granted her wish.

That was the first day.

On the second night, at her emphatic request, Frere moved, temporarily, into another room.

It was not merely the weather that made the Decoy Lodge feel gloomier, more shadowy than Louisa remembered, not merely the damp that left her bones so chill. The rooms were hollow about her, unresponsive, as though, resentful of her absence, they had returned to desuetude and would not lightly be chivvied back. It was dispiriting, and Louisa found it hard to settle to her work. For too long she gazed at the rain across the lake. It swooped and gusted, then hung impermeably, aspiring almost to a solid state. There were moments when it felt like a portcullis downward-slammed between herself and the human community.

She had not expected this. As soon as the ice broke on the lake she had returned to the Lodge with an appetite for work, for solitude. On her way to the boathouse that dawn—before the rain began and too early for her father to rise in protest—thin panes of ice had snapped beneath her feet. She saw leaves of the last fall encased inside them and, yes, it was cold, but there was a fine frosty light, and the mist over the lake made her think of a stoat's white fur. With a sense of release, of invisibility almost, she slipped within its folds. Only out on the water with Pedro panting in the prow had she dared to admit that for the first time in her life she had felt herself a prisoner at the Hall.

Not one peaceful night had passed since Emilia Frere exacted her promise; not even after she and her husband were gone, back to whatever wretchedness awaited them in the Rectory. Alone in her room, Louisa had been unable to put them from her thoughts. She found it painful to anticipate the poor man's misery, and was dismayed to recognize how ferocious was her dislike for the woman. Never had she experienced such negative intensity of feeling. It would not square with any value she had taught herself to cherish, for she believed herself above such petty sentiments, and could cope with them now only by turning her dislike upon herself. What sort of creature was she after all who could feel only loathing for a woman who had suffered so? Emilia had been long sick with pregnancy; she had lost the child; and somewhere she was terribly afraid. Having experienced none of these things, what right had Louisa to judge of this? Who knew what an unhappy woman might say in such straits, and how little she might mean it?

The memory of that cold hand on hers spoke otherwise.

Louisa had slept badly and dreamed ill. On waking each day she had been out of temper. She wanted only to be free of this, for the lake to clear, so she could retreat to her task. Her invisible companions at the Lodge were pure hearts all. She longed only to be one among them.

And now she was here, and her mind was still shadowed by that unsolicited intelligence. Staring at the rain, she recalled her first conversation with Emilia, how they had discussed *The Tenant of Wildfell Hall* and the woman had protested a righteous indignation at the thought of a wife deserting her husband. Yet with how much less justice than Helen Huntingdon did she contemplate it now!

Louisa strove for charity. It would not come. What displaced it was a sense of outrage that a man as kindly and compassionate as Edwin Frere should find himself shackled to a vixen. Almost it made one doubt one's trust in the Divine Intellect that decreed such things.

There was no profit in these thoughts. They served only to make her own heart sore and to mar her concentration. She reached for her pen and dipped it into the well so fiercely that when she lifted it a blot fell across the page. She sighed crossly, was about to dispose of the paper when a wicked thought possessed her. Under the black splodge of ink she drew the neck and shoulders, then the severe, aloof posture of the woman she despised. It was a few moments' work to have her sitting with her baggage in a gig, to crown the blot with a ridiculous hat, and to write the word CAMBRIDGE on a downward-sloping signpost. At the rear of the speeding carriage, she inked in a cloud of dust.

'Be gone, Emilia Frere,' she found herself thinking. 'Get you from this parish. Abandon Munding Rectory and your husband. I shall keep my promise.'

It was in the realm of pastoral care that Edwin Frere believed himself most truly priest. After a discouraging start he had begun, he thought, to win the confidence of the villagers. He had hit the right note of playful yet dignified affection with the children—mischievous Sam Yaxley had proved an ally there; and even throughout the days of his own distress he had comforted the sick and sorrowful, acting in the simple trust that, however removed those impoverished lives might seem from his own, they were members of one another.

Long before his ordination Frere had been persuaded that the human heart was held in common and, therefore, a word truly spoken either way could touch and move it. Forgetful of the silence which prevailed over his own most troubling experiences, he believed that direct and gentle questioning might embolden even the least articulate sufferer to speak all the grief and rage of the heart, and so dispel it. In this conviction, he tried, as priest, to stand open to meeting, for it was in the ground of meeting that true comfort grew. He heard all patiently, taking the pain within himself in the hope that he might show by his own fallible example how much greater was the patient love of Christ.

So, yes, with a neighbour he would have known precisely what to do. With his own wife he scarce dare attempt it.

He stood before her wretchedness like an incompetent at the scene of an accident. *Flowers,* he had thought; *surely they must lift her heart.* But this was a lean season for flowers, so he had gone out into the rain looking for snowdrops. He had found them and he loved them: the little heads like frail iron, withstanding this wolf-month cold; and, when you opened the white petals, there were the green veins, promise of the Spring to come. They were, surely, the perfect emblem of Emilia's need? He had attempted a verse on the theme, but the lines lacked grace. He had abandoned it and taken the flowers to speak for themselves at her bedside, but she did not hear them. What he had seen there Emilia failed to see; when he pointed it out, she turned away.

She would accept no other visitors and yet, he sensed, she did not want him near. His very tenderness seemed a burden to her. But this was not the hardest thing to bear.

Alone in the room where he passed his nights, Frere closed the chapter of the Bible which had long ceased to occupy his thoughts. Tomorrow, he decided, he must press her to a full disclosure of the grief harboured in her heart. Yet no sooner was the decision taken than he quailed at the prospect, for he knew that a full expression of the rage lying at the root of Emilia's melancholic condition must quickly overwhelm him.

Unspoken though they were, the facts of the case were plain, and he could no longer conceal them from himself. His wife hated their life here in Munding, and what had happened in the ice-bound park at Easterness had become for her the final bitter vindication of that hate. Munding was a place where her vitality bled away. There was nothing for her here; and if this was admitted between them it must swiftly prove an admission with only one exit.

Morose and fretful, Frere contemplated a further defeated return to Cambridge—his promises unkept, his congregation resigned to a curate's care, his mind racked by remorse and a crippling sense of his own twice-proven inadequacy. No, it was intolerable.

She had promised him obedience. She had vowed to honour him for better or for worse, just as he must honour her in sickness as he did in health. His marriage to this parish was inviolable in its own sacred vows. He was as little free to renege on them.

So what was he to do but bear with her? Accept her cold rebuffs without anger or impatience; be there for her as best he might in the fond hope that this dreary rain must cease, that Spring must come again, and she might wake one day to that glorious span of light across the water-meadows. As he turned back the coverlet of the bed where he must sleep alone, Frere consoled himself with the thought that what he was incapable of accomplishing himself might be accomplished for him by time and that providential hand, of which, in his earnest efforts outside the home, he was the faithful instrument.

It was perhaps a coward's answer, and he was honest enough to admit it. But he would pray—both for Emilia's recovery from affliction, and for the strength he would need throughout the long thawing of the ice about her heart.

One person at least had emerged from the unhappy events at Easterness with a renewed enthusiasm for life. Alone at his desk in the library, Henry Agnew put down his pen, blotted the page and placed it neatly atop the growing stack of paper at his side. Then he looked up at the portrait of Sir Humphrey Agnew and smiled. What a day of work this had been!

For some time now he had been certain that he had at last evolved a diction appropriate both to the requirements of classical epic and to the subtleties of the alchemical process. No mean problem, this, in a time largely deafened to such sober music, and were it not for the incomparable examples of Spenser and Milton, he might finally have despaired; but what they in their day had achieved for their grave themes ought (he had long believed) to be possible for the richer store of myth and symbol at his disposal; and now the lines had begun to move with the majesty he desired. He too now soared 'in the high region of his fancies with his garland and singing robes about him.' He too was poet. If only Louisa were by to share the joy of it.

Yet even the fact of her absence was cause for congratulation, for what she had presciently foretold had come to pass. He had indeed allowed himself to become too dependent on her, and he had paid the price of it. He had been so blinded by his need for her light that he had failed to see how deeply he stood in her shadow, and his work had been frustrated thereby. For a time, when she first took to the seclusion of the Lodge, days had been wasted in a sort of restless grief, but it had passed, resentment fell away, and gradually he found his way back into his own strength. It was he, after all, who was the master of the Art, and now that Louisa had taken upon herself the task of preparing his way he was freed from the immediate pressure of time. He could work more calmly, and had even—so surely had his confidence returned—felt free enough to step outdoors to watch the skating, though the grip of the cold at his lungs had troubled him. Then he had thought all lost in the sudden distraction of the parson's wife's misfortune. All might have been ruined there, with that nervous, alien presence in the house, the comings and goings, the servants all of a huff. Yet considerate as ever, Louisa had shielded him from the worst of the intrusion. He had pressed on with the work, permitting no more interruption than common courtesy required, and had joined in the prayer of thanksgiving with a truly heartfelt gratitude not occasioned only by the woman's departure.

Something in the quality of Frere's devotion had touched him. Bumbler the man might be, but his unaffected tenderness reminded Agnew of the care he had lavished on his own wife in her dying days. He remembered his own great grief, and how he had finally emerged from it with a renewed sense of purpose; for though his epic *was* intended to address the spiritual crisis of the age, it had also been conceived as a requiem for his lost wife and a celebration of her unwavering faith in his ability. Reflecting on the parson's fortitude in distress, his manifest care for his wife, and his humble acceptance of divine will, Agnew had felt a sense of shame that his original impulse had been clouded by the passing years. It returned now as an act of re-dedication; and suddenly the work progressed.

So intense was the flow of inspiration, he had barely noticed the rain at his window, and was amazed to be told later of floods and drownings. He had been elsewhere, rapt in meditation, as the harvest of his long withdrawal from the world came home. Verse after verse had sprung from silence to run in fiery lines across the page. Never had he known such rapture. Gratefully he might echo the joyful cry of Trismegistus in *The Golden Treastise*:

Approach, ye sons of Wisdom, and rejoice: let us now rejoice together; for the reign of death is finished and the son doth rule; he is invested in the scarlet garment, and the purple is put on.

Across the lake, in the Decoy Lodge, the mood was less exalted, for eventually all the demons of solitude came to visit Louisa Agnew where she worked alone. How well she was coming to know them: the Mid-day Demon of Accidie who dulled her mind and drained the words of meaning; the Seraph-Serpents, ever hot upon his heels, whose bite flustered her to panic and anxiety; then, by dark, the Ochim—doleful screech-owls whose appetite always demanded more than she knew how to give. Every anchorite had known and suffered from these phantoms of the mind: how naïve she had been to imagine herself exempt.

Yet the visitations had begun innocently enough. The first indeed had presented itself as no more than vivid memory, though—if she were honest with herself—she would admit it had arisen from a kind of fear.

As had not been the case throughout her first sojourn at the Lodge, she would start from her thoughts at some unexpected sound—a movement of the timbers, a mouse stirring in the wainscot, a drenched thrush fluffing its feathers in the thatch-eaves. Even Pedro, pattering nervily about the room, seemed more restless than usual, and when he slept his dreams were troubled. Gradually Louisa began to wonder whether her father had been right after all, whether she had been as unwise as he claimed to shut herself away in this sequestered place. At moments when her concentration was disturbed, when dusk came too soon and its shadows flittered dismally about the room, almost she might think she was afraid.

Once, when the shock of alarm thrilled through her with more than usual intensity, she began to sing, softly, to keep her spirits up, and several phrases had passed her lips before she realized that the song came from her childhood—that she had not sung those words for almost twenty years, had forgotten them even until this moment when, with startling clarity, her memory travelled back in time.

It was a summer afternoon—she could barely have been more than eight years old—and she had come to the Lodge with her brother and their cousin, Laetitia, who was visiting the Hall with her parents. Henry was thirteen then, Lettice a year younger, Henry had not wanted to bring Louisa on the expedition but she had cried to go, and the adults insisted that she not be left behind. No one had known that Henry planned to take the skiff and voyage across the lake into the forbidden territory of the Decoy Lodge.

If the Lodge was not quite ruinous then, it was in poor repair. No one had used it for years. The reed-thatch was spiky and unkempt, windows were broken, one of the doors unhinged. Breathless with a sense of violation, the three children had entered.

At the time Louisa was more impressed by the fact that Henry had lied to their father than by the dreariness of the place. Irritated by her presence, Henry had mocked and teased her nevertheless, for he could be quite beastly when the mood took him that way. He found a rusty man-trap in the cupboard—an evil contraption of chains and springs and teeth—and assured her that it had taken the leg off more than one poacher in its day. 'Look,' he said, pointing to some darker smudges of rust, 'you can still see the bloodstains here, and here.' Gratified by his sister's distress, he then whispered that he had a dark secret to tell them: *the place was haunted.*

What the girls had to understand, he whispered, was that his father's father had used the Lodge for very wicked purposes, things so wicked that he had gone quite mad and died in a madhouse. From there, no doubt, he'd gone straight to Hell; but there were times when he and his wicked mistresses were still to be seen walking here, their shades drawn back from Hellfire to visit the scene of their sins.

The lie had a pronounced effect upon Lettice who immediately ventured on a small excursion into terror. Louisa found her cousin's whimpers more unnerving than the story itself, but Henry, older, shrewder, discerned an encouraging element of titillation in Laetitia's fear.

'What sort of sins?' Louisa innocently asked, for this hitherto untold family news greatly interested her.

The sins were far too wicked to be named, Henry had answered with a confidential glance at Lettice who held her dainty hands at her mouth, wide-eyed. Moreover, that was not the only spookish thing about the place: Henry knew for a fact that hundreds of years before, there had been a magician in the family. His name was Sir Humphrey Agnew, and he had consorted with a witch hereabouts.

Louisa had heard of Sir Humphrey, but not that he was a magician.

'He most certainly was,' Henry insisted, 'and the witch's name was Janet. Everyone for miles around lived in terror of them. I've seen the cauldrons that they used to cast their spells. Father keeps them hidden away in a room off his library.'

This was impressive. Had Humphrey and Janet been very wicked too, Lettice wanted to know, and did they too haunt the Lodge? Henry said that he wouldn't be at all surprised; but Lettice need not be afraid as long as she stayed close to him.

'Are you very brave?' Lettice asked.

Henry assured her that he was. Much braver than Louisa—who was offended by this comparison and declared that she was not at all afraid.

'Oh yes you are,' said Henry.

'Oh no I'm not,' Louisa had protested then with all the virtue of truth in her small voice. She had been undaunted even when Henry said he'd wager that she dare not stay alone in the Lodge while he and Lettice explored the woods outside.

The stake had been set at a silver thruppence—a thruppence which (Louisa remembered smiling now) she had never seen, for the afternoon had ended in disaster. She must have sat alone there for a good quarter of an hour, singing to herself, before Henry and Lettice came crashing back through the woods, squealing that they had seen Humphrey and Janet and must take to the skiff at once. Genuinely frightened by their fear, little Louisa had rushed after them and sat trembling beside Lettice in the skiff while young Henry rowed for all he was worth. When she dared to look back, however, she saw nothing more alarming than Jem Bales, the woodman, and behind him, in the shadow of the trees, a woman who might have been Audrey, the kitchenmaid, though she could not be quite sure. Perhaps Henry and Lettice had seen something else? Whatever the case, the exploit cost Henry a thrashing later that day, and Louisa had too much heart to ask about her thruppence.

Emerging from those rapt moments of remembrance, Louisa put down her pen. The work had been far from her thoughts all evening. She had written little in the hour before the sudden sound had startled her and she began to sing to herself, the words of that same song she had sung so long before in this same room. How clearly it had all come back to her—even the piping treble of her own childish voice.

The lamp guttered a little in the chimney draught. She was returned to the present now, to the papers at her desk, to the rain barracking against the window-glass; but her thoughts were wandering still.

Had Henry spoken truer than he knew, she wondered, for at a dismal time like this the Lodge was a shadowy place. It had been a part of her intention in coming here to banish those shades: already it seemed they were darkening her mind as surely as they still lowered across her father's. She sensed that, even in contesting her decision to make use of the Lodge, her father had found it impossible to speak his full revulsion for the place. The mere thought of Madcap Agnew—a name rarely mentioned in the Hall—appeared to stultify him. What could the man have done that had been so vile?

Her only reference was the behaviour of Huntingdon and his set in Acton Bell's novel—the gambling, the womanizing, the drink, and the meanness of temper such vices induced. Those activities were so evidently a waste of spirit that Louisa had never understood how men were so easily lured by them. Yet lured they were, even deeper into the toils of matter, and women with them too. Was it only lovelessness then that made an evil of the flesh? For in the Hermetic Art—symbolic though its language was—the mating of Sol and Luna was a moment of great joy and exaltation. It was the healing of ills, the great *mysterium*. That humankind had been created male and female was, of itself, the promise that such mystery might be made flesh. Yet if the density of her father's silence spoke true, then Madcap Agnew had used this place to make of that mystery something vile indeed.

Alone with the pages of her book, Louisa felt depleted by the knowledge that the world for which she wrote was so completely estranged from the values she cherished. It preferred, apparently, to revel blindly in its senses, as though life were no more than a rout of appetite and sensation rather than the dream of gold she sought to share. And then she recalled the words Emilia

Frere had spoken: *You have not known a man . . . you have not suffered at their nakedness.*

If the words had chilled her at first hearing it was more because of the cold light they cast on the woman's most intimate life than for any reference to her own innocence. They troubled her more deeply now. From whatever inaccessible pit of bitterness the words reached out to touch an empty place in her own life. In these matters Emilia Frere knew more than she, for the woman had crossed the threshold of the married state; she had delivered herself over to the meeting of the flesh as Louisa had not been called upon to do; she had experienced what the uninitiate could only surmise. For Louisa this crucial moment of a woman's life—the very act by which life itself was assured of continuity—remained a mystery. In her preoccupation with other, larger and less accessible mysteries she had been too certain of the supreme value of her endeavours to attach great value to the consequent deprivations; but now she remembered also how Tom Horrocks had lightly berated her celibate condition while they skated with Edwin on the frozen lake. In their different ways both Tom and Emilia had alluded to the same experience; and before that experience she was utterly virgin. Yet her work touched on it at every point; and without such experience, without the knowledge of such suffering—if suffering it was—what authority did she possess to speak a word of meaning in the world?

With a pang of dismay she saw how everything she knew came only from a marriage between native intelligence and the wisdom of old books. Though the books were sound, her apprehension clear, the meeting joyful, could that possibly be experience enough?

She looked back through the many pages she had written, and saw the great names glitter there—Proclus, Plotinus, Iamblichus, Ficino, Pico, Agrippa. Ardent spirits all. Men who had known and endured the world. These and the adepts of the Art were her fiery masters. Apart from her father and her brother, these were the only men she had ever deeply known. She loved them all and, yes, she could write of them. Out of her mating with their books a small book of her own would be born. She had set her mind to it, and it would certainly be accomplished; but in that winter dusk, as the rain fretted at her window, as she recalled the innocence of the child who had once sung alone in the house where her grandfather had done such wrong, Louisa

Anne Agnew, already twenty-seven years old, wondered whether her life had yet properly begun at all.

'As far as I am concerned,' said Dr Horrocks, 'the matter is plain enough.'

'I am greatly relieved to hear it,' said Edwin Frere.

The noise in the doctor's throat might have been a groan or a growl. 'I am afraid you misunderstand me. The plain fact of the matter is, there is nothing I can do for your wife.' Then he saw from the sudden anxiety on the parson's face that this too might be misunderstood. He hastened to add, 'Physically, Mrs Frere is sound as a bell. There is no good reason why she should remain in her bed, and the darkness of the room can only aggravate her melancholic condition. She must stir herself, Mr Frere, and if she will not, then *you* must stir her.'

From the despair in the parson's eyes the doctor saw that this remedy had already been tried to no avail. Clearly the dose had not been severe enough. But how, delicately, to suggest as much?

'At the very least, this taste for laudanum must be discouraged. The tincture has its uses, but restoration of active vigour is not among them. It does not help, Mr Frere, it does not help.'

Frere's eyes were now wandering unhappily.

'Come, sir,' the doctor pressed. 'You must take her firmly in hand. In so far as decorum allows I have tried to do so myself, and at some cost to my reputation for a sympathetic bedside manner. As you will have observed, your wife was not pleased to see me; she remained impatient of my attentions throughout, and the only profit from the visit is my own. I need hardly say that I don't care to have things so. Don't care for it at all.'

Frere murmured an apology which Horrocks hastily dismissed. 'Dammit man, I know these things can be difficult but some people must be bullied back to shape. And there are occasions—this is most certainly one of them—when it is the husband's place, not the doctor's, to do the bullying. You must learn to sharpen your tongue, sir. Even in the pulpit there are moments when mildness of manner is not enough. It is certainly the case in bed.'

Frere's face reddened—a blush, yes, but also a hint of anger too. 'I have exhorted my wife to the point where I am at a loss for patient words,' he protested. 'Would you have me take a crop to her, Dr Horrocks?'

The doctor smiled. 'You might show her one. A touch more of the spirit that is in you now can do no harm.'

Sighing, Frere flapped his hands at his sides like a seal. 'You will forgive me if I insist that I understand Mrs Frere better than you do yourself. It will only turn her to stone, I promise you. It would do the same to me.'

'Stone against stone sparks fire, Mr Frere. Set a fire beneath her bed and I warrant she'll be out quick enough.' Tom Horrocks had scented something suspect in Emilia Frere's continuing frailty—it had been too sharply belied by the animus in her eyes. Yet he saw that this rough humour would not serve.

'It is not in my nature,' Frere appealed.

The doctor weighed his man. 'Perhaps, after all, you are in need of help. Mrs Frere needs company, stimulus . . .'

'She will see no one but myself.'

'What about her own family? Has she no sister perhaps?'

'Indeed she does, but she will not have me write to her.'

'Good God, man, you don't need her consent. Do it at once. Have her come. The surprise alone will be restorative. Take my advice, sir—put pen to paper instantly.'

The thought of Harriet fussing about the Rectory held little charm for her brother-in-law. In his opinion, though it had never been openly expressed, she was little more than a flibbertigibbet whose thoughts rarely ranged further afield than the next gratification. Neither was at ease in the other's company. But the doctor was right: he stood in need of help, and where else was there to turn?

'Perhaps it would be wise,' he said. 'I shall do it today.'

'Excellent. See to it that the resolve does not expire with my departure.' Dr Horrocks turned in search of his hat and crop, then decided that a further word was needful. 'We are friends, I think, Mr Frere?'

'I have been happy to think so.'

'Then, as a friend, let me ask you to have a care for yourself as well. My manner can be a little brusque, I grant you, but there is a reason for it—a sound professional reason. The care of others can be a wearing business. One must take steps to preserve one's own virtue—I use the word in the classical sense, you understand. I advise you to take some such steps yourself. Otherwise, my dear fellow, you will soon be of no use to wife, man nor beast. Remember—I saw you on the ice. You did not falter there. You displayed a rare vitality. I am certain that your wife is not the only one who would profit from its wider deployment. Delight and laughter, sir, delight and laughter! If you hear tell of better tonics I should be glad to hear of them.' But the doctor discerned no more than the ghost of either in the Rector's smile. 'Well, you must excuse me now,' he sighed. 'I have other calls upon my time.'

Outside, Tom Horrocks stood for a moment stroking the nose of his great bay. He was fond of the man who fretted beside him, and a touch impatient with him too. But when ears were deaf what use were admonitions? He put a foot to the stirrup and swung himself into the saddle. 'Fish or mend nets, Mr Frere,' he said. 'One or t'other and I don't mind which.' And with that he reined the mare's head about and was off down the lane, brandishing the crop, significantly, above his shoulder.

Frere watched him go, and such hopes as he might briefly have entertained receded with the clop of hooves. For an instant envying his friend's unmarried state, he turned into the house to pacify whatever agitated waters the doctor had left in his wake.

Sometimes far into the evening she kept herself locked at the desk, writing, writing. No longer could she take any pleasure in the act; almost she had come to hate the interminable travail. Her wrist was stiff, her fingers calloused by the pen. And yet, as though not she but some other invisible agency were the true author of the work, page after page was done. It was a process of automatic writing such as she had heard tell of in the sillier drawing-rooms of the county where idle men and women amused and, she suspected, sometimes alarmed themselves by tinkering in realms they did not understand; except that this was very different, for the entirety of her intellect was engaged. It danced in consort with whatever power it was that provoked her thought, and so energetically at times that, when a day's work was over, she felt as weary as one of the dancing princesses from a fairy-tale, exhausted by their demon partners.

Then, at what was to her the crucial moment of the work, the music began to fail. At the beginning of each new paragraph she must summon her strength to overcome enormous resistances. A voice whispered that the work was nonsense, too far removed from the interests of the age to be of value. It would be mocked, scorned, spurned. She merely revealed herself for what she was: a cloistered innocent, lacking the fashionable touch, too earnest by half in her endeavours to persuade a jaded world that she knew best. Still worse, her mind was recurrently invaded now by carnal fantasies.

She had reached the point in her argument where she must examine and explicate the emblems offered by the masters for the *Coniunctio Solis et Lunae*, the redemptive marriage-dance of sun and moon. Such emblems were manifold and she was embarrassed by their riches. Only after considerable thought and a number of false starts had she decided to take for her key reference the mysterious poem called the *Enigma Philosophorum* from Elias Ashmole's 'Theatre of Chemistry':

> There is no light but what lives in the Sun,
> There is no sun but which is twice begott;
> Nature and Arte the parents first begonne:
> By *Nature* t'was but *Nature* perfects not.
>   *Arte* then, what *Nature* left, in *hand* doth take,
>   And out of *one* a *twofold* work doth make.
>
> A *twofold* work doth make, but such a work
> As doth admitt *Division* none at all,
> (See here wherein the secret most doth lurk)
> Unless it be a *mathematical*.
>   It must be *two* yet make it *one* and *one*
>   And you do take the way to make it *none*.
>
> Lo here, the primar secret of this Arte,
> Contemne it not but understand it right,
> Who faileth to attaine the foremost part,
> Shall never know *Arte's* force or *Nature's* might,
>   Nor yet have power of *one* and *one*, so mixt,
>   To make by *one fixt*, one unfixed fixt.

It was, she thought, perfect for her needs. Gnomic, succinct, its puns and allusions introduced all the themes she must develop, yet it remained abstract enough for her mind to keep firm purchase on her errant feelings.

Such was her hope and her intent, but once launched upon her exposition she quickly found herself confused by the royal actors of the Art. They were not to be chastened by homilies like children at a Sunday school. Flamboyant, mercurial creatures, they had passionate wills of their own; they exercised a devious, seductive fascination. She struggled to preserve detachment, yet even as her mind appeared to perform its duty, covering page after page with swiftly written words, elsewhere it found ever more disturbing ways to misbehave.

Nor was it the mind alone. Her body had reached a climactic moment of its cycle, and felt famished and restless. Its clamourings against solitude were a constant distraction from the cooler processes of thought; yet even as her spirit chafed at this conflict between body and mind, Louisa understood that such stress was specific to her task and not to be avoided. Body and mind were among the contraries to be reconciled, and the true union of opposites was always preceded by bitter conflict. If her treatise was to fulfil the expectations raised by its prologue, she must make this difficult passage now—though it was, at times, an agony merely to remain seated at her desk.

The turns of the work became even more perplexing as the themes she must address became ever more entangled with the tensions she endured. In former ages certain masters had solved the problem by avoiding words entirely and resorting to pictures alone. There had been nothing either prurient or arbitrary in their choice of frankly sexual emblems to embody the mystery of the Conjunction; but even in times less hypocritical than her own such pictures had proved subject to misinterpretation. How much greater then the difficulty of conveying the mystery in words, and to an age reluctant to contemplate those experiences where the pathos of our animal nature stands in greatest tension with the highest aspirations of the soul! Nor was she herself exempt from confusion. In the erotic landscape on which her thoughts now opened, the illusory and the actual were so intimately twinned that only the most cautious eye might distinguish between them; and at each passionate encounter the symbolic and the literal seemed to enfold their embrace more tightly. Day by day her bewilderment increased, and, such was the fascination exercised upon the mind by these anarchic powers, she might find herself at any step allured in folly, and dizzily unaware of her plight.

She had, in part, been prepared for this. After all, Mercurius was the tutelary deity of the Art, and it was of his very nature to beguile and confuse in this manner; but she could take no comfort from the knowledge, for she must pursue him as through a hall of mirrors, from one bride-chamber to the next, and at each remove he shifted shape with such dispiriting agility that, again and again, she might have cried out loud for rest. And then, one afternoon, with the rain still beating down outside, appallingly he assumed the face of Madcap Agnew.

Aghast, incredulous, she craned to see more clearly if this was indeed her own mad forebear toying there inside her thought; and he turned to leer at her.

Louisa recoiled. The image vanished, but for several minutes now she sat in shock. It had been his face. Those features were familiar from the portrait in the Hall—the raffish eyes, the shining cheekbones, the lines about the lips and nostrils, that air of derisive irony. All were unmistakable; but if the crazed face of her grandfather had elided with the beckoning features of Mercurius then something had gone very wrong.

She looked back over what she had written: the words were empty, devoid of all vitality. It was not merely a matter of correction here and there—these were ashes; at best a discord such as some chained bear might pound on a piano. She released her breath in a sigh of exasperation. It was an attempt to preserve her objectivity, but it could not suppress a rising panic. She had deluded herself; she had believed that innocence of spirit and a devout purpose were adequate guides through this treacherous domain, but the facts were clear enough now: she had diminished mystery to pious platitude, and some devious element at work in the deeps of her imagination was scorning her efforts even as she made them . . . *Did you truly believe,* it seemed to say, *that I was to be so easily pinned down?*

Suddenly she felt cold. Half-consciously, she reached to pull the wrap more tightly round her shoulders; and still some seconds passed before she realized. The fire was still burning in the hearth; all the draughts had long since been stopped; but the room itself had gone chill around her. The cold came like the dowsing of a light. It was like a smell on the air. She was surrounded by it. Her palms, she saw, were damp.

Simultaneously, it seemed, there had been a change in barometric pressure. The room was unnaturally still about her, but the stillness might shatter at any second. It was waiting for something to happen; as she too was waiting for something to happen—something which must, at all costs, be forbidden.

Then it felt as though the world was sliding inside-out as, slowly, noiselessly, a panel swivelled in her mind. A hand somewhere might have touched a secret spring, for a whole wall was

turning on a hinge to reveal a hidden chamber. There were figures in there, sounds.

Either she must close her eyes against this or she must enter.
Unnerved, stricken with terror now, there was no choice; but
the darkness of her tightly shut eyelids offered no release. It
brought the images to sharper focus.

The chamber was candle-lit. A man was there, reclining on
a Récamier sofa, one booted leg slung along its length, the heel
of the other cocked against the floor. His shirt was casually
unbuttoned at the chest, the trousers high at the waist and tight
about his hips. They were, she observed, of a cut long since
outmoded. A ringed hand held a thin cigar which—as if in impatient expectation of her arrival—he stubbed in a silver tray.
The Lodge had altered around her. She recognized none of the
hangings, the furniture, the instruments scattered about. It was
like a disorderly tack-room, smelling of saddle-leather—except
that the air was also heavy with some dry exotic odour, dense
and sensual. And everywhere—an emanation of the cold itself—
there was a sense of incipient evil.

Distantly she could feel the tremor of a heart still recognizably
her own—though whether it shook with terror or from the first
stirrings of a ferocious excitement was hard to distinguish now.
Her mind was no longer entirely her own. Every nerve smouldered on a short fuse. There was an insatiable need for action.
With what remained of her objective consciousness Louisa strove
to tell herself that this encounter was not of her reality, not of
her willing . . . but even as she struggled she felt herself drawn
under the influence of a mind at once alien and familiar—a mind
resolute to lacerate its own fine sensibility, and with a perverse,
intellectual *sang-froid*. Slowly, as under the scientific patience
of a practised tormentor, all things were disfigured now. Around
her and—more terribly—within her, everything which had once
promised exultation and delight was warping to extravagance
and vice. Everything—however vile—was possible, and nothing
forbidden. The consequences left her sick with shame.

So far did the experience lie beyond the normal province of
time, she could not later tell whether it lasted for moments only
or extended into hours. What was certain was that throughout
its duration she felt wasted by an emptiness that no extremes of
violence, and no throes of humiliation, could even remotely
begin to fill. Bedevilled so, and moaning at her desk, she might
have frozen there had not Pedro come fretfully to her side. He

pushed his muzzle into her lap, wagging his rump, pleading to be let out. Louisa crashed back into time.

Instantly she knew that she too must get out of the Lodge. Even in the heavy rain she had to be out in clean air, running among the trees, anywhere other than inside the hot chamber of her skull.

As soon as the door was opened Pedro was gone. Louisa snatched her cape from the peg, banged the door shut behind her and leaned against it, panting. She saw Pedro disappear among the trees, called after him vainly, then stood in the rain, hands holding the hood tight over her ears. Then she too was gone, running, making for the trees.

At that same moment, many miles away, Harriet Frogmore—Emilia's younger sister and wife of a Cambridge gentleman-of-leisure—sat in what she was pleased to call her study, pondering the letter arrived that day from Norfolk.

Hattie was not the kind of woman ever to be troubled by demons. Her social calendar was far too full to entertain such disagreeable company, and should any turn up inadvertently among her guests then someone else must deal with them. Her own vague, frankly scatter-brained manner would always get away with it. Chatterboxes do.

Regrettably, however, she felt that Edwin's importunate letter must be taken seriously. No doubt he exaggerated (such was his wont where his conscience was concerned); yet the only news she had received from Em herself had not been happy; and now—to learn that she had suffered a miscarriage in that desert place at such a time of year, and that she had not felt able to share the grief of it with her own affectionate sister . . . Well, something was plainly wrong, and it was evident that Edwin was far too feeble to cope with it alone.

Hattie read the letter again, and sighed. As if her father's interminable complaints were not enough, no matter how she put herself out to please him. He had ever favoured Em—there were no two ways about it—and Em had been quite wrong to post herself to Norfolk in the first place. Sydney Smith had been wrong too; it seemed that the country was not even a *healthy* grave; though, judging from Edwin's pusillanimous letter, Smith might have been in the right when he suggested that there were three sexes—men, women and clergymen!

What qualities Em had ever seen in Edwin Frere quite beggared comprehension. The thought of several days cooped up with the man in some dreary Rectory was . . . Well, it was uninspiring, and Hattie needed inspiration. But she must go. Plainly she must go. Her appointments for the following week could, at a pinch, be postponed. Frogmore must hold the fort.

Hattie opened her writing-case, took out a sheet of paper and her pen, then sat gazing wistfully out of the window over Parker's Piece while she wondered whether or not to co-operate with Edwin's stratagem that this must appear a chance visit. How complicated the man made everything! Emilia would never be deceived; the sisters knew one another far too well. In fact, on second thoughts, would it not be far more sensible to invite Emilia to come to Cambridge? Surely, to get her out of that tedious place—if only for a time—must be a better answer. And that way she need cancel nothing. Em would enjoy the stimulus of old friends. It would cheer her no end, and it would delight their father too. Of course!

My dearest darling Em, she penned.

Then it occurred to her that this new plan would require two letters—this first and an explanatory note to Edwin, which was tiresome. Yet not half so tiresome as a February expedition across the fens.

How clever of her to think of this! She would remind Froggy of it the next time he ragged her for a noodle.

Calling vainly for her dog, Louisa pushed on deeper between the trees. She longed to encounter some other human presence and could not bear the thought of it. She felt contaminate. She would infect even the trivialities of conversation with the vileness of her thought. So she kept to the woods, following the way Pedro had led, until she came at last to the clearing at the head of the ride. It was the place where her grandfather, indulging some pharaonic whim, had planned to raise an obelisk. He might have done so, she reflected bitterly, had not madness made him its own monument first.

She stood with the cape drenched about her, the rain at her back, and knew she would never go back to the Lodge. The memory of what had happened there defied all thought. She had been too long the creature of thought, and now she had seen. She refused to think, to see, again.

She looked down the long ride to where, at the distant foot of its slope, the lake shuddered in the wind. She stared into its surface, which exercised a deep downward draw, as when one peered into a well and felt one's thoughts involuntarily plummet. She stared and stared until there was no division between the lake and her mind. Both were unappeasable. Here, like the mingled waters of a flood, was the first chaos of things. It was the dead sea of being female. Here one drowned.

A gust of wind tugged the hood to her shoulders. Freed hair fluttered about her eyes in soft, damp lashes. She must toss her head to see the lake clear again, and the action recalled how differently she had felt on the day when she skated there with Edwin Frere and Tom. She wanted to feel the world real around her again. She wanted to touch and be touched. She wanted to be comforted with closeness, to forget everything in such immediate intimacy, to be told that it was all right, that the world was real, and she had woken from a bad, bad dream . . .

And there was nowhere to turn. Even Pedro had fled from her. And if she abandoned the search for him, and hurried to the Hall, back to her father, what comfort there? A *forty-year madness*, he had called it, one which had laid waste the best years of her young life; yet he was back in the thick of his obsession now, and so elated by his own recent progress that he lacked the time to ask about her own. A wave of rage assailed her. He was a self-absorbed old fool. He had drained all the virtue from her. He had taken her innocence and beguiled it, filled her childish head with enthusiasm for his own mad fantasies, and left her depleted, a high-minded virgin on the rocks of her own barren dreams. A monstrosity.

There was so much anger in her she could not see what might be done with it. And how had all this happened? Because her father was afraid of life. As a child he had been unable to cope with the passions around him; he had hidden himself away in books, consoling himself with golden reveries. And then, as a man, he had needed a fellow-conspirator to make those consolations real, to confirm him in the righteousness of his seclusion from the world. Wisely, her brother had refused; but she . . . She had wandered innocently into this self-sealing labyrinth of fantasy until she was afraid of life herself. As now, in this terrible rain, she was afraid.

Emilia Frere had been right after all. To be a woman was to be a shell-less creature, bereft and vulnerable. It was to be the sport of men's insensitive obsession, raw matter tormented for the truth. One could survive only by silence and a strict refusal of complicity. One survived by guile.

But the thoughts sickened her. She was as much their victim as the naked flesh she had seen in that bleak vision had been victim to the flail. They did not fill the emptiness inside her; they only scarified it. She recoiled from the ugliness of it all, for the bitter reflections felt part of the epidemic of hatred she had encountered in the Lodge, and to brood on them was to remain its passive prisoner.

Had her father not tried to warn her after all? She should never have shut herself away in that dreadful place. And in another matter he was right: she had possessed no knowledge of the rigours of the task when she so confidently proposed it. On both counts he had tried to stay her impetuous hand. As always she had won her way, and now she was paying the price of it. She was suffering as he must have suffered; and if he knew her pain might he not come to her, as she had so often come to him, gently reminding her that despair was an unavoidable but essential ordeal, of the quest?

He might; but would she believe him if he did? In this miasma of voices, which were to be trusted? And if she tried to tell her father what she had experienced in the Lodge, what then? He would, she knew, be terrified himself. He would immediately forbid her return.

But was that not what she wanted—for a voice outside the clamour of her own head to tell her that she need not go back, that she *must not* go back? That it was folly to persevere, a needless risk. What she wanted was permission to cease.

Was she a child then still, that she could not take the decision for herself?

In confusion again, Louisa looked up and saw that the light was performing wondrously now across the lake. The billows of cloud were gleaming as they moved through the rain, and briefly her senses lifted at the sight, but there was no instant consolation there—only, inside a crowded mind, a sudden increase of space. Animate or inanimate, indifferent or not, there was something luminous and terrible about these clouds, raining as they did on the just and the unjust alike. Willingly she would have surrendered the gift of consciousness if only she might drift like these in a blind passion of being, exempt from question; yet even as she yearned wistfully so, another voice inside her agitated mind was whispering the old caveat from the *Rosarium*:

that all error arose from failure to begin with the proper substance, from a proud forgetfulness that the magisterium is Nature's work and not the worker's. She had no desire to hear it but the voice was insistent. It required a calmer appraisal of her predicament.

If she returned to the Hall and told her father what she had endured she would be forbidden to return—that was what must happen. And what then would become of her days? The task would never be resumed. She would have no heart for it. She would drift listlessly about the rooms, her dreams extinguished. It would be the end of all her high ambitions, and though the world would not greatly suffer thereby—for by now she had lost all confidence that anything she might say would alter the course of things—that crisis which was privately her own would remain for ever unresolved.

If she did not return to the Lodge she might never experience such terror again, but the memory of it would never leave her. It might diminish with time, secreting itself away in some irregularly attended cranny of her brain, but it would be there, waiting, finding its moments. Somewhere, for ever, she would be afraid. Her sanity might be preserved, but wherein would its value lie?

Yet if she went back . . .

Again she found herself trembling at the thought. Nothing could persuade her to enter the Lodge again. Yet she could not remain here, huddled against the rain which ran down her face and still would disguise from no one the humiliation of her tears.

She was still sick at heart when she passed down through the last glade and found herself staring at the Lodge's covert thatch, its closed door. She stood for a time in the yard outside, afraid to enter. She walked away, around the house to the jetty where her skiff bobbed on its painter, puddled with rain. She must bail before she could leave if she was not further to dampen her skirt; but what did that matter? She was already drenched. That alone might account for her shivering.

And still there was no sign of Pedro.

With more bravery than she had ever mustered before, Louisa retraced her steps. She pushed open the door on silence. The fire was dead in the hearth, the shadows gathering. She stepped inside and, still wearing the soaked cape, ready at an instant to flee, sat down at her desk. The pages of her book stared back at her. She waited.

For a long time she waited, and nothing more terrible came to enter that silence than her own dark imaginings. A decision was taken then. And Pedro's continued absence insisted that she act on it at once.

Half an hour later, driven by a resolve almost beyond her comprehension, she was across the lake, informing Tilly that it had become necessary for her to take up more permanent residence at the Lodge. The wet journeys back and forth were, she explained, a weary imposition on her time, and she had decided that until the work was done she would pass the nights there. Provisions must be laid in, now, that day. Sheets and blankets would be needed, candles, food.

More alarmed by her mistress's drawn features and wet clothes than by her brusque manner, Mrs Tillotson wondered aloud whether this could possibly be wise.

Wise or not, Louisa insisted angrily, it was essential. She would be grateful if Tilly would stir herself about it.

'I should be a deal happier,' Mrs Tillotson protested, 'if the master were consulted first.'

'By no means must he be disturbed,' Louisa snapped. 'Nor will I have you worry him behind my back. I am about his business and must accomplish it as best I may. Is that quite clearly understood?'

Astonished but not dismayed by this severity, the housekeeper surveyed her bedraggled mistress. With that homely air of perplexed affection that had so long endeared her to Louisa's heart, she gave voice to a remaining consideration. It seemed, at that moment, to distress her above all others. 'But there will be no one by at night to dress your hair.'

Louisa laughed then, though her laughter was close to tears. 'Then I shall be a fright,' she answered. 'Forgive me, Tilly, I don't mean to dismay you, but you have no understanding of how urgently these matters press. You must trust my judgment. I am safe enough at the Lodge and with your help I shall make all snug. Now come, waste no more of my time. I must be back before light fails.' And how deeply she wished she could feel the confidence impressed upon her voice as she added with forced lightness, 'Apart from any other consideration, I still have a wet dog to find.'

Unconvinced, shaking her grey curls under the mob-cap, Mrs Tillotson did as she was bidden.

* * *

The bedroom was insufferably dark, though if he insisted that the drapes be further drawn they would open only on to a dour and leaden sky.

'You have heard from Hattie?' he enquired.

'I have.'

'And what does she have to say?'

There was a long silence. Which he must finally break. 'My dear?'

'Did I not ask you that my family not be troubled?'

'Indeed you did, Emilia, but . . .'

'Do my wishes count for nothing in this house?'

'You know that is not the case. All of us desire nothing more than that you should take hold of your life again . . . more freely exercise your will. There is no future in this confinement from the world.'

'Do you think I would choose to be so?'

'Indeed I do not,' lied Edwin Frere. 'Yet you must have help to free you from this condition and, frankly, I have found myself at a loss. When the good Doctor suggested that I override your wish and write to . . .'

'That man was behind this then? I might have guessed.'

'He has only your best interests at heart.'

'The man has no heart. You have no conception how deeply he distressed me. He would be better employed as beadle, or as taskmaster in the Saxburgh Union.'

'Nevertheless, he wishes you well. If his manner was a little rough . . .' The sentence was stifled under the thick cushion of Emilia's sigh.

'Well, the harm is done,' she said, and placed the letter at her bedside-table next to the sal volatile.

'No harm, I am sure of it. Only good can come from loving company. Tell me, what does Hattie say?'

Frere was unaware of it but his sister-in-law had spared herself the burden of a second letter. He was, in consequence, in an agony of apprehension.

'She wishes the impossible.'

'She does?'

'Though she seems most eager to see me.'

'But why not? We have plenty of room here at the Rectory. It would be a delight to have her bright spirit about the place.'

'I know you do not greatly care for her, Edwin. Do not patronize me. I am not yet without my wits.'

Chastened, Frere said, 'Hattie would be excellent company for you. You could take the country air together. Surely your sister could do what I have failed to do . . . restore your cheer, your vigour?'

'As always you grasp the stick by the wrong end. Hattie wishes me to visit *her*, in Cambridge.'

For a moment Edwin Frere was stunned. How could the silly chit have so mistaken his intent? He had been at such pains. Never had a letter been more carefully worded.

'She is of the opinion that the loneliness of this place accounts for my condition. She believes that the respite of a holiday in Cambridge would speed my recovery. Of course, it is out of the question.'

'But I made it absolutely clear how frail you were . . . that it was imperative that she come here . . .'

Emilia looked up sharply in the gloom. 'Imperative? You used that word? Harriet mentions nothing of this.'

Caught in the toils of his own deceit, Frere's eyes scouted the room. He found its heavy odour suffocating.

'I thought . . . the surprise . . .'

'You would seek to conspire with my sister behind . . .'

Suddenly he was out of all patience. 'Dear God, Emilia, there is no pleasing you and your family. What am I supposed to do? Whatever motion I make you hasten to find fault. You terrorize the servants, insult the good Doctor, accuse me of sedition . . . Is all the world to blame but you? Why, you become as tiresome as your father.'

Had he smacked her across the face the result could not have been more devastating. Emilia stared at him with Medusa's eyes a moment then eased herself further into the bed where she lay gripping the coverlet with white fingers. On the stone mask of her face no tears appeared. Frere got up from his chair, hating himself, to prowl the room like a caged panther. Damn the woman, he would not apologize. He was almost of a mind to tear the sheets from the bed, heave her out, send her sprawling in an agony of humiliation across the floor.

Emilia said quietly, 'I think you have it in your heart to murder me.'

'Don't be preposterous, madam.'

But a hot darkness sweltered at his head. The breath was constricted in his chest and he found it difficult to swallow. Dear God, what had he done that things should come to such a pass as this? He turned to face his wife who lay, it seemed, transfixed with terror at his unprecedented rage, and hating him, hating him.

Violently he shook his head and slammed out of the room.

If Louisa had not dreamed badly on her first night at the Lodge it was because she hardly slept at all. Little enough daylight was left by the time Pedro came skulking back, and for most of the evening she had sat, talking to him, stroking the soft rug of his ear between tense fingers, and waiting for the fit to come again.

Nothing had happened. Louisa hardly knew whether she felt more relieved or cheated, for the act of summoning all the courage and then being able to employ it only against her own anxiety had depleted her to no useful purpose. She felt as a nervous duellist must feel when his challenger fails the appointment—angry, braver in the aftermath than in the apprehension, her stomach slightly queasy with unassimilated dread.

The truckle-bed had been narrow and hard, and she was profoundly unwilling to surrender herself to sleep. Though the Lodge was quiet enough, it would have been a too perilous lowering of her guard, so she tossed and turned until not long before dawn when her body took matters into its own exhausted hands.

The next day had been largely wasted. When she saw that her tense efforts to concentrate were getting nowhere she made a swift expedition back to the Hall. She wished to collect two items overlooked in the haste of her first departure: her deck of Tarot cards and, for wise consoling company, the porcelain figure of a Chinese mandarin which had stood for many years in her bedroom at the Hall. His face was smiling and, when you tapped the head, it rocked on a concealed axle so that he seemed to chortle at the absurdity of human antics. It was the smile she wanted with her, for she had felt its lack about her in the Lodge, and now that lack was remedied. Yet even under the Chinaman's cheerful protection the second night was little improvement on the first. Though she had slept longer, her dreams, if not alarming, had been most unpleasant, and she woke feeling unrested. Later that day she had been forced to catnap at her desk, having achieved little else of consequence there.

Brief as it was, the sleep did her good. On waking, it occurred to her with renewed conviction that the experience of two days

before might have been no more than a temporary aberration of
an exhausted mind. In the cool light of this brighter day it was
hard to conceive of it as a visitation of demons. She looked back
over the recently written unsatisfactory pages of her book, and
there was no doubt that her mind must have been tired. She
winced at their infelicities, at the clumsy way they beat about
the bush. She saw that it had been a mistake—an evasion perhaps?—to hamper herself with the abstractions of that cryptic
poem. Her attempts at explication had only clouded her own
contemporary voice, and led her far astray from the feeling heart
of the matter. She was fresher now, more confident; confident
enough to scrap the entire chapter and begin anew.

An hour or so was spent drafting a new outline for this second
approach on the mysteries of the *Coniunctio* and, when she was
satisfied that its thread was strong enough to guide her through
the maze, she took up again the pursuit of Mercurius through
the bridal-chambers of the mind.

Around nine o'clock on what was now her third night at the
Lodge she looked up from the page and saw a face at the dark
window staring in at her through the rain.

Instantly the entire surface of her skin went cold. She stared
at the window aghast, and the woman's face stared back, shadowy and haggard, blurred by the streaming rain. She stared in
at Louisa like a crazed creature, silently beseeching help.

Several seconds passed before the face of the strange woman
dissolved into her own recognized reflection. Heart pounding
still from the certainty that here was the returning shade of one
of her grandfather's mistresses, Louisa slumped back into her
chair and dropped the pen. When she looked back at the window
there was the face again; but it was attempting now to smile.

She had been foolish to neglect to draw the window-blind,
but there was no comfort in this self-reproof. The plain fact was
she had been terrified by her own reflection, and this was not
lightly to be dismissed. Anonymous anxieties still swirled inside
her. Again the questions returned.

Why was she subjecting herself to this penal state of solitary
confinement? Why was she afraid? Of what? And then—with
final, frightening clarity—what inward turbulence of her own
soul might possibly explain this sense of Madcap Agnew's unrequited presence in the Lodge?

For a moment, like a scholar contending both with his own
conscience and the uncovered fact which calls an entire thesis

into question, Louisa gazed in fascination at the thought, then flinched from it. Surely it was disproportionate? What need to import further obscure perplexities into an already complex situation—particularly when simpler and convincing explanations lay to hand? She was a woman alone on a blustery night with no one by in case of need: here was reason enough for timidity. Were she not to experience such moments of trepidation there would be something strange in her nature indeed.

To calm herself she scrutinized the evening's work. Her heart fell again. If she had neutered the quick of mystery in platitude before, she was smothering it with symbols now. It was hopeless, hopeless.

Again panic seized her. Fighting it, she scrumpled the pages in her hands. There was no question but that something vital had been missed, ignored, neglected there . . . something scarily associated with the darksome presence of her grandfather. She was in flight from it—as she had imagined that woman in the rain in flight. And, like her, she was drawn back, again and again, to the very place of terror that she fled.

As her father had so often complained, to engage with this task was to enter a labyrinth, and it seemed that whichever way she turned she came to this *impasse*. Perhaps, like the frightened creature she had imagined in the night—it was after all herself— it would always be so until she turned and truly faced the thing she feared?

Louisa stared at her reflection in the drenched, dark glass. She stared until it was hard to know which was herself—the disconsolate woman in the chill room or the other sorrowful face in the night outside. Somewhere, it seemed, she was ignorant of both.

A further decision was taken then. She pushed back her chair, stood up and crossed the room to open her box of tarot cards.

Four hours later she had begun to understand. Almost the entire deck of cards—sixty-six of them—were spread out on the floor before the fire. At the centre of a triangle of twenty-two cards, within a rectilinear arch constructed from the rest, lay the single card she had consciously chosen to represent herself. It was The Queen of Swords. Louisa's solitude, the wary alertness of her face, the way—symbolically at least—she brought the bright sword of her intellect to her defence—these and many other factors required this particular card and no other as her ambassador in the court of *Le Grand Jeu*. This was the name of

the spread she had chosen, and it displayed an entire interior
self-portrait on a scale she had never attempted before. Reading
that wealth of images had tested her powers of concentration to
the utmost, yet this act of unremitting self-scrutiny had left her
more energized than exhausted, for much of critical importance
had emerged.

The reading had fully revealed a fact which she had dimly
apprehended before but lacked the courage to confront until she
saw it reflected in the mirror of the spread. The fact was that for
many years she and her father had been living with a dangerous
illusion; and the illusion was that they were entirely virtuous in
their endeavours, entirely on the angels' side. She had striven to
make her work perfect—forgetful that it was not perfection which
life required, but completeness. And what a failure of sensibility
this had been!

To make the recognition now was not to deny that she and
her father had been aware of their flaws and petty vices; but to
consider themselves only commonly fallible was less than half
the tale. They had ever been larger than common in their aspirations, and the shadow they cast was correspondingly deep.

In angry self-reproach, Louisa saw how much sooner it should
have been evident to her that in identifying so completely with
his most noble ancestor, her father had been at pains to exclude
all thought of his more immediate and darker legacy. Aware that
Madcap Agnew's name was scarcely mentioned in the Hall,
that the Lodge had been for many years a forbidden place, and
that her father's heart still quailed to reflect on the terrors he had
suffered as a child, Louisa had not dared to let her reflections
on this unhappy history reach far enough. Still worse, she had
allowed herself to be drawn into a conspiracy of exclusion. She
had made—and with far less justification than her father—the
same grave error as he. Had it not been for the ignorant impet-
uosity which demanded the Lodge as the most appropriate environment for her work, the truth might have continued to elude
them. Nevertheless, the facts of the case were now plain enough
in her spread: Madcap Angew remained as much alive inside
them as did the glorious seventeenth-century adept of the Art.
He was, perhaps, more powerfully so, and not merely as a matter of proximate generation but precisely because such strenuous
efforts had been made to exclude him.

In an enterprise such as theirs every aspect of the complex
inward theatre must be brought into play and assigned its proper

place; and this—though she shuddered at the consequence—included the daemonic figure of her grandfather. Refused admission by the front door, he had forced his way through the back—and with quite terrifying violence. It seemed that her brother had been right after all when he warned her that the Decoy Lodge was haunted. Madcap Agnew was still here. He was here because she was here herself. In part at least, she was his returning shade, and that shade was clamouring now to be embraced.

The truth was fearsome and unavoidable. She remained uncertain still what was to be done with it, though she consoled herself with the thought that in entering the court of *Le Grand Jeu* and submitting to its verdict, she had already taken the first tentative steps. Yet she knew that the ordeal to come must tax all her strength and, not impossibly, exceed it.

Nor was a reckoning with her grandfather's shade the only sentence imposed by the spread. Another and equally disconcerting presence had materialized there—one which she had attempted to diminish some time ago and send packing from her thoughts. Yet there the figure remained and was, in a way, still less acceptable, for the mean spirit it betrayed lacked stature. To acknowledge it—as the cards insisted that she must—a portion of herself, was to recognize features which were paltry and despicable; it forced the reluctant awareness that she was, in part at least, a smaller person than she believed herself to be. But there in her spread was Emilia Frere—afraid of life, querulous, cold-hearted—and they were, it seemed, sisters beneath the skin. Somehow she too must be embraced.

The whole picture ranged wider far, but two vital considerations immediately emerged. The first was that she and her book would have nothing complete to say to the age until her grandfather's misspent energy had been redeemed inside herself. The second gave cause for more personal concern. It was evident from the spread that enormous powers were available within her—powers which might be channelled into rich creation, or which might, if not subjected to correct restraint, become destructive. She began to understand how the bleak vision she had been shown was no more and no less than the extremes to which such powers might go if once they lost touch with the exactions of a loving heart. Hitherto she had experienced the unruly masculine spirit inside her soul as little more than a matter for jocular asides or occasional remorse to see it bound like Pedro into mischief; but notice had now been served. The powers of this spirit were immense and impersonal. Unassimilated, they might one day wreak havoc in her life.

How to engage with it then, when at the first glimpse of its potentially monstrous nature she had fled? It still terrified her—even more now that it was acknowledged as a portion of her soul. She was far from confident that she possessed the moral courage to endure further revelations from that dark side of her moon. Yet the process of reading the spread had been like mounting a ladder that vanished beneath her: once started there was no return. She could not now pretend that none of this was known to her, that she was still simply a diligent and faithful daughter, loyal handmaid of a noble art. Consciousness exacted its price: as surely as it increased freedom so it diminished it. She must proceed.

Congenial or not, the truth had been made evident to her in the spread. She had seen it there not in terrible isolation but as a part, a vital part, of a larger pattern—one that pointed the way towards completion of her task. Completion must be her watchword now, whatever admissions it entailed; and was not completion at the very heart of the *Coniunctio*—the central symbol which had proved the stumbling-stone of her work? It was the reconciliation of *Sol* and *Luna* after the violence of their strife, the chymical wedding of Sulphur and Quicksilver, the meeting of the dark and light in close embrace from which the golden stone was born. She had known this all along, but she knew it with a different knowledge now. It was a more than intellectual comprehension; and to write of it she must strive to become that meeting. She must submit to its ordeals.

Last time Madcap Agnew had stepped unbidden from the chamber of her mind. She must summon him now.

Unconscious of the hour, driven by a nervous certainty, Louisa crossed to her desk, smoothed her hand across a fresh sheet of paper, and took up her pen.

'Well, old fellow in the cellarage,' she whispered lightly to herself, though the breath was shallow in her throat, 'it seems I must speak with you at last.'

If the domestic servants at the Rectory were surprised when their mistress came downstairs the following morning, her husband was astounded. Had his violent loss of temper done the trick after all? Was his wife human again?

Under her cold regard Frere quickly saw that his outburst would not easily be forgotten. And why should it, he reflected, when a sullen anger smouldered in him still? He had scarcely slept that night. He had let the sun go down on his wrath and woken with it. Anger, he saw, had not been lightly numbered among the deadly sins. For Horace it might have been a short madness; in Frere it threatened to become a running sore. Not even George Herbert's counsel that the country-parson's rage might here and there be justified had comforted. Nor could he even remember now what he had said in that burst of spleen. He dreaded that it might be unforgivable.

'My dear,' he attempted, 'how good to see you up and about again.'

Emilia informed the maid that she would take a lightly poached egg and some toast.

Thereafter there was silence in the dining-room.

'I was about to visit old Will Yaxley at The Pightle,' Frere volunteered eventually. 'I fear he cannot last much longer . . . But I will remain here and keep you company if you wish.'

Again there was no answer.

Frere swallowed, looked about him. 'His will be my first funeral in Munding, I believe.'

'Then perhaps you had better attend to the mending of his soul. He is a spiteful man and a drunkard. One who appears to find more comfort in the Feathers than the church.' There was an absence of interest in Emilia's voice.

'Yes, perhaps I should go.'

'As you wish.'

Frere's breakfast was finished. He ringed his napkin, scraped back the chair, made to get up, then had second thoughts. 'You are feeling stronger today?'

'A little.'

'I am glad to hear it.' Again he made to rise.

'There is dust on the banister-rail, Edwin. You had not observed the servants' negligence?'

Frere sighed. 'My mind has not been on dust, Emilia.'

Studiously Emilia declined the implication. 'Then I must speak to Mary myself,' she said. 'When I have done so I think I shall retire again.'

'A little at a time is perhaps best. I would not have you overtire yourself.' Frere hesitated, cleared his throat. 'Emilia, about yesterday afternoon . . .'

'I prefer not to speak of it.'

'Surely we must?'

'You may speak if you wish. I shall not answer.'

'You will accept no apology?'

She regarded him without warmth. 'In my opinion, if we are to survive together here it is best that we behave as though that . . . incident . . . had not occurred.'

That such a policy was entirely unfeasible was evident in her manner. He was on the point of saying so when he despaired. No, thought Frere, *this* is my first funeral. Let us bury it and be done.

'Very well. If you prefer it so.' He got up from his chair.

'And how am I to respond to Hattie's letter?'

Whatever way you choose, damn you, he thought. He said, 'Can there be any question? You are not yet well.'

'That is true.'

'Then you must thank her for the invitation and suggest a postponement.'

Emilia nodded. 'You would have no objection to my going when I feel ready to do so?'

'Of course not. Why should I?'

'As you are not free to go yourself I merely wondered whether you might not feel my absence.'

Dear God, he was beginning to think he would be glad of it. 'Of course I should. But a few days . . .'

'I was thinking of a longer stay.'

'You were?'

'As you know, father has not been well and Hattie is not the most reliable of attendants. She says in her letter that he misses me dreadfully.'

She would not hold his gaze. A cold suspicion entered Frere's mind. He realized that he could no longer trust his wife. 'How long a visit did you have in mind?'

'Oh I cannot possibly say at this point. The very thought of the journey wearies me . . . Several weeks perhaps.'

'Several?'

'Two or three. Perhaps more. I really cannot say.'

What was this sudden panic round his heart?—as though he had stepped on a rotten floorboard and it had fallen through.

'Well,' he hedged, 'as this is not an immediate matter we must speak of it again,' and turned away.

'Of course, if you would rather I wilted here . . . ?'

And there was the rage again. 'Emilia,' he demanded roughly, 'what are you saying to me?'

'If you continue to speak to me in that cold manner,' she answered, 'I shall say nothing at all. Go to your dying drunk-ard—it is quite clear you are out of all patience with me.'

At which point the maid returned with a salver and a rack of toast.

'We will speak of this again,' said Frere.

'Do you sit up, Will Yaxley, and make yourself a bit more pleasant now, for Parson Frere is come to comfort you again.' The sick man's wife pushed a cushion behind his head and brushed a wisp of white hair back across his brow. Then she turned to smile uncomfortably at the priest. 'Will you take a cup of something, Rector?'

'No thank you, Mabel,' Frere answered. 'Don't trouble your-self. Leave me and this old sinner alone a while.'

There was an insanitary stink throughout The Pightle, but how should it be otherwise with the sick man, his wife, two sons, and a daughter-in-law and three children crowded here? Frere was in the bedroom at the top of a winding stair, and the door to the only other upper room stood open on a clutter of pallet-beds and dirty clothes. Through the tiny windows under the thatch-eaves he could see the bare boughs of an apple tree and, beyond, the turned sods glinting in cold sunlight—land that this sick man had worked for thirty years or more, cursing the soil he tenanted from King's to yield a narrow living. Some-where downstairs came a clatter of pails, and the outraged squawk of a chicken rousted from the table-top. There had been no sign of little Sam. If the child had sense he was out some-where in the fields, away from the squalor of this wretched hovel.

'How do I find you today, Will?' he said.

The eyes were barely open but they strove to see in the gloom, and the thin lips trembled as they shaped themselves into a grim smile. It was as though the man sought to focus him in his contempt. 'Same as allus,' he was answered, 'None the better for your comings and goings.'

'Do you say so, Will?'

'I do.'

'And have you said the prayers I taught you?'

'The only service I credit is the way old Parson Stukely served Amy Larner and the rest. That were honest man's work.'

'I think your mind dwells too much on sin, Will. You have a soul to think of now.'

The man gave a little panting laugh which became a spluttering cough. He leaned over the bedside and gobbed into a bowl.

'Come, Will, let us say a prayer together.' Frere closed his eyes. 'Hear us, almighty and most merciful God and Saviour; extend thy accustomed goodness to this thy servant who is grieved with sickness . . .'

'Ain't nobody's servant,' muttered Will Yaxley, coughing still.

'Sanctify, we beseech thee, this thy fatherly correction to him, that the sense of his weakness may add strength to his faith . . .'

'Free man. My own master. Allus have been . . . Die that way . . .'

'Give him grace so as to take thy visitation, that, after this painful life ended, he may dwell with thee in life everlasting; through Jesus Christ our Lord. Amen.'

Frere opened his eyes on the sick man's scowl. What of life remained there was no more than this surly defiance . . . the refusal to admit any need . . . a dogged going-under as he had doggedly survived, on his own bleak terms. Frere doubted that he would outlast the night. It were better to go and leave the man in peace—every nerve-end in his body shouted so. But this was the first death since he had come to Munding; he held responsibility for the man's immortal soul.

'Be patient with me, Will,' he said, 'for I have a Christian duty to perform.' He faltered, sought cover in the Order for the Visitation of the Sick. 'Forasmuch as after this life there is an account to be given unto the righteous Judge, by whom all must be judged, without respect of persons, I require you to examine yourself and your estate, both toward God and man; so that, accusing and condemning yourself for your own faults, you may find mercy at our heavenly Father's hand for Christ's sake, and not be accused and condemned in that fearful judgment. Therefore I shall rehearse to you the Articles of our Faith, that you may know whether you do believe as a Christian man should, or no.'

Frere looked up from the pages of his Prayer Book. 'Do you understand me, Will?'

Eyes glazed and watering, the sick man did not answer.

. . . *without respect of persons,* Frere thought.

Dear God, this was terrible.

'Will, dost thou believe in God the Father Almighty, Maker

of Heaven and Earth? And in Jesus Christ his only begotten Son
our Lord? And that he was conceived by the Holy Ghost, born
of the Virgin Mary; that he suffered under Pontius Pilate, was
crucified, dead, and buried; that he went down into Hell, and
also did rise again the third day; that he ascended into Heaven,
and sitteth at the right hand of God the Father Almighty; and
from thence shall come at the end of the world, to judge the
quick and the dead? And dost thou believe in the Holy Ghost;
the holy Catholick church; the Communion of Saints; the Remission of Sins; and everlasting life after death?'

Whence this despair as he read—the sense of the utter irrele-
vance of these questions to the haggard gaze in which he was
gripped like talons?

'You must answer me, Will. You must say: "All this I stead-
fastly believe." '

Would he have the man lie then—here, at death's door?

But Will Yaxley was not even listening to the parson. His head
was turned away, vaguely alert, as though he were trying to
remember something—a song out of his childhood, something
that had once stirred his bitter heart . . .

Frere's eyes shifted to the 71st Psalm: *In thee, O Lord, have
I put my trust; let me never be put to confusion, but rid me and
deliver me in thy righteousness . . . O Saviour of the world, who
by thy cross and precious blood hast redeemed us, save us and
help us, we humbly beseech thee . . .*

All out of order now, but the words had passed only through
the silence of his mind. It was to himself they were spoken.
Again he looked down on this stubborn, yes spiteful, hulk of a
drunkard. He saw only the crabbed meanness of that life, written across the features in an illiterate scrawl. Suddenly the stink
was overpowering.

'Do you hear that?' Will Yaxley muttered.

Frere frowned, bewildered, and listened. He could hear only
the changed song of the chaffinch in the apple boughs outside.

'That's what I believe in,' Will Yaxley said. 'That 'n' hard
frost. All the rest is squit. You hear me? Squit.'

Throughout that long night in the Decoy Lodge the contest
had been waged back and forth, sally following upon sally, with
vehement force at times, at times as no more than the lurchings
of an all but exhausted will. An eavesdropper peering through
the still uncurtained lancet-window would have observed noth-

ing more dramatic than a lone young woman sitting at a lamp-lit desk, staring at an empty chair across from her. Sporadically she bent to write—her pen reaching for the ink so urgently she might have feared the nib dry before it touched the page; meanwhile, in the chimney-corner by the dying fire a young red setter dreamed of chase. But when, later, Louisa came to read over what she had written she would remember that there are times when a mind struggling for greater consciousness must take risks which a less exacting soul might think insane.

That the dialogue could not be sustained in entirely rational terms became rapidly evident, and she found herself thrown from her first cool challenge into responses of anger and disgust. From there, gradually, she began to learn a grudging respect for her opponent. Diabolical he might be in his cold, ironical determination to twist her meaning and, wherever he saw the opportunity, defile it; but that icy heart was ruled by a formidable intelligence which took nothing on trust and subjected each of her assertions to sceptical scrutiny. Why—she was required to answer—should any authority be ascribed to her own limited experience when his own had a different and more bitter tale to tell? Not a weak spot in her argument passed unmarked; each dubious element in her motivation was rooted out and exposed for the sentimental evasions it concealed; the full exertion of her intellectual powers was required merely to hold ground she had long considered safe, and soon it became a fierce battle to survive . . .

Either a divine order rich with meaning, or an insane jumble of atoms in which nothing is forbidden: this was the ancient matter of the debate; though *debate* is too civilized a word for all but a few passages of the conflict she endured. Nor were the lines of the conflict clearly drawn. Seeing herself as the champion of light over against his dark, she was forced to recognize that Lucifer too is a light-bringer in his way; and there was, at the heart of much she tried to say, a dazzling darkness. There were long sessions too when both recoiled, or when they lay locked together in holds so tight there was an erotic, almost tender, intimacy between them. At such moments Louisa might yield a little, only to find the advantage lost. Her feelings injured and abused, furious again, she spat defiance—and heard him laugh.

At last she emerged from what had seemed a fathomless despair to admit this conflict endless. Point for point was answered; pawns, knights, bishops, castles fallen, until only her white confronted his black queen. Stalemate was reached, and not accepted either way. Staring unvanquished into his gaze she saw that it was time to fold the board.

Strangely she no longer reviled him. Aware, quailing, of his power, she saw pathos too. He was a devil, yes, but a poor devil—a devil wrought from injured innocence—and she could find it in her heart to pity him. She saw too that it was only fear that had made her fight: that fear, as much as cold indifference, was the contrary of love; and here—at the climax of their bitter struggle—she could fear and love him at the same time. If victory mattered to him so much then he must have it—but only as a gesture of her love, for that was to concede no defeat at all.

Then, in a sudden relaxation of the room's fraught air, he was gone.

She sat for a time, half-wondering whether this withdrawal was only the preliminary to some new, devious stratagem he had devised, for she was too exhausted to recognize the scale of her achievement. And then, when nothing came to disturb the sense of peace gathering like sleep inside her, she walked to the door, opened it, and stood, breathing in the damp night air. Far above the distant Mount the moon stood at full among a shoal of clouds. The rain had ceased and the night was a luminous silence, devoid of consciousness and consecrated only to itself.

She slept right through the following day and night, and when eventually she returned to her work the sole cruelty lay in the self-imposed discipline of those long hours at the desk. She ate little, rose from her chair only to mend the fire and answer her bodily needs, or let Pedro come and go, and worked on far into the evening until she dragged herself wearily to bed. Sometimes she fell asleep where she sat until her posture altered and she woke, startled, uncertain where she was. Day by day the stack of written pages mounted higher. It was as if their volume had become her only concern: as to their meaning and value she had lost all compass. In moments of detachment she wondered who, in their right mind, could ever bring themselves to read all this.

Then the nature of the visitations changed. They came as dreams still, or as waking dreams—vagrant experiences which might have lasted hours or moments only, so little did they have to do with time, and interpenetrating through the states of wakefulness and sleep. Light-headed once, emerging from her trance, she recalled the story of the old Chinaman who dreamed he was a butterfly, and so vivid was the dream that when he woke he wondered whether he was a man who had dreamed himself a butterfly, or a butterfly now dreaming himself a man. And that, she thought, is surely my condition now: I am a case of butterflies.

She tapped the bald domed head of the porcelain figurine on her desk and made it seem to laugh. Watching the old mandarin's sly nod, she fell to dream again.

She had come into the library where her father sat motionless at his desk like an allegorical statue of Contemplation, a hand at his brow, undistracted by and unaware even of her entry. She passed to the bookshelves, opened the glass door and took down that volume of the *Bibliotheca Chemica Curiosa* of Joannes Jacobus Mangetus in which were depicted all the illustrations from the *Mutus Liber*. In the still air of the library she could smell the leather of its binding, and she was a little breathless with anticipation of delights to come, for to open that book was like unlocking a casket in which the contents changed each time one meditated over them. Carefully, with due respect for its age, she placed the volume on her lectern and turned its pages until she came upon the first picture where, from a garlanded ladder, an angel sounded a trumpet to wake the sleeper at its foot.

She heard the trumpet sound for she was that sleeper, and when—still dreaming—she woke into lucidity, backwards she travelled in time, before her own birth, before the death and birth of her grandfather, back across the centuries until it was high summer at Easterness, the sun and moon stood in the sky together, and she knew herself returned to the golden age of alchemy.

And this was dream within dream, for she might have been turning the pages of the book still as she gazed on two figures who were bent at work before a furnace, sweating in the heat as they fed charcoal to its flame; yet unlike the figures in the illustrations these were present in rich colour and animated by lively enthusiasms of their own.

Then, with a gasp of sudden delight, Louisa recognized the man. Though he was younger here than in the portrait above her father's head, and wearing no cavalier finery but a simple, soot-stained workman's smock, she knew the lean, engaging features for those of her ancestor, Humphrey Agnew. He was scarcely out of his youth, in his twenties still, his eyes active and earnest, alert with fascination; and a calm, controlled energy seemed to flow through each sensitive movement of his hands. If he was at that age, and working with such ardent intensity, then this must be the very day on which he had made his successful projection of the Stone; and through the agency of this lucid dream, she had been granted the otherwise impossible privilege to observe . . .

And might do more than watch, for there was a woman working beside him who could only be Janet Dyball, his sweet *soror mystica*—she who had searched the mystery with him, and whose hands had stitched the sampler hanging in Louisa's room at the Hall, on which were embroidered the words:

> *ARTIS AURI ARCANUM*
> *ET MARE ET FEMINA CONSTITIT*

She too was instantly recognizable to Louisa, and not because any portrait of the young woman had survived, but because—and this was strangest of all—her face was Louisa's face. She and Janet were one and the same, though her own wondering consciousness remained apart; and she was, it seemed, observer and participant at once as Humphrey paused in his labours to peer into the hot glass of the alembick, then turned to smile at her.

Soon, he was saying, the dissolution of the first matter would be complete, and she would see the alembick turn to a black so deep she might fear their work all lost; but this blackness was rather to be desired, and they must persevere throughout the time when it prevailed, for only through that darkness which some masters called 'The Raven's Head,' and others the *Nigredo*, could the passions of their matter rightfully be ordered. If they observed it well, a seed of light would glister at its heart, and she would wonder then to see it wax and magnify. When every shadow of the black had fled before this light, the work would have achieved its second stage, the white of the *Albedo*, from whence a saffron hue would then appear, which was the passage from the white to red. At last, if Hermes smiled upon their toil, the sanguine colour of *Rubedo* would appear, and bring the passion of their matter to perfection. 'Therein, sweet love,' he said, 'doth lie the true sperm of our male. From thence the splendour of the sun shall rise; for here is the fire of the Stone, the King's own crown, the glorious son of *Sol*; and there these first of all our labours findeth rest.'

None of this was unknown to the Louisa who watched; yet to she who listened the words came virginal. She rejoiced to hear the golden promises renewed in that rich voice. The antique tongue was instantly familiar, and not only from her readings in old texts. It was the very language of her heart, as dear to her as was the voice itself—a gentle tuneful baritone she recognized from her own time, as though it had ever been a member of her dream.

Throughout that long day they laboured there, tending the fire from change to change, until at last the sheen of gold was brought forth to perfection from the flame. And then, what lovers they were, the young alchemist and his mystic sister—naked as angels, white among green shade; and such laughter echoing from tree to tree, as though the knowledge of sin had never been conceived, and both knew only now the dazzling appetite to meet.

Was this then how youth, how life should truly be? No endless poring over books and dusty manuscripts, but acting out the glory of the word made flesh. Such tenderness! Such breathless apprehension of the mystery in things! And, afterwards, such peace!

Louisa dreamed like Ariel, and when she woke, like Caliban she cried to dream again.

'I have been thinking about my . . . accident . . . at the lake, that day.'

Frere looked up from his Bible, startled that his wife had spoken at all, and doubly so that this should be the subject, for since the day of her return she had refused all reference to the miscarriage. His confusion was further compounded in that his own thoughts had been quite other—he was agonizing over the problem of redemption. Will Yaxley had been buried that day and was, if stricter minds were to be believed, in Hell by now; which was difficult to reconcile with Frere's own concept of a merciful Christ who would take even a stubborn sinner to his breast. Yet the fact remained: Will Yaxley had rejected such consolation. To the end—an end which had been delayed much longer than Frere would have thought possible—he would have nothing to do with promises and admonitions of the life to come. Stubbornly he had insisted that his flesh would rot in 'the owld mowld,' and that was the end of it. There had been a terrible cold certainty in the eyes of the dying man. It was impervious to words. And so in this, as in so much else, it seemed, Edwin Frere had failed.

'You have?' he said.

'It begins to come clear to me that this was a judgment visited upon us.'

Sitting in his chair, the Bible open before him, Frere felt almost dizzy with cold dread. Judgment—the second of the Four Last Things—had been much upon his mind; and now, at his wife's words, he too stood in the dock, and the mercy-seat was empty. Had Yaxley been right after all? Was it not far saner to conceive of a natural world devoid of judgment than of a heartless, black-capped Justice before whom all was bared, and who could pass such sentences on mortal flesh?

'How else,' Emilia pressed, 'may one make sense of it?'

'It is not for us to question the Divine Will,' Frere said hopelessly.

'Merely to suffer it?'

'With patience.'

'As I must suffer the judgment you have passed on me?'

'Emilia, I have passed no judgment . . .'

'Have you not said you find me contrary and tiresome?'

'Were we not to speak of that?'

'I cannot bear your silence.'

'It is you who have imposed it.'

'See, there is hatred even in your voice.'

'No,' Frere hotly exclaimed. 'What you take for hatred is despair.'

'Then you despair of me?'

'Emilia . . . I think that this will drive me . . .'

'Yes, what will it do? Come, out with it, sir. Let us see the selfish heart that lies beneath your parson's vestments.'

'Emilia,' he pleaded, 'we were never so . . .'

'In Cambridge?'

' . . . before . . .'

'We were not here before. In this dreadful place where there is not a soul that truly cares for me. How dare you seek relief in protestations of a coming madness? You have played that game before, sir. It is done. Yours is not now the need. If anyone shall go mad here it is I.'

'Emilia . . .'

'I am your prisoner here. You are less my husband now than judge and gaoler. You shackle me in a pretence of care and tell me I must bear all patiently while secretly you rejoice to see me suffer.'

'Dear God, it is not so.'

'Then take me away. Take me away from this barren wilderness.'

Frere's hand was clutching at his hair. Was he again to abandon his mission, to collapse in ignominious defeat as once in India? To turn tail and run, become again a worthless shadow of himself? Did the woman know what she was asking? Was she, in cold deliberation, unpicking every thread that held his life together? O God forgive him, for she was right—he had, in truth, begun to hate her.

'I cannot do that,' he said. 'I cannot do that.'

Hopelessly he looked across at her and saw only a stone mask. For a hideous moment it merged with the features of the abominable idol on his church. Here was the dreadful shadow that had always hung across his ministry. Here was the admission with no exit. He remembered the hollow thud with which the first shovelfuls of earth had fallen on Will Yaxley's coffin. Sweet Christ, was there no escape from this?

'You would rather see me suffer?' she demanded.

Frere looked up at her in desperation. 'You leave me no room to breathe . . .'

'O come sir, enough of this. It is I, not you, who lack air, scope . . . meaning in my days. Have you forgotten how you pranced about the ice while I lay bleeding? How you continued to spread sweetness and light through other homes while I lay in that darkened room alone upstairs? How you fobbed me off with that rude beast of a physician, and even conspired with my own sister to free yourself of me? And now you bid me hold my peace and suffer patiently the insults that you heap upon my family. You are unkind, sir. I have friends elsewhere.'

'Then be gone to them, damn you,' Frere shouted from his frustration, his misery and rage. 'If I have failed you so utterly be gone, for I am at my wits' end with your wretchedness . . .'

He fled, heart pounding, uncoated, into the pitch-black night outside.

Louisa put down her pen and read what she had written:

So confident now the vigour of our ingenuity, so beguiling its productions, that we scarcely pause to wonder how the Sci-

ence with which we so excite ourselves has added not a jot to, nor substracted any portion from, the Wisdom of Antiquity. Of another order, of another world even, that Wisdom patiently abides; and by its light the science of our age— investigative of, dependent on, the contingencies of the external world—appears a dark lantern indeed. Our earthly power, our speed, our comforts and the satisfaction of our mortal appetites—all these things increase. Yet ever the dreadful question rises: to what end? What profits all our ingenuity if this, the fundamental challenge, stands unanswered and unsearched?

As the very name attests, the ancient Doctors of Philosophy loved Wisdom; and Wisdom is in no manner to be found amongst externals. Wisdom's Law, writ plain upon the temple wall at Delphi, has but a single clause: it is to know thyself. Yet if the proper study of mankind is man, we have neglected it. Not so the alchemist; for Man, we boldly now affirm, is the true laboratory of the Hermetic Art. He is its subject, he the alembick, he the Stone; and true Self-knowledge is the motive, mode and object of the Work.

She sighed, pinched her eyes, then thrust the paper aside. Too densely writ. At once too abstract and too explicit. Neither allusive nor provocative enough. It would not do.

And who was she to speak of Wisdom—she whose thoughts ran ever counter to her argument? How had she ever dared to dream herself the equal of this task?

Once more she tried to summon her glorious ancestor to her aid. What would he have to say to her now in this pass? She imagined a hand at her shoulder, that gentle voice saying, 'Come, sweet chuck, plague not thy mind with doubt. You have but wrought yourself unto the pitch of weariness, which ever was the way with us philosophers.' But it was to the modern age that she must speak, not one long past. And the tone she had adopted in this passage was too Olympian for that. Her words must speak *personally* or they would have only the same effect as any general admonition: precious little. But when she wrote directly, person to person, there was only one face that with increasing frequency presented itself for audience; and, when she looked on him, all objectivity was gone. She erred, back from the symbolic plane to the literal. At the thought of him, forbidden though that thought was, she no longer wanted to *say* these things; she wanted to *be* them.

All error arises, she strove to remind herself, *when the worker works not with the proper substance.* And where should that be found except in venerable Nature? She had been too long in this chair. How long was it since she had been out to observe the motions of the light across the lake? Far too long.

Louisa tidied away the papers on her desk and went out into the day.

A sprightly breeze teased the surface of the lake, and though there was a frostiness to the blue against which a gull bent crisp white wings, at her own less exalted altitude the air was not so chill as to make her shiver. There was, rather, a surprising warmth to the afternoon sunlight, for the year had been unfolding while she worked indoors, and so exclusive had been her concentration, so absorbing each feature of the terrain on which her introspective thoughts had opened, she had failed to observe the alterations of the light, the comings and goings of the rooks, and the way—this day at least—all things were breathing easily. If the fresh, delectable smell that cleansed her senses now was not quite yet of Spring, it might soon, she thought, be made to answer for its promises.

Reflecting on the evident elation of the trees, one ought—she felt—to experience a responsive lightness of heart, yet she did not. She was too wistful for that; and though the emotion was accompanied by an almost pleasurable sensation, it was not enough to mitigate a suddenly oppressive solitude. Restlessness, which vented itself in small, intermittent and unoccasioned sighs, came between her and peace; and, strangely, for there were no censorious eyes about her, she was troubled by the thought of her appearance. She had been less fastidious of late than was her wont, and was weary of this dress which she had worn for three—or was it four?—days now. In a previous life such negligence would have been unthinkable. And there was a waxiness to her complexion which her fingertips detected, even if she had given the mirror no more than a passing, critical glance. She was becoming dull. Even her powers of speech might have rusted from long silence.

What, she wondered, did this long work profit her if at the end of it she was no more than a shadow of her former self? After the final sentence was written and the last page blotted, she could conceive only of a great emptiness in which she would be for ever at a loss for things to do. Time itself must prove a tiresome condition. She would fret among its opportunities like a returned traveller in the certainty that nothing in the familiar scheme of things could equal the intensities she had experienced here. For a man such as her father the satisfactions of the inward realm might be enough; but for a woman—at least, for one such as she knew herself to be—true vitality resided in confluence with energies outside herself, and she would no longer be able to content herself with the old, almost juvenile connections. The revelation of her powers had brought with it the desire that those appetites be met and matched by the equivalent enthusiasms of a kindred spirit; and completion—it seemed to her now—was not merely a matter of singularity: it must inhere *between*.

Yet such reflections returned her, as did so much else, into the insubstantial theatre of dream, which was the only world in which those yearnings could be explored and given form; and the price of that, on return to circumambient reality, was this vexatious restlessness. And, deeper—she must learn to reconcile herself to this—a sadness which was finally unrequitable.

For some time Louisa stood at the jetty, gazing out across the water but not towards the Hall. Her eyes were fixed in a more northerly direction, west of the Mount, to the tree-line which concealed the village of Munding. The breeze tugged at the skirts of her dress and disarrayed her hair. It seemed to carry on its breath no answer. She shook her head, then turned, her attention caught by the wings of a heron flagging slowly across the lake towards the distant heronry. She was so rapt at the sight that only after it was gone did she become aware that she too was observed. She turned, alert; then smiled to see Tilly standing arms akimbo on the lawn outside the Lodge.

'So this is how they deal with pressin' business this side of the lake?'

'Tilly, dearest. You have found me longing for company.'

'I thought that were time you had some fresh greens here . . . and a delicacy or two. And I did fancy a walk, though I had forgot how far a turn it is round the lake.'

'Then you must put up your feet and I shall serve you tea, and we shall talk and talk before I row you back the easy way.'

'Don't hold with boats,' said Tilly dubiously. 'What with the drownin' in the Bure 'n' all.'

'I promise I shan't let you drown. Not at least till I have all your news.'

Relieved that Louisa no longer looked quite so fraught and bleached as she had expected to find her, Mrs Tillotson smiled. Gossip was indeed on her mind—she had missed her occasional hour of mardle with the mistress—and as she sat down in the Lodge, tutting silently at its spartan comforts, she was pleased enough to embark on a long excursion into parish tattle. There was Will Yaxley's death to shake one's head over . . . and who was to keep a proper watch on that young scamp Sam now that Will was gone? Though he'd been an evil-tempered sot, the man had always kept a weather-eye out for the boy. Then there was the brawl in Shippenhall Crown last Friday night, with two men bleeding and the constable called out, and one of the injured Sarah Pye's young man. He were a wild'n that Jim Haycock— Tilly had grown tired of telling Sarah so, but would the innocent mawther listen? She would not. One might as well talk to the wall. Also Louisa would be relieved to hear that the boy Wharton was now making fish-eyes at Fanny Hethersett, the solicitor's daughter in Saxburgh, who was turning out a fine young madam with nothing more certain on her mind than the making of a handsome match.

Tilly saved for the last her prize piece of intelligence—after all, she was not one to spread mere gossip, though what else could one do with it? Nevertheless she had heard—though she couldn't for gospel-sure swear on it, because who knew what Mrs Bostock wouldn't say?—but her maid had heard Mrs B. tell Liza Waters that all was far from well at Munding Rectory.

It took a little time to establish the credentials of this information (it had come from the vegetable-hawker who was sweet on the housemaid at the Rectory) before Tilly came to the point. 'Now I don't say as it is so, but the talk is of Mrs Frere packin' her bags and makin' off her way for Cambridge. And that poor Mr Frere—why, such a gentle soul, wouldn't you think?—but there have been raised voices thereabouts and the parson driven to bad language by the woman's mobbin' him so.'

Louisa returned her eyes to the kettle where it hissed on the hob. 'I fear she has never settled here in Munding. After her misfortune . . .'

'Which she have made a stick to beat the parson's back with, if I may make so bold. To my way of thinkin' there's a hard woman lie behind that fussin' 'n' faintin'. If she be high-tailin' it for Cambridge then it's 'cos she wills it so.'

Louisa strove to inject into her tone no more than the appropriate concern. 'And Mr Frere? How is he coping with this distress?'

A little surprised not to have been berated for dealing in ru-mour, Tilly shook her head and clucked her tongue. 'Not half the man he were before that black day on the lake. He walk about like a soul stark-dazed. That's not a happy business, you can be sure. I'm told there's two beds slept in there at nights. And now there's a hard Lent lie afore that man.'

Louisa poured more tea. The cup chattered a little to the saucer as she handed it to Tilly. 'Has no one befriended him?'

'Why now, no one like to interfere. That's hardly anybody's place to come between a parson and his wife.'

Louisa was obliged to agree, and then fell silent. For the moment Tilly herself had nothing more to say, and both women might have been meditating on the woe that is in marriage, but one of them was not. Eventually Louisa looked up and stilled her breath. 'And is it certain that Mrs Frere will leave?'

'All I know for sure,' Tilly answered, 'is that there's letters come and gone 'twixt Munding and Cambridge, and that there's talk of it. As to the rest, the good Lord only know.'

That last remark of Tilly's was not quite accurate. Even as she made it, Mary, the parlour-maid at the Rectory, had her ear pressed to the panelled door of the drawing-room where Frere and his wife were coldly agreeing that things could not contin-ue so.

'I think it best,' Frere said, 'that you take advantage of Hat-tie's invitation now. You seem to be quite strong enough for the journey.'

'Is that what you wish?' his wife replied.

Frere paused before answering. Steady as his voice had been, he could scarcely believe that he was saying this. He knew that more than a temporary remission was imminent in his wife's departure. Who could say now where this would end? They had hurt one another badly, and forgiveness was no longer a simple gesture. Everything remained too hot and murky for that; and if it might cool with this separation it might also freeze over.

There was a sense in which Frere was already alone, and in bidding his wife leave for a time he was merely actualizing that solitude. Yet, frankly, the prospect unnerved him. Since his desperate return from India he and Emilia had rarely been apart. She had been the agent of his recovery, the guarantor of his continued well-being. Alone again, in this great Rectory which now housed such unhappy memories, who knew what shadows might return? Yet life was presently impossible. There appeared to be no choice between a sham solitude and the real.

'It is plainly what you desire,' he said. 'I shall not stand in your way.'

'You will not accompany me?'

To what end? Why must she complicate things so?

Such was his impatient thought. He said: 'We must pray that a time away from here will alter your present perspective on our life together, and allow you to return in a more affirmative spirit.'

'Then I am dismissed?'

'Dear God, Emilia, I would not have chosen this.'

'But you do. By placing your parish over me you have always done so. It seems I have no choice other than to comply.'

'I cannot believe,' Frere exclaimed, 'that there can be any prolonged and deep-seated conflict between love and Christian duty. I pray that in your absence you will come to agree.'

Emilia Frere, tight-lipped, conceded nothing.

'You will return for Easter, I presume?' he said.

'If you wish it. If you find my presence tolerable by then.'

'Emilia, is not this hard enough that you must injure me so?'

'Is that what you will tell the parish—that I have injured you? I see I shall have a cold reception on my return.'

'The parish shall know nothing other than that you are on an extended visit with your family.'

'Do you imagine that your hang-dog look does not already speak volumes more?'

'You have not been alone in suffering.'

Emilia sighed—perhaps in impatience, perhaps in belated recognition that all this profited nothing. 'Well I, at least,' she said, 'have some consideration for others than myself. How will you manage in my absence? I know you are less firm of purpose than you would have me believe. You made a poor showing the last time you were alone.'

What had he done that she should come to despise him so completely? He looked away, trembling, 'I shall have a care for myself.'

'You will need help.'

'I have my work.'

'You had your work before. It was not enough.'

Was this, he wondered, some further cunning effort to unman

him? Dear God, how well this woman knew his weaknesses, how completely he was delivered up into her hands! Had she preserved him from those demons only now to loose them back on him?

She saw her advantage in his frailty, and could afford now to soften her tones. 'You will accept a word of counsel?' she enquired.

Dumbly he waited.

'The good Lord knows there are few enough compassionate hearts in this parish,' she said. 'however, should you have need for comfort—and I greatly fear you will—it has been my experience that Miss Agnew is not without charity. If you are in difficulties you must approach her.'

'I would not seek to . . .'

'You must promise me that, or I swear I could not in good conscience leave at all.'

Frere weighed his present choices with a heavy heart. 'I shall remember,' he murmured, ' . . . should occasion arise.'

Emilia sighed once more. For a moment Frere might almost have believed that some hidden consummation was achieved, though he himself experienced no more than a vast emptiness.

Behind the door, in the hallway, the parlour-maid heard the movement of a chair and quickly slipped away.

11 ✤ Meetings

I must have been halfway down the drive away from the Lodge before anger surfaced. I had no torch, an unreliable moon flirted among clouds, I was tired from the hot work over the kiln, from the swim and the tensions in the Lodge. Suddenly it seemed a long walk back to The Pightle, and as I stumbled through the dark, resentment grew.

I was angry with Edward for stoking his rage at my expense; I was angrier at Laura for her lack of consciousness. That she might have some neurotic need to hug the dubious secrets of her gifts—this was just about acceptable to me; that she should flaunt her body and—when accused of its implications—retreat into injured innocence, was not. It was asking for trouble. Small wonder Edward had blown his top. And both seemed oblivious of the fact that I might have feelings too. In different ways I'd been used and abused by them both. The more I thought about it the less forgivable it felt.

By the time I reached the village it was after midnight. Most of the lights in Munding were out, there was no shady blue miasma from the television screens, I expected to meet no one; but I hadn't reckoned with the country hours kept at the Feathers.

Three men were standing outside the pub as the bar-room light went out. I recognized Bob Crossley and Bill Rush, the pigman. The other man I didn't know. I could hear their voices on the still air.

'That's as may be,' Bill was saying, 'but if you ask me it don't make no odds who get in. They all find ways of partin' me 'n'

my money and I don't hev no say. I'll stick with my ol' porkers.
They don't say nothin' but they got eyes and they got brains.'

'You won't get things changed that way,' Bob answered.

'Things change in their own good time.'

'Not always for the best though.'

'Oh I dunno about that,' the pigman cheerfully returned. 'I
hear tell there's now a fruit-machine at the Rabbit's Head what
pay out every time.'

'The Rabbit's Head?' the other man put in, '—where's that
then?'

'Opposite end from its arse,' Bill chortled.

Amid general agreement that that were a good'n, Bob spotted
me and raised his hand. I nodded and would have walked on,
but he called, 'Hang on, Alex. I'll walk up the lane with you.'

I didn't want company and it was unavoidable. Nor did I show
much interest as Bob moaned over the difficulty of raising the
level of debate in the village. I was pondering the pigman's joke
and the sardonic light it cast on my work with Edward. From a
glad-handed fruit-machine to the Philosopher's Stone was no
great step, and the chances of finding it about as slender.

'They never let you know what they're really thinking,' Bob
was saying. 'Too scared of what might get back to George Wharton at Home Farm, I suppose.'

'Perhaps they just wanted a quiet drink?'

He grunted, sensitive to my withheld sympathy. We walked
side by side up the dark lane, an old man wondering what this
young man really cared about, the young man wondering what
these old men—Bob, Edward—had to do with him. I felt beleaguered by their history, the sense that life had already been
inventoried, the choices mapped. Both at odds with a world that
had disappointed them, both in search of the new Jerusalem,
they laid their conflicting claims on me, and right now I didn't
want to know about either. I hadn't come to Munding to change
the world; I'd come to get off for a while. I'd come here to be
miserable, which—with some solitary practice—I could get really good at. I had a natural talent. I was thinking that if Edward
was going to walk all over me he could sort out that mad farrago
in the muniments room on his own; and if Bob tried to box my
conscience he might very soon get stung. I was thinking, *Marcus, if twenty years from now you see a sententious look coming
across my face, run . . .*

'So how are things over at the Lodge?'

'Fine.'

'Doesn't sound that way.'

'It's been a long day.'

'Working you hard, is he?'

'We've been firing a wood-kiln.' I took in his frown, ex-plained: 'Laura's a potter.'

'Is that so? That's not what I heard.' He waited for a question which didn't come, then volunteered, 'The gossip is she's some sort of medium. Table-rapping . . . stuff like that.'

'Who told you that?'

'It's all over the Feathers. Not true then?'

'I told you—she's a potter.'

'And likes playing with fire? No smoke without it, they say.'

I said nothing. Let him think what he liked.

'Well, I'm glad to hear one of them does something practical. What's her work like?'

'I . . . haven't actually seen any of it. The kiln was already loaded when I got there.' I sensed rather than saw the raised brow. 'I should imagine it's interesting. She has a strong feel for the natural world.'

'But not for the supernatural one, eh?'

'Bob, it's not like you think.'

He nodded. 'What is it like?'

Again I didn't answer. 'None of my business, I know,' he said. 'But I've heard him talk, remember. He can use words all right, though I didn't hear much more than words. Nothing solid. Nothing that Bill Rush or old Stan could get their teeth into. And over against what's happening at Thrandeston it doesn't amount to a row of beans. So what's in it for you, Alex?'

'He's my friend.'

'Which is why you're walking home after midnight with a long face?' He shrugged at my silence, changed tack. 'Listen, I've been trying to get in touch with you but you're never about these days. There's a meeting tomorrow night in Saxburgh that might interest you. A few weeks back one of our CND group got himself selected as a Community Controller for Civil De-fence. He's just been on a training course—learning the hoops he's supposed to jump through when the big bang comes. He's reporting back to the group tomorrow. If you really want to know about playing with fire you should come.'

'I told you, Bob—I'm not a joiner.'

'I'm not asking you to join—just to listen.'

'I don't think I could handle that right now.'

Bob sniffed. 'Has it ever occurred to you that if we put our heads in the sand they get away with murder? I've even persuaded Neville Sallis to show his face. I told him that if the church stands for anything it should have the guts to look the facts in the eye. So what about you? Bring old Nesbit along if you like.'

'I don't think he'd come.'

'Neither do I. That's my whole point.' He hesitated, glanced quickly my way, and pressed. 'Listen, Alex, it's your future I'm talking about. Yours and the girl's. . .' It's over for Nesbit and me. We've had our chances. But you . . .'

'Bob, I'm tired. I'm feeling pissed off. I just want to get to bed, all right?'

'This is one hangover we can't sleep off. We've got to do something about it or one day we'll never wake up. Is that what you want?' He waited for an answer and none came. 'Well if you don't care about yourself, what about your kids. Or don't they matter any more?'

'Sod it, Bob. Leave it out, will you?'

My retreating back was well past his gate when he called, 'There's a lift—seven o'clock—if you change your mind.'

I turned up late at the Hall the next day and Edward wasn't there when I arrived. Unusually, however, Ralph was in the library, looking through the papers on Edward's desk. He glanced up at my entrance, startled and, I thought, guilty. 'I was looking for Edward,' he said. 'Doesn't seem to be here.'

'He's probably sleeping off last night. We fired Laura's kiln yesterday and then he . . . He drank rather a lot.'

'I see.' Ralph pondered this news, frowning. 'Fired the kiln, you say?' He looked back at the desk and muttered, 'He might keep me a little more in touch with things. Like to have seen that.'

'He was caught on the hop himself. Laura went ahead sooner than they'd planned.'

'Still. Might have let me know.' There was a petulance to his stricken features. They seemed to insist that the damned place was *his*, after all. Perhaps he'd had a bad night too, for there was something irritable in the air, and peeved. 'Drank too much again?'

'Things got a little fraught.'

'Between the two of them?'

I nodded, reluctant to say more, and was surprised to see his face brighten. 'Firing not go well?'

'It was okay, I think, but we all got tired.'

Ralph nodded, drummed his fingers on the desk-top. 'Well, mustn't keep you from your work. Things to do myself.' Still flustered that I'd caught him spying, he offered a shy grin. 'Husbandry, you know—the land. That's what it comes back to when the shouting's done. You can always count on the land—though I sometimes think Marx was right when he said that to entail an estate makes a man the property of his property.'

'There are worse fates.'

'True.' And now he was ashamed of his complaint, and perhaps by the effort to impress me with his cultural horizons. 'I've been thinking. You must come to dinner. You and Edward. Include me in your conversations. I'd like that. Like it a lot. Are you doing anything this weekend?'

'No, but . . .'

'Capital. I'll talk to Edward about it.' Then he looked at his watch, sighed, and went off to count his barley or whatever farmers do.

When he was gone I crossed to Edward's desk to see what he'd been looking at and saw nothing more interesting than some barely decipherable notes on the stage of the alchemical process called the *Nigredo*. Motes of dust drifted down the beams of sunlight through the leaded window as they had done for centuries. Watching their progress, I recalled Edward's voice drily enunciating a line from 'that brilliant little cripple,' Alexander Pope—a verse that defined for him the vacuous cosmos of the Enlightenment: 'Atoms dispers'd and dancing in the great Inane.' But the dust would continue to drift long after these old books that argued otherwise had crumbled to join it, long after it had stopped our mouths—powder from Humphrey Agnew's wig, lint from Louisa's dress, ash from an old man's sleeve. I sat down at my desk, took more index cards from the box, and wondered why I'd come.

After a restless night I'd lain in bed a long time remembering how the previous day had been before it turned sour; and the days before that—days when a modest content had seemed a possibility. When I thought about it coolly nothing substantial had changed. In the hot afternoon, things had slipped out of proportion; Edward had got drunk, that's all; but he'd shambled

off to bed sweetly enough after his outburst, and Laura's first
thoughts had been for him. In different ways we'd over-reacted.
Blame it on the moon, the booze, the old anarchic impulses of
sex that made antics of us all. Let the crazy day pass, I'd decided, and be friends again; for the prospect of life without their
company was bleaker now than before I'd met them. It was
avoidable loss. So I'd come to the library, forgiving and forgetful, and the old sod wasn't here.

I picked up the top index card. Under the heading LUNA,
Noetic Aspect of, it contained a quotation from the *Rosarium
Pholosophorum*:

> *Nisi me interfeceritis, intellectus vester non erit perfectus, et
> in sorore mea luna crescit gradus sapienta vestrae, et non
> cum alio ex servis meis, etsi sciretis secretum meum.*

It was followed, in different ink and a less confident hand, by a
reference to Louisa's mystic brother—the first I'd come across
for some time. I roughed out a quick translation:

> *Unless you kill me, your understanding will not be perfect,
> and the degree of your wisdom waxes in my sister, the Moon,
> and not with another of my servants, even if you know my
> secret.*

I brooded over the result vaguely, irritably. It was like all the
other references: you construed it, the syntax was intelligible,
it was of a piece. In this case the Latin was more immediately
comprehensible than the English heading: I hadn't come across
the word *noetic* before and couldn't be bothered to look it up.
Yet for all the light it shed it might as well have been written in
Sanskrit.

This alchemical prose made me think of modern packaging:
you could see there were goodies in there, you wanted them;
but nothing could fight its way through the filmy stuff's contra-
ceptive attention to its duty. The incomprehensibility of this particular passage made the work seem futile. This whole baroque
hothouse of alchemical exotica had nothing to do with me. My
tastes were simpler. I preferred the straight truth told. And the
truth was that I'd volunteered for this chore only as a way of
including myself in Laura's life; and that wild goose was not
about to be caught either—not by this handy, hatchet-wielding,

already married scrivener who had once, in a previous incarnation, been a poet.

I stared out into blue day. Against the master's strict instructions I lit the first cigarette I'd smoked in the library.

I was stubbing it against my heel when Edward came in. He took off his jacket, hung it across his chair so carefully he might have thought the wood must wince at the touch, then stood, solemn-jowled. If he smelled the smoke he said nothing. Eventually I had to look at him. He was studying the map of his palm. When he glanced up the bags beneath his eyes were the saggy webbing of old sofas. 'About last night . . .' he began.

'Forget it, Edward.'

'Only wish I could. Behaviour . . . insufferable. Can't apologize enough.'

'You did—last night.'

'Don't know what possessed me.'

'The booze?'

'Yes, but . . . Well, it's not good enough, is it? I mean . . . abominable old fool, you must think. I couldn't argue.' He sighed, looked round the library as at evidence of his own impossibility. 'If you've had enough of me, I quite understand.'

'I'm still here, aren't I?'

Dubiously his eyes swivelled to check the claim. 'Then we are . . . still friends?'

'What do you think?'

'Dear man.' He quizzed me with contrite anxiety. 'Deserve a wigging, I know.'

A *wigging*!

It was impossible not to smile. 'Edward, I accepted a long time ago that you're a perverse old bastard.'

The glitter was back in his eyes. 'But that's too kind. I'm a recreant ingrate. A cullion. A contemptible zed. An earthworm even.'

'I'll stick with perverse old bastard. What about Laura? Has she forgiven you?'

An arm, gangly as an ape's, was lifted to his head. 'She took it in surprisingly good part, all things considered.' He looked away: subject closed.

'Has she opened the kiln yet?'

'The kiln? Oh no, too hot still. It takes time to cool down.' Then he grinned at me. 'I'm a fortunate man, Cambridge. Luckier than I deserve. I mean, look at you—no ill-will showing, hard at work already . . .'

'It is half past eleven. Also I've just turned up another Mystic Brother reference.'

'You have?' A brief frown suggested that this might be a regrettable development. He took the card and studied it. 'The *Rosarium* again.' He twitched his jaw as though sucking on a hollow tooth and muttered, 'Can't be right.'

'What can't?'

'Laura. She hasn't got her mind on it.'

'But she has ideas?'

He glanced at me over the card, was about to say something, then appeared to change direction. 'Look, if you don't mind, I think I'd better take another look at the *Rosarium*. I suppose I might have missed something.' He wandered off to the shelves, took down the volume he sought, and settled at his desk. Situation normal—so normal that several minutes elapsed before I realized how deftly his extravagant *mea culpa* had side-stepped serious consideration of the previous night. The ball was back in play, the game resumed. Only an oaf would make heavy weather of it now.

An hour or so later I saw him fidgeting among his papers, agitated. Then he went through into the muniments room, moved things about in there, and came back scowling. 'Damnation.'

Remembering that I'd caught Ralph at Edward's desk, I said, 'Have you lost something?'

'Not lost—left. The rest of the cards—the other references you found. I took them across to show Laura the other night and I've left them there.' He cast about again on his desk. 'Really don't want to leave this now—I think I might be on to something. I'll have to ring her and ask her to bring them over.'

'Won't she want to stay with the kiln?'

'Probably, but this could be important.'

'Why don't I go?'

Edward looked up. I expected a suspicious frown and found none. 'Would you do that? You could take Ralph's skiff. He won't mind. They're on my desk in the sitting-room. Green folder. It'd be a great help.' He picked up his pencil, scribbled something down, then turned back to his book. I was already on my way out when he looked up again. 'Laura's in her studio. Don't bother her, there's a good chap. I know she wants to be on her own when she opens the kiln. Okay?'

* * *

I rowed into the light of a clear day such as blessed that Spring. The wake glittered behind me. There was a blue hush above the Mount, the trees all birdsong. Again my mood swung. I recalled that I might have been stuck at the Poly, prising an interest in literature out of dozy students, waiting for the bell and a cigarette. Instead I was here, at liberty, answerable to no one. Edward might be incorrigible, the work pointless, but I'd tasted freedom. I breathed it in with the light. I liked the lake-smell, the water-gurgle beneath the keel, the rowlock's squeak. I liked my little ship of fools.

In those moments I felt that nothing really mattered, and felt it without cynicism, for it stemmed not from disappointment but from a kind of renunciation. It was a renunciation of desire made possible by that noble day. I stilled the oars, drew deep on the air, watched the light shimmering about me. There was no need to push and fret. Wherever things were going, I was first person singular, uncompromised, and needing no complicity. This singularity was to be prized. It was an act of secession akin to the feeling that had possessed me under the stars that first night at the Lodge, but calmer, less aggressive, with less of the lone-wolf about it. It was a quiet distancing from the claims of the unquiet heart; and if there *was* a secret, I thought, then this must be it—this freedom from constraint, the effortless capacity to float on life like a varnished skiff.

And then, there in the middle of the lake, a line of verse came. I caught my breath as it shaped itself. Then another. I fumbled for a pen, found none, so I sat in the middle of the lake, saying the lines over and over to fix them. They were to become, much later, the closing verses of *The Green Man's Dream*.

Edward's papers were easily found, where he'd said, on the desk. Beside the folder stood a porcelain figure of a plump mandarin with a hugely domed bald head. When I touched it the head began to rock with silent mirth. He too, it seemed, was in on the secret.

I was smiling back at him when I heard Laura come into the Lodge through the door to the lawn. She stared at me with surprise and, I thought, irritation. Her dungarees were smeared with clay, her hair tied back with the scarlet bandanna. 'I thought it was Edward,' she said.

I explained what I was doing there, looked away, awkwardly aware of intrusion, then asked if the kiln was open yet.

'Not yet.'

'Still too hot?'

She nodded, distracted. The shadows of exhaustion I'd noticed round her eyes the previous night were still there. They were greyer, almost blue. They made her look ill. She leaned against the door-jamb, frowning into the room.

After a moment I said, 'It was quite a night.'

She might have heard nothing more than noise, and glanced up at me, warily, as at a stranger who had solicited conversation. I was about to say more—some wry comment on Edward's contrition—when she said, 'Why did you come?'

'I just told you—Edward's papers, remember?'

The frown deepened its creases. Again I felt my presence resented. I was interruption. I had come between her and her kiln. Well, Edward had warned me not to bother her and I'd tried. I turned to pick up the folder. Before my fingers reached it I heard her say, 'Oh God.' It came too quietly for an exclamation, was little more than an audible release of breath. She wasn't looking at me but to my right where the mandarin's head still rocked. Her lips were drawn tightly back.

'Laura, are you all right?'

She didn't answer, closed her eyes briefly, then looked out again. Again not at me.

'You look terrible. Are you feeling ill?'

She shook her head impatiently, dazed, as though she'd been under water and was coming up for air. 'I don't think I can handle this . . .' The hostility in her glance was unconcealed.

'Look, if I've disturbed you I'm sorry. I'll get back.' Again I reached for the folder.

'Why did you have to come?'

I left the folder where it was, turned, and suddenly felt like an object under her psychometric scrutiny. Adrenalin swirled. In that moment I realized that I knew nothing about her. Nothing at all. The active, pragmatic kiln-tender of yesterday was gone. Here in her place was a tenuous, dazed and, yes, *fragile* creature, receptive to frequencies of experience beyond my range. I felt transparent and insubstantial under that gaze until it broke, became a wince, and normality—or a condition closer to it—clicked back in. She said, 'I'm sorry. Something really weird is happening . . .'

'Do you want to talk about it?'

'I don't think I can.'

'Look, why don't you sit down?'

'I don't want to sit down.'

The ferocity startled me. I remembered what Edward had said about the delicacy with which she must be handled, and stood uncertainly. She lifted the back of her hand to her mouth—a child in a corner, staring, unapproachable. She was seeing something that I couldn't see. I knew it, and the knowledge rattled me.

Then she said, 'I am in great fear for my mind.'

It came almost as much a question as a statement—either way appalling. And not only what she'd said but the way she said it, the cadences entirely un-American, studiously formal.

'Laura, what's happening?'

The breath shuddered out of her. She looked up in desperate appeal. 'Not me,' she said. For an instant her eyes shifted back across planes, but the contact was blurry. Again I had the feeling of a head surfacing, looking for help, sinking even as a hand was reached. 'What did I say?' she demanded.

'You said you were . . . frightened for your mind.'

She nodded, panting and, when she saw the anxiety in my eyes, smiled weakly. 'Just stay with me, will you? Stay with me, please.' Her wrists crossed at her collar-bones. I wanted to unfold those tensely clenched knuckles but her eyes glanced up and stopped me. It was like touching an electric fence.

If I couldn't hold her it felt important at least to persuade her into a chair while I did something ordinary and restorative like making tea or talking her quietly down. Again I spoke her name, but she wasn't listening, not to me. Her eyes wandered the room, not—as I first thought—watching movement, but searching, looking for a way. They came to rest on the nodding mandarin. She stared at it, smiling in a trance of sympathy. My eyes flashed between them. I reached out, put my fingers to the head, stopped it.

She blinked, looked up. Dreamer returned? Or not? I gazed across at her, completely at a loss.

'Say it,' she whispered.

'What? . . . What do you want me to say?'

With an impatient shake of the head, she closed her eyes again, trying to collect herself. Unsuccessfully. Then she seemed to shrug herself clear, looked round the room again, then at me.

Again her eyes were all appeal. 'Oh God . . . would you do something for me?'

'If I can. What is it?'

'Be honest with me.'

I hadn't expected this. I swallowed, nodded, though with none of the mandarin's composure.

'It matters.'

'Yes.'

'It really matters.'

My answer and her emphasis were a collision of clipped breath. She blinked again, her head jerking as though under the impact of a sudden change of mind. It was left in distress.

'What is it?' I urged.

'I don't know how to . . .' Again her eyes were averted. 'Look, this is going to sound really strange . . .'

I waited, was startled by a soft cooing that echoed down the chimney-liner; a wood-pigeon must have alighted on the chimney-pot outside and was warbling to itself. I said, 'Go on.'

She held the silence until it collapsed in a sigh which passed right throughout the tense length of her body. But when they opened again, her eyes were calmer, resolute. 'Do you want me?'

'What?'

'Now, I mean. Right now.'

'Jesus, Laura!'

As though I'd slapped her she turned her cheek to the door-jamb. 'This is really difficult for me.'

'You're not the only one.' But the attempt at levity was misplaced. In the silence that followed I could hear us both breathe.

She glanced back, distraught. 'I got it wrong . . . I must have,' and turned her face outdoors towards the lake. 'I'm sorry . . . I don't think I can stay with this. I'd better get out of here.'

'Laura.'

'What?'

She stopped, the fingertips of one hand still at the jamb.

'Look, bear with me.' I tried to keep my voice calm. 'I don't understand what's happening.'

'Do you think I do?'

'I don't know. I really don't.'

'I thought you wanted me . . . I thought . . .'

And I too was in utter confusion.

Of course I wanted her. Ever since I'd seen her in the glade it had been impossible to be in her presence without the memory returning. Alone, those lonely nights since—the previous night in the lake—it left me hunted by the dogs of sense. And if, for a few moments in the skiff, I'd thought myself beyond desire, I knew differently now.

Be honest with me. Christ! Yes. Now. Whenever. But . . .

'Do you mean this?'

'Yes. I don't know. I think so.'

'Laura, I think I'd better leave.' I turned back to the desk.

'You've been brave enough to come,' she said. 'Be brave enough to remain.'

Again that eerie feeling of an alien voice, formally phrased and non-contemporary; yet it was all invitation, and when I turned she was looking at me, lips slightly parted, whispering, 'Don't go.' It was her own voice now, and the shift was unnerving.

'Are you doing this to hurt Edward?'

'What?'

'After last night . . . the rows you've been having?'

'Oh for God's sake.'

'He's my friend, for God's sake.'

'I know,' she said. 'I know.' Again she was biting her lip, eyes closed.

'Laura . . .'

'I don't know what's real, don't you see?' A hand pushed through her hair. 'There are all these feelings and I . . .' Her eyes were beseeching now. 'Be honest with me. Please be honest with me.'

I stared at her, tense and flushed, and knew that whatever delirious influence she was under it spoke to something entirely as irrational inside myself. Something prior to words, derisive of them. Yet it was a word she wanted. A true word to dispel the unreality around her, to make it real again. But once that word was uttered everything would change.

My thoughts were not thoughts at all; they were gongs, pulse-beats, measurements of moments passing; a needlepoint awareness that to act on her displaced, half-crazed condition would be irresponsible folly. And still I said, 'You know I do.'

Her eyes closed in a shudder of relief. A hand reached out.

Then, as I approached, 'Not here,' she said. 'Out there. On the lawn. Where the book was burned.'

* * *

For a moment that last demand stopped me in my tracks, but she was already out on the lawn, loosening the bandanna at her hair, and from the first opening of her mouth at mine I was lost. Hesitations, anxieties went to the wind, and what began as a fast coupling of limbs, hands everywhere, mouth on mouth amid the thick tangles of her hair, rapidly became much more than lust.

Though not immediately.

For a while I might have been exacting vengeance there—vengeance on Jess, on Martin, on—more obscurely—Edward, my friend; but she caught my head on her hands—no, this was not what was intended. Her gaze was asking me to listen to some sound, some call she heard; yet even there, in that plaintive searching of eyes, the meeting remained impersonal. It was as though we'd slipped our names with our clothes, and entered an anonymous dream where there was elegance, simplicity, a kind of carnal refinement in the way her lithe body moved around mine.

Not a word was exchanged. In a dazzle of sunlight and green trees, the lake lapping at the jetty where the skiff knocked and bobbed, we were, it seemed, almost dancing—softly and fiercely, the way swans might dance. Slowly, the dance became a third presiding presence from which we were indistinguishable. It was where and who we were—and to realize this I must have stepped outside it. Immediately she sensed my absence. As though to prevent some inconsolable loss that must otherwise be sustained, her hands clasped at my back like a fragile thing. I heard her gasp at the sudden loneliness; then, for an instant, the *thought* of her lying beneath me was more compelling than the fact. I was briefly exulting in the sense of control it brought, when I met the strength of her resistance.

It came as a refusal of shallow excitement; and then, more powerfully, as undertow. There was a swift, unnerving realization that she was no more in control than I, though readier to submit to whatever impersonal forces were gathering around and between us; then the waters closed over my head. I heard the cries as her body shuddered and softened, and I lurched over her, hovering there, wide-eyed, before pulling away to lie panting on the grass.

The entire surface of my skin was glowing. The sky seemed very far away.

* * *

Somewhere among the trees a bird piped two notes over and over, sharp as the bright tines of a fork.

We lay for a long time not even looking at each other. Not speaking. Had they even occurred to me the customary intimacies would have dried at my lips: the lawn was no homely marriage-bed, and what had happened there neither a casual encounter nor the consummation of a long-premeditated affair. It felt closer to a state of possession from which, only slowly, like a diver sensitive to pressure, the familiar self emerged.

When eventually I turned my head I saw the hair still streaked across Laura's face. Her eyes were closed, the long lashes unmoving. There was no tension anywhere about her. She might have lain in relaxation after a yoga class—the soft exhaustion that exertion brings. I smiled uncertainly, expecting her to sense my gaze and meet it. Only her breath rose and fell. There was no intelligible expression on her face. I was aware suddenly that she might have been lying quite alone.

As had never previously been the case after making love I felt entirely vulnerable. The longer I looked at her unturning head the more it seemed that whatever she was thinking about—if she thought at all—it wasn't me. She lay unmoving even as I reached out to touch her hand. I turned away, eyelids closed with the sunlight blazing through them. I could smell the grass very close. It stirred memories of adolescence and, with them, a sense of interminable loneliness.

Was this then what women felt when they complained of being used—that their own essential nature, their individuality, was of no intrinsic interest, a discard? Or did their disappointment run deeper still? I didn't know. It didn't much matter to me, for the glow was fading from my skin, and I felt brittle. I felt exposed, as though somewhere someone—Edward? the Green Man?—had been watching, was watching still, would shortly come out from the trees, grinning at my discomfiture.

Nothing happened.

And I remained uneasily aware that all these thoughts were counterfeit; that they sought to diminish the experience, to make it manageable as my will retrieved what it could from the forces that had confounded it. I badly wanted her to speak. I was looking, I suppose, for some word of acknowledgement that I had been real to her in my own right. She said nothing. The bird piped on, like an unanswered phone.

An insect nuzzled among the hairs at my shin. My back itched a little against the turf. And then I thought of Edward as he really was, in the library at the Hall, fretting over my delay, ignorant of this swift betrayal. I remembered his face as Laura climbed from the lake. I remembered the way he'd held the axe.

I said, 'So what happens now?' and broke her solitary dream. She looked across at me as if at last remembering. She smiled. A hand reached out. Too late.

Why was I angry? Why that, when so much else should have been possible?

'Well?'

She frowned, bewildered by my tone, then raised herself on one elbow to look down on me. A breast hung close to my chest. I flinched from its soft touch. Again the puzzled frown—candour amazed by the world's equivocation, a dreamer waking to find the dream unshared. I shifted my eyes away, possessed by the cold thought that I'd got what I'd long wanted and had little to show for it now but the prospect of more trouble than I could handle. I said, 'I have the feeling that had absolutely nothing to do with me.'

She didn't answer. For as long as I could I endured that troubled appraisal, then looked away. 'It's true, isn't it?'

'I don't know how you can say that.'

Because—I thought—I wanted it denied and she hadn't denied it. I was watching her face as she spoke, and saw the flicker of uncertainty. I was spying on her. I was spying on the machinations of my own mind. For a few moments out on the lake my life had been simple: now, not half an hour later, the twists were endless. If I was angry it was because I'd so quickly compromised the glimpse of freedom I'd been given. It was because I felt incompetent with the ensuing complexity, and remorse was mere indulgence. It was because I was still unnerved, and because anger itself wouldn't serve. And when, naked above me, she observed these ticking thoughts and said, 'It was beautiful, wasn't it? Be glad. Please be glad,' I was left feeling like a man too small for an honour conferred on him.

It shamed me, shifted the grim mood, but the edge of frustration was still in my voice as I said, 'Laura, I haven't the faintest idea what you're feeling . . . where you are.'

She looked at me, her lips slightly ajar, waiting for words to present themselves. She looked down at her hands, pensive, then plucked a stalk of grass, put it to her lips, and smiled. She was smiling as a nurse might smile, as an older woman might smile at a young inexperienced lover. I turned away.

'But you were there,' she exclaimed. 'I know you were there. You must have been or it couldn't have happened . . . not like that.' She took in my disconsolate frown. 'You don't know? You really don't know.'

What began as question had become realization. Then, amazingly, she laughed. Not loudly or long, but a bright involuntary peal of amusement that a moment before would have left me feeling mocked; but it was clear now that she wasn't laughing at me. It was at the sky, the moment, the spellbound day itself in which she seemed to see for the first time how she too had been tricked into ecstasy and was delighted by the joke. Naked against the vivid green of the grass, against the green shadow of distant rhododendrons, she was entirely alive, entirely enigmatic. And her delight made me want the rapture back, to cancel what I'd said, forget the spleen—it already tasted sour on my lips—and simply rejoice in the naked excellence of our being there. I began to see the anger for what it was—an evasion of vulnerability, a clumsy way of reasserting control; and that to persist in it could only forfeit something infinitely more precious.

'You asked me if I wanted you,' I said, 'and I was honest. And I know it was *you* that I wanted. I wanted you last night. I've wanted you for a long time.'

I looked up and saw her shy from this intensity. One of her hands was soothing the other. She was looking down at the grass.

'You wanted to know what was real,' I said.

But the sudden soft confusion in her face already showed how little purchase even true words have unless they arise from, and are met by, a shared sense of the real. There was tenderness there, but not the kind I solicited.

'Don't you have anything to say?'

'Our bodies were honest,' she answered. 'I trust that.'

'And that's all you feel?'

She lifted a hand to shoo a fly from her face. A long way away, like the sound of the heat breathing, a cuckoo called.

What I wanted to hear was easily said; it required no thought; but she was thinking. In the silence I was thinking too. I was thinking how tenuous her grasp on reality might be, of the way she seemed able to act with an oblivious disregard for consequence, as though there was no reality beyond her own experience. I was thinking as anxiety returned that, whatever had been happening in the Lodge, I might be, for her, no more than a means of precipitating drama in an arrested life, an unconscious adventure into change.

'I don't want to say the wrong thing,' she said.

'Then say the right one. Tell me what you're thinking.'

'Look, what you said . . . it means a whole lot to me . . .'

'But not what it means to me.'

She hesitated, looked away, dismayed to find herself under this unexpected pressure. 'Alex . . . what was happening to me in the Lodge . . . It was tearing me apart. If you hadn't been there I don't know what I would have done. But you *were* there. You had to be. It needed both of us. But if we get it wrong now . . .'

'And you think I am?'

She didn't answer.

'For God's sake, Laura, you just gave yourself to me. I've never known a woman give herself so completely.'

She looked away.

'Either that or you were using me.'

'I wasn't using you,' she said quietly.

'Then?'

'We were used.'

'I don't understand that.'

'I know.' She sighed, then looked back in an appeal for understanding. 'But you were right—I did give myself.'

The omission was as eloquent as the quickly averted eyes. She was invoking factors beyond my comprehension, and I didn't want to hear about them. They were no part of a sane world. To believe that she had privileged access to insights beyond my reach demeaned more than my intelligence. It underpriced the efforts I'd made to keep panic at bay during that phenomenal meeting. I was carrying an unrequited conviction that after such a plunge a man must emerge, however briefly, on paradisal shores, not find himself floundering in confusion. I looked away towards the lake where gnats scribbled themselves on the air— *atoms dispers'd and dancing in the great Inane.*

'Alex, I have to be honest.'

'Then what about honesty with Edward?'

It seemed that the thought had not presented itself until I posed it. His name cut the air. It closed her eyes.

'He's waiting for me. Right now this minute. What am I supposed to do? Walk in whistling and say, "Laura and I have just had a remarkable experience—you might like to hear about it"?' I saw her wilt under the sarcasm, and softened instantly. 'Laura, he's no fool. He's bound to sense something.'

I felt her thoughts move away and was imagining a further regression into unconsciousness when she said, quietly, as though in reassurance, 'But he won't want to know. Not from you.'

'*I* know.'

The retort was charged with all the significance I could give it, but even as it hung unanswered on the air I knew its conviction spurious. Any true statement of what I knew must comprehend many confusing ambiguities: that she had given herself to me and not to me; that she had been at once with me and elsewhere; that I'd tried to resist the full exactions of the meeting I'd desired, and could lurch like a drunkard afterwards from ecstasy to anger, through devotion to sarcasm, and back now through the muddle of it all to the disconsolate place where I said in a demand that was also plea, 'Laura, I can't leave it at that.' And that, at least, was true.

But with Edward's name spoken her focus had shifted. The perplexity was gone, and she was a pragmatist again. She gazed calmly across at me, said, 'I think you'll find you can,' and reached for her scattered clothes.

I watched in disbelief. The sunlight was bright on her body as she slipped the T-shirt over her head. I saw the thin white flash of the appendectomy scar. Then her face appeared above the blue folds and looked down at me. 'Don't worry. I'll talk to Edward.'

'I don't just mean about him.'

'I know you don't.' She bent, picked up my shirt and tossed it across to me, smiling warily. 'But it's my responsibility.'

'What about us? Don't we have a responsibility to one another? Christ, for all I know you might be pregnant.'

The smile broadened. 'You don't have to worry about that either. But you're right—we do have a responsibility, and if we act on it things will work out.' She found her pants, pulled them on, then reached for the dungarees. 'You should get dressed.'

'You mean that's it? That my feelings don't count?'

There was an amused reproach in her glance as she pulled the straps over her shoulders. 'Do you really know what they are, Alex?'

'Haven't you heard anything? I told you, Laura—I've been dreaming about this for weeks.'

She gazed at me steadily as though at last I'd uttered the needful, clarifying thing. I was sure I'd got through. Then she said, 'Perhaps you're still dreaming,' and smiled.

I could have beat the earth in exasperation. Hating myself as I did so, I said, 'I thought you were the one who's confused about what's real.'

'I was,' she answered unruffled.

'But not now. Now you know, right?'

'If I try to tell you you don't listen.'

It was like arguing with a mirage, and somewhere, with a falling heart, I knew that if the claims I made were sound there would be no argument.

'Alex, we don't need to fight. It's the last thing we should be doing.' There was no reproach in her gaze now, only tenderness. 'I'm glad it was with you. I really am. But I don't want to hurt you, and I don't want you to hurt yourself. I just want to get the meaning right.' If she had been half-crazed inside the Lodge, now she was as sane as the light around her, and as calm. 'Listen,' she added after a moment, 'a few days ago something happened. It was a very simple thing but it stayed with me. Can I tell you about it?'

Chastened, preparing myself for some further unwelcome revelation, I nodded.

'I was in the big greenhouse at the Hall—Ralph's gardener lets me keep some plants there and I like to look in on them every now and then. While I was in there a butterfly came to rest on an arum lily. Its wings were white but for splashes of orange at the edges, and it had very fine, very delicate green veins.'

'An orange-tip,' I supplied, wondering what this had to do with anything.

'You know it? Well, the point is that the colours were exactly the same on the lily. A perfect match—the orange pistil, the white petals, the same filaments of green. Do you think the butterfly knew that? Or the lily?'

I looked up at her bemused, and said, 'I don't know.'

'Neither do I. But what I do know is that it happened at precisely the moment when I was there to see, and I knew.'

'So what does it prove?'

'It doesn't prove anything. But there are symmetries. If we impose meaning on them we unbalance them. We have to listen for it. I'm listening, Alex. I'm trying not to miss any of it.'

The candour came from a place beyond earnest sincerity. It too proved nothing: was simply there. I could receive it or not. But her smile when she said, 'Now stop pushing and put your clothes on,' was irresistible. It altered the air.

I stood up, said, 'Come here.' She tilted her head, pursed her lips, hesitated a moment; but she came. I held her, felt her hands at my back, whispered, 'You know I have to see you again? Alone, I mean.'

'Yes.'

'When?'

She didn't answer. I pulled back to look at her face, and saw a hunted look about her eyes. 'Will you come to The Pightle?'

'If I can.'

'You have to.' I smiled, pushed: 'I'll come looking for you if you don't.'

'Don't do that. Promise you won't do that.'

'Then promise to come.'

'I will. I can't say when, but I'll come.'

I knew she was thinking of Edward, of the imminent consequences of her unquestioning trust in feeling. In that moment he was more present to her than I was. I felt a quick pang of jealousy, of which I was instantly ashamed. But, 'Soon,' I urged.

'As soon as I can.'

She pulled away, as conscious as I was of the resurrection taking place between my legs, and wandered away towards the lake's edge. I looked at my watch, frowned, and turned to gather my clothes. I was slipping into my shoes when she came back. As she reached to smooth down my hair I pulled her gently towards me, a little dazed still by the speed of it all and the way my feelings had swirled from one extreme to another. The embrace was chaste but I could feel her tense in my grasp. Then she loosened my hands.

'Listen,' she said. 'when you get back . . .'

I had been trying to put the thought from my mind, was wincing inwardly as she held me to it.

'Tell Edward I was right. Tell him to think in French.'

I found the shift utterly dislocating.

She smiled uncertainly. 'It's all you need . . . to get you

through meeting him again. He'll work it out. Tell him Louisa told me.' Then she leaned towards me, placed a swift light kiss on my cheek, and turned away towards her studio. For an instant I was stunned, and would have made to follow her, demanding explanation, but she was gone round the corner of the outbuilding. I heard a door shut, the click of a yale lock.

I looked at my watch again, cursed under my breath, and made, flustered and confused, for the skiff. My mind was so full of other things that I was well out into the lake before I realized I'd forgotten Edward's papers. When I got back to the Lodge again there was no sign of Laura.

Recrossing the lake, mooring the skiff and, at last, entering the library, I understood what it means to be beside oneself. Edward, however, was so preoccupied with his studies that he seemed barely aware how long my errand had taken. If anything he was mildly irritated by the interruption.

'I'm sorry if I've held you up,' I said. 'Laura came in while I was picking up the papers . . .'

I put the folder down on his desk and saw that he was looking at the same ancient volume which had lain open on the lawn at the Decoy Lodge on the day of the picnic. I thought it was the same illustration even, but then—despite my immediate dismay—I noted the differences. Under the heading CONIUNCTIO a man and a woman, both crowned, but wingless here, were making love. What's more, they were making love on, or perhaps under, the water of a small lake. A little sun shone over the full moon, as the king lay over the queen, and all four faces wore expressions of orgasmic ecstasy.

Though I managed to restrain my gasp, I felt stark naked there. It was as though Edward had been poring over an image of Laura and me in the mirror of the crude woodcut. It felt a certainty that he must know. I could scarcely believe his rapt preoccupation.

After a moment he looked up and saw me staring at the picture. 'The white queen and the red king,' he explained. 'Quicksilver and Sulphur. There are some verses from Merculinus to accompany it. Look.' He pointed to the quotation on the page:

> *Candida mulier, si rubeo sit nupta marito,*
> *Mox complexantur, complexaque copulantur,*

Per se solvuntur, per se quoque conficiuntur,
Ut duo qui fuerunt, unum quasi corpore fiant.

He looked up into my face where I strove for an expression of dispassionate scholarly interest, *'Enfolded in the bliss of their copulation they dissolve into each other as they approach the consummation—they that were two made one now, as though they were of a single flesh.* Right?'

I nodded.

'But look at this.' He pointed to the margins of the text where, in a faded sepia-brown ink, three letters were inscribed: *FMM*. 'Hadn't taken it in before today,' he said. 'Obviously Louisa wrote it there: *Frater mysticus meus*.' He smiled almost sheepishly up at me. 'I owe that to you. Would have come across it sooner or later, of course, but the fact is you found it.'

'But where does it get you?'

He screwed up his nose, twitched his moustache. 'Can't say yet. It's an emblem of the chymical wedding of course. It's got to be close to the heart of the thing. Must tell Laura about it.'

'I've got a message for you.'

He looked back at me, irritably—expecting, it seemed, some unwelcome intrusion from his domestic life.

'She says she was right. That you should think in French.'

'What's that supposed to mean?'

'She said you'd work it out. She said,'—I took a deep breath—'she said to tell you that Louisa told her.'

Edward took off his owl-glasses and looked up at me through narrowed eyes. They were also, I thought, suspicious. 'She said that?'

I turned uncomfortably away. 'You don't think I'd make it up?'

He put both elbows on the desk, held his head in his hands—the tendons were tense and gnarled among the hairs—and stared down at the woodcut in a frown of concentration. 'She can't be right,' he muttered under his breath; and then, louder, as though in challenge, at me: 'It's too literal, dammit! She's got to be projecting.'

'Don't look at me,' I said. 'I haven't the faintest idea what's going on.'

Edward did not avert his gaze. I felt as though the smell of sex was still on me, grass in my hair—which, it suddenly occurred to me, there might well be. In my confusion I hadn't thought to check. It was too late now.

'We had a row the other night. Not last night—earlier.'

'She told me.'

'It was about this—in part, at least. That was what it turned on—this mystic brother business.' He sniffed, shook his head, scowled down at the book again. 'Laura's convinced that Louisa was emotionally involved with a man. Not her father. Someone else. She thinks it became the most important thing in her life . . . that somehow it lay behind the conflict over the book.'

'Isn't it possible?'

I winced under a withering glance. 'Louisa was entirely devoted to her father and their work. The references she makes to the young men around here—in the journals. I mean—they're funny, satirical, scathingly disdainful. She was amused by their antics, that's all. Annoyed by them sometimes. There isn't a shred of evidence of any emotional involvement.'

'Apart from Laura's feelings.'

'I'm sure she's projecting. On just about everything else I trust her implicitly, but this is nonsense. It's Hollywood. It's romantic novels. Louisa lived from the spiritual intellect. She was too aware of the symbolic dimensions of the *Coniunctio* to get confused by the other thing. Anyway, apart from her father there wasn't her intellectual equal in the whole damn county. I just can't see it.'

Whatever else she was doing, Laura's stratagem had worked: Edward's thoughts were more than a century away from the present moment. Until much else became clearer, it felt wisest to keep them there; but even as I said, 'She seemed very certain,' it occurred to me that the past too was now treacherous ground.

Again that penetrating glance. 'What exactly did she say?'

'Only that she was right and you should think in French.'

'And that Louisa told her?'

'Yes.'

'How?'

'I don't know,' I snapped.

It was true but it was beginning to be a lie. And then, as I thought about what had happened, it became one. *Can't you see, you damn fool?* I was thinking. *Isn't it obvious. It's you who's wearing the horns now. Use them.*

'I'm sorry,' he said. 'Didn't mean to snap . . . It's just that . . .' He looked away, screwing his eyes in concentration again. 'She must mean about the mystic brother. It can't be anything else.' And then, after a moment's puzzling: 'My God!'

Jumpy as I already was, the exclamation almost had me out of my shoes.

'No,' he said, shaking his old head, scowling. 'It's not on. It can't be.' He threw me an incredulous glance that was almost malignant—the messenger blamed for the message.

Heart in my mouth, I asked, 'What?'

'The French for brother,' he murmured, scowling still.

'Frère?'

'Frere,' he said. 'Edwin Frere.'

Sticky and agitated, and overwhelmed with a kind of grief, I sat at my desk throughout the afternoon, trying to decide. I kept glancing across at Edward where he sucked his pencil over the *Rosarium*, grunting every now and then when he was driven back on the Latin dictionary. Lunch had been silent torment as he mulled over the implications of the pun and dismissed them. It was a relief to get back to work, but I accomplished nothing. I ran and re-ran the tape. Fast-forward, rewind, hold. What had really been happening there? Was it more, or less, than an aberrant excursion into the twilight zone? More to the point, why had I let it happen at all?

Because I wanted it. Because more or less consciously I'd been lusting after Laura for weeks, and the hectic glamour of the moment had been stronger than any thought for the consequences. And that meeting on the lawn . . . the forces I'd encountered there. Sexual or supernatural, their reality revoked all question. For a few timeless seconds they'd plucked me out of my head and plunged me back into dream, back into the light of the retorts. A light subtler than electricity. Not chemistry but chymistry. *Coniunctio.* If that was what ghosts brought, I was for ghosts . . .

But what did you do with it when the woman who'd opened those doors disappeared through them? When you recalled how primitive your response had been? And what did you do with feelings that yearned and recoiled and ducked their heads in shame? I could have bitten off my tongue to remember some of the crass things I'd said. They made me sweat with remorse as the sight of Edward made me sweat with guilt. He was my teacher and my friend, my magister and my fool. He was Mercurius shifting shape around me, not to be pinned down. I knew

that for all his faults he was grander than I was. He had a larger
sense of life. He was like an old Lagonda hogging a byway,
monumental and ridiculous and huge of heart. He was richer
than me and I'd stolen from him. I could sit here pretending that
nothing had happened, or I could cross the floor, confess, and
take the consequences. At least then I'd feel clean.

But mine weren't the only feelings at stake. It would be Laura
who took the real aftermath. By the time Edward got back to
the Lodge the first shock would have passed, and I knew what
happened next. So, I guessed, did she, which was why she'd
insisted he be told on her own terms, in her own time. She was
mistress of the situation now. I saw she had always been so,
quietly manipulating both of us on to her own ground, for all
the significant events had happened *outside* this library where
Edward and I burrowed vainly for the key. And whether it was
done for her own ends or—as I was quite certain she would
protest—in service of some higher principle, remained unclear.
I admired, desired and distrusted her, aware that if everything
felt unreal it was because she made it so. I could be no more
confident of the reality around me now than Edward could and,
at the moment, my feelings for him were clearer than my feelings for her.

Then he was standing over me. 'Do you think I should trust
Laura?' he asked. And, as I swallowed, added, 'About this
business I mean.'

'Edward, I don't know.'

'I've been thinking it over. She's been right before. But
this . . .'

I would have liked to be honest. Failing that, I wanted to be
helpful. 'I suppose it couldn't hurt to find out more. About
Frere I mean.' He frowned down at me in some consternation. '. . . Unless you really are on to something else.'

He shrugged, sighed impatiently. 'I thought I was, but . . .
God damn it, I don't know.' In what seemed a reluctant adher-
ence to the truth he added, 'There is an old Kabbalist tradition
that the sexual act can do something to heal the wound in the
heart of God, but only if it's performed in full spiritual awareness. Louisa would have known about that. But she chose the
other way—the way of denial. Abnegation. Spiritual ascesis.
Otherwise she would have married, right?' He looked for confirmation. I shrugged. 'It won't wash,' he said, and started to

walk away. Then stopped. 'I suppose there must be parish records . . . though I still don't see how they could help.'

'Didn't you say that Louisa mentioned Frere in her last journal entry?'

'Not Frere. His wife. He was married and he was the parson. It's preposterous.'

Then another fact surfaced in my memory. 'I seem to remember that Frere wasn't in Munding long. It struck me when I was looking at the list of Rectors in the church. I suppose something could have happened?'

Edward saw where my thoughts were going and scowled. 'A village this size? Victorian England? Anyway, what possible bearing could it have on the Agnews' work?'

'I don't know. But if Laura's right . . .'

He turned away, appeared to be studying his own reflection in the glass of a bookcase.

'These things do happen, Edward.'

'*Now* they do. Anything can happen in this contemporary madhouse. But we're not talking about now.'

'Human nature . . .'

'. . . is a pretext for all manner of irresponsibility. That was precisely the ground of the Agnews' work—deep self-knowledge; not some scatter-brained acting on romantic impulse. These were serious people.'

I retreated to safer ground. 'If there are records Neville Sallis might have access.'

'That dunderhead! He won't have anything to do with me. Not after last time. His grasp of theology could be resumed on the back of a Sunday-school text. The imbecile had the gall to ask me if I'd read my verses at some damned concert-party he's organizing.'

'Me too.'

'I trust you told him what to do with it.'

'Not as colourfully as you. I could ask him if you like.'

'I doubt it's worth the trouble. Anyway, God knows when the next service is. They seem to be organized like a sort of spiritual meals-on-wheels these days.'

'I know where he'll be tonight. At a CND meeting in Saxburgh. Bob Crossley goaded him into going.'

Edward eyed me dubiously. 'Will you be there?'

'I hadn't planned to but . . .'

'Then don't bother. I'm sure there's no point. I still think she's

got it wrong. Even in everyday experience it's difficult enough
to tell when you're connected to something real and when you're
just projecting. For Laura it's an even more delicate balance
between what's real and what's a sort of static, I suppose.'

'You mean she gets confused?'

'Sometimes.'

'It's happened before?'

'In a way.' But his voice lacked conviction. He sniffed, said,
'Anyway, the whole point is there aren't any short-circuits to
the truth,' and walked away.

His back was towards me, my wince invisible.

Bob was surprised when I turned up for the lift, but gratified
as well. I told him that his last remark about my kids had hit
home, and I wasn't lying; but it wasn't the whole truth either.

I'm not proud to admit it now but my reasons for attending
the meeting were narrower than anxiety over thermonuclear catastrophe, about which—I was resigned to this—nothing I could
do would make much difference. I had no appetite for brooding
alone in The Pightle that night. Any company was better than
none, and if Edward had no interest in pursuing Laura's intuition
about Edwin Frere, I needed to know whether or not it had any
substance. I could see no other means of establishing some objective reference on her behaviour that day. I had questions, and
Neville Sallis might, just possibly, supply the answers; and so—
despite Edward's caveat—I was looking for short-circuits.

Around twenty people had gathered in the upper room of the
Black Boys Hotel in Saxburgh. For a small market-town in Tory
heartland this was, I suppose, a reasonable attendance. There
were a number of young faces, though most were middle-aged
and ordinary—friends, professional people, well-known to one
another—and two older women in their sixties looked prepared,
when occasion demanded, to be dignified and difficult with embarrassed policemen. There were perhaps a few more women
than men, one of them well-advanced in pregnancy. The faces
were cheerful and indomitable—the kind of decency that violence betrays. Otherwise, apart from the fact that they were there
at all, there was nothing distinctive about them.

When Bob and I arrived Neville Sallis was chatting with the
old ladies. He was at pains to explain that he was not a member
of CND but felt it his responsibility to stay in touch with all
sections of opinion in his parishes. 'Also,' I heard him say, 'it's

not impossible that I might be able to play a conciliatory role in future demonstrations at the Thrandeston base. I'd like to think so.'

One of the old ladies smiled and said, 'I do hope you're not still sitting on the fence when we cut through it.' Sallis laughed, looked away and spotted Bob. He excused himself, came across to join us, but Bob had already been button-holed by another member of the committee, and Sallis and I were left alone in each other's company.

He ran a finger round his glass, aspiring to invisibility, then wondered aloud whether he'd been right to come.

'I'm glad you did. There's something I wanted to ask you.' It wasn't hard to persuade him of my interest in local history as he shared it. Did I know, he asked, that he and a few other people were talking of forming a society? No, I didn't know that, and had to listen to his enthusiasm until he gave me the opportunity to say that my own interest had been aroused by the church—Munding St Mary's.

'Gypsy May and all that?'

'Right, but I think I've come across the name of one of the previous Rectors before, as a minor poet. I wonder if you know how I could find out more about him?'

'A poet? That's interesting. Who are we talking about? I don't remember turning up any poets.'

'Frere. Edwin Lucas Frere. 1848 to '50, I think.'

I saw his expression change before his eyes shifted away.

'I was wondering if there are any records that might help.'

'Of course. The Diocesan Archivist has charge of them. However it's unlikely you'll be allowed access.' I saw that his relief at finding himself on uncontroversial ground had quite evaporated.

'Have you looked at them?'

Clearly he had. He looked severely now at me. 'What precisely is the nature of your interest?'

'I told you. I seem to remember coming across a poet of that name. I wondered if it was the same man.'

'Is that true?'

I was not prepared for this. 'I might be mistaken of course.'

'I think you are.'

'You know about Frere then?'

Sallis nodded uncertainly. 'A little.'

'Can you tell me about him?'

'I'm afraid not.' He nodded at an acquaintance across the room.

I swallowed, said, 'Why not?' as lightly as I could.

'Frere was . . .' He changed his mind. 'I'm afraid it's a question of confidentiality.'

'But the man's been dead for a century or more.'

'Where matters of confidence are concerned that makes no difference,' he answered sternly. 'Now if you will excuse me I must have a word with . . .'

At that moment a young woman called the meeting to order. Uncomfortably Sallis sat down next to me.

There was a certain amount of branch business to get through before the main purpose of the evening. It passed over me as I sat wondering what Sallis knew, watching him fidget beside me. If the church had closed ranks it looked, distressingly, as though Laura might be right. Only then did I realize that I'd hoped to prove her wrong. If I could show that Frere had been a respectable man of the cloth who'd slumbered away a quiet life in mildewed vestments, or that he'd been elevated to a bishopric and thence to Heaven without a blemish on his record, then Edward would at least have the consolation of knowing he was right, and Laura . . . Laura would have to come to terms with the here and now. Things might still work out that way, of course, but I had an uneasy feeling that they wouldn't.

I forgot Frere, forgot my surroundings, and was back in the confusions of the Lodge. For a few apocalyptic seconds the power of our meeting had estranged me from myself. I'd entered a magnetic zone where all the compasses were crazy, and to think about it filled me with a queer mix of desire and dread. The mind wandered gingerly around the experience, and the way my hidden shallows had been exposed. Then, from somewhere in my reading, it came up with the story of a European in India who, in service of no other deity than his own desire, had cynically taken advantage of a temple-prostitute. The woman was very beautiful and very intelligent. Aware of what the man was doing, she had exhausted him with all her incendiary skills, and then—by the simple act of refusing to give herself again— left him distraught. He'd wandered the world afterwards, endlessly haunted by her memory, a sexual cripple.

It was the kind of story that Edward might tell. In other circumstances he would have chortled at me: *'You've made your bed, sweet pie, so die on it; you might reincarnate as something*

more sensible—something harmlessly green; a cucumber per-
haps!' But there was little enough for him to laugh at here.
Whether he knew it yet or not, his tower was down, and it
stopped my heart to think of it.

I was brought back by the introduction of the principal
speaker. Bob had told me about George Hodgkiss on the way
into Saxburgh: he was a local character, a bearded former teacher
with a nice line in irreverence, who now ran an organic market-
garden on the edge of the town, using alternative technology
wherever he could. He was famous for the opening words of a
talk he'd given to the Women's Institute: 'Some people feel that
a shit-heap is the unacceptable face of country life. I say that the
future is in shit.' Evidently he was aware of the ambiguity.

Drily he now explained the process by which he'd been selected as one of the team of Community Controllers. 'I didn't
make any secret of my membership of CND. In fact, I positively
flashed my badge at the interview. But there wasn't much com-
petition for the job and, on this occasion at least, dear old England didn't seem to mind. Major Alsop seemed to think I'd be
a handy chap to have around after the event. That's what he calls
it, by the way. An event. Like the World Cup, you understand.
He thought I'd be useful till normal services were resumed—
building windmills, things like that. Also I'll be put in charge
of food. So if you're feeling peckish after the event you'll have
to come to me. Just don't expect my spuds to be additive-free.'

The laughter quickly faded as he went on to explain the finer
points of a Community Controller's duties. They were the ex-
ecutive arm of the Regional Seat of Government which would
be kept busy in the blast-proof vaults under County Hall doing
the thinking for the rest of us. 'The thing is,' he said, 'we're
working on the assumption that we'll be given fair notice of the
event. Forget that old four minutes chestnut: this fixture will be
advertised a week to ten days in advance. After all, it took seven
days to make the world and we don't have God's advantages, so
we need at least that long to organize its dissolution. I'm afraid
it can't be done without some inconvenience. Most of our troops
will already be in Europe but we'll have to find room for about
half a million American servicemen who'll all have to be fed,
housed and moved about. The Immigration Authorities aren't
expected to raise any difficulties and those of us who do—or
might—will be interned in camps. Of course, as CND members
that means you.'

'What about you, George?' someone called.

'Ha—well, I'm what you might call an anomaly. Major Alsop and the Parish Clerk were a bit at sea on that one, and it seemed impertinent to make suggestions. They finally decided we'd cross that bridge when we came to it. No doubt some accommodation will be reached. Now where was I? Ah yes. Living as close to Thrandeston as we do we're in a GDA. I bet you didn't know that, but you are. A GDA is a Ground Defence Area, so we must expect our patch to be put under military control, and that'll mean rather more than having a hard time fighting your way to the bar in the Thrandeston Arms. For instance, if your house happens to stand in the line of fire from the base—well, I'm sorry, but we'll have to pull it down. A nuisance, I know, but do put up with it because otherwise we might have to use what's called ''deadly force.'' All right? Now, when things get really sticky we're also going to have to accept that the other team are going to take a jaundiced view of this region. There are an awful lot of installations hereabouts so it might save a lot of heartache if you start off from the assumption that once our missiles are launched this area will be written off. We'll have to learn to look after ourselves, because all the doctors, for example, will already have been packed off elsewhere!'

'What if they refuse to go?' someone asked.

'Oh we can't have that. More defensible locations will have a use for them, and—it would be a waste, but if we have to shoot one or two *pour encourager les autres*, well . . . you can't mess about with martial law. Of course, other people might catch on that's it's a good idea to get out of the region, but you know what the roads are like round here. Think what a muddle it would be if the A47 was jammed with traffic while the military were trying to sort themselves out. No, the roads will be blocked. If you live here, you stay here and you take your chances. We'll do all we can to make your stay as comfortable as we can and, chances are, it will be brief. There are bound to be some annoying little hitches, but as you can't go anywhere the fact that all the fuel will have been requisitioned shouldn't cause too many problems. As for food—there won't be a lot of it about. You can't expect GIs to defend you on empty stomachs. The supermarkets will be empty or under guard, but the rationing system will be entirely fair. Major Alsop and I will see to that. In any case, even before the event there should be fewer mouths to feed. One of our first jobs—we'll get down to it this week—

is deciding which field will be most suitable for a mass grave. It's the old and sick, you see. No point wasting food on them; so, among our other sensible precautions, the hospital and the old-folk's home will be emptied and the contents planted in the field of our choice.'

One of the old ladies stood up. 'Would you care to explain that?'

'Certainly, madam. They'll be shot. The old and sick will be shot.'

'I see. Before the bomb has dropped?'

'Well, we'll hold off as long as we can, but we'll all be far too busy afterwards—probably wishing that we'd been shot too.'

'Suppose it doesn't happen,' someone said. 'I mean, what if they shoot all these people and then the politicians back down?'

'That would be embarrassing,' Hodgkiss conceded, 'but we'll do our best to see it doesn't happen.'

'The shooting or the war?'

'The backing-down, of course.'

Gallows humour, but without it the presentation would have been insupportable. It was barely so anyway. There was question, counter-question, argument, and even the gallows humour dried. A kind of black alert fell over the room. Everyone was numbed by the ghastly pragmatism of it all. If I wasn't among those who sat in silence wondering whether they should stock-pile food and fuel, it was only because I was wondering how I'd get back across the country. I imagined myself stuck in Munding while Marcus and Lily cried 200 miles away and I not knowing whether they were blind or burned. Neville Sallis sat, white-faced, beside me. I saw Bob glowering grimly at the floor. Even those who gallantly began to suggest ways of publishing this dreadful news, of dramatizing it to stir the township from its acquiescent sleep—even they must have had the feeling that they were scratching at iron doors. Power was always with the others, with the death-dealers and those who had obediently evolved the tunnel-vision it takes to organize atrocity. The room was already iced in nuclear winter.

And what nonsense this made of Edward and me poring over the Agnew papers, of all high talk of reconciliation of the op-posites. If the war became civil war before it went nuclear, if there were people prepared to shoot their neighbours in the name of efficient defence, what hope was there for a reconciliation across frontiers? It made nonsense of all values, this fear sizzling like radiation on the air. It corrupted thought. It corrupted everything.

The meeting fragmented into small anxious groups. Neville Sallis stood up, looked down at me, shaking his head. 'The whole point is it won't happen. That's why we need them. They've guaranteed nearly forty years of peace after all.'

He saw I was not about to ally myself with this attempt at public reassurance and looked away. The pregnant woman had heard him. Quietly she pointed out there wouldn't be much satisfaction in that once the guarantee expired. Someone else asked whether he took such a low view of human nature that he thought we could only control our own violence by frightening ourselves into this frigid peace. I listened to the clash—the old, endless, point-counterpoint failure to meet.

Nobody wanted it. Nobody in their right mind really wanted things this way. Yet here it was, an ultimatum to ourselves, a death's head hoping against hope. I realized how little thought I'd dared to give to our bleak predicament. I wasn't even sure that real thought was possible. Fear froze it. We were all scared, and what we were frightened of was *us*.

That, at least, I could see clearly. It was no use thinking in terms of *them*, the potential enemy, *them*, the designers of this hideous programme of civil defence, *them*, the trigger-happy hawks of either side. George Hodgkiss had been right to stick with the first person *we*. This was us made naked to ourselves. We were all members of this demented dream. Nobody exempt. Why else had the authorities made Hodgkiss privy to their dreadful secrets if not because somewhere, secretly, they wanted us to know; they needed to share the shame of it? *We* were the matter. The evidence was in, the jury out, and this the treason-trial of all time. Innocence was not an acceptable plea, and a judgment of *Guilty but insane* would bring no commutation of the penalty. For a species that had also conceived of Paradise it would be a miserable epitaph. But where, beyond such sardonic distancing, could you take these thoughts? For even as you thought, even as you made love, not five miles away the engines turned.

I couldn't bear the silent faces of those too appalled to speak. I couldn't believe in the stratagems devised by others to take on the warlords. Not then. Not that night. I could only think that if my children demanded to know why things were so I had no answer.

I looked round, saw an open window overlooking the market-place, moved and lit a cigarette. There was no structure to the meeting now. My move disturbed nobody and, listening to the debates, the shared anxieties, I knew I had nothing to add but my own portion of the gathering gloom.

In the night above the market-place the Great Bear prowled. So many other galaxies, other planets, spinning indifferent to the pathos of it all. I remembered Edward telling me about the Many Universes Theory, and wondered whether it didn't at least have a metaphorical value. So many worlds were possible—why this one then, this death-camp prospect on the future? If we were capable of such deep nightmare fantasies we were also, by the law of contraries, capable of equal heights of exaltation. Blake had known it. The alchemists had known it. Edward, my friend whom I'd deceived, insisted on it. Why then did we deafen our ears to these visionary spirits, preferring the grotesque 'realism' of our darker dreams? Why did I myself do that?

I turned back to where people argued, fretted, planned. We were all trapped in a machine of our own making. We were all trapped in time, in this old room of history that must once have been the Saxburgh Assembly Room. Louisa must have come here in her day. And it was much older than that. Those chamfered beams were already raised before the days when Humphrey Agnew passed his task down time. I remembered his epitaph from Virgil, and saw how terrifyingly true it was: to enter Hell is no problem—the door is ever open. It's getting out again that comes hard. *Hoc opus, hic labor est.*

Well this was hell now. We were well across the threshold. We could smell the fire.

Afraid for my children, with anxieties about Edward and Laura swarming through my mind, scared of the future, I thought: God damn it, Louisa Agnew, if you had an answer to all of this why, in the name of all that's human, did you burn it?

But Louisa Agnew was long dead and gone. Back in the womb of time, of the Great Mother. Silent and cold as Gypsy May, that other ever open door among the flints of Munding church. The lines were dead.

12 ❧ The Hanged Man

At the first discovery that he did not greatly miss his wife's company, Edwin Frere was a little ashamed. He would not permit himself to feel light-hearted, but neither were his experiments with grief a demonstrable success. It felt fraudulent to persevere with them; so he searched his heart and found philosophy. He and Emilia had suffered together and it had been managed badly. Each had been compromised by the inadequacy of the other; they might never have found room to move without this brief separation; and to recognize this was to admit failure, yes, but one that might be turned to good advantage. For on Emilia's return they would begin anew. She would be fortified by the vacation; he would have recovered tenderness. The sad loss of that winter season would recede into the past. With the Spring, with Easter, they would recommit themselves to their vows, and they would do it here, in Munding.

In the meantime there was work to be done, and he applied himself to it, lavishing on his parishioners all the care he had been unable to show his wife. He was aware that their regard for him was tainted with a kind of pity; but if it eased communication he could bear with that. Pity, after all, was not so far from true Christian love.

With the arrival of Emilia's first letter his mood darkened. The tone was formal, almost cold; her account of the restorative pleasures of life in Cambridge carefully worded to leave him in no doubt that his preference for rural seclusion had been, and still remained, a queer error of judgment. About events in

Munding she expressed no curiosity other than a mild hope that all was well.

The main burden of the letter reflected on her father's condition. Emilia had not previously permitted herself to realize how sorely his spirits had declined on her removal from Portugal Place. His need of her now was very great, and it was a joy to her, therefore, that in seeking her own recovery she had found it in attendance upon him. They prospered together. Her main, indeed her only expressed anxiety was for the effect upon her father of a second departure.

Frere read the letter many times and at each reading his foreboding grew. It took a number of drafts to pen a reply in which his worries were concealed, her hints ignored, and the emphasis placed firmly on the good wishes expressed in the parish for her speedy return. And still the letter answered neither Emilia's innuendoes nor his own qualms. When Eliza Waters next asked after his good lady he found himself wishing that she would not enquire so persistently. Sometimes it felt as though the women of the parish knew more of his domestic life than he understood himself.

He was yet more uncomfortable answering Miss Agnew's enquiries in the church porch one Sunday morning after matins. She had failed attendance for two weeks now and he had become concerned that she might be ill. It had been a relief, therefore, to see her next to her father in their pew once more. Henry Agnew was talking to Mr Wharton in jovial vein as Louisa presented herself before the surpliced parson with apologies for her earlier absences. He was about to enquire into their reason when she took the conversation in another direction.

'I understand that Mrs Frere is with her family in Cambridge?'

'Ah yes. We thought a brief visit might confirm her recovery.'

'You have heard from her?'

'Oh yes.'

'And she is well?'

'It appears so. Well enough . . . though there is some cause for concern in her father's condition, I believe.'

'I am sorry to hear that. Pray send her my good wishes. And you, Mr Frere? You are keeping well?'

The gaze was earnest. In this company, Frere was reluctant to mouth pleasantries that would fall vacuously on his ears; but it was his duty to ease the troubles of his parishioners not burden them with more. 'I was about to ask the same of you,' he said. 'You are looking a little drawn, I think.'

'I have been working very hard.'

'In your den by the lake?' She nodded. Almost shyly. Untypically so, he thought. 'You do not find it rather lonely there?'

'On the contrary.'

'You have guests?'

She smiled then, puzzlingly. 'I have a host of companions.' She took in his quiz, smiling still. 'Some of the noblest men and women who have ever lived . . . though few of them as celebrated as they merit.'

What a sprightly mind dwelt in those tilted eyes! It had taken a moment to realize that she referred to the authors of her books. 'Do I know their names?' he asked.

'Some will be familiar—Zosimus? Synesius? Plotinus, of course.

'Elevated company, Miss Agnew. I should be quite awestruck among them.'

'I too, I assure you. Yet I find their conversation patient and provocative. One must try to rise to it.'

'I trust you will not overexert yourself in the effort. The present has need of you too. You must endeavour to save some portion of yourself for we lesser mortals.' He hesitated, dared. 'One wonders whether others might share some of your discoveries among the mighty even?'

'That is my intention, Mr Frere. Perhaps you would care to read my little book when it is done?'

'So that is what you are about? I shall eagerly anticipate the fruits of your labours. May one know how it is titled?'

'In good time, Mr Frere, in good time. If all continues well you shall have an inscribed copy in your hand in a matter of weeks.'

'So soon? I am heartened to hear it. And then perhaps we shall see more of you about the village?'

'Indeed,' she answered, 'though should anyone have need of me in the meantime they know where I may be found.'

The remark was offered lightly enough, yet momentarily it discountenanced him, for he was aware of others waiting to share a word.

Then, 'Good day to you, Mr Frere,' she said. 'I am pleased to have found you well,' and drifted away to join her father at the lych-gate. Frere's eyes followed her progress a moment before turning to smile down into Mrs Bostock's iron gaze.

The next day brought a further disturbing encounter. He had been in Saxburgh to visit Canon Ivory and was returning through the market-place when a young woman accosted him. She stood in his way, holding a basket at her hip, smiling. 'It's Amy,' she reminded him. 'Amy Larner.'

Since Amy's tearful departure from the Rectory Frere had seen nothing of her. He had been touched to receive an ill-spelled note, thanking him for his help in finding a new position, one in which, he was assured, she was 'enormus happy.' Later, on one of his visits to Emilia, Tom Horrocks had spoken well of Amy's progress, but since then Frere had not spared the young woman a thought.

He covered his confusion now, asked after her welfare, and was regaled with an account of the good woman for whom she now worked and her adorable children. 'That's a family of angels, Mr Frere. I count myself ever so lucky to be among 'em.'

'I am delighted to hear things have proved for the best, Amy. Now if you will . . .'

'I do hear that your good lady is in Cambridge now.'

'Yes, that is so.'

'They say she'nt been at all well.'

Frere could not believe that Amy had any greatly charitable interest in his wife's welfare. It was also to exceed her station to enquire as closely as she did. His brisk, though polite, answer was intended to convey as much.

'Must be awful lonesome in that girt Rectory,' Amy Larner opined, undeterred.

'With so many needs to attend to a parson's life is rarely lonely.' He might have added that there were times when he longed for greater privacy, but she spoke again.

'That weren't what Parson Stukely used to say.'

'You mustn't ask me to answer for my predecessor, Amy.' Frere reached, significantly, for his watch.

'Well, I just wanted to say that you was ever so good to me, Mr Frere.' She fixed him with candid, tender eyes—a heifer's mild stare. 'Us Larners don't forget such things.'

'I know that, Amy. I found your note most touching. But you must think no more of it now.'

Again that glance, with a perhaps deepened suffusion of the cheeks.

Belatedly Frere realized what this might be all about. And blushed.

He looked away, cleared his throat, nodded at young Frank Wharton who drove his gig through the square with Fanny Hethersett laughing beside him, then said, 'Well I really must be on my way. It was a pleasure to see you.'

A hand placed softly on his own stopped him as he turned. Amy Larner held her nether lip in her teeth and smiled. Hotly conscious of the touch, he too contrived to smile. Then she lifted her skirt to cross a puddle and walked away, the basket swinging at her side.

His bed that night was enormously empty. He had not made love to his wife since the first advent of her morning-sickness. It was some considerable time since he had even slept beside her, and he thought he had grown accustomed to his lonely bed, was sure that he had done so, until with her sincere if unorthodox interpretation of Christian charity Amy Larner had seemed to suggest that he need no longer lie alone.

Not that he was tempted. Not by Amy. Heaven spare him, no. It would be an act of monstrous irresponsibility—one that Stukely might not have blinked at, but he (with George Herbert's little book on the pillow beside him) was made of sheerer stuff.

Yet in all innocence—if such a word could possibly be apt— the plump young woman had unleashed a demon in his mind. Celibacy was not his natural inclination. He was no anchorite, no ascetic, but a parson of the Anglican faith—a faith that had ordained marriage as an honourable estate for the priesthood, signifying the mystical union between Christ and his church. Even for the clergy it was better to marry than burn. But how if one married and burned also?

He lay on his bed recalling the reasons why marriage had been ordained: for the procreation of children; for a remedy against sin and to avoid fornication by those who lacked the gift of continency; for the mutual society, help and comfort that the married couple ought to have, one of the other, both in prosperity and adversity. Sound reasons all. Yet what if mutual comfort had turned to rancour and resentment; if the marriage was not blessed with children; the marital bed refused? What then if one lacked the gift of continency?

Not for the first time Frere began to pity himself. Trying as

hard as he did to bring comfort to others, wherein lay comfort
for himself? Not, for certain, in Amy Larner's arms; yet she had
set his mind raging elsewhere like a beast of the field.

Carnal lusts and appetites: how potently the language of those
Tudor divines nailed the beast. Yet the more he sought to resist
them, the harder they pressed. Better to shift his attention entirely. To contemplate next Sunday's sermon which must have,
he reminded himself, a little more of the common touch if it
were not once more to miss its mark. The parables were the
clue—the language and the experience of the common man rendered magnificently apposite. He recalled how he had approved
of Wordsworth's preface to his *Lyrical Ballads*. What was the
phrase? 'A selection of the language of ordinary men and
women'—something of that order. He too must find some appropriate correlative of the rural idiom. How did they speak
among themselves?

The nearest example he found was the memory of Amy Larner's sing-song cadences. He must remember to pray for her.

'Dear Lord, you who sit in the deeps of all our hearts, who
made us flesh and knows how flesh is weak, consider the soul
of thy servant Amy, and find it in your heart to . . .'

Dear God, such pious evasion!

It was not Amy Larner who came into Frere's chamber that
night, nor did the woman even look like her. The figure was
darker, more slender, sinuous even. She moved with un-English
motions, bejewelled, filmily dressed, Indian. She had stepped
from the temple-wall, stone made flesh, one of the crowd of
provocative nymphs that lingered there. Tender and indolent,
her gaze was turned towards him. It spoke of her yearning to
become a *maithuna* figure—to be coupled, like those pairs of
lovers that stood at the entrance to every temple, serpent-twined,
endlessly making love in public view, unabashed and rapt. She
was a silent, miasmic dancer whose every gesture uttered only
a single word.

The next day a second letter arrived from Emilia. She was
surprised and (she confessed) a little injured that Edwin had
proved so insensitive to the feelings she had tried so delicately
to express in her first message. She had hoped he would read
between the lines and voluntarily give her leave to remain longer
in Cambridge than originally planned. The case for this alteration was not selfishness on her part but a response to the dire

need of her father. She went on to describe at length the symptoms of his distress, which read strangely similar to those Frere had encountered in his wife, and angered him. He guessed what Tom Horrocks would make of this. Must he go to Cambridge and drag her back by the hair?

Then the tone of the letter changed. This was a voice he recognized from their early days—winsome and thoughtful only for his welfare—a voice he had ever found impossible to refuse. She knew how very hard it must be for him alone. She was sure that those regrettable moments of bitterness were occasioned only by mutual distress. They had been right to believe that a separation would rekindle a more feeling apprehension of one another, for this had certainly been the case with her. If she asked now for a longer leave of absence he would understand that it cost her quite as much in grief as must be the case for him. With her loyalties divided so she hardly knew which way to turn. Would Edwin not remove at least one anxiety by acquiescing in another's greater need? If her heart could find an easier way she would not ask it, for she was always his affectionate and obedient wife.

Frere read the letter and was ashamed. He had woken in shame and this had deepened it. Immediately, without pause for selfish reflection, he reached for his writing-case and penned an understanding answer.

At the Decoy Lodge Louisa put down her pen, blotted the page, and stretched her slender arms widely away from her shoulders. Aches and cramps unwrinkled as she splayed her fingers in the air, playing a trill on an impossibly wide and high piano. It was done. The last word of the first draft was penned. She had achieved the end.

She perused the final paragraphs once more:

This then is the secret entrance to the shut palace of the king of which great Irenaeus spoke. This is the sixth celebratory day of the Chymical Wedding, and the seventh glorious action which transpires in the eighth chamber of the tower, from which, like Rosenkreutz, we had thought ourselves for ever excluded. Here may Christian and Pagan, Mahometan and Jew stand reconciled to hear the Warden of the Tower inform us that 'no man never knoweth how well God intendeth him.'

For here is the final key of Eudoxus, the last great act of

the Hermetic Mystery; and those who have attained to this
Perfection of the Stone speak always with a single voice. How-
ever shrouded in darkness their rich store of metaphor; how-
ever bewildering each gesture of their Art; and however
fraught with inconsistency the legion of their volumes may
appear to be, here is light unto our darkness, an end to all
perplexity, and the reconciliation of those contraries which
give the human heart no peace. Here in the wedding of the
Red King and the White Queen, of our Sulphur and our Mer-
cury, of Sun and Moon, here is the grave and lovely celebra-
tion of true union which is the desire of every heart.

It is the present author's earnest wish that all who must now
judge with what sincerity it is offered, will accept this humble
invitation to attend.

Did she need that second *here* in the penultimate sentence,
she wondered. Well, for the moment, let it stand. There was
much in any case that must be revised, and it would take time;
but that was secondary work, the fettling of her stone. The main
burden was lifted now, the long ground covered, her truth told.

She put the last page with the others, got up from her desk,
and stepped out of the door of the Lodge. It was a clear, sharp
day. She could hear the coarse bustle of the rooks among the
elms. The crisp Norfolk air lucidly revealed all things.

Louisa was at peace with herself and very tired. She would
sleep long and let her mind lie fallow before returning with fresh
vigour to completion of her task. In the meantime she was sure
her father would be pleased by her achievement. Sure too that
the other for whom, of late, the book had secretly been written,
would soon find comfort there.

It was impossible to think of him without a smile, though the
smile was wistful, touched with sadness, for the brief meeting
in the porch had brought her gently back to earth. It had returned
him from her dreams to where he belonged in the waking-world.
It declared him Rector of the parish, married man, and friend.

Not for a moment did the realization diminish her devotion, but that too was returned to its proper place within the
secrecy of her soul. That was where it had first struck root, and
so covertly she had scarce been aware of it herself; but it had
grown there and sustained her as she worked alone. It had heartened in the knowledge of what was truly possible between a
woman and a man; and no more than she would question the

generality of that knowledge could she deny its source in the particular individual who had inspired it. But in his living presence that day at the church—his *unconscious* living presence—Louisa saw how she had allowed herself to confuse the possible and the inevitable. Desire, bred of her own solitude, had occasioned that confusion. It was her wilderness-temptation, and she had withstood it.

She had done more than that: she had converted its energy to the enrichment of her book. It flowed through the pages like an underground stream, though none but she would ever divine it there. Without that flow she would have accomplished no more than a stimulating but finally arid tract, and if it was fecund now then the harvest was entirely due to his unconscious presence in her heart. If no more than a word of polite affection might ever pass between them in the waking world, she lived now in the modest hope that the world would profit from the words they had exchanged in dream. And if, in consequence, she must seem to invite the world to a wedding where there was, for her, no actual bride, no actual groom, then this was the price exacted of her. She would not shrink from payment.

Somewhere she had always known her destiny a lonely one, and she would be less than human if the heart failed to ache at its acceptance; but from the very moment of her birth life had gifted her with privilege. *This one shall be fortunate,* it said, *for though she will know the pangs of solitude she will find riches there, and prosper in the sharing of its joys.* And what she might openly share with him was solace in *his* loneliness, and the promise of great meaning in the trials he endured. It would be bound there in the pages of her book. He would open it between his hands and there he would discover himself.

Standing on the jetty, Louisa Agnew looked into the waters of the lake. No, this was no dead sea, though tideless now and lonely; and in this moment there was nothing to be seen there but her own reflection shaking like a banner in the wind.

Darkness inhabited the mind of Edwin Frere. The impulse of tender regret with which he had answered his wife's last approach had not long survived the arrival of another letter from Cambridge.

It came from a college friend who had encountered Emilia at a *soirée* in the Frogmore house. He was writing to express his sympathies that the Munding living had proved so ill-starred.

Though the loss of the child was a great sadness it must be patiently borne; but that Norfolk had proved so singularly dismal did not greatly surprise the writer. Had he not expressed his own reservations at the time? Yet it must be duller even than he feared if Edwin was considering the abrogation of his well-known views against absentee incumbency. Nevertheless, he was sure that the appointment of a curate was the wisest course. He was relieved to hear of it, for Edwin's excellent mind would be better employed in Cambridge circles and, as far as this correspondent was concerned, he had been sorely missed. Could he look forward to an early resumption of their encounters over the chess board? It had certainly given him much pleasure to play the rattle with Emilia again.

Frere stared at the letter aghast. So that was what she was about! He had been beguiled. At this very moment perhaps Emilia was smiling over his contrite response to her last letter, satisfied that her hidden—how long-laid?—plans were proceeding apace. She had abandoned him here in cold deliberation, knowing that sooner or later his will must weaken, and that, if she held out long enough in her Cambridge fastness, he would join her there with his tail between his legs. Well she was wrong. His affectionate and obedient wife must be taught a lesson.

Yet could he write again so soon, countermanding the ignorant act of generosity and insisting upon her immediate return? To what end? To resume hostilities again? To have her sour the atmosphere of the house? To play upon his guilt by harping on her father's need? It would be intolerable. No, now that he was apprised of the facts, he too must be cunning. He must stay his hand, allow her sufficient rope whereby she would eventually be embarrassed by the long separation. And then, in his own good time, he would draw her back.

As to the friend's letter, let it go unanswered. If truth were told, he had never greatly cared for the fellow. He suspected that the man quietly smirked to see Frere once again turn tail. He should not be given the satisfaction. Let them both stew in their juice.

Yet Frere's was not a calculating spirit. The energy required for silent intrigue demoralized him. He had been compromised out of character by anger and circumstance, and fretted uneasily, for there was no constancy in him. When he considered how even his own good nature had proved treacherous he recoiled from righteous anger into gloom. What a vacillating mind was his, how unstable the motions of his heart!

Beyond the sham of his public appearances he was now immensely lonely. His wife was more than a few score miles away—she inhabited a different world. He felt deeply abandoned, and there was a self-regarding sensuality to his loneliness which left him increasingly distraught, for once he had opened the door of his bed-chamber upon demons it would not close again. There too he had been beguiled. With what charms, what consolatory allure, the first of them had come into him! Such a harmless creature to dally with! But she had friends, and they were not so harmless. He knew because he had encountered them before, in India.

Yet like the host of a party sliding from control he seemed powerless to eject them. They were too subtle for him. Even when he opened his Bible he found himself drawn to the rapturous verses of that Song of Songs which is Solomon's. Try as he might he could no longer persuade himself that its sensual hymn was to be taken only as a metaphor of Christ's love for his bride, the Church. He could not truly believe it. No more than he could believe his own restless stirrings a displaced desire for spiritual union with his parishioners—with Mrs Bostock, with Eliza Waters, even—God help him—with his own absent wife.

When he turned from this profanation of the Scriptures it was to seek solace in what had long been a secret love and vice—his affection for the verses of Catullus. They seemed to answer the passion of his soul. They gave voice both to his frustrated tenderness and to the obverse rancour of his spleen. Yet he was terrified by the dreadful plea at the end of the *Attis*, and could cry out with the poet that madness be kept from his door.

Night after night he was compromised by the treason of his dreams, though not all those dreams were vile. There were moments when he sensed the possibility of an innocent nakedness again, a stripping away of all that had fouled the appetite for life. Briefly the sense of a separate self dissolved. One luxuriated in sunlit exuberance like the leaves and tendrils of some exotic vine. It was a condition where one made no demands, for there were no demands to make. One experienced no lust, for all that was needful was there, available, unresisting. In that realm nothing was calculated, and the only speech was sensual speech. But they were moments only. When one woke it was into yearning again, and loneliness.

His greatest need was simply to be touched. Physically touched. For weeks, months now, his body had inhabited a sensory vacuum in which he touched no one and no one touched him. Even in the sacring of the mass there was no immediate contact save through the medium of the wafer and the communion chalice. There were times when his heart longed for the restitution of that ancient sacrament, the kiss of peace; but it was not to be, and in his daily life no more than a brief handshake actualized his membership of the human race. In the house the servants skirted round him, considerate enough, but keeping their distant station. His body wilted in long quarantine, and it was for that reason that the gentle momentary press of Amy Larner's hand lingered in his memory. In a world devoid of touch, its impact had been devastatingly sexual.

Yet how innocent was his need, and how perverse the consequences of its frustration. Amy's touch had felt like transgression, and it opened the door on darker transgressions. He was intoxicated on his own loneliness. He crowded it with phantoms—a dissolute concubinage of dreams from which he woke in shame and despair. It was despicable, this reeling between appetite and disgust. Humiliating, for his narrow sin was worse in its way than Matthew Stukely's. At least the old reprobate had not lacked the courage to act on his desire; in taking Amy Larner to his bed there had been some gesture of relationship. Frere made love to no one but himself.

He had hoped that this temporary separation would restore his integrity. He had hoped to cleanse himself of resentment, to recover his singularity so that he might rededicate himself to his marriage. It was not happening. Each night, and sometimes now by day, a throng of lechers revelled in his brain. His virtue was exhausted by them. The secret knowledge of it vitiated every word he spoke.

A third letter came in answer:

My dearest Edwin,

You will be sensible how great my relief to receive your last most welcome reply. I wish you also to know how abundant my joy to hear you speak as your noble self again. Surely this restoration of tenderness must justify events? Though indeed, could you see how my dear father prospers in my care, no other vindication of our sacrifice would be needed.

*He remains, however, frail. In all good conscience I dare
not yet set a date on my return. It is a consolation to know
that you are well, and that you have been strengthened in your
understanding of the need for this unanticipated prolongation
of our time apart.*

*Be assured that every night you are remembered in my pray-
ers as I know I am in yours, and trust that in all things I
remain,*

                    your affectionate and obedient wife,
                                                Emilia

Frere read the letter twice, and scrumpled it.

Even as the days began to lengthen into Spring his nights grew
darker. He was tempted once—just once—to seek some comfort
in Amy Larner's embrace. He had wondered whether a note
might not be sent by that same hand which had once delivered
one. It might be phrased innocently enough—a regret that he
had seemed a little brusque on their last meeting . . . an interest
to hear more about her progress . . .

He was reaching for his writing-case when he recoiled in
revulsion. Great God, what was he thinking of? But it required
no more than a moment's self-scrutiny to recognize this hasty
scurrying for virtue as mere sham. His revulsion was not moral—
it was aesthetic. Amy Larner with her dumpy figure and crabapple cheeks was not the Shulamite of his dreams. And even as
that bleak thought crossed his mind he saw an ironic demon grin
at his distress.

He was contemptible, and there was no one to whom he could
open his heart. Even were someone by, his tongue would scald
in his mouth before it could utter his degradation. It was this
knowledge which prevented him from seeking counsel through
his fellow-clergymen. Cuthbert of Thrandeston would merely
remind him of the fires of Hell; Jackman at Shippenhall had
time for no one's cares but his own; and the meek heart of Canon
Ivory would quail at the first word.

George Herbert might have understood—he must himself have
experienced such inward clamours to speak of them so aptly.
But George Herbert was long dead, and his little book had become for Frere no more than a rebuke to his failure. He was
alone.

Of late he had found himself washing obsessively, as if soap and water could cleanse a soul that wallowed nightly in the sensual mire. Yet the ablutions had been performed almost unconsciously, and when he woke to the futility of the thing, despair renewed itself. He was a whited sepulchre. He was abomination, for he knew that if Christ himself stood before him now saying, 'Go thy way and sin no more,' he could not do it.

He despaired, and despaired at his own despair. And that too was indulgence. The circles of this hell were endless, for each time he thought he must have plummeted the depths a further twist appeared. Then he hit upon a desperate remedy—to be athletic in his viciousness in the hope that it might be exhausted. If the demons would come whether he willed them or not, then let them come. He would dance on their pitchforks, willingly embrace their petticoats of flame.

On those terms they would not play. He was merely observing himself trying to be sinful. For a brief elated moment he thought he had banished them and won; then he saw that only a kind of mortal coldness had come from his effort at acceptance.

These days his words rang emptily. Service after service was conducted without reverence or feeling. He might as well have recited the logarithmic tables as read the liturgy. He made use of sermons not of his own composition, and whatever meaning they may have held for their composers they held none for him. And none, he suspected, for the grave white faces staring up at him. This was service that was no service. He served nothing. Alone he was without meaning, yet he dreaded, each Sunday at the church door, that someone might invite him into their company. In particular he found the troubled smile and gentle enquiries of Miss Agnew scarcely possible to bear.

Prowling his study one night, he saw that this sham must cease. The secret war with Emilia must end. He must write to her, not in anger or rebuke, but plainly begging her immediate return.

And if she would not come? If she used his sincere confession of disarray as a further weapon in her campaign to bring him back to Cambridge, what then?

Dear God forbid it, but she might in the end be right. It might be necessary once more to concede defeat. But not yet, not yet. With his wife beside him again he might yet win through. At least he must try.

He took out his writing-case from the desk-drawer and stared

down at the blank sheet. Each sentence he rehearsed in his mind
was a lie. Any sentiment that did not rankle with bitterness was
a lie. Finally, with a strict, despairing pang of honesty he saw
that it was because he did not truly wish her back.

There could be no comfort in her. No more than Amy Larner
was Emilia now the lady of his dreams. She was barely even the
wife of his bosom. She would bring nothing but sedition back
from Cambridge with her. If he took her to his bed their bones
would rattle together. She would repine beneath him like an
invalid. He would never dare to unlock the secret of his heart
and it would burn and fester there, for neither of them dared
address the truth. They would lie together as they lay together,
effigies on the catafalque of their marriage. Better to burn alone.
He would not beg for what he did not desire.

He thought again of Louisa Agnew; of her words in the church
porch; of Emilia's parting counsel. Yet it was unthinkable to
inflict his shame on her. Hers was a maiden spirit, untouched
by the vileness in the world. Even the astonishing candour with
which she had first discountenanced him so long before was an
earnest of guileless simplicity. He could not sully it.

Until that moment his reveries over women had been rank
with the impersonalities of sense. Only in form were they human; otherwise he had diminished them to provocative and re-
cumbent flesh, skin over appetite, no more. Yet even as he
revelled in it that lack of human tenderness disgusted him. His
dreams had indeed been an expense of spirit in a waste of shame;
and now, in thoughts of Louisa Agnew, he saw how little such
excesses answered to his deeper need.

There was that in the quality of her presence which distinguished the need of his heart from those of the flesh. Lovely in
form as she was, the spirit within spoke of rarer delights, and
when he thought of her now he saw—he had always somewhere
seen—that she was a special presence in the world, apart but not
aloof, distinctively herself. He saw her smiling up at him in the
shelter of the porch—the eyes bright and enquiring, yet warm
also with the tact of her compassion. Wistfully he watched her
turn and walk away. She was a baronet's daughter, carrying in
her very air a patrician grace of which her cavalier forebears
would have approved; but what a parson's wife she might have
made! She loved this place, this parish; she shared its delights
and felt its woes. Far from shocked at Amy Larner's frailty she
had discerned the generous heart within; for what in others might

have appeared mere nonchalance was, in Miss Agnew, ever
warmed by care. You could see it in her lively dealings with her
servants, who were closer far to friends. You could see it in
her affection for her feckless dog, and in the tender diligence
she brought to her father's needs. And there was humour there,
an inspiriting, sometimes breathtaking vivacity. How wrong he
had been a moment before to think her simple, for there was
also the extraordinary fact of her intellectual endeavours. Yes,
in both his private and his public life what a fine companion she
would have been! How well they might have worked together
here; and then, alone by the fireside at night, what conversation
they might share! With Plato and Plotinus for their friends, he
would urge her on in the adventure of the intellect, while she
perhaps might encourage him to pick up his pen once more and
try for verse. Why, in such domestic serenity, he would need
no encouragement.

Frere sighed. Pleasant as they were, such reveries were disgraceful too. Always, whether dwelling on the flesh or on the
more tender yearnings of his heart, his thoughts approached
adultery. What else should be the case when he abandoned duty
to his wife and pondered endlessly on selfish need?

He must try to think beyond himself, to look outwards, into
the world. He tried to fix his interest on his parishioners. He
thought of the other men in Munding, they who were not wed-
ded to the church, the free men. They who had a purchase on
the world. In their secret hearts, he wondered, were they too
desolated by the knowledge that life as *meeting* always eluded
their grasp? Was such despair the common lot? He could not
conceive of Mr Bostock and Mr Wharton agonizing out their
nights in dread.

Was it possible then that he had been elected to live out, in
stricter suffering, what was common to all yet evaded by most?
Perhaps that was it? Perhaps this was a cross he carried that
others might be spared what he endured? For a moment he saw
meaning so. His distress was suddenly suffused with pride. There
need be no shame in his suffering if that were so. It was a special
destiny.

And there the ironic demon grinned again. From lust to shame
to pride—a vicious circling deeper into sin. Always, at the heart
of it, this sensual obsession with the self. His *reflections* were
only ever precisely that—as though the darkness into which he
peered was no more than a mirror figuring back his inward

emptiness. And yet he must reflect, for what other guarantee remained of his continued spiritual existence? Not the bewildered smiles on the faces of his parishioners as he passed them, distracted, in the lanes. It was merely the animated black of his vestments that they saw, and the oddly white flesh of his hands and face. No, only this capacity for desperate thought was a serviceable spirit here—even if the twists of its mazes were where his demons dwelt.

In an agony of apprehension he saw how closely Easter loomed on the calendar before him.

Dimly at first, then with mounting alarm, he saw that in rejecting the vision of himself as paschal-lamb suffering on behalf of others, a catastrophic doubt had entered his mind.

Was it possible for anyone to suffer on behalf of others?

Easter was coming and he must profess it so. Yet the empty tomb on which his thoughts were fixed was not that of the risen Christ. It was a further reflection of his own hollowness. Intellectually he knew that he should take comfort from the Easter story. What he could not accomplish for himself had been done for him already through the passion, death and resurrection of the Lord. Here was the very heart of the Christian mystery. It was the miraculous fact which had invested almost two thousand years with meaning. It had made the crucial intersection between time and eternity. Since Adam's fall man had been born in sin, yet Christ had redeemed that sinfulness. All was washed clean, Hell harrowed, the gate of Heaven opened. It was his duty to assure the congregation of this truth. Yet did he really believe it?

From a long time before he remembered the voice of Henry Agnew at the Hall: *All that could be done for the world he did. Yet it remains a sorry place, sir, and man a sorry creature within it.*

Frere shied away from the implications of his thoughts. He tried to imagine himself in the garden of the holy sepulchre. He tried to imagine himself standing there outside the tomb and marvelling at the impossibly rolled stone. He found himself staring into empty rock—a dark cave, cold and empty.

He tried again to pray and prayer proved futile. Christ—that pure and sexless radiance—had no answer to the empty cave which was his own heart. He was ashamed even to come into that presence. He himself was absence, and in absence was it possible to believe in anything?

Only his demons came to keep him company. In them he could believe.

On whose authority did they come to torment him so? What principle of life had he so abjured that they should come now—as once before in India—to exact such vengeance? What lay behind all this agony? Where were its roots? How to lay hold of them and tear them from his soul?

The answer came as nightmare. He woke, sweating and shouting in his chair. He had been walking round and round his church only to find that it had no door. All the walls were sealed with flints. He had walked widdershins, faster and faster in mounting panic, until he came upon an entrance. It was a cave. The cave of the holy sepulchre. He flooded with immense relief, put his hands together in prayer, and entered. And then the cave had closed round him. He was shut in, walled up in stone, and it was not a cave—it was the womb of the hideous idol on his church. She had swooped down over him and engulfed him there.

He sat up, trembling. He was still half-crazed with the fear of it, and with the terrible awareness borne in on him. He had asked and she had answered. It was she who lay at the back of all this torment. She, the goddess who squatted naked across his church. Eostre, Cybele, Beltis, Ashtaroth, Kali, Gypsy May—the goddess of a thousand names. It was she who was his mortal enemy.

Therefore Sheol hath enlarged herself and opened her mouth without measure.

And Sheol, she of the hollow place, the underworld, was Hell. Was that what he had meant when he told himself he was in Hell—that she had swallowed him alive? Was it she who punished him so? And was it before her that he must grovel for mercy now?

Frere was not the only man in Munding experiencing crisis.

All that afternoon Henry Agnew prowled his parkland glowering at the premonitions of Spring. The library had become unbearable—all those damned books unforgivably complete, their places securely taken on the shelves of time, while his own once more groaned like a wagon in the mire.

For a time his verse had taken wing. Ground had been covered with mercurial speed and, yes, he had been aware of flaws, but surely it was wiser to make sail while the wind was at his back rather than lie close-hauled, tinkering over detail? Page after page of couplets mounted on the desk beside him. He was so infatuated with his progress that he found no time to miss his daughter, was glad rather to remain undistracted. Then the wind dropped. He found himself yawing, finally gravelled. He had tried to be philosophical, had seen no choice but to go back over what had been achieved and fettle it; and he had been appalled by what he found.

How could he have allowed so many false quantities to pass muster? How could he ever have taken for other than the grossest botches those clumsy inversions by which rhyme after rhyme was clinched? And the diction on which he had prided himself— inflated, sententious, dull. Shock made him perhaps a severer critic than the work deserved, but what grimaced back at him from those quick-scrawled pages seemed disaster. As contemporary witness to the Hermetic Mystery the lines might be unique; as verse they would be mocked out of court. Only an innately conservative temperament saved the papers from immediate destruction.

With Louisa still in exile at the Decoy Lodge there had been nowhere to turn other than to the works of Nature. Perhaps by immersing himself in her creative power he might find the strength to begin anew? His heart a dense lump at his side— itself a fragment of fool's gold now—he strode out into the park.

And soon found himself breathless and afraid.

He was an old man and he had failed. That was the cruel truth of it. Staring into the flawless light as though into a narrow tunnel, he saw that his epic would never reach completion now. None of the joy that Helvetius must have felt to see his projected gold successfully abide the assayer's test would ever be his. His own work was no gold, common or otherwise. Apply the *aqua fortis* of objectivity to it, or a septuple of critical antimony, and it crumbled. His work was dross.

He looked up and saw that with no conscious intention on his part his steps were taking him towards the Decoy Lodge. There, in that dreadful place, Louisa worked in patience, committed to her task, and utterly innocent of his failure. It might be some consolation to come there, to hang his head in his hands, and make a full confession of his wretchedness. Louisa would understand. She would know what must be done.

But even as he quickened his pace through the beech-wood glades he felt revulsion rise. Why had she insisted on making use of that infernal place? It was the place to which he had been dragged by his father once, when he was still a mere boy, unready for and undesirous of that barbaric initiation into the appetites of the adult male. The ordeal had been terror and humiliation. Its cruelty appalled his heart. He could still hear his own boyish voice tearfully beseeching release, the hideous laughter round him and his father's rage. Even now, more than half a century later, the memory was insupportable. He could not go there.

Then a new thought crushed his spirit like a blow. Even were he to overcome these phantoms from his youth and go to her, what must happen then? To confess his wretchedness would be to confess his failure. To confess his failure would be to render futile all her own laborious weeks of solitude, for her work had meaning only as a prologue to his own. Without his epic, her treatise would be an overture divested of the operatic drama. It would invite the world to a chymical wedding where there would be no marriage-feast. It would be mere mockery. She would see it instantly, and she would be desolated.

He could not do it. Sooner have murdered her in her cradle than mortify her days like this. Yes, she loved him dearly enough not to chide him with her useless sacrifice. Her own loss would count as nothing over against her grief for him. *But he would know it*. Each gesture of her sympathy would be intolerable reproach. He doubted he could long survive such bitter knowledge. For both their sakes it must not come to pass.

Yet how to prevent it now?

There was only one answer to his ills and that was work. Work, work, and yet more work. Had not all the adepts averred no less across the centuries? They had lost fortunes in their endeavours. They had suffered imprisonment, scorn and torment. Year after year they had wasted following new and fruitless lines of enquiry. They too had grown haggard and distraught on the labyrinthine quest. Only those who had endured to the end had seized the golden prize; and, even then, not all. Had not Norton himself died in poverty and despair? Agnew was spared the pauper's shame at least; and if his spirit expired of hopelessness then his daughter must never know.

He would return to his desk. He would smother all doubts, all fear, in work. He would outstare the empty page; and if nothing of value ever appeared there he would not admit it to the world. It would be his secret.

* * *

The little silver clock on her desk stood at twenty minutes to ten, and it was very dark outside, a moonless night, when Louisa heard someone moving in the yard at the rear of the Decoy Lodge. Alarmed, she put down her pen and listened. Pedro lay sprawled asleep before the fire. He had not stirred. Perhaps it had been no more than a figment of her own weary mind. It was, in any case, time that she stopped work. She put her papers aside. The first draft and the almost complete revision of her script lay in two neat piles. She was about to rise from her chair when she froze once more to hear someone stumble over a bucket in the darkness. And this time Pedro woke. Startled, he lifted his head, one velvet ear cocked, then stretched to his feet. He did not bark but every hair on his back seemed alert. They were no longer alone at the Lodge, and this visitor was real, material.

Had she remembered to bar the door?

She got up, walked quietly across the room and out into the back hall. The door was unlocked. The bolt was rusty and could not be shifted without a noise, yet it must be done. Pedro was with her now and, at some sound too quiet for her to hear herself, or at some strange scent perhaps, began to bark. The loudness of the noise intensified her alarm, as if the barking alone betrayed her presence when already her light must have been visible across the yard. She reached for the bolt and struggled to budge it. It shot home with a force that hurt her finger.

She stood, breathing quickly.

Pedro had his paws up at the door, still barking. Under her breath she hissed him to silence, then heard the sound of footsteps moving away through the darkness outside.

No violence had been intended then. Suddenly she was ashamed at her own needless fear: it must be someone who knew her, knew that she was here.

'Who's there?' she cried.

There was a long silence, into which she called again, then heard the sound of footsteps on the cobbles once more.

'Miss Agnew, it is I, the Reverend Frere.'

A great wave of relief passed over her. Without pause for doubt or question, as though a moment long expected had at last arrived, and with it reprieve from a long and tiresome solitude, she struggled to free the bolt again, opened the door, and admitted her lamplight into the darkness of the yard.

Edwin Frere squinted in the sudden brilliance. She saw how

bedraggled his appearance was. She saw how anxious his gaze among the shadows cast across his features by the lamp. Pedro bounded out to greet him and was called, with difficulty, to heel. The man looked up in bewilderment from the excited setter to the woman at the threshold.

'You have come,' she said.

He frowned, perplexed. This was not the response for which he had steeled himself. It seemed almost as if she had been waiting for him while he approached the Lodge through the darkness in such uncertainty.

'I have been out walking,' he improvised. 'I lost my bearings in the darkness . . . and then I saw your lamp . . .'

'Walking? At this late hour?' There was no reprimand, only wonder in her voice. She realized that she was whispering, a little breathlessly, and that he might be discouraged by her answer. She added, 'It was a very great relief to hear the voice of a friend.'

'I must have greatly alarmed you.'

'A friend is no cause for alarm.'

'You are alone?'

'Pedro is with me.' Which had, of course, been apparent from the dog's first commotion, and was therefore an otiose reply. She must collect herself; but she hesitated, divining his thought, then seized the moment before confusion could increase. 'Will you come in, Mr Frere?'

He shook his head, demurring, then looked up, and the appeal in his eyes belied the words he found. 'But if you are alone here . . . It might be thought . . .'

'There is no one here to think but myself,' she answered.

His eyes scouted the darkness as though testing the truth of her claim. He remembered that he had omitted to remove his hat and did so now, holding it by the brim at his chest, his glance downcast. He might have stood in mourning at a grave. Then, startlingly, beyond the gloomy outbuildings a barn-owl cried. He looked up, alarmed. Her mild eyes held his for a moment, and her heart faltered to see the desolation in his face.

'Miss Agnew,' he said, 'I am in great fear for my mind.'

Her first sense of joyful expectation quickly expired. She had thought she knew precisely how she would manage this encounter when it came—for come it must, she had long known that. She had known it even as Emilia unfolded her secret thoughts;

she had known it before that even, for something in Frere's very presence had always commanded the attention of her soul. Of course she had resisted it—he was a married and virtuous man, the Rector of the parish, beyond reproach. Except as friend and pastor he was inaccessible; and so it must be resisted, whatever way she might. She had tried to make him a figure of fun with his awkward, ear-tugging ways, his earnest diffidence. Certainly she had tried to outgrow her own juvenile fantasies, for they had been a disgrace to one who was, after all, Louisa Anne Agnew, kinswoman to Hypatia and Diotima, faithful handmaid of the Hermetic Mystery. She was no lovesick chit of a girl to fritter her life, like her cousin Laetitia, in daydreams over the opposite sex. No, her concern was only with the sacred marriage of spirit and matter, the chymical wedding of the androgynous human soul.

Yet, Rector or not, married or not, Edwin Frere had entered her world like the exacting memory of a previous incarnation. He had shimmered into focus as he skated on the ice. Her soul knew this man, and the knowledge had deeply troubled her. It swung her heart from fits of exaltation into a profound, sometimes petulant gloom. Almost she might have hated him for his intrusion on her inward peace. Yet all the long weeks of her work, and all the happier visions that had possessed her sleeping and her waking mind, had revolved around the thought of him. He had been present to her in the Decoy Lodge throughout. He had inspired her thoughts. The work had been done for him, and it should be possible to announce it now; to admit how much she knew of Emilia's motives, how conscious she had been of his increasing distress in recent weeks, and how she had longed for this moment which she knew must come.

On all these things she was constrained to silence. She saw that the man would be instantly overwhelmed by such admissions. He sat across from her, stiff, muddy-booted, scarcely daring to acknowledge the fact that he had entered, such was the temerity of presenting himself at this late hour in such a lonely place. How grave must his crisis have been to permit this to happen at all! Were she to behave as though considerations of propriety were trivial, he would be embarrassed and amazed. He would drag himself away in confusion, back into the night, to be lost to her for ever. And that must not happen. The fear of it filled her with cold dismay.

She had made tea which they sat drinking together, as though this were four in the afternoon and he on a pastoral visit to a parishioner, except that the cup and saucer rattled a little in his hand, and he had forgotten all the platitudes that might grace the opening of such an event.

'Miss Agnew,' he ventured at last, 'pray assure yourself that only a great loneliness of heart would occasion this intolerable importunity on your privacy . . . on your kindness.' She tried to put him at ease, to assure him that this was no imposition, that she considered his visit a privilege rather. He seemed hardly to hear. 'I had nowhere to turn, you see . . .' His eyes were bereft of hope. 'I was walking the woods for a long time . . . for a very long time . . . And then I remembered my wife's parting words . . . how, if I should find myself in need of company, yours was known to her experience as a charitable heart . . . Yet I felt I could not seek you out at the Hall. I have walked and walked, and came by here only because I was sure that at such a late hour the Lodge must be empty. I wished only to sit here for a while.' He looked up, smiling in a wan attempt to lighten his confession. 'Perhaps I was thinking that some of the wisdom you have uncovered here might cast a little light on my darkness. I did not think to find you here . . . and when I saw your lamp . . .'

'I am most happy that you did. It seems your need of company was very great.'

'Indeed.' He stared into his empty cup, then looked for a place to put it aside. She took it from him—no, he would not take more. 'I think perhaps that I should . . .'

'Will you not venture to share something of your troubles with me?' she encouraged and, when she saw the doubt in his glance, added, ' . . . in the knowledge that a burden shared is a burden halved.'

He sighed and shook his head. 'I would scarce know where to begin.'

It was evident that he was reluctant to begin at all, and for reasons quite other than his native diffidence; but having extended her hand—however metaphorically—Louisa would not lightly withdraw it. 'With your wife's departure for Cambridge perhaps?'

He searched her face, then every corner of the room, as he rubbed his fingers at Pedro's soft ear, for the dog propped its muzzle on his lap, gazing up at him with an expression quite as soulful as his own. 'It is an older tale than that, I fear.'

She waited. He withdrew into frowning silence. She saw how

white were the knuckles of his free hand against the arm of the chair.

'But one must begin somewhere?'

Was it wrong not to admit that she had been privy to Emilia's plans? The confession might prompt a more fluent revelation of his unhappy thoughts; but it was for him to speak; her part was to listen, to make speech possible. She must be delicate with her exhortations.

He pulled himself stiffly upright in the chair. 'I have been gravely in error to trouble you,' he said abruptly, and would have made to stand; but—so quickly that he was amazed into immobility by the act—she leaned forward and put out a hand to restrain him. For a moment it rested at his knee. He stared down at it as though burned by the touch.

'You have been brave enough to come,' she said quietly, 'be brave enough to remain.'

Having made its point, the hand was lifted. Involuntarily he moved his legs away. Pedro, thinking his advances rejected, turned to curl himself before the fire. Frere stared across at the young woman's gentle eyes. She saw the contest in the muscles of his face. 'I am not brave, Miss Agnew,' he said brokenly. 'I am not brave at all.' And suddenly this burly, mud-bedraggled figure of a man was trembling.

Told of a piece, from the first flickerings of dismay in India to this last dreadful night in the Rectory, it would have been impossible for him. The language did not exist in which an unhappily married parson could impart to an unchaperoned spinster of the parish his sense of degradation. Therefore much must remain in the lonely province of silence. Nor could he afford to reveal more than the merest hints of the wretchedness between himself and his wife. He must skate across the trembling surface there, though alas with none of the command he had brought to the ice at Easterness. So no more than clues, allusions, fragments of confession left his lips. But he was speaking, speaking.

And someone was there who listened. She listened without judgment, with concern and a tender regard for every difficulty in which he struggled. There were moments when he dared to look up into the searching blue of her eyes and he might have believed it possible to say anything—anything and everything of his shame and rage, his fears and his fathomless dread. Never had he felt himself in the presence of so receptive a spirit. She was more truly priest than he was himself. She would silence nothing, forbid nothing. She would exhort nothing but such measure of honesty as he felt able to share. She would exact no critical penance. Yet he withdrew from each rash impulse of trust. He told himself that she could not possibly understand. She was too young, too innocent. And, in any case, *it did not matter*. What mattered was that for these moments while he spoke he was human again, and not entirely alone.

He could not guess how much Louisa already knew of his wife, and the pain of their life together. Still less was he aware how much this young woman did understand of mental, spiritual and carnal anguish. She listened, aware of her untapped resources, of how much she might offer if only he dared to hear. And, as his story unfolded in fragments, the man became ever more visible to her. Nothing he might have said would shock or bewilder. She was seeing him whole, the dark and the light of him. He would have been mortified to silence had he known how nakedly he sat before her. He could not have believed how all that he took for his most secret ignominy appeared to her only as the passionate self-torment of a precious spirit entangled in matter. What she saw was the darkened star-fire burning in his soul.

How brave and bright it was to speak, however covertly, of its most anguished yearnings! Yes, the man had been weak. Yes, he must have wrought confusion in India, just as India had wrought confusion in his mind. Yes, Emilia must herself have suffered, and suffered grievously, at his many misprisions in their emotional life together. But theirs had been no true marriage, no irrevocable meeting of souls. It had been no more than a frail alliance made expediently from fear; and, like all such alliances, when the community of interests ceased, the hidden rancour was revealed. And how bitter were the terms of the treaty then, how costly that hour of vows and rings!

None of this escaped her. And none of it deeply mattered. With every word he uttered, with each new gesture of delicate evasion, every weakness fallibly revealed, she felt herself ever more deeply committed to this man. Emilia had not understood what she was doing when she consigned him to her care.

Neither—it was evident—did he. Nor did he discern it now as he sat staring into the fire, speaking his way tentatively back towards some sense of dignity. And Louisa could not tell him.

She must be silent there; and that was the only silence that deeply hurt. It was like flame at her throat, for she knew herself elected into love, and there was no possibility that her love could be returned. For the rest of her life she must learn to live with this knowledge. Here was her durable fire.

She might have despaired at the loneliness of the thought were it not for an invincible certainty that love is not a fixed condition of the soul but its motion: returned or not, it was a directed impulse outwards into life, into ever richer renewal of meeting.

Yet it burned. How painfully it burned.

Frere sat with his elbow at his knee, pinching the bridge of his nose, eyes closed. The little silver clock chimed midnight. He righted himself, gazed across at her, dazed with relief, and with perplexity.

'I am so grateful,' she said, 'that you should repose such trust in me.'

He shook his head. 'The gratitude is all mine, Miss Agnew. I . . .'

'Louisa,' she corrected, smiling. 'I think we are true friends now. I think perhaps we should . . .'

'My dear Louisa,'—the name rippled uncertainly on his tongue—'you cannot know it but I think by bearing with me so patiently this evening you may have saved . . .' He faltered from the extremity of the thought.

She saw the eddy of distress, sought to ease it with a light touch. 'Not your soul, dear friend. Your soul was in no danger.'

'But my mind . . .'

The murmur was half lost in the dry well of his throat. He was suddenly aware how little he had said to justify the first terrible claim with which he had won admission to her intimacy. Strangely he could not quite believe it now himself.

Yet his mind *had* been endangered; even—when he remembered the doubts that had engulfed him—his Christian soul. And he had said nothing of this, not truly. And with the full confession withheld he saw how things might merely be in remission, pacified by her gentle company, only to wait for him again in the empty Rectory.

A further thought flickered across his troubled mind: that in making this young woman his confidante he might only have exacerbated his guilt. Once apart from her, he might swiftly regret this exchange. Bereft of her patient sympathy, he could quickly relapse into new agonies of mind, wondering whether he had said too much. Already he was severing himself from her at the prospect.

She felt him drift from her. It was as though the room grew colder. She knew that if she let him leave now he would not dare to return. She might earnestly embolden him to do so, but it would make no difference. And the loneliness left in his wake would be insupportable.

However illicit this love she felt for him, however it transgressed all bounds of honour, order, rectitude, a truth burned there that might never be spoken but must never be denied. To let him walk off into the night, muttering sincere yet distant protestations of gratitude only to revert, later, into mere formality and separateness, would be such a denial. It must not happen.

'The mind is often our most intimate enemy,' she said. Then added quietly, attempting to hold his gaze, 'I would have you know that I feel myself to be your intimate friend.'

His quest for a gracious retreat was arrested by this quiet profession. He saw that she could not hold his gaze, that her cheeks were suffused, her breath quickly drawn.

As immediately now were his own. It was as if every motion of his metabolism suddenly chimed with hers. He looked at her, unable to draw his eyes away, unable to answer. Between where she sat, gazing down upon her folded hands, and where he trembled a little now, the air was mute. Then her eyes were raised again, modestly, but changing, widening, as they too entered on the spell that held him there. The merest dragonfly of breath hovered at his throat. To hold the gaze would be calamity; yet to break it must do injury both to her delivered spirit and to his inward conviction of his own existence, for it was like looking into a bright glass mirroring his soul.

Something must be said. Both knew it, and both were panicked by the thought.

'I think,' she began uncertainly, 'from the moment of our first true meeting . . . that morning in the park . . . when you were so discountenanced by Gypsy May . . .' She looked up in appeal that the memory was alive and present to him also.

It was, but without the fondness she had hoped to find, unless she had misunderstood his quick gasp of withdrawal; yet she had begun and must continue now.

' . . . I think I recognized yours as a questing spirit . . . one which must traverse many dark passes on its quest for . . .' But

she faltered there. Already, in her uncertainty, she had ventured
too far. She shook her head—the ringlets momentarily danced
about her shoulders—then looked down where she fidgeted with
the ring on her right hand.

The knock of Frere's heart demanded that she unfold this
thought, but he was appalled at where it might lead. That she
had spoken that name—as though she had divined the darkest
corner of his secret mind . . . No, this must cease. Already he
had permitted too much. A frown clove his brow.

And shadowed hers. She had erred, was losing him. Some
way must be found to speak again.

'Perhaps I overstep . . . ?'

'My dear Miss Agnew . . .'

'Louisa.'

'Yes . . .'

'Some thought has troubled you?'

'It is . . .'

'Yes?'

' . . . nothing of which I may permit myself to speak . . .'

He was wearing the face she had first seen that morning in
the park at Easterness; and—as then—she found herself smiling,
though less confidently, just as his own frown was yet more
troubled. 'I think, dear friend,' she said, 'that we have arrived
at such a moment before . . . on that very morning . . . and did
we not find our way through?'

He too remembered how lightly she had dispelled the fear
brooding over him. If it had been possible then might it not be
possible again? His heart and mind were in collision now; but
a response was required. He could not rise and leave. 'It is
strange,' he ventured, 'that you should mention . . .'

'That morning?' She saw how difficult his breath; saw more.
'Gypsy May?'

He nodded, silenced, looked down where his fingers wres-
tled.

'Why so?'

And still he could not speak.

'Why so, dear friend?'

'The image has been . . . much upon my mind of late . . .'

'And does she still discountenance you?'

'I had thought not, but . . .'

'Yes?'

He looked away. Silence swarmed like fog. A silence he must

break or choke. 'She has returned to haunt some of my darker hours . . . We are not at peace with one another.' He looked up, stricken; and sought to avoid the damage he might do. He sought for some lightness to dispel the panic in him. 'I have not grown up with her as you have . . .'

'Yet I think she has always been with you.'

The words had been uttered quietly, and she had not even looked at him as they were spoken, but their impact devastated. She saw it on his blanched features, hastened to add, 'She is with us all. Always.' And then, more softly still, 'Though I who lost my mother at my birth may be more conscious of her than most . . .'

When she looked up again she found no comprehension in his face, only a white bewilderment of anxiety, as though he were afraid she might speak some word of blasphemy. Bravely she held his eyes. 'She is our Mother. The Mother of All. We are part of her, and she of us.'

'But Miss Agnew . . .'

She winced at this further retreat to formality. 'Louisa,' she whispered again, though wistfully now, as though it was *his* name she had uttered as he vanished towards some distant horizon.

'As a Christian . . . a clergyman . . .' he mumbled, 'I cannot admit . . .'

She waited but he did not continue. How much could not be admitted, she thought; how much must not be denied. And saw how she must answer. 'She will not be denied, Edwin.'

'But . . .'

Again she watched him flounder. Then, in a voice that now staked everything on his response, she declared, 'It is a great sin to deny her. She *belongs* on your church. A church consecrated solely to the Father is but half a church.' And having dared so much, her sadness could not restrain a further thought: 'As a life devoted to the father is but half a life.'

Now he thought he understood. Regret for her own unmarried condition must explain all this. The confusions of an unwedded female mind had somehow misconstrued the quirks of an eccentric father . . . his dabblings in obscure systems of belief. Or again—more charitably—this strange profession might be no more than the yearnings of a child for her lost mother. Yes, she had admitted as much.

He was about to find some appropriate, corrective word of

sympathy when she added, 'She is completion, Edwin. Without
her we are less than ourselves. As you, I think, have been less
than yourself.'

He sat, stunned by the power in her, stunned by a fierce
lightning-flicker of illumination in his mind. Then he recoiled,
for every Christian cell in his brain was now rising in indignation. He saw his earlier extenuations inadequate. The power in
her face would not be reduced to such simple form. Dimly he
remembered that first evening at Easterness—the way he had
lightly remarked to Henry Agnew that, if Apuleius was to be
believed, even asses had been initiated into mystery. It was, after
all, no joke. The man would not have seen it so. What a blind
fool he had been not to recognize the forces at work inside the
Hall! Such professions were taken seriously here. An entire
world, an entire universe, was suddenly in question. Seriously,
seductively, she was asking him to place that monstrous figure
in the mercy-seat. To venerate it.

And this was heresy.

He got to his feet, a hand at his temple, the fingers punishing
the roots of his hair.

Was it possible then that this woman to whom he had foolishly
opened his heart was *pagan*? That she had come to his church,
singing and praying along with the rest, listening patiently to his
sermons, yet all the time secretly revering not God the Father,
God the Son, God the Holy Ghost, but the obscene, aboriginal
goddess that bared her parts to the world above their heads? The
realization appalled him.

Yet, when he looked back at her, he saw such innocence,
such apparent purity of soul. He remembered how his thoughts
had dwelt on her in solitude, how he had imagined the life the
two of them might have shared; and again his mind recoiled.
His eyes ranged the room—the languid setter, the fire, the clock,
the porcelain figurine. Thinking furiously, he took some steps
towards the desk where her sheaf of papers lay. Her book. Was
this then what it had to say? This her secret store of wisdom?
With as little respect for privacy as some inquisitor he reached
to seize its pages, but before his hand arrived there his cuff
brushed against the figurine. The head began to rock. He recalled himself, stared down into the Chinese face which he had
thought, for a moment, broken by his touch. It rocked on its
axle, smirking up at him.

He turned to stare at the still-seated woman. Strive as he might,

he saw only modest beauty there—the vividly blue, angled eyes
that held his gaze, patient and perhaps, now, a little afraid. Was
this then all she knew of sin? Had she no knowledge of the perils
among which she walked?

'Miss Agnew, I cannot permit . . . Do you not see? Would
you deny the Christian faith?'

'I deny nothing. Least of all what the New Testament teaches
us of love and merciful forgiveness.'

She was smiling a little, if sadly; and this evidently sincere
avowal brought some respite to his agitated heart. All was not
lost.

But she had more: 'It is the dark cloud of denial I resist. What
I seek is admission, completion. And without her there is no
completion.'

His alarm returned with greater force. No, there was power
there. Behind the demure features there was power. She had
accrued it from years of study among those old Hermetic books.
Those were her true scriptures, those occult texts, that dabbling
with magic. This woman was in danger. She *was* danger. And
how innocently he had bared his soul to her. Had it not ever
been the serpent's way to disguise iniquity behind the fairest
face? Already he had fallen prey to that seductive power. What
sort of spell must she have cast across Emilia's mind to persuade
her that he might find comfort here? He must not hear this. He
must not hear . . .

For she was saying, 'If she has troubled you, I think it is
because inside your deepest heart you know it to be so.'

'I cannot allow this. I cannot allow it.'

'But who is speaking, Edwin?' she demanded quietly. 'Who
is the I who cannot allow? Is it truly your voice . . . or the voice
of the jealous father in you?'

He looked down on her aghast. His head was reeling. How
had he come into this place? Who was this woman who had
enchanted his tongue only now to lead him into chaos? There
was an impulse to hammer at his temples where a dreadful voice
was roaring out its commination: *It is a fearful thing to fall into
the hands of the living God; he shall pour down rain upon sinners; snares, fires and brimstone, storm and tempest, this shall
be their portion to drink* . . .

He saw Louisa Agnew looking up at him as Gypsy May looked
down. Before his bewildered eyes the two faces blurred—the
fair one and the foul, the monstrous stone and the delicately

chiselled bone behind the flesh. Two smiles melting into one;
and within that already confusing blur a third appeared—the
thin, conniving smile of his wife, thin as a sexton's spade. He
stared and saw only descending darkness there. The smiling
dark, which must, at all costs, be resisted. Yet it swam before
his vision, a vortex of engulfing energy, smiling, inviting, taunt-
ing him.

Before he knew it was about to happen, it was done. In two
strides he was across the space between them, his hand raised
and, with a crack that horrified him, brought down across that
face.

Her head was wrenched round on her neck, tears jerked by
the impact to her eyes. The breath broke from her. Pedro was
up at her cry, bounding towards Frere, his mouth reaching for
the frozen hand. Louisa leapt to her feet, calling the dog's name,
pulling him off. It was all hideous muddle as she found the
collar, and the dog was dragged, yelping, to the door, straining
his head back at the man. She thrust the animal out into the
night, then turned, leaning against the slammed door, panting,
staring at Frere.

Who stood in horror, hands arrested in the air before him, a
cuff torn.

'You must listen to me now,' she gasped.

His head was shaking, hair and eyes wild, hands reaching to
cup his ears. 'I . . . I am so . . .' His face was all ruin now, the
hands helpless as though trying, vainly, to lift an immense load
of stone. 'I must go from this place . . . You must let me
out . . .'

Her head ringing still, she pressed herself closer against the
door. The breath shuddered through her.

'Please . . . you must let me pass . . .'

She did not move, but the shock was passing and, even in the
midst of the remaining rage, she saw the man must choose. He
must be free to choose. For a moment longer she panted there,
then stood aside.

Stupidly he cast about for his hat, found it, took a stride towards the door.

'If you leave now you will never forgive yourself.'

He heard the truth of it, stopped. He stared at her, saw how
pale the face except where his hand had crazed the veins, and
something collapsed inside him. He could scarcely breathe, but
said, 'I am already unforgivable.'

'That is not so.'

'You do not know. You know nothing of me. Nothing.'

Still she was panting, but inside herself was sudden stillness. Even her fury was a stationary flame, fierce but still. Out of that stillness she heard her own proud voice. 'My knowledge is the knowledge of the heart, and you will hear it. You have laid hands on me, Edwin Frere, and I have suffered it. You will listen to me now. And you will listen with the whole of yourself, for if you do not you will go empty from this place.'

Something vital on which his balance relied had sheared. Everything was shifting, on the move. Under no conscious direction—as though seeking its own safety from the general fall—a hand scrambled for his brow. His throat was an opened fault from which, as no more than a seized creaking sound, the years of grief convulsed. He turned away, and there was nothing certain beneath his feet. His hand felt for, and found, the chair.

A woman was kneeling at his feet. She was holding his hand in hers, and he could have swooned almost to be conscious of the touch. Again the terror of transgression seized him, but it was a gesture from the past, a shade that carried no great weight within the turmoil of his soul. And still the world was insubstantial round him, a glassy place, a hall of mirrors, where nothing was constant save the sound of a soft voice speaking above the din of his wreck.

'I know how terrible she appears. I know how to the uninitiated eye she seems to offer only immolation, dismemberment, the dark. But that is only the face of her own hurt. She has other faces, Edwin. She is our Mother. She is our Mother and her other face is love. And she will not be denied because she too is truth. I promise that there is great peace to be found in her. Hers is the peace which passeth understanding. It was hers long before the Christian church claimed it for its own. It is her service that is perfect freedom.'

The world was turning upside-down. He might have been hanged by the heels and swinging, so little was space firm around him. Everything was inverting now, like a mirage that shivered over desert air.

'I promise it is so. All true men, at all times, have known it to be so . . . have known that without her power they are less than men, mere shadows of their finer selves. And such powers never die. They are always immanent within us and ask only that we enter into new relations with them. She is around us always, dear friend, around and within, because she is Nature, the very matter of our being, the mistress of the elements. And whether she is revered as Pessinuntica or Artemis, Dictynna or Aphrodite, Cybele, Isis, or humble Gypsy May, she is always one and the same. She is alive here now in you, and asks only to be loved and rightly feared.'

Yes, fear was possible, for beyond that face everything was swinging still. Yet he was soothed by the gentle voice. The old names out of Apuleius lapped the air about him with their poetry. Archaic and strange their sounds, yet also immediate and familiar—and so blessedly soft in contrast to the harsh comminations of the jealous, isolated God.

And this woman across from him . . .

More priest than he was himself, he had thought; but how very wrong he had been. No priest but *priestess*, her face vivid with the living presence of the goddess for whom she pleaded now. He saw his own reflection in those eyes and, around it, unfathomable darkness. A dark where one might finally lose oneself for ever. And this was puzzling in the contrary emotions it aroused—for at moments he sensed the possibility of a long-sought consummation there, and at others he panicked at a kind of death—a drowning to be resisted, held at bay, refused. Always before he had thought of drowning in another's eyes as merely figurative, some fancy of the poets; but no, it was possible. And how then should one be saved? In that place there could be no will, no breath.

Yet the small reflection of his face was shining there undrowned; inverted somewhere deep inside the recesses of her brain, yet set aright within the bright field of her vision. Was this then where he deeply belonged? Was it possible that through such utter deliverance of the self into the dark, the self itself might shine?

How strange that from the tumult of his mind such glassy calm should grow; such void of all inhibiting commandment that now, slowly, he might reach out his hand to soothe the flushed cheek he had struck, and seek forgiveness there.

Eyes closed, wondering, she received its touch. She leaned her face into the soft cruck of his hand. And then, after a long moment, she eased her head away to look at him.

This was, and was not, everything that had been intended. So deeply had she prepared her heart for loss she could not quite believe that this had come to pass so quickly. She was perplexed and speechless now. No longer—no more than he—was she in command. With the breath arrested in her throat, she waited.

13 ❖ The Keepers of the Keys

We wander through experience like dreamers, and what should be obvious at once too often becomes so only when the harm is done. We know it, and we forget it; then we wake in shock.

In that way the meeting at Saxburgh shook me back to consciousness, for nothing I'd learned there was, in essence, new. That world was a dangerous and unstable place which continued to exist only because those with the power to decide otherwise permitted it to do so—this was birthright information. It had always been there, like the certainty that I must, at some point, die. It was a condition of existence, and to think on it too closely induced numb panic, an almost pathological despair. But I tried that night; I tried, and thought warped back upon itself.

Nobody wanted things this way; this was how things were; and though there was a reasonable case to make against such a state of affairs, it was not about to change. Reason, it seemed, was not enough. On both sides of the argument the premises were older far than reason. They would not be reconciled. And so—when thought failed—you were left with feeling.

The bleak news from the meeting jammed my feelings as it jammed my mind. That night I began to wonder whether the very capacity to feel was so impaired by exposure to atrocity that men like me could only bungle the music now, pounding out a few crude chords on a diminished register. Guilt we could manage; rage was still a possibility; and always, underlying everything, the deep bass note of dread. Beyond that—what? Something flute-like and tremulous, trying to phrase its breath. Small sound against the engines' roar.

My own most recent display of feeling had not been impressive. Regardless of the missiles pointed at my life, I'd rowed from shore to shore of the lake as to a marvellous island, and emerged from the encounter on the lawn with little on my lips but petulant demands. Where had I been? What did I imagine I was doing? What—the question presented itself here as in the graver, unthinkable matter—what were my real feelings?

Primarily guilt. It was after midnight, I was alone, Edward's agents were hammering at my door, and they knew I'd sing. Dragged in for questioning, I pleaded guilty. Guilty to loitering with intent. Guilty to being an accessory before, during, and after the fact. Guilty because Laura fascinated me, excited me, and, yes, unnerved me. But it was also evident that she was not in love with me.

I remembered her smile as she'd suggested I was still dreaming, and knew now, as I'd guessed then, that she was not in love with me. And neither—it should have been obvious before as it was obvious now—was I in love with her. I had been dreaming— a dreamer dazed by gratified desire who had woken, empty-handed. We had made love but we were not lovers. We were both about other business, the nature of which remained unclear. So here, as in so much else, the real crime was unconsciousness.

Alone in The Pightle I faced the incredulous challenge in the eyes of my children: *We don't understand why the world should be like this. Why have you allowed it to happen? You're our father, you made this world before we came. You brought us here and abandoned us. How do you explain all this? What do you intend to do about it? We deserve an answer.*

I could frame only their unanswerable demands.

I was in no shape for facing truth and knew that truth was unavoidable. Knew too that it was not enough merely to admit the truth—one had to act on it. But how?

I reviewed my life and found I had no practice. I was a father on the run, a failed husband, a faithless friend. I was a poet who couldn't write, a teacher with no store of wisdom, a loveless lover, uninitiated male. It wasn't meant to be like this and this was how it was. Always—whether in the realm of feeling or of thought—it seemed the unintended consequences of our own intentions took the trick.

Eventually I slept. I hadn't gone to bed—I fell asleep where I sat on the old Chesterfield, and even as sleep closed round me I was talking to my children, trying, vainly, to explain myself.

In the dream that came a woman had seen how to unlock the world's terror of nuclear war. I didn't recognize her. There was nothing distinctive about her. She was just a woman and her idea was simple; the leaders of the nuclear powers must surrender the keys that would trigger nuclear war. They must surrender them to her.

They were all old men and they were very tired. Mistrustfully, one by one, they handed over the keys. When they were all surrendered, the woman placed the keys on a cushion and took them to the Pope. (And, yes, even in its dreaming state a part of my mind sat up and said, *The Pope?*) But for a long time the Pope looked down where, in his hands, on the cushion, the possible destruction of the planet innocently lay. Finally, in a voice of absolute authority, he said, 'The Quakers shall hold the keys.'

I woke, agitated, and could make no sense of it. But I remembered Edward's advice, found pencil and paper, and there, at two in the morning, as faithfully as I could, I wrote its details down, then went to bed.

Well after nine I woke in anxiety. Throughout much of the morning I waited for Laura, expecting her at every sound in the lane. There was no sign.

For the first time I regretted my lack of a phone. I needed to know what was happening and feared that it was something bad. Why else didn't she come when she had said she would? I dithered, wondering whether to break the implied if unspoken promise not to seek her out. She had begged me not to do that; but wouldn't it be best—bravest at least—to have things out and ride the consequences? Or was I only forcing things with my own rough demands again?

The dithering was intolerable, and typical. For a time I floundered in self-contempt until I saw that out of the previous night's diagnosis of my life one thing might be done. Weeks had passed and I'd taken no final decision about the job. The deadline was soon due and I had to make up my mind. I did so, for though the thought was scary I'd seen it already—I couldn't go back. Even in sharing my students' disdain for the institution that each month paid my bills, I'd exampled them only in hypocrisy. The agenda of the job was acquiescence, and I could no longer acquiesce. It took ten minutes to write, sign and seal a letter of resignation.

There on the table I found the pencil scrawl in which I'd written down the dream. It read like nonsense, and my thoughts shifted away. My eyes fell on the sealed envelope. As long as it remained unposted nothing had changed. Also there was a phone-box outside the Post Office.

I set off down the lane, and even as the letter dropped through the slot it felt like madness. There was a *Victoria Regina* monogram embossed on the red box in the wall: that black mouth had been waiting since Louisa's time for just this crazy moment. It had swallowed my past.

I went into the phone-box and when I picked up the receiver it was dead. I couldn't believe it—having got the guts together to ring the Lodge, and then, I thought, my kids, the bloody box was dead. I hammered at the cradle and it made no difference. Mrs Jex came out of the Post Office. I had to listen while she explained at length about the endless trouble she'd been having with it. She took in my scowl, offered me the use of her phone; but I wasn't about to stand under her nuclear siren talking to Laura while she cocked her ears. I said it didn't matter and managed, finally, to get away.

When I walked back up the lane Bob was out in his front garden tidying his hedge. 'Feels like a waste of time,' he said, '. . . after last night, I mean. But I had to do something. Hardly slept a wink. Kept tossing and turning, wondering how the hell we ever got ourselves into this mess, and how the hell we're ever going to get out of it.'

'Me too.'

'Sometimes I'm grateful that Doris and I couldn't have a family . . . that there are no grandchildren to worry about.'

'I woke up wanting to talk to my kids but the bloody phone's out of order.'

'Use mine.'

'It's long-distance, Bob. I suppose I could get the operator to . . .'

'Don't worry about it. Hardly ever use the thing. The bill's neither here nor there. Take your time. You know where it is.'

Again the photograph of Bob's wife approved of me as I sat down by the phone. 'Forgive me, Doris,' I whispered, and dialled the number of the Decoy Lodge.

I let it ring for a long time but there was no answer. Not Laura, not Edward, just the moronic twinned buzzes, stillborn on the silence. I sat for a while, collecting my thoughts, before I picked up the receiver again. Saturday morning—they too might be out.

It was Martin who answered. My place, his voice.

'It's me—Alex.'

There was a short, I assumed stunned, silence before he said, 'Thank God. Are you all right?'

'I'm fine.'

'The kids got your letter. It meant the world.'

'I'd like to talk to them.'

'Yes, of course . . .'

I heard Jess's voice, thin, from the kitchen probably: 'Is that Alex?'

'He's okay. He wants to talk to the children.'

'Let me talk to him first.'

'He asked for them.' And then, into the receiver: 'Look, Alex—Jess wants a word. The kids are out in the garden. I'll go and call them, okay?'

'If you would?'

'You're really all right?'

'Really.' I heard how edgy my voice was. 'Relax,' I said. 'It's okay. Go and get them, will you?'

The receiver changed hands.

'Alex?'

'Jess, I really wanted to talk to the kids.'

'I know, but . . . listen. Are you really all right?'

'God—the pair of you! I'm okay.'

'You don't sound it.'

'I'm nervous dammit. I feel bad about . . . What about you?'

'We're okay.'

'That's all?'

'Well . . .'

'I mean, be happy, for God's sake. What's the point otherwise?'

'Alex, it's not that easy . . .'

I didn't want to hear their troubles; decided: 'Listen, I've been thinking things over. I accept things. Okay? It's for the best. It has to be. I don't think I could handle seeing you just yet, but as things are . . . it's all right. If you want a divorce, that's all right too. In fact, it's the best possible thing. Get a solicitor to serve me some papers or whatever they do. I'll sign.'

There was a long silence in which I heard the children come in from the garden. 'Alex, we can't talk about this now.'

'Okay, but get on with it, will you? I need to simplify my life. The only thing . . . money. That could be a problem. I've just resigned from the Poly.'

'You've what?'

'You heard. By September I'll be broke, so no point suing for maintenance. Anyway, you've got the house. Martin can earn. He can probably have my job if he wants it. I'll get some money to the kids as and when I can . . .'

'Alex, money is the last thing on my mind. We have to . . .'

'Listen, I'm on someone else's phone. I really want to talk to Marcus and Lily. Can I do that?'

'You're different. You sound different.'

'I am. I'm in Norfolk. They do different here. Haven't you heard?'

'What's been happening to you?'

'It's a long story. I'll tell you some time. Give me the kids.'

'Okay, but stay in touch, will you? Don't disappear again.'

'Yes to the first. I don't know about the second. Now will you please get off the line?'

Had she been a few years older Lily might have proved difficult. As it was, almost four, she mainly wanted to know about the pheasant, which had been some distance from my thoughts. Improvising, hoping it was true, I told her that the brood was hatched and learning to fly. Was I enjoying my holiday, she demanded, and why hadn't I taken her and Marcus with me? Because they both needed to be with their mother, I explained, and anyway wasn't Martin looking after them? He was and, heart swimming, I had to listen to tales of their adventures until we told each other that we loved each other and would be again together before too long.

Marcus was tougher. For a child not yet seven he had an unnervingly pensive face which was mobile enough when he giggled but otherwise observed the world with a detached mien that, in an older person, might have suggested incredulity. I was sure he was wearing that face now.

'Where are you?' he demanded.

'You know where I am. I'm in Norfolk. I told you in my letter.'

'When are you coming back?'

'I don't know yet. I still have things to do here.'

'Soon?'

'As soon as I can.' I tried to lighten the tone. 'How you doing, tiger?'

'I'm all right.'

'I know you're all right, but what have you been up to?'

'Nothing much.'

'How's school?'

'Boring.'

'Is that all?'

Marcus sniffed. 'The other kids . . .'

'What about them?'

'Gary Watson says you've run off.'

He was the next door neighbours' son, three years older than Marcus.

'Well, we all know what Gary Watson's like,' I evaded.

'Is it true?'

Once you admit the truth there's no ending, I thought; but wasn't all confusion in children finally traceable back to the untrue, the unreal? And not only in children.

'Listen,' I said, 'sometimes grown-ups get confused too. They need to be on their own for a time, to think. To try and sort things out. That's what I'm doing, Marcus. I know it must be hard for you to understand, but it's important, I promise you, and I wouldn't be doing it otherwise. Hasn't mummy talked to you about this, and Martin?'

'Yes.'

'And didn't they explain that I haven't run away from you?'

A silence so sharp I could feel the pricking of his eyes.

'Well it's true,' I said. 'I love you and I won't ever run away from you. I'm your daddy, right, and I always will be. That's what's true.'

'Are you coming back?'

'I told you—as soon as I can.'

'To stay, I mean.'

And, for a long time, I was silent now. 'Marcus,' I said at last, 'I can't promise that. When I see you we'll talk some more. It's hard like this, on the phone. I can't see your face and you can't see mine. And there isn't time to . . .' I faltered. 'Listen, I want you to hear this, and I want you to remember it. Mummy and Martin and me, we all love you. We're going to keep you safe—you and Lily—until you're old enough to look after your-selves and to understand properly what has happened to us now.

And you will. I promise you, one day you will. So don't be frightened, right? There's nothing to be afraid of. Other things might change but love doesn't. It's always with you whether I'm here in Norfolk or right beside you—it doesn't matter. The love is with you all the time. Do you understand that?'

Down the phone, two hundred miles away, I heard Marcus begin to cry. Dear God, why was the truth so invariably cruel?

There was a crackle as the receiver changed hands. Martin again: 'Alex . . .'

'I know,' I said. 'I tried to tell him . . . He asked . . . you heard. I didn't want to lie.'

'It's all right,' he answered. 'Jess is with them.'

For a time nothing but the sound of our breathing down the line and, distantly, the cries of weeping children.

'God,' Martin said, 'I'm sorry.'

'Don't be. It's done. You were right. For God's sake just take care of them.'

'I will.'

'I know,' I said, 'I know,' and put down the phone, and sat there in my tears.

As I came out through the garden Bob switched off his strimmer. 'Did you get through all right?'

'I don't know,' I replied. 'I really don't know.'

He looked across at me steadily, troubled, then sighed. He would have said something but I shook my head, thanked him for the use of the phone, and was walking away when I heard: 'By the way—while you were in there—I saw your friend go by.'

'Edward?'

'The girl. She drove up the lane, then back down again. I suppose she might have been looking for you. I tried to flag her down but . . .'

'She didn't stop?'

'I don't think she understood . . . seemed to be in a hurry.'

'Damn!' I was at his gate, about to pass through.

'And, Alex—I might be wrong about this, but . . .'

'What?'

'Well . . . I thought she had a black eye.'

From the gate of The Pightle I saw the note folded into the horseshoe that served as a knocker on the front door. I had never seen the handwriting before. It was strangely childish, without sophistication:

*Came but you were out. Couldn't have stayed long. Things
are difficult but we're surviving. I'll try to see you soon.*

L.

And underneath, a swift afterthought in capitals:

DON'T COME. I WILL GET BACK.

I stood there at the doorstone, the note trembling in my hands,
wondering what the hell was happening at the Lodge.

At the Decoy Lodge Louisa Agnew gathered the pages of her
manuscript into their binder and tied it neatly in a knot of green
ferret. She laid it down on the desk.

It was oddly separate from her. The book authorized itself.
She was only the vessel through which it had passed, out of the
dark latency of things into the phenomenal world. But for this
moment they were alone together with their secrets.

Throughout the day she had worked in a dream to complete
the fair copy of her script. She was weary from the long labour
and from that previous night in which she had scarcely slept at
all. Soon she would feel the first pangs of dissatisfaction that
swiftly follow any sustained expenditure of mental energy, but
such considerations were far from her thoughts. There was,
rather, a glow of certainty about her.

Louisa turned in her chair to survey the simple room. The
light was failing outside where wildfowl called across the lake;
she had not yet lit her lamp, and she was a grey shadow among
shadows. For so many weeks she had been alone there. Ice had
come to drive her briefly away, into that encounter on the frozen
lake, and later into the fraught, finally mysterious conspiracy
with Emilia. Her shades had come, stepping from the dark places
of her mind to engage her in sometimes harrowing, sometimes
joyous conversation. Tilly had come, bringing gossip and supplies, bewildered by Louisa's reclusive life, disapproving of it,
and utterly unaware how important to her mistress was the news
she shared. At last, as though invoked by her deep need, Edwin
had appeared at her door, dishevelled, distraught, yet knowing
somewhere—how could he not?—that a momentous beckoning
of providence had brought him there.

She had absented herself from life to write down all she knew
of life, and now, at the end of her labours, life had caught her

by surprise, saying, 'Everything that you have written here is true, but now you must *know* it; and with a knowledge that is no longer pallid intellectual *idea* but the very quickness of my touch.'

And so, as she had copied out the pages, her book had seemed more magical than, to a child's eye, those unfolding volumes where prince and princess, demons and fairies, rise in paper pageant as each leaf is turned. The images opening from her cabinet of dreams were subtler, far more tender. The words had proved an exact analogue of experience; and not of experience past, but that which—when the words were written—was yet to come. Words and experience, experience and words: each was a validation of the other. It was, of itself, a chymical wedding; and in her *Open Invitation* Louisa saw unanticipated resonances now. For, joyous as the previous night had been, how greater even than she had imagined was the cause for celebration there.

It was borne in upon her most forcefully as she copied out the passage which reflected on what was, for her, a crucial error in the history of the European soul. The passage examined that Vatican debate in which the Church had missed the opportunity to wed its spiritual vision with the natural magic of alchemic lore. For a moment, there at the height of Renaissance humanism, Trismegistus might have been preferred over Aristotle as the cornerstone of Christian philosophy. A powerful case was made for the immense spiritual values that would accrue; but the debate was lost. Sternly the church turned its back—and at what cost! The split between mind and body was re-opened. The palace of matter was laid waste, and a soul allowed only to human existence. The female knowledge of the heart was ever more mistrusted and reviled; and—where it might have been made whole—the consciousness of man shattered between the tragic contraries. In these rejections lay the crisis of the European spirit. Without the social strength of Christianity, Hermeticism lay in chains; without the regenerative power of Hermetic knowledge, Christianity was moribund. It was vital for the contraries to meet again. And now, in this strange unanticipated love that had brought Louisa and Edwin Frere together, it seemed to her that the reconciliation had at last begun.

He was the true spirit of the Christian church; she the handmaid of the Hermetic Mystery. How long had the sad world waited for this union! Yes, it was a seed only; but who knew what might grow from such a seed? If one had faith as a grain of mustard-seed then mountains might be moved. Was not the Kingdom of Heaven itself likened to a mustard-seed? And this small seed had scarcely yet begun to germinate.

She remembered that cryptic fragment from the Gnostic Gospel According to the Egyptians which had survived only because Clement of Rome had quoted it: *When ye have trampled on the garment of shame*, it began, *and when the two became one, and the male with the female is neither male nor female* . . . And there it ended. She had long been intrigued by its inconclusiveness. Perhaps the rest had been deliberately lost by some ancient bigot terrified of matter? It made no difference; truth would always survive censorship, and she knew now how the promise ended. For once the garment of shame is shed, and the male and the female become one together, *then shall ye enter the kingdom*.

She exalted in the knowledge; but strangely there were shadows too; an unease for which the exhaustion of mind and hand could not entirely account.

One regret was already identified. Dearly she would have wished to pen an inscription additional to the one declaring the book her father's property; to make some acknowledgment, however cryptic, that the book was also a gift to the man whom, for the purposes of the inscription, she might call her mystic brother. It was not possible. That dedication must remain a secret within the secret. It was enough that it was known to her heart. The secrecy enriched it, and this was accepted. So there was something else.

Some moments passed before she realized.

Her work was finished now. There was no further pretext for remaining sequestered in the small kingdom of the Lodge. She had worked all day to complete her task, to be free of it that more life might arrive; and the very act of completion spelled the end of all it had come to signify. She had been shown the gate of the Garden even as it closed before her.

The unease enlarged itself to panic.

Could she keep up the pretence that the book was unfinished? Work of this order was never wholly complete—it was only abandoned. Need she abandon it yet? There were always improvements that might be made. Its expression might be yet more finely tuned, its subtleties made subtler still. Out of her own dissatisfaction many weeks of work could be contrived. If time had laid siege to her kingdom she had invention enough to delay its fall.

Immediately she saw how ignoble such stratagems were. She had assumed this task out of the world's urgent need for her good news. She had accepted the grave responsibility of preparing the way for her father's greater work—he who was driven almost to despair by time, she who had ever been friendly with it. To fabricate delay would be more than selfishness: it would be an act of apostasy.

Striving to control her feelings, she remembered what she herself had said: 'We know that the Lord will hasten all up at last, and quickly enough.'

Well, the Lord was moving quickly now, and she was caught up in his haste. To procrastinate, to deceive and lie would vitiate the very meaning of her work. Rather than quickening the appetite for life's great mystery, the book would begin to smell of the lamp, of mortality. It would betray the love its present quickness celebrated.

And yet to leave the Lodge . . .

There was nowhere else he might come—not in honesty, not in the declared truth of who they had become. The confines, the secrecy of the Lodge was the entirety of their world; everywhere else they were estranged. And to seek refuge in the kind of renunciation with which she had earlier accepted loss would now itself be betrayal. It would be impossible.

Anguished minutes passed before her mind was calm enough to receive a further thought: if the Lord was importunate with her now, there was a Lady also. In Her she must place her trust.

The childish hand was uncompromising, its promise made. *DON'T COME. I WILL GET BACK.* So what do you do? When eyes are being blacked not to act is also to act, but cravenly. I couldn't leave it at that.

I think you'll find you can.

I'd already found that out once. But again? Caught between contrary impulses, I started and stalled like a fitful engine, for if Laura didn't want me to come she had her reasons. I remembered how Jess had kept Martin away from me at the start of my own crisis. And with just cause. Was that what Laura was afraid of then—irrational male violence? Was I afraid of it myself? I remembered Edward with the hatchet in his hand.

How did you defuse it? How did you stop the violence, the

fear? I was back in the meeting at the Black Boys Hotel. I was back with the dream of keys.

I looked at it again. Again it read like nonsense. But when my thoughts lurched back to reality, a voice—Edward's voice—insisted that I take dreams seriously—however preposterous they seemed.

Impatiently, as once working at the riddle so long before in the Lodge, I reapplied myself.

The first thing that struck me was that the prime mover was a woman. She had taken control, as Jess once, and now Laura, had taken control. But this woman wasn't Jess or Laura. It was no woman I knew. And no powerful political figure either. An ordinary woman, yet persuasive enough to win the confidence of the jealous male leaders and—which was absurd—talk them into giving up the most devastating symbol of their power. The Lady Alchimia, I thought, in twin-set and pearls? Absurd. Absurd. What was I doing wasting time like this?

Nevertheless a deal had been struck. The key to the situation had changed hands. However mistrustfully a deal had been struck between the male and female principles. Interesting! But having got the keys why should the woman turn them over to— of all people—the Pope?

I saw him smiling from the Pope-mobile, two fingers up, declaiming to the multitude, 'Thou shalt use no contraception; thou shalt not commit abortion; and, no, thou shalt have no divorce.' No friend to women he. No priestesses in his church, only nuns. It made no sense. He was the archetype of *male* spiritual authority, the latest in a long line of dubious fixers that ran right back through Pius equivocating over the holocaust, the Borgias who were not notable for compassion, the burners of heretics, all the way to old St Peter himself who was . . . the keeper of the keys!

Odd!

And then it occurred to me that the present Pope was also a Pole—representative both of the Catholic faith and of his particular nation, of a country pinned between east and west, where two totalitarian systems, one secular, one spiritual, were in deep contention. It was one of the places where the earth might end in flames. So the keys had passed back not only across the sexes, but from the political to the spiritual domain. Edward's thesis. The key to the situation was back in the hands of the male spirit.

But it didn't stop there.

Again I was faced with the absurd. The Pope, supreme head of the most authoritarian church in Christendom, takes a look at the cushion and decides that his apostolic role as key-keeper is over. What's more, he passes the buck to a protestant sect which, in its silent priestless gatherings, stands at the antipodes of the Roman hierarchy. *Pontifex Maximus* he might be, but that particular feat of bridge-building struck me as improbable.

I remembered the two old ladies in the Black Boys Hotel—Quakers or not? What did I know about Quakers? They were pacifists, of course. They were followers of the inner light. They were a socially-committed spiritual sect which seemed to have exercised a moral influence on the life of the nation out of all proportion to their numbers. I thought of Elizabeth Fry and the Cadburys. They seemed to have made a lot of money out of chocolate, which was dubious; still, they were pacifists. The keys should be safe enough with them.

Except, of course, that none of this could happen.

I woke to what I was doing, looked at my watch. Christ, anything could be happening at the Lodge while I dizzied my brain with a dream and did nothing.

What had happened at the Decoy Lodge had unfolded horizons on the secret, most intimate yearnings of Frere's heart. It had also—he knew it as soon as he stepped out into the darkness—been unforgivable. All that night and throughout the following day his mind swirled in confusion. Daring to face no one, scarcely touching his food, he was faint from guilt and adoration.

Had it been guilt alone he might have managed with more composure. Guilt was his constant companion—they were cellmates learning under compulsion to endure one another; and the fact was, nothing irretrievable had occurred. But it was not guilt alone: he was consumed also by a reckless desire for the irretrievable. Desire and guilt were indissolubly linked, and each was a violation of the other. In the ensuing turmoil only two things were clear: that Louisa Agnew had become the very air he breathed; and that any further intimate relations between them were utterly forbidden him.

Though again and again he did so, there was no need to rehearse the circumstances which defined impossibility—that he was married, a Christian, a clergyman; that she was virgin, one of the souls whose care he had undertaken, the beloved daughter of a friend. Not only the fabric of the social order, but his own vows, the sacred nature of the faith he professed, and the specific commandment of God, all had but a single answer to his railings against fate; and that answer was righteous and unremitting: *No, this is forbidden.*

He heard it, and could not believe.

Belief evaded him because never as on that night had he experienced so intense a certainty that he was in the presence of the sacred. The air itself had been numinous; from the moment he had entered the Lodge it had been so. He had striven against its power, had trembled there, until at last it was undeniable. And he was sure that this sacral quality inhered in her—that it was the crystallization of her open heart, her lucid mind, her bright exacting spirit. It was, he had come to think, the very condition of her being. Yet when, in tender awe, he spoke of this, she gently demurred. She would not have it so. Nor, she insisted, was it a figment of his desperate heart. What was sacred there inhered *between* them. It was the love into which they were now elect.

He had heard and known it to be true. Yet such a love was an abrogation of every law that held the world in place; and she seemed not to see it. For a space that night he had scarcely seen it himself, so innocent was its touch, so vast the sudden increase of space it seemed to bring. It was beyond all choice. He had not made up his mind that this should happen. When he walked through the dark wood towards the Decoy Lodge it was with no expectation of finding himself transfigured so. Why then had he gone?

Yes, Emilia had counselled that Miss Agnew was a charitable friend, and he had been sorely in need of friendship. He had remembered his wife's words and acted on his promise. But he must be absolutely honest here, for nothing less would answer before the stern judge at his heart. There was more. It reached deeper.

There could be no denying now that since they had first met in the Hall—from the very moment perhaps when he had heard her sing—Louisa Agnew had been, for him, a person apart. She was special, of another order, of another world almost. And it had not been her beauty alone that so distinguished her, though he had never been blind to that. Indeed, so intense had been its effect upon him he had scarcely dared look her too long in the face lest his susceptibility betray itself. With the same evasive tact he had tried to avert his mind from thoughts of her, never recognizing—fool that he was—how the effort required for each corrective withdrawal spoke to an almost magnetized condition. So in going to the Lodge that night he had been drawn by an intimation that, alone in all his parish, Louisa Agnew was the one person of importance to the survival of his soul.

It was evident now. So expert had he made himself in the concealment of his true feelings, they had become inaccessible under layer upon layer of pretence, and would have remained so had not recent events precipitated a geological convulsion in his being. His world had crumbled in the quake, but there, among the ruins, this buried treasure was revealed. Yet he would swear on the book his thoughts profaned that he had not gone there in search of it. It had possessed him. And it remained a calamitous impossibility.

These contrary truths were tearing him apart. They were—and he quailed at the blasphemy—the cross on which he was now nailed. And, for his unworthiness, he was nailed like Peter upside-down. How else to account for this total inversion of his world?

But this was disproportionate. He was no biblical apostle, faithless or otherwise. He was an insignificant Anglican parson overwhelmed by the clamour of his soul. If Satan had taken an interest in him, it was a minor diversion only, a crumb fallen from the communion plate, not to be gloated over, not to be missed. Thousands had fallen so.

He must try to keep his head cool.

But how to do that when every fibre of his being lurched between ecstasy and dread? He had been wise at least to insist that they not meet privately again; that, yes, they must treasure what had unfolded between them but they must not presume on it.

And what a lie, what a pious lie was that!

Had she known it even as, reluctantly, she agreed? Had she known that everything in his heart must clamour to live out that joy? To shout of it? And there was no one to whom he could even murmur it save her.

Should he break his own edict then and return to the Lodge? If perspective were to be restored it could only be done between them; and perspective must be restored. *Eros* and *agape* were not to be confused, for only disaster could result from such

confusion. He must go to her. They must speak of this. They
must . . .

That was to play with fire. It was to disguise recklessness as
sobriety, not even deceiving himself as he did so. He knew the
power he would encounter there, the power he would bring with
him. He knew it, desired it, and feared it. No, he must fight this
out alone. Apart from normal intercourse of parson and parishioner, he must avoid her—though simply to think of placing the
communion wafer between her lips brought his heart to his
mouth.

Until he had brought this tumult under control he must not
see her at all. He must see no one, for the effect of her touch
must announce itself like a sign to any observant eye. He would
betray himself. He would betray her. The parish was full of eyes.
Even the servants in the Rectory were not to be trusted. He must
be alone.

With fine, untypical calculation, he saw that it might not be
difficult to convince his servants that he had decided to enter a
brief retreat in preparation for Easter. It was Lent and his needs
were simple. He was capable of providing his own frugal meals.
Quickly, while the resolve possessed him, he gave his servants
leave. They would be paid in their absence, of course, and they
must not concern themselves for his welfare: he wished only to
be alone with his soul.

Surprised, but not displeased, the servants left the house. Its
silence closed about him.

I told myself I'd wait till nine; then I'd ring the Lodge to warn
them I was on my way. It would still be before dark, and the
nights, I knew, were the worst of it. I'd hold it together here
until nine, and then I'd act.

Throughout the afternoon I dug. I'd done nothing that Clive
had asked me to do in return for the cottage, and it was late in
the season, yes, but I found a fork in the shed and dug. The
ground was hard, the couch-grass rampant. When you pulled at
the roots almost always a shred snapped off, slunk away into the
soil to breed again. Like evil in a fairy-tale, never quite extinguished. Perhaps because its energy was needed, I thought,
because an entirely happy ending would be untrue. It would
leave the lovers iced like figures on a wedding-cake, pretty but
sterile. The Garden needed snakes.

I turned up earthworms. They wriggled in the sods, blinded

by the sudden light. A blackbird joined me, a few spits away. He was my overseer. He had uses for my labour.

I remembered Ralph talking about husbandry, thought about the difference between husbandry and rape; about Gypsy May, earth-goddess, each comer's whore and mother. About the male desire to possess, exclude trespassers, conquer and control— Napoleon in Wellington boots. I thought about my own futile efforts to assert rights of possession—*my* wife, *my* house, *my* children. I thought of Edward struggling for ownership of Laura, become Giant Holdfast now himself; and whatever he did, no matter how he raged, nothing would alter the facts.

In the crude language with which the sexual life seemed cursed, I'd *had* Laura; and it had left me wanting her. She was not to be had, not unless she chose to give herself, and she was not about to give herself to someone who behaved as I'd behaved. That love had been absent from my love-making was evident in the very nature of my response. I'd behaved in much the same way as Edward must be behaving now, for in the matter of the heart it was no great leap from the petulant demands of post-coital possessiveness to the blacking of eyes. It was all depressingly male—not only my responses then, but the way I tried to think about them now. It brought the delicacy of a mechanical digger to the subtle realm of feeling. It lacked grace. It shunned the willingness to live with risk, to trust the unwritten promises of care.

I put my foot to the shoulder of the spade and saw what must have long been evident to an outsider's eye: it was time I grew up.

I dug till the blister on my thumb was raw again. Then I waited. Waiting felt like a part—a very slow part—of growing up. But I waited like the box in the Post Office, red alert shifting to black.

Though the image was disproportionate, it felt scarily apt, for the box was the black hole in all our heads. It occurred to me that if there was such a box here, in Munding, then there must be one in every village—every hamlet's hot line to hell among the groceries and the greetings-cards, the bottles of boiled sweets and the notices about Social Security benefits.

I wondered if Edward knew it was there. I wondered how he would interpret its symbolism. He had been looking for a key; I had tried to help him; and I had found only the box. That and a dream of keys. About which—again it was as if Edward stood at my shoulder insisting—I should think symbolically.

I had half begun to do so when I looked at it the last time. The woman and the Pope I knew about. The keys were obvious. So what about the Quakers? What did Quakers symbolize?

Porridge Oats.

I saw the fat grin on the Quaker Oats packet, scowled, shook my head. The flippant mind jamming the waves with static. Think again.

Why were they called Quakers?

Because they quaked.

Why did they quake?

Because, I remembered, they were moved to speak.

In the silent spellbound meditation of the Meeting-house, sooner or later someone would feel compelled to speak. And not simply because they had something to say but because something demanded to be said through them. As, it seemed, this dream insisted on speaking now through me.

I'd had something of the same experience at public meetings—the tension between wanting to keep silent, inconspicuous, and knowing that something must be said. It happened at difficult moments, when you were least sure of yourself yet certain that the thing should be said. You quaked. It was a little like the birth-pangs of a poem. It clattered and banged until the words were out, and even then it didn't stop. It was what was happening to me now as I was torn between the contrary impulses to dismiss this dream and to engage with it; to wait here as I'd been told to do, or rush headlong down the lanes to the Lodge. One quaked.

It was—it occurred to me—like the forces at work inside an alembick, threatening to blow up in the alchemist's face unless those warring tensions could be reconciled. So that was it—people who quaked were alembicks. They were Pelicans. They were members of the chymical wedding.

With that realization I saw how the whole dream was elegantly structured around the tension of opposing forces: male, female; capitalist, communist; secular, spiritual; Catholic, Protestant; hierarchy, equality. It was a dream about conflict and reconciliation. Of fission and fusion.

It was about holding together. If we were to find a key to the explosive condition of the world it could only be done by holding contraries together. That *was* the key.

It was also obvious.

For a moment I recoiled from the banality. It was like saying, 'You really should love one another.' Of course we should, but we don't.

Then I saw what was not so obvious: that the holding together could only be done by *quakers*. And that meant not only the Society of Friends, however aptly named, but men and women everywhere who were prepared to quake. For quaking was what happened when you endured inside yourself the tension of divisive forces. It was what happened when you refused to shrug them off, neither disowning your own violence nor deploying it; not admitting only the good and throwing evil in the teeth of the opposition, but holding the conflict together inside yourself as yours—the dark and the light of it, the love and the lovelessness, the terror and the hope. And as you did this you changed. The situation changed—though whether it changed enough was another question. Perhaps a meeting of quality and quantity was also needed. Perhaps, in the end, what mattered was how many people were prepared to quake this way, for such quaking spirits were the keepers of the keys.

I woke from this trance of thought to find myself conscious of a beating heart. I saw it quaking in its blood—the auricles and the ventricles, the right side and the left, the upper and the lower chambers pulsing together—like the interlaced retorts of my first big dream.

Edward had called it a glimpse into the thalamus—the bridal-chamber of the brain. And perhaps it was. But I saw it differently now. I saw the retorts as a hologram of the heart. I watched as the bright bulbs of glass melted and fused into soft, muscular flesh, beating blood-red, alive and palpitant; and I wanted to share this dream. I wanted to share it with Edward.

A knock came at the door.

'What is it?' Henry Agnew demanded, loathing all the world and wishing only to be left alone.

'It is your long-lost daughter. May she be permitted to come in?'

For a moment he sat in the silent library, eyes closed. Then he sighed, removed his spectacles, and got up to open the door.

In a simple dress of grey watered-silk, she stood, holding her arms behind her back, looking up at him uncertainly. He was confused by her eyes: there was delight and anticipation there, but also, he thought, at the corners, above the fine bones of her cheeks, a glimmering of tears. Instantly an answering blur started to his own. 'My dear,' he said, 'it has been so very long.'

The admission almost overwhelmed him. It revealed too much. He turned to find his chair, to compose himself. Whatever she said in reply was lost in the contemplation that, however else he might vainly have lived his life, here, in his daughter, was his finest work.

He sniffed, essayed a smile. 'There have been days when it felt as though you were in Botany Bay rather than the . . . the other side of the lake.'

'I have half believed it so myself.' She stepped towards him, hands concealed still. Already she sensed that things did not go well with him. Yet he had tried to be light with her and she must respond in kind, for truth could only be approached by stealth now; and some truths—if they might be obviated—not approached at all. 'Dearly as I have come to love the Lodge there have been moments when it felt like a penal colony.'

It was that, and more, and worse, he thought, but murmured only, 'Did I not warn you of the rigours of the work?'

She heard the bitterness. Was it intended simply to discourage further mention of the Lodge, or was he speaking to other troubles? No matter now. Whatever the loss aching at her own heart, she had a great joy in store for his. 'You did,' she answered, 'but I do not return empty-handed.' She took a further step forward, planted a kiss on his freckled crown, then placed her ribboned binder on his desk. 'The prolegomenon is written. It awaits only your approval.'

For no more than a moment he stared down at the pages crowded there in that leather folder, then averted his eyes. 'You have completed it?' He was unable to keep the quaver of dismay from his voice.

She nodded, smiling, though the smile came hard. Had her father known the sacrifice this gift entailed the shadow of bewilderment at his eyes would have been darker still. Yet he was ignorant of it; so where was the cry of acclamation, the quick surprise of joy?

He turned his face from her. The binder with its neat green bow was easier on his sight than her gaze of eager expectation. His mottled hand strayed towards it, hovered above the knot; and then, as though he were afraid it might shatter at the touch, withdrew.

The air of the library was as still as dust.

They were both looking down on the book—she with a concealed yet enormous sense of bereavement; he as though on the
mortal remains of an extinguished dream.

He cleared his throat. 'I had not expected it so soon.'

He might have been speaking of some dreadful news.

Uncertainly she said, 'I was conscious of your urgency. Perhaps too conscious. It may be that in my haste I have made some
foolish errors . . .' She knew that this was not the case, but only
a failure of his confidence could account for this deficiency of
pleasure. She must do what she could to restore it. 'I am certain
only that the work will not be truly complete until it bears the
stamp of your correction and approval.'

Unaware that an attempt had been made to humour him,
Henry Agnew stared down at the leather binder. Then he saw
that some response was required. 'I am sure that it is . . . quite
excellent.' There was an attempt at conviction in his voice, but
no satisfaction.

She had foreseen none of this. She had prepared herself for
the collision between his excitement and her own secret grief.
She had schooled herself in enthusiasm, borrowing from what
belonged to another realm in order to conceal her loss in this.
All the lines were learned—and now none of them was apt.

What had happened? The last time she had seen him he was
so committed to his work, so sure.

'That remains to be seen,' she said.

He was elsewhere, pensive, unhappy.

With a pang of alarm Louisa wondered whether he was apprised of her secret. Had someone seen Edwin come to the
Lodge, returned to the Hall with gossip, scandal? Had it somehow reached her father's ears? There were no secrets in Munding. But it had been so late, the night so dark . . .

There was one other possibility. She clung to it. 'Your own
work,' she asked, 'how does it progress?'

He gathered himself in the chair, patted his fingers against the
edge of the desk. 'Well enough. Well enough. I have a draft of
the first Canto almost complete.'

'Progress indeed!' she said, disbelieving him.

So that was it.

A moment's relief was followed instantly by bitterness. Why
had she done this thing? Must she exchange the golden secrecy
of the Lodge only for hourly attendance on his dour humour?

Then she regretted the regret. Surely it could not be so? Surely her light must spread? Otherwise her sacrifice was meaningless. Perhaps in perusal of her own achievement this unhappy man might find fresh inspiration for his own? That must be the way, for it was the only way she could see open before her.

'I would not impede your progress,' she hazarded, 'but you will understand if I am eager to hear your response to my efforts. May I hope that you will read it soon?'

His eyes returned from staring at the window-glass to stare, equally estranged, at the folder on his desk. Had she no conception what an insult to his dignity this was? What order was there in the universe if she, a mere slip of a girl, could accomplish a task of this magnitude in a few short weeks while he had laboured in vain for years? No order. No justice. Only endless reproach for his own unworthiness—as these bleak thoughts reproached him now. He saw it and could not silence them.

'What need for that?' he answered coldly. 'I have said it already. I am sure it is quite excellent.'

She stared at him, shocked, but his eyes were averted. She too turned away. They were no longer of the same world. Far more than the span of the lake had been the measure of their separation. She had left her home to return home and found herself homeless now.

Her own voice too was cold. 'You have greater confidence in my powers than I have,' it attempted. 'Perhaps it is misplaced.'

'What do you know that I did not teach you?' he snapped. 'If you have been faithful to my teaching there can be nothing to correct. I have more urgent uses for my time.'

And then—he was amazed at himself as he did so—he stiffened the back of his hand at the spine of the folder and pushed it away.

In disbelief she stared down at the object—for such it suddenly was. A thing, to be moved from place to place; apparently no more than an encumbrance here.

And Henry Agnew loathed himself. Only with appalling difficulty could he prevent the utter ruin of his face. Yet he could not leave things so. For the life of him, for the love of her, he could not leave things so. 'Forgive me, my dear . . . I have worked too long today . . . My mind . . .' Despair crowded at his throat.

The old habituated response rose in her. She ought to comfort him, to encourage him to speak his wretchedness, to dispel it;

but with so much that must remain unspoken inside herself she lacked the heart. She was unsure even of the will.

Yet somehow this terrible silence must be filled.

'It was wrong of me to interrupt you. I was . . . insensitive.' Her voice was almost as hoarse now as his own. She sighed, closed her eyes. 'I think we have both been too much alone.'

'It may be so,' he answered dully. A man ashamed, he was striving for greater openness of heart. 'Rest assured, my dear; I have every confidence in your ability. I know you would not place before me a work that failed to meet your own exacting standards. My own are no higher than they.'

'But it would put my mind at rest if—'

'Have no doubts,' he interrupted sharply. 'If anyone alive understands these matters it is you.' Inwardly he recoiled from the bitter truth of that. 'Let your book go to the printers. Let it address the world entirely as your own.' And still he dare not look upon the pain he caused. How to admit that he could not endure the fact of her success while failure consumed him from within? It was impossible. He could not bear to read her book. He could not bid her destroy it. There was only one alternative. His bitter mind sought relief in practicalities. 'I informed Howgego of our intentions some weeks past. He promises me that our manuscripts will receive prompt attention, and it was always plain that yours would be the first to reach his desk. Let it go to him immediately. He'll be glad enough to apply his press to something other than hymnals and evangelical tracts.' From the corner of his eye he glimpsed her incredulity, and winced. 'The book will be back with us shortly, and it will be easier on my eyes to read your work in print. You shall have the entirety of my attention then. And—I am sure—my heartfelt commendations. Now, if you will forgive me.' He reached, blinking, for his spectacles, fearing she might argue longer; but she was already elsewhere.

Out of nowhere, like a chill wind from empty space, had come a premonition of solitude. It was as if the whole world might evaporate around her, and she be left entirely alone, entirely afraid.

She could not remain in the library. She nodded, involuntarily, like the tapped head of her Chinaman. Fighting the panic that closed from all sides now, she tried to smile, reached for her book, clasped it to her breast, and turned, leaving this old man who was her father quite alone.

She withdrew to her room. The familiar hangings, pictures, furniture, the sampler on the wall, were strange about her; former friends re-met by chance for whom, amazed, one feels: *I do not now belong to you; you have no claims; do not define me by the past.*

She crossed to the window, gazed through its leaded lozenges of glass, out across the parkland and the lake. The Lodge was invisible. It might no longer exist at all.

At ten to nine a car drew up outside The Pightle. I rushed to the door, saw Laura coming up the path, the anxiety in her eyes made spectacular by the yellowish-blue bruise rainbowed around the socket of her right eye. As she saw me she halted, hands clenched at her sides and, before I could speak, said, 'Is Edward here?'

Appalled by the bruise, remembering the blood I'd once brought to Jess's nose, and thinking what bastards we are, I shook my head. I saw a fist lifted to her lips, said, 'Laura . . . For God's sake, what's happening?'

'I don't know where he is. I fell asleep and when I woke up . . . I thought . . .' She turned again, but I was off the step, reaching for her. She didn't want to be held. She looked haggard as her eyes pulled away from mine and she said, 'I have to find him.'

'He'll be all right. I'm sure he'll be all right.'

'I'm really scared for him.'

'I was scared for you. I know what it can be like . . .' But she was too distraught to hear. 'Look,' I said, 'you're in no shape. Why don't you come inside and . . .'

'No, I can't do that. He might . . .' Then she was shaking her head, on the edge of tears. 'Will you help me? Will you help me find him?'

For a moment I stood looking down at her, saw the urgency there, then said, 'I'll get my coat.'

When I suggested that I should drive she put up no resistance, sat in the passenger-seat, smoking the cigarette I gave her, staring out through the windscreen as though Edward might be seen at any moment tramping up the lane towards us. I switched on the engine. 'Where do you think?'

'I don't know.'

'The Hall?'

'I rang. There's nobody there. I got the answering-machine.'

'If he's walking he could be anywhere.'

'I have to find him.'

'Then we'll go back to the Lodge. He might be there by now. But listen . . . He's going to be all right. He'll come through, I promise you.' I looked for and found no sign that she was reassured. 'I know what you're thinking,' I said, 'but don't. When we're hurt we lash out and threaten all kinds of crazy things, but we don't mean it. Not really. Laura, this isn't the first time this has happened to him.'

'You don't understand.'

'I think I do. I've been there, remember? He's hurt. We've hurt him.' I tried to hold her eyes. 'He can't bear the thought that he might have lost you.'

'You don't understand him,' she said. 'You don't understand him at all.'

Gradually, as we drove the lanes looking for Edward, I learned.

Village life has no secrets. By the time Edward had left the Hall that day, Friday—only the day before though it felt like several lifetimes ago—he already knew about me and Laura. We had been seen. George Bales, the gamekeeper, had seen us. When he got back to the Hall he told Ralph, and Edward had talked to Ralph before leaving.

He'd wanted to find out whether Ralph knew of any connection between Louisa and Edwin Frere, but his ancestor's past was not what pressed on Ralph's mind at that moment. He was no actor and Edward no fool. Sensing that his friend was holding something back, Edward had pressed. Finally, perhaps deciding that the shock might come gentler so, Ralph told him.

When Edward arrived at the Lodge he found Laura sitting beside her opened kiln surrounded by smashed pots. One of her hands was grazed and bleeding slightly. He can't have been prepared for this and, whatever his feelings had been a moment before, he softened instantly at the sight of her evident distress. For a few moments he fretted over the broken shards, trying to piece one or two of the pots together, then crossed to Laura, took the grazed hand between his own, and said, 'My dear, there was no need to hurt yourself like this.'

'He'd known, you see,' Laura told me now. 'He'd known all along that this might happen. Right from that night at the Hall when he fooled around with the Tarot cards. He saw that the card you chose was his as well—your past, his future.'

'You mean he thought it was bound to happen?'

'No. They don't work like that. The future isn't fixed, but the card showed which way things were going if he let them drift. That was why he asked me to take him away when he did. He was in as bad a state as you were, but he didn't tell me. He didn't talk to me about it. I wish to God he had.'

Listening, I began to see how Edward had been talking as much to himself as to me that day by the weir, and how it was not only me with whom he should have shared those thoughts. I saw why he had been rattled when I turned up at the Lodge with my dream, why he'd tried to freeze me out, and—when Laura wouldn't let that happen—how he'd tried to suborn me with his friendship. But the friendship had become real, and he must have thought himself secure—except that I too had been walking in a dream, and Laura also.

She was still in a distracted condition, and if it was hard to piece together a picture of what had happened in the Lodge, then the confused account she gave of it was not the only reason. My own assumptions clouded things—I saw no need to look beyond the sexual betrayal for the cause of Edward's rage. Yet his first feelings seem to have been of remorse and self-reproach. He blamed himself for having become so obsessed with the work that he'd lost touch with his feelings . . . Small wonder he'd been getting nowhere; but Laura shouldn't punish herself this way. The fault had been his; but now she'd freed his feelings again. Things would change. They would start over, recover what had been lost between them . . .

No, it wasn't Laura's actions he found unacceptable—it was her attempt to explain them. And, here, I too found myself in difficulties.

Like the pots around the kiln Laura's experience was now in fragments, and I had to listen carefully for understanding as she described what had happened to her that day. Already before I arrived at the Lodge she had been confused by what felt like an elision of her own thoughts with Louisa's. They had taken her into some very dark places and for the first time she felt afraid to be alone at the Lodge. All morning she had been slipping in and out of a trance-like state which left her nervous and distraught, uncertain of her own sanity. Things only clicked into focus when she went into the house and saw me there—though even then nothing was constant. She felt herself shuttling back and forth through time, from one experience to the other, unable to hold them together. On all previous occasions when this faculty had been invoked she'd remained aware of her own distinct existence as observer; but not this time. As never before she was implicate and, with voices and faces shifting round her, she'd felt a desperate need to know what was real. She could find, in both dimensions, only one certain criterion, and she'd acted on it. Only afterwards did she understand what it meant, and that I had not understood.

Some of this I had already guessed, and was uneasy with it. Edward's response had been, at first, more sympathetic. Again he found recourse in self-recrimination. He should have seen that Laura might become confused by her exposure to rare frequencies of experience. He was concerned that by exploiting her gifts he might have strained her contact with reality, and they must be very careful now. He tried patiently to talk her down, and met with absolute resistance, for whether he believed it or not Laura now knew what she had only guessed earlier—that Louisa was deeply involved with a man; a man she thought of as her mystic brother, both because of the intensity of their communication, and because that was his name. Laura had seen and heard it. She knew.

I don't know how long Edward patiently disputed this before his temper snapped and he accused her of using events on one plane to justify those on another. Was Laura asking him to believe that Louisa and Frere had made love, like us, on the lawn of the Decoy Lodge? To her own further confusion, Laura had been uncertain there. She didn't know; she doubted it even; but the physical facts of the case were beside the point. What mattered, she declared, was the love, the spiritual intensity of the commitment. Louisa had delivered herself over completely to Edwin Frere, and in some way this was bound up with the meaning and fate of her book. Didn't Edward understand that?

Edward did not. Alarmed by the implications of that impassioned declaration, the sympathy in his voice gave way to derision. He knew of only one woman who had thrown herself at a man in these parts, and that had happened very recently. This was all projection on her part; perhaps deception even; certainly self-deception. It was refusal to accept responsibility for her own actions.

'I could see,' she told me, 'that he didn't want to believe and it really frightened me. It was much harder than with you. I mean, if you *know* something and the person you trust most of all doesn't believe you . . . It's one of the worst feelings in the world. I felt completely isolated and it brought back . . .' She faltered there, lifted her thumb to her mouth and was biting the nail. 'I knew I had to tell him what happened after you left, and if he didn't believe that then I *was* crazy.'

'*After* I left?'

Her already harrowed face wilted further. 'About an hour after you'd gone,' she said, ' . . . everything changed. It was the change itself that frightened me at first . . . after what had happened earlier, those first feelings . . . It had been like a lot of doors all opening at once—doors on the past, on the present, maybe on the future even. It was like space increasing round me. And then, out of nowhere, this feeling of everything closing down again. I was fighting it all afternoon. I tried to think of it as guilt—about Edward, about what I'd done to him—but it was crazier than guilt, blacker, as if there could be no possibility of meaning in it at all. I tried to do things to make it go away. Even opening the kiln didn't work. I couldn't think straight. The pots seemed ugly, lifeless. And then I was smashing them as they came out. I just smashed them against the bricks and threw them away. Then I had to stop. It completely overwhelmed me—the most frightening feeling I've had since . . .' Again she faltered, shook her head, eyes closed, until she recovered herself. 'It was like fainting into blackness, as though all the oxygen had been sucked out of the air. Like having the life torn out of you. And I knew that something terrible had happened. It had happened to them—this intolerable feeling of life being cut off from itself . . .'

She broke off, at the limits both of language and her capacity to sustain the memory. Her face belied all argument. I knew—as Edward must have known—that this was real. Her fear was real, and it frightened me.

'I didn't know how bad it could be,' she was saying. 'I had no idea. I thought I understood some things. But it's terrible, Alex, it's truly terrible. And now . . . what happened to Edward last night . . . It feels the same. I'm really scared that what I felt wasn't just about the past. That it's now. The disaster is now, and I've caused it.'

When the bell rang that night, jangling throughout the silence of the Rectory, it seemed as though the very house had become an extension of his mind and was subject to the same convulsions. Other than the small sounds he made himself it was the first noise he had heard for many hours, an alien invasion, familiar only in its plangent anxiety. At first he could not bring himself to answer, for the prospect of being called out on some urgent pastoral mission utterly unnerved him. He lacked the stillness to contemplate his own infirmity let alone attend to another's. Yet he remained parson enough to know that only great need could summon him at this late hour. Should he fail to respond, the consequent remorse could only aggravate this already intolerable solitude.

He caught a glimpse of his face in the hall mirror—a wild man with frantic eyes and hair ruffled in a standing mane. Hurriedly he sought to smooth its wisps between tense hands. The bell jangled again above his ears. He stared at the vibrating spring, steadied himself, and opened the door on the damply caped and hooded figure of the woman who had come between himself and his demons, between his duty and his heart.

He stood at the door wide-eyed, unable to comprehend how she had stepped from the very instant of his thought to substance, here, at his threshold. Not a word was spoken. She might for a moment have indeed been a phantom conjured from his lonely mind. But there were raindrops dripping at her hood, and she was muddy-booted.

'Miss Agnew,' he exclaimed, then immediately—her eyes demanded no less—'Louisa.'

'I have departed the Lodge,' she murmured. 'I could not bear to remain alone in the Hall . . .'

'Your father . . . ?'

'Is alone . . . in his library. He will not ask for me.'

'I am . . . alone here. The servants . . . I have . . .'

'I know. I would not otherwise have come.' She looked up at him, for she had heard the reservation in his voice. 'You wish me to leave?'

'Dear God, I wish only to see you again, but . . .'

'Then may I come in?'

A moment longer his dark figure with the lamplight at his back blocked the door. Then he stood, uncertainly, aside.

How perilous things were between them now. He assisted with the removal of her cape, and saw, when she turned again, how a raindrop glistened in her hair. Then he ushered her through into the parlour, and she sat down at his invitation, arranging her skirts with tense hands. He remained standing, wondering aloud whether he might offer her some refreshment, but it was declined. She smiled at his uncertainty, said, 'I beg you to be seated for I feel at some slight disadvantage if you stand over me so.' He did as he was bidden. The room bated its breath around them.

It was some moments before they recovered their powers of speech and, as they did so in the same instant, they must disentangle themselves from the brief collision that ensued. He deferred. Hesitantly she disclosed the nature of her feelings on leaving the Lodge, and though these feelings were edited a little in the telling—the resumed formality between them seemed to require such discretion—he listened attentively also to the spaces between her words. She gathered strength, and went on to recount the painful encounter with her father that same day. Her confusions were apparent; Frere wore the face of receptive sympathy which he knew from previous experience assured his interlocutors that they might trust his patient understanding. Even as she spoke, however, both were aware that the Rectory was not the Decoy Lodge. They were no longer sequestered among dark woodland by the lake; they were in the heart of the village with neighbours all around; they were in the house he had shared with his wife, who might have reclined across from them now, watching, listening.

Yet they were alone; and if Emilia was not present in those difficult moments, neither were the gods. It was only the two of them—a bewildered, married parson and a confused young spinster of the parish, both yearning now for what terrified them both. The air might shatter at a truly spoken word.

He sought refuge from the irretrievable, striving for a detached yet concerned interest, for control. Somehow this thing must be controlled. She must forgive him, he tried, but he was unfamiliar still with the precise nature of the work on which she and her father were engaged. He would be better placed to understand her distress, and respond to it, if she might say more.

She looked up in incredulous appeal, scarcely masking the pang of disappointment. Surely he must know? She met only a gaze of mild intellectual curiosity which would have frozen speech at her lips had she not seen also the unconcealable tenderness fretting at his eyes. Momentarily it encouraged her. She tried—how lamely—to speak of the Hermetic Mystery and its complementary relation to the Christian faith. She intimated at its vital importance as a remedy for the crisis of the age. She watched him nod, trying to comprehend. But what did any of this matter? Either they *were* it or it was nothing. Even as she spoke another, detached portion of her mind was listening. It shared his uncertainty. It wondered whether she had, after all, deluded herself.

His fingers were at his earlobe now. Wanly she smiled as her heart went out at the familiar, bewildered gesture. She wanted to cross the great space of this green room, to kneel beside him, take that hand in hers, be held again, for she was utterly certain of her love if of nothing else. And utterly unable to move.

Then—in an instant of devastating clarity—she saw. The gift of love had been given, yes. Both ways it had been offered and received. It had become her life; in breach of all propriety, it had emboldened her to come by night to the house where she knew he waited alone; yet he could not rise to meet her and fold her in his arms any more than she could cross this final space to him. The limit had been reached. She must learn to live with the knowledge that their love must remain eternally an inward thing, never to be expressed except as a modest sharing with the world of the radiance it lent.

Yet it was so charged with power that the act of containment must soon prove insufferable. It was not to be borne. Her spirit refused to believe this love a mere Midas curse, turning the whole world to gold at its touch, yet rendering it impossible to breathe.

It seemed, at that moment, to have turned him to stone. Neither was capable of the movement that both desired. They sat, like Dean and student, untouching, saying nothing to break the spell that held them there. The further he questioned and the more she answered, the deeper gathered gloom about them. The words fell emptily like dropped tin trays. Mystery spoken thus became nonsense, noise, absurdity, until she could bear it no longer and her eyes were a flash-flood of tears which left him astonished and distraught. He fished for a handkerchief and found none. Neither could he bear this grief. He stood, hesitated a moment, and then, relinquishing all but the present moment, he crossed the room to sit on the couch beside her, put a tentative arm about her shoulder and, as she fell against his breast, heard himself saying through a silent welter of tears, 'Dear God,

Louisa, however terrible the consequence may be, I love you
so.'

For a space there was no further motion, yet what had been
intended as a gesture of comfort was already more than that. In
crossing the room Frere had overcome immense resistances with
an ease that astonished him; in speaking his word a new and
irrepressible flow of energy had been released. The consoling
gesture became embrace, the embrace a sudden confluence of
need; the need beseeched completion in a meeting of their lips,
and that the kiss itself was no more than the first quiet chord in
an unpremeditated music was now entirely evident. Even then
he might have withdrawn in confusion but she had passed beyond that possibility. Her mouth was raised again to his, and
gazing into her eyes he saw space enlarge itself around him like
the unrolling of waters across an otherwise impassable sea.

There was silence—a long moment less of decision than admission—then, holding his gaze, she released the clasp of his
hand from her waist, and stood. Her fingers reached for the
button at her throat, and quietly, without modesty or shame—
as though she were at last proudly shedding the case of matter
itself—garment after garment was laid aside until she stood naked there. Unpinned, the hair fell in a mantle about her shoulders. Her hands were crossed as if to hold it fast. Then she
turned away, trembling a little, and stepped closer to the fire
where she sat with her arms loosely gathered at her knees, and
smiled at him.

Though void of words to name it, Frere knew that a more
than physical transformation had taken place before his eyes. He
was all wonder now, for though they were here, in his house,
he sensed himself more a stranger to this realm than she: and
if, shyly, he too stripped himself as bare as Adam once, it was
an Adam shown the garden after his own fall. Yet, astoundingly,
the gate stood open.

His thoughts—for he lacked her facility to free the mind of
them—dwelt much on Paradise. These were its meadows and
its vales, this the very fragrance of its air. From some moment
long before, he recalled the presence of a snake—green-headed,
crackle-glazed, and flickering its tongue. He marvelled now that
he should dare to let it bite him so. Yet bite it did. He felt the
swirl of venom in his blood, and might have fainted there; but
then came power. It came as a sense of singularity, of having
stepped, re-minted, hand-outstretched, from the first chaos of

things to where all manner of new joy was possible. Power then; and with that power a desire for the absolute perfection of this moment.

He heard her cries. The arsenic-green walls of that still room in the Rectory swayed about him.

Then it was done. He looked down where she lay beneath him, heard her breath, saw its rise and fall, the long, closed lashes at her eyelids, the torrent of hair intimately unfurled around the rapt brow, the soft folds of her ears. He saw the smile that seemed no smile at all but the serene composure of a face in which each muscle was so relaxed that the spirit might have quite departed from it. He saw the eyes open, the unfathomable wonder in that gaze, its welcoming . . .

And terror struck.

When she looked up, amazed, she saw him cowering across the room, holding himself.

The only light in the Decoy Lodge was the one Laura had left burning; there was no sign of Edward. She telephoned the Hall again and, when the machine answered, left a message: 'Ralph, this is Laura. If Edward comes by have him ring me please. It's urgent.' Then we looked at one another, uncertain which way to turn, intimate only in our shared anxiety.

'He's probably out in the woods somewhere,' I said, '—clearing his mind. I think we should wait here. He's bound to come back.'

'And if he hurts himself?'

'He won't.'

'You weren't there. You don't know.'

In the silence of the Lodge we were almost whispering, yet the words might have come from opposite corners of the galaxy. Laura stood by a window, staring out into the night, withheld from me. Feeling responsible and useless, deciding that whatever else that meeting on the lawn might have meant, this wary distance from one another could not have been intended, I said, 'Edward once told me that everyone has to find their own way out of hell. He said that the real danger is falling asleep there, and I can't believe he'll do that. Right now I'm just as worried about you.'

She turned her head towards me, for the first time that night conscious of me as more than a man with questions. I tried to smile and added, 'I also think he was right when he said you shouldn't blame yourself. You were looking for what was real—trusting to it. We have to trust Edward now.'

Her eyes appraised me for a long moment, the right one bloodshot and curled a little against the bruise; then she said, 'You feel different.'

'So my wife tells me. I was phoning her when you came this morning.'

She received this information, nodding, lips slightly ajar. 'Something's changed . . . in you, I mean.'

'I hope so. Look . . . your eye . . . Shouldn't we do something about it?'

'It looks worse than it is.'

'How did it happen?'

She sat down then, a hand at her temple. I lit cigarettes for us and, after a time, seeking relief from tension in narrative, she described how Edward had recoiled from the first shock of her revelation into silence. He wasn't arguing with her any more, not trying to substitute his own explanation for hers. Nor was he at all sensitive to Laura's distress. Eventually he had retreated to the bedroom and, when she sought him out there, shouted at her to go away, to leave him alone. He came down later, unspeaking, in a state of furious gloom, and then began to drink. He sat, ignoring her approaches, drinking his way down a bottle of whisky; and then, when she tried to touch him, hit out with a violence that knocked her to the floor. Laura was dazed by the blow and when she recovered he was gone, out of the house. She found him sitting on the jetty, trembling. At her approach he collapsed into tears.

Neither of them had slept that night. Laura stayed with him throughout, trying to talk to him, trying to make him speak. He remained unreachable, lurching between incoherent extremes of feeling—laughing sometimes, grimly, to himself—and at each lurch descending deeper into a trance of despair. There was one moment when he looked across at her with eyes so malevolently cold she might have run from the room had he not spoken then; and what he said was, in itself, frightening. He said, 'I feel evil. I feel absolutely evil.' But the mercy was that he had spoken it, for the sense of evil seemed literally to express itself, and then, for a time, he was capable of only tears.

It had been mid-morning before he fell asleep, and Laura too was drained by then. She was afraid to leave him but dreaded that I might come looking for her, and knew I must be kept away from the Lodge till this was over. As I wasn't contactable by phone, she'd driven quickly to The Pightle while Edward slept, only to find me not there. Edward was still sleeping when she got back, and she sat for a long time, waiting for him to wake, hoping he might be reachable again. Then, without intending it, she too slept. She woke, hours later, to find him gone.

'I've seen him in a bad way before,' she said, 'but never like this. He could scarcely breathe at times. He was fighting for his breath as if his throat was blocked, and I couldn't do anything but try to hold him. He'd hardly talk at all and when he did I couldn't understand a lot of what he was saying. It was about other people . . . *to* them sometimes . . . people I don't know, the past, things he's never talked about. And he wouldn't explain. He wasn't really talking to me. A lot of the time it was as though I wasn't even there. Just this chaos of feeling, as if his whole life had collapsed around him, and nothing made sense.'

Then, like the lid of a box clicking shut, I saw what should have been obvious from the first—that this wasn't just to do with us, with Laura and me, with sexual betrayal. Edward had worn the horns before. He knew how to use them. Though they might for a time play pitch and toss with anyone who got in their way, he was familiar with this savagery as the first, primitive stage in the renewal of feeling. He knew it and had tried to act from the knowledge; but it hadn't worked. It hadn't worked because this was more than a matter of mere cuckoldry.

'Do you remember what he said about the Tarot card? About the tower—how it represented both my past and his future?'

'I've thought about that, but . . .'

'I think he got it wrong,' I said. 'The lightning wasn't us—or, at least, we were only a small part of it. It didn't really hit until he realized you were telling the truth about Louisa.'

'But he never accepted that.'

'I think he did, Laura. We were talking about it earlier that day, and he was trying to rationalize it away. I could see him doing it. It was as if he couldn't afford to believe that you might be right.'

Laura was still dazed from exhaustion, and her frown showed only bewilderment. 'Think about it,' I pressed. 'He's staked his life on trying to understand the alchemical secret. After poetry had failed, after whatever else he's been into, this was the key, right? Alchemy became the obsession. And this place was his best chance—perhaps his last chance—of unlocking it. He was sure that the Agnews had kept the tradition alive, that Louisa had the key.'

'Yes, but I don't see . . .'

'Suppose you were right. Suppose that the real secret behind the burning of Louisa's book was a sexual secret—a scandal—one that rocked her father's Victorian heart. If it was that, and only that, then for Edward it was the end of a dream. It made everything meaningless. All those years were waste. And the way you found it out . . . intuited it . . . whatever . . .' My eyes shifted away from her gaze as I said, 'He couldn't argue with that. It was over for him. Don't you see?'

I looked back at her, saw the bruised eye seem to squint for focus. She said nothing. 'He'd locked himself in,' I said. 'You were outside, looking for the real, and you found it. I think he knows that now and he can't handle it. I suspect he wasn't even hitting out at you—he was punishing Louisa.'

Laura sat for a long time in silence. She wore that bruise like a badge of her endurance, and I regretted speaking that last thought. It stole something from her as I had not intended to steal; but I was sure I was right. I watched her recollecting all Edward had said and done, assessing it in the light of this interpretation. Eventually she looked across at me. 'You really think that?'

Her voice was flat, dull. 'It makes sense,' I said. 'I thought it was just us at first. I was so sure I could understand him from my own experience. But he's larger than that. He's taken bigger risks . . .'

'That's not what I mean. I mean about Louisa. You really think that's the whole of it?' There was a glacial calm about her now.

Uncertainly I said, 'I was trying to understand Edward . . .'

'I'm trying to understand you.'

I was on trial and had not expected to find myself there—not by her. 'Laura, I think it's possible. I talked to Neville Sallis about Frere . . . following up on your intuition. He wouldn't say anything. He knew, but he wasn't saying. I think there *was* a scandal, and if the church still won't talk about it, then . . .'

'A scandal.'

'I think that must be it.'

'And this is how Edward sees it?'

'I'm almost sure of it.'

'Then you're wrong,' she said. 'You're both wrong.'

The statement was absolute, the confusion gone. Then, in sudden exasperation, she exclaimed. 'What is it with you men? Why for God's sake won't you see?'

I was dismayed by the sudden anger. I'd been so sure I had the picture together; the evidence had gathered force even as I rehearsed it; I thought I was reinforcing her own position. Yet her response made the insight seem purblind.

'Laura, I think you have to . . .'

'Do you know how many times you've used that word? You think this, you think that. It's like a leaking faucet—*think, think, think!*'

We were both still racked by worry for Edward; it left us both on a short fuse; and her expression—it seemed to say that if I was changing, I hadn't changed enough—unleashed exasperations of my own. What was it with these women that they must have everything all ways, were unappeasable in their expectations? I said, 'Isn't it obvious what happens if we act without thinking?'

She heard the cold accusation in my voice, and tossed back her hair. 'So tell me—what were you thinking yesterday?' And, when I did not immediately answer: 'That it was too good a chance to pass up? That it was your lucky day? Is that it? Is that the whole of it?'

'If you were listening you'd know that's not true.'

'But I did listen and I don't know. I don't know what's happening here.' She drew fiercely on her cigarette, then glared at me again. 'For a time yesterday—and listen carefully to this, I don't want you to get me wrong—for a time everything felt clear. *Felt*, you understand, *felt!* And I don't just mean about Louisa, though she was part of it, she was there. I mean about *me*. I felt freed by what happened. It was like coming into possession of myself. For a time I felt absolutely sure of who I am, of why I'm here. And whatever you think that means you're wrong, because you can't know. It was obvious yesterday that you didn't know, and if the feeling hadn't been so strong I could have wept for that. As it was, I didn't know whether to laugh or cry when you came at me like you did. And the way I found that freedom—yes, if you like, there was something reckless about it—a kind of appetite for life, to be *in* it, *of* it, *for* it. After all the tension, the confusion, years of it—not just now, years before that—I felt *single*. I felt to be *me*. And not just selfishly me, on my own, but me as part of things, belonging here . . . *given*.

I've been trying to hold on to that. Through everything that happened afterwards I was trying to hold it, to act from it, in the full knowledge that whatever freedom I'd found was conditioned by care—real care for everything else. Then when Edward first came back . . .' The ardour in her eyes was displaced by perplexed despair. 'He was so gentle with me at first . . . I was sure he understood. I thought we'd be able to hold it together between us . . . that if we were true with one another . . .' She shook her head, her eyes closed, and when they opened again they were all tears. 'It's hopeless,' she said, 'hopeless. It practically killed Louisa and it still goes on. It happens all the time. What are you frightened of, for God's sake? What are you frightened of?'

Though it was addressed to all men the question went through me like a spear. I'd been struggling for calm, for understanding, to make sense of what was happening around me. I thought I'd grasped it, that—intellectually at least—I was in control. But I *was* frightened, and not just for Edward. Laura's impassioned reproach dragged me to dark ground where I was night-blind still—or where, more accurately, I saw just enough to realize how fathomless that dark might be. It was the realm of feeling and of dream, and I was afraid of my own dreams, of my own feelings. I was afraid of the charge they laid. I could think about them, yes; I could even try to act on those thoughts. But step beyond that brink and nothing held. You were in an unreliable region where—why not?—the dead might walk and speak; where the reason might undergo a dissolution so complete, a man—as perhaps Edward had already found—could go quite crazy there. In such lunar territory we were bat-fowlers at best, stumbling about, struggling to keep our lamps alight because the moon could not be trusted.

Yet if one refused to go . . . if one refused to *be* there, to suffer the dissolution that came with full feeling, to undergo it . . . then was any real renewal possible?

I remembered how the loss of Jess had overwhelmed me; how I'd cut and run from the giddy baselessness of things, from the feeling that I might drown in chaos. I remembered the panic which had seized me when making love to Laura, and how I'd recoiled from it. I remembered the sense of loss which came with that recoil; the abdication to resentment, rage, demand. And still, after all I'd been through—*because* of all I'd been through—this dithering on the brink; which was, I realized, still absorbed in its own interminable business while a woman sat across from me in silent tears.

I crossed the room, crouched beside her chair, offered a hand to her shoulder, and felt her flinch away. 'If we knew,' I said, 'if I could answer that, maybe we wouldn't be afraid.'

'Then why won't you learn?'

'We're trying, Laura—me, Edward, all of us. If it was easy, if it was a simple thing, don't you think we'd all be dancing? But the old ways of being male . . . they don't work any more. The meaning's drained from them. And there are no easy options, so we *have* to use our minds. It's a precious thing, this capacity for thought. We have to use it.'

'To the exclusion of everything else?'

'No, not that. I know you're right . . . that even to think well we have to tune our intelligence to the flow of feeling. And we get it wrong. Again and again we get it wrong, because the feelings hurt . . . they're injured . . .'

'And that's our fault?'

'Laura, the heart's a complicated thing.'

'It's simple,' she protested. 'At heart it's very simple.'

But any poet could tell her that simplicity is the hardest thing of all. To marry thought and feeling, to let them flow together through the imagination in the full reach of its sympathy so that right words came like water from the rock—it might look simple when it was done but there was nothing harder in the world. And the heart might be no more than a simple pump keeping the flow of sympathy alive until it seized, but beyond that first essential duty its operations were endlessly complex, endlessly mysterious, or why else were we here?

'Laura, what might be light to you is dark to us. It comes hard.'

'But it's necessary. You need it.'

'Yes.'

'Then why be afraid of it?'

'Aren't you frightened now?'

'Yes, but not of that. I'm frightened by what you do with it . . . by what Edward's doing with it . . .'

'Laura, we're trying. We do try.'

'Sometimes,' she said, 'I think you'd rather die.'

Her eyes were damp still but the tears had stopped, arrested by their own bewilderment. I was close to her, holding that gaze; we were both caught in a flow of sympathy that was also fierce resistance; yet it must have looked anything but that as we heard the latch click, turned our heads, and saw Edward standing there.

I stood up instantly. As Laura raised herself from the chair I could sense the relief in her. She started to cross the room but Edward lifted his hand, pointed a finger, and stopped her in her tracks. The first surprise had vanished from his face. His eyes swivelled in my direction, narrowing. Beneath the moustache his lips curled in a derisory smile. It came at me like a splash of black paint. 'I see you weren't expecting company,' he said.

'Edward, Alex came to find you. I went . . .'

'Had he mislaid me then? Overlooked me somewhere?' He was wearing a long poacher's coat, weather-proofed, an oily olive-green, with the collar turned up at his neck, as though it was raining out there, or cold. It made him look taller than I remembered, more louche. I stood, weighing the perverse smile, weighing the possible words.

It was Laura who spoke. 'Edward, I've been out of my mind . . .'

'I don't think so,' he answered, and crossed to a stickback chair where he sat down with his shoulders hunched, his hands in the large pockets of the coat. 'I've been out of *my* mind. He's been out of *his* mind. But you . . . No, I don't think so.' His eyes flickered back at me. 'Feeling good are we, Cambridge? Feeling like a man . . . like a green man, are we? All shaggy and wild and . . . what's the word I want? Ah yes, *instinctual*.'

Before I could answer he sniffed and looked away. 'I gather you've been privileged with a mystical experience . . . a little Tantric trauma on the lawn. On *my* lawn.' He fumbled in his pockets for a cigarette packet. 'Also that you were too stupid to make the most of it. But then . . .'—he struck a match, lit the cigarette—'against stupidity even the gods are helpless. So what chance was there for a blind old fool like me?' He coughed over the first full gasp of smoke.

Laura said, 'Edward, we have to talk.'

'But I've heard it all, my dear. I've heard it all before, and far more elegantly phrased. What about you, Cambridge? Don't you find they're all much of a muchness—Laura, Louisa Anne? I could list a score more but I'll spare you the tedium. I mean, once they've got into their stride . . . once they've put the pincer-grip around your legs . . .' He grinned up at me like a malevolent elf. 'But no . . . I forget. You haven't seen it yet. All you see is Laura coming at you with the *Rosa Mundi* opening up between her thighs and you just can't wait to jump because you have not yet observed the teeth.'

I steadied my breath, held his stare. 'Edward, you can say what you like about me but . . .'

'I lack the words, dear man. My dictionary fails. Perhaps you have suggestions? I mean, you're the poet, aren't you? You're the one who dips his wick in ink.'

Laura glanced anxiously across at me. 'Alex, I think you'd better leave.'

'He's not going anywhere. Not yet. Not till I've finished with him.' His eyes had never left me. 'The pity of it is,' he added, 'I could have loved you, you treacherous little shit. I really think I could.' Then he did look away, the cigarette pressed to his lips. I saw that his fingers were trembling.

'Edward . . .' I faltered a moment as he looked back at me, brows innocently raised, like a man addressed across a dinner-table. 'You once told me that I'd chosen what happened to me. That whether I knew it or not it was my choice. Well, I think you've been doing some choosing too. If you won't listen to us, you should listen to yourself—to your best self.'

'Dead, dear man. Stone dead. Laura, have you offered our guest a drink? You should. He's going to need it.'

'Your words, Edward,' I urged.

'I know. And they bore me. They bore me to extinction. Have you none of your own? Laura, make yourself useful. The drink.'

'You've had enough,' she answered. 'You don't need it.'

'Don't tell me what I need. Just bring the bottle and shut up while this memorious parrot and I finish our game.'

'It isn't a game, Edward,' I said. 'It never was.'

'Oh I think so.'

'Then if it was, you've won. I'm . . .'

'But it isn't over yet.'

'As far as I'm concerned it is.'

'Oh no, sweet pie. It's not that easy. You can't walk out on this one.'

'I'm not walking out. I came here looking for you. I want to talk about what's happened.'

He snorted on his cigarette. 'Do you think I care about your little hour of splendour in the grass? Do you imagine that in the great sum of things the adventures of your tiresome cock amount to anything more than a puddle of spilt seed? Over which, if I

may say so, it's far too late to start crying now. What a sentimental oaf you are! Laura, the whisky.'

'If you want it you'll have to get it yourself.'

Edward released a heavy sigh, shrugged, then got up and
crossed to the table where the whisky bottle stood by a single
glass. He poured a large measure, left it there, and sat down
again. 'I told you,' he said, 'it was for him. I don't need it. He
will.' And then, mildly, as if picking up the threads of a conversation, to me: 'Do you remember the poem?'

'Which poem?'

'You know—the one which, typically, you couldn't write.'

'I don't know what you're talking about, Edward.'

'Yes you do. The one about the Green Man. The one you
couldn't write because a better man had already written it a long
time ago. I mean the Gawain poem. *Gawayne and the Grene
Knyghte*.' He enunciated the title in impeccable Middle English.
'You have read it, I suppose?'

'Of course I have, but . . .'

'Then you'll remember the story—how the Green Man comes
with his axe into Arthur's court and demands a game. You can't
conjure up Green Men without playing their game, and you have
to play by the rules. Do you remember the rules, Cambridge?'
Again Laura tried to intervene, and again his finger silenced
her. 'Forgive me,'—he spoke over her—'but as you haven't the
faintest idea what we're talking about I think you'd better keep
your mouth shut. Our friend, on the other hand—he knows. He
knows we're not just talking books now. So why don't you en-
lighten her, Cambridge? Why don't you show her your stuff?'

'Edward, I don't see . . .'

He sighed impatiently. 'It's simple enough, but let me remind
you. The rules are these: if any of the knights is brave enough
to lop off the Green Man's head he's free to do so—on condition
that he shows up for a return match at the Green Chapel a year
later. Well, the odds look good, don't they? There's the axe,
there's the bared neck. One quick stroke'—with a hissing breath
Edward brought down his hand in a slicing action—'game over.
So Gawain, rashest of knights, steps forth, takes the axe, and
the head rolls. But what happens then, Cambridge? What next?'

I swallowed, said, 'The Green Man puts his head back on.'

'That's right. The game's not quite over after all. Do you
begin to see now? It's a talking head. "See you at the Green
Chapel," it says. "If you're a man of honour you'll come." Are

you a man of honour, Cambridge? Do you know the meaning of the word?'

'Edward, there are things you have to . . .'

' " 'Tis the finest sense of justice that the human mind can frame.'' Even that old windbag Wordsworth, who behaved not entirely honourably in his youth, knew that. Honour and justice, Cambridge. Do you see now why we haven't finished yet?'

I held the derisory flash of his eyes, refusing to believe him beyond all reach. 'Didn't you once tell me that when a man's head is off he might start to think with his heart?'

Edward snorted. 'Well, he might, I suppose. He just might. On the other hand, he might not. We'll have to see, won't we? I have the axe. I have it right here.' He tapped one of the pockets of his coat. I heard the sound of something hollow in there.

Laura shook her head, distraught. 'Edward, what is this?'

'It's the key we've been looking for, my dear. I've found it. We needn't look any more.'

'I don't understand. I don't know what you're doing.'

'You don't need to. You've played your part. Consciously or not, you did it admirably, and now you can leave the stage. From here on in it's a man's game.' He turned again to me. 'Well, old son, you took my head off all right. Neatly done while my back was turned. Can't say I felt a thing at the time. But are you going to play by the rules now? I wonder if you have the balls.' He coughed over his cigarette, his eyes watering a little, and then, a sickly smile scarcely distinguishable from a wince passed across his face. 'It's my turn now. I have the axe. I know where the Green Chapel is, and you're luckier than Gawain—it won't take a year to get there. We can drive there in ten minutes. So if you're half the man you think you are, you'll drink your drink and we'll be on our way.'

I was in no hurry to go anywhere with Edward, not like this. I picked up the glass and sipped at it slowly, taking in the feel of him. He sat in the chair like a cold lunar shadow of himself, glittering and sinister. He found it difficult to look me directly in the eyes, as though an instant's true meeting might displace the caricature he'd made of me and allow reality back in. I could feel his will in there, hating my youth, hating the fact that he'd ever admitted me to his intimacy; hating, perhaps, the image of himself reflected in my gaze. But at least he was speaking, not locked away in impenetrable silence. Somehow it must be sustained. It felt vital to keep him talking until that cold will broke,

and the injured heart might be reached. Yet reason wouldn't
reach it, and sympathy neither. It would take an entirely irrational approach, a risk.

'Wasn't there another bargain in the poem?' I said. 'Didn't
Gawain promise to hand over whatever he'd gained in the days
before the second meeting?'

Momentarily he squinted at me through narrowed eyes, then
drew on his cigarette. 'Well, we all know what you've gained,
Cambridge. Nothing I haven't had myself, so there can't be
much interest in that.'

'There's something else. Something you don't know about.
Something I think you need to know.'

'Now what could that possibly be?'

'I had a dream last night.'

'Ha! Now there's a funny thing. I had a dream as well. And
so did Bottom once, poor fool! And my dream was somewhat
like his in that it hath no bottom. Shall I tell you about it?'

'Let me tell you mine first.'

'No. I think we're all much happier if you keep your dull little
dreams to yourself. I should have thought that was obvious by
now, and my dream tells you why. It's a dream about how the
world was made. It was made by a demented angel. Crazy with
loneliness he looked into a mirror and the mirror cracked, and
thus the world was made. We can wander about picking up the
pieces if we like, but all we ever see is our own face squinting
back. Through a crack. Darkly. It's a cold place, you see. A
place of question and cold wind. And with such poor lighting
that we can only see at all because the mirror's back is black. It
was a botched job, Cambridge. The Gnostics knew it. They
knew there's Gnothing for us here. So your father and mine
would have been much wiser not to bring us here at all. They
should have left us where we belong—out across that milky way
which begins beyond the rim of the universe and ends between
our thighs. But crazy angels that they were, they made us crazy
angels too. And here we are, and we have a thing to do. Now
are you ready? He leaned over and stubbed out his cigarette in
a plant-pot on the window-sill.

Laura said quietly, 'That's a betrayal of everything you've ever
taught me.'

He laughed. 'I don't think bed-swervers are in any position
to deliver homilies on betrayal.'

'All right, Edward,' I said. 'I've listened to your dream, now you're going to hear mine. And you're going to think about it.'

'I think not. Haven't I just demonstrated that there's nothing duller than other people's dreams? You have humiliated me, young man; that does not give you the right to bore me. Time's up. We should go.' He got up, patted the bulges in his pockets and crossed the room. 'The torch,' he said. 'Where's the bloody torch?'

Laura stood in front of the door. 'Edward, this has to stop. You're not going anywhere. Not like this. We have to talk.'

'But I don't have anything to say to you. It's him I want.'

'Isn't it enough that you're hurting me?'

'Ah yes . . . your eye. Your poor eye.'

'I don't care about that. It's you I care about.'

'That, if I may say so, is a great mistake.' He looked round—'Ah there it is'—and picked up a torch from a shelf by the door. 'Now if you'll let me through.'

'Where have you been?' Laura demanded helplessly. 'What have you been doing?'

'Merely following your intuition. It led all the way to perdition.' He stared at her for a long moment, not in menace, nor with any degree of warmth—just staring, as if trying to recognize a dimly remembered face. Then his own face hardened. 'Laura, get out of my way. I really don't want to black your other eye.'

She shook her head, refused defiantly to move. I saw his eyes narrow.

I said, 'Let him through, Laura. I'll go with him.'

'Not without me.'

'There's no place for you,' Edward said. 'Not now. You've spoiled everything else, but you won't spoil this. I told you, it's a man's game now.'

She stared at him in disbelief. 'All right,' she said coldly, 'kill yourself if you like. That's what you're doing, isn't it? And I can't stop you. Not for ever. But remember—you're killing me too.' Still she did not move.

Edward held her stare for several moments. I was sure he must come back from whatever arctic region of the mind his thoughts had frozen in; but he leaned forward, kissed her lightly on the brow, whispered, 'No, that's your choice. Entirely yours,' and pushed her aside. He opened the door, turned to me and said, 'Are you coming?' then walked out.

I glanced uncertainly at Laura. 'I won't let him hurt himself.'
'You can't stop it,' she answered.
'I can try.' I walked out into the yard and saw the moon step
out of cloud. Edward was sniffing the night air. I said, 'I think
I'd better drive.'
'You don't know where we're going. This is my trip.' He
opened the driver's door and climbed in. As I walked round the
other side of the car I heard him curse and mutter, 'Bloody
keys.'
A jingling sound came from the direction of the Lodge. Laura
was standing in the doorway. She had put on a jacket and was
holding the keyring.

Alone in his study at the Rectory Edwin Frere sat at his desk
by lamplight, his pen poised above the first of several sheets of
paper. He was staring at the fire in its narrow grate, watching
the flames as though entranced by them. After a time he sighed,
dipped his nib in the inkwell once more, and began to write.

*If I commit these words to paper it is because only so shall I
know my thought; only so may I calmly reflect on it; and so
at length win from this bewilderment some gleam of understanding. As a letter written from myself to myself it is penned
in confidence; one which, once accepted, only flame can keep.
The flames are waiting as I write. I warm my hand by them.
Tonight it is very cold.*

A further period of long thought followed before he wrote again.

*In the beginning, says the Evangelist, was the Word, and the
Word was with God; and the Word was God: the* Logos; *the
great* I Am, *of which no predicate shall suffice. This I have
believed.*
    Now I remember also Hesiod in his Theogony, *who tells us
there that* Chaos *was the first of things, and then wide-bosomed*
Earth, *dim* Tartarus, *and* Eros, *fairest of the deathless gods.*
    *Thinking on this, confined between chaos and the word, I
puzzle over what must once, and not so very long ago, have
appeared an impossible question: how if both accounts are
true? How if, in our distinction of things into the* either *and
the* or, *we but perplex ourselves? How if only such an account
which embraces* both *this* and *that—however paradoxical the*

conjunctions—how if only such an antinomian account can
be complete?

This she would have me believe.

This the contradictions at my heart would seem to say is
so.

He put down his pen and went to warm his hands at the fire.
He loathed the cold damp of this late winter, early spring. It
chilled each thought. It left him still more deeply a stranger now
inside in his skin. Only an immense effort of the will brought
him back to the desk, for it was not just from cold that his hands
were trembling. As if sipping on some rare, medicinal substance, he heard himself breathe.

At that same moment in the Hall Louisa sat in one of the two
chairs drawn close to the fireplace in her room. Some minutes
earlier one of the chambermaids had mended the fire which was
blazing warmly now and, though it was impossible entirely to
relax, Louisa was relieved at least by the knowledge that she
would not be disturbed again that night, for she too experienced
the pain of contrary emotions.

During the course of the day her menstrual blood had begun
to flow, and what she had taken previously as a matter of course
now filled her with unfamiliar feelings. If she attempted to think
about sensations that had, of their own deep nature, nothing to
do with thought, they presented themselves as a commingling
of relief and loss, though of the two the latter weighed more
heavily in the ache about her breasts. And neither word was
adequate. Relief and loss: like twin streams risen from a common source, they flowed throughout the flux of feeling she had
now become, and of which her silent tears were the merest
intimation. It seemed impossible that the room could be so entirely still around her. It seemed impossible that she could be
so entirely alone.

For two days now she had instructed herself in patience. It
came with greater difficulty than she who had ever been at ease
with acceptance could have imagined; yet no other solace for
this grief availed itself. She was denied his company; and the
company of others was no more than a gross intrusion on the
tense state of dream in which she sought to recreate and understand that moment which had been the most liberating and,
subsequently, the most deranging of her life. Once more confined in silence, her mind sought also to conceive of futures,

and did so in full awareness of the risks it ran. Yet her powers of solitary reflection had become a hapless instrument, for solitude itself was the one inconceivable thing. It made no sense. It was as much a violation of her altered being as the closing of a cage around a full-fledged lark. Yet he who had shown her how those wings might soar insisted upon solitude—as if such a state were viable now for either; as if he, any more than she, could experience anything other than injury there.

He must be suffering now. They were united only in their suffering, and perversely so, for the sovereign remedy for that pain was to be found in meeting. There was no solace in this patience with the unacceptable, only a malingery of grief. Some means of communication must be found.

Louisa released the tight grip of her hands at the arms of the chair. She relaxed the dense armoury of muscles at her shoulders and her neck. She closed her eyes and concentrated upon the process of breath until its rhythms were no longer a matter of volition and she had become a vessel for the passage of air, a shell in which the sea might hear itself, rising and falling like the thoughtless tide.

Carefully Frere wiped the nib on the brink of the inkwell and wrote down his thought:

Living our human experience, learning to know ourselves, we disclose the variety and ineffable nature of Mystery. It is, rather, disclosed to us; and in that disclosure are revealed the contrary impulses at its heart. Thence comes responsibility; for either we must enlarge ourselves to embrace them, or they shall tear us apart.

He pondered nervously on that for a time and then, impelled by the logic of his earlier thought, and by the inexorable logic of his experience, added:

Or we must both enlarge ourselves to contain them and they shall tear us apart.

His hand was trembling again. He put down the pen and lifted the fingers to his brow. The mind was a fearful thing these days. It had always been so, but more than ever now. It was his most intimate enemy and somehow he must try to make it his friend. Then he remembered whence that thought had sprung, and sat back, shaking, beyond all thought. The room dissolved around him.

It was like the change that comes across the air with the chiming of a clock, but no clock had chimed. There was a sense of sudden warmth, and without having to open her eyes Louisa knew that she was no longer alone: he was sitting in the chair across from her before the fire. Without having to utter the words aloud it was now possible to speak.

'I knew that you must come.'

'It was impossible to sustain the separation on which I so foolishly insisted.'

'Not foolishly, my dear; but, yes, impossible. I too have found it so.'

'And it was not your choosing.'

She sighed then, smiling. 'But then, in some things, we are now beyond all choice.'

'That is true,' he conceded, 'but only in some things, and everywhere else choice is waiting for us, and with no great patience. My dear, there are lines which must be drawn.'

Her heart quailed at the gravity in his voice, but she strove for lightness. 'I do not think I believe in lines. Look as I might, I can find them nowhere save in constructions of the mind.'

'But you know very well what I mean.'

'I know what you *are*.'

'I am a man, Louisa, and it is choice which makes us human.'

'That too is true, but choice has much to do with listening.'

'To what?'

'To the gods in us, for they too make us human.'

'I have a great fear that they are utterly indifferent to our humanity.'

At these words they might, for a moment, have been adrift in space, his statement was so cold and airless—except that it was touched too with the breath of human pathos. She strove to recover confidence, to be true both to the impersonal dimensions on which his words had opened and to what was true in her. 'They have their own needs,' she said quietly. 'They are larger than ours and perhaps more terrible. We must be careful therefore how we answer them.'

'And we must choose, surely, which of them we answer to at all?'

'Or is it rather that the gods choose us? You must try not to take too much upon yourself.'

'I feel it is my duty to receive it all. For a time . . . the other night . . . I sought refusal. I was afraid. I had a terror of transgression, and—deeper still than that—of the price my actions must exact, and not only upon myself. But I know now there is no escape from that except into oblivion.'

'And perhaps not even there.'

'That may be so. But there is a thing that weighs more heavily upon my mind.'

'Then share it with me.'

There was a long silence in the room before he sighed and said, 'I have listened to you, my dear. I have listened with more tender attention than ever in my days, and so you must hear my entire presence in the words when I say what I must say.'

She heard her heart beating as she said, 'Which is?'

'That whether we choose among the gods, or whether the gods choose us, each has their rite; and once the choice is made it must be undergone.'

She was silent then, listening for the meaning in his words; and the effort was almost too much for her, for in her deepest heart she wished to consider none of this. She wished to be free from the intransigence of words, which must always prove too dense, too earthbound. Were they not both creatures now of dream, who might pass through language as less happy shades might pass through walls? Yet she could feel the resistance in him as he said, 'Even those who serve only Mammon will, in their more honest moments, tell you that.'

'But they are only men . . . only male. They could not serve him else. And you, my dear, are more than male, as I myself am more than female now.'

'I cannot speak to that.'

'I think if you will free your heart you can.'

'Free it,' he exclaimed, '—when it is bound as on a rack between a sense of what is sacred in our love and an unremitting knowledge of its sin? We are illicit, Louisa. This is an illicit love.'

'Illicit love?' she said gently, smiling, struggling for calm. 'I think, my dear, that must surely be a contradiction in terms.'

'Which is the very rack on which I find myself. There is nothing which more deeply confirms my sense of what is sacred here than the knowledge of my own unworthiness.'

'I too feel that. But it is not the only knowledge. If we were indeed unworthy, surely we would never have been elected into love? Can you not take comfort there?'

'Can *you*? Are you too not racked by this intolerable loneliness?'

'We are not now alone.'

'Louisa, we are always alone.'

'I do not believe that.'

'However deeply our beings may have touched one another,' he said slowly, 'whatever knowledge of the sacramental unity of things we may have been briefly blessed with, we are also always alone.'

'It is not true.'

'Reach out to touch me then.'

'I already have. I am holding you. I feel your presence warmer than this fire.' But even as she spoke the room grew colder round her. She opened her eyes and saw that the chair across from her was empty. The breath came quickly to her lips. She must calm herself, be still. Quietly she must summon him back.

Alone in the Rectory, Frere scratched the nib across the page:

As Idea knows itself in man, and man knows himself through Idea, so Mystery knows itself in woman, and woman knows herself in Mystery. Male and female they were created; for the idea divested of mystery is empty, and mystery unshaped by idea is formless.

He hesitated for a moment, wondering where this might lead, but the thought dissolved inside his mind, became a hot chaos flooding everywhere. She was mistress both of Idea and Mystery; he master of neither. As if the action might itself build dikes against the flood engulfing him, he returned the pen to the page and scribbled:

As I now am empty and without form, and therefore neither idea nor mystery, neither male nor female.

For a time he stared at that in horror. Either it was nonsense or it was true; or it was *both* nonsense *and* true; and what salvation for a mind in such confusion?

Only in the unquestionable clarity of her presence did meaning now inhere. Only because, in the tumult of his passion, he had permitted them to come together did chaos overwhelm him now. He had banished himself from her company that order might return; yet, apart from her, in this insufferable solitude, there was no order, only an internecine conflict between the anarchies of feeling and of thought—from which now both heart and mind recoiled into an agony of fear.

And she must struggle to hold him with her. She felt him slipping from her grasp as though, perversely—for there was nothing less on earth he wanted—he was resolute to prove his own insubstantiality. And if she strove with him he would only resist more fiercely, so she must still herself, let go, in the hope that the primary imperative of his own being must bring him back. For a time the room was very cold.

'Let it be ice then if it must,' she thought, 'for even there we know we can stand together.'

'I am so cold,' he said—and not in answer—'I am so very cold.'

Though she too shivered at the touch, she said, 'There is warmth with me.'

Then there was long silence.

'In another world,' he said quietly at last, '—perhaps in another age even, we might—you and I—have been able to sit so, side by side, before a blazing hearth, with the wind trying the window-latch and yet unable to enter where we shared our peace. I have dreamed of this. One night—even before I came to you at the Lodge in such disreputable condition—one night, alone inside the Rectory, I dreamed of this. How we might sit there quietly with our books—you deliberating over the profundities of some old Hermetic sage; I pondering my chosen text, or—better—counting out the numbers of a verse . . . our two imaginations hard at work in silent sympathy until the clock should chime, a log shift among the embers in the grate, or some night-bird call above the billows of the gale . . . Then we would look up, and catch each other's eyes, and smile . . . And this, my dear, remains the entire and utterly impossible longing of my heart.'

She might have wept to hear the sadness and the tenderness of that voice, but the vision it invoked corresponded with such total intimacy to yearnings of her own, and filled her so completely with the warmth of her returning presence, that it was less grief at those closing words which possessed her now than a hope, however tentative, for the recovery of lost joy. Somehow it must be possible to transfigure this experience. Whatever bars the world might seek to place between them, they had proved it now: it was possible to meet, if only so, in this ethereal domain where heart might speak with heart without concealment. No one could reach or touch them there, and none divide. Was not the realm of the spirit the one region where they had always truly belonged? Was not this perhaps the very meaning of his swift and agonized withdrawal from their meeting in the flesh? They had proved its joys, and proved them in a manner that belied all grossness. Now they must pass beyond. Their element was elsewhere, rarer, more refined.

'Do you know,' he said, 'what date it is today?'

'It is the 25th of March.'

'The Day of Blood.'

Her perplexity was compounded by the response. Where had he gone while she was lost in thought seeking the one way through?

'It is the *Dies Sanguinis*,' he said, 'the day when the dead Attis rises from the dead.'

Now she thought she understood. They had not, after all, strayed so very far apart, for his thoughts, like her own, were seeking images of resurrection. With a confidence that surely must share itself she said, 'The day also when once, according to a very old tradition, the date of Easter Day was fixed.'

'No longer so. The feast is movable.'

'Yes, and it is a great loss. That it moves in relation to the phases of the moon was the only wisdom in the change, for otherwise pagan and Christian might still have shared that celebration of renewal which was, for the worshippers of Attis, *Hilaria*, the Festival of Joy.'

'When the world was turned upside-down in carnival,' he said, '—the feasting of the flesh.' And then, after a moment's silence, in a voice that chilled her soul: 'As you and I have turned the world upside-down.'

'But only that it might be righted.'

'Out of chaos?'

'Which is,' she answered swiftly, 'the First Matter of things, whence all shall be reborn. That is the promise both of the cross and the Attis-tree. These days about the solstice have ever been a hallowed time. And—do you not see it, Edwin?—Mary and Cybele, the two grieving mothers, are one and the same. This is the day when both their sons shall rise.'

'Easter is not yet, and nor do I think that I can bear its coming.' His voice was hoarse and fearful now, more distant. 'Today is the Day of Blood and what I see is a milling crowd. I hear the sound of laughter and savage music. I hear the cries of women selling violets. I can smell slopped wine. I see a drunkard piss-ing in the open drain, and there a masked clown strokes a giant phallus strapped about his loins. Among the cymbals and the flutes, the detonation of the drums, I see the long procession dance, and everywhere there is a lascivious sense of dread.'

As possessed now by the terror of the vision as he was him-self, she strove, gallantly, to answer. 'I say to you: our love can only make this holier.'

He laughed quietly, and she could not bear the note of mock-ery. 'I would have you speak that thought,' she said.

'It is only that you have overlooked something.'

'I am trying as best I may,' she cried, 'to hold the whole of this together, and you must help me, Edwin. It cannot be done alone.'

'I think,' he said, 'that it can only be done alone.'

Alone in the Rectory Frere had abandoned his attempt to write. In the contest between chaos and the word, the word had lost; yet chaos must not win. The irretrievable was done, and he could not deny the truth of the experience. He was committed now—committed both to the saving grace of it and to the guilt. He could conceive of only one point where these contraries might converge.

Unable to find a shaping word of his own, he must turn else-where for guidance. Two books lay open on his desk: one of them, the larger, was the Holy Bible, opened at the nineteenth chapter of St Matthew's Gospel; the other was his small, secretly long-cherished volume of the verses of Catullus.

Even dumb objects have their destiny. Rarely given a second thought, they perform their unconsidered duty day by day until their moment arrives and everything seems to hang on their location. Such now was the case with the keys to Edward's car. Unthinking, I'd put them down on the table when Laura and I entered the Lodge; Edward wanted them, Laura was in posses-sion, and the ensuing muddle in the yard would have been com-ical had it not been vile. Laura was resolute that she'd throw the keys in the lake sooner than let us drive off without her. Edward was equally determined that she should not come. With the two of them shouting at one another, we jangled together like the

keys on the ring until she threw them across the cobbles and—
when Edward went to search for them by torch-light—opened
the rear door of the car, got in, and refused to leave. Already
regretting the impulse which had led me to take up Edward's
challenge alone, I was glad enough to see her there. 'Come then
and be damned,' Edward snarled, and switched on the ignition.

He drove in rage, would answer neither of us, stared ahead,
crashing through the gears, but was alert enough to stand on the
brake when a hare jumped from the hedge and froze in the
headlight-beams. We were all thrown forward. When I looked
up, the hare crouched there in the moonlight, pricking its ears,
staring back at us, before bounding off to be lost among the
trees. The shock shifted Edward's mood, but not pleasantly. I
heard him chuckle beside me, and felt a *frisson* of dread as he
muttered, 'Enter these enchanted woods who dare.'

He didn't stop again until we reached the centre of Munding
where he parked the car outside the churchyard. It was Saturday
night, around eleven-thirty. People were still drinking in the
Feathers. He picked up the torchlight from the floor, patted my
thigh with it, and said, 'Get out. I'm going to show you something.' As he slammed the door behind him, I turned to look at
Laura. She was white-faced, her nerves in ribbons, biting her
lip. I said, 'As long as we stay with him he can't hurt himself.'

Her reply was a tense whisper, so thin on her breath I had to
strain to hear it. 'Something terrible's going to happen,' she
said.

'Not if I can help it.'

'Nobody can stop it now.'

'I don't believe that. Are you going to help me?'

The breath shuddered out of her as she opened the door.

Edward was waiting for us at the lych-gate. Ignoring Laura,
he pointed the torch-beam at me. 'I'm going to show you Gypsy
May.'

'I've seen her already, Edward.'

'I know that. You've *seen* her. But have you really looked at
her? Have you let her take a long hard look at you? I think not.'
He turned away along the gravelled path, chuckled, and began
to sing. I recognized the song from my rugby-playing days at
school—a bawdy variation on an air from Gilbert and Sullivan:

There's a portion of the female that appeals to man's depravity,
  It's fashioned with considerable care—able care;

And what at first appears to be a simple little cavity
  Is really quite an intricate affair.

Now doctors of distinction have examined this phenomenon
  On very many experimental dames—lucky dames,
And have given to this portion of the lower female abdomen
  A series of delightful Latin names.

The tune was flat on his throat, the words elegantly obscene. He stepped away from the path into the grass among the gravestones, then directed the torch-beam upwards. It scanned the flints until its circle of light came to rest on the crudely carved features of the idol. The bulging eyes and the mouth's grimace were thrown into shadowy relief. More hideous than it had been by day, the figure was no longer comical. The torch might have been a magic-lantern projecting this single slide for a mind obsessed with its own disgust. In the otherwise dark night it turned the church into a lavatory wall.

'Ugly old bitch, isn't she?' Edward murmured. 'And what *is* she saying? What is the *son* to my little *lumière*? How about: "Would you rather have me foul and faithful or fair and faithless?" And what's the answer to that little puzzler, Cambridge?' He moved the beam slowly down until it was centred where the hands clutched at the open groin. He gave a perverse grunt of satisfaction. 'You don't know? Well, here's another one for you. Do you know what *that* is?' he demanded. 'Have you given it any thought?' Uninterested in any answer I might have found, he left a second or two for the question to sink in, then said, 'It's where we start and where we end, and we spend the time between trying to scramble back inside. Why do we do that, do you imagine? What *is* the fascination of the thing? I suppose Laura knows. She *is* it. But she can't tell us. Those particular lips can't talk. They can only open and shut like the mouth of a fish, without intelligence; and the only sound they make is a sort of munching.'

Quietly Laura said, 'Why are you hurting yourself like this?'

Edward gave a little chuckle and ignored her. 'Shall I tell you what I think it is? I think it's the Black Hole. It's the Singularity. It's where all the laws break down. It's where, if we dare to look, the universe turns inside-out. Gravity is infinite here. Space and time come to an end. It's the crunch, Cambridge. It's the big crunch.' He stared up for a long time and then, in a changed voice, hollower, more abstract, added, 'Theoretically speaking, it might constitute the entrance to another world, another universe—a kind of cosmic Happy Valley. Regrettably, however, the equations governing this hypothesis are so unstable that if they are disturbed by other factors—a body, for instance, approaching the Singularity—they collapse. The door closes. It shuts in our face. So we can never know. We don't know how to think about it, you see. It can only *happen* to us. Like this.' He switched off the torch and plunged us into darkness. 'What does that make you think of, Cambridge?' And, when I didn't answer, 'Precisely,' he said. 'Your silence hits the nail on the head.'

He switched on the torch again but it was placed beneath his chin now and the shadows made a hideous grinning mask of his face. 'Of course, Laura would have us think of it otherwise. They have to. It's their ace in the hole. They're under zoological compulsion to make it look as inviting as they can. And, I grant you, it can be beautiful. It's of its antinomian nature to be at once beautiful and ugly; seductive and repugnant; rarely seen and evident everywhere; silent and summoning . . . I could go on and on because, as instruments of torment go, this one is singularly well-designed.' He lowered the torch. 'You might say it's one of the cleverer tricks in Death's Jest Book.'

By now I was scared, and less of Edward himself than of his absence. He was gone from his own face, and from his own voice. Something cold and vile had usurped his place, had seized the opportunity to corrupt his dreams. And this was only the preliminary. I began to feel that Laura was right—that a terrible thing must happen unless it was stopped now.

'I don't believe any of this,' I said. 'This isn't you speaking.' I held his stare, casting about for the ounce of civet that might sweeten his thought, but he lifted the beam to my face, momentarily dazzling me. 'Then you haven't seen it yet. You just haven't got it.' He swivelled the torch-beam back up to Gypsy May, and spoke to her. 'You're going to have to try harder, lady. This one is denser than poor Frere.' Then he looked back at me. '*He* saw it—your friend Frere, our mystic brother—yours and mine, sweet pie. He knew. Listen to this.'

He fished in one of the large pockets of his coat and brought out a book. It was small, ledger-like, with a scarlet spine and marbled cover, and the contents—I saw them briefly in the torch-beam—were hand-written. Edward began to read aloud from a page he had marked with a spill of paper:

> *In his loneliness the poor fellow's mind seems to have been unhinged by thoughts of Gypsy May, though how a man of his culture and intelligence—to make no mention of his faith— could fall under the spell of such superstitious, corn-dolly nonsense is quite beyond me. Perhaps his unhappy stint in India accounts for it, for there was also much confused mention of that. Whatever the case, take her seriously he did, and to what lunatic extremes!*
>
> *Try with our scalpels as we might to unlock its secrets, the brainbox remains a mysterious job-lot affair in which, for aught I know, the rude aboriginal savage still stamps his dance next door to the respectable Anglican parson at his prayers; or, for that matter, on the hither side, your free-thinking man of medical science who sits scratching his pate, posing questions to both his neighbours—questions to which, it seems, there yet wants a reasonable answer.*

Edward looked up from his reading, snapped the book shut and replaced it in his pocket. 'It's about Frere, of course. It's from the casebook of Dr Thomas Horrocks, physician and surgeon of Saxburgh. It's dated in March 1849. You might have got on well with him, don't you think?'

'Where did you find it, Edward?'

He gave a sardonic chuckle. 'Never you mind. Here it is. What every bad boy needs to know about blind justice.'

'Ralph,' Laura said. 'You got it from Ralph.'

Edward stared at her. 'You really are quite remarkable. Yes, Ralph had it all along. He was the keeper of the key after all. But that doesn't matter now. What matters is the end of the game. Are you with me, Cambridge?' Swinging the torch across the night-sky he began to walk back towards the lych-gate, picking up the words of the song.

'Where are you going?' I called after him.

He swung the torch so that it illuminated the red brickwork and the white window-casements of the old Rectory. 'To the Green Chapel,' he said. 'Where else?'

Inside the Rectory Frere's fire was burning low. He rose from his desk, took a log from the basket and dropped it among the embers. A brief constellation of sparks rose and sparked against the hearth-back. He put his shoe to the log, thrusting it among the small flames and, when he was sure that it had caught, returned to his desk. A third book waited there, splayed open on its spine on the pages of the opened Bible. It was the Book of Common Prayer. He had been studying the Order of Service he must shortly observe for Easter.

On Good Friday morning—no more than a few days hence—he must address the God of the Christian faith before his congregation, asking for mercy on all Jews, Turks, Infidels and Heretics. He must read that Epistle to the Hebrews in which it was acknowledged that the blood of bulls and goats had never been an adequate sacrificial offering, and what was finally required was that the human body of Christ become the paschal lamb. He would be obliged to bid the congregation draw near with a true heart, in full assurance of faith, having their hearts sprinkled from an evil conscience and their bodies washed in pure water. 'Let us hold fast our faith without wavering,' he must exhort, 'and let us consider one another to provoke unto love.'

Even now, alone, how his heart stopped at the word.

Before Easter was over he must announce to the parish that Christ, the passover, was sacrificed for them: 'therefore let us keep the feast. Not with the old leaven, nor with the leaven of malice and wickedness, but with the unleavened bread of sincerity and truth.'

But which truth? Whose sincerity?

'If ye then be risen with Christ,' he must command, 'set your affection on things above, where Christ sitteth at the right hand of God, not on things on the earth.' And this with his own eyes painfully averted from that beloved face in the nave before him—but not turned upwards, away from it, towards the goal he must set for his parishioners.

'Mortify your members,' he must instruct them, 'which are upon the earth; fornication, uncleanness, inordinate affection, evil concupiscence, and covetousness which is idolatry. For which thing's sake the wrath of God cometh on the children of disobedience, in the which ye also walked some time when ye lived with them.'

As he himself still walked, still lived.

He was the child of disobedience. He was idolater. His tongue must turn to stone sooner than speak these words.

Had he been wrong then not to heed his wife, not to respond more completely to her complaints and grief, not to abandon this place where—he had known it from the first—disaster must come upon him, and to return to whatever sober and safe life they might contrive in Cambridge?

It was still possible.

It was still impossible.

He closed the pages of the prayer book, looked back at the words he had written earlier, shook his head over them, and took them to the fire. For a moment the flames burned brighter there. Then, with the poker, he broke the blackened remains to ash.

In the night outside, the wind gusted, and he heard on its wing the sound of singing from the Feathers.

'It's empty,' I said. 'It's been empty for years. There's nothing in there.'

Edward had already pushed open the iron gate to the Rectory garden and passed through. He turned now, glanced our way, and smiled. 'You think so? Then take a look at Laura's face. It seems she doesn't agree.'

She stood beside me staring across the dark garden at the upper windows of the derelict building. Her face was like tallow. It was numb with dread; with the same terror she'd experienced after I left her alone at the Decoy Lodge. I reached out a hand but she flinched away.

'It's the Green Chapel, Cambridge. Perhaps I should dress for the occasion.' Edward crossed to a holly bush, tucked the torch under his arm and, with difficulty, snapped off two green sprigs which he threaded through his hair, one above either temple, like green antlers. He side-lit his head with the torch and grinned at me. 'Regrettably, I lack the whetstone to sharpen the axe's edge. The noise was rather effective as I recall, but never mind.' He tapped the bulge in his pocket. I heard the hollow sound again before he said, 'Are you coming—or must I add cowardice to the sins already heavy on your head?'

I summoned the resolution to meet his sneer. 'Call it what you like, but it's a very real concern for what's happening to you.'

He gave a derisive snort, and turned to Laura. 'Here he is then—the dreamer who was going to make all the difference. I don't think he wants to know. Do you?'

Laura stared at him, and said nothing. I saw that she was trembling.

I said, 'This feels fake, Edward. I think you're big enough to carry your own pain, not splash it around like this.'

'Slippery,' he replied, smiling. 'Very slippery. But it's not me who's in question now. You've started something, Cambridge, and it would appear you lack the guts to finish it. And as for this feeling "fake"—I promise you, it's real. The moment you decided to have your way with Laura—and don't misunderstand me, I'm not whingeing about that—in that moment it all became very real. You conjured powers there, sweet pie, and they don't greatly care for those who practise *coitus interruptus* of their rites. So tell me—are you going to funk it again?'

We stared at one another to the exclusion of the whole world. It was akin to the moment long before over the Tarot card, but far more dangerously charged. I sensed Laura's fear beside me, and was dry-mouthed at my own. Shadowed by the torch-light, Edward was a barbaric, barely human figure in the long coat, under those green horns, as unnerving as the masked priest at some savage initiatory ordeal. The three of us were frozen in silence—the dense silence of the East Anglian night in which there was nothing to be heard but the faint crepitation of the trees in the Rectory garden. The silence reached along the lane, across the churchyard and the water-meadows. It inhabited the Rectory. It entered my head—a silence impossible in cities. It veered upwards between the stars.

Then Laura spoke. 'Edward, I can't go in there.'

'Your presence is not required,' he answered. 'I told you not to come. Take the car. Go home.'

'Not without you.' Edward turned, dismissively, away. Laura's voice was shaking as she said, 'We'll talk about it. We'll talk about it at home . . .'

'Haven't you seen it yet?' he said. 'This is where words stop.' He sniffed, shifted his eyes to me. 'Either he comes with me, or I go in there alone.'

'You're wrong,' she pleaded. 'You're wrong about Alex, wrong about me. You're wrong about Louisa. But most of all you're wrong about yourself. I've never lied to you and I won't take your lies now. I won't even listen until I can feel you real inside what you're saying. All I've heard tonight is death and lies, and it's withering everything you touch. Is that what you want? Is that what you really want?'

Edward was holding his head at an angle from her agonized plea, but at that moment a car came down the lane from the direction of The Pightle, headlamps illuminating the rosy brick-work of the Rectory and the ivy reaching round its window casements. It passed on, round the bend, towards the Feathers and out of sight, but for an instant Edward had been spotlit by the beams. What I saw was a pathetic old man with holly in his locks standing outside an empty house. Shorn of darkness thus, he was more grotesque than menacing, ageing almost visibly as he stood there; and—as his eyes met mine—I caught a kind of desperate beseeching on his face.

With the car gone, the dark returned, but its spell was broken. There was a silence, then Edward's free hand reached up, took the holly sprigs from his hair and let them drop. The action seemed to cost him an enormous effort. For a moment he cast about, disoriented, then he said, 'Take her away. Get her out of here,' and staggered away. He was making for the Rectory, alone.

Utterly distraught now, a hand clutching at her hair, Laura called after him. When he didn't respond, she turned to me. 'Help me. Please. I have to get him away from here.'

It was evident both in her face and her voice that her fear was not only for Edward. In this condition her judgment was no more to be trusted than his. I glanced back where Edward stag-gered down the gravelled drive like a man under compulsion, towards an arched gateway that must lead to the back of the building.

To drag him away or not? Either way was risk; but the dread had gone and in its place was a cold curiosity. He had a reason for bringing me here—a crazy reason, wrong; but words wouldn't reach him, and if he wasn't made to *see* that he was wrong . . .

I heard the gate creak open and, as Edward disappeared into the darkness, felt certain that the real disaster—for all of us— might lie in not seeing this thing through with him.

'I have to go with him,' I said. 'If you can't bear to come, wait here.' I was halfway towards the gate when I heard the sound of Laura's feet on the gravel behind me. Then the crash of breaking glass.

He was standing under a window at the back of the Rectory with a flint-stone in his hand, staring in fascination at a small cut across his fingers. He glanced up at my arrival, an exhausted old man who had gone too far. Then he saw Laura at my back. Empty of his demons, almost weeping, he said, 'Go away. I don't want you here.'

I shook my head, said, 'I'm not leaving you. You wanted me here and I've come. It's an empty house, Edward. You're coming in there with me and you're going to see that. Then we're going home.'

I saw the stone fall from his fingers, heard the breath panting out of him; then Laura spoke.

'It's not just an empty house.' Her voice was barely more than a whisper on the night air. I turned to look at her, saw the struggle on her face; her voice gathered strength as she said, 'But you're right—we have to go in. We have to try to see it whole.' She brushed past me, stood in front of Edward and said, 'It's not just a man's game. It never is.' Then she turned to me. 'Can you let us in?'

Uncertain now, alarmed by Edward's haggard condition, excluded from the resolve that seemed to have taken possession of her, I hesitated.

'It's all right,' she said. 'We can do this together.'

I saw Edward shaking his head, cursed beneath my breath, reached through the broken window for the catch, then shinned up and through into a dark room. I caught the smell of damp on my lungs, and turned back to demand the torch. Edward tried to resist but even his physical strength was failing. Laura prised the torch from his grip, handed it through the window, then turned to comfort him.

Oppressed by the gloom of the place, I flashed the torch and saw a large porcelain sink with brass taps jutting from iron pipework. Across the pammented floor was a hearth with a stepped brick chimney-breast and, next to it, an old washing copper with a wooden lid. I'd broken into a whitewashed laundry-room, cobwebbed now, and damp. The door opened on to a passage which led eventually through to the rear lobby where I unshot two bolts and opened the back door. Laura came in, turned, and held out her hand to Edward.

'You shouldn't be here.' His voice was hoarse and laboured. 'I've been wrong . . . I've been very wrong, and I'm tired, Laura. Take me home. We should go home.'

'We can't,' she said quietly. 'Not now. We have to end this.'

'Laura, you don't want to know . . .'

She turned to me, drawing her breath deeply, and said, 'Give

me the torch.' Out of the struggle with her fear she had won
authority. There was an almost glassy calm about her as she
took the torch and shone it through into the front hall with its
closed, panelled doors and walls that were stippled with rising
damp. I looked back at Edward who stood with one hand leaning against the door-jamb, his breathing terse, gazing into the
Rectory as into his own bad dreams. 'Alex,' he gasped, 'you
have to stop her.'

'Why did you want to bring me here?'

'It doesn't matter now. I was wrong . . . But she shouldn't
have come. You've got to get her out of here.'

Laura had moved away along the corridor, making for the
stairs. She was no more than a shadow against the torch-beam,
and it was like watching a somnambulist—someone derisive of
risk, pushing on into a darkness rank with the fungal smell of
rot.

'I'll stay with her,' I said. 'Are you all right?'

'Don't worry about me. Just get her out.'

Laura was already climbing the bare boards of the staircase.
At each step the torch-beam danced across the banister and
walls—too small a light, I suddenly thought, to penetrate the
past, which was itself a place where the mind might lose its
bearings. I put a foot to the bottom stair and called after her.

Without turning, she gestured with her free hand to silence
me, then took the turn of the staircase up on to the railinged
landing. The sound of my shoes on bare wood echoed in the
stairwell. I heard Edward panting along the corridor below and,
when I reached the landing, saw Laura open a door and shine
the torch up a further narrow stair which must have led to the
old servants' quarters in the attic. She closed the door without
entering, then turned along the landing. Convinced that the
higher we went in this derelict house the more perilous it must
become, I felt a moment's relief that she had declined the attic
stair, but she pressed on, opening other doors, shining the torch
into room after room.

She came to the back stairs which descended, I guessed, to
the kitchen and laundry-room where I had entered, and halted
briefly as a call from Edward startled us both. Shaking her head
as if to free it from distraction, she turned the torch on another
door. I saw the light gleam on the brass handle. She turned it
and had to push hard before the door jerked open. I was left in
darkness, feeling my way along the landing towards her, and

when I reached the doorway she was sweeping the beam around the bare walls of a room too small by the standards of this vast house to be a bedroom. It might have been a study once. There were ashes in the fire-grate still. In the far corner a length of damp wallpaper drooped from the picture-rail.

'It's like a mind,' she said. 'The whole house is like a mind. It's hurt and frightened of itself.' Then she sighed, glanced across at me, and for a moment I thought she was about to come out again; but she stiffened. I could feel the change in her.

'What is it?'

She lifted a hand as though to fend off my voice. Then—it might have been an intrusion from a different century—a car passed down the lane outside, its headlights swooping through the window, travelling across the ceiling as the car took the bend. In the brief radiance I saw a bare bulb dangling from the ceiling-rose, and Laura beneath it with her eyes closed in a tight frown. It was the face of someone reaching for a difficult thought, or—had the eyes been even slightly open—to see across far distances. The room darkened again with the passing of the car.

'It's here,' she whispered. 'This is the place.' Another quick glance sought reassurance that I was still there. Edward called her name along the landing, and she frowned again, biting her lip. A moment later he was beside me in the doorway, a hand at my shoulder for support. His breath, short and stertorous, was the only sound.

'I can't hold it,' Laura said. 'It's there but . . .' She gasped, looked across at us, said, 'Shut the door,' and—when neither of us moved—the demand was repeated, fiercely. Determined not to leave her alone in there, Edward pushed past me. Hating this place, loathing its rank stink, yet sure now that, having gone this far, the thing must come to its conclusion, I too went inside. The brass knob was loose on its screws, and the door so swollen it jammed against the frame. It felt as though I was shutting out the air.

Laura stood in silence. Her hands were at her sides, the torch pointing to the floor so that her feet were brinked on its small pool of light. 'I can't . . .' She shook her head in frustration. 'No, it started here, but . . .'

In a voice that was little more than a hoarse croak, Edward said, 'You can't see it because it shouldn't be seen. Come away now. I can't talk about it here.'

Laura drew in her breath quickly and raised the torch high

enough to illuminate his face but not to dazzle him. 'The thing you brought with you. You said it was the key.' Edward shook his head and drew away. I saw a rime of sweat glistening at his temples. Laura held out her hand. 'I need it. I can't get through without it.'

Diminished, shrinking upon himself, Edward leaned against the wall. 'Come away. I'll try to tell you . . .'

'But you don't know. You haven't seen it all. You couldn't have been like that if you'd understood. Give it to me, Edward.' As he turned away from her, looking in appeal at me, she said, 'You're trying to protect me from something you wanted Alex to face, and it won't work that way.'

It was hard to tell in that uncertain light whether the pain in Edward's face was more mental or physical. Either way, he was vulnerable, old—older than his years. Without the support of the wall he might have fallen. For a time a silence empty and cold as the room around us was accented by the friction of his breath; then he seemed to summon strength, turned on his shoulder, still leaning against the wall, and said, 'I've been in hell, Laura, and I'm trying to keep you out of there. You can stand there in your ignorance and tell me that I'm wrong, but I'm telling you there are things you don't even begin to understand. I haven't turned my back on anything. I've looked at it. I've stared it in the eyes. And it won't hold together. It's the mirror—what I said about the mirror. It's cracked and the crack runs right through everything. And once you've seen that—once you've looked through the crack—you know we're capable of absolutely anything, and nothing makes any difference. It can't be mended.'

'I don't believe that,' she answered softly.

'Because you haven't seen.'

'Then let me see. If it's the truth why protect me from it?'

'Take my word.'

'I took your word before. It was a better word.'

A wince passed over Edward's face. 'A dream, Laura. The last illusion. And it's over. I'm tired. I'm tired of all this.'

'I know. But it's not over. Not yet . . . And in this moment I'm stronger than you. Let me take it from you.' She held out her hand again.

Edward's face was ash-grey in the torch-light. 'It'll tear the heart out of you.'

'If you can't do that,' she said, 'nothing can.'

'God damn you then,' he snarled in sudden fury. 'See for

yourself. See what we can do.' He reached into his pocket and took out a thin black box. At first sight it seemed nothing more harmful than a case for a musical instrument—a flute perhaps— but it was too short for that, too narrow. Trembling, Edward threw two small brass clasps. The plosive clicks were loud in the empty room. Then he turned away, fumbling in the darkness.

The breath hissed out of me as he turned to face us again. He was holding a cut-throat razor by its ebony handle, the blade extended, glinting as it turned in the torch-light. 'Do you see now?' he demanded. 'Do you see now where the dream ends?'

He held the razor upright, close to his own throat and, in that small room, within striking distance of both hers and mine. The blade gleaned what little light there was, an incision on the darkness so fine and morbid that it seemed to make the dark complete. Sick with the fascination of the thing, numb with apprehension, I stared at it and saw the possibility of all three of us lying in our blood in that dark room.

He had wanted to bring me here alone. If my stupid, contentious pride had let it happen, he would have brought me here into this derelict place, and the blade would have been between us. And when I looked into his eyes now I saw that he too did not know what might have happened next. We are capable, he had said, of absolutely anything. Even in that moment, with Laura gasping beside us, he was still uncertain, as though the blade might have a will of its own, ready, at a wrong word, to wreak havoc there.

No word was spoken.

Old man, young man, rivals and friends, contemporaries in love and pain, Edward and I were frozen in that intimate exchange. He must have seen the incredulous question in my eyes, and neither in words nor yet in action could he bring himself to answer. The blade quivered in his hand. Otherwise everything was motionless. Whatever it might be, the next thing had enormous leisure in which to decide, with cool detached curiosity, whether or not to happen. Then Laura reached out her hand.

Her wrist was very narrow beneath the blade, very white; too frail a thing to put between a man and his despair. I watched her fingers fold around his knuckles where they gripped the black handle.

'Let it go now,' she said. 'This isn't yours. It's out of your hands now.'

Edward stared down as she released the soft clasp and straightened her palm. There might have been nothing in the whole world but his own hand holding the razor and this other, vulnerable hand waiting to receive. Long seconds passed before the last of his will was expended in a scarcely audible groan.

As she took the blade from him, Laura closed her eyes. I heard a sharp intake of breath as though her flesh was seared with cold. She seemed to reel, and for a moment I thought she might faint, but with a little moan she turned away from us towards the open window. Reflected against the dark panes, the torch-beam blazed there like a planet, sending webs of light back across the ceiling. They circled round us as the torch shook in her hand.

Then, in a voice of infinite pity, a voice that was her own and not her own, she murmured, 'Oh my dear, what have you done . . . what have you done to yourself?'

All that he needed here was assembled. Everything was ready now. Only the self must be prepared.

Trembling, Frere returned to his desk.

At the end of all thought there was but one word that answered to his need, and the word was *sacrifice*. He whispered it aloud, and then, intrigued by the sound, repeated it: 'Sacrifice.' Like the noises of his fire, its sibilants and fricative crackled and hissed across the tongue. Its purity annealed the mind.

It was a word radiant with great beauty, yet filled also, when approached in nakedness, with dread. It was a word he had tried to live with all his days, yet only now, after the brief burnt offering of all the other words by which he'd failed to still his heart, did he begin to understand how such a word might summon angels; for angels, like the word itself, were both beautiful and terrible, and carried immolation on their breath.

To sacrifice: to make sacred, to do the holy thing. It must remain a possibility. For however deep his transgression, if this love was sacred then one might make it more so in the act of sacrifice.

That there were occasions when a prized value must be sacrificed to the claims of the higher—this was part of his stock-in-trade as clergyman, a weekly adjuration to the Bostocks and the Whartons of this world, as nightly to himself. Yet how little he had lived its meaning, contaminating sacrifice with resentment, or forgoing it in preference for solace that did not long console. Those days were past. They had receded like the days of infancy when angels were the guardians of sleep, gentle as the tester's drapery, merciful as his mother's smile. How, as a child, he had puzzled over Jacob's violent encounter with an angel, for who could believe that an angel might find it in his heart to maim a man? What an innocent he'd been to carry for so long the sentimental illusion that such powers were appointed merely for his protection!

Well, he knew better now. He was coming to understand the nature of true sacrifice.

He was coming to understand also how dubious was the distinction between the old law's sacrifice of blood and the bloodless offerings of the new. The new law had been born in blood as everything was born in blood. There was blood on the stable-straw, blood on the cross, blood—if one truly dared to taste it—in the chalice of the mass. It was the very currency of life, and therefore the only food acceptable before the gods. This was the knowledge every woman carried in her loins. It had always been so under the old law and the new; and he—poor quaking fool—was caught between them both. He had shed his cloth and entered the Garden; he had thought it Paradise, but he knew now that its true name was Gethsemane, and that the roses of Isis flowered there among the violets of Attis.

To sacrifice: to be at once the priest, the altar and the offering. Much was already immolated in his passion's flames, and a lifetime of prudent abnegation would recover nothing from the ash. Nor must he regret it; for if he had lived at all it was in those moments when, like a dancer on the ice, he had surrendered narrow consciousness to the rhythms of the flesh, and thereby shook a fist at fate. Yet was it possible to live without regret? If Catullus were to be believed not even the first initiate could answer yes to that.

He turned again to the pages of the *Attis*. Its closing cry was already deeply scored, but what seized his attention now was the crucial line of the poem where the gender of its subject shifts. How well Catullus understood the nature of the sacrifice required; how terrified the poet had been of it! And Frere himself was suddenly aware, in contrast, how remote he remained from the terror of the thing.

He closed his eyes, and realized that though his shoulders were cold his palms were clammy; for the body knew. It understood the action it must undertake and undergo; the nerves vibrated with premonitory alarm. Poor Brother Ass—it had ever been his faithful servant, save only in the matter of its carnal

appetite; and even there the mind had been the true seat of
contention. So what reward was this?

Here, in the hour of their collision, there was a curious oth-
erness about the body's operations, as though it sighed and trembled now without consent, fretting in its traces while the mind
hummed and hawed like an indecisive master. With the fingers
of one hand he stroked the palm of the other, trying to catch his
senses sensing themselves; and all he apprehended was a faint
tickling sensation utterly remote from the place where he watched
and waited. A hand may not embrace itself, he thought, nor the
eye see its own seeing, any more than a mouth could bless itself
with kisses. How strange that we should be so identified with the
flesh that housed us, and yet feel so separate from its palpable
existence! Yet its pain was our pain, and it could shrivel us. Even
the pain of the mind was a physical pain, like the action of a vice
sometimes, and sometimes like the cleaving of an axe.

And all of this was again evasion. What was needful now was
the one thing solitude could not afford: an impulse from outside
the self. The encouragement, the momentum, the hysteria—
however one conceived it—that came from drum and tambou-
rine, the wailing of the priests, the incitement of a crowd hungry
for vicarious expiation. One might be seized in such a tide,
drawn on, spring forth, and with a savage shriek of *Ololugmos*
do in an ecstatic instant what a century of solitary meditation
might never accomplish. Yet except in a few brief and precious
moments of his life Frere was no ecstatic. He was a stolid pil-
grim who had erred. He was a man of books, who closed the
pages of Catullus now, in fear, in an orgy of self-contempt; and
saw, beneath its binding, the pages of his Bible lying open there.
Here was the book of all the world. Exactly and unfailingly, it
spoke to every aspect of the condition of man—even to such a
terrible condition as his own had now become.

Had this same fear, he wondered, thrilled through the nerves
of Origen, those many centuries before, when he, in his dark
time, meditated on those same enigmatic verses in St Matthew's
Gospel? He must imagine so, for there was nothing new under
the sun, and even here, in the particularity of fear, he had been
preceded. Even perhaps in the realization which had come to
him at last: that there *was* a rite in which a man might make his
sacrifice to God and Goddess in a single act.

For if a priest was unworthy to share with his congregation
Christ's sacrificial passion, there remained a way whereby—in

service to all the powers prevailing in his church as in his mind—
he might take another sacrifice upon himself. A moment exquisite with pain; the self swiftly severed from the self; and thence
a peace that passed all understanding might at last be found.
The gods might there be met on their own terms. Within himself
the opposites could at last be reconciled.

And this, surely, she must understand?

At his desk under the curtained window Frere began to read
aloud, to calm himself, to know that even here in this extremity,
he was also in the presence of his Lord. He was reading Christ's
words from St Matthew's Gospel: 'For there are some eunuchs
which were born so from their mother's womb; and there are
some eunuchs which were made eunuchs of men; and there be
eunuchs which have made themselves eunuchs for the Kingdom
of Heaven's sake. He that is able to receive it, let him receive it.'

He closed the cover of the Bible, repeated those last words to
himself, and then, trembling in that cold March night in 1849,
Edwin Frere took his razor from its leather case and held it for
a time in the crocus of the candle-flame. Sitting quietly naked,
he sought to compose his lonely mind until there was nothing
of Cybele and Attis there, of Origen and Matthew's Gospel;
nothing of Gypsy May. All images were displaced by the face
of the woman he had loved with the entirety of his flesh and
soul, and with a love that was finally forbidden. *In her name*,
he thought, *do I make this offering*; and that calm which is the
fortitude of a mind in resignation descended over him. When he
saw that the steel had cooled, he made a slow inspiration of his
breath, then cupped himself in his left hand, and with the other
drew the blade across his flesh.

Later, when he saw that his fumbling efforts to stitch the
wound had failed, he staunched the blood with napkins, drew
on his clothes, went out to the stable and harnessed his horse to
the gig. Then he drove slowly along the dark lanes to Dr Hor-
rock's surgery in Saxburgh.

Priest to both God and Goddess now, never again to be the
lover of Louisa Agnew, he had become, and would for ever
remain, her mystic brother.

14 ⊠ The Gesture of the Secret

Ten minutes after midnight Ralph Agnew's man Talbot was driving back to the Hall after an unsatisfactory evening in Norwich when he found Munding Street blocked by a small and, at that time of night, unexpected traffic-jam. Beyond the three cars halted ahead of his own he saw the blue light of an ambulance whirling its lurid flicker across the faces of those who watched from doorways and the few people standing in the street. Among them he recognized Bill Rush, George Bales, and Mrs Jex wearing a topcoat thrown over a dressing-gown and carpet-slippers. His first thought was a street-accident—probably someone rolling home from the Feathers knocked down by a drunken driver. Then he saw me: one arm around a figure huddled in a blanket, I was approaching the rear door of the ambulance through the gateway of what, to the best of Talbot's knowledge, was the empty Rectory.

His curiosity further aroused, he switched off his engine and was no sooner out of the car than he was ordered to get back in and reverse, like the cars ahead of him, into the carpark of the Feathers. From there he watched the ambulance wail around the bend by the Post Office, making for Saxburgh and the main road. By the time he joined the small group outside the Rectory gate disturbing rumours were already taking shape.

A quarter of an hour later Talbot was back at the Hall reporting to Ralph what he now knew—that his friend Edward Nesbit had suffered a heart-attack and was dead.

This devastating news would later be confirmed by the one person who, in what had been ill-lit and frantic circumstances,

438

was best placed to observe precisely what was happening; but in those shocked moments Ralph needed no confirmation. Incapacitated by grief and guilt, he tried to take in Talbot's confusing account of the night's events, and then, having sought to clear the brandy from his head with coffee, he changed his slippers for shoes, covered his informal evening-wear with a trenchcoat, and drove against the blur of approaching headlights down the long miles to the hospital.

Most of what Talbot told Ralph he had learned from the pigman, Bill Rush, who had been walking away from the Feathers with Bob Crossley less than half an hour before when he spotted a light in an upstairs window of the old Rectory. He was puzzled by it at first, and then a little unnerved. It was Bob who insisted that they investigate.

The two men came through the Rectory gate at the moment when, with time swirling round me like the torch-lit air of the room, I heard Edward gasp, saw him clutch at his chest and then—as fast as if an axe had truly fallen—topple to the floor. I heard Laura's clipped cry, then the sound of the razor clattering to the boards, and I was down beside Edward, pulling back the collar of his coat, loosening the throat-buttons of his shirt. I felt, before I saw, the tears rolling down his face. I felt them on my hand. Then, outside, like the return of sanity itself, someone shouted, 'Who's in there?' and I recognized Bob Crossley's voice.

By the time Bob and Bill Rush had found their way up to where I crouched over Edward's prostrate body and Laura shivered across the room, Edward's mouth was already turning blue. Dazzled by their torches, I squinted up at the two men aghast, and said, 'He's not breathing. I think . . .'

Bill stood in the doorway, wide-eyed, and the questions froze at Bob's lips as he recovered from the first shock and bent down over Edward. He put a finger to his throat and found no pulse; then lifted an eyelid, looked at the pupil, whispered, 'Damn,' and turned to me. He must have seen I was in no state to act because he looked back over his shoulder at Bill and snapped, 'Ring for an ambulance. Don't stand about. Now.'

'The box is dead,' I said.

'Sod it.' Bob reached into his pocket, held out a key to Bill. 'It's for my front door. Use my phone and for God's sake be quick about it.' Commanded out of astonishment, Bill grabbed the key and turned for the landing. 'Tell them it's a heart-attack,' Bob shouted after him. 'Wait for them outside. Show them where to come.' Then he looked back at Edward, took a deep breath, raised his fist and brought it down with a sickening thump on the breastbone. He shifted his weight, pinched Edward's nostrils with one hand, lifted his head back with the other, then bent and began to blow into his mouth. After several breaths he felt again for a pulse, cursed under his breath, then looked back at me. 'How long's he been like this?'

'Two minutes? Three maybe. I don't know.'

'No longer than that?'

'It can't be.'

'Then there's still a chance.' Again he blew into Edward's mouth, then shifted to press urgently on his chest. It was like watching a man trying to kindle fire with nothing but bare hands and breath. Three or four times he lurched from mouth to heart, muttering, 'Try, dammit, try,' and then—as once more he felt for, and failed to find, a pulse—I watched my mind reel through calamitous thick dark, and heard my own words yearning for denial as I hissed in a breath I hoped Laura would not hear, 'Is he dead?'

'There's no pulse,' Bob said, 'no ventilation. I think he's gone but we've got to keep trying. It'll be easier with both of us. Look, I want you to work on his heart. Press on the chest— here, at the sternum. No, a bit higher or you'll break it. That's it. I'm going to give him more mouth-to-mouth, and as soon as you see me stop push down hard—use both your hands—four, five times, then I'll try to get more oxygen in him. We'll keep it going like that—alternating. Are you ready?'

I nodded, knelt beside Edward and, as Bob raised his mouth, began to push at Edward's unmoving chest. Crossed hands mimicking the simplest, forgotten action of the heart, battering at Edward's door, I was shouting in silence, cursing him, begging—a fervent muscular beseeching that he not persist in this refusal of his duty, until—no longer knowing whether I was trying to pump life into him or pump death out—I could manage no more than an abject iteration at each push upon his heart of the one word *please*.

From a place somewhere close to the ceiling Edward is looking down in mild perplexity that we should be so alarmed by what is to him an entirely acceptable predicament. He feels no pain, no panic at this abrupt severance from a body which is no more than an object of remote and declining interest. He watches as Bob presses his lips to what had once been his own mouth, and I lift and drop my weight like a plunger at his chest. He wonders that this stranger and I should take such pains to drag him back into the pathos of the flesh when he has been liberated from its toils with such simplicity. It is, admittedly, a little odd to be floating here in such detachment while things are so frantic below, but the sensation is not unpleasant; indeed, were it not for our obvious distress, it would be mildly amusing even. Then his attention shifts to where Laura watches, her arms crossed at her chest, hands at her shoulders, shivering. With a pang of dismay he recognizes her profound state of shock.

His first thought is that there should be some means to comfort her, but from this airy altitude nothing is quite tangible. He is powerless to touch or speak, and he does panic a little then, but only for a moment. Even more forcibly than when he'd gazed from inside the skin, he is struck by how very young she is, and how very beautiful. He observes her at last without demand or desire, as though a series of film-thin screens have been withdrawn—screens of thought and fancy, ideas mirroring his otherwise invisible soul—and she is simply *there*, beyond all yearning, and beyond—as the last of those screens is removed—the merely circumstantial fact of her material existence.

So this was what the ancients had meant when they spoke of star-fire! He has never entertained any of the pallid, Sunday-school illusions of the soul as a wispy length of cotton-voile floating about in inner space; but that her centre should be so crystalline and igneous, shining like struck flint, and, yes, burning with a cool sapphire brilliance—this ravishes his feelings. It fills him with a pure rejoicing; and so excellent is the revelation that—when he remembers her contingent self once more—it is with a tenderness that could dream of asking nothing save the small effort of consciousness which would show her to herself as she is visible here to him.

But then, as though he is ascending with astonishing velocity or—because there is no sense of motion—she is receding with equivalent speed, he sees her diminish even as he seeks to communicate these thoughts. She is becoming smaller and ever more remote until all the illuminated figures gathered about his body have quite disappeared, and the light itself has dwindled to a single distant star.

* * *

Ralph arrived unseen in the waiting-room of the Casualty Ward at the moment when a young doctor was reporting to Bob and me on Laura's condition. Dazed, half out of my mind still, I heard him say that she had been in a severe state of shock on admission but was under sedation now. They'd decided it wisest for her to stay overnight. He assured me that a good night's sleep was quite the best thing, and saw no reason why she should not be discharged the next day—though she would be delicate still and need careful handling.

The doctor rasped his hand across the stubble of his chin and blew out his breath. 'As for the old man . . . I'm afraid it looks like an extensive heart-attack. In fact, if you hadn't known what to do . . .' The sentence expired in a shrug. 'Anyway, he's with the coronary unit now. His blood-pressure's on the low side, and the next 24 to 48 hours will be quite critical. But the longer he goes without another attack the better his chances. If you ring tomorrow we might be able to give you a clearer picture. Did you leave your number—just in case?'

Bob said, 'I left mine. I'm there most of the time.'

The doctor glanced back at me in an effort of encouragement. 'You did a good job. All being well he could be out of here in a week to ten days. I hope this doesn't completely mess up your wedding plans.'

Anxiety, ringing in my ears, made it hard to hear even the words intended to dispel it, so I was slow to realize that this last hope was also addressed to me. And that it made no sense. The doctor must have seen bewilderment deepen on my already dazed face. 'It's not you who's getting married?' and—when I shook my head—'My mistake. I'm sorry. It's just that he kept muttering something about being late for the wedding, and I thought . . .' He glanced in embarrassment at his watch. 'Well, there's not a lot more I can say. I should go home and try and get some sleep if I were you.' He raised a dismissive hand at our thanks, and turned away.

Bob released his tension in a sigh. 'He's right you know. There's nothing we can do here. Come on, I'll take you back.'

I turned uncertainly and, for the first time, saw Ralph. Wondering with vague dismay how he could possibly be there, I saw him ease himself on to a bench and, with an expression too fatigued among the stresses of his face to believe in any other possibility, say, 'I thought he was dead.'

And so, for a time, had Bob, who admitted as much to Ralph now. And so had I; and though I'd listened to the doctor's report with the critical attention of a jealous lover, I was still uncertain, for I'd heard no final reassurance there. It was as little absolute as the first faint shrug of Edward's heart beneath my hands had been, as that first vomited gasp of breath before Bob turned him on his side. Speaking or not, Edward was in limbo still; and I in that tense and rarefied condition where the nerves believe that sleep is something only other people do.

To leave Edward and Laura there felt like dereliction. It seemed to forfeit what little superstitious pull I had to stop him changing his mind again in the night; to make sure that Laura did not wake alone to the news that his heart had risen in rebellion once more. But there were no beds in these wards for the guilt-crippled and the lonely worriers; and Bob was not about to let me pass the night in this waiting-room where there was no comfort in the knowledge that mine was not the only grief that Saturday night.

Ralph too was in poor shape, his eyes watery in their pouches, the patrician calm quite lost in the ticking of his cheek. He pushed his fingers through the thin silver sweep of his hair, and diffidently suggested that we might like to come back to the Hall. He would, he said, appreciate our company.

'I blame myself for this.'

Tactfully, embarrassed by our gratitude, and with many of the questions that must have crowded at his lips like pressmen still unanswered, Bob had slipped away. At Ralph's request I'd stayed on at the Hall in full expectation of his retribution. I would have welcomed it; but he sat over his brandy for a long time in silence, not even looking my way, before making this abrupt admission. His chin was tucked in his jowl, the tips of one hand stroking his temple. He might have been sitting for the portrait of an elder statesman pondering a lifetime's failure to mend the ills of the world.

'But you didn't even know what was happening,' I said, '—not till it was too late.' I looked up and met the pained smile of an old man sensitive to youth's tendency to forget that life is not its exclusive property.

'Edward and I,' he said, '. . . we had the most appalling row earlier this evening. It should never have happened. My fault, you see. Entirely my fault. It's not the first time.' His eyes wandered the elegant room, stopping to hold in doleful regard the portrait of Sir Humphrey Agnew above the fireplace. 'Secrets!' He grunted, shook his head. 'They're killers, you know. Learnt that in the Intelligence Service during the war, but we don't care to admit it in our own lives. Families like mine . . . they have all kinds of secrets. They have their secrets and they have their pride, and the one often protects the other. Eventually, of course, it all comes out . . . usually in the wrong way, at the worst possible time . . . Then your pride goes to the bloody dogs, and you wonder why you didn't . . .' He sighed, opened the palm of his hand, and smiled warily across at me. 'Not being clear, I know, but it's a little like Louisa's story . . . been lying around for a long time like an unexploded bomb. Sooner or later it had to go off . . . Leaves you dazed when it does.'

I said, 'You knew the truth about Louisa all along?'

'And you're wondering why I didn't tell Edward from the first?' There was a long silence which ended in a deep but not yet decisive sigh. 'Edward and I . . . we go back a long way. A friend brought him up to Cambridge in the old days . . . I'd never met anyone quite like him. Some people found him brash and uncouth, and he was difficult, yes. But I liked his contempt for the place, his refusal to be awed. And that farouche wit.' Ralph looked up and added, as though in extenuation, 'his origins are quite humble, you know.'

'He's never talked about it.'

'No, he wouldn't. Likes to give the impression he sprang fully-grown from a mating of Hermes and Aphrodite.' If there was a touch of bitterness in his voice it was displaced by sad affection as he said, 'Most of all I was taken by the way a whole aviary of birds seemed to sing under his hat—a rather disreputable hat as I recall. Then there were meetings in town. Paris briefly . . . This isn't the first time we've . . . what? Disappointed one another, I suppose. And deceived, of course. Yes—always the deception.' He got up, offered me the decanter and, when I declined it, poured more brandy into his own snifter. He returned to his chair, seemed to drift into reverie, though not happily so, and I saw for the first time what Bob must have noticed earlier: that he was already drunk.

'Let me put it this way: suppose you had a friend—a very old and once very dear friend whom you'd lost touch with years ago in circumstances which were . . . which you'd long bitterly regretted. And suppose, as you'd often wished he would, that

friend suddenly wrote to you again wanting to renew the friendship. Suppose also—though this might come harder—that you
were old and rather lonely when the letter came. Are you with
me so far?' He glanced up quickly, shyly, took in my nod and
the thoughts behind it. 'Then you begin to understand. Of
course, I knew that Edward must be after something—when was
he not? But one didn't really mind, you see. You're a poet yourself; you must have observed that Edward is quite the visionary
. . . a man of enormous gifts who might, in the right emotional
environment, have . . . Well, that's neither here nor there. Not
now. The point is, I was more than happy to hear from him
again. And when it became clear that he was more interested in
the dead Agnews than in their sole survivor, it didn't greatly
matter. He would be here at Easterness. We would be together.'
He sniffed, swirled the brandy in his glass, then looked up again.
'I should explain that in our correspondence he made no mention of Laura.'

Under eyes intent for my response, I said, 'That sounds like
Edward.'

'Does it not? Though—in the light of what I've said—you'll
imagine my dismay when they turned up together. A research-
assistant, yes—advised of it, who could object to that? But a
love-nest in the Decoy Lodge was not at all what I had in mind.
Nor, to be perfectly frank, did I have any great faith that their
researches would uncover anything of importance. I was left
with the hope that Laura would soon find the work tedious, as—
I felt rather sure of this—she must quickly tire of Edward.' A
thin, ironical smile reflected over vain wishes. 'I felt reason to
be optimistic. He was excited by the library . . . obsessed by it.
He was talking in terms of a long stay. I had seen what happened
before when his enthusiasms rode roughshod over the claims of
relationship. And this particular relationship . . . Well, the girl
was almost too young to be his daughter even. A somewhat
vague creature, I thought. Beautiful, yes, but ill-educated, with
an almost barbarous disregard for culture, history . . . I saw no
future there. It could only be a passing involvement. So I had
hopes, you see. And means to preserve those hopes. Means
which, at the time, I thought not entirely self-serving.'

Dazed as I was, it occurred to me that Ralph's interest in first
inviting me to the Hall might have been more complex than I'd
guessed. Though the invitation had been to meet Edward, he
might well have been fishing for the complications that could

arise from a meeting with Laura. Observing my frown, he glanced away, then said, 'I want to show you something,' and pushed himself to his feet a little unsteadily. He crossed to a shelved alcove, removed the first of a number of identically bound volumes, and began flipping through leaves of charcoal-coloured card. Towards the end he found the leaf he sought. 'Ah yes. Take a look at this. It says it all.'

He handed me the open album and I was looking at a snapshot of two young men reclining on a lawned river-bank, one with his head in the other's lap. Both had open-necked shirts and wore baggy flannels. A blond quiff fell across the brow of the seated youth, who smiled down where his fingers tilted the pet-ulant chin of his darker companion towards the camera: Edward. It was recognizably he, though unlined, clean-shaven, and glamorous as a lean-visaged gypsy. He held a cigarette between his lips, and frowned, impatient of the moment. A wine bottle and an open volume of verse lay on the grass beside him: high summer, more than half a century ago, twenty years before I was born.

'That was in Cambridge,' Ralph said. 'On the Backs at King's. Shortly after we first met. As you will have observed, the years have not been kind.'

It was true. Outside that context I would not have recognized Ralph's features in that blond young man. He took back the album, gazed down at the picture for a moment, then snapped the covers shut, and returned the volume to its place on the shelf. Then he paused beside a small framed portrait on the panelled wall, snorted, and arranged his own face at the same angle as that of the old man portrayed there. 'Do you see the likeness? It may not be so obvious now—since my stroke, I mean—but Edward was not the first to comment on the resemblance. This is Henry Agnew, of course—Louisa's father. Do you believe in reincarnation?'

The abruptness of the demand took my already confused mind by surprise. Before I could answer, he said, 'I don't. But I do believe in blood. And, in a way, I suppose I believe in ghosts. We carry them inside us. We are all haunted houses. Henry was haunted. His father certainly was—atrociously so. And I sup-pose I too am a haunted man. You can't live alone in a place like this and not be haunted.' His glance surveyed the high ceiling, the costly drapes, the antique furnishings. Suddenly the atmosphere of the Hall was claustrophobic: centuries of privi-

lege, and the price of privilege, hanging on the air like jaded
regalia; the portraits, varnished against time, but gazing down
on life like exiles. 'I've made arrangements to leave it to the
National Trust,' Ralph said; and then, with a dry melancholy
smile: 'Perhaps democracy will exorcize it.'

I felt myself beginning to dislike him as much as I now mistrusted him, but as I watched him return to his chair and swig
at his brandy, I remembered that I can't have cut much of a
figure myself at that moment; that we were complicit in our
separate guilt over Edward; and that my judgment was so confused by the night's events it was no longer reliable.

'Where was I?' he asked.

'Your feelings when Edward turned up here with Laura.'

'Ah yes. So, the fact is, when Edward began questioning me
about Louisa—what I remembered of her, what I'd learned from
my parents and elder brothers—I took a decision. I decided to
keep a secret. A secret, you understand, not the secret. The
Hermetic secret I couldn't keep for the simple reason that I
didn't have it. Nor was I even persuaded of its existence . . .
although I suppose I engaged in a little self-deception here.
Edward clearly believed in it—which surprised me a little because the first time we'd talked about my ancestors many years
ago, he'd shown not much more than a sceptical curiosity. But
now he needed the belief—it was what brought him here, and I
was not about to discourage him with my own scepticism. In
fact, his enthusiasm delighted me. I became rather intrigued by
it myself—knowledge that might give us greater purchase on the
lamentable fiasco in which we are all condemned to play our
impotent part these days—and here, at the Hall, among my family's papers! Improbable, I grant you, but intriguing. So I told
myself that if my ancestors had indeed possessed knowledge of
such a secret then the purely circumstantial factors of their private lives could have no intrinsic bearing on it. I went further. I
told myself that such information might only confuse the issue
. . . though you will have guessed by now, of course, I was
afraid that if Edward knew all there was to know about Louisa
then his interest in remaining at Easterness might not long survive the knowledge. There has been scandal enough in his own
life. He has scant curiosity about the emotional difficulties of
others.' He sighed, glanced wanly up at me. 'A secret within
the secret then. At the time it seemed harmless enough. Indeed,
I'm still not sure that I was so very wrong. As Edward himself

will tell you, secrecy is a great enticer.' Then he favoured me
with a rueful smile. 'I had not anticipated that Laura would
prove to be a person of such singular abilities. Nor that events
would unfold quite the way they did.'

Again he withdrew into silence, negligent of my existence.
Part of me wanted to be out of there, alone with my own feelings; but there was a kind of justice that Ralph and I should be
consigned to each other here. We had both deceived Edward,
and were both agonized by the harm we'd done. In those moments we deserved one another. We had no one else.

'The point is,' he resumed eventually, 'when Edward came
into the Estate Office yesterday demanding to know whether I
was aware of any connection between Louisa and Edwin Frere,
I could scarcely believe my ears. The only evidence of such a
connection was in my private possession—as it had been for
many years. I had found it among the things left behind by my
brother Hilary when he went to Flanders. No one had touched
them—for a long time his room had been a sort of shrine, a
dreadful sort of reliquary—until I took over here and sorted it
out. Did you know that Hilary had the makings of a fine poet?
I was always rather envious of him. Envy and admiration are
rarely far apart.' Ralph sighed; I thought he might lose his thread
once more, but he recalled himself and said, 'You will imagine
my consternation then—particularly as at that moment I had
more pressing matters on my mind—something my gamekeeper
had told me only moments before.'

I coloured and said, 'That's why you shouldn't take all this
on yourself. You weren't the only one who lied to him.'

'No, but I told him the truth, and sometimes that is the greater
crime. You must have been blaming yourself, of course, but
take my word for it—your little misdemeanour may have been
the occasion of Edward's crisis but it was not the cause. I made
use of it, you see. Not then. Not at that moment, though the
seed was planted. But later—when he came back—when, finally, I threw the facts in his face. The facts about Louisa and
Frere, yes . . . but that, I'm ashamed to say, was less than the
half of it . . .'

He averted his eyes from my puzzled gaze, then pinched them
with the thumb and finger of his right hand. He sagged back in
his chair, wincing from the memory. After a time I asked him
what had happened.

'I was on my own here earlier this evening . . . listening to music. I didn't hear him arrive . . . wouldn't have known he was here but I went out to get something and heard the noises in the muniments room. Talbot was out and it frightened me a little . . . the security here isn't very good. I was about to phone for the police when I heard him swearing and recognized his voice. I went up, saw the frightful mess he'd made there. Papers everywhere, Edward in the middle of them, looking like death. He was behaving . . . abominably . . . strangely, and I was very worried for him at first . . . but then, once the truth was out, he was violently angry with me . . . offensively so . . . hurtfully. And suddenly I was furious with him . . . angrier than I knew until the rage started to take its own disastrous course. There were almost fifty years of anger that had been waiting for this moment . . . anger, resentment, injury, humiliated and wounded pride . . . the vicious brand of rancour that only the rejected know how to wield. I made him face it all—his own endlessly disastrous folly over women, his talent for treachery and betrayal, for using other people as, once again, he had made use of me. I dragged him back over what I well knew had been quite devastating experiences. With a cruelty of which I would not have believed myself capable I forced him to recognize that most of his life had been a monstrous exercise in self-deception . . . that I was not the only one who had suffered from the lies he told himself. I told him that to the best of my knowledge there was only one secret behind existence and he was excluded from it, and would always remain so because his heartless self-absorption rendered him incapable of love. I could see that I was lacerating an already wounded man, but I couldn't stop myself because I too, you see, am a very selfish old man. The ugliness of it all was appalling. It ended with my handing him Frere's razor and inviting him to make use of it—to do to himself what he'd long since done to his verse, and what, for all the good I am, he'd done to me . . .'

Ralph was trembling as he spoke. With a hand covering his face he turned away, and we sat in silence together for a long time.

When he had recovered a little I tried to talk to him, but he took no comfort from my efforts to understand. Exhausted and confused as I was I had little to give.

It was after two in the morning when I got up to leave. Ralph offered to drive me to The Pightle, but he was in no state for that. In no state either—it was evident from his earnest suggestion that I sleep at the Hall—to be left alone that night. He argued that my staying overnight would make things simpler in the morning—we could learn together how Edward was, and drive in together to pick up Laura from the hospital. I dreaded returning to the emptiness of The Pightle, but it was the expression on his face that finally persuaded me to stay.

He showed me up to a room overlooking the park and the dark lake. The moon was high and clear. Calls of wildfowl echoed across the water. On the wall next to the window was a framed linen sampler, but instead of the usual biblical text or homiletic counsel for moral improvement, within its carefully hand-stitched garland of flowers were the words:

ARTIS AURI ARCANUM
ET MARI ET FEMINA CONSTITIT

But if the secret of the Art of Gold consisted in the male and the female, it seemed that we had all failed to find it.

Ralph saw me pondering its rubric. 'It's very old,' he said. 'The tradition is that it was stitched for Sir Humphrey by Janet Dyball in 1645, the year he attained to the Stone. Louisa had it reframed and placed here. This was her room once.'

Her father has come to her room. It is the first time he has been here almost since she was a child, and he is pale, grim-lipped. He is calamitously old, and so distraught behind the effort of composure that it seems impossible that he knows nothing of what has befallen her.

'Louisa,' he begins, 'I thought it best that I visit you here because . . .'

But it would appear that he has forgotten his reasons, for he falters there. He can scarcely bring himself to look at her, yet what he has glimpsed from the corner of his narrowed eyes fills him with still greater trepidation. She is so pale, so utterly wan that he might believe her own spirit quite as broken now as his. Like a frail monument she stands absolutely still, and waits.

He clears his throat and says, 'I wonder if I might sit down,' then crosses to a chair. 'Will you too not be seated, my dear?'

She seeks to soften the distracted shaking of her head with a smile, then looks away out of the window. She had noticed what she had failed earlier to observe: that the book in his hand is a printed and bound copy of *An Open Invitation to the Chymical*

Wedding, and she has no appetite for this unsought conversation. She has no appetite for anything.

'I have completed my reading of your book.' He too contrives a smile, and glances up at her. Her face is strangely empty; nothing for which he has prepared himself is to be found there—neither anxiety nor joyful expectation. With a deepening of the foreboding at his chest he wonders whether it is possible that she who knows so much has already seen the secret at his heart, and steels herself against it; but he shies from the thought. 'My dear, you have worked so hard . . . And your book . . . It is a great marvel.' Again he looks up and sees only the palest shadow of a smile about her lips—a smile which, in one of a more worldly disposition, might seem almost sardonic and dismissive. It troubles him, for she is as little given to the sophistries of self-deprecation as she is to braggadocio and there is something wrong here. Something beyond the equivocations lodged in his own throat.

He takes his spectacle-case from his pocket, and applies the lenses carefully to his face, a little fussily. He opens the book with its handsome green and gold binding, and presses his palm to the title-page. 'And the inscription,' he says, ' . . . I was most deeply touched.'

'It *is* your property.'

'And never has a father been given such a gift.' Her response had been less warm than he anticipated but, encouraged that she has spoken at last, he launches on an enthusiastic review of her achievement. There is much he can commend with heartfelt admiration before he brings himself to say what he must finally say; and he devotes himself with such vigour to his strategy that he remains unaware how little attention his words receive.

She is looking out of the window where the clouds are bustled by a gale across the park and the light appears to shift at every buffeting. Why, she wonders, must he talk at her so? Why can he not, as Tom Horrocks had done, simply rise from his chair and gather her silently in his arms? But then she remembers: Tom, dear Tom, had known. He had known that there were no words for such great grief. In holding her so, he had given her all that he had to give—some portion of his strength—before admitting her to Edwin's presence. And her father knows none of this; must never know it; as he does not know that she is no longer really present in this room.

For days now she has been present nowhere. She has become

strangely insubstantial, making the same limited motions day
by day, coherent and outwardly unchanged, yet touching nothing and untouched. She has become mere appearance, like some
ghostly revenant so harmless and regular in its manifestations
that life must seem incomplete without it. Tilly has noticed, of
course, and is concerned; but that there should be some link
between her mistress's distraction and the disappearance of the
parson is a contingency so remote that her imagination will not
stretch to it. And her father, apparently, has noticed nothing.

She is close to presence in one moment only, and that now
past. Time has already been at work upon it. Each day it grows
a little harder to recall what was said, and how it was said, the
delicate inflexions of their silences. She remembers the hangings
in that upper room at Tom Horrocks's house, and the faint smell
of ether as she passed up the stair. She remembers how the room
itself became an island, a world unto itself, where the air floated
strangely, and the noises from the market-place outside were so
alien that they scarcely impinged at all. Yet she remembers them
now—the flower-seller's cry, the rumble of the dray, the church-
bell quartering the hours. Why should it be so much easier to
hold these trivial things clear than to recall the words that must
stand between her and emptiness for the rest of her days?

'You must try to forget all this now,' Tom had said afterwards.
'Your secret is safe with me and we must bury it together. The
Bishop assures me that a place will be found for Edwin . . . but
it must not be here, not in this county even. You must understand and accept that. And time *will* pass. You must engage your
mind with other things, for nothing—absolutely nothing—can
repair what has been done, and you will only make your heart
sore by a prolongation of useless grief. You *will* forget, Louisa,
and you *must* forget.'

'I will forget nothing,' she had answered.

Never was declaration more passionately felt; yet already her
mind has begun to blur. It is a faithless friend. Only the feelings
remain unadulterate: they can be summoned instantly, as now
when she feels her heart sway again, a cloud in wind, a reflection
in the lake, whatever insubstantial thing it is that can seem to
hold everything and be entirely empty.

Her father is speaking still, but clumsily. He is absent from
his words as she is absent from their hearing. He is trying to say
something that he finds very difficult to say, as though there is
either too little or too much energy of truth behind it. 'My dear,

my dear,'—she hears the dolorous appeal in his voice—'surely
you must have seen it for yourself?'

What should she have seen? These eyes have seen too much.
But they must try to see him now, to return themselves to this
moment which appears to have, for him, great import. The colour has risen among the shattered blood-vessels at his cheeks.
He has removed his spectacles and his eyes are restless. Something has greatly agitated his mind, and she must try to listen.

Eventually it becomes clear: he is telling her that she has
written so lucidly of the inmost secrets of the Art that her book—
which has, he swears, the radiant beauty of a sacrament—must
pose a danger to the very life it celebrates. She has done the
work too well. She has been too generous in her appraisal of
human nature. If all were of the same purity of heart as she then
they would find only a mirror of their own potential in these
pages; but sadly such was not the case. He is trying to suggest
that though her understanding of the mystery is complete, she
has little understanding of the world. It will corrupt and defile
what she has offered it. It will seek to use the power invested in
her work for its own cruel ends, for she has dared too much. He
is saying that he greatly fears the world must never have it . . .

What does she care about the world? What does she care now
whether it defile itself or no. She knows only that in the moment
when her own life truly began it was already over. As to the
book itself—she has forgotten it. It is the excrescence of her
mind, no more than that. Why then should he trouble over it?
Better that the paper had stayed rags for some poor wretch to
warm himself against the wind.

Her father is looking hopelessly up at her. He expects her to
weep. She can see that, and he cannot know that all her tears
are shed. She is dry and brittle as a stick. And he is suddenly
transparent to her. Every weakness sapping at his life is evident.
She sees now what he is doing; she knows why he is doing it;
she can rifle his mind like an unlocked casket for it is as open
to her; and nothing she finds there really matters. It might leave
her quite untouched were it not that she loves this sad old man
who sits before her, waiting for her word, and dreading it.

'I feared that must be so,' she lies.

Relief, visible relief, enlarges him. 'The fault is mine . . .
You asked that I should read your work before committing it to
print. I was remiss . . . preoccupied . . . selfishly preoccupied.'

Already she regrets the lie. It was no more than complicity

with the death already at work inside him . . . with the one inside herself. Then she sees how the lie might be redeemed.

She speaks across his abject sentences. 'I feared that what I sought to share was impermissible. I feared that the world must wrong it.'

He nods, caught now between relief and a suddenly more bitter knowledge of his own deceit. 'I felt sure,' he tries to comfort himself uncertainly, 'I felt sure from your face as I entered that you must already have seen it.'

'I sought only to be true.'

'I know, my dear, I know.'

But this is not all he knows, and her truth impugns his falsity. Only further speech might bury it more deeply. 'I should have seen earlier that the duplicities of the Art are not your element, for you were never the equivocator. Truth, plain truth, has always been the very air you breathe, and to withhold it when it might be spoken . . . it is not of your nature.' He is speaking, and breathing, too quickly. One of his eyelids flutters like a moth.

And almost she might smile at his words, for what an innocent he is! Soon, when the first flush of his shame has passed, he will come to believe his own lies.

And yet there is a paradoxical truth in what he says. The meaning of her book was bound up with her love for Edwin: apprised of either, the world would demean and revile them both, for was that not always the way when it felt its own foundations tremble? He was speaking truer than he knew.

A great sigh shudders through his frame. 'My dear . . . what is to be done?'

She stands in thought for a long time, for his question resounds throughout the remainder of her days. How are they to be borne? What indeed is to be done?

It seems that, after all, the last of tears is not shed. These remain. She will hold them at her eyes between herself and the world which blurs around her now. She stares out of the window: its lozenged panes, the park, the wind-fretted span of the lake, the scudding clouds—all blur, as though relinquishing the vain and painful effort to sustain their form. Yearning for the unity whence they sprang, they are dissolving in it—and yet, after all the dreams, the visions and the revelations, the promises passed from flesh to flesh, what a sad *unio mystica* is this! All things blurring from shade to shade of grey, sadder than widows' weeds, less palpable; and nowhere in this grey dissolving world to stand . . .

Faintly, as from a great distance away, her father is murmuring. 'I cannot see . . .' he sighs, 'I cannot see what is now to be done . . .'

She draws breath, turns her head, holding the locket at her throat, and takes in the pathos of his downcast frown. He knows himself observed, and cannot raise his eyes.

Then it comes to her. She sees how the secret which embraces the secret weds, like subtle chemistry, with her father's secret need.

Quietly, amazed how calm her voice, she says, 'This at least is not irrevocable.' She gazes on him but his eyes have closed. 'You must not concern yourself unduly. I hear you and I understand.' Her voice gathers strength as a kind of certainty returns. 'I understand that there are things at once so marvellous and dreadful that they must never take a fixed material form.'

She is thinking—but she does not say—that such things must remain for ever alive and for ever invisible, an inward secret between the spirit and the soul; that their otherwise destructive fire must burn quietly there like a Pentecostal flame which, in its time, might bring the precious gift of tongues.

She raises her head, and the power accruing to her now demands his closer attention. 'I have erred,' she confesses. 'I have greatly erred. I have wished to fix that which of its very nature must remain for ever volatile. In that I was wrong. And perhaps in only that.' She sighs then, holding his eyes as he raises them. At last she is present. 'I see now what must be done.'

He looks up at her, filled with new doubt.

'We must recall the book,' she says; but even as the words are uttered she is aware of how much of herself that book contains, and how wrong she had been to dismiss it with such frigid indifference. Like stragglers from a demoralized and scattered host, the first of her feelings begin to return, and the news they bring is pain. Even as she tries to focus on what has now become the problem of her book, she sees that to sever herself from it will be like sundering her own life.

But her life is already sundered. It was sundered in the moment when Edwin severed the threads of his flesh. It was sundered again, irreparably, with the realization that he intended to withdraw from her, never to return. All that remained from this

passionate winter was her book; and now, it seemed, she was
required also to let go of that.

Then, with a further access of liberating clarity, she remembers what Edwin had tried to say as they sat together in that
upper room while the sounds of the world chimed around them.

'I have sought,' he had murmured quietly, 'to make a sacrifice
on behalf of all men. And now that the sacrifice is made, none
other need make it.'

She remembers how, for an instant, her heart had raged against
him then—for he was wrong, wrong to the very depths of the
despair on which he had entered. In silence she had raged, but
for an instant only. She had held his eyes, beheld the old, familiar diffidence there—but no despair. Not now. Already he
was something other; something which to her eyes—whatever
their grief, their yearning for the now eternally impossible—was
utterly beautiful. There was a softness to his skin, a tenderness
in that shaking hand, and in the eyes a gentleness which—
whatever they had seen—saw clear. For that brief moment he
might, like an emblem from an old text, have been winged and
crowned, and rising as the harvest of his wound.

But there were no wings, no crown. The room, like the sounds
outside, was commonplace; and he was neither priest to the
God, nor priest to the Goddess either: he was simply the fallible
man she loved and, in that, priest perhaps to the great sea which
lies between us all.

She turns to take in her father's troubled gaze.

'We must recall the book,' she says, 'and we shall burn it.'

Her voice is absolute, practical; and he is awed and shamed
by this sudden enthusiasm for what had been his own intolerable
desire. Shocked, he recalls how often he had sat in the library
willing the whole world to flame as he himself was in flame. He
knows the desire, and understands it. He knows it a lust for
destruction, and fears to see it unfettered now in her. Was this
to be the end of all his labours then—to see the star-fire at his
daughter's soul turn smoke and ash?

'No.' In a rage born of insupportable remorse the word leaps
to his throat. 'No, that must never be.'

She watches as his face slowly dissolves before her. He is all
tears, the breath breaking from him, and with it—however in-
coherently, however difficult its stammering—the admission of
his falsity, his bitter truth. Where she has succeeded, he is striving to say, he himself has failed . . . He has failed from the

dismal ignobility of spirit which lacked the courage to endure. His soul was craven, his will abused. 'And if,' he confesses, quaking, 'I have sought to deny your work it is because I cannot bear the light it casts upon the irredeemable failure of my own.'

She is standing beside him now. She takes the sobbing head into her embrace and presses his brow against her. 'Now all that you have said today is true,' she whispers softly, 'and we are free of it.' But he weeps on as though the quiet deluge of his grief might quench the fire in which she means to burn her book.

'Everything is changing now,' she says, 'and I think the time has come when we must both be brave. We have failed . . . we have both failed, and there is nothing that can mitigate the pain of that. But we are changed by it . . . already we become other than we were. And if we act aright, then a new thing may arise from our failure—a spirit beyond our conception, larger than we are, less confined by the personal—one which may endure, invisibly, and prevail long after our own small, personal failures are forgot. Have we not always known that it is in the realm of the invisible where the true powers work? I think we must consign our failure to their care.'

Her father does not answer her; she is not even certain that he hears her words; but her own thoughts are already elsewhere. She is remembering the Collect for Easter Eve—those words which had been read in a voice other than Edwin's, and with no great feeling; but she understands now why, even through the baffle of her numbed condition, as she had sat in the church from which the man she loved would be for ever absent, those words had stirred a premonitory tremor in her heart: 'Oh God, who through thy Son, who is called the cornerstone, hast brought the fire of light to the faithful, make holy for our future use this new fire struck from the firestone.'

Our future use. For the first time since her world had ended—if vaguely still, and with a trembling spirit—she begins to conceive of futures. She had thought herself quite drowned in tears; though their agony had been a mortal agony, the body had refused to die; and yet a death of sorts, a death by water, had been undergone. She knew it, if none around her knew it. She reflects upon the words from the Easter Collect, and knows also that what is now required of her is a fiery passage back into the feeling world. And what is her book if it is not her Stone—a stone of fire, her shining flint, her firestone?

She takes her father's face between her hands and lifts his

gaze to hers. 'It is now my own earnest desire that we shall burn the book,' she says. 'There, at the Decoy Lodge, where all the hopes and fears invested in our work were first conceived, we shall make a burning-ground together.'

Her father looks up at her, shaking his old head, unable to understand. 'But the loss . . . It is too high a price . . .'

'No loss,' she says. 'We only free it so.' She is smiling down on him, a smile in which immensities of sadness are comprehended now. 'That *is* the price,' she adds; and then her expression changes. Her face may be no more than a place indifferently found by a ray admitted through the lozenged window, but it brightens with reflected light as she speaks—in a whisper so slight and wistful that the words escape his hearing—one final consoling thought: 'People have burned for less.'

Ralph woke me shortly before one in the afternoon of a calm Sunday. Even before he drew the cream curtains I saw sunlight streaming through them and felt the June heat, but the sense of change was so profound there might have been a fall of snow in the night.

My first thought was that we must ring the hospital. Ralph had already rung and, having failed to secure more than a formal assurance that Edward was doing as well as could be expected, he had called the home-number of a friend who was a consultant there. The friend had made enquiries and reported back that Edward was in reasonable shape physically but giving the nurses a hard time with his bad temper. 'Apparently,' Ralph said, 'he's been insisting that he's earned the right to be dead and deserves it. My friend suggested that severe heart-attacks can sometimes cause personality changes, but'—Ralph tried to smile—'it rather sounds as though Edward is very much the same.'

'There haven't been any more attacks?'

'No, thank God.'

'And Laura?'

'She woke very confused, but they're satisfied with her progress and she'll be discharged later today. Do try to relax—they're both in good hands. I would have brought you the news sooner but I thought you should sleep . . . Also I was held up by an unexpected caller. Neville Sallis came by after Matins at Thrandeston. He's only just left. Apparently his phone was ringing this morning with complaints that Munding Rectory had been used for rites of black magic.'

'What?'

'I believe the term "witchcraft orgies" was used—and, if I know this area—I'm afraid that's the story that will stick. As you can imagine, poor Neville was quite put out, and he didn't find my explanations entirely satisfactory. It seems he already knew of your interest in Frere, and that caught me off guard a little . . . Still, I think I smoothed his feathers. He's had rather a bad weekend of it . . . hasn't been sleeping well after some meeting he went to.' Ralph took in my dishevelled features, shaking his head. 'You must be hungry. Why don't you get yourself sorted out—we'll snatch a bite to eat, and then we'll drive in for visiting-hour this afternoon?'

'How are you feeling?'

'I didn't sleep too well either . . . but what matters is Edward. I'm just enormously relieved that he's still with us.' He sighed, went to the door, and turned there. 'Alex, about last night . . .'

'It was a confidence,' I said. 'I'm grateful for it.'

Ralph nodded, smiling weakly, then left me alone.

The phone rang while we were eating. Ralph took the call in his study and came back with a distraught face. 'It was Laura . . .' He raised a hand to still my evident alarm. 'She's been with Edward. Apparently he's dreadfully depressed. He doesn't want visitors. He won't see us, Alex . . .' I watched him sit down and push away the plate from which he'd eaten very little. 'For my own part, I can understand it . . . but Laura asked me to convey the message to you. He doesn't want to see either of us . . .'

I had not been prepared for this. Nervous as I was of the meeting, I'd been searching for ways to find touch with Edward again, to prepare the ground so that—if we were given the glimmer of a chance—something new might grow from the ruins. I didn't know how I'd do it, but I knew that I had to try; and to be banished this way made everything feel hopeless. Only the news that his heart had suffered another attack could have come harder.

Ralph took in my distress. 'It's probably for the best,' he murmured. 'God knows, neither of us wants to put him under further strain . . .'

'How was Laura?'

'Very tense . . . but then we've never been at ease with one another. She says she's over the worst of the shock.'

'And she thinks this is the right thing?'

'She was rather insistent on it. In the end I felt I had to trust her judgment. She's planning to stay close to him until he's discharged. There's a small hotel close to the hospital . . .'

'But that means a lot of time on her own.'

'I know. But it seems to be what she wants. She can't face being alone in the Lodge, and she declined my invitation to stay here. Edward will see no one else and she feels the need to be as close to him as she can. Also I rather gathered she has to sort out her own feelings . . .'

'She'll need things—money, clothes . . .'

'We talked about that. She also needs their car to pick them up. As far as she knows it's still parked in the village.'

'It's outside the church,' I said. 'I could drive it in.'

'She'll be waiting for you,' Ralph smiled. 'Outside the hospital, at five.'

She was pale, a wan figure in the sunlight, scanning the traffic. Relieved that the appointment had been kept, she asked, tensely, if she might drive, and did so hurriedly, anxious only to get back to the Lodge, pick up the things she needed, and return. When I asked about Edward she added little to what I already knew—perhaps because, like myself, she hardly dared to believe that he was alive at all, and was afraid that words might provoke a capricious fate. She dismissed my concern for her own condition, and when I questioned the wisdom of staying alone in a hotel, her mind was firm: Edward needed her; she must be close by, and with him for as much of the time as possible; for the rest, she preferred to be alone. For a time it was like talking to a stranger. And then—as we drove under sun-dazzled arcades of trees in full leaf—we did not speak at all.

Instead of taking the turn to the Lodge she drove on through Munding and pulled up outside The Pightle. Only when her diffident smile expressed the wish to go to the Lodge alone did I recognize how far my own tension had been responsible for the atmosphere in the car.

'Listen,' she said, 'I don't know when I'll get to see your friend—the one from last night . . .'

'Bob. Bob Crossley.'

'But will you thank him for me? . . . I was in no state last night . . .'

'Of course. But I'm sure he understands.'

'And you, Alex. Without you . . .' She held my eyes a moment, then looked down where her hands gripped the wheel.

'Without me it would never have happened.'

She heard the self-recrimination in my voice and glanced back up at me, shaking her head. 'You're not to blame yourself. It can't help.'

'It's hard not to.'

'I know, but . . .' She faltered there and looked up in appeal. 'Alex, I don't think I can talk about it yet. I need time.'

I saw then that what I had taken for an almost cold distancing was the only way she had found to contain emotions that might overwhelm her. I wanted to hold her, simply, just for a few moments; but there was an inhibition in the air between us, like that of former lovers re-met, who remember the intimacy yet are no longer able to touch one another with the old freedom. So I said quietly, 'I understand.' And then, sighing, 'When you get back to Edward . . . will you give him my love?'

She nodded, tried to smile; and was on the edge of tears. 'I don't know if he'll hear it . . . It's as if he still thinks of himself as dead . . . is almost nostalgic for it. It's why I have to . . .'

'You don't have to explain.'

But once having begun to speak, the words would not be stopped. 'Look, I know you must be feeling terrible . . . and I'm no help right now, but . . . I'm trying to hold it together—all of it. And it scares me even to think this way with Edward lying hooked up to that machine, but . . . I can't believe that what we did was wrong . . . even after what's happened. Somehow we have to try to see it whole. I think Edward needs us to do that. I think he needs it more than ever now. Do you understand?'

I nodded uncertainly, wanting to comfort her with agreement; but if things were to be seen whole there was a darker side to acknowledge too. I said, 'I can only speak for myself, Laura, and I think I've been wrong . . . Wrong in the way you said, because I was dreaming, but still wrong. Morally wrong.'

She shook her head. 'It was necessary—all of it. I'm not talking about morality—I'm not even sure what that means. All I have is my feelings and I have to trust them. I'm talking about things coming to completion . . . of making room for everything that belongs, however confusing . . . And I only began to see it because of what we did . . . because you were there.'

I tried to hold the impassioned plea in her gaze, and again

found that I couldn't lie. 'Laura, I wasn't even with you there. Not really. The whole thing scared me half to death . . . I couldn't control it, and so I was pulling away. That's why I behaved the way I did afterwards, and there was nothing right about that.'

After a moment I glanced up to see the effect of my words, and found that she was smiling. It was a sad smile, affectionate and without reproach. A woman's smile, responsive to the truth, and realistic in its adaptations.

'You didn't pull away last night,' she said. 'When I'd lost touch . . . was feeling scared . . . you decided to see it through, didn't you?'

'And look what happened.'

'I know. But you weren't to blame for that. Edward had got it wrong. What he'd found was real and terrible, but it wasn't the whole truth. He knew the facts but he got the feeling wrong, so none of it made sense to him. All he could see was pain and injury and failure . . . but there was love there, Alex, and courage. There was a sense of deliverance through all the pain. It doesn't deny what we were looking for, it confirms it.'

I very much wanted to believe her, but there was only one thing of which I was sure: that she herself had changed. Yes, she was pale and distraught still; the anxiety in her face was accented by the yellowish bruise at her eye; and what she was saying was not so very different from things I'd heard her say before. But the manner of the saying was different, and the quality of her conviction. Where a stranger might have heard only a scared woman seeking to rationalize disaster, I was awed by her sober willingness to persevere when everything appeared to have gone terribly wrong. I saw why she had been reluctant to speak, and why she had felt compelled to do so, for if Laura had always known the value of experience, she now knew more of its price. She spoke—and I heard her speaking—from its full authority.

'Do you understand?' she asked quietly.

I understood for her. For myself, excluded from her experience, there was only one truthful answer. 'Laura, I just don't know.'

I heard the intake of her breath, saw the fingertips trembling where the palms of her hands rested on the wheel. After a moment she said, 'So what are your feelings now?'

'Shame. Grief. Anxiety.' The words were out without thought.

'I'm ashamed of the callow side of myself that's been so pre-occupied with its own hurt it doesn't know how to relate any more. I'm ashamed of the way I behaved with you, of what I've done to Edward, and that I couldn't be truer with either of you. I'm filled with grief and anxiety for him . . . He won't see me now and, God knows, I can't blame him . . . but it feels as though he were my father and he'd died before I found a way to say I loved him. It feels as though I only ever learn anything about myself through the hurt I do others. And as long as things stay that way I'm a million miles away from knowing how to live . . .'

There was silence in the car. Outside I heard the calm, throaty call of a wood-pigeon among the chestnuts. Through the window I saw the sunlight warm on The Pightle's thatch, the roses climbing against white walls: a small enclosure; elfin space; briefly, magically mine; and not mine at all.

'And those feelings hurt?' she said quietly.

'Yes.'

'So what are you doing with the hurt?' And, when I didn't answer, 'Holding it,' she suggested. 'Being true to it. Letting it change you.'

I glanced briefly across at her, and saw the smile again.

'Then it *was* right,' she said. 'Thank you.'

'For what?'

'For the confirmation.'

Bewildered, I held her gaze a moment longer, then looked away. 'It feels as though all I've done is add my troubles to the ones you're already carrying.'

Her hand reached for mine and rested there. 'Does it really feel that way?'

I looked at her again and saw how much of the nervous tension had passed from her. Her question calmly insisted on the real, and there was encouragement, a candid affection, in her smile. It brought a wan smile to my own face as I shook my head in answer.

'I think you've stopped dreaming,' she said. 'I think we can be friends now. Loving friends.' She leaned across from her seat to kiss me lightly on the cheek. I held her for a time, saying nothing, feeling the warmth of her, the brief simplicity of our being together there.

A few moments later I was out of the car and she was gone.

* * *

I was left waiting, each hour fraught with anxiety until, on the following Tuesday, I learned with a relief as great as if I too had been reprieved from a capital sentence, that Edward's condition was no longer considered critical. Relief came as exhaustion as much as thanksgiving; and as the knowledge, for the first time fully accepted, of how completely we are at one another's mercy.

When I rang Laura at her hotel I gathered that there had been no great improvement in Edward's emotional state. For much of the time he was still remote in depression, and otherwise crotchety and ill-tempered, as though taking exception to his own recovery. Any certainty that Laura had felt in the car was gone from her voice, and when I tried to encourage her I met only a weary gratitude for my care and an insistence that she was best alone. She described her own condition as thoughtful, and would say little more. My own first relief became worry again.

With the intention of prodding me from gloom, Bob invited me to a meal. He too had been thoughtful, for by now all the gossip around Munding had reached him. He'd heard George Bales's account of what he'd seen on the lawn of the Decoy Lodge, but—possibly because he'd thought it inevitable all along—he made no heavy weather over it. The other rumours bothered him more, and not because he believed them but because he was having a hard time conceiving what possible truth they might distort. With the food eaten and some of his homebrew inside us, Bob released his questions now.

As honestly and completely as I could, I tried to answer. I told him about my dream and how its images had undermined my own first scepticism about alchemy. I shared what I had learnt from Edward about the contemporary relevance of alchemical symbols to the confusing processes of personal evolution. I told him about Louisa Agnew and her father, and how Edward had been convinced that their lost work might have crucial light to shed on the crisis of our own time.

With greater patience than I might earlier have expected, Bob listened. His dismay after the meeting in the Black Boys Hotel had left him receptive to any evidently serious effort to think about the intolerable questions it raised; but he was a practical man, unimpressed by symbolic dimensions when the brutal facts stared him in the face. 'That's all very well,' he said eventually, 'but at the end of the day you won't change anything till you've changed the social structures that govern the way people think.'

'And who's going to do that, Bob?' I asked. 'What sort of people are going to do that? And is it just a question of thinking? What about imagination? What about feeling?'

By a vigorous statement of his own position Bob required me to refine my own, and it came hard. Like that of the alchemists before me, such conviction as I had was grounded more in experience than reason. It had been nourished by dreams, which are elusive and ambiguous at best, and not the sort of testimony that carries public weight these days. I felt a little as women must sometimes feel trying to hold their ground against male logic—that the terms of the debate were not inclusive enough, and that there were values being discounted and ignored. Delicate values, ones that found it hard to speak their word. There were moments when I might have lost heart except that I felt to be arguing as much for Edward's sake as for my own.

The conversation drifted back and forth from the intractable issues of the age to more immediate examination of our personal experience—education, social conditioning, the tensions of marriage, the degree to which we took refuge from uncertainty in fixed systems of thought. Time and again we got stuck until one or other of us made some admission that had the force of personal revelation behind it, and we were off once more, conceding here, asserting there, becoming firmer and deeper friends. It was contest not compromise, and it was more than words. I came away late at night, convinced that it must be possible—if there was time—to build new bridges between an affirmation of the spirit and a sane, social pragmatism increasingly aware of its own unconscious roots. I was aware too that all opposition would not be as tolerant and congenial as Bob's, and that an immense faith was required in the power of the small.

The next day I went across to the Hall to clear up the papers I'd left and found Ralph in the library. He was re-reading Edward's early verse, remembering the occasions from which various poems had sprung, and he was able to cast light on some of their surrealist obscurities. 'He was always slippery,' he commented in a kind of sardonic resignation, '. . . slipped through your hands like water. If he's angry now it's probably nothing at all to do with you and me, you know . . . simply frustration that he's failed to pull off a final spectacular vanishing act.' He took a silver box from his pocket, placed a pinch of snuff in the cruck of his thumb and sniffed it. When I remarked on the many images drawn from fire in Edward's verse he said, 'That's his infernal angel at work. I used to think it rejoiced to see him burn. In fact, I've often wondered whether that wasn't his real attraction to Louisa—that her work went up in smoke . . . The fascination of the flame.'

'Do you know why he abandoned verse?'

'No,' Ralph sighed, 'not really. I'd already lost touch with him by then. We no longer had friends in common. I simply waited for the next volume to appear and it never did. I tried to ask him when he turned up here at Easterness.' He snorted, smiled. 'Slipped away again. Wouldn't say.'

'He told me once that his sanity was menaced. He took cover behind Rimbaud but the feeling was real.'

Ralph nodded but said nothing.

'He also said that poetry wasn't enough.'

'Then we must believe him, I suppose. He tested other things to the point of destruction. Whatever it was that stopped him writing, it must have been terrible. I suspect there's a death in there somewhere—symbolically for him, and perhaps literally for someone else. But I don't know. Edward's secret is known only to him.' Ralph smiled mournfully. 'Not a coward's secrets though. Not like mine.' He tapped his fingers on the arm of his chair, then glanced up at me again. 'Shall I tell you a truly sad thing? When he first came here during the winter, he was trying to write again—verse, I mean. Didn't tell me about it, of course. I wouldn't even know but I went poking about his papers here one evening . . . Disgraceful, I admit. But it was a way of . . . feeling closer. I came across a sheet of paper so angrily obliterated that only a sentimental old fool like me would recognize that the scorings hid a verse; and that, if one held it against the light, the words were just legible.'

'Do you remember them?'

'Of course. I have them by heart. But I don't think he'd want me to share them with you. Do you?'

'I suppose not.'

'I can tell you they weren't very good. I quite see why he was impatient with them. But I was rather touched . . . What mattered to me was that he was still trying . . . after all these years. And what he seemed to be trying for was a new simplicity. He failed and—to my eternal shame—that failure was one of the things I threw in his face the other night.' Ralph winced from the memory, and there was a long silence before he said, 'I've wondered, you know, whether this wasn't behind his frustration during the past weeks . . . Not just the difficulty of the work on my family's papers or the state of his unsatisfactory relationships, but his failure to recover the gift that you still have.'

'I haven't been able to write for ages.'

'But you will. And Edward knows that. He must have found it hard to . . . what? Forgive you for it? No, not that. He's not envious that way. But it must have sharpened the sense of his own sterility. There was a moment once—he was talking to me about Laura—trying to persuade me of her finer points—when he said that if he could still do with words what she was trying to do with clay, then everything else could go out the window.'

'Even though poetry isn't enough?'

'My dear man,' Ralph gave me his wry, canted smile, 'when Edward ceases to contradict himself—to be a kind of walking oxymoron—then we'll know he's breathed his last. And the world will be a poorer place.'

On the Thursday morning a letter arrived at The Pightle. I recognized Jess's handwriting on the envelope.

Dear Alex,

Thanks for ringing at the weekend. I know it can't have been easy for you, and I'm sorry it went wrong—but there was more than one reason for that, which is why I'm writing now.

I wonder if you've forgotten that it's Marcus's birthday on the 23rd? He was too proud to remind you, and I know it upset him that you didn't think of it when he asked when you were coming back. We have to decide what to do about it now.

Martin and I would like you to come if that's what you want, and so would Lily of course. But I can't promise it will be easy with Marcus. I'm pretty sure he'll punish you as he's punishing us, and perhaps we all deserve it. On the other hand, I don't know—he grows more like you every day so I suppose he could surprise us all. But it's up to you. If you can let us know one way or the other it would help.

I've wondered about whether I should respond here to your

*mention of divorce. You're right, of course—it's the best thing
now, and I'm grateful to you for bringing it up. But I think we
need to talk about what it means for Marcus and Lily, and
how we can carry them through it in the right way. I don't
think we can do that by letter, and I don't think we should let
it go by default. Will you make time for that? It matters very
much.*

*I promised not to make demands and I seem to be making
them, but I think you'll see that they're not just for me. Also
I've just read through this and it sounds colder than I mean.
I hate this awkwardness, the loss of the old fluency between
us. I wonder if, one day, we might be the good friends we
should always have been?*

                                                    Jess.

*P.S. Thinking about it, I'm glad you've chucked in the job.
You were always a caged beast there, and I used to feel guilty
about it . . . though how you plan to survive . . .*

Well, none of my business now.

                                                    Love,
                                                    J.

I went for a long walk that day, back across the water-meadows
and into the trees, and saw that the season of the Green Man
was over now.

Yes, I'd forgotten my son's birthday; yes, I hated myself for
it; and, yes, I knew I would go. It might be hard for Marcus to
cope with a father turning up like a vagabond with gifts, but it
would be much harder if I abdicated in action from everything
I'd tried to tell him on the phone.

The arrival of the letter was like a bell ringing 'time,' for I
knew that once I left Munding I would not come back. Return
was not impossible—Clive had no immediate need of his cottage; but The Pightle had been intended only as a temporary
refuge; and everything was changing now.

I had changed. Somewhere among these glades I'd spied on
an old man and a naked girl. Briefly I'd become the lover of the
girl, and now she was my friend. I had made Edward my friend
and I'd betrayed that friendship—doing the wrong thing in the
right way, or the right one in the wrong way—I didn't know
which. I lacked Laura's clarity there. But I had changed, and I
couldn't just cut and run this time. I couldn't blame Edward for

not wanting to see me; I couldn't bear the thought of leaving without seeing him; and I would soon have to go. If the sight of my face was still unacceptable to him, some other way must be found of acknowledging both the injury I'd done him, and the great debt I owed.

I could write to him, I supposed, as I must now write to Jess, and in neither case would it be easy to convey my sense that the man who had come to Munding and the man who was leaving were not the same. Jess knew me so well that any new performance would have to be spectacular to impress her jaded eye. She knew also that words are cheap coin. Yet, if nothing else came of all of this, there ought to be some way to answer her hope that, one day—across that most difficult of divides, a misalliance—we might recreate the friendship I too missed.

First we must talk about divorce. It was the old alchemical procedure—*solve et coagula*. The elements must be resolved into their separate identities before they could meet each other in the right way; and I knew something now of the problems posed by that simple formula. Still, for Jess and me, divorce might hold the possibility of renewal: but for the children . . .

Marcus was seven years old, Lily four. They were infants, novices, from whom—however carefully we approached them—the doves of innocence were about to fly. Not for the first time I wondered whether Jess and I had come together in marriage only so that these two particular children might be born and suffer at our particular hands their first initiation into pain. Yet everything I'd learned—everything I'd dreamed—insisted on a larger view.

I walked through the woods thinking about marriage—about the way we settle for an intimate conspiracy of two against the world, or a sad compromise of disappointed hopes, when—with a little patience, a little more self-knowledge—we might discover mystery made flesh. This was the directive of my first big dream. It pointed inwards and outwards at once. Somehow the ring must be held between our conscious choices and the dark imperatives of dream, for they would settle for no less. I wondered whether Jess and Martin had discovered this for themselves, were holding on to it throughout the difficulties they faced. But that—in Jess's tactful phrase—was not my business. For me, for now, and probably for some time to come, the chymical wedding must remain an inward process; and one that

my children would severely test before I could look for fresh
connections with the world.

A thought occurred which would have been impossible when
I first walked in these woods: that the growth of self-knowledge
might bring an increase of freedom, but the more one had of
both, the less one had, it seemed. Smoking, I leaned against the
silky green trunk of a beech, and saw that someone had carved
two sets of initials there a long time ago. A lover making this
tree his book. Unmarried and childless. Still inside the dream.
Then an aircraft roared across the roof of the wood, and I was
startled to fury, shouting what the trees could not shout, that I
hated the bloody weapons, I loathed and abominated them; but
the plane was already far away and, even more than distance,
the noise of his own engines deafened the pilot to my shout. So,
for a time, there was nothing this silly sod below could do but
quake.

Eventually the walk brought me through the glades towards
the Decoy Lodge. I hesitated, uncertain whether to go down. It
felt like indulgence—a wallowing in nostalgia—to invite the
feelings that would meet me there; but not to meet them would
be an attempt to close accounts too soon.

The Lodge was locked and oddly bereft of life—no washing
on the line, the old car absent from the yard, and—when I peered
through a lancet-window—things tidied away inside. It might
have been waiting for new tenants. I walked round to the lawn,
over the innocent grass where Laura and I had made love, and
looked around me. No ghosts, no presences. Not even—I winced
wryly at the thought—the gamekeeper watching among the trees,
a shotgun under his arm, wide-eyed. Whatever else, we had
provided hours of conversation in the Feathers! One day, I hoped,
Edward might be able to laugh over all of this.

I went down to the jetty and was surprised to find the skiff
tied there. Edward must have rowed back from the Hall after
the confrontation with Ralph, brooding across the dark lake with
Tom Horrocks's case-book in his pocket, and Frere's razor. Had
he really meant to come looking for me, I wondered, or had my
unexpected presence in the Lodge tipped him over into that
darkness? Unless we met again and found a way to talk, I would
never know.

I stepped down into the skiff and sat in the stern, staring out
across the lake. The two swans—Humphrey and Janet—glided
on their own reflections, preening themselves, dripping their

elegant necks beneath the dappled surface. A breeze fretted among the reeds.

I took a notepad from my pocket, and my pen. I had meant to write a reply to Jess, but I found myself thinking of words for Edward. Poetry, I thought. *Poesis*—a word that was originally derived from the sound of water. I stared and stared at the lake. And, after a time, I began to write.

The sun was well past the meridian when I stood up again, and I was hungry. I walked back by way of Laura's studio and looked in through the windows for the first time: cool, white-washed walls of wattle and daub, a line of plastic buckets with bags of clay stacked beside them, a workbench on which stood a small blue turning-wheel and a neat array of tools. There was a high stool at the bench and a battered old armchair was placed beside her view of the lake. I saw a collection of pebbles in a dish of water, a swan's pinion-feather, and the salt-stained piece of driftwood we had found on the beach. A cork pin-board was covered in sketches and photographs. Mostly they were of flowers and trees, but there was a polaroid snapshot of a handsome, rather Nordic man with an arm around a dark-haired woman who smiled uneasily at the camera—Laura's parents presumably, standing in the garden of their clapboard house. I saw only one alchemical image: a photocopy of an illustration from the *Mutus Liber* in which the adept and his mystic sister worked at their furnace as Laura and I had sweated once over her kiln.

I walked round the shed to look at the kiln and was startled by the ruin there. Bricks from the kiln-door had been stacked neatly enough among the muddle of split timber with shelves leaning against them, but all around the ground was littered with shards of smashed pottery. So much had happened since that I'd forgotten Laura's state of mind on opening the kiln, but here its relics lay in pieces. Vandals might have been at work.

As Edward must have done before me, I knelt down, picked up shard after broken shard, trying to piece them together as though the world that had existed on the day of the firing might be made good again. So much entrusted to the flame, and so much ruin. For a time, once again, none of it made any sense.

Bob came round to The Pightle shortly after I'd got back. 'Laura rang earlier,' he said, 'but you were out.'

'Is she all right?'

'She's okay but . . .'

'Edward?'

Bob waved his palms to calm me down. 'They're both all right, but apparently she's had enough of him playing the voice of doom. She's talked to the nursing-staff and they all agree he needs to reconnect with life, and that he might have to be pushed. Laura wonders if you'll go in to see him this evening.'

'Does he know about it?'

'She says he'd only get worked-up if he did.'

'I'd like to see him. I need to . . . But if he still doesn't want to see me . . .'

'We talked about that, and she came up with what I think is rather a good idea. She thinks I should go in with you. Cushion the blow. If you're agreeable that is.'

I thought about it, saw the advantages and the disadvantages, and that the former might outweigh the latter. 'It might make things easier . . . if you really don't mind.'

'Oh, I warmed to the idea. I was rather looking forward to it. I've only ever seen him shooting off his mouth or speechless, and'—Bob grinned—'I feel I've sort of got shares in him now. I want to find out if it's a good investment.'

'So long as you don't expect gratitude.'

'Laura warned me about that. I'll settle for a good argument.'

Though Laura looked tired when we met her outside the hospital, her smile had none of the tension I'd expected. She seemed cheerful even, and amused by my trepidation when she announced her decision not to come into the ward with us. 'I was with him earlier and I think he's seen enough of me for one day. He might behave himself if I'm not around. I'll wait for you here.'

Bob and I joined the small crowd of visitors waiting admission to the wards. I took in the antiseptic smells, the anxiety and the relief around me. Everyone else seemed to know where they were going so we were left surveying the array of beds, screens and machines until I spotted Edward at the far end of the ward. He looked up, frowned, glanced away, then pushed a notebook and pencil into his bedside drawer, and turned to nod at my greeting, old and frail.

Bob said, 'We represent the world. You're supposed to connect with it.'

There was a glimmer of a smile.

'Do you remember Bob?' I said. 'You met him that first night at the Hall.'

'You called me a naïve materialist,' Bob prompted, 'and a builder of public conveniences, as I recall. We've brought you some grapes. Can I have one?'

Edward made a weak gesture of largesse with his hand. 'You have me at a disadvantage,' he said. 'I'm in the embarrassing position of owing you my life . . . I'm afraid I don't quite know what one does with a debt like that.'

'One forgets it,' Bob answered immediately.

Edward studied him for a moment, then said, 'I rarely repay debts but I never forget them.' A touch of the old spirit was there, but the voice was weaker.

'It wasn't a forgettable experience,' Bob conceded. 'You're the first person I've kissed in nearly ten years.'

Edward smiled. I began to relax, ventured to ask how he was feeling.

'Feeling?' He was still finding it hard to look at me, and his eyes wandered around the ward before he seemed to remember that he had been asked a question. 'I suppose I should know. I mean, we're all experts here—in the heart and its problems.' He looked back at me through slightly narrowed, embarrassed eyes. 'Not a nuance of ventricular fibrillation escapes us. Ask us about myocardial infarction and you will receive a lengthy answer. But ask me how I'm feeling and I'm at a bit of a loss . . .'

Bob filled the silence. 'You seem to be making good progress.'

'Oh, if it's our progress you want to know about, you need only observe our position in the ward. We're all on a Wheel of Fortune. You start over there when you're in no state to understand the system, and they walk you to and fro and swing you round till you get over there where our infarcted hearts are supposed to lift at the imminent prospect of return to life's mercies. Always supposing, of course, that you don't fall off on the way. Some do. Some do.' It was hard to tell whether there was more of sadness or envy in his voice. 'I, as you see, still have a few more spokes to go.'

Bob smiled. 'Your tongue doesn't seem too infarcted. You must be feeling better.'

'My principal feeling,' Edward answered, 'is that if I hear another wag say "Blessed are the pacemakers" with a grin of invention on his face, I might expire of boredom.'

'Do they think you'll need one?' I asked.

'A pacemaker? I already have one. Where is she tonight, by the way?'

'She thought it best if . . .'

Edward looked away, discouragingly. Then, before I could speak again, 'I could have done with a whole new engine, and all I'm offered is a sort of de-coke. I'm forbidden to smoke. What they don't explain is how, in those diminished circumstances, one is expected to breathe.' He offered a bleak smile. 'It appears I'm stuck with this particular heart—doubtless because any substitute would reject me.'

And so it went on. I was grateful that Edward was speaking at all, yet aware how distanced was this sardonic banter. I could find no way through it, and caught myself covertly examining the colours of his skin, the quality of light in his eyes, the pace of his breathing, as though at any moment he might tire of this and send alarm-bells ringing round the ward.

At one point a young nurse stopped at his bed in passing and said with cheerful, ironical surprise, 'So you do have friends after all, Mr Nesbit!'

'These are mourners,' Edward answered.

'Then I hope they're prepared for a long wait.'

'Not at all. They're grieving over the demise of my youth.'

The nurse smiled. 'They should have got over that years ago,' grinned at Bob and me, and passed on.

'Saucy baggage, that one,' Edward commented. 'I made the error of calling her a tight-arsed bitch when she was being stern with me. She replied to the effect that the flexibility of her rectal muscles was a mystery on which I was unqualified to speak, and that I'd never get to the bottom of it unless I cheered up.'

'It's a good incentive,' Bob suggested, then looked at his watch. 'You two must have things to talk about. Edward, when you're up and about again you're welcome to visit me at my convenience.'

Momentarily Edward looked alarmed, but he recovered himself and said, 'I shall do so, dear man. And I'll endeavour to put the breath you lent me to sweeter use.'

'If you don't insult me,' Bob replied, 'I'll think that one or other of us is getting past it,' then winked at me, and left.

Edward regarded me with a wintery eye. 'Were you a party to this conspiracy of tact, or are we both its victims?'

'I did want a chance to talk.'

'Well here I am—a captive audience, as you see.'

There was an embarrassed silence which we both tried to end in the same breath. I deferred to Edward, but he insisted that it was my responsibility to entertain him.

'I don't have many jokes, Edward.'

He sighed then, assessed me sadly, and said, 'Neither do I. But I can offer a nice line in regret.' For a moment the past lay between us like grief. I wanted to reach out for his hand and say simply that I was sorry, but that was impossible as long as his eyes refused to meet mine. Which they did, for an instant, as he murmured, 'For God's sake, don't agonize. I've done enough of that for both of us.'

'Edward, I . . .'

'You were a young fool,' he interrupted, 'which is tolerable. I was an old fool, which is not. But unless we're to grovel before one another in an orgy of contrition, I think there's a verb that should remain understood in all our sentences.'

'To forgive?'

He nodded, smiling warily, then said, 'There are only two things I've held against you, and I think I've just let them both go.'

I looked up and saw the remission. The air had changed between us. Neither of us had moved but the distance was diminished. I felt freed to speak.

'About the first . . .' I began.

'You don't know what it is.'

'Laura?'

'But not what you think.'

He was smiling at me more broadly now, amused by my bewilderment as I said, 'Then what?' He shook his head again with a kind of affectionate despair, then relaxed back on to the piled pillows, staring up at the ceiling. 'It wasn't the rogering that bothered me,' he said eventually, ' . . . not in itself. It was the consequence—the fact that you, a mere novice, were chosen to do what I had failed to do.'

I puzzled over this and could see only one possible context in which it might make sense. 'To put her in touch with Louisa, you mean?'

Edward scowled impatiently. 'We are alive *now*—in my case regrettably so. It's the present that matters.'

'Then I don't understand.'

In a voice hoarse and wistful, Edward murmured, 'You made her virgin.'

'Laura?'

'Who else?'

'That's not the word I'd have chosen.'

'It means more than you think it means—though I may have confused the issue by saying that *you* did it. It wasn't you, of course, but it came to her through you . . . and I found that a little hard to take. Particularly as your face would seem to suggest that you still don't have the faintest idea what I'm talking about. Do they teach nothing sensible at Cambridge?' He sighed with exasperation, the corners of his mouth tucked in a weary frown. A teacher impatient with a talented but lazy pupil. Or just a tired old man? 'There are times when it's a rite,' he said, '—a rite by which a woman becomes one-unto-herself. Single. And she does it not by giving herself to a particular man but by committing herself to life without reservation.' He looked away again. 'Laura was able to do that with you as she was not able to do it with me. It shines out of her now. If you're not quite blind you must have observed it.'

'Yes, but . . .'

'That is a fact beyond buts. There's now another Virgin woman in the world, and God knows it has need of them. I would have preferred to accomplish it myself, but I'm deeply glad for her. And if that was the only, right and best way of getting the job done, then blessings on you both.'

It was as if he was consigning Laura to me, and I couldn't believe that he was left with this misunderstanding. 'But she must have told you . . .' I began.

'She didn't have to. I could see for myself.'

'I don't mean that . . . I mean, that we're not together . . . Laura and I. It wasn't . . .'

Edward sighed impatiently. 'That's utterly beside the point. If you *were* together it would be a completely different kettle of fish. It would be marriage, and neither of you is ready for that—especially you.' He shook his head. 'I have no idea what you are now, but Laura is virgin.'

Smiling with relief, I said, 'She's certainly her own person.'

'She was that before. She's her own *woman* now. There's a difference.'

'God knows what the feminists would make of that,' I said after a moment.

'That, fortunately, is none of our business. They have their mysteries and we have ours. One day perhaps the twain shall meet, then the sparks will turn to confetti and we can all have a party.' He grinned at me then. 'That might be fun.'

I was encouraged by the mischievous light in his eyes, but it was brief. Almost as though he'd remembered that he was supposed to be unhappy, or—more likely—because he was reflecting on the impossibility of communication across different experience, his face clouded again. He muttered something about gasping for a cigarette, and looked at his watch.

Thinking that I'd taxed him enough, I prepared to leave. 'You're in better shape than I expected,' I said. 'I can't tell you how much that matters to me.'

'God knows what I thought I was doing that night . . .' His eyes were closed, grey about the lids. The breath was released in a long sigh, and it carried an enormous grief that had not, until that moment, expressed its own enormity. 'Madness . . .' he whispered. 'Went too far . . .'

'It's past, Edward.'

'Despair, you see . . . It can be absolutely ruthless . . . savages everything. And the hell of it is, it feels just as real as the other thing . . . as if they belong together, and you can't have one without invoking the other . . .'

'You told me once that we're the case for hope as well as the authors of our own despair.'

'I said a lot of things. Too much . . . Trying to convince myself. To hold it here.' He held up his empty hands. 'It's always larger, subtler . . . You make statements like that at your peril . . . find yourself turning into something you wouldn't believe.' He gave a weary shake of his head. 'I'm tired, Cambridge.'

'Do you want me to leave?' But no, he wasn't ready for that, not yet.

'The second thing,' he said. 'Don't you want to hear about it? It was harder to let go.'

'If you want to tell me about it.'

'That you brought me back.'

I tried, and failed, to hold a grave gaze that contained no reproach but was unbearably sad. 'Without Bob I wouldn't have known what to do,' I said. 'It was a close thing. I'd never have forgiven myself if . . .'

'You don't know?' There was a note of perplexity in his question, and when I looked up the corner of his mouth was twitching a little.

'What?'

He searched my face and saw that I too was genuinely puzzled, then looked away. And back again. 'You really don't know?'

I shook my head. 'I'm not with you.'

He smiled then, still a little baffled, and said, 'It takes more than breath, you know.'

'You'll have to say more.'

He studied my intent expression steadily for a moment, then sighed. 'Perhaps another time.'

Then I realized what had been at the back of my mind throughout the conversation. 'Edward, there may not be another time—not unless you want me to visit you here again.'

'Why not? I should be out of here in a couple of days.'

I told him about the letter from Jess, about Marcus's birthday, and why I had to go. 'But you'll come back?' he said.

'I don't know, Edward, but I doubt it. I have some reconnecting of my own to do. And now that I know you're all right . . . that the verb is understood . . .'

'Your dream-quest is over—is that it? Time to return to the tribe?'

'I can't imagine that you'll be going back to work on Louisa's papers?'

'No, there's no need for that.'

'Then . . .'

'There's nothing to hold you here?'

'I think it would be evasion. Another tower. I have to get a purchase on the world. Most of all I have to get back in touch with my kids. Jess and I are getting divorced, but the kids will still need both of us.'

'And you have your dream.'

'Two dreams,' I said. 'And you to thank for both of them.'

'Two?'

'Yes. The other night—Friday—I went to the CND meeting I told you about, and that night . . .' But Edward raised an admonitory finger.

'Don't tell it,' he whispered. '*Become* it.'

'I'm not sure it was about me.'

'They always are,' he said. 'They're the secrets we whisper to ourselves. And if it's a secret the rest of us should know then make something of it. Remind us.'

'If I can.'

'I think you will.' Then his lined face unfolded in a smile! 'Show us that Zosimus was right.'

'Zosimus?'

'One of the texts I didn't show you. Thought it might inflate your ego, but I don't suppose it can do too much harm now. If I can get it right he says, "For the priest, the man of copper, whom you see seated in the spring and gathering his colour, do not regard him as a man of copper . . ." ' He hesitated, frowned, remembered, ' . . . "for he has changed the colour of his nature and become a man of silver. If you wish, after a little time, you will have him as a man of gold." ' Then he smiled at me again. 'Mind you, there's still a coppery tinge of green about you; and in the spiritual calendar a little time may be as much as a half a century or more.'

'I can wait. It might give you a chance to get there first.'

'And, doubtless, I shall continue to example nothing but my own perversity. However, apart from Laura's transformation, two other things appear to have happened: I've been brought back from the dead, and your Green Man seems to be a less shaggy beast. One might almost mistake us both for human beings. These developments should perhaps be celebrated. When do you say this birthday is?'

'The 23rd.'

'So you needn't leave till the 22nd?'

'I'd planned to leave earlier. I should see my publisher, Clive Quantrill. I have to thank him for the loan of The Pightle—and tell him he should spend more time in Munding.'

Edward sniffed. 'Publishers can wait—especially when they're on to a good thing. Will you bear with an old man and promise you won't leave till the 22nd?'

'No, but I'll bear with *you*.'

'Don't patronize me, you little shit.'

The woman by the next bed started at his growl. I smiled at her disapproval and said, 'One has to do something to stir your stumps.'

He eyed me shrewdly. 'A bargain? I'll stir my stumps if you'll stick around till our next meeting.'

'Will my head be safe?'

Edward grimaced. 'My dear man, in this day and age nobody's head is safe.'

'A bargain then.' I put my hand to his. He gripped it, held it for a long moment, very tight. So tight I could feel the pricking of my eyes. Then he narrowed his, and growled. 'Stay out of my way till I send for you. I've got more important things on my mind.'

I learned later that what he had in mind was a celebration of the summer solstice. Discharged, he'd secluded himself in the Lodge, and it was Laura who brought my invitation to The Pightle. Also she was looking for my help.

She told me that Edward was insisting that the time had come for her to return to the States without him. He argued that she was her own person now, young, with the whole promise of her life before her. In his words, there was neither sense nor justice in tying herself to the geriatric future of a tiresome old man with a heart condition.

'But it's precisely the condition of his heart that makes me want to stay with him,' she said, '—and I don't mean its weakness. It may sound contrary but it's precisely because he's let me go that I feel I can stay. Freely stay. Does that make any sense to you?'

'If you're sure it's what you want . . . that you're not just doing it for him.'

'It's what I want and need. I know we need each other. He won't see it—he denies it even. But it's only a kind of obstinacy, as if it was enough just to know we love each other without doing anything about it.'

'He's thinking of you.'

'I know he is, but he won't admit it. He knows he's on shaky ground, so he says he's making his soul—that it's like making your toilette—you do it on your own. He says he has a thing to do before he dies and he doesn't want me under his feet.'

Uncertainly I said, 'If you make allowances for the rhetoric . . . I mean, have you considered the possibility that he might be right?'

'I've been over and over it. I've examined my own motives and I've thought about his. I've listened seriously to everything he has to say, and in the end it's the feeling that convinces me. I know what I feel, and all the logic in the world isn't going to alter that. As for him . . .' She shook her head in exasperation. 'He's not going to get rid of me that easily.'

'Has he told you what it is he wants to do?'

'No, but I have a damn good idea, and I know he'll do it better if I'm around.'

'What do you think it is?'

Laura smiled. 'His business.'

'His real business?' Her smile broadened. 'God, I hope so. It would be the best possible . . .'

'Yes.'

'Does Ralph know this? It would really matter to him.'

'They've talked. They spent a long time together. I don't know what was said, but Edward was smiling when Ralph left. I guess the two of them must think I'm ignorant or something—about their past, I mean.'

'You know about that?'

'It was obvious the minute we turned up here. One of the many things Edward wouldn't talk about. Ralph neither. It put me in a terrible position. Anyway, it seems to have changed now. Ralph was really sweet with me. He thinks I should stay.'

'And that hasn't made any difference to Edward?'

She shook her head, gazed up at me. 'I wondered if . . .'

'You want me to talk to him?'

'As a friend.'

'I doubt he'll listen.'

'I think you matter to him more than you know.'

'But after all that's happened . . .'

'Because of. Look how easily you cheered him up.'

'He did that. He made it easy.'

'But you brought him back—and not only out of gloom.' She held my eyes for a moment then looked, pensively, away. 'How much has he told you about what happened?—after the attack, I mean.'

'He did say something that puzzled me, but then he shied away.'

Laura nodded. 'Then make him talk about it.'

'Has he told you?'

'Yes. And I think you need to know. From him.'

'I'll try . . . and, if you're sure it's what you want, I'll talk to him about you too. But at the end of the day only you can convince him.'

'I know.' She smiled up at me again. 'But you can soften him up for me. Will you do that?'

'Look at me like that and I can't refuse you anything. But it'll cost you a hug.'

'Payment in advance.'

When, after a long moment, we let each other go, she said, 'Edward tells me that you're leaving.'

'The day after the party. It's my son's birthday.'

'And you won't come back?'

'To visit perhaps . . . if you're both still here.'

'I hope so. We'll both miss you.' She looked away towards the window where light slanted down into The Pightle's shade. 'The Weeping Fig's looking good. You've been talking to it?'

'All the time.'

'What does it say?'

I thought for a moment, then said, 'It speaks Latin. It says, "*Sunt lachrymae rerum.*" '

'Which means?'

'Untranslatable, but it has to do with the sadness in things.'

'And what about the joy?'

'That's Advanced Level. I haven't quite got there.'

'You will.'

'Perhaps I should come back for lessons. I think I might need them.'

Her smile lightly disparaged the remark. 'Shall I tell you your fortune? Give me your hand.' I did, and watched, smiling, as she studied the map of my palm.

'Do I want to know?'

'Oh I think so. It says: beware of American women, cantankerous poets, Tarot cards and stone effigies. Pelicans are to be trusted, and ghosts are not what you think—they come from the future. I see . . . mmm.'

'Well?'

'I see a lot of ink.'

'And scrumpled paper?'

'Heaps and heaps. But that's not all.' There was a change in her tone of voice, then another thoughtful hum.

'What else?' I demanded.

The smile became more sibylline. She folded my fingers on to the palm. 'Don't you know by now?' she said, '—the future comes when we're good and ready for it.'

* * *

All that blue midsummer afternoon the sky over Easterness and Munding was loud with aircraft targeting their subtle, interlaced assault-manoeuvres on the tower of the ruined church at Shippenhall, then zooming out across the calm North Sea. They sortied like mating pairs, frisky and metallic, as though impelled by an excess of exuberant vitality. So much care, intelligence, precision. Such expensive skill.

By the time I walked across to the Decoy Lodge that evening their trails had evaporated against a deeper blue. Less harsh than it had been by day, the Norfolk light solicited the best from everything, and even at the time—as now in recollection—it seemed to draw into its soft, enveiling blur the trees around the Lodge and the full palette of rhododendrons flowering beside the lake in pinks and whites, magenta and raw gold. With more to celebrate than the solstice, I sensed already how much I must miss this place, the light, the high expansive sky that never quite darkened to black that night though the stars were visible.

There were more cars in the yard of the Lodge than I'd expected and many people already gathered on the lawn. Bob was there, of course, and Ralph, but many others I didn't know—Estate-workers and their families, children scampering about among the bushes, and old friends of Ralph and Edward invited up from town. Among them, to my amazement and delight, I saw Clive, who informed me that he'd been drawn by rumours of witchcraft orgies in the old Rectory. The remark was overheard by someone else I hadn't expected to see there, but Neville Sallis seemed to have recovered from his indignation. He gave me what my mother would have called 'an old-fashioned look,' and resumed his debate with Bob.

'Well, mooncalf,' Clive said, 'you must tell me all before I go to bed tonight, and don't expect to leave before I've checked the silver.' We were joined by Ralph who gave me his shy, lopsided grin saying he hoped I would enjoy this party more than the last. 'Edward's been forbidden the Tarot cards,' he promised, 'and if he's more than traditionally rude to anyone I shall terminate his lease.' He glanced across to where Edward sat in state on a high-backed whicker chair, wearing a raffish neckscarf and a cream silk shirt above his scarlet-bracered corduroy trousers. He was surrounded by old friends.

I said, 'I gather things are happier.'

'I'm happy that he's on the mend,' Ralph answered. 'The rest is bonus.' Then, with a twinkle, 'Have you seen the spread over there? Laura's outdone herself.'

After a time I went looking for Laura and found her sitting alone in the kitchen of the Lodge. The sheer cotton dress of dark blues and greens, the silver dangle of earrings and the subtle use of make-up, all spoke to breathtakingly successful care over her appearance, yet she seemed—as I suggested—to be hiding herself away.

'I've looked forward to this so much,' she said, 'and now I'm too nervous to enjoy it.'

'Don't be. It's a triumph.'

'Is he happy?'

'I haven't been able to get close to him yet, but judging by the chortles, yes, I'd say so . . . very. He's sitting there like the Grand Cham. It's not going to be too much for him?'

'It's the way he wanted it. I've made him swear to tell me when he gets tired.'

I spotted her empty glass and asked if I could bring her another drink. 'In a minute,' and, when I offered her a cigarette, 'I've stopped—to encourage Edward. But have one if you like.' I shook my head, put the packet away, and said, 'Perhaps I should do the same—though I think I may need at least one vice.' There was a brief, uncertain silence in which I caught the scent of her perfume, slight but delicious, on the air.

'Alex,'—I turned my gaze back from the window—'what I asked you to do . . .'

'I haven't forgotten.'

'There's no need.'

'You mean he's woken up to how lucky he is?' I saw that he had, and added, 'Perhaps it's just as well. With the way you're looking tonight I might have had second thoughts . . . I mean, friendship's fine, but . . .'

It was said lightly enough but the air between us was delicate. Then she smiled and looked away. 'Edward tells me I'm virgin now. I suppose he knows what he means.'

'Do you?'

She said, 'I think you had better get me that drink,' and stood up, sweeping back her hair. 'On second thoughts, I'd better come with you.'

We were standing very close. Involuntarily my hand reached for the cigarette packet again as I said, smiling, 'You can be a very disturbing person,' but her grin arrested the gesture.

'I'm trouble, I know. Edward encourages it in me. But then . . . it must have occurred to you that life is a very disturbing business.'

'Some such thought has recently crossed my mind.'

Still she didn't move; and then, with a demure, flirtatious solemnity, she said, 'Then I advise you to meditate on it, Mr Darken; for women as creatures are passing strange, and I suspect your life still has much business with them.'

Laughing, I said, 'I didn't think the party could be quite complete without her.'

'You don't know it yet,' she answered, 'but we still have a couple of things to do on her behalf.'

'Which are?'

'You'll see.'

'Enigmatic as ever.'

'Not really. At heart we're very simple.'

At that moment Ralph came through into the kitchen. 'There you are, Laura. Edward's been asking for you.' Then he took in how close we were. 'I hope I didn't interrupt anything?' Momentarily he was dismayed by our laughter as I assured him we were being good this time, then he recovered and said, 'It seems we are all becoming expert at renunciation. I do hope it's good for our health.'

Out on the lawn Edward rose slowly from the chair and stretched out his hands to receive us. 'Midsummer night,' he announced. 'The dream time. Time to light the fire against the dark.'

On the grass close to the lake's edge and well away from the thatched roof of the Lodge, the brushwood pyre stands ready. It is tall, pyramidal, well-constructed to sustain a blaze. Jem Bales is waiting beside it, staring down at the piles of handsomely bound books he has unloaded from the cart. His leather gaiters are the colour of chestnuts, and he is scratching his grizzled head. Jem is no reader, has no use for books, but she can see that even to his woodman's eye a lot of good money is about to go up in smoke, and to no reasonable purpose. Then Pedro is bounding ashore towards him.

Louisa lifts her skirts, steps from the skiff to the jetty, and turns to assist her father. He is staring in fascination—not at the pyre but at the Lodge itself, and within the wrinkles of his harrowed face she discerns the wary expression of an uncertain boy.

If the hand he lifts is trembling, it is not only with the infirmity
of age.

'Come,' she says, 'we promised to be brave.'

'I was wondering why it should be that every occasion of my
coming here is an unhappy one.'

Because, she thinks, you first learned to suffer here, and have
never quite forgiven or forgotten that. And who is she to judge
of this, when her own novitiate in pain is incomplete? In that
respect Edwin is already far ahead of her, and there is further
pain to be accrued before she gains on him. She has persuaded
herself that any unhappiness this day may hold can only diminish the distance between his experience and hers, and thus—
through a paradox—might even convert itself to its own
opposite.

None of this can be shared with her father, though she says,
smiling, 'Unless we choose to see it so, this need not be an
entirely unhappy day.'

'I cannot see it otherwise.'

'But it has scarce begun.'

Jem touches a hand to his temple as the baronet and his daughter approach, and Louisa wonders aloud at the way the woodman's command has stilled Pedro to untypical obedience. 'He
pays scant attention to a word I utter,' she complains. 'One day
you must teach me your secret, Jem.' The man smiles and
shrugs, says that if there is a secret he wouldn't know how to
explain it, then hopes that everything has been arranged to their
satisfaction. He casts an eye upwards at the scudding clouds,
comments that the breeze should make a good blaze, and that
even if it veers, the thatch should be safe enough. His reassur-
ances are addressed to the master, but it is the daughter who
answers.

'Thank you, Jem—you have done splendidly. Did you find me
the flints I asked for?'

Jem reaches into his pocket and brings out the twin halves of
a broken flint. He looks down doubtfully where the exposed
inner surfaces glint in his hands, and mutters that it seems a
painfully slow way to kindle fire.

'But the oldest and the simplest,' she answers, for the man
would have no understanding if she spoke aloud the words that
echo in her mind from an old text: *Certaine Divine Raies breake
out of the Soul in adversity, like sparkes of fire out of the afflicted
flint.*

Old the method may be, but Jem is unpersuaded of its simplicity, particularly at a young woman's uncalloused hands. Nor is he happy at the thought of her down on her knees blowing at a hard-won spark among dry leaves. He decides to speak his mind.

Though patience does not come easily, Louisa listens; then resists. She has made her decisions, however capricious they appear; but her father intervenes. 'Jem is in the right, my dear. Let him kindle a torch for you at least; and then—if you insist—you may bring it to the pyre yourself.' Reluctantly she sees the sense in this, and watches as Jem strikes the flints among the tinder he has laid ready in the lee of a ring of stones. Each click of the struck flints comes as a pang on the air. She sees now that it is, indeed, more difficult than she had anticipated.

Her fingers reach for the locket dangling at her throat. It contains a strand of her mother's hair, but it is also gold, and she has found an unexpected source of comfort there. Gold speaks to her now in richer language than before. Having been at pains for so long to stress its symbolic value, she is surprised each time her fingers close around the locket to sense a virtue in the actual element itself which is a mild but sovereign remedy for the disappointments of the heart. She understands why ritual objects are made of gold; she thinks it small wonder that men should hoard and covet it, unconscious as they were of what they deeply sought. The gold inside her hand is nourishment; it fortifies and heals.

Jem is blowing among the stones. He adds more leaves and blows again, then grunts as the new leaves catch and a small flame crackles and thrives among them. He adds the dry twigs he has collected, and the ring of stones becomes a hearth. Utterly unaware how Promethean his endeavours, he stands, and looks down on his fire in satisfaction. It will take a torch now, and if she wants to send things up in smoke it is not his business.

'Thank you, Jem,' she says. 'You may leave us now.'

But Jem is a woodman; he has no great trust of flame, and mutters that it might be best if he stand close by for a time lest the fire get out of hand.

'If you wish,' she answers, 'but all will be well.' She dips the reed-torch to the hearth, and when the fire has caught she lifts it to the breeze. It becomes a brand. Alarmed, her father worries for her hair, but she holds the torch confidently and steps to-

wards the pyre. With her free hand she lifts the first of the books
from the stack and allows it to flip open.

What a host of words were here! And were any of them true,
she wonders, or was her book no more than a consoling illusion
that she—like countless solitaries before her—had woven out of
dreams? No matter. It is her work. The harvest of deep feeling
and long thought. Silently she makes the dedication that she
could not write.

She lifts her eyes, takes in the bright day, then throws the copy
of her book into the brushwood. It falls open on its spine, the
pages fluttering in the breeze. At arm's length she holds the torch
to the paper. A fringe of coral appears at the corner of a page.
Flame blossoms and folds—coral blushing to purple, then saffron, and a paler glowing aureole like a feather's tip. The page
is rustling and flaking, mourning itself, until it is bent and ragged as an old crone in black tatters burning at a pyre.

All the colours of the Art, she marvels; then throws the brand
among the brushwood. The breeze gusts. Fire feels its way
among the branches, sniffs the air, then swoops. The pages of
the burning book turn quickly, leaf over blackening leaf, like a
shuffled deck of cards. Twig and branch combust in a gasp of
orange flame and she is pushed backwards by the sudden heat.
She reaches for another book, feeds it to the fire, then another.
The fire exhilarates. She is all enthusiasm. Bright-eyed, she
points to where the burning pages turn. 'Look,' she cries, 'never
was book so eagerly devoured. Never more completely understood.'

And she laughs.

He stands in vast, uncomprehending grief, unable to stop her,
unable to assist. The fire burgeons. Smoke bends in obeisance
to the breeze, rises and makes off across the lake.

Our fire had been built beyond the kiln, and Edward was
sitting in its ruddy glow talking to a small girl—an Estate-
worker's daughter who had taken a fancy to him. I listened as
he talked to her about fire, about how everything began there,
in the stars, and how one day everything would return to fire.
When she seemed disturbed by this thought, he told her about
phoenixes and salamanders; and then, eventually, he told her
about Louisa. He told how she had come here once, more than
a hundred years before, to light a fire which was a magic fire
because it never went out. In fact, he said, the fire was really

there all the time—it had been there long before Louisa lit her fire, and the fire in front of us now was the very same fire. It was just that sometimes it was invisible—a small flame burning inside each one of us—and at other times, like now, it became visible again so that we didn't forget it was always there.

The child was at once entranced and dubious. At one point, under question, Edward glanced across at me and murmured, 'What a critic have we here!' but at last he told her he had a thing to do, and promised as he left that if she gazed into the fire as into a mirror, and did so long enough, she would see her own small spark of star-fire reflected there. It was all a question of knowing how to look.

When he'd gone the girl favoured me with one of those exaggerated facial expressions by which the young practise their scepticism of the adult world. I said, 'But didn't you enjoy his story?'

'On the whole,' she conceded—I saw that she was grateful for the opportunity to employ the phrase—'but he's funny, don't you think?'

I agreed, and we stared into the fire together. Some time later I became aware of Edward and Laura standing over me. The little girl had gone.

'Didn't she believe me then?' Edward asked.

'She thinks you're funny.'

'It's a pity Laura wasn't here. She could have shown her that fire doesn't only destroy things—it transforms them.' He looked at Laura who glanced down at me. 'There's a gift for you,' she said. 'I thought you should have it. It's on the window-sill in the sitting-room.'

Giftless myself, I stood up, embarrassed. 'Well, aren't you going to see?' Edward encouraged after a moment, smiling.

'You're not coming with me?'

Laura shook her head and sat down by the fire. Edward joined her. A little bemused, I went back to the Lodge and through into the sitting-room, where the curtains had been closed. I drew them and found what was in the window-alcove, waiting for me.

Its form was flower-like, opening like the outward reach of a corolla, the rim serrated and uneven where thin sheets of clay had been folded and pressed together, shaping the delicate cup of a vase. It might have been growing there from the white window-sill, stemless but poised on its own centre of gravity. The glaze was matt, earthy, yet shot with igneous colours—

shades of umber, ruddy irons and manganese, vivid and raw—
as though mineral elements had fused into botanical form, or
an ardent plant had been petrified by heat. This pot was a living
presence, discretely itself, yet a portion also of the natural world
around us, a member of its order. I lifted it and it felt good in
my hands. Then I saw the note:

> *This one survived, and it's for you.*
> *Think of us. Think of Louisa.*

Smoke billowed across the lake, and through the shimmer of
the heat-haze all the lovely parkland of Easterness betrayed itself
for what it was: illusion; a playful, momentary gesture of matter
in the immense symmetries of time and space. And yet substantial also, not to be negated; blessedly real in that moment of
immediate fire. What a mystery this was, the universal, pyro-
technic brilliance of things, ever contingent, ever the incarnation
of intelligence beyond contingency. Simply *there*.

One by one the copies of her book had charred, unfurled and
flowered, and now the last was in her hand—no different, in its
green and golden binding, from all the rest, save that it was the
last, and with it would expire the only record of her work. All
the others might be no more than soot, yet if this single volume
was held back, the fire would have no significance beyond the
enrichment of the soil on which it burned. Louisa stared into
the flame.

For a long time she stared and saw many things. She saw
herself crossing the lake that first winter morning, and the innocent enthusiasm with which she had inscribed the title page;
she saw the skating on the lake—the chestnut-fire, the snow—
and Emilia lying on her bed of pain; she watched Mercurius
dance like the elusive sprite he was, from chamber to fiery
chamber among the burning books; and she met her grandfather's face, lean and maliciously handsome, savouring the quality of her pain, and taking perverse satisfaction in her appetite
for the flames that licked him round. She saw the face of Edwin
Frere.

Should she live to be a hundred this great gap in her life, this
hollow, aching unassuageably inside her, could never be filled.
No flame could burn away its pain. And she would, she knew,
be philosophical. It was her nature. She would again be
calm. She would grow calm and wise and old. And—as was

surely the case with him—whatever service she might still perform to illuminate the darkness of her fellow creatures and to
lend them warmth, she would for ever be alone. But already—
as she threw the last copy of her book into the fire—she knew
that it was only a book she was burning there: it was not her
life.

So intense was the heat the pages instantly combusted. All
the life compressed within their binding was immediately transformed—fire reaching from the earth beside the water of the
lake, becoming air—all the elements celebrated change. And,
Benedicta Natura, she quoted silently to herself, *blessed are thy
works, for out of that blackness which is true putrefaction all
the many colours shall unfold.*

Yet it burned, it burned.

Sighing, Henry Agnew rose from where he sat shielding his
yellowed eyes from the heat and—before she understood what
was happening—with the wide, abandoned flourish of a man
inebriated, he flung the pages of his own manuscript to the flame.
Flame leapt to receive it. The pages became tongues.

And this was the hardest thing of all to bear that day.

Louisa watched him stare into the fire, tears rolling down his
cheeks, and learned again what she thought was already seared
upon her soul: that only the pain of those we love is unendur-
able. A body might withstand whatever torment for itself, but
to watch a loved one suffer tore the secret from the firmest will.
Helpless, one wished, impossibly, to take the entirety of pain
inside oneself.

In silence she reached for his hand, and they stood together,
observing the ineluctable processes by which matter consecrated
itself to matter, inherited itself. She felt his hand quaking under
hers, and for the first time admitted to full consciousness what
she had scarcely dared to glimpse before: that her father could
not now have very long to live. He had betrayed the secret as
she had not betrayed the secret, and the price of that was written
on his flesh. About this too there was nothing, absolutely nothing, she could do.

If there was tragedy here, it was surely his, for her own work
was not lost. It had simply become invisible inside her, had
taken less palpable and more translucent form that it might endure, entirely on its own impassioned terms, throughout her
days. She had merely followed the alchemists' final advice to
destroy the books, which were, in any case, no substitute for

experience, and might—if too much value was attached to them—consume the heart. But he . . .

Had there been any tears to shed she might have wept for him as his papers turned to soft black moths scribbled on the air. There were none, and so she turned again to the fire, wondering what must now become of the world they had sought so long and patiently to address. It would never, in any case, have heeded them. It was too addicted to fascinations of its own; one day, as matter was tormented ever more insensitively for its secrets, and apparent mastery over the elements increased, one day it might also consign itself to flame. And then, on this small planet would be universal suffering, and, in the Universal Mind, a sadness that one of the great experiments of Nature had failed.

Louisa contemplated this with an equanimity that frightened and astonished her; but what it might mean for the unfolding of a greater plan lay far beyond her powers to say.

Then she felt the grip of her father's hand tighten, and a tremble pass through his frame. She saw him staring in a rapt trance of concentration at the flames, and there was awe in that gaze. Wondering, she looked back in the fixed direction of his eyes. She looked towards the fire which seemed to hang on the wind, almost without motion, like a candle flame.

The wind gusted again, the flames bent before it, and resumed their dance. A great sigh passed from her father's lips. And he was whispering.

He was speaking aloud the ancient words in which Hermes Trismegistus, the father of the Art, had once spoken of his encounter with the Divine Intellect. *'He looked me long in the face,'* he whispered, *'so that I trembled before his gaze. Then as he raised his hand again, I saw how in my own spirit that light which consists of countless possibilities became an Infinite All . . .'* And there his old voice faltered. His eyes were watering against the heat, and his frown might have been expressive of intense physical pain, or of the difficult efforts of a failing mind to recover lines once known by heart and half-forgotten now.

For a moment Louisa wondered what he had seen in the fire to call forth these words. Had he seen anything at all—anything other than the phantom of his own lost hopes? There was no means to tell; but she saw the difficulty in his face as he struggled to remember; and prompted him.

'And then,' she offered, trembling now herself, *'while I remained utterly outside the sense of a separate self . . .'*

'. . . he spoke again . . .' Instantly the old man had seized her cue, and he was smiling now at the returning memory. *'. . . He spoke again, saying, "Thou hast now seen in the true intellectual spirit the origin and first form of all things . . . and that beginning to which shall never be an end."'*

His eyes were still fixed on the fire, and the smile had gone, replaced by a wistful yearning, troubled by nothing now, it seemed, save the vast invisible distances between where he stood and where he wished with all his heart to be. And so, hands tightly clasped, father and daughter stood for a long time, golden together in the light of the flame, while there, in the embers of the blaze that burned their secret, the secret thrived.

'There are things that fire won't burn,' Edward said, 'and we have one more duty. I think it's time we took to the skiff.' He put an arm to my shoulder, the other to Laura's, and pressed us towards the jetty; but when we arrived there Laura drew in her breath and said, 'I think the two of you should do this alone.'

'Why so?' Edward asked.

Smiling she said, 'Because it's the end of a man's game,' and, before Edward could demur, turned away. We watched her walk along the lawn, away from the fire with its ring of chattering people, to sit alone on the lake-shore. 'I'll wait for you here,' she called. Edward shrugged, raised his brows at me and said, 'I think you'd better take the oars.'

Reclining on cushions in the stern, he trailed a hand through the water as I rowed out into the lake. The sky was a deep, refulgent blue, ruddied at his back by the bale-fire's glow. Someone had brought a guitar and people were singing. The sound travelled across the water. Woodsmoke mingled with the green lake-smell.

'I suppose she was right,' he said.

'If this is what I think it's about.'

'What else.'

We were silent for a time. Edward lay with his eyes closed, feeling the motion of the boat, listening to the sounds. Then he smiled, and said, 'How very odd!'

'What?'

'That you should be my ferryman now.'

'I promise it won't cost you an obol. And it's a return trip.'

'Another?'

'Less dramatic, I hope.' I took in his dry smile and said, 'Laura told me to ask you about that.'

'She didn't tell you herself?'

'No. She thought you should.'

Edward sighed and stared down into the dark water. 'One had heard of such experiences, of course . . . but when it happens . . .' He gazed wistfully across at me. 'Rest your oars. Listen.'

He gathered his thoughts, and then, quietly, without drama, he told me his experience of the heart-attack—how the pain in his chest and arms had exploded into blackness, then the calm awakening to detachment from his body. In exact detail he described the frantic scene in the room at the Rectory; he told me how, for a few instants, Laura had appeared translucent to him, and then how he had moved swiftly away towards the light. Like a man remembering a dream, he paused there, musing. I sat in rapt silence, waiting for his words.

'I recognized the place I came to,' he said after a time. 'It was one of those impossible palaces out of the *Splendor Solis*. I knew the chequer-board tiles on the floor, the entablatures, the marble statues in their niches, the arcades with their prospects of distant towers and gardens . . . There was a lovely balance between masonry and air . . . a sense of a presiding architectural vision that was at once whimsical and informed by the classical spirit . . .' He paused, reached into his trouser-pocket, and took out a packet of cigarettes.

'Edward, for God's sake..!'

He made a moue, put a finger to his lips, and hissed. 'My secret,' then struck a match and drew on the cigarette. 'Don't tell her,' he said, exhaling. 'And don't look at me like that.' After a time he resumed.

'There were people waiting for me. My arrival was expected. I was told that a wedding was about to be celebrated . . . that I was an honoured guest . . . and I knew that the other members of the wedding—people I once knew well—were all delighted I had come. There were genial smiles, jokes, the sound of convivial laughter . . . But I was in poor shape, dishevelled—a bit of a disgrace as usual—and though they weren't surprised by my condition I felt badly about it. They were prepared for that . . . I knew the cleansing would be uncomfortable at first, like shedding skin, or the first sensation of stepping into a hot bath . . . But I'd never felt so welcome, and I wanted the scouring. I wanted to be new, cleansed, to have fresh raiment, not to soil in any way the candid light around me . . . I wanted to be at my best for the bride and groom.

He sighed again, then snorted, shrugged. 'I don't know how long I was there—time was immaterial—but eventually I became aware that there was some consternation around me. It was as though everyone but me understood that a difficulty had arisen. Then I was informed that someone had come for me. There had been some error . . . A friend of mine was here demanding to see me. I looked up and who should I see standing there but you?'

Edward smiled ruefully across at my astonished gaze. 'You were not a welcome sight, I promise you. And you were very insistent, embarrassingly so. You claimed that I had unfinished business . . . that I had no leave to depart. There was much shaking of heads, regret, and the next thing I knew I was rammed back inside this wreck of a body and the shock was appalling— much worse than the physical pain, though that was bad, very bad . . .' He closed his eyes again, drew deeply on his cigarette, exhaled. 'I was, as I think you may begin to understand, extremely displeased with you. Also, when I finally brought myself to accept your presence—back here, I mean—amazed that you appeared to be entirely innocent of what had happened.' He looked away across the lake. 'So here we are,' he said, 'and what do you make of all of that?'

I sat in the skiff, marvelling uncertainly at this strangest of all his traveller's tales. The sound of laughter came from the shore, and Edward was smiling as though he'd heard the joke. Behind him the fire's reflection wobbled in the lake.

'You're quite sure it was me?'

'Unmistakably. Who else would have been so tactless?'

'Then if it was, I'm not sorry.'

'I might have guessed you'd lack the grace to apologize.' An eyebrow was lightly raised, the smile ironical.

'I seem to recall your telling me that everything in a dream is an aspect of the dreamer's own psyche.'

'But I wasn't dreaming. I've dreamed dreams and I've been through this experience. I assure you they are not the same.'

'Then are you telling me there's an after-life?'

'I'm telling you what I know. Not a tittle more, not a jot less.' Again he smiled and looked away. 'Of course, you're at liberty not to believe me.'

'The difficulty is,' I said after a moment, 'I half believe I do.'

'And, putting aside the fact that I'm a famous liar, why should you not? After all, others have experienced something similar. They insist, as I do, that they were dead at the time.'

'Alchemical palaces?' I queried.

A gesture of his hand took in the lake, both shores, the stars. 'Don't we live in an alchemical palace? But, no, the nature of the zone we enter appears to shape itself in sympathy with our individual tastes. Some are welcomed by long-dead relatives, some see Shiva in his glory, others are met by gentle Jesus himself. I was invited to attend the chymical wedding—an invitation which I was required, unfortunately, to decline. It took a little time to forgive. Beyond that, I make no claims.'

'But you must have given the matter thought?'

'Thought has its limits.' I thought for a moment he would say no more, but he sighed and looked back at me, and I knew now that he was absolutely serious, speaking with no urgent desire to persuade but out of calm conviction. 'There are only three things I'm quite sure of. Firstly, that the mirror of experience is more mysterious than I'd even begun to imagine. Secondly, that I would much rather have stayed where I was . . . Yes, still . . . for all this happiness. Even now.' He drew again on his cigarette.

In the silence I said, 'But this evening has been a kind of wedding, Edward. A better one, because it's alive. That fire over there—we lit it against the dark.'

'Yes,' he answered quietly, 'and I don't for a moment demean it. But the third thing . . .'

'What is it?'

He smiled again, a little sadly. 'I hesitated only because you can't yet know it for yourself, and thus my words will make no difference. But the fact is, whatever fear I had of death has quite disappeared. It's gone. There's nothing to be afraid of there.'

'But you can't want it. Not now.'

He gave a little laugh. 'Don't you know yet?—I want everything. I want it all. Including a quiet smoke every now and then. And don't understand me too quickly—I'm entirely conscious of the many privileges of being alive . . . even without that final consoling certainty.'

I shook my head in affectionate exasperation and said, 'I'm sure Laura will be pleased to hear that.'

'I'm not speaking to Laura now. I'm speaking to you, and I'm only doing that because you—or whatever exacting spirit took your form—were quite right. I do have unfinished business here.'

'I hear you've been busy.'

'One has to pass the time.'

'You're writing again?' I risked. And, when he nodded and glanced away, 'Verse?'

'It's the only serious answer to the silence, wouldn't you say?'

'And it's enough now?'

'Of course it's not enough. But you may recall me suggesting once that we are children sent on an errand who forget our instructions . . . ? For a long time I've been stupider than most, and there's not a great deal of time left . . . One has to perform one's duty as best one can.' He examined the tip of his cigarette, allowed a moment to lapse, then said, 'And you?'

I took my cue from his casual nonchalance. 'Oh, I've managed a scribble or two.'

He nodded, blew a smoke-ring. 'Any good?'

'A start. What about yours?'

'The same.' A breeze ferried more laughter across the lake. 'Not before time.'

'Impertinent little shit,' he muttered lazily.

'Perverse old bastard.'

We beamed at one another before he looked away, upwards at the sky where still, at this late hour, the dense blue was suffused with sunlight. There was an ease between us more complete than I'd experienced before, no contest, no need to prove anything. Though Edward's manner was recognizably his own, he seemed less identified with it and by it. Such was the nature of his new repose, he felt more immediately accessible, yet also—and with no evident change in his demeanour—more subtly elusive. Thus I could look at him and see a mild old man reclining in a boat, or I could look across and see a figure who appeared to have passed beyond the fascination with ideas into a realm of knowledge where even the last duality of life and death raised no insuperable problem.

Edward glanced at his watch. 'Well, we've seen the sun at midnight, and it's way past my bedtime. We should do what we came to do.' He fished under the cushions and brought out the black razor-case with the initials E.L.F. stamped in gold. 'Such a small thing,' he said, 'to contain such pain,' then held it balanced across his palms, studying it in silence. 'A votive offering,

I thought,' he said at last, '—to the Lady of the Lake. Better than my last idea, don't you think?'

'I've never quite dared to think what that was.'

Edward sighed, shook his head, and his breath came as a little wince. 'I had the *tremor cordis* on me. Who knows? Perhaps I was just trying to make us both feel something.'

'It certainly worked.'

'To the point of overkill.' He tapped the case against his palm. 'There are gentler ways. I look forward to exploring them. And yet . . .'

'What?'

'What I said that night . . . The feel of it was all wrong, of course—hideously so. But the gist . . . I don't know . . .'

I took in his quick, wary glance, and said, 'Say it.'

Edward smiled. 'It's just that if the art is to hold two absolutely contradictory truths inside you at the same time, then that may have been one of them. And about that we will say no more. As for this'—he held the case towards me—'it belongs elsewhere. Will you throw it for me?'

I held the case for a long time, feeling its weight in my hand, studying its black, its gold.

'Throw it,' Edward said. 'You never know, an arm in white samite might rise to catch it.'

I stood up, balancing myself in the skiff, and hurled the clasped case far out into the lake. It turned in flight, was lost against the shadow of the Mount, then we heard the distant splash and the whirr of a coot's wings as it scuttled across the surface before settling again. The skiff rocked a little. Water slapped against the varnished wood.

The end of Edward's cigarette sizzled in the lake as he said, 'Poor Frere.'

'I wonder what became of him.'

'I know a little about that. Ralph followed it up for me through a friend of his in the Cathedral Close. It seems that with some encouragement from King's the Church took care of him. A parish was found in the London slums. Apparently it was what he wanted . . . I see him as an unassuming, rather saintly figure among the gin-palaces and stews of the Dickensian fog. He died in a cholera epidemic. And I rather suspect that a pile of letters was found amongst his remains.'

'You mean . . . ?'

'Oh yes, I think they kept in touch. Ralph tells me that shortly before Louisa died a maid found her in her room burning a large number of letters. He remembers the rumpus it caused.' Edward grinned across at me. 'Playing with fire at her age—she might have sent the Hall up in smoke. They must have been from her mystic brother, don't you think?'

'I wouldn't accept any evidence to the contrary.'

'Me neither. Just as well we're not scholars.'

'What about Frere's wife?'

'God knows . . . I wonder if she ever even knew. Can't imagine it—not in those days.'

'Either way, she must have been pretty embittered.'

'Or glad to be rid of him? Anyway, they're all at peace now.' He stretched his arms in a yawn, and said, 'Shall we get back?'

I reached for the oars, pulled on my right to turn the prow and, as I looked over my shoulder, caught a prospect of the Hall in the fading light. I said, 'I'm going to miss this place so much.'

'Then take it with you,' Edward answered. 'Carry it invisibly inside, the way Louisa kept her secret.'

'I wonder if there really was one—beyond the one we found, I mean.'

'What do you think?'

'I'd like to think so. But it's a pity we didn't uncover it.'

I tightened my grip on the other oar and smiled up at Edward expecting his agreement; but he too was smiling. Provocatively.

'You're looking very sphinx-like,' I said.

His smile broadened.

'Edward, are you holding out on me?'

'Would I do that?'

'Of course you would.' And, as he made a small tutting noise and muttered something about mistrust, 'You know something I don't know.'

He tilted the lined head, twitched his moustache.

'And you're not going to tell me.'

'I wouldn't want to spoil your fun.'

I shipped the oars and said, 'I can always keep you out here till you sing.'

'And miss your son's birthday? Anyway, the Lady Alchimia responds only to gracious requests.'

'Forgive me. I'd forgotten. Would she be so gracious as to give me a clue?'

Edward smiled and nodded. Then he raised the index finger

of his left hand upright in the air beside his shoulder, and with the other sealed his lips.

I recognized the ancient gesture of the secret. It was the enigmatic position adopted at the completion of their work by the adept and his mystic sister in the final illustration of the *Mutus Liber*—the silent book, whose title Louisa had chosen for her epitaph. In Edward's version there was something both comical and solemn about the posture. I waited, studying him from under a raised brow until he lowered his hands.

'That's all I get?'

He nodded and glanced away.

'Are you telling me the secret is there is no secret?'

'Did I say anything so dull?'

'I didn't hear you say anything at all.'

'Precisely.'

He snuggled back among the cushions, the red socks crossed at his ankles, one freckled hand resting on his stomach, the other loose at his thigh. His head reclined against the cushion, eyelids closed, quietly serene, with perhaps the faintest suggestion of a smile at his lips. So many years of experience were charted there you might almost navigate among their reefs and shoals, past islands where his monsters dwelt, and others where the Graces sang. Here were the burial grounds of lovers and of friends; here a contented resignation to fresh happiness in store; and somewhere, perhaps, behind those lidded eyes, a prospect even Mandeville had been denied on paradisal shores. For though all seven deadly sins had left their evidence across those windrow features, it seemed also that a kind of innocence had been resumed, and it was younger even than the indolent, elusive glamour of the youth in Ralph's old photograph.

Reflecting on this, I recalled how in the late portrait of Louisa Agnew innocence and experience had been brought to gentle reconciliation like the lovers of my dream; and I wondered whether—if Louisa and Edward did hold a secret in common now—it was because they *were* what they knew, and in that identity was no distinction such as words must seem to make.

But Edward raised his hand as though to shoo a fly, then sighed and murmured, 'I'm tired, Cambridge. Take me home.'

Smiling, I dipped the oars again. I might pester him with questions on our way back to the shore but I'd get no larger answer. Nor—in a sudden, wiser preference for silence—did I wish for one. Edward was right: it was getting late, Laura was waiting for us, he needed rest, and I had a long journey ahead of me; and once you begin to admit the truth there is no ending.

Acknowledgments

If the Stone of the Philosophers was a stone rejected by the builders of European culture, then no one has worked with greater intellectual courage than C.G. Jung to recover and illuminate the values it represents. The influence of his later works—*Psychology and Alchemy, The Psychology of the Transference,* and *Mysterium Coniunctionis* is evident everywhere throughout this romance. I owe much also to the way Jung's friend and student, Esther Harding, has patiently demonstrated the contemporary relevance of the ancient rites of the Mother Goddess. It was in the pages of her *Psychic Energy* (2nd edn, Princeton/Bollingen 1963) that I found the seed of what was to become Dárken's dream in Chapter 5.

Stanislas Klossowski de Rola's *Alchemy, The Secret Art* (Thames & Hudson, 1973) enlarged my acquaintance with the magical world of Hermetic art, and its illustrations furnished some of the contents of the library at Easterness. For the history of alchemy I have relied on E.J. Holmyard's *Alchemy* (Penguin, 1957) and H. Stanley Redgrove's *Alchemy Ancient & Modern* (first published in 1911, and re-issued by E.P. Publishing in 1973). For insight into its meaning and significance I was helped by essays in Alan McGlashan's marvellous book, *The Savage and Beautiful Country* (Chatto & Windus, 1966); and, as a provocative corrective to the Jungians, I found Titus Burckhardt's *Alchemy* (Stuart & Watkins, 1967) invaluable— particularly in its insistence on the vanity of trying to describe the essence of alchemy in solely psychological terms.

Devotees of the Hermetic art will have recognized a much larger debt. I should explain and acknowledge it.

I was still looking for a form for this romance when my friend, Richard Lannoy, introduced me to a rare edition of a book with a curious history. *A Suggestive Enquiry into the Hermetic Mystery* was written and published by Mary Anne Atwood (née South) in 1850, and then immediately withdrawn at the behest of her father, an Hermetic poet, on the grounds that it revealed too much. Even more than the book itself I found the circumstances of its appearance and disappearance very suggestive—though in ways quite other than its author can have imagined or intended. Like all the characters of my novel, Sir Henry Agnew and Louisa are creatures of fiction, and are in no way offered as portraits of Thomas South and his daughter. I have borrowed what I needed—the bare outlines of their intriguing story—and adapted it to the demands of my imagination. In consequence, the events of Louisa Agnew's life are far removed from the quiet, meditative, happily married career of that remarkable Victorian Hermetic, Mrs Atwood. She and Louisa have a middle name and the authorship of a withdrawn Hermetic text in common, and little else. Nevertheless, without the real Victorian (who lived in Hampshire, not in Norfolk), the fictional one would not have been conceived, and I owe her shade my thanks.

Fortunately, Mrs Atwood's work was not completely destroyed and, even while I was making use of her story, the *Suggestive Enquiry* was reissued by the Yogi Society in Britain and the Julien Press in the USA. It came as a relief to know that she was free to speak for herself once more, and that her attempt to share the wisdom of the Hermetic tradition has now been honoured on both sides of the Atlantic.

I am indebted to Richard Lannoy for much more than this timely introduction. He first interested me in the Tarot many years ago and, since then, both as colleague and friend, has freely (and often hilariously) shared with me his extraordinary range of learning and experience. Also, though they are in no way accountable for the use I made of it, Dr Alan Blandford and Dr Phil Harvey gave me professional advice on the matter of the heart, and there are many other friends for whose confidence and support I am very grateful; but, as always, the greatest debt is to my wife, Phoebe Clare.

About the Author

Lindsay Clarke was born in Halifax, England, and educated at Cambridge University. He now lives in Somerset.